LARAMIE DUNAWAY

By Laramie Dunaway

Hungry Women
Wicked Women
Women on Top

702714

Hungry Women
Wicked Women

Laramie Dunaway

CORONET BOOKS
Hodder and Stoughton

Hungry Women copyright © Laramie Dunaway 1990
Wicked Women copyright © Laramie Dunaway 1991

Hungry Women first published in Great Britain in 1990
by New English Library Paperbacks

Wicked Women first published in Great Britain in 1991
by New English Library Paperbacks

This collected volume first published in Great Britain in 1994
by Hodder and Stoughton Limited,
a division of Hodder Headline PLC

A Coronet paperback

The right of Laramie Dunaway to be identified as the Author of
the Work has been asserted by her in accordance with the
Copyright, Designs and Patents Act 1988.

10 9 8 7 6 5 4 3 2 1

British Library C.I.P.

A CIP catalogue record for this title is available from
the British Library

ISBN 0 340 62331 4

Printed and bound in Great Britain by
Cox & Wyman Ltd, Reading, Berkshire

Hodder and Stoughton Ltd
A Division of Hodder Headline PLC
338 Euston Road
London NW1 3BH

HUNGRY WOMEN

PART ONE

Live Wires

**In Which the Differences
Between Sex and Death
Are Finally Revealed**

1

Barcelona Lee sits at the wobbliest table in Hamburger Hamlet waiting for her best friend to arrive so she can lie to her. Lying makes Barcelona anxious. She thinks of the radio news report she heard on the drive here that claimed each year more women than men attempt suicide, but more men actually succeed. She wonders if that means women are more incompetent or just smarter. To pass time, she decides to test the radio's accuracy by taking an informal tally of her friends who have threatened suicide. It is either this or grade freshman essays.

For each friend who has openly offered to kill herself but would never really do it, Barcelona places a fried zucchini on the lip of her plate. Four zucchinis are stacked upright like crusty vertebrae. For each friend who had threatened and might someday try it, she rips a hunk of lettuce the size of a rose petal from her hamburger and places it in a separate pile. Two. For those who have dabbled at it and failed, she stacks pickle slices. Two. For those who have done it—slashed, gassed, or pilled themselves into oblivion—she uses maraschino cherries. Actually, there has been only one woman she knows personally who has succeeded. Darlene. Darlene hanged herself with an extension cord in the guest bathroom on August 16th, the anniversary of Elvis Presley's death.

Barcelona plucks the neon-red cherry floating in her

9

Diet Coke and twirls it by the stem, deciding where best to place it.

Suddenly ashamed of her own morbidness, she pops the cherry into her mouth and sucks out the delicious sweetness. For once she doesn't worry about what the Red Dye No. 45 is doing to her insides.

'Did you order yet?' Trina asks, appearing suddenly and sliding into the booth opposite Barcelona. The wobbly table jiggles and the stack of fried zucchinis tumbles over. Trina exists in a perpetual state of being harried. Her clothes are elegant Liz Claiborne and Anne Klein II suits, but she always looks rumpled, like a hastily made bed. Her makeup is uneven, as if applied with a putty knife while running up steep stairs. Even her hair looks anxious, frizzled black curls yanked and tugged grudgingly into submission. Yet she has a lusty, sensual look that men always seem to notice. Trina eyes Barcelona's half-eaten hamburger and frowns. 'Yeech. How late am I?'

'Twenty minutes.'

'Shit, that's not even late for me.'

'It is for me. I still have to go back to work.' First lie.

'You can always fake it. Not me. The Candidate wants me to dig up something on Councilwoman Bennington.'

'Dirt?'

'What else? Dirt is what fuels the machinery of modern politics. I just made that up. Profound, huh? Hey, waitress.' Trina wiggles her chipped fingernails at a slender young woman in a short skirt which flares over her hips but doesn't quite cover the matching maroon panties underneath. 'Soup and salad. Ranch dressing. Glass of white wine.' She hands the waitress the menu and waves her away. Trina watches her walk away and makes a face. 'Christ, I hate staring into some eighteen-year-old's twat when I'm ordering food. Who designs their outfits anyway, lifers at San Quentin?'

'So how's The Candidate doing?' Barcelona asks. Trina is a publicity flak for Cory Meyers, Kennedyesque candidate for Los Angeles City Council, one of the most powerful political offices in the state. Trina alternately refers to him as either The Candidate or The Great Pretender, never by his name.

'He's up in the polls. Another half a percentage point.'

'That's terrific.'

Trina shrugs. 'Not good enough to win.'

'Well, if he doesn't, it won't be your fault.'

'Doesn't matter who's at fault, kiddo, just who gets blamed.'

Barcelona raises her left arm to look at her watch, remembers she'd taken it off back at her office because it ticked too loudly during the faculty meeting. She reads Trina's watch upside down. 'Where's Diva? She's never this late.'

'Oh, I forgot to tell you.' Trina snatches the pile of pickle slices on Barcelona's plate and stuffs them into her wide mouth. She chews as she does everything in life, vigorously. Barcelona always has the feeling that Trina fears someone is after her seat, her car, her food, that everything in life must be consumed immediately before stolen. Trina swallows the half-chewed lump and says, 'Diva can't make it today. Rehearsal.'

'What is it this time? Some soft drink?'

'Ketchup, I think. Or mustard. Relish, maybe. I don't know, some condiment.'

'She'll be there tonight, won't she?'

'Natch. We'll all be there. Where else would we be?'

Barcelona shrugs. 'Dixie's still working Vice. They may have her on hooker patrol again.'

'Not anymore. I had breakfast with her this morning. She's now undercover in a high school busting students. Can you imagine? I mean, high school was awful enough

11

the first time around.' Trina reaches again into Barcelona's plate and grabs the fried zucchini slices. She sticks out her tongue, lays a breaded zucchini on the wet gummy membrane, and pulls it back into her mouth.

'Every time you do that I expect you to give change,' Barcelona says.

'The Candidate told me it reminded him of a bullfrog snagging a fly.'

'What were you eating when he said this?'

Trina grins and looks Barcelona in the eyes. 'Him.'

'Oh?' Barcelona doesn't permit herself to look surprised. 'I didn't know he'd issued a position paper in that regard.'

Trina folds a napkin and sticks it under the table leg to keep it from wobbling. 'It just happened. No big deal. We were in Burbank taping an interview show—"L.A. Morning," "Wake up, L.A.," "Pick the Sleep Crud from Your Eyes, L.A.," something like that. They had some problems with the video equipment. We went out for a snack and ended up in some motel doing it standing in the shower. We didn't plan it or anything.'

'How was it?'

'Okay, I guess. Thing was, the whole time we were bouncing away, I kept wondering if this position would give me varicose veins. Kinda distracted me, you know?'

'What about his wife?'

'She already has varicose veins.'

'Yuk, yuk.'

'Okay, so she doesn't really. She's truly gorgeous, like out of *Vogue* or something. They stand us next to each other. I'd be the "before" picture.'

'Then what's going on between you two? Love or sex or boredom?'

Trina laughs and starts choking herself with both hands. 'God, I'm the last one to ask about these things. Definitely not love. More like curiosity, I guess. We've worked so hard together for the past year, maybe it was just inevitable. Besides, they're getting a divorce. Keep that to yourself, Barcy.'

'The sex part or the divorce?'

'The divorce.'

'Who would I tell?'

'She's staying with him until after the election, then they're splitting up. She doesn't want to hurt his political chances right now. They're both so adult and civilized about the whole thing it's nauseating.' Trina shakes her head and laughs. 'She's who I want to be when I grow up.'

Barcelona reads Trina's watch upside down again. 'I've got to get back. Students will be lining up outside my office in about twenty minutes.' That too is a lie, but she isn't quite ready yet to tell Trina the truth. Not until she knows the extent of the bad news. Maybe tonight, at dinner, when they are all together. She'll tell them then.

'Hey, I met someone who'd read one of your books,' Trina says.

'Which one?'

'A guy over at the mayor's office.'

'I mean which book?'

She shrugs. 'I don't know, the one about the planet where there were too many women so they had to undergo forced sex-change operations to balance the sexes out.'

'*Balancing Acts.*'

'Whatever. He got off on that idea. He was shocked as shit when I told him B. Evans Lee was a woman.'

'Was he at least cute?'

'Looks like that scruffy actor who never shaves. The one in *Barfly*.'

Barcelona rolls her eyes. 'Mickey Rourke.'

'Yeah, him.'

'All my fans look like Mickey Rourke.' Barcelona stands up.

13

'Hang on,' Trina says, sliding quickly out of the booth as if she's just discovered it was on fire. 'I'll walk you out.'

'What about your food?'

'I gave them fifteen minutes. They can't bring a lousy soup and salad in fifteen minutes, fuck 'em. I'll pick something up at the deli.'

This makes Barcelona very uncomfortable. Guilty. A coconspirator. Certainly there must be some kind of law about ordering food and leaving before you are served. But she knows there is no way she will change Trina's mind. To make up for it, she leaves double the tip she'd planned to leave.

Trina sees what she is up to, shakes her head, grabs one of the dollar bills from the table, and stuffs it back in Barcelona's purse. 'Don't encourage incompetence.'

All the way back to the car, Barcelona feels badly. Despite Trina's chattering about The Candidate's newest TV commercials, Barcelona keeps thinking of all the possibilities of why the waitress had been slow to serve Trina's meal. The cook, perhaps a recent emigrant from Baja, had misread the order slip. Maybe the waitress saw the soup was not steaming and had handed it back to the cook with a firm scolding, 'I can't serve cold soup to my customers.' Maybe she'd started her period today and had run to the bathroom to change her tampon. Maybe . . .

'You want me to run by and pick you up tonight?' Trina offers.

'I'll drive.' She hesitates before telling her why, but knows she'll have to tell her eventually. Besides, one secret a day is all she can handle. 'I promised Eric I'd stop by tonight before dinner. Just for a minute.'

'Christ, Barcy!' Trina gives her a disgusted look. 'I didn't realize tonight was your night for self-torture. Why not slam your head into your refrigerator and save the mileage?'

14

'Give me a break, okay?'

'Will *Luna* be there?' She says the name as if it were a venereal disease.

'I don't know. It doesn't matter.'

'Yeah, right. It doesn't matter.'

Barcelona unlocks the door of her blue 1977 Chrysler, an oversize car that she'd inherited last year from her deceased grandmother. The Geezemobile, the others called it. She slides behind the wheel. No bucket seats, just a benchlike seat as long and hard as a Catholic pew. She could seat the cast of *Twelve Angry Men* in here, give them something to really be pissed about.

'Don't be late again, okay?' she tells Trina. 'We only do this every two weeks. Coming late makes everybody feel you don't care.'

'I care, I care. Honestly, I'd rather be with you guys tonight than on a date with a disease-free rich man who loves children and is not afraid of commitment.'

'Really?'

'Almost.' She winks, squeezes Barcelona's arm, closes the car door. 'Tonight, kid. It'll be wild. I promise.'

She watches Trina march purposefully across the side-walk, heels clacking cement as if sparks should fly with each step. Trina is one of the fried zucchinis, a threatened suicide six months ago. She'd called Barcelona at home, a little after one in the morning, catching her watching TV while grading student papers. David Letterman was still on, cackling at Stupid Dog Tricks. Barcelona had hit the remote switch that shut the TV off. 'Life sucks,' Trina had said, not waiting for a hello. 'Life sucks but I don't.' She'd laughed sadly. 'Get this, this will kill you. The miniseries of my life. I just come home from a date with this guy, an assistant d.a. I met last week at that dinner for the governor. Anyway, this is our first date, we've had dinner at some swank French place out in the Valley. He brings me

15

home in his new Mercedes, still has that new-car smell. Did I mention that he was wearing a goddamn tuxedo? Looked gorgeous, like Harrison Ford getting an Oscar. Anyway, we're back at my place. We're sipping this modest white wine I've been saving, nibbling some brie. We kiss. Kiss a little more. A little light tongue action. Okay, so far so good. What do you think would follow? Huh?' Barcelona had started to say something but Trina cut her off. 'You figure a little grab and stroke, some tender buildup, hands running along thighs, some ass-squeezing, ear-nibbling, buttons suddenly falling open, music swells, so does he, and eventually some serious humping. No, sir. This guy kisses me twice. Two fucking times. Half-assed kisses at that. Next thing you know, he asks me to go down on him. Not later. Right now. Pulls his fly open and whips out the hairy beast. Doesn't even want to get undressed, for God's sake.' A long weary sigh followed. 'I mean it, Barcy, if this is what it all comes to after thirty and divorce, I'd rather check out now. I fucking mean it.' And she'd hung up. Barcelona had called her back immediately. They'd chatted a few minutes. Trina seemed to calm down. Barcelona had offered to go over, spend the night. Trina had laughed, said she was too old for a pajama party. She'd be fine, she'd go to bed now, had a million things to do in the morning.

Unable to sleep, Barcelona had turned David Letterman back on but couldn't concentrate. She'd call Trina back but the line was busy. Next day she found out from Diva that Trina had called Dixie and told her the same story. Dixie had rushed over and stayed with Trina that night. 'I would have gone over,' Barcelona had explained to Diva. 'She told me not to come.'

'Told Dixie the same thing,' Diva had said. 'Dixie went anyway.'

Ever since, Barcelona feels a little guilty when seeing

16

Trina. Perhaps she should have rushed over too, ignoring Trina's protests. Isn't that what a true friend does? But Barcelona isn't that pushy. She takes people at their word. Dixie, on the other hand, is a cop. She's used to taking charge. She thrives in emergencies.

Barcelona turns on the radio. Janis Joplin is singing 'Get It While You Can.' Afterward the news comes on and repeats the story about suicides. Barcelona thinks of Darlene, the successful suicide. Not a friend really, a vague neighbor about the same age. Occasionally Barcelona would be pulling into her garage just as Darlene was out walking her dog, a tan Lhasa apso named Foxy. They never looked at each other when they exchanged greetings, chatting about the homeowners association or such. Instead they would speak to each other while staring at the dog as he raised a leg and peed or squatted to defecate, which Darlene would immediately scoop up with neatly cut squares of newspaper and stuff into a brown lunch bag. Barcelona smiles at the memory of Darlene standing there with a lunch bag full of shit discussing the parking problem. She realizes now that if asked, she could better describe the dog's features than Darlene's.

Every once in a while Barcelona runs into Darlene's husband, Dave, and they have almost identical conversations to the ones she and Darlene used to have, each still watching the dog, the dog still squatting and grimacing on the greenbelt, Dave holding a lunch bag of shit.

Barcelona pulls into the heavy Westwood traffic, concentrating on maneuvering the aircraft carrier Geezemobile so she won't think about Eric. But every store she passes is one she and Eric had been in at some time or other in their frequent visits here. There is the Nike store where they'd bought matching running shoes. He'd worn his out in six months. Hers were still practically new in the back of her closet. With the new tennis racquet

17

and the skis and handball gloves. He'd wanted her to become more competitive, like him. Enter mixed-doubles tournaments. But she'd never enjoyed that aspect of herself. Didn't like how it made her feel squirmy and edgy.

Now that they were split up, she went to the health club every day and took a jazzercise class. She'd lost her six pounds she'd put on after the split, plus another eight she'd been meaning to lose for the six years they'd lived together. Dixie has been trying to talk her into lifting weights with her. Dixie is in remarkable shape. She once demonstrated the benefits of weight lifting by picking up a quarter from the floor between her buttock cheeks. Barcelona doesn't think she is quite up to that yet. Her stomach is flat, her butt firm. What more could she expect from life?

She follows Wilshire Boulevard past the San Diego Freeway entrance that would take her back to her home in Orange County. No need to tell Trina that there is another reason she is in L.A. today, other than to have lunch together. Not until Barcelona finds out what this mystery is all about.

Yesterday afternoon the strange phone call had surprised her. 'Can you buzz in tomorrow?' her agent had asked.

'I teach in the morning.'

'After lunch then?'

Barcelona rarely spoke to her agent and even more rarely actually saw her. This was very unusual. 'Why? What's up?'

'We'll talk about it tomorrow. Two o'clock, okay? It's important.'

So here she is, carefully piloting the Geezemobile through Beverly Hills among the Porsches, Mercedes, and Jaguars until she finds the parking lot behind the Banana Republic. She parks, walks the two blocks to her agent's building, where they have underground parking, which

18

she purposely avoided. She doesn't like the hollow echo of her heels down in those places. The sound of emptiness amplified.

She walks past the sleepy security guard who waves his soggy sandwich at her. She smiles at him, catches a strong whiff of tuna salad, and hurries to the elevators. She waits for the next car with two tidy young men in business suits. They are in their late twenties, about five years younger than she. Their suits are drab but expensive, indicating some important corporate position. She still isn't used to seeing so many people younger than she in responsible positions.

When the elevator door hisses open, one man enters first, the other holds the door open for her. She nods, walks in, feels his eyes behind her starting at her ankles and finger-walking up the backs of her thighs, curving over her buttocks, lingering there a moment, wondering, then moving up, jumping off midway up her back. When the door closes and the three of them are alone, sliding up the shaft, the two men return to their discussion of some investment property over in Riverside County, completely ignoring her. This is a recent phenomenon, something that has happened more and more often in the four years since she'd turned thirty. Young salesmen in their twenties who used to vault over three older customers to wait on her, now let her wait her turn with the other adults. She is still attractive, still a big hit with men her own age and older, but she misses that special attention she'd always gotten from the young. When had she stopped being one of Us and become one of Them?

Barcelona gets out on the eighteenth floor. She looks around a moment, disoriented. It has been so long since she's been here, she isn't sure this is the right floor after all. She starts walking the halls, reading nameplates. Nothing looks or sounds familiar. J. G. HEIM, PRODUCER.

19

LAURA LISTER, DDS. HAROLD K. BARRETT, AT-TORNEY. Some of the office doors are open and she can see massive color-coordinated suites with several young secretaries, all of whom are dressed better than she is. The whole floor smells of new carpeting.

Her armpits are dripping now, cool drops of sweat skating down her ribs. Her stomach rumbles. She must be getting closer. This anxiety is the reason she never meets with her agent. Barcelona considers herself lucky to have an agent. Though she has written six published science fiction novels, none has been much of a success. Modest advances and modest sales keep her living slightly better than her assistant professor's salary would afford, but not enough to help support an office in a building like this.

When she finishes a novel, she sends it to Grief, her agent. Within a few months to a year, she receives a letter, some contracts in the mail which she signs without reading, and a year later the book appears in the paperback section of bookstores. Like magic. Barcelona prefers to think of it that way. Not muck around with the voodoo of publishing. She never expresses disappointment than the advances aren't higher, or that her books don't sell more copies. She is pleased to be published at all, enjoys the minor celebrity status it gives her among her students, the occasional fan letter from Kansas City or Jacksonville usually addressed to *Mr*. B. Evans Lee, the look of respect from someone new when they find out she is a writer.

She sees the corner office down the hall and knows without reading the gold plate that this is Grief's office. She hesitates, knowing full well why Grief has asked her down here today. To dump her. Toss her out of the agency. Take your stupid science fiction books and peddle them yourself. They don't even pay for my stamps. Barcelona leans against the wall, rummages through her purse until she finds some spearmint Breathsavers, scratches the lint off the top one, pops it, and bites down hard. A rush of bittersweetness stings her mouth.

She continues down the hallway. The office door is closed, the lettering on the gold plate in lavish medieval script: *Grief Fenton-Happs, Literary Agent*. Barcelona pushes open the door and enters.

Grief's young secretary, who looks a lot like the waitress at Hamburger Hamlet, is on the phone telling the caller that Ms. Fenton-Happs was out of the office for the afternoon but would call back first thing in the morning. Barcelona feels a cold shiver as she wonders if she's gotten the day wrong.

But suddenly there she is. Grief doing an exaggerated tiptoe past the secretary who is still on the phone denying her boss's presence. She waves for Barcelona to follow her into her inner office. Barcelona does, noticing that Grief is in her stocking feet. Also noticing a knobby bunion bulging on the side of her left foot like a toadstool. As soon as she gets close to Grief, the taller woman grabs her in a firm shoulder hug and says, 'It's so good to see you, Barcy.'

'You too.'

'That yutz on the phone thinks I'm going to sell him this hot new author I just started handling for popcorn and a fingerfuck. Forget it.' She collapses into her chair behind her huge and unbearably messy desk. She looks at Barcelona for a long minute as if wondering what this meeting was about. Finally she leans forward and smiles. 'So, Barcy, what do you want first, the good news or the bad news?'

2

Trina storms into The Candidate's office without knocking. She waves the memo from him she just found on her desk. 'What the hell does this mean?'

He looks up from behind his desk and smiles. 'Hello to you too.'

'This says you want me to fire someone.'

'Right. I don't care who. Your choice.' His perfect smile widens to reveal even more perfect teeth as square and white as Chicklets. Trina realizes it is his teeth that make him a successful politician. Someone with teeth like that is very cautious, practices preventive hygiene. People admire that in a leader.

'What are you talking about?' Trina asks. 'Why fire anybody?'

'Because we can't afford five full-time people on staff anymore.'

'Donations are way up,' she reminds him.

'Yes, and I know I have you to thank for that.' Impossibly, his smile widens even more and she sees yet another group of perfect teeth. She wonders if his teeth continue down his throat, line his stomach, intestines large and small, all the way through his body. If she pulled his pants down and bent him over would his asshole snap at her like those chattering teeth you buy at novelty stores?

'Then what's all this crap about firing somebody?'

22

'You sound like Jack Lemmon in *Mr. Roberts*. Remember at the end when he bursts into James Cagney's office and says, "What's this crap about no movie?" God, I loved that.'

'Save the charm for the voters, slick. We're not exactly broke around here. I mean, it's not like you're spending all your money on my salary.'

He laughs. 'We both know you're underpaid and overworked. Don't think I'm not appreciative of everything you've done.'

She thinks maybe that 'appreciative' crack and this smug smile refer to their shower sex the other day, but she's not sure. Suddenly she realizes that she's not really sure they even went to a motel or had sex or if she just dreamed it. She thinks about asking him, but decides not to.

The Candidate yawns long and loudly. He is the only man she's ever met who looks startlingly handsome even while yawning. He leans way back in his chair, tilting it off balance, webbing his fingers together and stretching them over his head. Several fingers crack. The sound seems to surprise him and he looks closely at his knuckles as he laces the fingers and slowly cracks them again, his eyes so intent as if looking for the exact moment the knuckle swells up out of the socket under the tight skin. Two knuckles pop and he leans back with a sigh, his scientific curiosity satisfied.

Trina sits down on the leather sofa away from his desk. Her head hurts. She doesn't even remember driving here. The last moment she can clearly picture was walking away from Barcelona at the Hamburger Hamlet in Westwood. She must have gotten into her car and driven here, but she can't recall sticking her key in the ignition, fastening the shoulder harness, driving here, parking. She looks down and sees the red cardboard parking stub from the lot down the street wrinkled and twisted in her hand. Her thumb is red from rubbing it. That is where she must have parked her car, though she doesn't remember.

'You okay, Trina?' the Candidate asks, getting up from behind his desk and walking toward her.

She stares at his desk, one of those ultramodern jobs, smoked glass top and black wire baskets for drawers. She can look straight into each drawer and see what's in it. Part of his open, nothing-to-hide image.

'Trina, you okay?' he repeats. He sounds honestly concerned.

She notices he is not wearing socks with his Topsiders. She has warned him against this habit. 'Where are your socks?' she asks suddenly. It is the same tone she uses with Karyn, her twelve-year-old daughter. The Candidate is forty-two.

'You look a little pale,' he says, bending over her.

'You could get away looking like that when you were campaigning for Jerry Brown. But we don't want to happen to you what happened to him. The Flake Factor. Makes people think you're laughing at them. People won't stand for that. You can lie to them and steal from them, but you can't laugh at them.'

He walks over to the Sparklettes tank and draws a paper cup of water. He carries it back to her. 'Drink this.'

She sips from it. 'Let's learn from his mistakes, okay?'

'Sure. Wear socks, don't date rock queens.' He sits beside her on the sofa. He smells faintly piney. 'You feel better?'

'I'm fine. Just a little light-headed. I skipped lunch.' She finishes the water. He takes the paper cup, crushes it into a ball and shoots it across the room at the Plexiglas wastecan. The paper wad bounces off the rim and rolls under his desk.

'Plexiglas isn't as forgiving as metal,' he says.

'You mind if we put your jump shot on hold and discuss

24

this stupid memo? With the campaign in its final months, we need more people, not fewer.'

'And we'll get them. Later. Right now we need to do two things. One'—he holds up his thumb—'we need to reduce the staff so we can afford to send this newest mailer. Hopefully the mailer will get us more money to hire more people. And two'—he jackknifes another finger—'we need to remind our employees that that is exactly what they are, *employees*. Sometimes they act as if they were crusaders.'

'What's wrong with that?'

'We haven't been rising in the polls as fast as we'd all hoped. They're depressed, slowing down. They need a shot of inspiration.'

'This is more like a shot through the head.'

'Damn right. Remind them that we pay them a salary, and if they want to keep getting that salary, they'd better start working for it. From now on around here, it's blow job or no job.'

Trina laughs. 'Can I quote you?'

'I already sent it to Bartlett's.'

Trina sips her water again, dabs some on her eyelids with her fingertips. It helps. She likes the staff, knows they all need the money. She can't bear having to fire any of them. 'Can't you just talk to them? Give them one of your famous pep talks?'

'I'm not famous for my pep talks. I'm famous for my . . .' He pauses, then laughs. 'Actually, I'm not famous for anything. That's why I'm losing this election.'

Trina kicks off her shoes, rubs her toes against the carpet. 'Give them a talk anyway.'

'Actions, as any voter can tell you, speak louder than words.'

'Even shitty actions?'

'Especially shitty actions.'

Trina sighs. A sudden picture of herself getting into her

car in the Hamburger Hamlet parking lot flashes into her mind. Her hand reaching for the ignition. Turning on the radio. The image vanishes.

'You having a drug flashback or something?' he asks. 'You look zonked.'

She glances over at him and shakes her head. 'The Great Pretender to the throne of L.A. sees all.'

'I like to think of myself as The Great Contender. Thanks to you.'

Suddenly Trina has another flash: she sees herself pulling into the parking lot down the street, getting the stub from the young Mexican kid with the porcupine moustache who stares openly at her breasts. The image fades and she concentrates on The Candidate. 'So, who should I fire? Do you have a sexual or ethnic preference?'

'You pick,' he says. 'It doesn't matter. Except Trudy. She's the only one who gets the lunch orders straight.'

'You can be a real bastard sometimes,' Trina says.

'Yes, but a bastard for the right side. Isn't that why you're working for me?'

'I'm a hired gun. In it strictly for the money.'

'You'd like to be. But I know you better.'

'You do, huh?' She stares directly into his eyes.

He gives her a long thoughtful look. 'Maybe I don't.'

His smile snaps away like a rubber band and she can see he doesn't like this firing business any more than she. She also can see that he is right. The staff has been slacking off as they get closer to the elections and their man doesn't look like a sure winner. Firing is a cheap incentive program.

He picks up a pencil and begins drumming on the edge of his coffee mug. 'So, factoring in the latest polls, the media editorials, and what you've overheard in the various women's rest rooms, what are my chances of actually winning this damned election?'

26

'You want the truth or a pep talk?'

'I'm hoping they're the same thing.' He is smiling again, but she can glimpse the flicker of fear in his eyes. She has seen it at some time or other in the eyes of every candidate she's ever worked for, even the ones way ahead in the polls. It is as if they glimpse a picture of themselves losing everything, humbled, stripped naked and shivering in front of millions of laughing people. Trina admires men and women who run for office, even the ones whose policies she doesn't agree with. What tremendous courage it takes to put yourself through all that. She doesn't have that kind of courage, never had. The only courageous thing she ever did was have Karyn.

'Well?' he asks. 'Just how thick is the soup?'

'You want charts and tables or just the bottom line?'

'Depends whose bottom is on the line.'

'You've got a pretty decent chance. With some luck.'

He thinks about this for a minute, nodding to himself as if he were carrying on a lively interior debate, still clacking his pencil on the mug rim. When he looks up at her his face shines with resolve and determination. 'Then we'll just have to make some luck, won't we?' he says. 'Work harder.'

'Meaning dig up more dirt.'

'The harder you work, the luckier you get.' He changes the tempo of his drumming and sings, 'Work all night till de morning come.'

'You're nuts,' Trina says, laughing.

He reaches over and plucks a piece of lettuce from her lapel. 'This is so much more practical than a carnation.' He tosses the lettuce into his mouth and chews loudly.

Trina laughs again. She admits that he is fun to be around, not only handsome, but good-natured, witty, caring. The kind of man you'd remember having sex with. Yet, still she isn't sure. She seems to recall the hot water

27

sluicing down her spine, trickling between her buttocks. Her hands pressed flat against the wet tile, her feet spread slightly, squatting a little as he entered her. But she can't remember what he felt like inside of her. Did she come? Did he? Maybe she had dreamed it.

He reaches over again and she thinks he will find yet more food on her. That is not uncommon. She always returns from meals wearing a sampling of whatever she ate. But his hand rests on her shoulder in a friendly, concerned manner. He squeezes his fingers and she can feel their strength even through her shoulder pads. 'Maybe you need a couple days off, Trina.'

'Yeah, right. Perfect time to take a vacation. The peak of the goddamn campaign.'

'A day or two won't make a difference to the great city of Los Angeles. Me neither. Drive down to Palm Springs for the weekend. Dayna can take over.'

Dayna is his wife, officially his campaign manager. But despite her good wishes for her husband's success in the election, lately she has abdicated more and more of the daily responsibilities to Trina. No one has even seen Dayna at the headquarters for weeks.

'I think you've been working too hard,' he says.

'First you think the others aren't working hard enough, then you think I'm working too hard. Make up your mind.'

'They're employees, Trina, you're a friend.'

We must have done it then, she thinks. 'I'm fine. Really.'

'You look like you just got out of bed. Like you dressed last night, went to bed, and just got up, fully dressed and came to work.'

'Hey, that's my look. I work hard for it. That decadent, anyone-can-have-me look.'

He gets up, returns to his desk, scratches the bare ankle above his Topsiders. He looks at the papers on his desk. 'Whoever you fire, you can hire them back again in about a week. But don't tell them that. Blows the whole purpose.'

He opens the top basket drawer of his desk, reaches under some papers, and takes out a pair of argyle socks. Even the glass desk has secrets, she thinks. He kicks off his shoes and starts putting on the socks. 'Look, Ma, socks.'

Trina gets up and goes to the door. She is closing it behind her when she impulsively pokes her head back in and says, 'Just for the record, did you and I screw in the shower the other day?'

3

'Make up your mind, Barcy,' Grief says. 'I need to tell him something.'

'I don't know what to tell him,' Barcelona says.

'Think of something, dear. He'll be here any minute.'

Barcelona tries to concentrate, but she can't take her eyes off Grief's feet. The plump bunion that bulges from the ball of her left foot fascinates her. It strains against the stocking like a robber's face. She imagines it may be the petrified fetus of the twin sister Grief has always longed for but never known. She glances up and sees Grief staring at her, expectant. Barcelona shrugs. 'What am I expected to do?'

'Do? Do whatever you want, dear. It's your life, your career. It's all up to you.' Grief looks amused. Her tone is always condescending. Maybe this comes from being so tall, Barcelona thinks, forty-plus years of looming over others. She is over six feet, though all of it built solidly as a marble column. Her skin, by contrast, is pale and delicate, taut as Saran Wrap. She wears pleated black slacks and a white pirate's blouse and Barcelona realizes that this is the same color combination Grief wore the other times they met. Black slacks, white blouse, or white slacks and black blouse. Sometimes pearls. She has fine silky hair so blond that it is almost white; and white-blond eyebrows that are invisible from more than two feet away. The

30

invisible eyebrows and tight skin give her face a slightly scalded look.

'You look different,' Barcelona says.

'Yes?' Grief says encouragingly.

'I don't know how, just different. Maybe not. I just haven't seen you in a couple years.'

'No, no, you're right. There is something different. You're the first to notice. I should have known you would.'

Barcelona feels some pressure how to guess what is different, scans Grief's face for some sign, finds nothing. She shrugs. 'I don't know.'

'The eyes,' Grief prompts, delighted. She leans forward so Barcelona can take a closer look.

'New makeup?'

'Eyeliner. It's not makeup. It's a tattoo.'

'You had your eyes tattooed?'

'Do you like?'

Barcelona leans closer. Her own eyes water and burn at the thought. 'It looks like makeup, maybe a little thicker than before.'

'It's great. I never have to put eyeliner on. And it never washes off. I go swimming, I come out of the shower, it's still there.'

'But the needle, so close to your eyes. I don't think I could do that.'

'Nonsense. Nothing to it. The only thing I miss is when I cry, there's no more smearing and smudging that makes me look like a harlequin. Used to drive my husband into instant apology and an expensive gift. I noticed I cry a lot less now. What's the point?' She laughs as if to show that she's just joking.

The phone on her desk buzzes and Grief picks it up. 'Yes, Bette? Okay, give us a minute, then send him in.' She hangs up the phone and smiles at Barcelona. 'He's here. Anything you want to ask me first?'

31

Barcelona thinks hard. There are a thousand questions colliding in her head like carnival bumper cars, but none stays in focus long enough for her to snag it. The good news, Grief had told her fifteen minutes ago, was that they were about to meet with a film producer who is interested in optioning one of her novels for a feature film. Barcelona had broken out into a huge smile. 'That's great! What's the bad news?'

'I don't know yet,' Grief had said. 'But with these guys, there's always bad news. Sooner or later.'

Barcelona looks toward the door. She feels like a matador awaiting the release of the bull.

'Are you ready?' Grief asks.

Barcelona nods. 'Olé.'

The door opens and Bette leads a man into the room. Barcelona is startled. Though she has never met a real producer before, her mental image of one is of a fat, double-chinned man puffing a thick wet cigar and smiling too easily. What stuns Barcelona is that that's exactly what this man looks like. Rotund, thick lips, little hands, he walks in with a big smile and grabs Barcelona's hand as she rises from her chair.

'So this is the young lady who's going to make us all rich,' he says. He releases her hand and puffs the cigar again. 'Pardon the cigar, but my doctor's got me on this strict diet and it gives me bad breath. Ketosis. This kills the taste.'

'Roger,' Grief says, pecking him on the cheek, 'this is Barcelona Lee. Better known as B. Evans Lee. Barcy, this is the infamous Roger Carlyle.'

Roger Carlyle chuckles as if he likes the roguish image Grief's introduction implies. He points a plump finger at Barcelona and grins. 'Read your book, Ms. Lee. Read the whole thing in one sitting. Grief here sent it over to me two years ago, I stuck it up on some shelf, never read it.

I'll be honest with you, I don't even like to read. I especially don't like to read science fiction. Space ships, warp speed, crazy stuff. Christ.' He makes a dismissing gesture with his hands. 'But last week I get a call from a friend of mine, a source really, a spy. If you're going to be successful in this business you need to have spies. It's like a fuckin' war. You think I'm kidding. I'm not.' He laughs a gravelly laugh that is part chuckle, part gargle. 'Anyway, my source tips me that Lynda Kramer is coming to town to look over possible film ideas.'

'Lynda Kramer,' Barcelona repeats, impressed. Lynda Kramer is the classiest young actress around. In her mid-thirties, she has already starred with every major actor in a variety of films, most of which called for her to look mysterious and vulnerable and use an exotic accent. Academy Award nominations are automatic.

'Lynda took a year off to have her daughter and stayed pretty holed up in her husband's London apartment. Wouldn't even look at any scripts. Now she's on her way back and has let it slip, at least to my source, who is part of her entourage, that she'd love to do some kind of futuristic film, something classy, with a message. Like *On the Beach* or *Clockwork Orange*, something along those lines. Not just the usual cowboy rip-off, and no *Star Wars* flicks where special effects dominate. Something simple, but with heart.'

Roger Carlyle has said all this still standing in front of Grief's desk. Barcelona is standing less than two feet in front of him, reeling a little from the combination of cigar and ketosis. Like having her face ground into an ashtray.

'Sit, Roger, sit,' Grief says, waving him toward the chair opposite Barcelona. She looks at Barcelona, 'You, too.' Barcelona is already in her seat as Roger lowers his bulk into the chair and the bones in his pudgy knees crackle. Barcelona notices he is wearing stiff dry-cleaned black jeans with razor creases and a black polo shirt, perhaps in an effort to hide his girth. There is a sprinkling of dandruff on his shoulders and Barcelona imagines him getting dressed that morning, naked, looking at himself in the mirror, trying to decide whether to go with the white shirt to hide the dandruff, or the black shirt to hide the gut. How long had he stood there staring at his naked flab and snowy scalp, weighing the pros and cons?

'Anyway, I call Grief here, remembering at the back of my head some sci-fi stuff she'd tried to peddle a few years ago. She tells me about an even better book you wrote—'

'*Live Wires*,' Grief says.

'Yes. *Live Wires*. Great title. So I read it, one sitting like I said. Love it. Every page. My wife wakes up in the middle of the night, can't believe I'm reading. And worse, not even a script. She thinks it must be pornography, rips it out of my hand, reads a few lines, nods, gives it back, goes to sleep. It was hysterical.' He laughs again and Barcelona smiles to show she appreciates the compliment.

'So what did Lynda have to say?' Grief asks.

'I went over there two days ago, pitched it to her, left her a copy of the book. She called me yesterday, wanted to talk more. I went right over.' He stops suddenly to return to his cigar. A move, Barcelona realizes, designed to add suspense. It works. She wants to scream at him to tell her what Lynda Kramer said.

'Anyhow,' he continues, 'Lynda wants to see a script.'

'Ah,' Grief says and leans back in her chair smiling.

'Yes.' Roger Carlyle nods.

Barcelona waits for him to continue, but he too leans back with a satisfied smirk. She looks over at Grief, who is nodding to herself. They both look like two people who have just finished having sex.

'What happens next?' Barcelona asks.

'Well, that depends.' Roger Carlyle stubs his cigar out

in an ashtray shaped like a sleeping cat. He takes out a pack of Velamints, removes two, and thumbs them into his mouth. 'It could go a lot of ways from here. We give her a script, she doesn't like it, we either get a rewrite, or we drop the project. Or she likes it and wants a rewrite. Or the studio doesn't like it. Or everyone likes it but before it gets made the studio changes heads and we get put in turnaround by the new studio head. But'—he crosses his pudgy fingers and smiles—'if God is smiling on us, we go into production and the three of us sitting here are suddenly hot properties in this town.'

Barcelona likes the idea of being a hot property. When she'd first walked into this office this afternoon, Grief had made some offhand comment about a hot young writer and Barcelona had felt a jealous gnawing in her stomach. Her own writing had started as a lark, a break from the academic tedium of graduate work. Her speciality in school was Middle English Literature, the medieval writings in England from 1150 to 1500. The late hours she had labored, poring over Old English, reading the small print dissertations of obscure scholars on the homosexual rhythms in the London dialect of Chaucer. The toenail motif of Malory. Studying the dusty texts of Lowland Scots, the ballads, folk lyrics, and miracle plays that were passed down for centuries orally before they were eventually written down, often incompletely. Then at the end of the fifteenth century William Caxton set up his printing press at Westminster. This is what Barcelona had gladly spent her life reading and writing about.

But during her last year of graduate school, when her dissertation on John of Trevisa's translation of Higdon's *Polychronicon* was finished, she found herself scribbling short stories, poems, character sketches, anything to amuse herself, remembering what it was like to just love the story, before she began toe-tagging and autopsying each work.

35

One short story she started just wouldn't end. She had never read science fiction, except for a few of the classics her friends had pushed on her with fanatic fervor. She had remained lukewarn to their charms. Yet her story, merely an updating of an anonymous thirteenth-century ballad, began in California and soon drifted off the planet into another galaxy. Suddenly she was a science fiction writer.

'Our plan, then,' Roger Carlyle is saying, 'is to present Lynda with the best possible script and go from there.'

'Who are you getting to write it?' Barcelona asks.

'You,' Roger Carlyle says with a wink.

Barcelona looks at Grief. Grief smiles, nods. Barcelona uncrosses her legs, bangs her ankle on the edge of Grief's desk. Pain corkscrews through her leg then shoots into her stomach, splashing hot acid around. She shows no outward sign of discomfort.

'I've never written a film script before, Mr. Carlyle. Actually, I've never even read one.'

'Easily fixed. I'll have a dozen scripts sent over to you from my office. Jerks with a lot less talent than you are making a fortune writing movies. Imagine what you could do with all your talent.'

Barcelona isn't worried about the script. She has faith in her ability to conquer any form. She's not even thinking about that. She is thinking about Lynda Kramer, gorgeous, intelligent, talented. She imagines herself on the set, chatting with Lynda, maybe going on a shopping trip, holding her child on the set while Lynda goes off to perform another scene. She would never admit this to anyone, but she thinks of Lynda Kramer as a woman with secrets to share about being a woman. Whenever men see her photo they sigh the sigh that translates, 'If only . . .'

She asks, 'Do you think Lynda Kramer might actually do it? Make this movie.'

'She's interested,' he says. 'That's the first step.'

Grief goes to work then. She stands quickly, guides Roger Carlyle to the door, promises to get in touch with him tomorrow about the deal memo. He winks again at Barcelona, not in a sexual way, in a way that suggests he has everything under control.

When she is alone with Grief, Barcelona asks, 'What do you think?'

'The money's shit and he's an asshole.'

Barcelona is surprised. 'He was lying?'

'Lying is relative.' Grief sits in the chair that Carlyle was in. She shifts uncomfortably as if he had somehow done something awful to it. 'He was telling the truth in that Lynda Kramer probably is interested. But there's no studio involvement, no development money yet. That means Roger's putting up the money. That's one of the reasons he's willing to hire you. He can pay you off in pennies.'

'How many pennies?'

'Ten thousand dollars.'

'That's more than I got to write the damn novel.'

'Half of that goes to your publisher, dear. They retained fifty percent of the film rights. You get five grand, minus my ten percent.'

Barcelona thinks of her $163 in her checking account. 'I'm not complaining. At least it's a chance to make more, isn't it?'

'Sure. If the film actually gets picked up, you'll get another hundred thousand. Split with the publisher, of course.'

'And minus your ten percent.'

'Minus my ten percent.'

'So are you saying I shouldn't do this?'

Grief laughs. 'Your naïveté is charming, Barcy.'

'What does that mean?'

'Of course you should do this. Carlyle is scummy, but he's willing to plunk down some of his own money to bring this off. That means he really does have a shot. If, by some miracle, the movie gets made, you will be the next golden child of Hollywood for about forty-eight hours. Plus your novels will fetch more money. But until we see the green of his money, it's just what is known in Hollywood as "good air."'

Barcelona finds 'good air' is heady stuff. She is excited by the prospect of making more money. She hadn't ever really considered it much because it never really seemed a possibility. Now that it is, she is surprised at how feverish she feels. She wants to go right home and start the script.

'Goodness,' Grief says, pointing at Barcelona's leg. 'You're bleeding.'

Barcelona looks down, discovers the scab on her ankle where she'd nicked herself shaving yesterday is bleeding. It is where she had earlier banged herself on Grief's desk. The blood sieves through the panty hose like a Rorschach ink blot. The pattern reminds Barcelona of a sea urchin. She wonders what that means. Nothing good probably.

Grief offers her Band-aids and peroxide, but Barcelona refuses. She returns to her car, looks around to make sure no one is coming, then rolls off her panty hose. In the first aid kit in the glove compartment she finds gauze and adhesive tape which she applies to the scab, though it has already stopped bleeding. She keeps her skirt bunched up across the tops of her thighs and feels wicked as she drives down the freeway without underpants or pantyhose, the car vent blowing cool air between her thighs. She feels her pubic hairs rustle and she begins to sing 'Get It While You Can,' imitating Janis Joplin's crushed-larynx style.

After two verses, Barcelona's throat begins to sting at the back. She can only do Janis Joplin for short periods before she becomes hoarse and unable to speak. She digs a Breathsaver out of the ashtray where she also stores loose coins, individually wrapped toothpicks, and a plastic box of mint-flavored dental floss. She begins to plan how to turn her novel into a screenplay. Lots of ideas come to her. She realizes how much of the book she will have to change, whole characters will have to be axed, entire subplots ignored. She doesn't care. She is thrilled by the challenge. She imagines Lynda Kramer shaking her hand and saying, 'This is the script I've been waiting my whole career to play.' She makes a mental list of the people she will thank on Academy Awards night.

She turns on the radio and switches the channels around. She flies past Jackson Browne, Willie Nelson, Stray Cats, Bon Jovi. None of them are right for this special moment. She thinks this is what it is like orchestrating a movie, matching music to mood. She jabs the Seek button which plays five seconds of a station before automatically moving on. It slips past Phoebe Snow, Iggy Pop, Tom Waits, The Bangles, jazz, commercials. Suddenly Janis Joplin comes on singing 'Down On Me.' This is not one of the songs she likes, but the coincidence is such that she feels it would be bad luck to skip past it. Barcelona presses a button to keep the station.

For some reason she begins to think of Darlene and her dog, Foxy. She pictures Darlene and herself watching the dog squat and shit. The dog looking over his shoulder, his face contorting with effort. She laughs at the image until a couple of tears drip down her cheek. Barcelona suddenly feels depressed. This dark mood catches her by surprise, makes the air thick and stuffy. She turns the air conditioner on.

To shake the mood, she focuses back on her screenplay, Lynda Kramer, The Ideal Woman. But mostly she concentrates on how she imagines Eric's face will look when she tells him the news this evening. More than anything else,

this breaks the sad mood and makes her smile. She begins to sing 'Get It While You Can' again, though using her own voice now.

4

Trina sits on the cracked wooden toilet seat and pees. When she is done she spreads her knees and looks down into the toilet bowl. Her urine is bright yellow, like lemon meringue. She smiles because that means her vitamins are working. Dixie has had her taking Joe Weider vitamins for six months, ever since that night she mentioned suicide. Not that she would ever, ever, ever have gone through with something so asinine; she just liked saying it. Hearing it aloud made it a real option.

She explained all that to Dixie, but all she got in response was that skeptical cop's nod and four giant jars of vitamins. Dixie is convinced there are no problems that vitamins and hard exercise can't fix. Each morning Trina gags down six rat turd pellets with a can of Diet Cherry Coke. Trina admits that now that her urine looks so bright and cheerful, it makes her more cheerful too. Visible proof of self-improvement. Trina also knows that she is bullshitting herself, but since bullshitting is what she does for a living, she admires her own technique rather than questions the results.

Trina pulls off a huge fistful of toilet paper, much more than is necessary, and dabs herself dry. Rob, her ex-husband, always complained that she used too much toilet paper. 'Half a roll,' he'd say, grinning, standing over her while she sat on the toilet. 'Half a roll to blot your pussy

41

and another three-quarters of a roll to wipe your ass. It's getting so we can't afford your bowel movements anymore.' Then he'd laugh, thumbs hooked in his back pockets. Thing was, even though he was laughing, Trina knew he was serious. 'It's not the goddamn paper,' he said. 'I make over a hundred grand a year. We can afford toilet paper.' Somehow Rob always managed to work the magic number 'hundred grand a year' into most of their arguments. A hundred thousand dollars a year was exactly twice what his father had earned the best year of his life before dying of prostrate cancer three years ago. 'It's not the paper, it's what it reveals. A wasteful attitude. Like leaving the lights on all day when you go to work. Or leaving the iron on. Which is not just wasteful, it's dangerous. What if the iron didn't shut itself off?' 'But it does shut itself off,' she'd reply. 'What if?' he's say meaningfully.

Trina stands up carefully, her panty hose bunched around her calves, and hops from the bathroom to the bed. She feels like a bound liquor store hostage who's worked her gag free and is making a break for the back door. It's uncomfortable stripping on the toilet. The oak seat has a crack the same shape as the one in the Liberty Bell and if you turn a certain way, it pinches your left butt cheek. She plops down on the edge of the bed and rolls her panty hose off her feet. The skin on her calves feels prickly from the sudden rush of fresh air. Her dress is already off and hanging from one of the posts of the four-poster bed. Each post is decorated with an assortment of her clothing. Her entire wardrobe from the previous week can be traced day by day by walking clockwise around the bed.

Trina lies back on the bed wearing only a bra. When she is alone she likes to be naked except for her bra. Her breasts are large and pendulous with white stretch marks like cartoon lightning bolts zigzagging back from the

42

nipples. The bra offers her support and hides the fault marks. Someday she plans to get them surgically reduced.

She looks at the clock radio. Five-thirty. Two hours before she meets Barcelona, Dixie, and Diva. She's relieved that she won't have to tell Barcy that she'd been mistaken about The Candidate.

Three hours ago she hadn't been so certain:

'*What*?' he'd squawked when she'd asked if they'd had sex. 'What did you say?'

'I have this memory. You and me in a steaming shower. Thing is, is it real or is it Memorex?'

'Are you kidding me?'

'No.'

He didn't even smile, he just raised one cashmere eyebrow. 'You realize how amazingly unflattering this question is? I mean especially if we'd had sex.'

'Right now, I don't really care. I'm more interested in where I parked my mind than in flattering you.'

He smiled. 'Seems to me the most prudent answer would be no, we did not shower together.'

'Don't screw around here, Cory. I'm serious.'

His face looked suddenly concerned. 'You really are serious.' He sat up, crossed his hands in a formal pose behind his desk. 'Yes, Trina, we made love in the shower of the Travel Lodge. We were going to do it again in the bed, but we had to get back to the studio.'

Trina had sighed a long relieved gust of air. She wasn't losing her mind, just small memory lapses. Fifteen minutes later, as she'd left his office, she'd been able to picture the whole event for the first time. Everything came to her at once. She could feel him inside her, his penis wide and insistent, trying to go deeper than physically possible, a gold-crazed miner searching for the Mother Lode. That's what she'd thought at the time and had started to laugh, the laughter squeezing him out.

Suddenly Trina realizes why she had been so forgetful. What is causing it. Of course, it's so obvious. She is pregnant! Her period is not due for another week but she knows without any doubt that she is pregnant. She just knows. And she knows who the father is.

'Hi,' a familiar voice says and Trina looks around the bedroom and sees no one. Then she realizes her eyes are closed. She opens them, looks at the clock. Six-fifteen. She has been sleeping for forty-five minutes. She sits up quickly and holds her head as blood rushes to her brain and makes her dizzy. She pulls the bedspread over her naked body. 'What are you doing here?' she asks without looking at him.

'Dropping Karyn off,' Rob says.

'Thanks. See you in two weeks.'

'You look good. How's it going?'

'I use too much toilet paper.'

'I should've bought stock in Charmin.' He laughs at his lame joke and she peeps an eye at him.

'See you in two weeks,' she repeats. She finds an earring on the bed that must have come out while she napped. She works it back into her lobe.

'I get the feeling you're trying to get rid of me,' he says with a smirk.

'For a guy who only makes a hundred grand a year, you catch on quick.'

His smirk disappears. Trina makes $125,000 a year now and he knows it. 'Fuck you, Trina,' he says and walks out. His new leather jacket makes crinkly sounds as his sleeves brush against his side. She hears Karyn saying good-bye to him at the front door, the door closing.

'Karyn!' Trina calls.

Karyn comes running. She jumps on the bed next to Trina. 'You made him mad again.'

'Sue me.'

44

Karyn looks at her mother's nakedness, the forest of clothes surrounding the bed. 'This is gross, Mom. It's like a bear cave.'

'I need you to keep me in order.'

'You need a maid.'

'Maybe I'll hire you for the job.'

Karyn tilts her nose in the air in a snooty pose. 'Speak to my agent.'

They both laugh. Trina hugs Karyn to her. Karyn resists hugging at first, part of the game she plays. Then she gives in and hugs back, her body collapsing against Trina, her head falling just so in the same place on Trina's shoulder it has for twelve years. Trina imagines the shoulder bone to be slightly curved in that spot, a permanent sway to cradle Karyn's head. Karyn's left ear is next to Trina's nose and Trina can smell Karyn's special scent, a scent so light yet earthy it reminds her of some exotic Chinese tea. Blindfolded and bound, Trina could sniff Karyn out of a crowd of a thousand little girls.

'You'll be late,' Karyn says, breaking away.

The hug is over too soon but Trina knows better than to try to recapture her. If she does, Karyn will be stiff and impatient and that feels worse than anything else in the world to Trina.

'What'd you do in school today?' Trina asks.

'Stuff.'

'What kind of stuff?'

'You know, school stuff.'

'Oh, you mean useless cramming of information that can't possibly have any relevance to anyone in the whole world?'

Karyn nods. 'That's what I said. School stuff.'

Trina makes a parental face and Karyn giggles victoriously. Neither ever grows tired of this game.

Trina stands up, aware that Karyn is studying her body.

Sometimes she catches Karyn staring at her boobs with something like fear, as if they were an affliction, giant tumors Karyn prays would never curse her. The rest of Trina's body is relatively normal. Her ass isn't as trim as Dixie's or Barcy's, but not as jiggly as Diva's. Her legs are legs. Not thin, but not fat either. Her waist isn't exactly skinny, but it curves in appropriately. She has what men call the voluptuous look. She thinks of herself as overripe.

'Mom?'

Trina walks into the bathroom and starts the tub water running. 'Hmmm.'

'What's affectation mean?'

'How was it used?' She asks this because Karyn often asks the meaning of words but sometimes mispronounces them. She might mean affection, affliction, asphyxiation.

'Someone at school said my name was an affectation.'

'Why?'

'Because it had a "y" where there should be an ".""

'What'd you tell them?'

Karyn hesitates and Trina knows she is trying to think of a lie. 'Come on, the truth. What'd you tell them?'

'To eat shit and die.'

Trina laughs. 'Did you tell your father that?'

'No.'

'Good.' Instantly Trina feels a little pain in her side that quickly vanishes. Nothing more than an invisible poke really. It is the feeling of loss she gets when she wants to share something funny with Rob but remembers she can't. The pain is always in the same place as if there is a physical scar there where they'd been surgically separated when divorced. 'Karyn with a "y" is an old and revered name with a long and honorable tradition. You were named after a princess from Austria who had three blue dogs and twelve red cats. All the people of Austria loved her madly.

46

One day this handsome knight rides into the village—'

Karyn isn't listening. 'I told them that Lynda Kramer had a "y" where she should have an "i" so I could have one too. Did you name me after Lynda Kramer?' She says this hopefully.

Even though, according to *People* magazine, Lynda Kramer was an unknown theater major at Yale when Karyn was born, Trina nods yes because that will make more sense to the kids at school than an Austrian princess with blue dogs and red cats.

Actually, Karyn's 'y' *is* an affectation. Rob's idea to make her special. He is in advertising and decided on his daughter's name the same way he would a product. 'Research shows people prefer products that begin with K. You know Keds, the sneakers? What's that word mean? Nothing. They were originally going to be called Peds, you know, like peds for feet. But market research found out the public prefers "Ks".' Trina hadn't argued much because of the difficulty she'd had with her own name, Trina Bedford, Jr. That had been her mother's idea, the junior, because her mother thought that would help Trina be taken more seriously in business. Her mother was, still is, a vice-president at Prudential Insurance. Trina had kept her maiden name of Bedford even after marrying Rob Barre, so she could keep the junior. Her mother had been right. People did take her more seriously.

Trina walks into the bathroom, and turns on the water. After the tub is filled, she shrugs off her bra, and climbs in.

The ledge around the tub looks like an explosion in a chemistry lab. Spilled puddles of cream rinse and different colored shampoos polka dot the white surface. Three soap slivers thin as credit cards are glued to the tub. A brown plastic scalp massager clogged with clumps of gnarled black hair sits like a furry mutant, perched on the hot water knob. Once again she is reminded that she needs to hire a new cleaning person.

'Can I wash your hair?' Karyn asks, kneeling beside the tub.

'I'm not washing it right now. I'm already running late.'

'Boy, that should shock them.'

'Smart ass punk,' she says, flicking water from her fingertips into Karyn's face.

Karyn giggles, a sound so sweet and moving, Trina feels tears in her eyes. She dunks her hair under the water and hands Karyn the aloe vera shampoo. 'Wash away, kid. Go crazy.'

Karyn's fingers dig into Trina's hair like hungry worms nibbling at her scalp. Occasionally Karyn scrubs too hard and yanks a hair or two out at the root. Trina helps. 'Hey, you want me to be bald.'

'Yeah. Daddy's getting bald, you can be bald together.'

There was a time Trina wouldn't have minded even baldness if it meant they'd be together. That was the old her. The pre-vitamin her. Before her urine became cheerful. Now she closes her eyes and leans her head back against the tub. Karyn's fingers dig and claw with such intensity that she wonders if she might be bleeding. She opens her eyes and a drop of shampoo leaks in and stings her. She doesn't rinse it, she doesn't move. She doesn't want to disturb Karyn's concentration.

Her scalp tingles and a shiver works it way down her spine and legs to the tips of her feet. The shiver is icy despite the steaming bathwater. The feel of Karyn's fingers washing her hair is the best definition of happiness she can think of. She thinks about telling Karyn that she is pregnant. Sharing her own delight. Maybe she should wait until she's had the medical tests. Maybe she should test the waters on Barcy, Dixie, and Diva tonight at dinner. She tries to imagine their reactions, the expressions on their faces. Diva and Dixie will be enthusiastic, offer up toasts. Barcy will ask probing questions, reveal no emotion.

'We'll see,' she says aloud.

'You're mumbling again, Mom,' Karyn says and digs her fingers deeper into Trina's hair.

'The miniseries of my life, kiddo,' Trina says, closing her eyes.

5

As Barcelona approaches Eric's street, three military helicopters appear ahead rising up over the horizon. Framed by the setting sun, to her they seem frozen in the sky like fat preening flies. Sunset flickers off their blades. She is reminded of *Apocalypse Now* and Martin Sheen lying in bed drunk, listening to The Doors sing 'This Is the End.' She begins to hum the song, thinking this is appropriate music for her visit to Eric's house.

The helicopters are from the nearby El Toro marine base where the young pilots are being trained. Every day these drab green helicopters circle over Orange County, usually in loud packs like growling dogs. There have been several crashes lately and yesterday Barcelona read in the newspaper that there will be a federal probe of the company manufacturing the helicopters. The manufacturer in question is also in Orange County and residents are afraid that the investigation will force the plant, which employs thousands of people, to be closed down. Residents are also afraid that a defective helicopter will crash through their roof and drop into their living rooms. Residents aren't sure which to fear most.

Barcelona is not so much afraid of the helicopters as she is of how crazy people around here have been acting over them lately. Ever since the *Twilight Zone* crash that killed Vic Morrow and those children, everyone has been nervous about helicopters. Last month 'Sixty Minutes' did a story about the frighteningly high crash rate of emergency medical helicopters. The pilots interviewed blamed their long shifts, and described how they would fall asleep while flying. On the news there have been numerous reports of mysterious bullet holes in the police helicopters from random snipers, kids they think. Last week two police helicopters chasing a teenage car thief accidentally crashed into each other and both pilots were killed. They've charged the teenager with murder. Fear of the sky has made people vindictive.

Right now Barcelona is pleased to see the three helicopters because they add drama to the moment. Good production values. 'Production values' is a phrase she picked up that afternoon from a book about writing scripts she bought at the mall. She's not sure exactly what the phrase means, but she knows these helicopters escorting her to Eric's house have something to do with it.

She is on Eric's street now and sees the security gate to the parking lot of his apartment complex. The black iron gate is wide open. Barcelona carefully guides the Geezemobile in and drives around the perimeter of the buildings looking for a parking space large enough for her car. The huge car rolls over each speed bump with a mysterious rattle and Barcelona hopes this means the car is finally dying. She wants to get rid of this albatross and buy a sleek new car, preferably Japanese, but this is the only thing she has of her grandmother's and feels compelled to keep it until, like her grandmother, it dies too. The only change she's made on the car was to put in a new stereo, and she feels guilty about that.

Barcelona eventually finds a parking space not just for compact cars. Even so it is a tight squeeze, her car sucking up all the room between the cars on either side. The driver's door opens just wide enough for her to struggle out, banging her ankle on the edge of the door. It is the same ankle she'd cut shaving, the one she'd banged in Grief's office. She stoops over, peels down her lime green sock. A tiny pinpoint of bright blood peeks through the crusty scab. She pulls the sock back up.

She hurries through the apartment complex, past the giant palm trees and spreading ferns, the loud streams and brooks that wander throughout the place. Over a thick bush she sees a lean young man in a tight Speedo bathing suit dipping his toe in the Jacuzzi. A girl laughs, but Barcelona can't see her because of the foliage. The laugh sounds teasing, definitely sexual. Even from here she can see the outline of the head of his semi-erect penis through his skimpy bathing suit. She thinks of Eric's penis. 'Eight inches of tempered blue steel,' he used to say in a mock-Bogart voice, standing naked in front of her, aiming it like a gun. 'Die, Commie bastard,' he'd say. 'Rat-a-tat-tat.' And she'd grab it hard and yank and they'd both fall to the bed laughing.

Barcelona thinks this is a bad time to be thinking about Eric's penis. Someone else is yanking his tempered blue steel now. Luna.

She decides it is a good thing that she has purposely timed her arrival so that she has only twenty minutes to spare before she must leave to meet Trina, Dixie, and Diva. She forces herself not to picture him standing there, holding it, pointing it at her. Rat-a-tat-tat. She notices her hand has curled involuntarily as if it were holding him now. She brushes her palm against her jeans.

Up the stairs, second floor. She knocks. The door opens almost immediately.

'Hey,' he says. There is an awkward space after 'Hey' because he used to always say, 'Hey, baby' or 'Hey, honey' or 'Hey, sweetheart.' Now it's just 'Hey' and those two empty syllables are choked off like a smothered baby.

'Hey yourself,' she says and enters.

They hug clumsily, though she thinks it is she who is clumsy because she is unsure where her hands should go. He seems perfectly comfortable holding her close, then releasing her with a peck on the cheek. He used to hold her, squeeze her ass, then release her. His hands now, however, remain politely above waist level.

'Where's Luna?' She had promised herself she would not be the first to mention the name, but somehow it slipped out.

'She'll be here any minute. She has a late class tonight.'

'Oh? What class?'

'The Women Followers of Freud. An unfortunate title, but the course is pretty solid. Ruth Mack Brunswick, Anna Freud, of course, Helen Deutsch—'

'Melanie Klein, I would imagine.'

'Sure, the English School.'

Barcelona nods. She is comfortable with academic subjects. She is knowledgeable, widely read, remembers almost everything she's ever learned. Discussing psychology is much easier than thinking about eight inches of tempered blue steel.

'Drink?' he asks.

'Alcohol?'

'White wine. A buck-a-gallon brand. Luna drinks it.'

'Pass.' She looks around the living room. Though she has never been here before, everything looks familiar. It is small, dimly lighted with one table lamp and one floor lamp. The furniture is old and beaten, longing for retirement. Against the wall is a cinder-block-and-particle-board bookcase jammed with scholarly textbooks on psychology, anthropology, language. Barthes's and Lévi-Strauss's names are prominent on many of the book spines. The room looks just like the one they used to live in at graduate school. It is a student's apartment. She supposes that is appropriate since Eric is technically still a student, though he is thirty-five. Barcelona owns a town house in Irvine, a planned community eight miles south of here. In Irvine, people pick up their dog's shit immediately or pay a fine to the Homeowner's Association. People in Irvine have overhead track lights so the rooms are always bright. Barcelona is not embarrassed that she likes bright rooms and no dog shit.

'So what was so important?' she asks.

'Boy, you get right to it, don't you. Enough with the pleasantries.'

'I'm meeting Trina and the others for dinner in a few minutes.'

'Ah, the bimonthly meeting of the Gourmet Mafia.'

He is smiling, but she recognizes the disapproving tone. He doesn't think her friends are smart enough for her. He wants her to join Mensa as he did. She taps her watch and says, 'I don't want to be late.'

'I just thought you should know,' he says, not finishing the sentence, walking over to the Formica counter that separates the tiny kitchenette from the living room. He picks up a bound typewritten manuscript, hefts it lovingly, and hands it to her. 'It's done. Finally.'

'Oh, Eric,' she says, truly pleased. She smiles, kisses his cheek. 'That's wonderful. My God, you must feel so good!'

He laughs. 'Well, I've been working on this bastard for five years. At first I used to imagine how good it would feel to have written a brilliant scholarly text lauded by experts. After a couple years I imagined how good it would feel to have written a text mildly appreciated by an adoring few. These last few months, though, I just imagined what it would feel like to be finished. Just done.'

'Well? How does it feel?'

He grins. 'Good. Very fucking good.'

'Is this my copy to keep?'

'It's the least I can do. You did a lot of the research for me. If it wasn't for you, I'm not sure I'd have finished it.'

Barcelona is embarrassed by his honest expression of gratitude. It makes her feel shoddy and mean after her earlier thoughts. She looks away from him and studies his manuscript. The title is *Toward a Semiotics of Battered Women*. This is his doctoral dissertation, five years in the making. The typing looks very professional. Good production values.

Eric's field of study is somewhat complex: the use of language in violent households. He believes that from studying the patterns of speech, violence can be predicted. It doesn't matter what the educational backgrounds are of the household members, or the extent of the vocabulary, simply by the juxtapositioning of certain words, images, phrases, the potential for violence can be uncovered. He makes a very convincing case and for that reason has always been the darling of his professors. He is also extremely handsome, black hair and lean rodeo cowboy's body, which has always made him the darling of women. But Eric doesn't exploit his good looks, Barcelona admits, he doesn't even seem conscious of them.

'Can you believe it?' he asks. 'Finished.'

'Hard to believe.'

'I still have to defend the damned thing in front of my committee, but Dr. Goulart says it's only a formality. I'm in. Dr. Eric Jasper Fontaine.'

'I'd lose the Jasper,' she says, then kisses his cheek again. 'That's great, Eric. It really is.'

Eric will now get his Ph.D. in psychology. He finished all his course work five years ago and has been struggling with the dissertation ever since. To support himself, he works full time at a refuge home for battered women. He counsels, comforts, helps them find jobs. He has also been instrumental in establishing day-care centers within several

55

local companies. Over his left eye is a thin white scar that cleaves his black eyebrow. He received the scar when an angry husband tried to drag his wife out of the refuge home. Eric wouldn't let him take her and the man clubbed Eric with a stapler from the desk. In return, Eric smacked the man in the face with a heavy tape dispenser, breaking the man's nose and slicing open his lip with the serrated edge that cuts the tape. The woman stayed, the man left. Eric gives them books to read, suggests composers, rents foreign videotapes for them. The women there love Eric.

Barcelona hates to admit it, but Eric is a better feminist than she is. They espouse the same principles, but he does something about them.

She turns the page and sees her name. This is the dedication page. It says: 'To Barcelona, without whom this would not be possible. And to Luna, without whom this would not be valuable.' She is both flattered and insulted. Better not to be named at all than to share billing with Luna. In her book on screenwriting, she read a passage about screenwriters who have unwillingly shared billing and have had to go to arbitration to settle who actually wrote the produced script. Perhaps she could do that here. Who deserves most of the credit for helping Eric finish this manuscript, Barcelona, who encouraged, flattered, critiqued, and researched for four of the five years? Or Luna-come-lately, who has only been in his life for the last year, and at twenty years old, is still too young to have been much help on the actual manuscript?

'Well?' Eric says, grinning happily as Barcelona stares at the dedication page.

She looks up at him, his boyish smile beaming, and realizes he has no idea that she is hurt. He thinks only of the compliment he has given her. For all his work with women, all his empathy and support, he is finally insensitive to what goes on deep inside. He doesn't see that their six years of living together has some priority. Although they'd separated out of mutual agreement, Barcelona feels that his meeting and marrying Luna within three months of their split-up, trivializes their former relationship. Especially since during those six years he'd been as adamant as she about the faults of the institution of marriage.

Barcelona has seen Luna only once, at a distance, in the shopping mall. Eric and Luna were eating at Forty Carrots, splitting frozen yogurt and fruit, both reading and discussing a magazine spread out on the table in front of them. It was the same thing she and Eric had often done. From where she stood, she could see only that Luna was young and pretty, with long black frizzy hair and thick pouty lips. Bee-stung lips. She had been tempted to walk over and join them, but was able to control such high school instincts. Barely.

'It's lovely, Eric,' Barcelona says, closing the cover. 'I'll read it later.'

'Let me know what you think. Your opinion means a lot to me.'

'I will.' She makes a show of looking at her watch again. 'Better be heading out. The gang's waiting.'

'You can spare a couple of minutes.' He sits on the sofa and gestures to the nearby chair. 'What have you been up to? How's the balancing art of writing and teaching?'

Barcelona knows she should walk out the door now, but her feet move over to the chair and her butt sinks down into the too-soft cushion. The chair smells greasy, like a combination of the last five hundred meals cooked in the kitchen. Kitchenette. 'I'm still teaching, of course. Can't give that up.'

'Still power-crazed, huh?' He laughs.

She smiles, loads her bomb, sights, fires: 'And the writing is going well. In fact, I was just hired to do a screenplay of *Live Wires* for Lynda Kramer.'

He nods, but not in an impressed way. More like a professor whose prize student has given an answer that is close, but not exactly what he wants. 'Just be careful of priorities.'

'What's that supposed to mean?'

'You're still a teacher first. You have a responsibility to those kids.'

'Don't tell me my responsibilities, Eric. I know what I am. I am a teacher and a writer. Not one over the other. A combination. Teacher, slash, writer. Like being both a woman and an American.'

'Relax, Barcy, I didn't mean anything. I'm just talking about balance, that's all. You don't always have to control everything.' His gaze is calm, benign, that of a therapist. 'Will you be using your own name?'

'I always use my own name.'

'You know what I mean. Your full name. So readers will know you're a woman.'

This is an old argument between them, but she falls into the trap anyway. 'What the hell difference does it make, Eric, as long as they like my work?'

'Who are you fooling, Barcy?'

'It's a business decision, nothing more. Don't try to turn it into a moral issue.'

'Don't you think forcing yourself to conceal your sex, hide your true self, is a moral issue?'

She ignores his question. 'Have you even read *Live Wires*?'

He looks away toward the kitchen, then looks back, eyes fixed directly on hers. 'You know I don't have the time for that kind of stuff. I have serious reading to do.'

'Ah, so my stuff isn't serious.'

'That's not what I said.'

'That's exactly what you said.'

He shakes his head. 'You're trying to turn this around,

58

Barcy. I meant that I don't have much time for recreational reading anymore. Just because you feel some guilt at having wasted your talents on genre writing—'

'Die, Commie bastard,' she says, holding her hand out the way he used to when playfully aiming his dick. 'Rat-a-tat-tat.'

'What's that supposed to mean?' He is angry, flushed.

'Figure it out, Eric. You're the psychobabblist.'

'Don't play games, Barcy.'

'Then don't use your education like your dick. It's a tool, not a weapon.'

He stands up, walks slowly to the kitchen, jerks open the refrigerator, and leans his head inside. He returns with a can of V-8 juice. 'Maybe we should drop it.'

'Maybe.'

The front door opens and a young girl with long frizzy hair and bee-stung lips stands in the doorway taking her backpack off. She is younger-looking and more beautiful than Barcelona remembered.

'Ah, honey,' Eric says. 'Barcy, you've never met my wife.' The way he emphasizes 'my wife' shows he wants to get one last dig in. 'Honey, this is Barcelona. Barcy, Luna.'

'Hello,' Barcelona says.

'Hi.' Luna smiles with what appears to be genuine pleasure. She tosses her backpack on the floor and rushes over to shake Barcelona's hand. 'I've read all your books, you know.'

'Oh?' Barcelona is surprised. She looks over at Eric, but he is looking at something in the distance, pretending he hasn't heard.

'God, yes. I started reading you when I was in high school. Way before I met Eric. I used to read them in the cafeteria during lunch. I just love them. I don't mean to gush, it's just that I've asked Eric a dozen times if he would introduce me to you, but he never gets around to it.'

Barcelona doesn't know what to say. She says, 'Ah.'

'I don't want you think I'm one of those sci-fi nuts, like a Trekkie or something. God, that must sound awfully smug. Forget it. Let me start over.' She plops down on the sofa next to Eric. Eric reaches for her as if to kiss her, but she slides away as if she didn't see him. Barcelona realizes Luna has done this so as not to embarrass their guest. It is a compassionate gesture and Barcelona appreciates it. Eric leans back with an annoyed expression.

'Isn't it shitty,' Luna says, 'the way they brainwash you about art? What is and isn't art. Speaking of which, I'd talk to somebody about the cover art on your books. God.'

'I know.' Barcelona nods.

'When my girlfriend first gave me one of your books to read, I took one look at the cover with this naked nympho with a sword straddling some dragon's tail—'

'*The Beauty Circuit.*'

'Yes! And I told her no way will I read this sexist shit. But she made me promise to give it a try. I read it that night, cover to cover. Great stuff.'

'You wrote that your first year teaching, didn't you, Barcy?' Eric asks. 'When we had that apartment over on Hudson Street.'

'Yes. You thought the book was too long. Too much plot.'

'That's not what I'd said at all. Writers have such selective memories. I said the characters did too much running around without thinking about what their actions meant.'

Luna laughs. 'That's the point, Eric. Not everyone analyzes everything they do first. Then they have to suffer the consequences. Like life.'

'Like some people's lives,' he says.

She laughs again, the sound deep and throaty like a lawn mower. 'God, Barcy, was he this bad a snob when you lived with him?'

'I think he's gotten worse,' Barcelona says.

Eric seems to enjoy the attention now. 'Sure, pick on poor Eric. Easy target.'

'Deserving target,' Luna says, patting his knee affectionately.

Outside the front door, someone screams in terror. The voice is so high and crazy that Barcelona can't tell whether the screamer is a man or woman, young or old. 'Help! My God, please help!' the screamer cries. 'Help me!'

'That's Mrs. Finney,' Luna says, running to the front door. Eric is right behind her as they rush outside. 'Mrs. Finney, what's wrong?' Luna calls down the stairs.

'Please, oh please. Please . . .' she sobs. 'Please help.'

Luna and Eric run down the wooden steps. Barcelona can feel the apartment shake with each step. She goes outside, sees Luna and Eric following a plump woman in her sixties. The woman is wearing a pink quilted bathrobe and no slippers. Barcelona also runs down the stairs and follows after them, not certain why she is tagging along but knowing whatever they will find will not be pleasant. No one says 'please help' the way that woman did until it's too late to help.

The three of them round a corner ahead and Barcelona loses them in the lush foliage. When she rounds the same corner they have disappeared. She looks around. She can see the Jacuzzi now, but the young man with the tight trunks is gone; so is the giggling girl. The Jacuzzi is empty, but she can see the steam rising.

'Please! Please help him!'

Barcelona turns and sees the open door under the stairway. She hurries toward it and enters the apartment. She smells cat urine and something sweet and sour, like baked ham with pineapple rings.

Somewhere down the hall the old woman is wailing, her words incomprehensible again. Barcelona takes a deep breath and plunges into the hallway. The smell is beginning to bother her. She enters the bedroom. The bed is neatly made, with a handmade quilt covering it. A fluffy calico cat sits on the bed licking her tail. She takes long deliberate licks, as if it were an ice cream cone. The sobbing and wailing don't disturb her.

'What's happened?' Barcelona asks. She sees Eric holding the old woman by the shoulders, comforting her, murmuring soothingly to her. Their backs block the doorway to the bathroom, but she can see Luna on the floor, bent over something. Barcelona walks toward the bathroom. She looks over the old woman's pink-quilted shoulder and gasps.

An old man with cottony tufts of white hair lies sprawled facedown on the floor. He is naked and wet. One leg is bent against the tub sticking straight up into the air. One hand flops into the kitty litter box next to the toilet. Green pellets stick to his arm like candy sprinkles.

'Get her out of here,' Luna says.

Barcelona backs up a step, thinking Luna means her. But Eric guides the old sobbing woman into the bedroom and sits her down on the bed. The cat looks up, then jumps off the bed and runs down the hall.

'We were getting ready to go out for dinner,' Mrs. Finney says. Her speech is slow and awkward, her eyes unfocused. 'Henry likes the Malibu Chicken at The Sizzler. I usually get the soup and salad bar.'

Barcelona looks over at the straight-back chair by the closet. Slacks, a shirt, underpants, socks, belt, and shoes are neatly laid out awaiting Henry.

'It's my fault,' Mrs. Finney says, sobbing again. She burrows her face into Eric's chest. He pats her gray head.

'It's nobody's fault, an accident,' he says.

'No, no, no,' she says, shaking her head, though her face is still pressed against Eric's shirt. She looks up into his eyes. 'My fault. I took my bath first. I always took mine first, then left the water in for Henry. I always take so long with my hair.' She looks away, embarrassed, then stares at Barcelona. Until that moment, Barcelona had felt invisible. Now the old woman speaks directly to Barcelona, ignoring Eric. 'I took two towels to dry off. I always take two towels. One for my body, one for my hair. Always two.'

Barcelona nods, glances into the bathroom, sees Luna flipping the pale bloated body over. There are feces and urine on the floor, running down the side of the tub, down the man's legs. Luna arcs the man's neck, pinches his nostrils closed, then places her pouty bee-stung lips over his. She breathes into his mouth.

'Two towels,' Mrs. Finney says again, her voice trailing off as if she'd lost her train of thought. But her eyes stay on Barcelona, bright and glittery from the tears. 'After I dried my hair off, I laid the towel on the counter next to the sink. I always do that. Right next to the sink. I came out here to pick out Henry's clothes. He's color-blind, you know. Can't match anything. If it weren't for me, he'd dress like a circus clown.'

Luna is still breathing into the man's mouth. She looks up at Eric. 'Call the goddamn ambulance, Eric!'

Eric looks around the bedroom. 'Where's your phone, Mrs. Finney?' He sounds calm, but Barcelona is surprised to see that he is so shaken.

'In the kitchen. We can only afford one phone.'

Eric nods to Barcelona, who takes his place on the bed, looping her arm around the old woman. Luna is still breathing into the man's mouth, counting, breathing again. There is a string of spittle hanging from Luna's lower lip and Barcelona wonders if it is hers or the old man's.

Mrs. Finney doesn't pay any attention to what Luna is doing. She has already accepted Henry's death. Now she must tell her story, that is all that she has left. Her story. 'Usually there are three towels in the bathroom. Two for me, one for Henry. He only needs one. He never towels his hair because he says it damages the follicles. Maybe he's right, I don't know. But today there were only two towels. The third one was in the wash. Henry always wipes his mouth on it after he brushes his teeth. I tell him to rinse off first, but he just goes over and wipes all that white foam on the towel. Then it dries and gets hard. I don't know about you, but I don't want to put a towel like that to my face, would you?'

Barcelona thinks this is a rhetorical question, but when Mrs. Finney continues to stare at her with a questioning look, she finally says, 'No, I wouldn't.'

'Me neither. So there are only two towels. One lying on the counter, and one wrapped around me out here in the bedroom. Henry is ready to get out of the bath, he doesn't see a towel, he starts hollering at me for a towel. I tell him to wait a minute and I'll bring him a fresh one from the linen closet. Not that we're poor people with only three towels in the house. But you know Henry, so impatient. He must have taken one step out of the tub, gotten a hold of the towel by the sink and yanked it toward him.' She does a yanking motion, banging her elbow into Barcelona's rib. She doesn't apologize. 'Underneath the towel was my curling iron, which I was waiting for to heat up. The towel must have snagged the iron and pulled it into the tub.'

Eric returns to the bedroom. He is holding the calico cat in his arms, petting and comforting it the way he had Mrs. Finney. 'The ambulance is on its way.'

Luna stands up, shakes her head. 'Sorry, Mrs. Finney.'

Mrs. Finney looks at her, then down at Henry. She starts to sob again and Barcelona hugs her close. She can feel the woman's tears soaking through her blouse, stinging her skin. Mrs. Finney stops crying. 'I'm sorry,' she says, wiping ineffectually at the damp spot on Barcelona's blouse.

'No, don't be,' Barcelona says.

The cat jumps out of Eric's arms and runs into the bathroom, walking across Henry Finney's wet chest to hop into the litter box. She squats, pees, scratches the box, hops back out, scattering green pellets from her paws like BBs.

'Nature calls,' Mrs. Finney says. Barcelona isn't sure whether she's referring to Henry or the cat.

'You were very good in there,' Barcelona tells Luna as they walk back toward the apartment. Police and paramedics are in Mrs. Finney's apartment. Luna has called Mrs. Finney's niece who is on her way over now. 'I was very impressed.'

'Luna is pre-med,' Eric says.

'Oh, a doctor.'

Luna shrugs. 'I don't know. Maybe. Right now I'm not feeling too keen on medicine.'

Eric slips his arm around her and kisses her cheek. She leans wearily into him. 'You handled yourself very well, sweetheart. I have to admit, even I was a little frazzled by the sight of Henry lying there like that. Christ.'

'Would you like to stay for dinner, Barcy?' Luna asks.

'Thanks, no. I'm supposed to be meeting some friends. I'm already late.'

'Another time,' Luna says.

'Sure.' Barcelona hurries away. As she rounds a rather lush and fierce-looking bush, she glances over her shoulder and sees Eric kissing Luna. He is squeezing her ass.

6

Barcelona hurries through the dimly lighted restaurant drawing stares from several of the startled diners. There is less light in here than in Eric's gloomy apartment and she has to grope her way among the tables, diners, and waiters. In her hurry, she knocks her sore ankle against the edge of a booth. Sudden pain blooms through her leg. She can feel the crusty scab fold back under the sock. But she hates being late worse than pain and rushes ahead, determined to at least shave a few seconds off her tardiness.

'Sorry I'm late,' she says, still ten feet from the table. Trina and Diva and Dixie are already sipping red wine, their menus open in front of them. A half-empty carafe sits in the middle of the table. Her place setting is undisturbed, the pink linen napkin folded like a tulip still nested in the clean wineglass. Barcelona pulls her chair out and sits, grabbing the napkin and spreading it across her lap. 'A guy next door to Eric electrocuted himself in the bathtub.'

'Jesus,' Diva says.

'Never mind that,' Trina says. 'Let's stick with the important matters first. Sign this.' Trina hands Barcelona a pink linen napkin. There is writing on the napkin in bold black letters from a eyeliner pencil: WE THE UNDERSIGNED ATTEST TO THE FACT THAT ON THIS DAY, THURSDAY, APRIL 23, BARCELONA EVANS LEE WAS NOT ONLY LATE, BUT LATER THAN

TRINA BEDFORD, JR., BY MORE THAN FIFTEEN MINUTES. The three of them had each signed it with elaborate flourishes. It looks like the Constitution.

Barcelona takes the offered mascara waud from Trina and quickly signs her name. 'Okay,' she says, handing the napkin back to Trina, 'but I'm not paying for the napkin.'

'Neither am I.' Trina winks, stuffing it quickly into her purse.

'Unh uh, Trina,' Dixie says. 'Don't force me to make an off-duty arrest. You wouldn't like prison life. No henna to cover the gray hairs.'

'Whoa, look who's talking.' Trina reaches over and lifts a lock of Dixie's sandy-blond hair. 'These roots were made for walking.'

They all laugh, including Dixie.

Diva laughs too but then says, 'I don't get it.'

'The song,' Dixie explains. 'Remember? "These Boots Are Made for Walking."'

'Yeah, Nancy Sinatra. But what's that got to do with roots?'

'Jesus, Diva,' Trina says and shakes her head.

'She means I bleach my hair so often that the roots are so brittle they could walk.'

'I didn't know you bleached your hair.'

'I don't,' Dixie says.

Diva frowns. 'Then I still don't get it.'

Barcelona pours the red wine into her glass. 'Ridicule and humiliation. It's a male bonding technique.'

Trina nods. 'Yeah, it's like in the movies when two guys beat the shit out of each other over nothing, then afterwards start laughing their asses off and are instantly best buddies.'

'Yeah, their faces all swollen and bloody and they toast each other with beer.'

'A beer sounds good,' Diva says.

'I heard this joke today over at City Hall,' Trina says. 'Why does a woman have a cunt?'

'I heard this one,' Dixie says.

'I haven't,' Diva says. 'Why?'

'So men will talk to them.'

'I heard it a little differently,' Dixie says. 'I heard it was so men wouldn't put a bounty on women.'

'My version is dumb,' Trina says. 'Yours is ugly.'

'Yeah,' Dixie agrees, 'I heard it at the station. Either a cop or a felon, I can't remember.'

Barcelona laughs and realizes how happy and comfortable she is right now. Her anxiety about Eric and Luna is practically gone. Her depression over the old man's bizarre electrocution is waning. Her nervousness over the screenplay job is melting away.

'You notice how most of the jokes you hear lately are about AIDS?' Trina asks.

'That's sick,' Diva says. 'I never hear any jokes about AIDS.'

'People don't tell you jokes because you never get them.'

Diva nods. 'That's true. Makes me feel stupid.'

'You're not stupid,' Dixie says. 'The jokes are.'

Barcelona looks at Dixie, impressed by how supportive she is at all times. It's almost eerie.

'But it's weird how jokes go in these cycles,' Trina says. 'Remember all the dead baby jokes when we were kids? What's the difference between a truckload of babies and a truckload of bowling balls? You can't pitchfork bowling balls. Jokes like that.'

'I remember all the Polish jokes a few years ago,' Diva says.

'And now the AIDS jokes. And condom jokes. I heard a bunch of condom jokes the other day from Senator Grodin's press secretary, Herman Fordham. Why did the guy put condoms over his ears?'

'Over his ears?' Diva repeats, confused.

'Because he didn't want to get hearing AIDS.'

Barcelona blows a raspberry, Dixie laughs. Diva says, 'I get that one. It's not funny, but I get it.'

'I heard a combination Polish and condom joke,' Dixie says. 'A Polish cop I worked with on Vice told it to me. Why did the Pollack put ice in his condom?' Pause. 'He wanted to make the swelling go down.'

They all laugh.

'Fine,' Barcelona says, still giggling, 'now we're bigots.'

Barcelona pours wine in everyone's glass, finishing the carafe. She thinks of Eric squeezing Luna's ass the way he used to squeeze hers. She wonders if he also draws cartoon characters on Luna's breasts the way he did with her. Somehow he always managed to work the nipple in as the focal point of the drawing. Bugs Bunny chewing a carrot, the tip of which was her nipple. Elmer Fudd chasing Daffy Duck, Daffy's tail with a target painted on, the bull's-eye Barcelona's erect nipple. If it wasn't already erect, he'd lick it erect, 'for that 3-D effect.'

'Are you ready to order, ladies?' the waiter asks. He is young, mid-twenties, with blond hair moussed into a curly pile on top of his head like a plate of thin noodles. He smiles with confidence, like a gigolo. He knows he is handsome and he also thinks he is charming. He is obviously anxious to practice this charm on the older, more mature women at his table. They run into this often. Boys who act as if they are doing these elderly women a favor by lavishing attention, flooding them with sexual vibrations. He smiles at Barcelona and she smiles back because she knows Trina will not let this boy's smugness pass.

'I think we're ready, aren't we, *ladies*,' Trina says. She lingers on the word ladies.

'What will you have?' the waiter asks, slowly removing

his pen from his jacket, as if writing it down were a mere formality required by the management. A man like himself would never forget a word spoken by such women as these. His smile roves around the table like a sniffing dog, his eyes finally resting on Trina, eyes flicking off her chest to her eyes, not wanting to seem obvious. Poor baby, Barcelona thinks, everyone looks at Trina's chest first, even women. Especially women. It is the perfect chest, the size and shape that every magazine, movie, novel, and dreamy-eyed man ever described as perfect from the moment they knew what breasts were.

'We'd like more wine,' Trina says.

'Of course,' he agrees, writing. 'And an appetizer perhaps? May I suggest some Calamari Marinati or the Lumache Borgogno? The former is, of course, marinated calamari on a bed of lettuce. The latter is our own escargots with garlic butter and white wine. Delicious, ladies.' He smiles broadly now, really rolling, thoroughly enjoying his part.

Trina looks up at him, her smile lovely and patient. 'You're a very good-looking young man,' she says.

The waiter's smile widens, but his face reddens a little. He is clearly embarrassed. This is not how the game is played, not so overtly.

'High school sports, right?' Trina continues.

The waiter is confused. His smiles winches down a few turns. 'Baseball, some football.'

'And you plan to go to college when you graduate?'

'I am in college,' he says stiffly. 'Part time at Sand Coast College.'

Barcelona, feeling embarrassed for him, pretends to wipe her mouth with her napkin to hide her face. Diva, too, pretends to drink, though Barcelona can see her lips are closed tight against the tilted glass to keep from

70

laughing. Only Trina and Dixie stare directly at the waiter, both with pleasant but steady expressions.

'You know, young man,' Trina continues. 'I'd hate to see a boy like you, his life ahead of him, making any mistake that might jeopardize his whole life.'

'What are you talking about?'

'About serving liquor, young man. You do know that you must be eighteen to serve alcoholic beverages?'

'Of course.' His voice is a ragged blend of annoyance and fear. Trina's voice is authoritarian, hinting at secrets she knows. 'I'm twenty-four,' he blurts out.

'You can prove that to Officer Cooper here, can't you?' Trina nods at Dixie, who flashes her badge from her purse.

'Hell, yes.' The waiter reaches for his wallet, drops his pen into the basket of garlic bread sticks on the table, fishes the pen out, drops his order pad, picks that up. Finally he has his wallet out and flashes the driver's license at Dixie and Trina. They study it, look at the photo then up at him, back and forth like that a few times.

'Okay, Bobby,' Trina says.

'Robert,' he says.

'We're ready to order now.'

'So the old guy fries himself with his wife's curling iron?' Trina asks.

'Yes,' Barcelona says. She is cutting her *petti di pollo alla Marsala* into small bite-size pieces. She spears a piece of chicken and two mushrooms and slips it into her mouth. She presses the food with her tongue before chewing, enjoying the hint of Marsala wine.

'Maybe it was suicide,' Diva says. She is picking at an *insalata di spinachi Caldo*, a spinach salad. She is the youngest and pudgiest of the group and always eats salads. She hasn't lost a pound in the three years Barcelona has known her.

Dixie shakes her head. 'People seldom choose electrocution as a form of suicide.'

'I wish it had been suicide,' Trina says. 'Once the papers and TV get ahold of this story, there'll be all kind of snide comments and clever jump lines at the end. The whole implication will be that women and all their beauty crap are dangerous to men. Women's vanity is hazardous to men's health, something like that. Wait and see.'

'You're overreacting,' Dixie says.

'Dixie, publicity is my business. I know what will play and what won't with the public. I know this is a perfect little ironic device they love. You'll see.'

Dixie shrugs. She concentrates on her *bistecca al Pepe*, pepper steak with cognac and cream, which Bobby the waiter prepared sulkily at the table. She slices the beef, stares at it on the fork a moment before putting it in her mouth. To Barcelona, she looks as if she's examining evidence. Because Trina owes her a dinner, she told Robby/Robert to give her the most expensive dish on the menu. Dixie is the shortest of them. Five three. She also has the best body. Under her baggy blue sweater and white slacks, her arms and legs literally ripple with muscle. She lifts weights daily after her shift and even on her days off. The only time she misses her workout is twice a month when they all get together like this. Barcelona has seen her naked many times in the locker room after they've taken a jazzercize class together. She can't help but stare in admiration at the bumps and ridges, the rocky sinew of Dixie's body. She wishes she had Dixie's discipline.

'Was his hair all frizzed?' Diva asks.

'Frizzed?'

'Like in cartoons. When someone gets electrocuted, their hair frizzes out.'

Barcelona can only think of Luna's frizzy hair. 'He was bald,' she lies.

72

'That doesn't happen too often,' Dixie says, chewing. Most everyone else is done eating, but she has hardly touched her food. She pokes listlessly at it while she talks. 'I've seen a couple electrocution deaths, and the hair wasn't spiked either time. Although I did see this cat once that had jumped on one of those tranformers. His hair stood straight on end, like he'd just come out of a clothes dryer or something.'

Trina laughs. 'Maybe we can come up with a new home perm. Put a little metal thimble on your finger, stick it in the socket. Voilà. Which twin has the Toni?'

'The what?' Diva says.

'That old television commercial. Which twin has the Toni?'

'I didn't watch much TV as a child. My parents were very strict. Dinner, dishes, homework, the Bible, then bed.'

'You've been culturally deprived, child,' Trina says.

'Dessert, ladies?' the waiter says. He smiles, but there's no confidence now. He is merely polite.

Barcelona feels bad about what they did to him. She feels like a bully. She wants to make it up to him. 'What would you recommend?'

He gives her a careful look as if suspecting some trap. His voice is flat and tentative. He recites now rather than charms. 'Perhaps some sherbert to clear the palate.'

'Fine.'

'Sherbert all around,' Trina says.

'Except me,' Diva says. 'Just coffee.'

When the waiter leaves, Diva says, 'I've decided to become a vegetarian. No more meat.'

'Starting when?' Trina asks skeptically.

'Starting yesterday. I haven't had any meat since the day before yesterday.'

'Sure you did,' Trina says. 'Just now.'

73

'No I didn't. I had a spinach salad.'

'There's bacon in the salad.'

'Not real bacon,' Diva says, looking down at the place where her salad used to be. 'Nobody uses real bacon anymore.'

Barcelona kicks Trina under the table. Trina says, 'That's true. Most of them use a soybean imitation. I forgot.'

Diva finds a stray bacon bit and nudges it with her thumbnail. 'I can't tell.'

Dixie reaches over, presses her finger over the bacon bit. It sticks to her finger and she flicks it off onto the tablecloth in front of her. She picks up a spoon, crushes the bacon bit into a brown powder. She examines it closely, sniffs it as if it were a possible illegal drug, tastes it with a loud smacking sound. 'Soybean,' she pronounces.

Diva relaxes with a smile. 'That's a relief. I just can't stand the idea of eating other animals anymore. I keep seeing their faces. I know it's childish and that this will only confirm your already low opinion of me, the only living species that feels guilt about what we eat. Can you imagine any other species worrying so much? The anteater saying, "Gee, I keep picturing those poor little ant faces in my mind every time I slurp them up."'

'That's an easy answer, Trina,' Diva says.

'No it's not. It's a sane answer.' Trina finishes her wine. 'We're all part of some gigantic cycle. We all feed off each other, die, turn to fertilizer, then the whole process starts again. Like a big house of cards. Sometimes the queen of hearts is on the bottom, but eventually the house collapses and when it's rebuilt, she may be on top. It doesn't matter, because no matter how often it's built, how much prettier or complex the structure is, it always falls and is always rebuilt. That's the great chain of life. We're all pissing into the same pot.'

74

'No more wine for you, Trina,' Diva says.

'Barcy knows what I mean, don't you?'

Barcelona shrugs. She doesn't want to get into this now. She often feels the way Diva does but so far has managed to push it out of her mind when the steaks are served.

'What about vegetables,' Trina says. 'They were alive, had offspring.'

'That's different. They don't think.'

'How do you know? It's been proven they like classical music and being talked to, just like humans. Maybe they're thinking up a storm.'

'Come on, guys,' Barcelona says. 'What's the difference? If Diva wants to eat vegetables, let her. Diva, enjoy.'

Dixie, who's remained curiously quiet during the exchange, dabs her napkin in her water glass and scrubs her lips. 'I don't like eating anything anymore.' She say it so matter-of-factly that everyone thinks she's kidding.

Diva laughs. 'It's not like you have a choice.'

'You don't like eating?' Trina says. 'What's not to like?'

'I don't know,' Dixie says. 'Food doesn't appeal to me. I'm never hungry.'

'You order a twenty-buck entrée I have to pay for and you weren't even hungry?' Trina pretends to be mad.

'That was revenge.' Dixie smiles. 'You bet no guy would offer more than fifty dollars when I worked Vice. First john out of the chute is ready to pop for a hundred.' She leans back in her chair, pushes the sleeves of her sweater up over her forearms. Barcelona looks at the muscles of her arms. The skin is tight over them, the veins protrude slightly. 'I have to eat, I know that. I'm not starving myself or anything. It's just that I don't get any pleasure from it.'

'Try chocolate,' Diva suggests. 'Chocolate cures everything.'

'Maybe you should see a doctor,' Barcelona suggests. She is uncomfortable with Dixie's confession. She feels helpless, the way she felt when Trina threatened suicide.

'There's nothing wrong with me. Food is just boring.'

'Maybe you're overtraining at the gym,' Trina says. 'Pumping too much iron and not enough men.'

'You're not taking steroids, for God's sake,' Diva says.

Dixie laughs. 'No, I'm not taking steroids. I want strength, not a moustache.'

'Could be an allergy,' Barcelona says.

Diva agrees. 'I read an article somewhere about certain reactions to food allergies.' Diva is famous for her tidbits of information from obscure articles in even more obscure magazines. Because singing in commercials requires a lot of sitting around during technical adjustments, she always has a magazine in her purse. 'You may be having a reaction to white flour or something.'

'You think?' Dixie asks, intrigued. 'Like white bread or something?'

'Could be. They have to run some tests on you to be sure.'

'I'll check into that,' Dixie says and Barcelona knows she will because Dixie always does whatever she says she will do. Of the four of them, she is the one most capable, most in control of her fate. Barcelona admires that in her. They met three years ago when Dixie took a medieval poetry class from Barcelona at the college. For contrast, Barcelona had brought in a dozen contemporary poems with similar themes. Dixie had liked the poetry, though had no particular feel for its complexities. She didn't like the contemporary poems that didn't rhyme, that weren't strictly metered. In class, she'd made a joke about herself as a Meter Maid of Poetry and everyone had laughed. Barcelona had admired her self-awareness. Analyzing poems bored Dixie, an intellectual crossword puzzle, she called it.

Once they'd been discussing a poem by W.D. Snodgrass,

'Mementos I.' The poem was a sometimes bitter account of the narrator's divorce, but ended with a longing for his estranged wife. Dixie raised her hand immediately after the poem had been read aloud by another student. Barcelona expected her to comment on the poem's clever use of rhyme and rhythm. Instead, Dixie said: 'The problem with this poem is the guy is pissed at his ex-wife because he blames her.'

'For what?' Barcelona had asked in her teacher's voice.

'For not making him happy. Men blame us because nothing in their lives make them truly happy. Even if they achieve success in their careers and whatnot. They know something's missing. They think women are the answer. They expect us to make them happy and we don't. Not in the way they expect.'

Another girl raised her hand. 'Are you saying we deserve their contempt?'

'I'm just making an observation. They think of women as mind-altering drugs. We'll change reality, make it all better for them. Ain't gonna happen. You have to learn to live with that, treat men as suspects in a drug bust. Perpetrators.'

They got a laugh. After class, Barcelona invited Dixie to join the group.

'What kind of group?' Dixie had asked.

'Just some women friends.'

'Not a support group or anything like that. I'm not into bitching. That wasn't bitching back in class, that was just an observation. I don't hate men.'

Barcelona had laughed. 'None of us hates men, Dixie. Men have nothing to do with this. We're just friends who get together twice a month and have a fabulous meal at an expensive restaurant. Nothing more to it.'

Diva had not been a part of the group then. Glenda Carson had been the fourth member. But she had moved to Tucson when her husband's parents were killed in a burglary and he inherited the family children's clothing store. Trina brought Diva in after they met during a local charity telethon Trina was publicizing. Diva had been a singer on the show. Diva was a nickname given her by Trina. Her real name was Dianne Klosterman.

Diva pulls a cigarette from her purse. It is gnarled and black and looks like a freshly dug up tree root. She roasts the tip with her Bic. Lighting it seems to take a long time.

'I can't believe you're still smoking those things,' Trina says, waving the smoke away from her face. 'Healthwise, you'd be better off eating a dozen cows. Probably even cow dung.'

'They help make my voice throatier.' Diva lowers her voice and sings a few bars of 'Girls Just Want to Have Fun,' only she sings it slow and sultry, in Marlene Dietrich's accented voice; 'Girls juz vant to hahv fun.'

'That's pretty good,' Dixie says.

'I'm pretty good,' Diva says. 'I'm especially good as peanut butter. That's what I'm doing now.'

'The radio commercial,' Barcelona says. 'Trina told me.'

'Yeah, I'm doing backup with three other white girls while some black chick gets the lead. They wanted a soul sound to capture the black market or something. Shit, man, I can do goddamn soul.' She puts her brown cigarette in the ashtray and sings the melody of Aretha Franklin's 'Respect': 'P-E-A-N-U-T, show your little nuts to me. B-U-T-T-E-R, eat you while we're in the car.'

Everyone laughs but it's true that she doesn't sound very soullike. She sounds like Petula Clark.

'Well, can I do soul or what?' It is not a question but a statement so no one replies. Diva puffs frantically on her cigarette.

'I've been asked to write a screenplay,' Barcelona announces. She says it quickly because she doesn't know how to share the news without making it sound pretentious.

'Jesus,' Trina says, grinning. 'That's great.'

'You're kidding,' Diva says. There is a hard edge of envy under the smile.

'When did this happen?' Dixie asks.

Barcelona tells them the whole story. She resists embellishing it to make it sound like more than it is. She finishes with, 'It's a long shot.'

'A long shot at Lynda Kramer is better than a sure shot with most others,' Diva says with authority. Because she is a professional singer, she has always been their resident expert on show business.

'Oh God, I just thought of something,' Trina says with a melodramatic gasp.

'What?' Barcelona asks.

'That scene in *Live Wires*, the one where the woman has sex with the alien ambassador in the space shuttle. That was me and Rob on the shuttle from L.A. to San Francisco. I should never have told you about that. Now everyone will see it.'

'That was you?' Diva says, surprised.

'Rob's idea. The only good one he ever had. I think that's when Karyn was conceived.'

The sherbert and coffee arrive. Diva sips her coffee and lights another twisted black root. Barcelona and Trina eat their sherbert. Dixie digs her spoon into hers carving a face, but never eating any.

Trina is already finished with her sherbert and takes Dixie's away and starts eating it. 'Shit, if you're going to make snowmen from it, I'll eat it.' She spoons some into her mouth and talks, her tongue and lips orange. 'I kinda like the idea of being immortalized. Having Lynda Kramer play out something that happened to me. Maybe they'll hire me as a consultant, you think?'

Barcelona smiles. 'I wouldn't count on it.'

'Fuck them then.' She spoons the rest of the sherbert into her mouth.

'Any new perps in your life?' Dixie asks no one in particular.

Barcelona looks at Trina. Trina winks but doesn't say anything. Barcelona realizes now that The Great Pretender is to remain a secret between the two of them.

'Same-o-same-o,' Diva says, lighting yet another black root. Diva has a live-in boyfriend named Calypso. He claims to be half-Jamaican, but Diva has expressed some doubts about that. Calypso is a drummer with a local band, Fast Lane. 'Calypso wants me to marry him, have kids.'

'Jesus,' Trina says. 'There's a frightening thought.'

'He's not so bad,' Diva says halfheartedly. Then she sighs. 'He has the names of the kids picked out already. Sport if it's a boy, Spring if it's a girl.'

'Sound like dog names,' Dixie says.

'Doesn't it? That's what I said. He laughed, said maybe we should get dogs then. I think he just wants something to hang those names on.'

Trina yawns. 'No men talk tonight. Too boring.'

'Be right back,' Barcelona says, rising. She grabs her purse and heads for the rest room. The wine is expanding by the second in her bladder. She takes a couple of wrong turns before she finally finds the hidden corridor that leads past the telephones to the rest rooms. A silhouette cutout figure is on each door, but they look so similar, she isn't sure which is a man and which is a woman. An old short woman with elastic wraps around her swollen ankles pushes past her and enters one of the doors. Barcelona follows.

She sits in the stall and is surprised that there is no graffiti. She is also surprised that there is no toilet paper. She makes both discoveries after she is already in the

80

process of peeing. She is thankful that is all she has to do. Under the gap between the two stalls, she can see the older woman's left foot. The wraps around her ankle look tight, the skin above the wrap puffing out over it. She is making a noise that sounds like crying, but suddenly the noise stops, the toilet flushes, and the woman leaves without washing her hands. Barcelona doubts that the woman even had time to go. When she finishes, she searches through her purse for a tissue, finds one crumpled up with lipstick on it, refolds it for a clean surface, and wipes herself dry.

She leans over the sink and washes her hands. She presses her palm against the soap dispenser. A few drops of pink lotion fizz out, but not enough to really lather up. She pumps the plunger a few more times but it too is empty. The door behind her opens, she looks up into the mirror. It's Dixie.

'What's all this crap about not eating?' Barcelona says.

'I didn't say I didn't eat, I said I was never hungry.'

'You should see a doctor. Really.'

'Maybe it's just psychological. I mean, sometimes I feel hungry, then by the time I cook something up, I've lost my appetite.'

'Go to restaurants.'

'That's even worse. I pay money and still don't want to eat it. Besides, it's not just the food. It's the process of eating that bothers me. The biting, chewing, swallowing. It'd kinda sickening if you think about it.' She steps up to the mirror and pulls down the collar of her blue sweater. There's a small bruise on her neck.

'What happened to you?'

'Just what it looks like. A hickey.'

Barcelona laughs. 'You? A hickey?'

'Part of my undercover assignment at that high school. I'm supposed to be infiltrating this group of kids they think sells drugs.'

'Do they sell drugs?'

Dixie looks at Barcelona in the mirror. 'The head kid, name's Joseph Little, does about two hundred thousand dollars' worth of business a year.' She points at her hickey. 'He likes me.'

'Sounds dangerous, Dixie.'

Dixie shrugs. 'Not really. I'm not going to bust him, just gather some evidence for a week or so, then disappear.' She pulls a folded toothbrush out of her purse, opens it, squeezes a dab of toothpaste on and brushes her teeth. She talks around the toothbrush. 'Your mom still getting those obscene calls?'

'I don't know. I haven't talked to her in a while.'

'She contact the local cops like I suggested?'

'I told her to, but who knows what she actually did. She has a mind of her own. Besides, they're just small-town cops. They wouldn't do anything except tell her to change her number and make sure it's unlisted. I've already suggested that.'

'But she won't, right?' Dixie rinses off the toothbrush, folds it, zips it back into her small black purse. She examines her teeth in the mirror.

'Right. I think she's worried some long-lost friend she hasn't seen in twenty years will suddenly get the urge to call and not be able to reach her.'

Dixie leans toward the mirror, examining the hickey more closely. 'Jesus, that little nipper has a bite doesn't he?'

'I've seen worse.'

'I've given worse.' She laughs. Her laugh is lovely, like unexpectedly overhearing a few notes of a favorite song. 'That was a long time ago, of course. I'm not that kind of girl anymore.'

Barcelona smiles. 'Of course. Me neither.'

'Of course.' She laughs again and they return to the table together.

'Diva met this guy,' Trina tells them as they sit down. 'You gotta hear this. Tell them, Diva.'

'No big deal, just a guy,' she says, but she is smiling wickedly.

'Yeah,' Trina says. 'Just a guy with a verifiable ten-inch tongue.'

'What do you mean "verifiable"?' Dixie asks.

'He measured it for me,' Diva explains.

'Start at the beginning,' Trina says. 'When he approached you.'

'Okay. This was last week when I was doing that loan company ad, you know, where I sing like Bette Midler?' She taps the ashes from her black cigarette. 'We were on break, some technical shit with the ad copy. Anyway, this sound guy who works at the recording studio comes up to me and asks me out on a date. He's not very cute, looks a little like that guy does the camera commercials on TV.'

'John Newcombe?' Barcelona asks.

'No.'

'Ben Cross?' Trina asks.

'No.'

'Laurence Olivier?' Dixie asks.

'God, no. He's too old. This guy was young, my age. Anyway, I tell him no, tell him I've got a boyfriend, I live with a guy. He tells me he doesn't care and neither will I. Then he sticks out the tip of his tongue. "Ten inches," he says. "Bigger than most men's dicks." I started to laugh, but he sticks it out again, only this time he sticks it out all the way and the thing just keeps coming at me, I swear I must've backed up a couple steps. Then he whips out this tape measure he has clipped to his belt and measures it. Sure enough, ten inches, just like he said.'

They are all laughing.

'I could make him president,' Trina says.

'He sure has the brass,' Dixie says.

'More important, he has the tongue.' Trina reaches her spoon across the table and scrapes up the last bite of Barcelona's leftover sherbert. 'Is it my imagination, or is it getting weirder out there?'

'We're just getting older,' Barcelona says.

'Bullshit,' Trina says. 'It's fucked up in Romanceville, kiddo.'

'Trina's right,' Diva says. 'I run into the strangest guys lately. I'm just lucky I've got Calypso.'

'Yeah,' Trina says. 'He's heaven-sent.'

'You don't like him because he's half black.'

'No,' Trina says. 'I don't like him because he's completely stupid. Barcy doesn't like him because he's half black.'

'I don't care that he's half black,' Barcelona says. 'I don't like him because he's a leech. Dixie's the one who doesn't like him because he's half black.'

Dixie shakes her head. 'That's the only thing about him I do like.'

Diva laughs. 'Well, to tell you the truth, I don't think he's really half-Jamaican like he says. You know those dreadlocks of his? He gets them permed. I promised not to tell, but I think that's so *strange*.'

They all laughed.

Diva sighs, puffs her black cigarette. Her fingernails are painted a metallic pink with tiny green palm trees growing out of the cuticles. 'I don't know. It's easy for you guys. You're all gorgeous. I'm too fat to get the really good men.'

'That's bullshit,' says Trina. 'You know why?'

'Because a good man won't care that I'm fat?'

'No. Because there aren't any good men.' Trina laughs loudly and draws stares from nearby tables.

'I thought we weren't going to talk about men tonight,' Dixie says. 'Your suggestion, Trina.'

'I was overruled.'

Diva points at Dixie's left hand, the ring finger. Dixie wears a simple gold band. 'I can't believe you wear that ring on that finger.'

'Why not? It was my mom's.'

'Why not? Because guys will all think you're married and stay away.'

'Not today they won't,' Trina says. 'I think it may even encourage them. They figure you're horny for some variety with no strings attached.'

'I wear it to keep the creeps off at work,' Dixie says.

'The cops or the criminals?' Trina asks.

'The creeps,' Dixie repeats.

Trina chuckles. 'I'm still hungry. Hey, Bobby.' She waves at the waiter as he passes. 'Let me see the dessert menu again.' He nods stiffly and hurries off.

'Are you drunk?' Diva asks.

'Why, am I too loud?'

'No more than usual,' Dixie says.

'That's too bad. This has not been a usual day.' Trina stops, looks at them in a funny way. Barcelona thinks she is about to say something important, but the moment passes and Trina smiles. She is not drunk.

The waiter returns and hands Trina the menu. He scuttles off again.

Trina licks her lips as she reads the menu. 'God, this stuff sounds good.'

'It's all fattening,' Diva says, lighting her third black cigarette.

'You ever notice how it always sounds better than it actually tastes?' Dixie says.

'I have,' Barcelona agrees. 'I mean, even if it tastes good, it never tastes quite as good as you've expected.'

Trina nods. 'That doesn't keep us from ordering, does it? Thing is, what we need is a menu of men that we could order from. That would make things so much easier.'

'Absolutely,' Dixie says. 'With guys listed according to their appeal. Like some guys are merely appetizers, some are desserts.'

'And some,' Diva says, grinning lewdly, 'are full-course meals.'

'How about something like this,' Trina says. 'Beef Ribs à la Jack. Huge slabs of meaty ribs that take all night to finish.'

Barcelona laughs. 'With juicy, buttery corn on a stiff cob. On the side.'

'That's the way I like it best,' Diva says.

They play with the idea for a while, each topping the others in their descriptions. They laugh loudly. When the waiter returns for Trina's order, she says she's changed her mind about dessert and asks for the check. They continue playing the Man Menu game while they divide the bill.

Diva lays a twenty in the middle of the table. 'Let's do it for real.'

'Do what?' Barcelona asks.

'Make this menu. With men on it.'

'That's crazy.'

'No, it's not,' Diva says. 'We all know and meet lots of men. Some of them you're interested in, but some of them you're not. Maybe one of us would be.'

'This sounds a little like high school,' Barcelona says.

'Not today's high school,' Dixie says.

'It doesn't sound like high school,' Trina says. 'It sounds like business. Diva's talking about networking.'

'Yeah, networking,' Diva says tentatively, as if uncertain what the word means.

'Exactly,' Trina says. 'We're all professional women. If

86

we were in the same profession, we'd be helping each other in business, giving leads to jobs or clients, that sort of thing. Why shouldn't we try to do the same thing in our personal lives?'

'Are you serious, Trina?' Barcelona asks.

'She's serious,' Diva says.

Dixie makes change for everyone and figures out a tip. She hands two dollar bills back to Diva. 'I don't know what you're so hot about, Diva. You're living with a guy.'

Diva stuffs the bills in her purse. 'We're living together but not really *involved*.'

'You were just talking about having kids. Remember Sport and Spring?'

'Yeah, that's a good point.' Diva lowers her head, stares into her purse a minute. Then she lifts her head and smiles. 'I can still look though. I don't have to date any of these guys, right? Besides, the only kind of sex Calypso is interested in lately is anal. I'm starting to think he may be secretly gay.'

'Jesus, Diva,' Trina says, 'we just ate.'

Barcelona says, 'Boy, living together ain't the thrill it used to be.'

Dixie hands Barcelona a five. 'What are we talking about? A physical menu with guys' names on it?'

'Yes,' Trina says. 'Their names and a description, in food terms only, of who they are. We can use the price column to describe their income. Expensive means they're raking it in. Moderate means they're able to pay their bills in Yuppieland. Inexpensive means they're artists and get ready to spend some of your own dough. I'll type the whole thing on my computer.'

'Count me out,' Barcelona says. 'This is too weird.'

'Come on, Barcy,' Trina says. 'It's just for fun.'

'Yeah, you could share some of those professors you know.'

'I can give you the rundown on them right now. "Chicken fried steak à la Tweed. Chewy and dry. Beverage and dessert not included."'

'That's pretty good,' Dixie laughs.

Barcelona looks at Dixie. 'You're not taking part in this lunacy, are you?'

'Why not? I know a couple cops might be of some interest. And, of course, there's always my new friends at the high school. You can come to the next sock hop.'

'Come on, Barcy,' Diva says.

Barcelona shakes her head, but then sighs. 'Okay, I'll contribute to the menu, but I'm not ordering anything from it.'

'Probably none of us will,' Trina says. 'But it's fun dreaming.'

'What about married men?' Diva asks. 'Should we include them if they're real hunks?'

'No,' Barcelona says.

'Fair game,' Trina says. 'If they have a steady income and a dick, good enough.'

'No,' Dixie says. 'I agree with Barcelona. No married men.'

'Unless physically separated from their wives,' Trina compromises.

Dixie shrugs.

Barcelona listens to them discuss it for a few more minutes as they walk through the restaurant toward the exit. They're having fun and she doesn't think it will ever get past the talking stage. Occasionally, Trina or Diva will give funny descriptions of a man as an entrée and they will all laugh.

In the parking lot, they hear the rotors of helicopters overhead. They look up but can't see the crafts, only their blinking red lights. There are three of them.

'The CH53-E Super Stallions,' Dixie says, looking up.

'That the one they're trying to ground?' Trina asks.

Dixie nods. 'Twenty marines dead so far in crashes.'

They stare up into the darkness a few more seconds before splitting up. Dixie and Diva head for their cars. Trina lingers to walk with Barcelona. 'It'll be fun,' she says. 'You're taking it too seriously.'

'People often refer to me as a saint,' Barcelona grins.

'Yeah, but they usually follow it with Bernard.'

They laugh, lean against each other.

'Shit, look at that asshole,' Trina says suddenly, breaking away. A red Porsche is parked at a diagonal across two parking spaces. 'I had to park in Cambodia because the lot's so full and this jerk takes two spaces.'

'He doesn't want his car scratched.'

'Fuck him,' Trina walks over to the car, stoops by the rear tire, uncaps the inflation valve. 'Find me a small pebble,' she says.

'What are you doing?' Barcelona asks.

'Here's one.' Trina plucks a tiny stone from the ground, stuffs it into the cap, and screws it back on the valve. Barcelona can hear the air hissing slowly from the tire. Trina stands and slaps her hands clean. 'Asshole.'

Barcelona sees a couple coming out of the restaurant and she pulls Trina away. 'Why'd you do that?'

'Trust, Justice, the American Way.' She smiles. 'And because it felt good.'

PART TWO

Networking

In Which the Friends Determine
How to Put the Men
Back in Menu

7

Diva wakes up because she feels her hand being lifted from her chest. She is too confused to open her eyes. Her hand is held by the wrist and is being moved upward until her knuckles scrape the sheet, then it moves horizontally, like those marine helicopters that are always crashing. Finally it is slowly lowered onto a very serious erection. She feels her hands being shaped around a large pole, her fingers being curled around it one by one. Both the hand shaping hers and the erection are very warm.

She sits up and looks over at Calypso. 'What the hell are you doing?'

He is grinning. 'I've got a hard-on.'

'How nice for you.' She pulls her hand away and gets out of bed. She is naked but not embarrassed by it even though she is only 5'4" and 160 pounds. Six inches shorter and ten pounds heavier than Calypso. The weight certainly isn't her breasts, which are small but pudgy. Her stomach sags a little, as do her arms, her butt, her thighs. She has been dieting for three years and has yet to lose any weight. She has gone to many doctors, hoping for some glandular excuse that medication would adjust. The last doctor just shrugged and said, 'Hey, you're just one of Nature's fatties. Live with it.'

Diva walks across the room to the battered old stereo. Officially, the stereo is in the living room. But since only a folding rice paper screen separates the bedroom from the living room, it is a meaningless distinction. She flips the stereo switch. One of the speakers has a low buzz which she has been ignoring for the past two years. She lets the record already on the turntable play, though she doesn't remember which album is on. When she hears Laura Nyro, she is pleased and sings along as she heads for the kitchen. *'Surry down to a stone soul picnic/There'll be lots of time and wine . . .'*

The refrigerator is nearly empty. Half a carton of nonfat milk two days past the expiration date, three nonfat yogurts, a jar of crunchy peanut butter they gave her from the commercial she did yesterday, and a couple of bulbous yellow squash. She'd left twenty dollars with Calypso yesterday to buy a few groceries but, as usual, he forgot. If she went to his jeans right now she'd find the two tens balled up at the bottom of the pocket with some guitar picks, loose change, maybe half a joint. He's not evil, not into booze or serious dope or any of that shit. He just forgets.

The chilled air from the refrigerator teases her naked skin and her nipples harden. For some reason she puts one hand protectively between her legs as she bends into the refrigerator. She finds an open can of Diet Rite Cola. She drinks. It is flat and syrupy. She finishes it anyway. Afterward she rinses the can in the sink before tossing it into the trash. They have to be very careful with the trash now. This is ant season.

The only window in the apartment is in the living room. The place is so small that this window is visible from anywhere in the apartment. It looks out onto the complex's east parking lot. The other side of the building looks out onto the street, a row of beach houses, and finally a little scrap of the beach and ocean. Those apartments cost $45 more a month for the view. Diva can't afford the view. It's

94

enough for her knowing the ocean is over there, this close.

The whole complex is pretty run-down. The hallway smells rancid, as if people have been storing dead fish and rotting vegetables under the already mildewed carpeting. The smell of dope is heavy. The laundry room is dangerous, not just to the tenants, two of whom have been raped in the past year, but also dangerous to the clothing. The washing machines are more like blenders, the dryers like flame throwers. The parking lot is like a swap meet of stolen goods and drug deals. But Diva, for the sake of her soul, must live by the beach and this is the cheapest she could find, even though it still takes most of what she earns every month. There's so much going on down here all the time. The energy is tremendous. Even now, glancing out the window on a weekday morning, instead of seeing a lot of people driving to work, she sees three boys in wet suit jackets with surf boards under their arms heading for the beach.

She returns to the bedroom area but Calypso is not in bed. There is a small passageway to the bathroom, about five feet wide. This is the closet. She walks through the closet to the bathroom. Calypso is sitting on the toilet, naked, jerking off. He is grinning at her while he does it.

'This turn you on?' he asks, stroking himself.

'Yeah. I'm all wet.' She leans over the sink, turns on the faucet, and splashes water on her bangs. They are too long and she's been meaning to cut them for a couple of days. Later this morning she has an audition for a car dealer commercial, singing the freeway directions to the guy's lot. She wants to look good. She opens her drawer but can't find the scissors. 'Where are the scissors?' she asks Calypso.

His eyes are closed as he slowly but steadily continues to thump up and down. 'I don't know.'

Diva roots through the drawer some more but comes up

empty. Finally she settles on a pair of manicure scissors. She curls several strands of wet hair around her fingers, pulls straight out, and whatever is leftover, she snips off. The sink fills with spikes of brown hair.

'Oh, man, Diva,' Calypso moans. 'This feels good.'

She continues snipping. She thinks of Barcelona, the movie deal with Lynda Kramer. She feels very jealous. Not that Barcelona doesn't deserve her success, but so does she. She thinks of all the years of singing, the endless auditions, the record companies she's been haunting the past few years. She deserves some success too. She doesn't want to be singing radio commercials all her life. She wants to rock 'n' roll. Have her own album. Walk into Tower Records and see her own CD up front with the Picks of the Week.

'Oooh,' Calypso says. His breathing is getting shallower, his hand is moving up and down his shaft faster. She glances over. His eyes are still closed. There are a few drops of creamy semen on the tip of his penis. His hand is jerking up and down in a blur. His mouth is tight with devotion. Goddamn, it *is* sexy after all. 'Oh, for Christ's sake,' Diva finally says, slapping away his jumping hand and replacing it with her own. She kneels down next to him, starts tugging up and down. He pumps his pelvis up and down into her fists, his skinny butt bouncing on the toilet seat. It takes only a few more strokes and he arches his back and shouts, 'Ihreeeeee,' which is Jamaican slang for 'Everything's cool.' His thick gummy come starts to shoot crazily, splatting Diva on her left breast. The rest dribbles over her knuckles, down between her fingers.

He leans back against the toilet lid, wiping himself with yellow toilet paper. Diva washes her hands. 'There,' she says. 'Happy?'

'Actually, yes.'

She laughs. It is not her nature to be angry about

anything for long. 'You should have seen your face when you were pounding away. You looked like a little boy doing it for the first time.'

'Every time is like the first time. Just as good.'

'Is that true? Really? It's always good when you masturbate?'

'Yeah, it is. It's like scoring a hundred percent on a test every time you take one.' He stands up and goes to the bedroom. He finds yesterday's underpants and puts them on. They are black Calvin Klein's. They are the only pair he owns, along with three pairs of jeans, four shirts, two pairs of shoes, three pairs of socks, and a white tuxedo jacket he found lying around after a bar mitzvah party he once played at. 'Isn't it always good for you?' he asks. 'Jerking off.'

'Not always. Sometimes it's hard to come. I have to concentrate real hard. It's difficult to concentrate and rub at the same time.'

'Hmmm, I see your point.' He pulls on his jeans. He is so thin that no matter how small the size of jeans he wears, they always sag at the butt. He comes back into the bathroom while she is rinsing off her toothbrush. He stabs his fingers at his dreadlocks, puffing them out. Against his pale skin and freckles, they look silly, like a Shirley Temple wig.

'How do you like it?' he asks.

She puts the toothbrush away and returns to the bedroom. She starts to make the bed.

'Seriously, mom.' He is starting to speak in his Jamaican accent now. 'How do you like de hair?'

'Your dreadlocks look more like dead lox.'

He studies them in the mirror for a minute, tilting his head this way then that way. He shrugs and laughs. 'I'll show you a dead lox.' He runs back into the bedroom and leaps onto the bed. He grabs Diva around the waist and

97

pulls her on top of him. His tongue is licking her everywhere: hips, legs, nipples, eyelids. She is giggling as he rolls her over and over, tongue lapping her skin.

'Stop,' she says, hoping and knowing that he won't.

'Dead lox patrol,' he says, licking, licking, licking.

She feels his rough tongue on her ass, then in the crack, then right up against her hole. She recoils at first, embarrassed. But he pulls her back and continues licking her there. When she realizes it is too soon for his dick to get hard enough to use on her there, she relaxes and enjoys what he is doing. He works his way even farther down and has somehow turned her onto her back without ever stopping his burrowing and licking. His head is between her legs now, the tongue drilling inside her, then playfully tapping at her clitoris. His tongue beats a pattern against her as skillfully as if he were playing the steel drums. He whips his head from side to side now, the tongue tripping over her clitoris repeatedly.

She is vibrating with pleasure. She is having trouble catching her breath. 'You skinny son of a bitch,' she yells, pulling his head tight against her, squashing his nose into her pubic bone.

He lifts his head and shouts, 'You pudgy pigorama!'

'Bony bastard!'

'Fat fuck!'

Her thighs tense against his head, her signal that she is ready to come. He picks up the pace, slips his thumb deep into her vagina and stutters his tongue on her clitoris. She moans, stiffens, her legs suddenly shoot straight out, her toes pointing downward toward China.

Afterward, she showers and when she comes out, Calypso is gone. The two tens she gave him yesterday are on the kitchen counter. A note lies under it. It says: *Pizza tonight*?

She sits on the sofa, still naked except for the towel

wrapped around her hair. She begins thumbing through an old issue of *Rolling Stone*. In the classifieds are ads for songwriters. None for singers. Wait a minute, she thinks. That's it! Every major decision in Diva's life has come in on a flash of inspiration, an epiphany of revelation so great she shudders on the sofa with almost the same intensity she had earlier with Calypso's tongue inside her.

A songwriter. That's what she'll become. She would still keep humping at singing, but now she would add songwriting to her talents, which would make her much more commercial to the record companies. She'd be like Joni Mitchell, Laura Nyro, Phoebe Snow.

She jumps up and begins cleaning the apartment. A new life decision always requires cleaning house. Starting fresh. As she changes the sheets on the bed, she smiles at how good sex with Calypso had been that morning. She'd had one of the deepest orgasms she'd ever had in her life. For a moment there she'd felt as if she'd vacuumed Calypso right up through her vagina and into her womb, and if she didn't fight her way back to consciousness, she would suck up the apartment building next, then the beach, the ocean, and more. Like a black hole of the universe. God, it had been terrific.

After she changes the sheets on the bed, she gathers Calypso's clothing and stuffs them into a plastic trash bag. The white tuxedo doesn't fit so she folds that neatly and lays it on top. She pins a note to the lapel: *Dear Calypso, Sorry no pizza tonight. And please move out. I'm changing my life. Diva.*

8

Dixie is eating lunch in the school courtyard with her new friend from algebra class, Melody Krauss. Melody is drunk from spraying the contents of an Opium perfume bottle from her purse into her mouth. The Opium bottle is filled with Southern Comfort. She has offered to spray Dixie's mouth a couple of times and Dixie let her once right after gym class.

'God, this is good stuff,' Melody says, spraying her mouth again after eating a Twinkie.

'I wish I could say the same about this,' Dixie says, listlessly stabbing her mashed potatoes with her fork. She had taken a bite of the corn and an even smaller bite of the roast beef. She pushes the tray away. 'We should've gone to Burger King.'

'Just needs some seasoning.' Melody giggles. She sprays Dixie's roast beef with her Opium atomizer. Southern Comfort mists the table. Some lands on Dixie's arm and she licks it.

'Yum. My compliments to the chef.'

Melody laughs but stops suddenly when she sees a teacher approaching their table. Dixie spots Mrs. Filborne's loud plaid skirt and clashing striped blouse and feels a tingle of rabbit fear. Once again she is surprised at how quickly she has fallen into the undercover cop's typical Us versus Them Syndrome. She identifies with the kids, shares their resentment of the teachers, even the ones they like. The same thing happened when she went under as a hooker. She could feel her fear of cops budding. It's not unusual; they warn you against it before each assignment. Still, she is surprised how easily it happens.

Mrs. Filborne, the history teacher, stops at their table. She is black with a two-inch Afro and a slight gap between her front teeth. 'Mr. Peterson wants to see you,' she says to Dixie.

'What about?' Dixie asks.

Mrs. Filborne narrows her sharp eyes. 'He didn't say. I'll write you out a hall pass.'

While Mrs. Filborne scribbles on the pink hall pass, Dixie shrugs at Melody to show she doesn't know what this is all about. Melody is busy stuffing her Opium atomizer back in her purse. She looks scared. Finally Mrs. Filborne finishes, tears the pink hall pass from her pad and hands it to Dixie. 'Right away, Dixie.'

'Yes, ma'am,' Dixie says.

Mrs. Filborne looks Dixie over with an openly appraising eye. She has seen Dixie only twice in class, and Dixie was careful not to volunteer any answers. But Dixie can feel the woman's opinion hardening like cement already. New girl, hangs around with Melody, a known lush, seen with Joseph Little the drug pusher. Short skirt and too much makeup. Tramp, dummy, druggie. Dixie feels Mrs. Filborne's eyes drawing a careful line through her name, crossing her out of the list of good students. Dixie even feels like a loser now, hopeless. Her anger toward this woman is suddenly fierce, made worse by the frustration of her position.

'Jesus, Dixie, what'd you do?' Melody asks when Mrs. Filborne has walked away.

'Nothing. I didn't do anything.' Dixie smiles nervously. 'Well, I'd better go see.'

'Good luck.'

'Yeah, thanks. See ya.' Dixie walks off toward the principal's office. Her anger lessens as she walks. She understands Mrs. Filborne's own frustration. Too many students, many of whom are drugged or drunk or just don't care. This isn't some urban school with forced bussing or welfare children. This is Newport Beach and the children are dressed in colorful but expensive clothing from the mall. Their parents are educated. The student parking lot contains over a million dollars' worth of spotless automobiles. The faculty lot is exclusively Japanese compacts.

'Come in, Dixie,' Mr. Peterson, the principal, says. He gestures at the chair across from his desk as he circles around her and closes the door. He is a good-looking man in his early forties, slightly balding at the sides. He is the only one in the school who knows who she really is.

Dixie sits. 'Yes, Mr. Peterson?'

He lowers his voice to almost a whisper. Civilians often do this when talking to cops who they know are undercover. 'What have you found out so far?'

'Not much that you didn't already know. You've got a lot of drugs and booze flowing through this school.'

'Damn.' He looks miserable.

'I'm not telling you anything new. You knew all this going in. That's why I'm here.'

'Yes, yes, I know. I just thought, hoped . . .' He sighs, leans back in his chair. 'I don't know.'

'You hoped it was some kind of mistake, maybe an isolated incident confined to one or two students.'

He smiles. 'You've been through this before.'

'Several times.'

They met only once before, briefly, at the police station. He had been very nervous:

'I'm just not so sure this is necessary,' he'd told Captain Janeway that day.

'Well, Peterson,' Captain Janeway had said, 'your school board members disagree. They called us in.'

'It's a tricky situation,' Mr. Peterson said. 'What with student rights. God, it's just so damn sneaky. I know, I know, things have gotten out of hand. I tried drug programs, teen AA meetings. They seem to be helping.'

'Not fast enough for the school board, I'm afraid,' Dixie said.

'Yes, the school board.' He nodded thoughtfully.

Captain Janeway explained the setup, how Dixie would go undercover, identify only the student pushers, possession with intent to sell, establish patterns when they would be carrying, and then let the uniforms come in and bust them. Hopefully that would be enough to scare some of the fringe users from continuing to buy. 'Probably not,' Captain Janeway said, 'but let's give it a try anyway. We're not out to bust the whole student body.'

Mr. Peterson stood up. 'I appreciate that.' Then he looked at Dixie, as if for the first time. He frowned. 'I know you know your business, Captain Janeway . . .'

'But?' Captain Janeway said.

'But I've been around high school students for the past twenty years. No offense, Ms. Cooper, but you don't look like a high school student.'

'You mean I'm too old?'

He stammered, embarrassed. 'You're not *old* old. I mean, you're very attractive. What are you, twenty-seven, eight?'

'Thirty-three.'

'Oh. Well, see, you look much younger. But seventeen, eighteen, that's a big leap even from twenty-seven. Certainly you have younger cops, kids just out of the academy.'

'You've been watching television, Mr. Peterson. Cop shows, right?' Captain Janeway asked.

Mr. Peterson grinned.

'I thought all you academic types watch PBS, those British imports.'

'Sometimes,' Mr. Peterson said. 'If the Lakers aren't playing and I've already seen "Murder, She Wrote".'

'Believe me,' Captain Janeway said, shaking his hand. 'You won't recognize Sergeant Cooper once she goes under.'

Now sitting in Mr. Peterson's office, Dixie could tell that he was replaying that scene too.

'It's remarkable,' he says, squinting at her. 'You look eighteen.'

'A lot of eye makeup, comb my bangs straight over my forehead to hide any wrinkles. Wear these long earrings to keep them from looking too closely at my skin. And the short skirt distracts them from my face a bit.'

Mr. Peterson glances down at her smooth stockingless legs. 'Works for me.'

Dixie stands. 'Anything else, Mr. Peterson?'

'Kevin. Please.'

'Better keep it Mr. Peterson for now. Helps me keep in character.'

'I understand. Perhaps I should give you an hour of detention, just to make it look good.'

She smiles. 'That's making it look too good.' Dixie starts for the door. 'It's probably best if you don't call me again, Mr. Peterson. Captain Janeway will keep you informed of our progress.'

'Okay, sure. Good luck.'

Dixie leaves his office. Good luck. It's what Melody had said to her too.

Dixie detours into the girl's lavatory. Two tenth-graders are sharing a cigarette. They are both a little plump. One has a sprinkle of acne across her forehead, the other has thick braces.

'He's pissed because I won't lend him my U2 album,'

the one with acne says. 'He wants to tape it and I told him to go buy his own.'

'What'd he say?'

The one with acne looks over at Dixie, takes a long drag on the cigarette, and blows the smoke out the side of her mouth. She returns the butt to her friend. 'He said, "Fuck me in the ass, cunt," and gave me the finger.'

The girl with braces giggles.

Dixie is applying more mascara to her eyes.

Another girl comes in, a senior with hair dyed so black it is almost blue. Other than that she dresses in very expensive sports clothes. The collar of her polo shirt is worn fashionably up. A white sweater is tied around her waist.

'Quit smoking in here,' she tells the two younger girls. 'You're stinking the place up.' She waves her hand in front of her face.

The girl with braces tosses the cigarette into the nearest toilet. It sizzles loudly. The two girls leave.

The senior leans over the sink, cups one hand under her right eye, and pops out her contact lens into her hand. She removes a plastic bottle from her purse, squirts the lens, replaces it in her eye, blinks rapidly, then leaves.

Dixie is alone for a moment, staring into the mirror, carefully applying mascara to erase fifteen years of aging. She realizes how rare and precious this moment of being alone is here. It is the way she felt when she had guard duty at the jail. Never alone. The thought isn't even completed when the door opens and three more girls come in chattering. Two go to different stalls, the third removes her earrings, replaces them with a different pair, shrugs, adds yet another pair, shrugs, then adds the original pair. Each ear has three earrings now. During the whole process of peeing and earring changing, the three girls have not stopped talking.

Dixie watches her eyes in the mirror as she circles them with eyeliner pencil. She is lucky and knows it. Her mother is Iowan, but her father is Chinese. His Chinese genes have given her the smooth skin and slightly tilted eyes that keep her looking younger than her years. This is one of the reasons Captain Janeway finds her so valuable working undercover. She has a range of ages from eighteen to forty. She could show Lynda Kramer, famous actress, a thing or two out here, where if you screw up your performance the critics don't kill you, the audience does.

Most people miss the Oriental heritage in her face because of the sandy hair. Her mother's contribution. That and eight years of piano lessons before she died of a malignant melanoma hidden in her pubic hairs. What was surprising about that was that Dixie's father was a doctor, an internist who had never noticed that his wife had a mole on her pussy that was turning black and ugly. Dixie had always sensed things were strained between them, but only after her mother died did she realize to what extent.

Dixie's father, despite his forty years in this country, still speaks with a heavy Chinese accent almost indecipherable to Dixie's friends. His practice is in Santa Monica. After his wife's death, Dr. Lo had abandoned his internist practice to devote himself to acupuncture. At the time, Dixie thought it might be some attempt of his to return to his Asian roots, as if he had somehow defiled his ancestors by marrying the blond piano teacher from Iowa. His practice became an enormous success. He was flown all over the world to stick needles in celebrities. He treated Teddy Kennedy's bad back, George Wallace's dead legs, Kareem Abdul Jabaar's migraine headaches. Once—and this Dixie read about in one of her father's medical journals—he had been flown to Mexico to see this wealthy man's wife who had been in a coma for two weeks. According to the article, because her father never talked about it, he had entered her hospital room, examined her for fifteen minutes, stuck a needle in her left foot, and she had immediately awakened from the coma. Her father had made several trips back to China now, bringing back photographs of women watching, smiling happily, while doctors performed a Caesarian birth on them. Even patients with eyes open, smiling, a thorny crown of needles haloing their shaved heads while surgeons poked through their open skulls at the exposed brain.

In high school, Dixie had typed her father's medical articles about Chinese herbal medicine for him. Occasionally, she tried making sense of them, but too much of it was steeped in the ancient philosophies. The world divided into five symbolic elements: Wood, Water, Metal, Earth, Fire. Each element generates another element while at the same time subjugating another element. Wood generates Fire, but Wood subjugates Earth. Dixie thought of it as the old hammer, scissors, paper game. Paper covers hammer, but hammer smashes scissors.

The only paper of his she can clearly remember anymore is the one she typed for him on *malva verticillata*, or *dong kui zi*. Also called farmer's tobacco. The seeds were said to help people having trouble urinating, but also facilitate secretion in breast-feeding mothers. Dixie had always thought that an odd combination. Surely piss and mother's milk weren't related. One was poison, the other nourishment.

As his business increased, her father's English worsened. They had never been close, but now visiting him was like seeing a complete foreigner. Except for an occasional phone call for his birthday and at Christmas, Dixie had no contact with him.

The name Dixie had been her mother's idea. A name

so utterly American, she couldn't be mistaken for anything but a homegrown native. Cooper was Dixie's husband's name. After the divorce, she kept it.

'You work out or what,' the girl with all the earrings asks, looking at Dixie's muscular legs.

'Yeah,' Dixie says. 'I go to the gym with my mom.'

One of the girls comes out of the stall zipping the back of her skirt.

'Aren't you afraid?' the earring girl asks.

'Of what?'

'I don't know, scaring the guys away. Getting too buffed.'

The girl zipping her skirt agrees. 'Tim says girls with muscles are too much.'

The other girl comes out of the stall. 'I think it looks cool. I'd love to have muscles.'

They have cut Dixie completely out of the conversation and they leave the rest room still discussing the matter. Dixie hears the word 'dikeoid' just as the door closes behind them.

She walks down the hall, stops at her locker for her history book, and continues toward her next class. She passes the cafeteria and wrinkles her nose at the medicinal smell of the institutional food. She thinks back on the meal last night at the restaurant and wishes now she'd eaten more of it. Then she remembers Trina's idea for the Men Menu and smiles. Perhaps she should put Kevin Peterson on the menu. He is nice looking, although he combs his hair straight back and the bald spots on the sides make him look a little like an eagle. He's intelligent, has a sense of humor, isn't a felon . . .

'Yo, Dixie Cup.' Joseph Little, purveyor of fine narcotics, is suddenly walking next to her. He is California handsome, sun-blond hair, colorful shirt with a silk tie carelessly knotted just so, royal blue suspenders, a shapeless linen sports jacket, an expensive trigold watchband to hold a campy Gumby watch. 'Where to?'

'History.'

'The World According to Filborne, huh?' His hand was on the small of her back.

'I don't think she likes me.'

'She doesn't like anybody who isn't dead or quotable.' His hand slips down to the top of her ass. His fingers scratch at the fabric of her skirt.

She twists away from him. 'I'm already on Peterson's shit list. I don't need anymore trouble.'

'You're still mad about that little hickey, aren't you?' He places his fingertip against her neck, looking for it. He rubs the spot and she winces slightly. 'There it is. You covered it with makeup. How modest of you.'

'I haven't been here that long, Joe. I don't need a reputation.'

'Reputation?' He laughs. 'How quaint. You sound like a Fifties movie.'

Dixie is worried she may be blowing it. 'Fuck you, man,' she says and walks quickly away.

'Hey, I'm sorry.' He catches up and walks with her. 'I can be a jerk sometimes. I don't mean anything. I just like you, that's all. No big deal.'

Dixie looks at him. He is truly gorgeous. He is also a straight-A student. His parents appear to be happily married, both working professionals. His older sister graduated three years ago and is studying architecture at San Luis Obispo. But if Dixie threw him up against the wall right now and patted him down, she'd undoubtedly find cocaine, marijuana, pills, and maybe even heroin on him. So far she had found no evidence that he took the stuff himself, only that he sold it. The question now was, who did he buy it from?

'I like you too, Joe,' Dixie says. 'But you are a jerk sometimes.'

He smiles. 'I'm working on it. I expect to be jerk-free by the summer.'

Dixie laughs, kisses him on the cheek, then ducks into the classroom. Mrs. Filborne is writing on the blackboard, 1873 in large letters. She takes her eyes off the blackboard to watch Dixie walk to her desk. Finally she faces the rest of the students and says, 'Now, class, what's so special about 1873?'

9

Trina sits behind two guys in rags. They smell like lemon-scented furniture polish. They are unshaven and scratch their necks a lot with dirty ragged fingernails. Watching them scratch makes her feel itchy and she finds herself scratching her own neck. She doesn't move, however, because she is nicely hidden by these two. She is spying.

At forty minutes after ten o'clock the city clerk once again calls roll. The Los Angeles City Council is supposed to begin its meetings at ten, but these meetings never begin on time. A quorum of ten of the fifteen council members is required to start. Only eight are here now, including the object of Trina's spying, Carla Bennington.

Councilwoman Bennington is sitting at her desk talking on the telephone. While talking, she peers down her nose through bifocals at the pink phone message slips her female aide is handing her one at a time. She laughs into the phone, her head thrown back with glee. Her laughter bounces off the polished marble surroundings. One of the other council members looks up from his newspaper, smiles, then returns to the paper. It is that kind of laugh. Trina finds herself smiling too.

Carla Bennington hangs up the telephone, hands two of the pink slips back to her aide, and begins to pore over some papers in front of her. Even from here, Trina can sense the woman's energy. She is forty-six, with long black

111

hair that drapes neatly over her shoulders. A gray streak two inches wide starts at her widow's peak and continues back, curves around to the left, and tapers off as it mingles with the rest of her hair. She parts it in the middle like early Joan Baez and wears unflattering suits that hang shapeless on her trim body. She wears no rings, a simple Timex watch, and earrings completely inappropriate to her face, hair, and clothing. She dresses like a mother completely outfitted in Mother's Day gifts from her small children.

Trina writes all this down in her notebook.

The clerk calls roll again and finally there is a quorum. A few more scruffy men and women shuffle in and take seats in the audience. Today is a discussion about the homeless. Several well-dressed businessmen from Chinatown are disturbed that the city is housing the homeless in hotels there. Both sides will plead their cases. The five-minute speaking limit rule will be strictly enforced.

Trina gets up and leaves. Now that Carla Bennington is occupied for the next few hours, Trina can get to work.

She climbs the stairs and walks down the hallway, stopping at a public phone to call her gynecologist. She makes an appointment for tomorrow afternoon. She already knows for certain that she is pregnant, but she wants to make it official. After she hangs up the phone, she searches for the office where she has her secret meeting.

'You're late,' Howdy says as Trina enters his office.

'How late?'

Howdy looks at his watch. 'An hour.'

'Hell, that's not late for me.'

'That's true.' He nods.

Trina goes around his desk, leans over, kisses him on the forehead, wipes the lipstick off his skin with her fingertips. She licks her lips as if tasting something. 'You using moisturizing cream now, Howdy?'

'Count the wrinkles, sweetheart. One for each birthday, plus two for every year we dated.'

'We dated for two months, kiddo. Two month over summer because we were in summer school and most of the rest of the kids in summer school were gorps.'

'Skags.' He laughs, stands up. 'Let's talk somewhere else, okay? Somewhere private.'

'Sure.'

She lets him lead her down the hall. He is making this more cloak-and-daggerish than necessary, but she plays along. Howdy White works for Councilman Nicastro, so it isn't exactly out of line for him to be talking to a representative from The Great Pretender, Cory Meyers. The twist, though, is that Howdy is engaged to Lila Steinmann, the shapely aide who'd been handing Carla Bennington her pink phone messages.

Howdy leads Trina down several dark corridors, the glossy marble floors reflecting the dim overhead lighting like lily pads in a scummy pond. They pass several council members' offices, with their little shingles hanging out announcing name and district. They don't speak. Hardly anyone does in the hallways. Voices carry.

Finally Howdy stops in front of a door with no shingle. He knocks. When there is no answer, he opens the door. Several desks are stacked on top of one another. Chairs and boxes are also stacked along the wall.

'We'd better hurry,' Howdy says. 'Councilman Shea likes to come in here and smoke a joint during break.'

'You're kidding?'

'No.' Howdy looks very serious. 'He has kidney cancer. The chemotherapy is wiping him out. The dope seems to help.'

Trina knows about the cancer. His seat is not yet up for re-election, but she's already been approached by two

113

hopeful candidates who are planning to run as soon as he dies or steps down.

Howdy gestures around the room. 'They're going to make this either a day-care room for building employees with small children, or another conference room, depending.'

'Depending on what?'

'The outcome of this election. All plans are on hold until we see who's in and who's out.'

'You're sitting pretty. Nicastro hardly has to campaign.'

'You want me to feel guilty?'

'A little, yes. He's such a schmuck.'

'Yes, but he's a Hispanic schmuck. And I'm the token Jewboy on his staff. He's running against two other Hispanic candidates, a black woman and two white businessmen this time. Any one of them would be better than Nicastro, but he's been in the office so long they'll have to catch him with his hand in the till before they can shake him out of office.'

'From what I hear, that's not impossible.'

Howdy smiles. 'That would put me out of a job.'

Now they were getting down to it. Trina unstacks one of the chairs and sits down. 'There are other people you could work for.'

'Oh?' He tries to look innocent, but the god of that had left him long ago. He merely looks more devious.

'I take it there's no room on Carla Bennington's staff,' Trina says. 'After all, you do have connections there.'

'She's happy with her current aides.'

'There will be new members of the council after this election.'

'Sure, but they already have a loyal staff.'

'There's always room for a smart, knowledgeable man.'

'Your word?'

Trina hesitates. She hasn't discussed this with The

114

Candidate yet. But she is sure he will go along with her suggestion. 'If what you have is helpful.'

'Ah, the big If.'

'What'd you expect? Unconditional surrender?'

Howdy hops up onto one of the desks. 'Your word is gold with me, sweetheart.'

Trina looks at him with curiosity. Yesterday she couldn't remember if she'd had sex a few days earlier with The Candidate. But today she remembers with unnatural clarity the only time she'd slept with Howdy White. In his dorm room at the University of Redlands. She'd fumbled with the foam contraceptive. He'd watched her inject it and made a kind of sour face. During the actual intercourse, her legs sticking straight up in the air, his roommate had stumbled in drunk, a six-pack of Coors in each hand. She'd looked up over Howdy's sweaty back, between her stiff legs upright as goal posts, and stared at the reeling roommate. She tried to tell Howdy, calling him, punching his arm, but he didn't seem to notice or thought her punches were signs of urgent passion and quickened his pumping. The roommate grinned at Trina, winked, then quietly left, locking the door behind him.

One of the reasons they'd split up was because they couldn't find anyplace to have sex again. Trina's dorm room was out because her roommate was a hypochondriac who never left the room except for class, and immediately rushed back for her medication and a nap. Motels were out because both were broke. Howdy's room was out because she couldn't stand the thought of seeing the roommate again. It all worked out okay. Howdy started dating Gretchen Fowler, whose roommate had dropped out midway through the semester with hepatitis and had a dorm room to herself. Trina had married Howdy's roommate, Rob Barre.

Now looking at Howdy, though, Trina finds him a

115

perfect candidate for the Menu. Lanky, dressed for success, a thick moustache, intelligent. Yes, he was engaged, but that only meant intentions to be married. Until a better offer came along.

'So when's the wedding?' Trina asks.

'We haven't set an actual date yet. Lila's waiting for the election to be over.'

'And you?'

'I'm just waiting.'

Perfect for Barcy, Trina decides. Smart but not brainy, manipulative but not a martyr. Not like Eric.

'I don't have much time, Trina,' Howdy says.

'Then tell me what you know.'

'Agreed that if Cory wins, I get a staff position commensurate with my current position?'

'Agreed.'

'With a ten percent raise.'

'Five percent.'

'Shit, Trina, we're old school chums.'

'Not quite. I went to the school of hard knocks, Howdy.'

'Hard knockers is more like it.' He frowns.

She grins. 'Five percent.'

He sighs. 'Okay, Lila isn't exactly a gossip about Carla. In fact, she's about as dedicated to the woman as you can be. Lila's still a little naive that way. If she'd been around when Eugene McCarthy was running, he'd probably been president. She even worked on Gary Hart's campaign before the big sexposé, boffing in Bimini.' He grins and shakes his head. 'She'll learn.'

'I thought you didn't have much time?' Trina says flatly.

'This is all I know: Carla gets up about five in the morning every fucking morning, weekends included, and jogs about eight miles. Her ex-husband Phil sometimes joins her, isn't that cute? They've been divorced for four years but that hasn't hurt her any. If anything, it probably

116

increased her popularity. Attractive, sexy woman on the loose.'

'I know all this, Howdy.'

'Let me do it my way, okay?' There is an edge in his voice, but he quickly smiles to show no hard feelings. Howdy does not like to be bossed, a condition common among those who know they are smarter and more capable than the person they work for. But Howdy is also smart enough to recognize he does not have the kind of personality that will win elections for himself. He is too direct and intellectual. This scares voters. 'She has two daughters. Erin is at UCLA, Alice is waiting tables in Venice Beach living with a performance artist.'

'Ah, an artist,' Trina says. 'Drugs?'

'Probably. I can't verify.'

'What's Carla doing about it?'

'What can she do? Lila says it's eating her up. Alice is twenty-two, quit college after one year, has lived with a variety of men, all artists of some sort.'

'Arrests?'

'She was stopped once for a broken taillight. Cops found a half-smoked joint on the car floor. Looked like she'd just dumped it. They took her in but as soon as they found out who she was they let her go with a warning.'

'Carla lean on the cops?'

'No. She didn't even know about it until Alice was out. Tell you the truth, even if she'd known I don't think she would've leaned on the cops.'

'Come on, Howdy. She has a say in overtime pay for cops. That's a lot of muscle.'

'And that may be why the cops let Alice go. I'm just saying Carla didn't ask and probably wouldn't have asked.'

Trina sighs. 'So far you're talking yourself into unemployment, pal. No one's that clean. She's good looking, sexy, bright, powerful. Who's she fucking?'

117

'She dates occasionally. Always very public places, always someone safe. One of three guys: David Kraft, the electronics millionaire; Stephen Pomadeer, the millionaire TV producer; Evan Frankel, the millionaire plastic surgeon.'

'I see a common denominator. Anything there? Private campaign loans.'

'None that Lila knows about.'

'What about the plastic surgeon? Some after-hours nip and tucking, a secret face-lift?'

'Not that Lila knows about.'

'What the fuck *does* Lila know?' Trina asks in frustration.

Howdy smiles and Trina knows he's been saving something. 'Carla does take off for weekends.'

'Gosh, wow. Stop the presses.'

Howdy laughs. 'No, I mean, she goes off on weekends, sometimes even during the week. She never gives a place or phone number. Instead she calls in her office twice a day in case something comes up.'

'How often does she do this?'

'Every month at least.'

Trina thinks about this. 'Could be she just needs to get away. City Council is a demanding job, she works hard at it.'

'Sounds like you like her,' Howdy teases.

'She's good. That doesn't mean someone else wouldn't be better.'

'Hey, no need to convince me. As far as I'm concerned, whoever pays my salary is better.'

'Where do you think she goes? Does Lila ever speculate?'

'Yeah, sometimes when we're naked in bed we make up scenarios. Secret Colombian drug connections to finance her campaigns, teenage surfers she picks up and

118

takes to Hawaii, two men in black socks with leather hoods and her alone in some basement in Pasadena. Afterwards, Lila and I make love.'

'Thanks for sharing that special moment.' Trina stands up and paces. 'This is very unusual. I wonder where she goes, what she does.'

The door suddenly opens and Councilwoman Carla Bennington is standing in the doorway. She looks first at Howdy, then at Trina. There is no expression on her face. She tucks her hair, including the gray steak behind her ear.

'Howdy, Howdy,' she says.

'Hello, Councilwoman Bennington.' Howdy is on his feet, standing straight and looking guilty. 'Do you know Trina Bedford, the Bedford Agency?'

'Nice to meet you,' Councilwoman Bennington says, looking at Trina.

Without hesitation, Trina walks over and shakes her hand. She is taller and bustier than Carla and uses her height and chest to overcome any awkwardness caused by the situation. 'Nice meeting you too, Councilwoman.'

Councilwoman Bennington glances at Howdy. 'I was looking for Councilman Shea. Have you see him?'

Howdy shakes his head. 'Not this morning.'

'Thanks.' She looks back at Trina but does not smile. 'Good luck,' she says. She leaves, closing the door behind her.

Trina is wondering what she means by that. Good luck with the campaign. Or good luck trying to dig something up on me.

'I'm in big trouble,' Howdy says, frowning. 'Lila is going to slice, dice, and julienne my nuts.'

'Tell her the truth, you were spying for me.'

'I'm better off if she thinks we were in here screwing. That's understandable. Betraying Carla is worse.'

119

'From what I can tell about the woman, she probably won't even say anything to Lila.'

Howdy considers that for a moment. 'You're right. I'm safe.' He opens the door, turns around, wags a finger at Trina. 'You're the one in trouble. Carla knows you're sniffing around.' He smiles at her. 'You are still sniffing around, aren't you?'

Trina playfully pushes him out the door. 'Every time I'm alone in a room with you, someone walks in. Explain that.'

'Because every time you're alone in a room with me, you're doing something nasty.'

Trina walks silently beside Howdy as they stroll down the corridor. 'Yeah,' she finally says, 'I'm still sniffing around.'

10

'I really don't understand, any of this,' Ben says. 'Maybe I'm too dumb.'

Barcelona says, 'Just be patient.'

Ben Leopold nods uncertainly. He is sixty-two years old, three years from mandatory retirement. He repairs photocopiers for Xerox. His fingernails are remarkably clean but slightly grooved, as if scrubbed regularly but with bristles that are too hard. He is in Barcelona's Early British Poetry course where they are currently studying John Milton's *Samson Agonistes*.

Barcelona sits behind the brown metal desk in her office in the Literature and Language Building. Ben sits miserably next to her desk holding his term paper about John Milton's imagery. His clean fingers have worried the erasable bond into permanent wrinkles. She recognizes the accountant-fine red pen marks on the front page of his paper, her scribbled notes in the margins telling him what's wrong. The grade is hidden on the last page, but she can see it plainly through the top five pages as if she had X-ray vision. C minus.

'Well,' he says, 'if I'm not too dumb, then I must be too old.'

'Come on, Ben, let's not play this game.'

He looks over his shoulder through the narrow strip of glass next to the office door. The glass runs floor to ceiling

121

and is maybe a foot wide. It is embedded with heavy wire mesh. Ben points at the Literature and Language secretary's office through the glass. 'I was fixing your department's machine last semester. You guys jam that thing up maybe once a month, don't ask me how. I overheard you talking about poetry to some kids and figured, what the hell, I'm gonna retire in a couple years and I don't really know much about anything except photocopiers, so I signed up for your course.' He runs his pale hand through his short grey hair. 'Dumb.'

'Is this where you say, "Can't teach an old dog new tricks"?'

Ben smiles. 'Would it help?'

'John Milton was sixty-three years old when he finished *Samson Agonistes*. And he was blind.'

'You're just like my son, won't let me get away with anything.'

Barcelona takes the paper from his hand and goes over the flaws in it point by point. Ben Leopold hunches over the desk and listens. He nods, asks questions, argues occasionally, laughs good-naturedly at some of his own statements. Outside the office, through the strip of wire-meshed glass, Barcelona can see another of her students standing, peering in. She holds up four fingers and waves him away, telling him four more minutes. Ben looks over his shoulder, sees the other student walking away.

'I should go now,' he says.

'No rush. You understand my comments any better?'

'Sure,' he says. 'I'm not blind.'

She laughs. 'Rewrite the paper and I'll change your grade.'

'What if the paper is worse?'

'Then I'll change your grade to a lower one.'

'You be nice to me, young lady. I'm a widower and there aren't that many eligible bachelors around anymore.

I read last week that after thirty there are eight women for every man. Couple more years, I'm gonna start looking pretty good to you.'

'See you in class, Ben.'

'Did I mention my substantial pension?'

'How substantial?' she says.

He laughs and leaves. The other student, Grant Treemond, enters. He is eighteen, gangly, very serious. He carries a battered skateboard under one arm. His hair is cut so short he looks almost bald, except for the eight-inch lock of hair that sticks out of the back of his head and is braided and tied with a lime green shoestring. 'I wanted to talk about my paper,' he says as he plops down in the chair. He sets his skateboard under his feet and rocks it back and forth on the blue carpet.

'You got an A on your paper, Grant,' Barcelona tells him.

'A minus,' he corrects her. 'I don't agree with some of your comments.' He takes his paper out of his backpack. It is folded into a little square the size of a baseball card. He unfolds it and lays it out on her desk. There are hardly any red marks on it. This was the best paper in the class. 'On page two,' he says, 'where I compare Homer's blindness and the blinding of the Cyclops with Milton's blindness and the blinding of Samson. You didn't like that.'

'I like the idea, but you never do anything with it. You mention it as being perhaps significant, but you never explain how or why. It's basically an aside that detracts from the main thesis of your paper. Either develop it or kick it loose.'

Grant thinks about that a moment then nods. He flips the page. 'What about this?'

Barcelona reads her note. 'Okay, here you compared Delilah in the poem with her biblical counterpart. You mention that in the poem Milton made her Samson's wife, though in the Bible they aren't married. But you fail to comment on why he did that. Why make such a drastic change?'

'Maybe he was having marital problems and wanted to say something about marriage, you know, a dig at his wife. The old goat was married three times.'

'Maybe.'

'Or maybe he thought the illicit nature of their affair in the Bible undermined the impact of the betrayal.'

Barcelona smiles. 'Maybe.'

Grant stares at her a minute, then smiles too. 'Maybe? That's like saying, "Look it up," right? Look It Up. The teachers' national anthem.'

'In the Peace Corps they have a saying: "Give a hungry man a fish and he eats one meal; teach a hungry man how to fish and he eats forever."'

'You in the Peace Corps?'

'Almost.'

He shakes his head. 'I should've figured you for an ex-hippie.'

The office door opens and Harley Buss, the English Department chairman, sticks his head in. 'I hear you're about to become rich and famous.'

'Hi, Harley.'

He steps in with one blue-jeaned leg. He is holding a steaming mug of coffee. He has sleepy blue eyes, perfectly coiffed gray-black hair, a low friendly voice. Barcelona and Harley have been dating casually for a few months, since Christmas break. Over Christmas vacation Harley's young girlfriend left him to become an actress. He is forty-five, the young actress is twenty-two, a former student from his Shakespeare class which he taught before he became department chairman. After she moved to L.A. he was so depressed that everyone in the department was

124

worried about him. One day after class, Barcelona had stopped by his office to try to cheer him up. They ended up going out to dinner. He is extremely bright and charming, handsome in a boyish way. They slept together after a couple of weeks, not that Barcelona wouldn't have sooner, but he'd never made the move. Finally when they did go to bed, the lovemaking had been somewhat lethargic on his part. Workmanlike, she kept thinking while he crawled around her body. As if he had a standard repertoire of techniques, a sexual Things To Do list that he completed and checked off. Afterward they lay in bed watching TV and he made funny jokes about the shows. She laughed until she ached, enjoyed that part of the evening much more than the sex.

'So you're on the brink of celebrity,' Harley says from the office doorway.

'Oh?'

'The screenplay. For Lynda Kramer.'

'Ah,' she says.

'You doing a script for Lynda Kramer?' Grant asks.

'Trying to.'

Harley sips his steaming coffee. 'Lunch later?'

'Maybe.' She isn't being coy, she just doesn't like it when faculty pop into her office during a conference and then talk around the student as if he isn't there.

'We're proud of you,' Harley says. He sips his coffee, winks, and is gone.

'You're going to make a fucking fortune,' Grant says, snatching up his paper. 'No more of these dumb Milton papers for you. Go for it, man.' Then he too is gone.

Word is out. Barcelona has mentioned it only to her office mate, Susan Mesa, as they had exchanged news that morning before class the same as they had every morning for the past six years. Now everyone knows. Barcelona doesn't mind; already she's been congratulated by half a dozen faculty members. This surprises her more than anything, because these are the same people who have never read any of her novels because they weren't 'serious' literature. When Barcelona had sold her first novel, she had been so excited that she threw a little party for her friends in the department. She had rented the recreation room at her apartment complex. Eric had placed a wooden door over the pool table and they used it to serve the cold cuts and dips and extremely cheap champagne. Everyone showed up, congratulated her. She thought that during the weeks to come they would mention the book, how they liked or didn't like it. Finally, after asking around she discovered that no one had actually read it or even bought it. 'I don't read science fiction,' a few had said. Others, 'Over summer vacation, I promise.'

And so it had continued ever since. The rest of the faculty thought she was wealthy because of her book sales, having no idea how small the advances are. When she joined the other teachers in an after-school drink, they always expected her to pick up the check. She stopped joining them.

She wrote, she taught. A full-time teaching load consisted of four courses. Everyone taught two sections of Freshman Composition, which was why they were so proprietary over the one or two courses they got to pick for themselves. Three years ago Barcelona had petitioned to teach an introductory creative writing course, but the faculty committee had turned her down, as they have every year since then. 'While we applaud your ambition,' Foster Malone, the novel writing teacher had explained, 'we don't think the publication of two genre works qualifies you to teach the complexities of the creative process. We are, after all, a college and should be focusing on relevant literature.'

Foster Malone is Irish with a rolling brogue and a gray-flecked beard and mussed long hair that shouts Writer! ten feet in every direction around him. He has had eight poems published in Ireland and six in this country in the twenty-two years he's been teaching at Sand Coast College. The other creative writing teacher, Hester Hoffman, had a published novel sixteen years ago, but hasn't sold anything since. Instead she opened her own literary agency and has sold five of her student's novels during those years. She agreed with Foster. 'It's not enough to have published,' she'd said. 'One must be able to teach the delicate craft of writing.'

So Barcelona has been delegated to the ghetto of pre-eighteenth-century British literature. The twentieth century was already staked out by Gary Lehman. Nineteenth-century poetry belonged to Barbara Foley; nineteenth-century novels was Arnold Dickey's domain. Shakespeare, which was within her allotted time frame, was the exclusive property of Marvin Endright.

Finally, Barcelona stopped her petitions. She continued teaching Milton, Chaucer, Malory, Marlowe, Donne, and the others as she had done since graduate school. No one else wanted them, they required too much preparation and weren't as popular with the students. Unpopular courses risked being canceled unless they had a minimum of twenty-two students sitting in their desks on the first day of class. If your class got canceled, you were assigned yet another section of Freshman Composition.

Now, however, Barcelona is thinking of quitting. The idea has come upon her suddenly and takes her by surprise. Never before has she even considered such a move. Such a drastic change. She is not fond of changes anyway, especially drastic ones. Still, she is thrilled at the daring of such a thought. Though she doesn't make as much money as the others imagine, she makes enough to support herself without her teaching income. And now that she is writing

127

a screenplay, opportunities seem to be everywhere around her. She gathers her papers into her briefcase and decides she could live without Grant's battered skateboard and Ben's grooved fingernails.

Barcelona is eating onion rings. They are called onion fritters by the fancy restaurant, but that is because they are very thin. In no way do they resemble any kind of fritters. Harley Buss is sitting across from her eating the wheat fettuccine.

'Why did you quit teaching, Harley?' she asks him. She figures it is okay to ask him this now because they spent the first thirty minutes of lunch talking about Debbie, his former actress-girlfriend. She came by last night to pick up a few clothes she'd left behind. She cried, said she missed him, that she wished they were back together again. When he suggested she move back in, she started screaming at him that he was doing it again, trying to 'kill her ambition.'

'Can you figure her out?' he'd asked Barcelona after they'd ordered. She realized now that they started every date with a discussion of Debbie or how well Harley was coping without Debbie. He always asked Barcelona's assessment of the progress of his split-up.

'Were you killing her ambition?' Barcelona asked him.

'What ambition? She wanted to be an actress.'

Barcelona didn't know what else to say. 'Shouldn't she be in Los Angeles then, or New York?'

'I wanted children. So did she. We both did.'

'Did she have an agent? She needs an agent if she wants to be a professional actress.'

'She has a portfolio. Photographs of her in different outfits and moods. She drove up to L.A. a couple of times for auditions but she told me she hated it. Too humiliating. I was trying to protect her.'

128

'Catcher in the rye, huh?'

'Maybe Holden had something there.'

The meal had come then and Barcelona said nothing. She ate the blackened Cajun chicken sandwich.

'You know,' he said. 'I saw her act a couple of times. Local plays. Chekhov's *Three Sisters*. Something else, uh, *Luv* by Murray Schisgal. To tell you the truth, she wasn't very good.'

'I don't think that's the point, Harley.'

He sucked in a stray fettuccine and nodded. 'I know. The point is I'm too old for her. I know some people talked about our age difference, God knows I sure would have. What was the talk around the department? That I was afraid of women my own age, doubted my own masculinity, wanted to play Big Daddy? What? You can tell me.'

'All of the above.'

'People don't understand. I mean, I've been married twice before, both times to women my own age, one had a goddamn Ph.D., the other made more money than I did, working in a loan company. So I'm not afraid of strong, smart women. I just wanted a fucking family. Wife, kids, house, the whole deal. Now all I've got is the fucking house.' The house, Barcelona thought, that really is the sad part. Harley had sold his old house and bought a large five-bedroom home in Laguna Hills with a large yard and plenty of room for children. He and Debbie had picked it out after a year of house-hunting. Escrow closed last month and now he was on the hook for the house payments. He'd moved in by himself last weekend. 'The house just makes things worse,' he said. 'Makes me think about the kids we were going to have.'

He mentions kids on every date. Barcelona always finds that topic uncomfortable. She feels he is somehow interviewing her, trying to get her opinion about having children. She doesn't have an opinion, which is why she feels uncomfortable. Some days she is certain she wants to have a baby, the next day she is relieved not to have one.

Barcelona repeats her question, 'Why did you quit teaching?'

'I didn't quit, I'm chairman of the department. The Big Enchilada.'

'But you don't teach anymore, you're an administrator.'

'You're not going to start in on me, are you? Teachers versus administrators crap.'

'No. I'm just curious. You were an excellent teacher. I constantly heard students praising your courses. They loved you and from what I could tell, learned a hell of a lot.'

He looks wistful. 'I was good. But the lure of money, power, sex, the awe of my fellow teachers, human sacrifices in my name. It was too much!' He cackles like a mad pirate then laughs. 'Why? You thinking about taking the money and running? Going Hollywood on us?'

'Fuck you.'

'Ah, a raw nerve.'

Barcelona shakes her head. 'The same bunch of faculty members who've always been so contemptuous are now congratulating me on writing a screenplay. A screenplay, for God's sake, the most mundane of forms.'

'They're impressed by the glamour, the bucks.'

'Swell. You don't see any hypocrisy here.'

'Sure, but you make it sound like a conspiracy. Let me remind you, I've only read one of your novels myself.'

'You don't try to hide your shallowness,' she says.

'Please, your flattery embarrasses me.' He laughs and pays the bill. She lets him.

Outside they sit by the fountain and enjoy the sun.

'I have to get home,' she says. 'Fame and fortune and Lynda Kramer are calling to me.'

'Just a few minutes,' he says, tilting his head back and

looking straight into the bright sun. When he looks back at her, he is squinting. They sit quietly for a few minutes and Barcelona thinks how pleasant this is. Not sexy, not heart-thumping panties-wet passion, just pleasant. Nice. For some reason she thinks of Trina's menu and wonders if she should include Harley. She imagines Trina or Dixie going out with him, Diva and he would never do. She feels absolutely no jealousy. She sees them in bed, Trina's large breasts swaying over his open mouth. Nothing. Dixie's oak-hard thigh muscles flexing as she lifts her hips to his. *Nada.* Still, there's no way she's going to get involved in such a ridiculous idea. Men-u. Christ.

She watches Harley as he watches the women walk by. The restaurant is nestled between two towering glass office buildings. The clouds are mirrored in the buildings, making them seem somehow reverent, modest about their own existence. Totems in awe of Nature. Barcelona smiles at such thoughts. Don't put any crap like that in the screenplay, she thinks.

Well-dressed women from the buildings walk by in groups of three or more on their way to or from lunch. Their high heels clack out a military cadence. Harley is grinning as he watches them.

'So this is girl-watching, huh?' Barcelona says.

'Yup. The real thing. Up close and personal.'

'That's all there is to it? Just sit and stare?'

'Well, some guys may shout things, make rude noises, but that's a rarity among the true aficionados. Mostly we just stare.'

'What do you think about? Screwing them?'

Harley looks at her with amusement. 'I can't tell you. That's guy stuff. Telling you would be breaking the code. It'd be like a magician telling how he made the rabbit disappear.'

'Consider it research.'

Harley sighs. 'I'm probably making a big mistake here, but okay. I will share my uncensored thoughts with you as I girl-watch. However, you must promise not to hold anything I say against me. Remember, everything I say comes directly from the id, unfiltered by super ego.'

'Christ,' she says.

Three women in their twenties walk by. Harley puts on his sunglasses and looks in the opposite direction.

'See,' he says, 'this is how you can stare at them without seeming like a lech. You have the sunglasses on so they can't see your eyes.'

'Obviously.'

'But the trick here is to look away from them, toward where they are walking. That way, when they walk into your sight, they are walking away from you and you can stare at their legs and asses but you don't look like you've been staring at them. They just happened to wander into your line of vision.'

'Ingenious.'

'Fucking A, kid.'

'Okay, but what do you think about when you stare at their legs and asses?'

He tilts his head at the three women as they walk away. 'They all have fat asses. The one on the left in the red has nice ankles. The one in the middle has too much hair spray, I'd have to be drunk to go to bed with her. The one on the end looks like she likes to give head, but she looks dumb too, giggles too much. Probably watches "Three's Company" reruns, Harvey Korman is her favorite comedian.'

Barcelona laughs. 'You're a pig.'

'Hey, hey, we made a deal.'

'I'm sorry.' Barcelona is not really offended, she thinks it's funny. More, she finds it oddly erotic to be listening to Harley's commentary on the women passing by.

Four more women come out of the same restaurant they just ate at.

'Uh oh,' Harley says. 'Here comes The Mild Bunch.'

Barcelona notices that, like the other women they've seen, these four all have extraordinarily complex hairdos. Lots of curls and swirls and puffing up. A blow dryer would not be enough for any of them. Electric curlers, a curling iron . . . She thinks of the curling iron that killed Eric's neighbor. The old man, naked, bloated, lying with his one foot propped up against the tub. Luna bent over him huffing air into his dead lungs. She is ashamed at how useless she was in an emergency. Luna, the young keeper of Eric's eight inches of tempered blue steel, knew just what to do. So did Barcelona. The difference, Luna acted.

'Look at that one,' Harley says, chuckling.

'Which one?'

'The blonde in slacks, the one with the panty line.'

'Oh.'

'She'd be my pick of the litter. The two on either end can barely fit into their panty hose. Those babies are on so tight they need an exorcist to get out of them.'

Barcelona laughs and the blonde turns and looks at her. Harley turns his head and pretends to be looking at the restaurant. When she looks away again, he returns his gaze. 'You're gonna queer the whole gig, baby.'

'Does this kind of activity make you talk like that?'

'It puts me in the mood, I pretend to be a poor, ignorant, happy relative. Distant relatives. Stop in for a beer every night at the same bar, talks about the girls walking by outside. I feel less guilty.' He points to the blonde again. 'She's the only one I'd actually want to get naked with. The others should be sent to the glue factory.'

'You're so arrogant. You assume all these women want to sleep with you.'

'Sure.' He stares silently at the women as they enter

the office building. 'It would never work out between us though.'

Barcelona is startled, she thinks he is talking about her and Harley.

'She's the kind of woman who has hobbies. Backpacking up steep hills. Bicycling with those dumb helmets with the little mirrors on them, wearing those tight pants that show the bulge in your crotch. Or worse, horseback riding. Yeah, that's probably what she does. Every Sunday we'd be out at some stinking barn fighting the flies, digging horseshit from their hooves. I'd look up and she'd be smiling, talking baby talk to a horse, kissing his snout. Is that what they're called? Snouts?'

'Muzzle, I think.'

'Whatever.' He shakes his head and Barcelona is surprised at how angry he seems. He is not joking now. 'Instead of lying around reading the Sunday paper, going to brunch, maybe taking in a matinee, I'm fucking shoveling straw or hay and busting my nuts on a horse. I love Sunday brunch and the Sunday paper and a Sunday matinee.'

'I didn't know girl-watching could be so complex,' Barcelona says.

He glances over at her and a smile slowly returns to his face. 'It's not as easy as it looks.'

And not very rewarding, she thinks. Harley doesn't daydream about sexual conquests when he ogles these women. He looks into the future, as if all of these panty hose-encased rumps formed some giant fleshy crystal ball. He looks into the future and sees conflict, compromise, and finally failure.

'Maybe she is married,' Barcelona says, trying to cheer him up. 'I think I saw a ring.'

'Maybe,' he says. 'But she's still single. Haven't you heard? Everybody's single, or expecting to be.'

Barcelona is tired of this and starts to get up. He grabs

134

her arm and gestures at the two women walking toward the restaurant.

'Oh, God, look at those two,' he says. 'That hair. My God, she must have washed it in a flushing toilet. She thinks she's real sexy, the way she walks. Those six-inch heels, the black stockings.' He looks at her a while longer. 'Hmmm, she is kind of sexy after all. The one with her though, nice butt and legs, but that face has so much makeup you know she's trying too hard. Too hungry.'

Barcelona looks at her. She is talking animatedly to her sexy friend, but she manages to catch a peek at Harley. Her eyes linger a moment, then flick over to Barcelona. She looks away as quickly as a camera blink. Barcelona tells him, 'She likes you.'

'Gosh, maybe you can call her brother and tell him Harley likes his sister. Then we can meet at the malt shop for a float.'

She ignores his joking. 'What do you mean "too hungry"?'

Harley stands up, takes off his sunglasses. 'Let's go. I've seen enough.'

Barcelona drives home thinking about the screenplay. A black Porsche convertible cuts her off as she tries to change lanes on the freeway. She honks her horn at him and he turns around, smiles, and waves at her. 'The asshole thinks I'm making a pass at him,' she says aloud. Probably all men who drive black Porsche convertibles think all women are making passes at them. She thinks about ramming his rear bumper, see what he thinks of that, but she knows she won't. Still, she drives close enough to him to give him a scare, she hopes. He has a red and black bumper sticker that says: GAS, GRASS, OR ASS. NOBODY RIDES FOR FREE. He waves at her in his morror, pulls out of the lane, and roars away.

Barcelona returns to her screenplay. She already has some ideas on what to keep, what to cut, and which characters need to be consolidated. She is very excited by this project. And not just the challenges of it, but the potential for her future. Her life has followed such a predictable routine over the past decade that she welcomes this new aspect. She has decided to postpone any decision about teaching until she finishes the screenplay. By then it will be summer vacation and she can think more clearly. By then, too, she'll know whether or not she can even write a screenplay.

When she arrives home, there is a UPS package on her doorstep from Roger Carlyle. She tears open the thick mailing envelope while standing on the doorstep. Inside are three scripts. Two are from movies she has seen, the other is a teen sex comedy she avoided. She unlocks her front door and hurries inside with her booty, anxious to get started. She wonders what Lynda Kramer is doing right now, right this second. Is she wondering how the script is coming? Is she having a quiet moment with her husband? Feeding her baby daughter? It seems to Barcelona that Lynda Kramer lives in a world where there are no bad decisions. No fear and trembling. Whatever she decides is the right decision.

Barcelona grabs a Diet Apple Slice and takes it upstairs to her study. On her way up the stairs she flips through one of the scripts to get an idea of proper format. Just as she is about to enter the study, her doorbell rings.

'Damn,' she says but doesn't move. She hasn't decided whether or not to answer it. She knows it is probably some school kid wanting to sell her a subscription to the *Register* or someone from the Fireman's Fund with thirty-three-gallon plastic trash bags for sale. The doorbell rings again and she turns around and skip-hops back down the stairs.

She peeks through the door viewer and sees a distorted pumpkin face. Immediately she opens the door.

'Eric?'

'Hey.' He comes in. They stare at each other a second. 'What's up? I haven't read your thesis yet.'

He shrugs as if his thesis was the least important thing in the world. He sighs sadly and reaches out toward her in a friendly way for a hug. She hesitates, then steps into his arms, gives him an awkward hug, and starts to back away. He doesn't let her. He hugs her tighter. His hand slips down and squeezes her ass.

11

Trina is driving to the house of the father of her baby. She hasn't seen him in three weeks, since the time he impregnated her. She hadn't really expected to see him ever again, unless by accident but she feels she owes it to him to tell him about the baby. Trina can't think of anything worse than one day discovering you have a grown child, realizing you missed out on its growing years. She remembers a few years ago reading about Hugh Hefner being told he had a teenage son. There were photographs in the newspapers of their reunion at the Playboy mission. Hugh Hefner had a pipe in one hand, his arm around the boy. They were both smiling. Hugh Hefner looked genuinely pleased. Months later she read that the blood test on the boy didn't check out and he wasn't really Hugh Hefner's. She wonders whether they still see each other.

Trina has no expectations from this man she is driving to see. Certainly she doesn't want his money, nor does she want to further any relationship between them. This is just a courtesy call.

Their sexual encounter had been totally unexpected. They had both been at the California Women's Press Associates' monthly meeting. Trina has been a member since her days as a reporter for the *Los Angeles Times*. He was one of a panel of three guest speakers, the only man in a roomful of professional women. Each member of the

138

panel was a foreign correspondent returning from some distant hot spot. One of the women, an old news horse with leathery skin and a cigarette constantly hanging from her dry lips, had just returned from Lebanon. The other woman, a young Japanese-American beauty, was a former weather girl, now a local anchorwoman. She had recently gone to Nicaragua with her camera crew. She had heard shooting down the street. They showed film of her reporting the sounds of gunfire, holding her microphone toward the window, then crawling under a bed in her hotel, whispering breathlessly while gunshots continued to crack down the street. The camera stayed on her throughout the brief battle. Afterward, they showed her crawling out from under the bed, looking very serious, declaring that she now knew what these people must be going through. Most of the women in the audience managed to keep a straight face, but a few chuckled. The anchorwoman didn't seem to notice.

Then Jamison spoke. Jamison Levy had just returned from El Salvador. He had slides, black and white, that he took himself. The film had to be smuggled out. Though he didn't say how he did it, he did imply that revealing the hiding place would be personally embarrassing. Some of the slides were humorous, some domestically touching, as if they could have been taken in anyone's home anywhere in the world. But others, the ones he had to smuggle out, they were heartbreaking. Most of them were bloody, small children wandering among piles of mangled dead bodies looking for their lost mothers. A woman arranging the pieces from several corpses, trying to puzzle together the remains of her ten-year-old son. When Jamison spoke of these things, there was the deep power of his convictions in his tone, but there was also the tremor of compassion. He had impressed them all.

Trina couldn't remember who spoke to whom first, or

if they'd even been introduced. Somehow they just wound up chatting together near the open bar. He was drinking ginger ale.

'Too early for you?' she'd asked him, sipping her own scotch and soda.

'It's always too early for me.' He'd smiled. 'I'm an alcoholic.'

'You and about half the people in this room.'

He'd looked around with an appraising eye. 'More like seventy percent. Fifty percent know it, the other twenty don't yet. What's your vice?'

'Toilet paper.'

'Pardon?'

'I use too much.'

He laughed so heartily that she had to laugh too. 'That's the first time a woman has ever admitted anything like that so soon.'

'Hey, get with it. This is the nineties.'

'I know I've been gone awhile, but I thought we were still in the eighties.'

'Technically,' Trina said. 'But I read in *Esquire* magazine that decades never start when they should. Some start early, others late. I've decided that the eighties is too boring and we should start thinking of this as the nineties decade. Maybe it'll be more interesting then.'

He'd given her a funny look and Trina knew right then that they would end up in bed together. They'd gone back to his house in Laguna, made love, and played Scrabble afterward, naked in bed. She won by three points. He had called her a couple of days later and they had talked for forty minutes on the phone about nothing really. Both had laughed a great deal. She had expected him to ask her out, but was relieved when he didn't. That had surprised her. He was a terrific man, witty and charming and pretty damn good in bed. But there was something about him that made

140

her nervous. Maybe his intensity. Maybe she felt a little intimidated by his dedication to his work. Here was a guy who walked among people whose lives were a daily tragedy. He was trying to make the world better. What was she doing? Trying to get a man with perfect teeth elected to the City Council.

She was being unfair to The Candidate. She wasn't just working on his campaign because she'd been hired to. She believed in him, found him to be strong, decisive, humble, intelligent, and informed. He cared about people but wasn't a naive idealist. Trina also knew that if he didn't win this election he would win the next. And after that he would slowly work his way up, perhaps to mayor, then governor, then senator. He had the stuff.

She is driving high up into the hills of Laguna. Some of the hillsides are spotted with the jumbled debris of crushed homes that slid down with the mud after last year's rainy season. She sees one new home being constructed on the ruins of an old home site. She can't decide whether she admires the owner's optimism or condemns his idiocy.

She remembers his street, but can't remember the exact address. All the houses look different, but in a way they all also look the same. The same manic attempt to look individual blurs any substantive distinction. It is like driving around in a huge art gallery filled with giant abstract sculptures. Finally she thinks she recognizes his car, a battered old Datsun with huge rust spots on the rear left fender.

As she walks towards the front door, three marine helicopters buzz overhead. She shades her eyes and looks up at them. They seem to be moving slowly, like green blimps. The little red lights flashing on their bellies seem to be some code meant just for her. She smiles at the notion. What would their message be? Stop where you are! Do not proceed! Go home, bitch.

141

She continues up the walkway and rings the doorbell.

She hears footsteps, then a pause at the door and she knows he is checking her out through the door viewer. She turns her face away and pretends to look at the birds of paradise bushes on either side of the door. She doesn't like the way those door viewers distort your face into something grotesque. Imagine what he would think if he saw her boobs through one of those things.

The door opens and she swings back around to face him. He is wearing a bath towel around his waist and is rubbing his wet hair with another smaller towel. Both towels are black with a single yellow strip running the length of each. They look thick and luxurious.

'Trina?' he says. There is surprise in the way he says her name, but not really in his tone.

'Hi,' Trina replies. 'Got a few minutes?'

He hesitates and makes a slight gesture with his left wrist as if he wishes to check his watch, but stops himself. Maybe because he remembers he isn't wearing one. 'Sure, come on in. I'm running a little late though.'

'Won't take long.'

Once inside, she realizes she has no idea how to tell him. Just announcing that she is pregnant sounds very spiteful or accusatory. If she acts too pleased, he might think she's trying to hook him. Trina now knows she hasn't thought this thing through nearly enough. What if he too is delighted and decides he wants to get married? She hardly even knows him and definitely isn't in love with him. Or he may want to share custody the way Rob shares custody of Karyn. Every time Rob comes for Karyn, Trina's heart contracts into a tight fist and stays that way until he brings her back home. Now that pain will be doubled.

She needs a couple of minutes to compose herself, figure things out. 'Got anything to drink?' she asks. 'Soda water or something. Plain water's fine.' No more booze, she reminds herself, not even beer or wine. Bad for the baby.

'Sure.' He walks out of the room. She watches his toweled behind, the firm tapering thighs, the bulge of calf muscles. No doubt about it, he's still great looking. Whichever one the kid looks like, he or she will be a looker.

Trina looks around the living room trying to get some fix on who this guy is. Last time she was here it had been dark and they had rushed right upstairs to the bedroom. She is impressed with the decor. The walls have salmon-colored textured wallpaper, the carpet is that thick nubbed cotton and still looks new though she remembers he said he'd lived here seven years. The artwork on the walls are original oil paintings, mostly giant brightly colored abstract forms merging with other darker, sharper-edged abstract forms. At the point of merger is a bright white line that looks like a tear in space, a flaming new sun trying to emerge. She recognizes the artist's name from some magazine article she's read someplace.

He returns with a glass of sparkling water and ice. 'You look a little dehydrated.'

'Thanks for noticing. You're looking good too.'

'So, it's like that, huh?' He grins. 'Should I slip into something comfortable, like a catcher's cup?'

Trina laughs. She can't decide what to say. Tell him or not? Yes, he's a goddamn charm machine, a juggernaut of suave. But if she didn't tell him, she'd have the baby all to herself, not have to share it with anyone. She smiles broadly at that idea. Jamison misinterprets the smile, thinking she meant it for him and he smiles back.

'I don't mean to be an ungracious host, Trina,' he says, 'but I really am running late.'

What to do? she wonders. She really doesn't know him

143

at all. Beneath the charm . . . what? Maybe nothing. There is no way to reason this out, no applicable logic. She can't leave and think it over because she knows if she leaves now she won't ever tell him, her own selfishness will take over. She needs to figure him out, now.

'I was in the neighborhood,' she says. 'Just wanted to say hi. I should have called.' She puts the glass down and gets up from the sofa. She starts for the door.

'No, I don't mean you have to rush out right now.' He follows close behind her. 'We still have some time to chat.'

As Trina turns back to face him, she lets her hand swing out a little and brush the front of his towel. 'Oh, sorry. You okay?'

It wasn't a hard hit and she knows it. He shakes his head. 'I'm fine.'

'You sure?' She reaches out, puts her hand on his waist, her fingers lightly touching his warm flesh. She drags her fingertips down a couple of inches and he shivers.

'Yeah, fine.'

'Well, okay.' She leans over and stands on her toes as if to give him a little good-bye peck on the cheek. He leans his face toward her and suddenly she steps into him, her hip nuzzling against his crotch. She kisses him on the cheek, but lets her lips linger while her hip rubs his lap. He turns, kisses her full on the mouth. His teeth nip at her lower lip and he reels her into his arms and hugs her. His hand is cupping her butt. He hikes her skirt up with one hand, rubs his palm across her panty-hosed behind. A callus on his palm scratches the material. His hand lifts her buttocks and forces his tongue deeper into her mouth. She can feel his penis stabbing against her hip and grinds a little against it.

'Let's go upstairs,' he says.

He takes her hand and leads her. His towel is poking

straight out in front of him as they climb the stairs. As they near the bedroom, she hears the television. She recognizes David Letterman's voice.

'He isn't on now,' Trina says, looking at her watch.

'Tape,' he says. 'I can't stay up that late anymore. I've lived in too many places with sporadic electricity. If you can't read at night or watch TV, you have to drink or screw or sleep. One is expensive, the others dangerous. That leaves sleep.'

'Which is expensive and which is dangerous?' Trina asks, unzipping her skirt and hanging it on the doorknob.

He whips off his towel and neatly peels back the white down comforter, folding and refolding it across the bottom of the bed. His neatness is mathematical, his concentration intense. Trina unbuttons her blouse and takes that off too. She looks around the room and notices it is as gorgeous as the downstairs. This is one of the best parts of sleeping with someone new, exploring their bedrooms. As she sits on the edge of the bed rolling off her panty hose, she feels like an archaeologist at a fresh dig. What mysteries can be learned about the inhabitants by examining these artifacts. The textured wallpaper, the earth tones of brown and white broken only by the bright explosions of color on the walls, the cracks of light behind the merging geometrical figures. Trina decides that not only is the room beautifully decorated, like a model home, but it is also the cleanest home she's ever been in. Even the baseboards are dust free.

David Letterman turns on the fountain in front of his desk and then they cut to a commercial.

'He interviewed this guy earlier,' Jamison says, climbing under the sheet, waiting for Trina. He has removed the towel but his penis is still poking up the sheet in front of him as he talks. 'This guy, they call him the wild man or something. He goes through Central Park eating the

145

plants. First they arrested him, now they've got him giving tours.'

'I read about him,' Trina says. She is naked now except for her bra. She unfastens the front, but turns her back to him as she opens it. She doesn't want him to see how her huge breasts pop out and flop against her chest. She tosses the bra on the floor and slides into bed next to him.

'The guy was showing Letterman some of the plants from the park. There was this one called gout weed. Used to be called goat weed, but over the years the name degenerated to gout weed. Thing is, people then thought it was called that because it had a medicinal effect on gout. So ever since they've been eating this weed just because they misunderstood the word. All these people eating this weed because they got the name wrong. Imagine that.'

'A rose by any other name,' Trina says, snuggling closer.

Jamison reaches over to the bedside table, glistening darkly with furniture oil, grabs the remote unit, and shuts the TV off. The tape machine continues to whirr faintly beneath the dark screen.

Compared with the last time, this sex is more urgent. Last time he had been inventive, resting between various maneuvers, chatting and joking. There had been a lot of stroking and patient fondling. Like a tub slowly being filled with water. This time it is more like a damn bursting and a flash flood. She likes this just as much.

He is inside of her within minutes, but she wants him to be, asks him to enter. She can feel the sheets beneath her buttocks soaking wet and cool against her skin, all the moisture leaking from her. When he enters her, he does so slowly, almost politely. Trina can't wait. She arches up with a quick hip thrust, swallowing all of him in a gulp. He moves in and out until she is panting, on the brink, then he stops a few seconds, starts in again. Her eyes are closed and she sees herself swimming toward shore. Her friends are picnicking in the sand. Barcy is there cooking something on a small hibachi. Trina can see the smoke, almost smell the barbecue sauce. Dixie and Diva are playing smash ball, whacking the little ball back and forth with their wooden paddles. Each hit is like the crack of a gunshot. Diva is wearing a bikini and looks like she's lost weight. Jamison is sitting on a towel, naked, his dark skin glistening from suntan oil he is rubbing into his thighs. He waves at Trina to join them. Trina is swimming harder and harder. Kicking her legs, thrashing in the water. The shore doesn't seem to be getting any closer. Then Jamison begins to rotate his hips in a circular stirring motion. The shore changes colors, has a yellowish hue. Jamison begins to thrust harder and deeper, his breathing tight bursts of air. Trina swims harder, her arms and legs exhausted. Suddenly a large wave swells under her, lifts her high above the water. It is an impossible wave, twenty, thirty feet above the ocean. The height makes her dizzy. It sweeps her toward the shore in a blur. She is certain she will be killed when the wave crashes against the sand, but she doesn't care. The speed is intoxicating, worth whatever happens.

Jamison comes in one long spasm followed by four shorter ones. His body jerks against hers. His spasms bring her the rest of the way and she comes with a loud holler that startles him. He lifts his head. Through half-opened eyes she can see his confusion at her noise. He looks embarrassed, as if she's farted.

'Don't look so surprised,' she says.

'You didn't scream last time.'

'First date. Nice girls don't scream on the first date.'

He laughs. 'You're incredible.'

She wonders if she's so incredible, why is he looking at the clock and getting out of bed. That is an unfair thought, she realizes. He'd warned her he was running late. She had seduced him. If he had to dress for another date now, she had known that going in.

She remains in bed and watches him as he hurries about the adjoining bathroom. He moves very efficiently, turning on the shower, then going back to the sink, setting out his toothbrush, deodorant, cologne like a police lineup. Trina knows that they are arrangéd in the order that he will use them. She thinks that his neatness is amazing for someone who spends so much time in war-torn countries. Perhaps that's why he is so neat back home, from chaos to order. His obsessiveness would be too much for her, but he might be perfect for Barcy. It's hard for Barcy to meet people her own intellectual equal, though she would never admit that Jamison, though, is very smart.

Trina decides to tell him about the baby. He deserves to know. Besides, as a foreign correspondent, he will probably be out of the country most of the time anyway and not want to share custody. 'Jamison,' she says.

'Speak, wench.' He tears open a new box of Tone soap and sticks it in the shower. He tests the water temperature, adjusts the knob.

'I came over here today . . .' She doesn't like that opening. 'I wanted to talk . . .' That's even worse.

'Uh oh,' Jamison says, looking down at his penis. He turns toward her holding it in his hand and she can see its bunched skin and bald head crusted in red. He touches it and a pink flake snows to the floor.

Trina looks between her legs, sees the blood on her thighs. The yellow sheet is also pink with blood. She has started her period. She is not pregnant.

'Why don't you hop in the shower?' he urges. Meanwhile, he is getting a washcloth.

Trina climbs out of bed and walks toward the shower. She feels tremendous heat in her stomach, as if she has just lost

148

a child. She knows that is silly, there was no child. Still, she grieves.

She washes quickly, soaking off the blood. When she emerges, Jamison holds the damp washcloth he's scrubbed the sheet with in one hand. In the other hand he holds a blow dryer and is methodically blow-drying the sheet. Obviously he is expecting to be sharing the bed again this evening and doesn't have time to change all the sheets and pillowcases so they match.

'I'll do that,' Trina says. 'Go shower.'

He hands her the blow dryer and she finishes drying the sheet. She remakes the bed. She finds an emergency tampon in her purse and inserts it. She is standing in a half-squat, pushing the tampon inside when he emerges from the shower and watches her.

'God, that's sexy,' he says. His penis starts to swell a little in confirmation.

'You're running late,' she says. She balls up her panty hose and shoves it in her purse. She dresses quickly. They exchange a few clever lines that she forgets as soon as she is out the front door. She is in a hurry to get home.

As she walks toward the car, the tampon feels huge and uncomfortable inside her. She starts to walk a little bow-legged, even though she knows she is exaggerating the size and discomfort in her mind.

12

Dixie sits in a cold concrete room with twenty-three teen-age girls in their underwear. Gym class. Last period of the day. The sport of the week is basketball. They are all changing into their gym clothes: a pair of maroon shorts with the school's name in yellow lettering on the right leg, and a yellow T-shirt with the school's name in maroon letters across the chest. Maroon and yellow are the school colors. The T-shirts also have a cartoon aardvark wearing sunglasses and riding a surfboard. The aardvark is the school mascot, a bit of whimsy from the school's first graduating class nine years ago. Recently parents have been trying to have the mascot changed because it isn't dignified. Some parents have actually shouted at school board members over this issue.

The girls are all crowded together on the wooden benches that separate the banks of red metal lockers. Dixie is amazed at the variety of underwear. When she attended high school, underwear was white, blue, or pink. To her right, a girl is taking her contact lenses out and storing them in a little white case. She is wearing a dark red lacy bra that shows the nipples. They are small breasts and small nipples, but in that bra they look provocative. The girl to Dixie's left is standing, reaching into her locker for her yellow T-shirt. Her buttocks are eight inches from Dixie's face. Her panties are cobalt blue, consisting of a small patch of fabric to cover her crotch and narrow blue elastic strings that ride high over her hip bones, meet at the small of her back, then disappear in the crack of her buttocks only to emerge again between her legs and connect with the patch of fabric. Dixie winces a little to think how uncomfortable it must feel to walk and sit all day in that.

Dixie realizes now she has made a serious mistake. When Captain Janeway gave her department money to buy clothes for her undercover assignment, she neglected to buy special underwear. She figured she could just use her own. Underwear is underwear, she thought. She was wrong.

She is still sitting in her short skirt and blouse, reluctant to get undressed. She fumbles with her combination lock, stalling. She can feel the mucky dampness in the air from the last class's showers. Fat drops of condensation dribble down the sweaty red lockers. Around her, girls chat, gossip, giggle. She sees one frighteningly skinny girl with sleepy eyes pop a Benzedrine into her mouth and swallow dry. The girl's ribs protrude against her pale skin like fingers poking against a plastic balloon. The bones seem to be the only thing keeping her body from completely collapsing in on itself.

The girl in the red bra tucks her contact lens case in her purse and removes a pair of glasses from her locker. She attaches an adjustable length of elastic to each endpiece and puts her glasses on, shaking her head to make sure the glasses won't fall off during any movement. She looks over at Dixie. 'What's the matter? You getting turned on?'

Dixie smiles. 'I'm just trying to think of some way to ditch.'

'Forget it,' the other girl says, the one with the panty strings in her crack. 'You can ditch any class in this school but gym class.'

'We always could ditch gym where I come from,' Dixie says.

'Where's that?' the red bra asks.

'Oregon.'

'Well, shit, this is California. Nobody ditches gym.'

Dixie quickly strips out of her clothing. Her own panties are women's Jockeys, pink. Her bra matches. She is the only one in the locker room whose bra and panties match. She might as well be wearing her badge.

Red bra stares at Dixie's body. 'God, what did you do in Oregon, move pianos?'

A few of the other girls look down at Dixie's underwear-clad body. Even relaxed, not pumped up from lifting, the muscles in Dixie's arms and legs twist and bulge like braided bread. Her stomach is as flat and hard as the tiles in the shower. She looks at the other girls' bodies, some thin, some shapely, some hefty, but all somehow un-formed, doughy. Like the half-formed pods in *Invasion of the Body Snatchers*. Dixie's body, however, is the result of many years of training, daily discipline. Only her face is as flat and unlined as theirs. Her character shows in her body; a California version of Dorian Gray.

'Fuck, man,' the girl with the string between her butt says. 'Look at those veins. Fuck.'

Dixie glances down at the ropy blue veins worming just under the skin of her forearms. 'I was on the dive team back home at school,' Dixie explains. 'High dive. Took a bad dive during competition and hit the diving board coming down. I was unconscious when I hit the water.' She parts her hair at the back of her head as if to show them the scar. But no one looks. 'I was in a hospital bed for three months. They thought I might not walk again.'

'God, that's horrible,' red bra says.

'They put me in physical therapy after that, you know, lifting weights and stuff, and after a while I started to get

152

better. Took me two years before I could get out of that damned wheelchair. My mom still makes me keep it up though. I think she's scared that if I stop, I might not be able to walk anymore. She's kinda superstitious and all. I graduate in a couple months and then I'll be going to UC Santa Barbara. Then I can stop.'

'UCSB,' red bra says. 'I hear that's a real party school.'

'Hope so,' Dixie says. 'After being crippled for two years, I'm ready for some partying.'

The girls turn away from Dixie, not wanting such bad luck to rub off on their own young and charmed lives. There is a general lacing up of Reeboks and L.A. Gears and Etonics. Dixie's matching underwear is forgotten.

Back at the station, Dixie leans over the drinking fountain. On the back of her tongue sits a white tablet, 500 mg of vitamin C. She sips some water, tucks down her chin, and swallows. Most people think you should throw back your head to swallow pills, but in fact that constricts the throat. Serious vitamin takers know to tuck the chin to the chest. Dixie has been telling people that for years, but still she sees cops tossing back their morning aspirins, head tilted toward the sky, grimacing as they swallow. People never learn.

Next is the green tablet, her favorite. It contains calcium, magnesium, zinc, iron, copper, kelp, and manganese in a base of trace minerals from montmorillonite and horsetail herbs. She places the tablet on her tongue, leans over the fountain, sips water, tucks chin, swallows.

'Dixie,' Captain Janeway says.

'Sir?'

He is carrying an armful of file folders. 'You wanted to see me?'

'Yes, Captain. Just for a few minutes.'

He hands her half of the file folders. 'Make yourself useful.' He starts off down the corridor.

She still has one vitamin left, a red-speckled table containing vitamins A, D, and E. She pops it in her mouth, steals a quick sip of water, swallows, and hurries after Captain Janeway.

'How's that Mustang of yours holding up?' he asks her as they near his office. He's been wanting to buy it from her for years. He would like to start restoring cars as a hobby. He has never restored a car, in fact knows little about cars. He told her he would like to learn on her '70 Mustang. When she sells it to him he will begin his new hobby, that way he'll have something to do when he retires in ten years. Dixie senses that, despite his many offers to buy the car, he would be more grateful if she never sells it to him and wouldn't have to start learning how to restore it. Of course, now she is stuck with the car. She can't sell it to anyone else or he would feel slighted. But if she sells it to him, he would start to resent her for forcing him to live up to his proclamations of restoring the damn thing. That's why Dixie never locks her car. Her only hope now is that someone will steal it.

'The car's fine,' she tells Captain Janeway.

'How's the carburetor?' he asks.

Dixie would be surprised if he even knew where the carburetor was. 'Fine, sir.'

'I'd probably start with the carburetor. Work on that first. Get the engine perfect before starting on the body.'

'Good idea.'

They are in his office now. He plops the file folders on his desk, takes her bunch and plops them on the desk also. He sits behind the desk, loosens the laces on his left shoe, and leans back with a sigh. 'How's the blackboard jungle going?'

'I need some more clothes allowance. About fifty bucks.'

'You really are starting to sound like a teenage girl.'

'Underwear, Captain. I need to buy certain underwear.'

He looks at her funny. 'They wear special underwear?'

'This school's a little more affluent than some of the others. Just take my word for it, you don't want to know.'

He laughs. 'Thanks for protecting my boyish fantasies.'

Dixie smiles at him. He has a daughter who just turned fourteen. Her photograph sits in a silver frame on his desk. So does one of his wife and a third of the three of them together at Disneyland on the Mad Hatter's Tea Party ride. Captain Janeway is spinning the saucer while his wife and daughter hold on to each other screaming and laughing. He smiles gamely, though he looks a little nauseated. Several times Dixie has been in here for meetings and caught him accidentally looking at the photograph and smiling contentedly.

Captain Janeway is the most decent man Dixie had ever known. Everyone in the department respects his honesty and integrity. He has been decorated twice for bravery. He served in Vietnam, was wounded twice, once losing three toes on his left foot. He returned to the States and joined the LAPD. He married and divorced twice, no kids. Both wives wanted him to be more ambitious, but Captain Janeway just wanted children. He began dating again. Though plain looking, slightly overweight, with sad eyes and a large nose that made him look older than his mid-forties, he was kind and caring and managed to meet a lot of women. None seemed right. Finally, frustrated with dating, he began corresponding through one of those Asian mail-order bride services with a Vietnamese girl living in Hong Kong. He wrote to her in Vietnamese, she wrote back in English. One day, without telling her, he took his vacation and went to Hong Kong. Embarrassed by his surprise visit, Trang confessed the truth she had kept from him: she could not have children. He brought her back anyway and they married. Two years later they adopted a four-year-old girl, half black and half Mexican. The little girl's right leg was permanently crippled from a beating with a broom handle she received from her drunken father. Captain Janeway had taken her to many doctors, had arranged several operations on her leg, sitting beside her hospital bed teaching her chess while she recovered from each one. To Dixie they were like some kind of miracle family, the kind they make TV movies about. Dixie had been over to their home many times for old-fashioned backyard barbecues. He actually wore one of those silly aprons with an American flag on it with the caption: RED, WHITE & BLUE. THESE COLORS DON'T RUN. Underneath he wore the last pair of madras shorts in the country and white socks and sandals. Captain Janeway and Trang seemed very happy together. Their daughter, Shawna, still limped slightly, but otherwise laughed a lot and hugged a lot and worried about her grades and dating like all the other girls her age. She called Dixie 'Aunt Dixie.'

Some of the women cops were offended by the mail-order bride aspect of the relationship. They speculated that Captain Janeway had been looking for an Oriental slave, an unliberated women he could boss around. But from what Dixie had observed, that wasn't the case. Trang raised Shawna, but also took classes at Sand Coast College several evenings a week. Her English now was much better than most native Americans, and she was on the verge of getting her real estate license. Orange County had hundreds of thousands of Vietnamese residents, which could make her a valuable asset to any real estate agency. Captain Janeway had encouraged her to pursue whatever interest she had.

'Anything shaking out there?' he asks.

'I've made contact with the main dealer.'

156

He points to the faint hickey on her neck. He doesn't miss much. 'I'd say you made more than contact.'

'He's a little rambunctious. Nothing I can't handle.'

'Don't let the fancy cars and clothes fool you. The kid's dealing, that means he has to buy it from someone. Somewhere down the line there are some very bad men with their hands on the bucks. They give hickeys with .44 magnums.'

'Thanks, Dad.'

Captain Janeway chuckles. 'Okay, okay, end lecture. What have you got?'

'Joseph Little is really the only one to worry about. There are plenty of drugs floating around the place. These kids can afford them. Some minor sales, just among friends, a few joints, some poppers here and there. But the big action goes through this Little kid.'

'Who's his ratboy?' Meaning who's his supplier, the one who checks the quality of the dope, the one they were really after. Street slang always sounded funny coming from Captain Janeway.

'I don't know yet. I've hung around him a few days now on and off, not enough to make it seem like I'm looking for him. He likes me.'

'Yeah, well don't get your prom dress out of moth balls just yet. I want this rapped up within the month. Find his connection and let's take them both down. I'm getting some pressure from the federal shines.' Shines are the bureaucrats, recognizable from the shine on the bottom of their pants from sitting all day. 'The new federal law means any sale within a thousand yards of a school is automatically one to forty years in prison. That makes the stakes a little higher, China Doll.' Captain Janeway rubs his left foot through his shoe, massaging the missing toes. He closes his eyes. 'How's Principal Peterson holding up?'

157

'Thinks this is "I Spy." Another week he'll be wanting to use passwords and decoder rings.'

'He's all right. I like him. Reminds me of me.' He opens his eyes and smiles.

'How about that fifty dollars?'

Captain Janeway scribbles on a form and slides it across his desk to her. 'Fifty bucks for underwear. Jesus.' He plops his hand down on the form as she reaches for it. 'Kidding aside, Dixie. Be careful. High school or not, when there's this much money involved, there's always somebody around who likes to play rough.'

'I'll be careful, Captain.' She takes the voucher and leaves. She can feel his worried eyes on her back and is grateful.

In the policewomen's locker room Dixie sees more women in their underwear. These bodies are nothing like the ones she saw earlier. These are more like their lockers: battered, rusted, and chipped. Most of these women have bruises on their arms or legs, fist-sized on the arms where they've been grabbed by men unwilling to be arrested by a woman, and foot-sized bruises on their legs where they've been kicked by kids, women, and weak men unwilling to be arrested by a woman.

Dixie mostly notices how much bigger these women seem than the girls from the high school, even though they aren't really. There is just something about the way they walk, sit, stand, an attitude that seems to take up more room. Whatever you've got to show me, I've seen, they seemed to be saying, so get the hell out of my face. Dixie wonders if that is just a cop attitude or an adult woman attitude.

Lena Walker comes from the shower with a towel wrapped around her waist. Both eyes are purple and she has a shiny metal cast taped over her nose. Her breasts are bare and the right one has a nasty bruise that extends from her collarbone down to the nipple. It looks as if someone has spilled tea on her skin and stained it. Dixie went to the Academy with Lena.

'Jesus, Lena,' Dixie says. 'What happened?'

'You want the truth or something interesting?'

'Is your nose broken?'

'Fucking right it's broken. You think I'm playing Liberty Valance or something?'

'I thought maybe it was a new fashion look.'

Lena laughs. 'The Bruised Broad Look. Maybe we can get Cybill Shepherd to do the *Cosmo* cover. I could do her makeup with this.' She makes a fist. For some reason no one understands, Lena hates Cybill Shepherd and never misses an opportunity to bad-mouth her.

'So what happened?' Dixie asks.

'Dumb. Goddamned dumb.' She reaches into her locker and pulls out her panties, slipping them on as she speaks. 'I stop this car, a blue Impala with Texas plates. Cracked windshield. No big deal, a quick fix-it ticket and I'm on my way to lunch at the Mexican restaurant over on PCH.' She steps into her jeans, which are at least a size too small. She struggles into them. 'I call it in, nothing on the computer. I go over to write him up and the bastard jumps out of the car like a madman. Slams the car door into me.' Her pants are stuck at the knees and Dixie can see the bruises on her thighs from the car door. 'I drop to my knees and the son of a bitch slams the car door into my face. Busts my nose and cracks my cheek. Drives off like some crazy guy.'

'Jesus.'

'He looked a little like Jesus. Long brown hair, beard. Ten-gallon hat.'

'I don't recall anyplace in the Bible where Jesus wore a ten-gallon hat.'

'If he had worn one of those babies, no way they'd have crammed some crown of thorns on his head.'

Dixie flips expertly through the combination on her lock and pops open her locker. 'What does Barry say about all this?' Barry is Lena's husband, a CHP motorcycle cop.

'He wants me to quit, as usual. Hell, someone cusses at me and he wants me to quit. That boy needs to get a thicker skin.' She lifts out her bra but doesn't put it on. She rolls it up and sticks it in her gym bag. Dixie notices the bra matches the panties. 'The damn things rub my bruise and stings like hell.' She pulls her sweatshirt over her head. 'Things work out the way we plan, me and Barry'll be buying a house in a year.'

'Really? That's terrific.' Lena has wanted a house for as long as Dixie has known her. But money has been tight and they haven't been able to save enough for even a small down payment. Dixie doesn't want to pry, but assumes they came into some kind of inheritance.

As she undresses she has a sudden rush of camaraderie with the other women in the locker room. She is happy to be naked among her own kind. The bruises, the lumpy butts, the sagging flesh. Despite her own chiseled body, she feels that this is where she belongs, among women whose bodies are broken in.

'Here's the deal,' Lena says abruptly, in a confessional rush. 'I'm going to have a baby . . .'

'Hey, congratulations,' Dixie says. She knows Lena and Barry have wanted children, but had decided to wait until they bought a house first.

'It's not what you think,' Lena says. 'I'm not pregnant. I'm going to get pregnant. But not with Barry's baby.'

Dixie doesn't want to know anymore. She is too tired for moral complexities. She just wants to change into her sweats and go upstairs and lift weights. Today she works her chest, back, and legs. She is looking forward to the exhaustion she knows she will feel when it's over.

Lena looks directly at her. The nose brace glints the overhead fluorescent light back in Dixie's face. 'It's going to be one of those in vitro deals. In vitro fertilization. Won't be Barry's sperm and it won't even be my egg. I'm just the incubator.'

Dixie opens her mouth to say something, but doesn't know what to say. She closes her mouth and thinks about doing lat pull downs.

'I've already had the blood tests, hormone injections, sonograms. They changed my oil and spark plugs while they were in there. I'm ready to race, baby.' She laughs as she ties her shoes. 'You should see this couple, the expectant parents. Nerds from Hell. Guy actually carries one of those plastic pocket protectors stuffed with pencils and pens. He's some kind of engineer. His wife looks like the one who always did the decorations for the high school dances but never had a date to one.'

'Why are you doing this, Lena?' Dixie finally asks.

'Yeah, yeah, I know it sounds crazy. But we're doing it for the same reason most of the people we arrest do what they do. For the money. We want a house, we want kids, we can't afford either. We've been saving for a down payment for five years, we've got about two fucking grand. Good luck trying to buy anything in Orange County for two thou down. The Nerdlys are paying me ten thousand bucks plus my salary for maternity leave. With that we can buy a house and start our own family. Makes sense, doesn't it?'

Dixie has to admit it does make a certain amount of sense. But there is something about it she doesn't like. 'What does Barry think about all this?'

'He says as long as I don't have to fuck the guy, it's okay.' She leans toward Dixie and grins. 'Hell, for ten

161

thousand bucks, I'd've even boffed the little squirrel.'

Dixie knows that's not true. Lena is a tough-talking cop, but she is also a practicing Catholic. 'Doesn't the Pope frown on this kind of thing?'

'Hey, the Pope can afford to frown. He already has a house.' But she looks down at the floor guiltily. 'I figure the kid's not any part mine, so it won't be as hard to give up. And God has provided a way for me to finally be able to build my own family. He gave me this body, this brain, my health, the smarts to figure this all out. This thing can't be a sin.'

Upstairs in the gym, Dixie does an extra set of each exercise. She lets out a strangled cry of exertion with each additional rep. Vaguely it occurs to her that she sounds as if she were giving birth.

Dixie sits in her evening law class barely able to hold the pen to take notes. The professor is lecturing on why those nasty little 'technicalities' that everyone is always screaming about aren't really so little. She has heard all this before in courtrooms during cases in which she has testified.

Dixie has a plan. Night school for another four years, then she will have her law degree. Passing the bar exam will be tough, but she will do that too. She has always accomplished everything she has set her mind to do.

She looks around the room. Randy is not here. Randy Vogel is her boyfriend, significant other, lover, whatever the hell you'd call it these days. Dixie prefers boyfriend, but Trina always makes fun of her when she uses that term. Trina says, 'We're adult women now, for Christ's sake, not on the pep squad.' Dixie agrees but still feels most comfortable with the word boyfriend. It's familiar, and somehow not too intimate. Significant Other sounds like a business partner. Lover is too personal, like he gives her gynecological examinations every night. Boyfriend means we date, occasionally have sex, share some meals, talk vaguely about a future together, but never get around to any specific timetable. Boyfriend.

The door at the back of the classroom opens and Randy enters, tiptoeing, looking embarrassed at disrupting the class. Naturally everyone's head swivels about to watch him creep to the closest desk. The professor's eyes lock on target, fire a quick blast of disapproval, reducing Randy to ashes, and he moves on, continuing his lecture.

Randy slumps down in his chair and winks at Dixie. She smiles back and returns to her note-taking. She can share them with him after class.

Dixie has been dating Randy for six months. They met last semester in Introduction to Criminal Law. Dixie wants to be a criminal law attorney; Randy wants to go into entertainment law. He was a child actor, having had a small but reoccuring role on the old 'Dennis the Menace' TV show. He played one of Dennis's Hillsdale neighborhood friends. Mr. Wilson, the put-upon neighbor, was originally played by Joseph Kearns. Randy says he was a real nice guy who used to joke with the kids all the time. But he died during the filming of the 1961-62 season and was replaced by Gale Gordon as his brother. The next season brought Gale Gordon back but not Randy Vogel.

Randy says he and Jay North, who played Dennis, used to get in a lot of trouble around the set. Jay was every bit as mischievous as Dennis. After Randy left the show, though, he never saw Jay again. Randy did a few cereal commercials, but he never really caught on again. As a red-haired freckled kid in a baseball cap he'd been cute. As a red-haired freckled adolescent he just looked gangly and homely. He went to USC, studied film editing, and got enough TV jobs to support his cocaine habit for six years. Now he was clean.

Dixie wonders why all the mothers on those old shows always seemed so old. Not the stars of the shows, of course, but all the neighbor mothers looked like they were fifty or sixty with ten-year-old children. At the rate Dixie was going, that's how old she'd be if she ever had a child. Trina says Dixie doesn't need to have a child, she just dates them.

Dixie looks up because she realizes she missed what the professor had just said. She glances over at the young man next to her and copies his last notation. He moves his arm so she can see it better and she whispers thank you.

Trina contends that Dixie finds the stray dogs, the losers, the weaklings, and nurtures them like some Sixties earth mother, then is disappointed when they can't stand on their feet. 'Why should they,' Trina says, 'when they can stand on yours?'

Dixie suspects there may be some truth in that. Not with Randy, of course, but with her past relationships, especially her ex, Karl. She remains friendly with Karl, though not as friendly as he wants. He calls often just to chat. Sometimes he casually suggests they give it another try. She ignores him when he says things like that, but he is determined.

Trina is not one to talk about relationships, Dixie concludes. Of the four friends, she is the most promiscuous. She remembers the evening she went over to Trina's. There was no real danger of suicide, Trina loves Karyn too much to do that to her, but Dixie had learned enough about people from this job never to take chances. They had talked, laughed, cried, eaten pizza and ice cream. The next day Dixie had to run an extra four miles just to work off the junk she'd eaten. She smiles at the memory. Trina is not just the most sexual of the group, she is the most passionate. Dixie envies that.

Diva is the dreamer of the group. Her eyes are always

164

focusing on the future, waiting for the Big Break. Record a hit record, make millions. She buys a lottery ticket every day just to hedge her career bets. To Diva, buying lottery tickets is the same as opening an IRA. Her relationships with men are chaotic, accidental. She meets someone, they move in together the next day, live together for a week, a month, a year, drift apart, she meets someone else a few days later, the guy serving her a hamburger at Coco's. Diva just knows things will work out, that she's heading for fame and fortune, even if there is no concrete indication of it in her life at a given time.

Barcy's the odd one. She is the smartest woman Dixie has ever known. Not just knowledgeable, but smart, quick-witted, intelligent. She is the conscience of the group, the one who weighs the cause and effect of every action. Dixie should have that role, considering her job, but she doesn't. Dixie realizes she isn't deep enough to grapple with some complex problems. Give her the rules, the laws, and she will enforce them. Ask her to write new laws and she is lost. She hopes these classes will change that.

Barcy's relationships are perplexing. She meets plenty of men, dates them, seems to like them. She has been proposed to several times. But something happens, she always says no. Dixie thinks Barcy analyzes everything too much.

The professor stops talking and people start to put their notebooks away. Several students hover around the professor with questions. The rest gather their books and leave. Randy is waiting by the door for her. As Dixie walks toward him her legs begin to feel leaden and slow and she wonders if that is just from the workout.

13

'The bar is closed,' Barcelona tells Trina.

'You're kidding.'

'Does this look like I'm kidding?' Barcelona holds up a glass of Diet Coke.

'Well, shit,' Trina says.

Trina is twenty minutes late, not bad for her. Barcelona, Dixie, and Diva are already seated at a booth in the festively decorated Hot Pepper Mexican restaurant. Life-size piñatas in the shape of donkeys and dancing women and banditos dangle from the high ceiling in bright tropical colors. Barcelona munches a couple of warm tortilla chips from the basket and gestures at the empty seat next to her. 'Sit, Trina. You can go on the wagon for one night.'

'The fucking bar's closed?' Trina says, sitting. 'I've never heard of a bar closing on a Friday night. No wonder the place is so dead.'

'It's not dead,' Diva says. 'We're here.' She is drinking Perrier, lazily poking her fingernail at the fetally hunched slice of lime adrift with the melting ice cubes. Her finger-nails are glossy water-melon red and have little white unicorns painted on each one. Some lime pulp sticks to one nail. In the ashtray beside her drink smolders a half-smoked black cigarette.

'No bar,' Trina repeats, shaking her head. 'They re-modeling or something?'

'Court order,' Barcelona says. She hands Trina a little placard that sits on the table. On it is a cartoon of a teddy bear in a sombrero. The caption reads: 'Please bear with us. The State Dept. of Alcoholic Beverage Control will not allow us to serve alcoholic beverages temporarily.'

'What gives? Were they caught serving minors?'

'Remember that discrimination suit some Chicanos brought last year?' Barcelona says.

'Yeah, they accused the place of turning minorities away from the bar at night. Mexicans, blacks, and Arabs.'

Dixie nods. 'This is a real pickup joint after work. Half the office buildings in Irvine empty out into here. There's so much cocaine snorted in the bathroom you can get a contact high just by taking a leak.'

Trina laughs. 'You take all the condoms from the guys' wallets on a weekend night here and you've got enough rubber for all the sneakers in the whole NBA.'

'So this is where you meet your dates,' Diva teases.

'Yeech. You sleep with any of these guys and in the morning you'd have to douche with a blowtorch.'

Diva frowns in disgust. 'God, Trina, where do you come up with that stuff?'

'When I was in uniform,' Dixie says. 'I came over a couple times to break up fights in the parking lot. Even three-piece suits like to go at it every once in a while.'

'Anyway,' Barcelona says, 'apparently they were turning away these ethnic guys—'

'Just the guys?' Diva asks.

'Of course,' Trina answers. 'These places don't care what a woman looks like as long as she has a pussy. Hi, do you know me? I cured cancer and did away with nuclear arms. But when I travel men don't recognize me. That's why I carry this.' Trina points at her crotch. 'My cunt. Welcome in more places than American Express.'

'Jesus.' Diva chuckles.

Barcelona grabs a few more tortilla chips. 'Turns out the whole chain of Hot Pepper restaurants was doing it. So the judge ordered their bars closed for one week as part of the punishment.'

Trina opens her menu, scans it quickly, and closes it. 'Well who picked this place then?'

'I did,' Diva says. 'I like Mexican food. I didn't know about all that other crap.'

'Don't you read the papers?'

Diva shrugs. 'If it's not in *Rolling Stone*, how important can it be?'

Trina playfully throws a tortilla chip at Diva and it gets caught in her hair. Diva untangles the chip from her hair and eats it. Everyone turns to their menus.

'Maybe we shouldn't eat here,' Dixie says. 'If this place discriminates, I don't think we should.'

Diva makes a face. 'We're already here, Dixie. I mean, we've already eaten two baskets of their chips. We can't just get up and walk out.'

'Sure we can,' Trina says. 'Want to?'

Barcelona recognizes the glint in Trina's eyes. The opportunity to walk out of a place, make the grand gesture, sizzles in her eyes. She lives for that kind of thing. Extravagant actions. Barcelona does not like grand gestures. She prefers quiet activism. Volunteer work, letter-writing campaigns, petitions. When she was in college during the Vietnam War, she was deeply involved in antiwar campaigns. She was in charge of the Coca-Cola boycott on campus. She hustled up over three thousand people to sign postcards to the Coca-Cola Company declaring that they would not drink Coke until the war ended. The theory was that they would force Coke to pressure Congress. Barcelona also worked in the student government spearheading a draft-resisters' advisory office on campus. Once she even drove two eighteen-year-old boys into Canada

168

over Christmas break. Their draft lottery numbers had been announced on television the week before, very much like the lottery shows on TV now. One of the boys, Jimmy Remo, had been in her French class. During the drive, he confessed to Barcelona that he had a crush on her and begged her to stay with him up in Canada. They'd get an apartment together, he'd find a job maybe in a bookstore. They could get married if she wanted. This revelation was news to Barcelona. When she mentioned that they had never even dated, he gave her a defeated look and nodded in disappointment. Already he'd become an expert in hopelessless.

She drove back from Canada in the middle of the night, her wipers brushing off a light eyelash snow from her windshield, her radio blaring, the heater working only intermittently. Sometimes the vents would pump too much hot air and she'd have to open the window, other times it stopped working altogether and she'd pull her scarf up over her nose and mouth. For some reason, as she got closer to home, she kept turning the radio up louder and louder, WOR from Chicago. Marvin Gaye sang 'Inner City Blues.' Slade sang 'Coz I Luv You.' The Chi-Lites sang 'Have You Seen Her?'

She never marched, never carried signs, never threw vegetables at buildings, never shouted obscenities at cops. No grand gestures.

'Whaddaya say, Barcy,' Trina encourages, 'should we blow this racist place?'

'They've changed their policy,' Barcelona says. 'And they've already been punished. Let's just eat, okay?'

Trina shrugs, returns to her menu. The others do too.

Barcelona is having difficulty reading the menu. The letters are furry. In her purse are a pair of cheap reading glasses she bought at Thrifty's drugstore a month ago. They are wire-rimmed and rectangular, like the granny glasses all the kids used to wear when she first went to college. Only those glasses were usually colored pink or blue or yellow to make the world look brighter and happier. These are just plain reading glasses. So she can read her own books as she writes them. She hasn't told anyone that she uses them. Except Eric.

The waitress comes over. She is wearing a short yellow skirt with a ruffled hem that stops at mid-thigh. The neckline plunges halfway down her breasts and pushes them together so they strain a little against the neckline. The blue veins beneath the pale skin of her breasts are so visible they look as if they've been traced with ink. The waitress is in her late forties and wears little makeup, just some eyeliner and lipstick. Her outfit seems to embarrass her, but she is very enthusiastic and helpful when they order. Diva still can't decide, so the waitress agrees to return in a few minutes. 'Meantime, let me get you a couple more baskets of chips, girls,' she says with a smile. 'The hot salsa should take your mind off the fact that you're drinking Cokes instead of margaritas.' She leaves, tugging down the back of her skirt as she walks.

'Well, let's get right to it then,' Trina says, snapping her fingers impatiently. 'Let's see what you've got.'

Diva taps the menu with her unicorn fingernails. 'You think I can get a decent vegetarian meal here?'

'You picked the place,' Dixie reminds her.

'Yeah, that's true.' Diva nods agreement as she scans the menu. 'This *chalupa* sounds good. Deep-fried corn meal cup, stuffed with beans, red beef chile . . . Shit, beef. Maybe I can get them to make it without the meat.'

Trina is incredulous. 'That's not the menu I'm talking about, kids. Let's see what gourmet delights await us out there in the real world. Who'd you select, Diva?'

Diva hesitates, flushes. 'I couldn't think of anyone.'

'No one?' Trina asks.

' 'No one I think any of you would be interested in.
Except maybe Calypso. We split up a couple of weeks
ago.'

'Really?' Dixie says. 'Why didn't you tell someone?'

'I told Barcy. But I made her promise not to tell you
guys. Just until I was sure we really were finished.'

Trina looks at Barcelona. 'I hate the way you can keep
a juicy secret.'

Barcelona sips her water so she doesn't have to say
anything. To be honest, she is able to keep Diva's secret
so well because she'd forgotten about it. Though she likes
Diva, even has a fondness for her ditsy life-style, Barcelona
does not feel close to her. Not secret-sharing close.
Yet, for some unknown reason, Diva continues to
confide in her, call her up to chat, ask for advice.
Diva is flighty, unpredictable, undisciplined—the opposite
of Barcelona. But still Diva treats her as if they
were soul mates, as if Barcelona would understand her
lunacies.

'So, are you two finished?' Dixie asks Diva. 'Calypso is
gone for good?'

'Yeah. I haven't seen him in over a week now. Funny
thing is, I never really missed him. I got myself all geared
up for depression and an eating binge, maybe some heavy
crying. Never came. You think it's delayed shock or something?'

'I think you're just glad to be rid of him,' Trina says.
'Now you can look for someone with an actual personality.
Or at least a job.'

'You sound like my mother.'

Barcelona laughs. 'She sounds like everyone's mother.'

'I *am* everyone's mother. Earth mother. With tits like
these I can afford to suckle the universe.' Trina turns to
Dixie. 'How about you? Any decent perps?'

Dixie pulls out a slip of paper. 'Against my better

171

judgment.' She hands it to Trina. 'My only contribution, so don't bug me later.'

Trina sips her wine and begins to read aloud: '"*Kevin Peterson. 6'2", approximately 175 pounds, slightly balding, black on black . . .*"' She looks questioningly at Dixie.

'Black hair and black eyes,' Dixie explains.

'"*High school principal, drives a 1983 Volvo, rents an apartment in Tustin, plays tennis and skis. Divorced, one male child, eight. No scars or distinguishing marks. No arrests, no warrants.*"' She grins at Dixie. 'Very thorough, Officer Cooper. But is he cute?'

Dixie ponders the question a moment then nods. 'Yeah, he's cute. Reminds me of a young Jimmy Stewart.'

'I love Jimmy Stewart,' Diva says.

'Promising,' Trina says. 'What else have we got? Barcy?'

'I'm not involved in this lunatic idea,' Barcelona says.

'Come on, you made a deal.'

'It's just for fun, Barcy,' Diva says. 'We're not conspiring against them for God's sake.'

Dixie touches Barcelona's hand. 'Don't make me the only one who actually brought a name.'

Barcelona smiles as she reaches into her purse. 'Okay, but if Gloria Steinem plasters our faces on wanted posters, you'll know why.'

'This isn't sexist,' Trina says. 'This is a group of women using their skills and know-how to maximize their companion-searching efforts. Think of it as if one of us worked for a large corporation in need of a good CFO. Of course we'd advertise in the usual publications, but we'd also put out feelers amongst our friends in the business world so we could be sure to get a highly qualified candidate. Why should dating be any different? This is matchmaking at its most efficient, nonsexist manner.'

Barcelona hands Trina a folded piece of paper. 'Here. It's the least I can do for feminism everywhere.'

Trina looks at the name. 'Harley Buss? Aren't you dating him?'

'On and off. Nothing serious and I don't think it ever will be. Not from me anyway. Maybe one of you will have better luck.'

Trina reads the paper aloud. '"*Harley Buss, forty-five, blue eyes, premature gray hair.*"' She grins. 'Every guy I know claims his gray hair is premature. When exactly is it mature gray hair?'

Dixie says, 'When they realize it won't go away on its own like a sunburn.'

Trina returns to the paper. '"*Ph.D. in English. Very handsome.*" I've seen him and can agree. He's a looker. What else have you got on him? *Divorced*, naturally. "*Two daughters in junior high school. Income about $50,000. Owns 5-bedroom house in Laguna Niguel. Likes sailing, theater, books, restaurants.*" Sounds good.'

'He's recently split with his girlfriend,' Barcelona warns. 'So expect some fallout.'

'How is he in bed?' Trina asks. 'A moaner or a screamer?'

Dixie laughs. 'Or a whimperer. I hate that the most.'

'Find out for yourself,' Barcelona says.

The waitress returns with another basket of tortilla chips and two bowls of hot salsa. She takes their orders and leaves, again tugging the back of her skirt as she walks away.

Trina sips a Diet Coke and spreads Dixie's paper next to Barcelona's paper. Then she removes a neatly typed sheet from her own purse. 'This guy's engaged, but I don't think it's a serious engagement.' She describes Howdy White.

'Sounds good,' Diva says. 'But how do you approach a guy who's engaged?'

'How do you approach any of these guys?' Dixie asks.

173

'I mean, you don't just walk up and say, "Hi, your name was on my take-out menu."'

Trina laughs. 'Why not? Just call one of these guys up, say you're a friend of whoever introduced him to our menu, and say you'd like to meet him for a drink after work. What's the problem?'

'We don't all have your balls,' Barcelona says.

'Most guys don't have your balls,' Diva agrees.

'We could have a dinner party,' Trina says. 'Invite four guys to Dixie's or Barcy's place, theirs are the cleanest, and we could mingle and choose then.'

Barcelona shakes her head. 'Count me out. I'd feel like I was back in high school. What if two of us go after the same guy, or two guys go after one of us. It makes the others feel shitty. I don't like it.'

'I agree,' Dixie says.

Trina thinks it over, shrugs. 'Well, then everyone's on their own. We just keep adding names to the menu and let each of us decide what to do with those names. Something or nothing. Okay?'

'Okay,' Barcelona says. She has no intention of using the stupid menu anyway.

Apparently, Eric had been waiting for her the afternoon she'd come home from lunch and lessons in girl-watching with Harley.

'I was watching from my car,' he said, still holding her. His hands cupped her buttocks in that familiar way. She thought she should say something, pull away, but it felt so good, so comfortable, that she didn't move, didn't say anything. His fingers kneaded her butt affectionately. When he spoke, his voice was a warm mist in her ear. 'I've been out there for hours.'

'Oh?'

'Okay, half an hour. But it felt longer.'

'You never liked cars.'

'I tried reading.' He broke away to pull a large paperback out of his jacket pocket, *Not in Our Genes*. 'About the invalidity of biological determinism. Really fascinating. You should read it.'

'Sure,' Barcelona said. 'Now?'

He laughed nervously. 'No, not now. When I'm done. I'll lend it to you.'

'Okay.' She looked up into his dark eyes. The crooked scar that cleaved his eyebrow caught the light from the window and gleamed a pure white. 'Anything else?' she asked.

'Huh? What do you mean?'

'You didn't wait in the car for all that time just to tell me about this book, did you?'

He looked confused, embarrassed. 'Yeah, well . . .'

Barcelona walked out to the kitchen, Roger's scripts still clutched in her arms. Eric followed. She set the scripts on the kitchen table and went to the refrigerator. 'Want something to drink?'

'What have you got?'

She tossed him a can of Diet Squirt. 'This or nothing.'

He popped the can and sucked up the foam. 'How can you still drink this stuff? Tastes like acid.'

Barcelona didn't know what to do or say. She felt like she was in a play she hadn't rehearsed and for which she didn't know her lines. The actor's nightmare, it was called, though she had only ever been on stage once, in her high school's production of *Oklahoma!* She was in the chorus. She moved around the kitchen straightening the toaster, wiping the counter, opening a can of cat food for Larry, her cat. She rarely saw Larry. Occasionally she would hear him enter the cat door and hear him eat. But he never hung around the house. He didn't like to sleep with her nor did he like to be picked up or petted. She wasn't even

175

sure why she fed him; she really didn't have any feelings for him. A year ago she'd agreed to keep him for some friends while they moved to Utah. Later they'd called to say they weren't allowed to have pets in their new apartment. They asked Barcelona to have Larry put to sleep. They'd reimburse her the thirty dollars. But Barcelona couldn't do that. It was easier for her to open two cans of 9 Lives Sliced Beef in Gravy every day than to have him killed.

Eric sat at the kitchen table making interlocking wet rings with his can of soda on the glass top. Finally Barcelona had no more props to fuss with and she sat in the chair next to his.

'What's the matter?' she asked. 'You look glum.'

He looked in her eyes, a gaze so direct and unblinking she winced a little. 'I don't know what I'm doing here,' he said.

She had the feeling he was about to say something that would complicate both their lives, make things sticky and sneaky and uncomfortable. She tried to head him off. 'How's Luna?'

He blinked. 'Fine. Great. She's a terrific woman. Well, you saw.'

'Yes.'

'And she's very smart. She doesn't apply herself as she should, but she has great potential.'

'For what?' Barcelona asked.

He blinked again, shrugged. 'For whatever she wants. She gets straight A's in her classes, has a 4.0 GPA. She's also on the swim team at school. Does the butterfly stroke. It's very beautiful, very sensual to watch. I go to all her swim meets.'

'Cozy,' Barcelona said and immediately regretted the snideness in her tone. This was not how she wanted to act, not at her age.

'I won't talk about her if it makes you uncomfortable.'

'No, I'm sorry. I'm just preprogrammed for sarcasm. I liked Luna, I really did.'

Eric nodded. 'She's something special.'

What am I, Barcelona thought, *yellow waxy buildup?* She said, 'She certainly is.'

Eric reached across the table and laid his hands over hers. 'Thing is, Barcy, I miss you.'

Barcelona's heart squirmed uncomfortably in her chest. This is what a baby must feel like jockeying for position in the womb, she thought. She concentrated on breathing, deep soothing breaths.

'I know it sounds funny,' Eric said. 'But it's true.'

Barcelona decided to play it casual, not fall into any traps. She removed her hands from under his and patted his arm in a friendly manner. 'I miss you too, Eric,' she said with a sisterly smile. 'That's natural.'

'You know what I mean, Barcy.' His eyes were slicked with moisture. 'I'm already squirming, no need to kick me too.'

'I don't know what you want from me, Eric. I really don't.'

He leaned across the kitchen table, pushed the pile of scripts out of the way. One slid off the top of the pile and splatted onto the wood floor. Eric ignored it. There was something so theatrical about the script falling and Eric ignoring it that Barcelona almost laughed. But then Eric leaned closer toward her until he was kissing her and she wasn't stopping him, not only not stopping him, but opening her lips, her mouth, receiving his tongue, not wanting to laugh anymore, not wanting to do anything but this, keep kissing him. His left hand cupped the back of her head and pulled her mouth even tighter against his. His other hand cupped her breast and she pushed herself tighter against his hand. His fingers found her nipples through her bra and he pinched hard, which she liked. A sudden moan vibrated up from her throat and into his mouth.

Even as they dropped to the kitchen floor, she knew this was a big mistake. Did she really want Eric again, or did she just want to get back at Luna? Was he leaving Luna or was this a quick fuck for old times' sake? They should talk about it first. But there didn't seem to be a chance. They were busy struggling out of their clothes, piling them under Barcelona's back and buttocks as a cushion against the hardwood floor. She wasn't in the mood for much foreplay, she wanted him inside her now.

He was rocking on top of her, her legs clamped over his hips, her ankles hooked together. The scab on her right ankle kept rubbing against the other with each thrust, but the pain didn't bother her. He said I love you half a dozen times but that didn't bother her either. Behind her she heard the heavy rubber flap of the cat door open. She opened her eyes, saw that Eric's were still closed tight in concentration. She glanced upside down over her shoulder. Larry, fat and gray, was sniffing the fallen script. He batted it once with his paw, then turned away and went over to his bowl of food. He ate noisily. Never once had he even looked at Barcelona or Eric.

Barcelona closed her eyes again and tightened her grip on Eric's shoulders. She felt a button from her blouse grinding into her shoulder blade and shifted. But the button was stuck to her skin and moved with her.

She was on the verge of coming but Eric was stopping a lot, something he always did when he wanted to last a long time. But she didn't want him to last a long time. She wanted to come and she wanted him to come. She wanted to feel him exploding inside of her, feel his body sag against hers, collapsing into her arms. She reached around behind him, between his legs, gently cupped her hands around his balls, and squeezed just a little. His body arched with pleasure and he began pumping faster. She stroked his tight sack a few times and he thrust deeper and harder against her. She slammed her pelvis up against his and he moaned. Suddenly he was coming, his hips spasming, his elbows wobbly. Feeling him coming made her come too and she clutched against him the way she imagined locusts cling to corn husks. Odd image, she thought as she heard the rubber flap of the cat door again as Larry exited.

They silently stood up and walked up to the bedroom, got in bed, and held each other while both drifted in and out of sleep for the next hour. It was the most comfortable Barcelona had felt with a man in a long time. She didn't worry that she would drool or snore in her sleep. Eric had seen it all before. He just held her tight. She had to admit, he was the best cuddler she'd ever known. He never grew impatient with the closeness and rolled away. He could sleep for hours while holding her in his arms, an attribute she found more desirable than sexual agility. Which he sometimes also had.

Finally, when they were both awake and staring into each other's eyes, he wound his finger through her hair and said, 'What about Luna?'

Trina dips the tip of her napkin in her water glass and tries to scrub the enchilada sauce from her blouse. 'Damn, this blouse is practically new.'

'It had to be christened sooner or later,' Dixie says.

'Why couldn't it have been a cream sauce?' Trina says, scrubbing.

The waitress arrives to clear the dishes. As she stacks them efficiently in one arm, she asks if anyone wants dessert.

'Want to split something?' Trina asks Barcelona.

'Like what?'

'There is only one thing worth pigging out over. Death by Chocolate.'

Barcelona made a nauseated face. 'God, Trina.'

'We'll have one,' Trina tells the waitress. 'Two forks.'

The waitress nods. As she reaches for Dixie's almost full plate she asks, 'Do you want to take this home?'

Dixie shakes her head.

The waitress stares at the plate. 'Something wrong with it?'

'No. It was fine.'

The waitress balances the plate on top of three others and whisks away.

'You still not eating?' Barcelona asks Dixie.

'I eat,' Dixie says. She takes a package of vitamins out of her purse, tears it open, and begins swallowing them one at a time, washing each down with water.

'Vitamins are okay,' Trina says. 'But they don't compare with Death by Chocolate.'

'Have you been taking yours?' Dixie asks Trina.

'Want to check my urine? Bright as sunshine.' She picks up her water, sees the junk floating in it from when she scrubbed her blouse, picks up Diva's water instead, and drinks the whole glass. 'God, I wouldn't mind some wine right now.'

'Causes breast cancer,' Diva says. 'I saw that on the news the other night. Some study said so.'

Trina nods. 'I read about that. One glass a week of booze ups your chances by fifty percent. Is there anything left in this world that doesn't go straight for our breasts? It's all a woman can do these days to hold on to these things for a lifetime.'

'Alcohol causes cancer,' Dixie says. 'So does diet soda. So do those cigarettes.' She points at Diva's black root in the ashtray. 'And that chocolate monstrosity you ordered will clog those arteries like hair in your drain. Half the

180

stuff we consumed right here at this table tonight is trying to kill us from the inside out.'

'Now what's the bad news?' Trina says and they all laugh.

Barcelona goes to the rest room. She doesn't wait to see if anyone wants to go with her. She wants to go alone. She's avoided Trina the past couple of weeks because she didn't want to tell her about Eric. She feels guilty enough, but Trina would also make her feel stupid.

Only the handicapped stall is available. Barcelona hates using it, though she has no reasonable explanation for feeling that way. She's not afraid of catching anything, being crippled isn't contagious. Mostly she's terrified that while she's in there someone in a wheelchair will come in who really has to go and can't use any of the other stalls. How would Barcelona feel stepping out of the stall seeing a woman wriggling frantically in a wheelchair waiting for her?

Barcelona pulls down her jeans and panties and sits. The urine starts to flow and it burns. Her vagina is sore, from membranes to muscles. During the past two weeks, she has made love with Eric at least a couple of dozen times. Baker's dozens. They have tried new positions and locations that they never did even when they lived together. Last night they had tried to make love but both were too sore. The head of Eric's penis looked inflamed and angry.

She washes her hands, and returns to the table. The Death by Chocolate has been served and Trina has eaten most of it. 'What a swine,' Barcelona says, pulling the plate away from Trina.

'I'm doing it for you,' Trina says. 'Every bite I eat is five hundred fewer calories on your hips.'

Barcelona eats a bite, makes a rapturous face at Trina.

'Go ahead, eat the rest. You're doing me a favor,' Trina

181

says. 'I took Karyn in to see the orthodontist last week to see if she needed braces. Son of a bitch says Karyn's teeth are fine but that *I* could use braces. Said I could look just like Kathleen Turner.'

Dixie laughs. 'What'd you tell him?'

'I asked him whether it bothered him having people look up his nose all day long. Did he worry about what they saw or did he pick his nose before each patient?'

Barcelona choked on her dessert, washed it down with water.

'Has anyone else noticed,' Trina asks matter-of-factly, 'that as guys get older, the hair in their noses gets bushier? Am I the only one who's noticed?'

'Maybe you've had more opportunity to make that observation than the rest of us,' Dixie says.

'Maybe. But it's true. Someone ought to tell them, though. Considering the position that women usually are in, we have to look up those things a lot.'

'Maybe that's why people close their eyes during sex,' Diva offers.

Barcelona leaves a few bites of chocolate and pushes the plate over to Trina. 'Here, you've grossed me out of the rest of it.'

'Good, it worked.' Trina gobbles the chocolate hungrily.

The check comes and everyone begins counting out cash. Diva throws her Visa card on the plate. 'I'll charge it, you guys can pay me the cash.' No one disagrees, but she hurries on with explanation. 'I'm getting my hair permed tomorrow and ever since I bounced a couple checks, they want cash from me.'

'I see on the news that The Candidate's up a couple points in the polls,' Dixie says.

Trina tosses a twenty on top of Diva's Visa card. 'Still not enough to win, but we're nipping at Carla Bennington's butt.'

'You able to turn up anything scandalous on her yet?' Barcelona asks.

'Not yet,' Trina says, but in a tone that Barcelona recognizes as meaning she is close. Trina is very good at her job; if there's something to find, she will find it. She turns to Barcelona, obviously anxious to change the subject. 'How's the screenplay coming?'

'It's coming,' Barcelona says. She turns away from Trina, a sign they all recognize as meaning she doesn't want to discuss it. Once Barcelona has started a project, she never talks about it with anyone.

In the parking lot, Trina tells them she will make copies of their menu and send each one a list. Three of them split up and hunt down their cars. Only Dixie has used the valet parking. Trina walks part of the way through the lot with Barcelona.

'What's with you lately?' Trina asks.

'What do you mean?'

'I haven't heard from you in a week. You can't be that buried in your work.'

Barcelona hesitates, wanting to confess everything, tell about Eric. She can't. Not yet. 'Screenplays aren't as easy as they look. I've had to do a lot of research.'

Trina looks into her eyes. Barcelona holds the gaze, not wanting to give anything away. 'Okay,' Trina finally says. 'Maybe we can have lunch this week.'

'Sure. Monday's good. I'll be in L.A. anyway. I'm driving my script up to Grief.'

'Fine. Stop by the office, we'll go from there. About eleven-thirty we can miss the lunch crowd.'

Barcelona agrees. She waves to Trina as she gets into her car. Trina waves back and squeezes between two parked cars on her way to the next row.

The drive home is unusual. She turns on the radio, presses every preset button but can't find a song she likes.

Several of the buttons are for oldies stations, but she doesn't recognize the songs because they are too recent. She considers that a bad sign. She tries using the Seek button, but nothing satisfies her. She gropes for a tape cassette from the glove compartment, slips it in. Smokey Robinson and the Miracles sing 'I Second That Emotion.' She immediately ejects the tape. Nothing seems right. Even dinner tonight seemed somehow off-kilter. Dixie still not eating, gobbling vitamins. Trina pushing that stupid menu idea on everyone. Diva depressed and jealous.

Barcelona takes a shortcut through an undeveloped section of Irvine. The wooden skeletons of clusters of new condos under construction hunker in the dark on either side of the road where eight months ago were strawberry fields. Deep gulches wide as a stream follow the contours of the narrow road like black rivers. This is where the sewage pipes will go. She can see the giant pipes stacked on the side of the road. In a year, these will all be homes for more young middle-class couples with little children. Barcelona does not begrudge the future owners their piece of the planned community of Irvine. She is happy for them. But as far as she knows, there are no plans to increase the number of supermarkets in the area. Lines are already intolerably long. Rather than shop for the week, Barcelona limits all her purchases to ten items or less and carries enough cash to go through the express lines. Lately, even those lines are long.

She is debating whether or not to stop by Von's right now to pick up some panty hose and Diet Squirt, when she feels something thud against her car. She is alone on the dark road and pulls over to the side, careful not to drive into the sewage gulch. Her heart is bouncing as she jumps out of the car. She knows it must be a small animal, a rabbit maybe or a gopher, but fears it may be someone's pet cat or dog. She looks down the road, sees a black blob of something on the road. It is screaming, leaping, heaving its mangled body off the ground, but each time it flops back to the ground with a tortured shriek.

Barcelona is running now, running down the middle of the road. In the distance, maybe a mile away, she can see headlights approach. She has only about a minute to do something. If it is someone's pet, she will have to take it to a vet, contact the owners. If not a pet, then what? Leave it?

She is within fifty feet and now she knows what it is. The scent hits her at first almost sweetly, then, halfway up her nostrils, it bites the membranes with a sour stench. Skunk. She stops running toward it. She watches the car in the distance approaching. The animal is not wrenching itself anymore, it is merely quivering. She can see the black liquid puddled around it. Barcelona doesn't know what to do. She thinks of Luna, how she had taken charge with Henry Finney's bloated body as he lay on the bathroom floor in his own waste. Barcelona had sat on the bed and watched, listened to Mrs. Finney eulogize her dead husband, his clothes all laid out less than five feet away for dinner at The Sizzler. Malibu Chicken.

The headlights flicker ahead, rounding a curb, then disappearing behind the bend next to one of the condo development sites. Barcelona inhales deeply several times, holds her breath, and runs the rest of the way toward the skunk. Even without breathing she can smell it, its scent seeping through her pores. She had read somewhere that skunk secretions are used as a perfume base. Perhaps the Tuxedo perfume she is wearing right now has skunk in it.

The skunk's eyes are open. She can't tell if it is alive, if it is breathing under all that blood-matted fur. It doesn't have a white stripe down its back like cartoon skunks. It has two stripes that curve back from the top of its head down along the side of its body, across the hindquarters, and disappear into its tail.

Barcelona's lungs are burning. She needs air. What she has stored in her lungs is seeping out of her mouth.

The other car's headlights are full on her now, coming down this straight stretch of road. She looks around the side of the road. Some jagged chunks of plywood are discarded in the weeds. One is flat and wide enough that she could use it to scoop him up like a pizza and moved him to the side of the road. If he is still alive, she will drive him to a vet. The hell with her car. The hell with the smell. She is not afraid; she can take action like Luna. She exhales the rest of her air and takes a shallow, tentative breath. Not as bad as before. This isn't that bad. Quickly she climbs down into the gulch, reaches into the weeds for the plywood, and scrambles back up to the side of the road.

Too late.

The approaching car whooshes by, the left front and left rear tires bouncing over the skunk's body. If it had been alive before, it definitely is not now.

Barcelona tosses the plywood into the sewage gulch and slaps the dirt off her hands. She hurries back to her car and drives away.

When she arrives home, she immediately turns on all the lights and the TV. She flips the channels until she finds a 'M*A*S*H' rerun. The phone answering machine is next to the refrigerator. She pushes the playback button and pours wine into a coffee mug while listening. The first message is from her mother: 'Hi, sweetheart. Nothing new, just wanted to see how my Hollywood girl is. Talk to you soon.' The second message was from a student: 'Ms. Lee? This is Trudy Cornelius. Um, I was in your class last semester. Thing is, I got a D. They're talking about taking away my Social Security for school. Can I do some extra credit or something now and maybe you could change my grade? My number is 678-0998. Thanks a lot.'

Barcelona sits at the kitchen table. Alan Alda is sniffing a pair of socks, making a face. She can still smell the dead skunk's scent and thinks it a funny coincidence that Alan is sniffing his socks.

The third message: 'Hi, Barcy, it's Luna.'

Barcelona turns and looks at the answering machine as if it were Luna and she had just caught her in bed with Eric. She feels her pulse thumping as much as it had when she'd hit the skunk.

The machine continues: 'I'd like to talk sometime, if you've got some free time. Give me a call.'

The voice is friendly, not threatening, not hurt. Not accusing. The machine shuts itself off, but Barcelona continues to stare at it until the theme song to 'M*A*S*H' plays and she turns to see the closing credits roll by too fast to read any names.

14

Diva lies in bed singing.

'*Cocktail waitress don't have a smile to spare/Gotta serve martinis then go fix her hair.*'

She stops, scratches her pubic hairs, thinks about the lyrics. She's been working on this song daily for two weeks. So far she has only these two lines, but no definite melody. She's been lying in bed for the past hour singing variations on the same two lines.

She sings the words again with a different tune, going higher at the end of each line rather than lower. She shakes her head unhappily. Something's not right. She tries it folksy, then rockabilly, then with a country twang. Nothing is right. She likes the lines but the melody sucks. She looks around for some paper and a pen.

She tugs open the drawer of the bed stand, rummages through the magazines, three old *TV Guides, Self, Vegetarian Times, Spin, Rolling Stone*, some coupons for free frozen yogurt at a new store down the street. A stub of a yellow pencil lies on the bottom of the drawer, sticky from God knows what. The pencil's point is broken so she picks and peels at the wood until a nub of graphite peeks through. It reminds her of a dog's dick unsheathing and she laughs. She picks up *Rolling Stone* and leafs through it searching for a page with an ad that has lots of white space. Page 72 has the perfect ad, one for Infinity speakers.

She begins writing her lyrics above the simulated oak-finished speakers.

Immediately, she gets another idea and starts singing: '*Cocktail waitress ain't got an easy life/She gotta talk like the devil and soothe like a wife.*'

She writes that down, looks it over, crosses out 'soothe' and writes 'serve' above it. She sings it with the new word. She isn't happy with that. She crosses out 'serve.'

'Fuck,' she says and scratches herself with ferocity. The crevices of her pubic region itch badly where she shaved them last night. The skin is stubbly and raw with red irritated splotches. She hates shaving there but the new bathing suit she bought yesterday is worth a little discomfort. After trying suits on in fifteen stores, this was the only one that didn't make her look pregnant.

Diva stares at the last line she wrote, but her eyes drift down to the stereo speakers in the ad. RS-4000s with polypropylene drivers and an EMIT tweeter. She could use new speakers, ones that didn't hum and buzz all the time. Something she could listen to without . . .

Listen!

She scratches out 'serve' and writes 'listen.' She sings it in her Bette Midler voice. '*Cocktail waitress ain't got an easy life/Gotta talk like the devil and listen like a wife.*' She sings it again. And again. She likes it. Her soon-to-be hit song, 'Cocktail Waitress,' is finally coming alive. She draws a couple of dollar signs next to the lyrics. Since she was in high school she has tried to write songs but never finished one. The frustration of not finding the right words, or having them sound too much like other songs, always sabotaged her determination. This time will be different, she vows, this time she's serious. Before she was immature, not ready for success. Now she is.

She scoots over to the side of the bed and reaches for her guitar. She strums the D chord and A chord. Back and

forth. Then the G chord and D chord back and forth. She
tries to sing the lines she has so far using these chords. She
doesn't like the way it sounds.

The laminated wood of the guitar is cold against her
breasts, making her nipples pucker into hard rubbery tips.
Actually, this whole songwriting thing has surprised her.
She always imagined the words would be the hardest part
and that the music would come easily. Maybe the lyrics
had to be worked out very methodically, then the melody
would come all at once in a sudden flash of inspiration. So
far it hadn't. She tries a dozen different combinations of
chords and melodies but doesn't really like any. She takes
the guitar off her lap and leans it against the night table.
Little red lines are cut into her thighs from the edge of the
guitar. She rubs them with her fingertips and they fade a
little but don't disappear.

Her song could be a big hit if she could only finish the
lyrics and get the right melody. She already knows how it
should be sung, with an exotic sensuality, the way Maria
Muldar sang 'Midnight at the Oasis.'

Diva sits and daydreams about her song while continuing
to scratch her pubic area. Absently her finger dips down
and bumps against the clitoris. Diva shivers. She looks
down, but her belly sags out just far enough to hide her
own crotch from her. She sucks in her gut and watches the
white unicorns on her red fingernails romp among
the forest of curly brush. She thinks of Calypso sitting
here a couple of weeks ago, whacking off with that
moronic cross-eyed grin. Still, she doesn't stop rubbing
herself.

Her middle finger is slicked with moisture, some of it
urine, but most of it thicker and stickier juice. She plunges
her finger deep inside herself, spreading her knees apart
to accommodate. She probes and stirs, surprised at how
good it feels. Feeling good always surprises her. She slides

another finger inside herself, not moving them around much, just enjoying the sensation of them inside her, filling her up. Calypso's penis felt this way, the few times he put it in this opening and not the other one.

Diva slides her fingers out and drags them slowly up the moist path to her clitoris. Lazily she massages around it, her fingers flat so her nails don't accidentally scratch her. The warmth in her lap is spreading up through her stomach and into her chest. Her neck feels flushed. She keeps rubbing but misses the full feeling of something deep inside her. She doesn't want to get up now to get her worn plastic vibrator with the dead batteries. Instead, she brings her left hand down and inserts two fingers as deep as they will go, until she can feel each knuckle inside her. With her right hand, she keeps rubbing, picking up speed, feeling the clitoris swell and throb. The heat down there is so great, each pubic hair feels like a live electrical wire shocking her with hot volts. Her head rolls back and she closes her eyes. She is rubbing so fast her hand is cramping up. But she can't stop. She pictures a door, big wooden doors, carved with grotesque creatures from the Middle Ages. The doors are locked but there is something on the other side, some powerful force. The doors bulge and stretch the way they do in cartoons as the force on the other side tries to break through. Diva rubs faster, her sharp fingernail nicking her sensitive membrane. She jerks from the shock but doesn't stop. The door is stretching thinner and thinner. She rubs, feels the heat in her chest spreading. Her right leg shoots out and grazes the guitar, the toes brushing the strings, strumming some strange chord. Her left hand burrows even deeper inside her. She continues, watching the door stretch, but it never bursts. She is getting sore now and stops rubbing, withdraws her fingers from inside her. She got close that time.

Diva sits there a minute catching her breath. Then she

stands up, walks into the bathroom, washes her hands in the sink, and brushes her teeth.

'Wanna beer?'

Diva shakes her head and drops her towel and bag next to his beach chair. 'Too early.'

'Early? Shit,' Coma says. He is leaning back in his chair, head tilted toward the sun, eyes closed. A white visor shades his eyes. His long legs are stretched out as far as they will go and his feet are buried up to the ankles in sand. A battered 18-panel Spalding beach volleyball sits in his lap. One hand spiders the ball with his fingers, the other holds a paper bag with a can of beer inside. It is only ten in the morning and Diva can smell the beer sweat on his body. She looks up and down his body. It is a magnificent body. Long and lean and tan and muscled. He is twenty-seven. His real name is Jarrod Reisner, but everyone calls him Coma because he seems to live in one. He is slow-moving, slow-talking. Except when he plays volleyball. Then he is the fastest, toughest, fiercest player out here.

'You off work today?' he asks her without opening his eyes.

'I have a couple hours free. Thought we might play a couple games.'

He opens his eyes and squints at her. 'That can be arranged.'

Only sex, drugs, or volleyball can rouse Coma from his beach chair. During their friendship, Diva has given him all three. The sex was only once and that was over a year ago. It was a cold overcast day and nobody had come down to the beach to play volleyball. Coma had been there for four hours, drinking and waiting. Finally Diva had shown up, just off a radio commercial in which she sang the radio station's call letters. Coma had been drunk and bored and horny. Diva had taken him across the street to her apartment to sober him up before he drove home. He made a pass at her over the instant coffee and she didn't resist. They'd screwed quickly and afterward napped for a couple of hours. When she awoke he was gone and neither had mentioned it since.

Coma's family had money. They owned several of the fanciest restaurants in Newport Beach. Last year his uncle had pulled out of his gated driveway, driven two blocks in his black Porsche with a cassette of Crosby, Stills, and Nash playing on the stereo system, stopped at a stop sign, and was shot five times in the head and neck by a passing car. Police reported it as a gangland-style slaying and the TV speculated on drug connections, but Coma never seemed to have any drugs of his own and was always bumming them off other people.

Apparently the family expected Coma to enter the family restaurant business once he grew out of this beach phase of his. Diva doubted that this was a phase. This was just who he was.

He sits up, tosses her the ball. 'New suit, huh?'

Diva beams. 'You like?'

'Cute.'

The suit is a one-piece, mostly white with some blue and white mountains at the abdomen and seven tiny blue kangaroos hopping across the stomach. Boxed in red across her breasts was the word Australia.

He stretches out, looks around the beach for some competition. The locals know not to challenge him unless they are at the top of their game. Coma doesn't have a beach rating because he never plays in tournaments, though several pros have asked him to partner with them. He turns them all down. In fact, he doesn't even bother playing at other beaches or even other nets. He plays exclusively at this net and everyone who plays serious beach volleyball knows where to find him. Occasionally the unwary, the uninitiated wander by and, in a friendly way, not knowing who he is, ask him to play. He just shakes his head and naps in his beach chair until worthy opponents came by.

Diva is an excellent player too, though nowhere near his league. She grew up around here, has played beach volleyball since she was a little girl, even played on her high school indoor team. Coed volleyball is not really taken seriously down here, but is played as a kind of relaxing intermission. For the guys. The women have to hustle their butts off or forever be banned.

Diva stands on the court and practices setting the ball to herself while Coma slowly saunters onto the court. He tosses some sand up to check the wind direction. He scans the beach looking for someone to play.

'Let's just warm up,' Diva suggests. 'Someone will come along.'

They set the ball back and forth a few minutes, then do some hot pepper spiking and digging practice.

'You want to hit some?' she asks him.

He shakes his head. 'Too hot.'

Surfers wander back and forth, toting their fiberglass boards. Some look over in Diva and Coma's direction, but they don't challenge.

After twenty minutes a couple of guys walk up, watch Diva and Coma set for a few minutes. From their short square haircuts, Diva knows they are marines from the El Toro base. One of them is big and muscular, with a neck as thick as his thigh. The other is skinny, not as tall, but also well built. They are bare-chested and hairless, both have tan lines on their arms and necks from their uniform T-shirts.

'How about a game?' the big one asks.

Coma doesn't even look at them. He just watches the

ball soaring back and forth between him and Diva. 'Sure.' He lets one of her sets drop through his hands and he butts the ball with his head toward them. 'Warm up.'

The two marines hit it back and forth a few times, practice their spikes. Diva thinks they are pretty good.

When the game starts, the marines serve only to Coma, which is a courtesy because that allows him to pass the ball, Diva to set, then him to spike. The theory is this makes the teams more evenly matched since he had to play with a female. After Coma crushes their first serve down so hard the ball bounces back up over their heads, they stop this courtesy and serve to Diva. However, she is also a good hitter, dinking, cutting to the sides, and even spiking a few into the back court. The game is over at 11-1. They play two more games. 11-0. 11-1.

The marines leave without saying anything. As they walk away the bigger one punches the thinner one in the arm, knocking him sideways. The thinner one rubs his arm, shouts 'Fuck you!' at his friend and walks down to the ocean and dives in. The bigger guy sits on the sand and watches his buddy swim.

'Beer?' Coma offers Diva. He opens his cooler and there are half a dozen 16-ounce 7-Up bottles inside. It is Coma's clever habit to replace the soda with beer so he can drink it on the beach. The one in the paper bag he'd been drinking when she first arrived must've been the one he'd been drinking on the drive down.

'Sure,' Diva says. She takes one and drinks a large gulp. She doesn't have much time. She has to be at her other job soon, the one she keeps a secret, even from Barcy, Trina, and Dixie.

'Hey, dude,' Cliff says as he and Bart walk up.

'Hey,' Coma said, squinting up from his chair. 'It's the fag patrol.'

'You wish,' Bart says, reaching into the cooler. He tosses

a beer to Cliff and takes one for himself. They are both about twenty, tanned, well built. They might have been Coma's little brothers. But then Diva thinks most of the guys on this beach looked as if they could be related. Hairless bronzed bodies with large pecs and narrow waists. They'd have made attractive girls.

'Hey, Diva,' Bart says, 'how's the singing?'

'Same,' Diva says. 'How's your job?'

'I quit, man. Fuck that shit.' He'd been a valet at a fancy French restaurant owned by Coma's family. 'It was cool driving those red cars, man, but they all thought, you know, that they were better than me, just because they drove a Jag or a Rolls or something.'

'They are better than you, man,' Cliff says.

Coma laughs. 'Yeah.'

After a couple of minutes, Ed Dortmunder and his girlfriend, Diedre, stroll by eating ice cream cones. Ed is almost as good a player as Coma, so they naturally are pretty good friends. Diedre is a knockout blonde with large breasts and long legs. She wears a bikini so small that Diva is certain she'd had to shave all her pubic hairs to wear it. Ed's parents own a lot of real estate on Lido Isle. He and Diedre both attend USC together, but come down to Newport Beach on weekends.

They all converse about nothing in particular, but Diva feels herself slowly being edged out of the picture. Not on purpose, but by virtue of some jungle instinct in these guys. They all face Ed and Diedre, directing comments to her just so they would have an excuse to stare at her. When they think she isn't looking, their eyes flick down to her breasts, the outline of her nipples against the thin fabric, or down to her crotch where the material creased in along the crevice of her hairless cunt. Diva feels herself getting fatter by the second. Her thighs are ballooning, her stomach puffing out like a blowfish. Soon her new suit would simply burst apart and she'd have to run home naked.

'See you,' Diva says, gathering her stuff.

'Yeah,' Coma says. 'Thanks for the games. We showed them marines.'

'See ya,' the others say, including Diedre.

'You can leave your panties on for now,' she tells Diva.

Diva does so, stepping out of the bathroom wearing only her panties, the rest of her clothes folded neatly in a pile in her arms. She sets them down in the usual place, the antique wooden rocker by the bay window.

This is only Diva's second time here. She is still unsure of herself.

Toni Hammond is carefully unwrapping the plastic cover from the half-formed figure. 'This is a water-based clay,' she explains. 'If I don't keep it covered, the clay dries out.'

'Oh.' Diva nods. She stands self-consciously in the middle of the studio. She knows it's ridiculous, but she feels as if she should cover her breasts until they start.

Toni continues to study the figure, touching it here and there, running her fingers along the clay, following ridges of cheekbones, the hollow of the neck, the jut of the jawbone. She chews on the inside of her mouth as she circles around the figure. Diva decides the face looks nothing like her own and that maybe Toni is not very good at what she does. Still, the pay is good, and Diva needs all the money she can get if she's to make this songwriting thing work.

'Don't worry about the face,' Toni says. 'It's not supposed to look like you.'

'How'd you know I was thinking that?'

Toni smiles. 'I've been doing this a long time.' She strokes the brow over the figure's left eye. 'Needs some shaping here.' She takes out some instrument with a

197

wooden handle and a metal triangle on the end and starts shaving some of the brow away. Toni is about forty. She is dressed in jeans and an extra large tuxedo shirt that is smeared with dried clay. At first sight she appears attractive, but after a while there is something about her that is slightly disconcerting. Her limbs are too elongated, like someone standing in front of a distorting fun house mirror. Her arms and legs and fingers, even her neck and face seem stretched beyond healthy limits, as if she were some sort of elastic doll whose extremities had been tugged on by a nasty child. 'What do you do, Dianne?' Toni asks. 'I mean when you're not doing aerobics.' They met in aerobics class last week. Toni had walked up to Diva in the locker room while Diva was struggling to peel off her sweaty leotard. 'Your body is perfect,' she'd said and handed Diva a business card. Now here she was.

'I'm a singer,' Diva answers. 'And songwriter.'

'Yeah, I used to be an artist/secretary. Then I was an artist/salesclerk, then an artist/seamstress.'

'Now you're just an artist,' Diva says.

Toni laughs. 'How sweet.'

'What do you mean?'

'Not many would call making mannequins an art. They think of it as something like illustrating comic books or something.'

'Looks like art to me,' Diva says. 'Anyway, you seem to work hard enough at it that they should give you the benefit of the doubt.'

'I'm afraid how hard one works is not always the main criteria for what constitutes art.'

Diva is getting in over her head here. She is not well read nor very intellectual. Her philosophy is if you like it it must be art. 'I don't know much about the visual arts,' she says. 'I'm mostly into music.'

'You said you sing.'

Diva nods. 'And write songs. I'm working on a tough one now. I don't care what anyone else says, when I'm finally done with it, I'm calling it art.'

Toni laughs, puts down her tool. She walks over to Diva and starts staring at her face and body, studying it in a way that makes Diva uncomfortable. Toni stares too long at Diva's plump belly. 'Perfect,' she says, placing her hand on it, sizing it like a melon in the supermarket.

'This is weird,' Diva says. 'I still don't get it. Why would anyone want fat mannequins?'

Toni doesn't say anything. She'd explained the whole thing the other night and Diva knows enough about the woman to realize she does not like repeating herself. All Diva remembers is that Toni designs the prototype mannequins from which the rest are cast. She works for an L.A. mannequin company whose visual director told her that there was a new demand for chubby mannequins, not just for specialty stores catering to overweight women, but even for the major department stores. Nordstrom's wanted a couple of hundred. Apparently, there are millions of fatties out there who were tired of seeing waifish mannequins with hollow cheeks, flat stomachs, and no rumps.

Toni starts arranging Diva into a pose. It is not a very difficult pose, hips a little forward, back arched slightly. 'I want to get the chest right today.' She stares at Diva's breasts and frowns. 'What size are you?'

'Dress size?'

'Breast size. What's your chest measurement?'

'Uh, thirty-six.'

'Hmmm.' Toni goes over to the drawer of a desk and pulls out a red tape measure. 'Probably a lot of those inches are due to the size of your back.' She lays the tape measure across Diva's chest, from armpit to armpit. Then

199

she shakes her head, thinks, and measures each breast, strapping the tape across each breast separately.

'I hope they're the same,' Diva says.

'Huh?' Toni looks up. 'Oh.' She smiles. 'Yes, they're fine. Breasts are very tricky in the mannequin business. Usually we make them different for each style of clothing. For example, with lingerie I want the breasts to look bigger, so I make the back smaller. It's different for sportswear, where they want the bodies to look smaller and younger, more active. Then I pull the rib cage out wider and flatten the chest. See?'

Diva nods. 'I didn't realize how complicated it is.'

'It's not really,' Toni says. She returns to her clay, starts forming the breasts with her hands, cupping and rubbing and building and smoothing, all with her fingers in muddy clay.

Diva finds it a little unnerving to have a woman staring at her breasts while fondling another pair, even if that other pair is clay. There's something weird about it. She doesn't say anything. She decides this is a perfect opportunity to work on her song. She quietly hums different melodies to the four lines she has written.

After twenty minutes Toni gives her a break. 'You're a good model,' Toni says, handing her a robe. 'Most models can't hold a pose longer than twenty minutes. You looked like you could just keep going.'

'I was thinking about my song.'

'Oh? Is it ready for public singing? I'd love to hear it.'

'God, no. Not yet.'

Toni nods, walks over to the mini refrigerator. On top of the refrigerator is a coffee maker with half a pot of coffee. 'Want something to drink? Juice or coffee?'

'Juice, please.'

'Apple, grape, tomato.'

'Apple.'

200

Toni hands Diva a can of apple juice. Diva pulls the tab and drinks. She looks around the studio at various mannequins standing against the walls. She wonders if maybe there's a song in all this. 'Now what?' Diva asks. 'I mean when you're done what happens?'

'The mold-makers come over here and pull a plaster waste mold.'

'Waste mold?'

'They call it that because it gets thrown away later, along with the clay model. See, they cast a fiberglass prototype that looks just like this thing. Then they cut it at the hip and leg so they can be more easily packed and dressed and undressed. You know. Then they use the fiberglass prototype to make the production mold.'

'Must be a kick to go shopping and see your mannequins in the stores. Like having a gallery showing of your work.'

'Not quite,' Toni says, sipping coffee. 'But it's rewarding.'

'What about men?'

Toni looked startled, her cup frozen halfway to her mouth. 'Pardon?'

Diva realizes Toni thinks the question is personal. That's why she looks as if one of her mannequins had just started speaking, like on that old 'Twilight Zone' episode. 'I meant male mannequins. Are there going to be any in this chub line?'

'Not yet. Frankly, I'm relieved. Male mannequins are the hardest. You can't do them in any type of motion or it's considered effeminate. Mostly you have them either leaning forward like bird dogs, or sitting down with their legs apart, looking tough. And with their hands in fists, always in fists.

Diva laughs. 'That seems so silly.'

'To us. But no guy wants to buy clothing from a mannequin that looks swishy.'

'Well, some guys do.'

Toni laughs. 'I'll create that line when they ask me.'

They go back to work. Diva is arranged in the same pose, Toni is back smoothing the breasts of her clay model. After a while she stares unhappily at the breasts, looks at Diva's breasts then back at her clay breasts. She shakes her head. 'The nipples aren't right. Each breast has a specific kind of nipple that is right for that particular shape.'

'And I don't?' Diva asks.

'Of course you do. I just haven't captured it yet.' Toni walks over to Diva, looks at her breasts, reaches out with both hands and pinches Diva's nipples. Hard.

'Hey!' Diva says. Her nipples swell out, erect.

'That's better.' Toni walks back to the model and re-shapes the nipples.

Diva doesn't know what to say. She never had a woman pinch her nipples before, not since elementary school anyway. She wasn't sure whether she should be angry or embarrassed or what. It was a strange thing to do, but Toni is an artist. She needs erect nipples. Maybe that's the difference between Diva and a real artist. A real artist thinks only of the work, concentrates only on completion, no matter what it takes. Even pinching some other woman's nipples.

Diva is flushed with new purpose. For two weeks she'd been dabbling at her song. What then? Would she jerk around looking for some way to record a demo? Then wait around record company lobbies hoping to get someone to listen? No, she would get more aggressive than that. Be more like Toni. Starting now.

Diva stands frozen in the pose working on her song. When her nipples flatten out, Toni comes over and pinches them again. Diva doesn't mind. This whole thing has been a valuable lesson.

202

15

'Hurry,' Dixie yells, 'they're getting away.'

'I'm hurrying, damn it.'

'Faster.'

Randy is stooped in front of the sink, rooting through the cupboard. He is wearing only a nubbled bath towel around his waist, which keeps coming undone and which he keeps reknotting. 'For God's sake,' he says in frustration.

'Hurry, hon.'

He snatches up a can of Pledge and tosses it to Dixie. 'Use this in the meantime.'

'Furniture wax?'

'All this shit's the same.'

Dixie tosses the can back to him. 'It's right behind the Brillo pads. Red can.'

Randy continues knocking cans and bottles over in his frantic search for the Raid Ant & Roach Spray. Meantime, Dixie stands guard over the ten thousand ants that have formed a black stripe that goes from the garbage disposal up out of the sink and across the kitchen wall until it disappears behind the built-in microwave oven. When Dixie wandered out from the bedroom this morning to fix some coffee, she thought the black stripe was some spray-painted vandalism, the work of neighborhood punks. Until she saw the stripe moving, flowing like a black river. The stripe bubbled and boiled and jitterbugged with activity as the tiny ants marched back and forth in neat and orderly lines.

When she called to Randy, he stumbled sleepily and naked to the kitchen, took one look at the crawling ants, and ran back into the bedroom to wrap a towel around his waist. Perhaps he thought the towel would protect his crotch from the deadly predators, Dixie mused. Men were paranoid about their crotches. Actually, she hadn't called him out here for help, she just wanted him to witness the amazing sight of all these ants strolling across her wall in an almost perfectly symmetrical stripe. It was almost an art form.

Dixie stands in front of the hordes and stares with admiration at their calmness in the face of imminent destruction. What must they think the blue-eyed chink hovering nearby will do to them? Such trust, or arrogance. She wonders if they are capable of feeling fear.

Dixie is wearing a long yellow T-shirt. There are no clever sayings on the T-shirt, no dancing animals, no icons from popular culture. To find such a blank shirt took her several days of shopping. Under the T-shirt, she is wearing very sexy red panties that she bought as part of her under-cover costume. She hopes she can keep them after the assignment is over. Randy especially likes them. She's noticed that he seems hornier when he sees her still in her high school clothes and makeup than when he sees her as she usually looks. This bothers her a little, though she's sure it's just a harmless fantasy. Most men her age had such a bad time in high school they relish an opportunity to relive those terrible times, only this time they actually get laid.

'Here!' Randy says finally. He stands, hands Dixie the can.

She shakes it, removes the cap, and starts spraying. The poison mist rains on the ants. They don't stop right away, though they do slow down, stagger about, seem confused by the sudden change in weather.

'Like Agent Orange,' Randy says, stepping back a few feet and making a sour face. 'Years from now the survivors will sue you. As a law student, I can guarantee it.'

'What's your advice, counselor?'

'Take no prisoners.'

Dixie laughs. sprays them again. They are slowing down now, wading through the sticky spray. Some are stuck to the wall, a few dead bodies drop to the counter.

'Yeech,' Randy says. 'Ugly little bastards.'

Dixie sprays the garbage disposal, runs some water, turns it on, lets it rattle and grind a few seconds, turns it off.

'Come on, let's get out of here,' Randy says. 'This stuff is making me sick.'

They retreat into the bedroom. Randy shuts the door dramatically, as if they were being chased. Dixie laughs.

'Hell of a way to start the weekend,' he says.

Dixie goes into the bathroom and shuts the door. Floating in the toilet is a used condom from last night's lovemaking. No matter how often she tells him, he never flushes them. He's still on a water conservation kick started a few years ago during the California drought. He stacks bricks in his toilet tanks and bathes in six inches of water. The condom is all stretched out and sickly looking. It reminds her of the molted skin of a snake. Bits of semen are suspended around it like tiny marshmallows in Jell-O. She flushes the toilet before sitting down.

Just as she reaches for *Time* magazine, Randy knocks on the door.

'What's the big secret in there?' he says. This is an old argument. He doesn't like Dixie to close the bathroom door when she goes. He thinks it's a barrier between them, some such Sixties nonsense.

'I'm pissing,' Dixie says. 'I'll give you a full report later.'

'Why the closed door? It's not like I haven't seen every inch of you before. Or tasted every inch of you.'

'You want a taste? I'll save some in a jar.'

'I never close the door when I go.'

'I wish you would,' she says and is immediately sorry. He will take that wrong, she knows.

There is a hurt silence. 'I see,' he says.

'No you don't. I just want this much privacy. It's not shutting you out, it's keeping me in. A moment to myself.'

'Yeah, right.'

'If it'll make you feel more intimate, I'll come out there and fart. Just let me pee alone. Okay?'

He pauses. 'Okay.'

She hears the mattress spring creak as he flops onto the bed. Good. He's in no hurry to go out and play tennis or go to breakfast or go to a matinee. They can laze around for a few hours, read the paper, watch HBO, make love again.

On the wall in front of her is a framed cartoon that Randy bought for her. It is one of those red circles with a diagonal line they use to tell you not to do something: no smoking, no skateboarding, etc. Inside this circle is a caricature of an Oriental man with slanted eyes and buck teeth, grinning moronically behind a steering wheel. No Oriental Drivers. This is a joke exclusive to Orange County, where so many Vietnamese families have settled. There are also large communities of Japanese, Koreans, and Chinese. They all have a reputation for being terrible drivers. Racial loyalty aside, Dixie knows this to be true. Every time she gets behind a car going 30 in a 55 mph zone, or changing lanes suddenly without signaling, or crawling through intersections at 5 mph, she knows it will almost always be an Oriental driver. Before the influx of Vietnamese, everyone ragged on the elderly and their driving habits. A few miles south was a planned community for the elderly called Leisure World. The locals called it Seizure World. The driving for a ten-mile radius around the place was always erratic. Lots of honking horns. Driving slowly is the only sin in Southern California.

When Dixie enters the bedroom again, Randy is lying on his back watching TV. He holds the remote control switcher in his hand and is flipping through the stations.

'Anything good on?' she asks.

He grins. 'Yeah, there's something good on. Take a look.' He points to the towel around his waist. His penis is pressing stiffly up under it.

'Subtle,' she says, smiling.

'There's no time for subtle. The Lakers play in half an hour.'

He is kidding her. Randy likes sports, but he is not addicted to them. They have gone to a couple of Lakers games together. They both like watching sports on TV. Dixie prefers boxing, Randy enjoys baseball. Both like basketball, neither likes football. Seems perfect. She looks at him lying there on the bed, his head propped up with pillows, the white towel around his waist. He is not very tall, about 5'7", but he is burly, thick chested. He is the hairiest man she has ever known, except on the top of his head. While the rest of his body is one thick waterproof pelt of buffalo hide, Randy's head is barely covered by a short cap of thinning hair.

Dixie kneels on the mattress and lays her hand on his chest. The hair cushions her hand so much that she can't feel his skin. She has gotten used to this and kind of likes it. She likes him. He is somewhat of a fugitive from the Sixties, still has his old Give a Damn button. The late Sixties was the last time he fully remembers being sober. Sometime after Lyndon Johnson, during Richard Nixon, he started into the drugs and booze, not just dabbling like

207

before. Finally, he ended up with cocaine as the drug of his choice, stealing film editing equipment from USC to hock to buy more coke. But he kicked it on his own. Dixie admires his courage. She's never had any addictions, never smoked, never drank except for an occasional glass of wine to be sociable. She rarely drinks more than a sip or two. She has never done drugs. She doesn't crave junk food or grease. She enjoys sex, but has gone for long stretches without. The only things she does habitually are eat and go to the bathroom. And lately the eating has been sporadic. It isn't that she doesn't eat; she forces herself to eat to keep her weight and energy up. She doesn't feel any desire for food. No appetite.

Randy has overcome so much. All she had to worry about was a little appetite.

Randy changes the channels again. Snatches of dialogue flash by in a jumble of interrupted sentences and images. Finally he settles on an old movie. Glenn Ford is a cowboy in this one.

Dixie looks at Randy, but his eyes are fixed on the TV. He is a good man, caring, honest, supportive. She likes being with him, having him here. But she realizes that she doesn't mind it when he's not here. She is pleased when he shows up, but doesn't miss him when they're apart. There is something wrong with that, she decides. Perhaps she is holding back; perhaps he is. She wonders if she should read one of those self-help books about women and relationships. Or maybe see the police shrink.

She lies down next to Randy, presses her nose to his neck. There is a faint scent of last night's cologne, Calvin Klein. The sweetness of the cologne has been dulled by Randy's own body odor. She likes the smell and inhales deeply. She watches Glenn Ford throw a drink in a man's face. Randy puts his hand on her hip and pats her lovingly.

The phone rings.

The doorbell rings.

'Shit,' she says.

'What the fuck?' Randy says.

They sit up.

The phone rings again. It is not Dixie's regular phone, it is her undercover phone. The number is different from her regular number. This is the phone number she gives out to her high school 'friends' so they can call her. The phone is red and sits next to her regular white phone. The red phone makes her think of Moscow or Washington. Hello, Mr. President?

'Get the door, okay?' she tells Randy.

He grumbles, gets up, tightens the knot in his towel. He lumbers out the bedroom toward the apartment door. Dixie stands behind the bedroom door looking through the crack at the hinges. From here she can see who's at the front door. She reaches for the red phone.

'Hi,' she says.

'Dixie?' It's Melody Krauss, her high school friend with the Southern Comfort spray.

'Yeah. Hi. What's up?'

Melody sobs. 'Oh, Dixie.'

Immediately Dixie thinks the worst. Child abuse, incest, rape. She has seen it all, five-year-old girls raped so brutally by their fathers that they needed stitches. 'What's the matter, Melody?'

'T-T-Toby.' She is crying freely now. The sobs catch in her throat and she coughs. Dixie wonders: Assault? Drug overdose? Attempted suicide?

Dixie peers through the crack of the bedroom door to see who is at the front door. Jesus Christ! It's Karl, her ex-husband. Randy is standing in the doorway holding his towel in place. Both men look uncomfortable.

'That rat bastard!' Melody cries.

'What's Toby done?' Toby is the yearbook editor. He

209

is handsome, wealthy, and drives a Jeep with more accessories than most luxury cars. Melody has a crush on him and has talked about him nonstop since Dixie met her. Although they share a chemistry class, Melody is certain Toby doesn't know she is alive. 'What's he done?' Dixie repeats into the phone.

'He *fucked* me, for starters.'

Dixie isn't sure whether this is literal or figurative. 'He raped you?'

'He fucked me. Then he fucked me over.' She is sobbing again. Her speech is slightly slurred. She's been at the Southern Comfort again. 'Please come over, Dixie. Please, Dixie.'

'Have you been drinking?'

Melody laughs nastily. 'Of course. What else is there to do?'

'Have you taken any drugs?'

'What're you, my mother?'

'Melody, answer me,' Dixie snaps. Her voice is so strange and authoritative it often surprises people.

'N-no,' Melody says. 'Just some booze. But I can get some shit if you want.'

Dixie sighs. Melody thinks she asked the question as a prerequisite of coming over. Dixie looks through the crack again. Randy and Karl are both inside now. They are talking back and forth. Randy gestures with his right hand, the left still clamped on his towel. Karl just stands still, his arms at his sides. They don't seem to be arguing. Dixie wonders what they are saying.

'Please come over,' Melody says.

'I don't know, Mel,' Dixie hedges. 'My parents want me to go over to my grandparents with them. It's a big deal.'

There's a long silence. Dixie feels lousy about this, but she's off duty now. She has a real life here, a boyfriend and ex-husband in the living room.

'Can't you get out of it?' Melody asks.

'Not likely. It's my mom's folks. She's heavy into family and stuff. Can't you call somebody else? I mean, you've only known me a few weeks.'

Melody sobs loudly. 'I don't know. I guess I trust you more.'

Dixie watches Randy and Karl sit. Randy keeps glancing anxiously at the bedroom.

'Okay,' Dixie says. 'I'll be over as soon as I can.'

'Thanks, Dixie,' Melody says happily. 'I mean it. I'm your friend for life. I swear.'

'Bye.'

'Wait, Dixie! Wait!'

'What?'

'Let's meet at the mall, okay? I've gotta get out of this place or my mom's gonna see I've been crying and want to have a mother-daughter talk. I'll wait for you in Nordstrom's. The shoe department.'

'Okay.' Dixie hangs up. She opens the closet. The clothing she wears for this undercover assignment are all neatly hung in one section next to the wall. She pulls on a pair of jeans and rolls up the cuffs, slips into a red plaid cotton skirt which she leaves unbuttoned to show her yellow T-shirt. She doesn't bother with a bra. She slips into rubber flipflops. In the bathroom she hurriedly applies makeup to her eyes and face, mousses her hair and scrubs her fingers through it.

'Hi, Karl,' she says as she enters the living room, still tucking in her shirt.

Karl nods formally. 'Dixie.'

Randy makes a strained face at her. 'I think I'll go change.'

'I've got to be going,' Dixie tells him. 'Business.'

'Fuck.'

Karl smiles. 'Some things never change.'

211

Dixie does not like this. It's bad enough to disappoint Randy, but to have Karl also being judgmental annoys her. 'What do you want, Karl?'

'We were supposed to go to lunch today. Don't you remember?'

Karl is always doing this. Claiming they have set up an appointment to do something, then acting hurt and insulted that she forgot. It is difficult to get mad at Karl, he is so good-natured and harmless. They met during Dixie's first year on the force. The department wanted some new computers and Karl was a salesman for a local computer store. He came in, looked over the department's needs and suggested they buy a dozen Macintosh computers. But Captain Janeway thought they looked like toys and went with the IBM PCs. Karl was busy around the station for several weeks, installing the new computers and training the personnel, rushing over whenever there was a glitch in the software or someone accidentally dumped their data.

One afternoon as Karl was leaving, he discovered one of his tires was flat. Dixie was leaving at the same time and saw him staring at the tire perplexed.

'You have a spare?' she asked.

'Of course,' he said. 'I think.' He lifted the trunk lid of his Honda. 'Guess not.'

Dixie peeled back the cardboard bottom and showed him the spare underneath. 'Haven't you ever changed a tire before?'

'Not really. Not on a car. On a bicycle once. I was twelve.'

She looked at him and shook her head. She had to smile, he looked so lost and confused. He was a handsome man, a couple of years older than her twenty-six years. He had the reddest hair she'd ever seen that didn't come out of a bottle. A cluster of freckles spilled down the side of his nose across one cheek, forming a constellation very much

212

like Orion. As he bent over the trunk trying to get the tire out, she saw a long piece of thread hanging from the inside of his pocket down across his butt. Very cute, she decided.

'Here,' she said, grabbing the spare and the jack. 'I'll show you how.'

They dated for two years after that, though they were engaged to marry after six months. Karl still lived at home, trying to save enough money for a down payment for a house. Dixie suggested they could live together and he could still save money, but Karl was a strict Roman Catholic and was determined they wouldn't have intercourse until they were married. At first, Dixie thought this was crazy and she was ready to split up. But soon she got used to the idea, kind of liked the discipline of it, the challenge. It was very much like weight lifting. Just when you want to quit most, when your body is shaking and burning for you to stop, that's when you have to pump out just one more rep.

For two years they masturbated each other, had oral sex, used objects from fruit to frankfurters on each other. But they never had intercourse. After two years, Karl had saved the money. They married, bought a small fixer-upper, had sex every day the first week. After that once a week, then once a month. Six months later she left him.

Now Dixie looks back on that time of her life as a foggy experiment, the way some of her generation went off to live in a commune or joined the Peace Corps.

She still likes Karl. He hasn't changed one bit. He would have made a good brother. The only problem is that Karl still wants to spend time with her, more time than she can spare. He still loves her in his own way. He was perfectly happy with the way things had been going in the marriage. He has more than once suggested they live together again, not romantically if she preferred. Just as friends. That is too complicated for Dixie.

213

'Karl,' she says patiently, 'we were not supposed to go to lunch today.'

Karl brushes a lock of fiery red hair from his forehead. 'Why can't you just admit when you've forgotten something?'

Randy takes a step toward Karl. 'She said there was no lunch date, friend. So why don't you just leave.' Randy's broad hairy body is menacing, but his voice is high, still sounds like the little boy he played on 'Dennis the Menace.' Still, Karl is impressed enough to back up a step.

'I'll call you next week,' Dixie says, taking Karl's arm and guiding him toward the door.

'Sure you will.'

'I will. Next week.'

'We'll have lunch?'

'I'll call you.' She nudges him out the door. As he turns and walks away, she looks at his behind to see if there's any thread strewn across it. Not this time. The seven years since they met have not changed him much. She feels as if she's changed so much it's a wonder he recognizes her.

Dixie closes the door and turns to Randy. 'Sorry about that. He's not really a bad guy.'

'He seemed okay.'

She smiles at him. 'What was with all that posturing. Were you going to deck him?'

'Me? I haven't hit anybody since high school. I was just trying to be firm, assertive. Women like that.'

Dixie kisses him on the cheek. 'Will you wait for me?'

'How long are you gonna be gone?'

'I don't know. A couple hours maybe. It's hard to say.'

'We're supposed to pick up Lonnie at two.' Lonnie is his son, who is living with his ex-wife in Huntington Beach. Today is Randy's day with Lonnie and he wants the three of them to play miniature golf.

'I should be back way before then.'

214

He scratches his heavy day-old beard. 'I'll wait.'

'Good,' she says, kisses him quickly on the lips and leaves. On the way to the car she tries to decide whether or not she's glad Randy will wait for her.

'That rat fuck bastard!' Melody says. She is sitting in a chair in the shoe department of Nordstrom's. Four shoe boxes are piled next to her. She had two different shoes on her feet. 'Which one do you like best?'

A man in his mid-twenties with too much mousse in his hair kneels in front of Melody. He holds the partner to each of the shoes she has on. He smiles at Dixie. 'I like the sandal, how about you?'

Dixie sits down next to Melody. Melody's eyes are red, probably from a combination of crying and Southern Comfort. Southern Comfort was a favorite of Janis Joplin, Dixie remembers. 'The sandal is nice,' she says. 'So's the pump.'

'Great! I was hoping you'd say that.' Melody kicks both shoes off. 'I'll take them both.'

The salesman hastily packs the shoes back into their boxes. 'Cash or charge?'

'Charge.' She hands him her Nordstrom charge card. He takes it and the boxes and walks over to the counter and begins ringing the sale up. Melody wriggles her feet into her Topsiders and stands up with a grin. 'Now all I need are a couple blouses, a few skirts, a sweater, slacks, and we'll be done.'

'Melody, I didn't come down here to go shopping with you.'

'Why not?'

'Because I had other plans. I came because you said you needed to talk.'

'We can talk and shop at the same time. Shopping makes me happy.'

215

Dixie shakes her head. 'I'm leaving.'

Melody suddenly grabs her arm with surprising strength. 'No, please, Dixie.' Her eyes widen pleadingly. 'I need you right now. That asshole cocksucker Toby.' She starts crying. Women circle around at a safe perimeter, pretending to examine the shoes on display, but looking out of the corners of their eyes, watching. The salesman is waiting at the counter with the shoes and the charge slip. Melody can't stop crying.

Dixie sits Melody down in a chair and goes over to the counter. She takes the charge slip and the brown Nordstrom's charge card. She tears up the slip and pockets the card. 'She's changed her mind. Sorry.' She hurries back to Melody and guides her out of the store into the parking lot.

They sit in Dixie's vintage Mustang, Melody sobbing silently, shoulders hunched and shaking, Dixie holding Melody's hands.

'It's stupid,' Melpdy says now. She stops crying just as suddenly as she began. Her face is streaked with tears, shiny and moist as snail trails. Her eyes are red and puffy. A thin bubble of mucus expands at her nostril as she breathes, then bursts. Melody wipes her nose with the back of her hand. 'No big deal I guess,' she says. 'You know I've been crazy for Toby since the tenth grade.'

'You told me.'

'I told everybody. Everybody except Toby.' She opens her purse, takes out a silver flask and drinks. 'Want some?'

Dixie shakes her head.

Melody swigs again. 'I was over at Licorice Pizza looking at some records, and he comes up behind me and hugs me. I mean, the guy practically lifts me off my feet and he's never even spoken more than five words to me in three years. I'm wearing just my Jimmy Z shorts and that bikini top, you know, the one with the pink and black

216

polka dots. I figure he's mistaken me for someone else.'

Dixie nods. She isn't really much interested in these details, but she knows from experience victims need to tell their stories in their own ways. The details are really for their own benefit, as if they thought that reconstructing the scene down to every detail would give them the power to change the outcome. Dixie has never seen the pink and black polka dot bikini top, or the Jimmy Z shorts, but she can imagine what Melody looked like in them. She is not a pretty girl, her face is a little too pinched, the nose, eyes, and mouth bunched together in the middle of the face rather than spread out proportionately. That leaves a lot of forehead, cheeks, and chin with nothing on them but an occasional cluster of acne. Not much, just enough to keep the cool boys away. But she has a shapely body, long slender legs, wrist-sized waist, and breasts a little too large for the rest of her. In that way she reminds Dixie a little of Trina.

'He's got me in this bear hug, right? I mean tight. I can practically feel his dick stabbing me in the butt. He puts me down, says, "Hi, Melody." You believe that? "Hi, Melody." Like we've been buddies for years. I say hi back and go back to looking through the records. I'm reading the jacket to Tom Petty and he's still standing there. He starts talking about the record, how cool Tom Petty is, and he starts in on other music stuff. The kind of stuff you talk about when you're hitting on someone. I'm standing there thinking, hey, he's got a girlfriend. So I ask him, I mean, I ask him straight out, "Where's Missy?" He looks at me kinda funny, like he's never heard the name before. I mean, he's been banging her for his whole senior year. Then he just shrugs, says, "I don't know. We're not married or anything." I don't know what that means. Is he telling me he's busted up with her or what? I can't figure.'

Dixie shifts in her seat. Sitting sideways in the bucket seats of a Mustang is very uncomfortable. She steals a glance at her watch and tries to calculate how soon she can be home again. Randy would be pissed if she didn't go with him and Lonnie to miniature golf.

'So he invites me over to his house, go for a swim. I ask him where his parents are and he says they're gone for the weekend. Santa Barbara or something, some golf tournament his dad's in. We go to his place. We're not even all the way in the house he starts scamming me. He's kissing me and all. I mean, just kissing, frenching of course, but he hasn't grabbed anything yet.' Melody swigs again from her flask. She smacks her lips. 'So we go out to the pool and swim. I'm in my panties and bikini top, he's got these cool Maui trunks come down to his knees. He comes on to me in the pool, hugging and all, kissing some. I guess I was feeling kinda horny too, 'cause I let him take my top off.' Melody looks over at Dixie, waiting for a reaction. Dixie gives none and Melody continues. 'Anyway, we end up in his bedroom fucking. He's got these colored condoms, red, blue, yellow. He lets me pick one. I didn't care, shit, I'd never actually seen a guy even put one on before, they always, you known, turn their backs or something. I thought it was complicated. So I pick the red one and he slips it on. Then we do it.' She twists the cap on the flask on and off, on and off. 'Afterwards we're lying there listening to his Peter Gabriel records and the phone rings. He answers, then takes the call in another room. When he comes back he tells me I've got to go, Missy's on her way over. My panties and top are still in the dryer downstairs. He runs down, brings them up, and tosses them on me. They're still fucking wet. I don't know, I guess I blew it, but I started screaming at him. Missy had to work this morning, that's the only reason he came on to me. He saw me, was horny, and wanted to fuck. I

218

wouldn't have minded so much if he'd just been up front. Shit, I'd probably have fucked him anyway, but I hate being lied to like that. Treated like a slut. You know?'

Dixie stares at Melody. It wasn't rape or incest or child abuse. No drug o.d. or teen suicide or assault. It was just the usual lesson in adolescent love. Not as dramatic as the crimes Dixie was used to, but just as heartbreaking to the inexperienced. Melody was in real pain, felt used and ugly. Her damp panties thrown at her while she was lying in the bed of the boy she'd wanted for three years. Dixie feels bad, not just for Melody, but because she had been impatient with the girl's pain because it was merely normal human suffering. Nothing criminal. Dixie starts the Mustang up and pulls out of the lot.

'Cool car,' Melody says. 'Where are we going?'

'I love nachos,' Melody says.

'Me too.' Dixie used a tortilla chip to scoop up some guacamole, sour cream, and spicy chicken. A long string of melted cheese hangs from the chips as she lifts it to her mouth. Melody reaches over and snaps the cheese string. 'Thanks,' Dixie says and eats the loaded chip. She is hungry for the first time in days.

They are sitting in the Atrium Court of Fashion Island. Fashion Island is like no other place in the country. It is an open-air shopping center that sits on a hill in Newport Beach overlooking the Pacific Ocean. As shoppers wander from Neiman-Marcus to Robinson's to Buffum's, they can actually see the ocean, the luxury boats sailing by. Many of the people who live near Fashion Island own large million-dollar homes. There are many stores here that cater to these people, but there are also a few that cater to the cheaper tastes of the upper middle class.

Dixie used to shop here only for special occasions. Back then the Atrium Court was J.C. Penney's, but most of the shoppers here couldn't imagine what J.C. Penney's might possibly have that they would want to own. The store closed down, was gutted, and a few years later remodeled to include three floors of small but expensive clothing stores, plus a fancy supermarket on the bottom floor that features a sushi bar and exotic fruits and vegetables. And in the middle of the supermarket is a circle of specialty fast-food restaurants. Diners sit in a cluster of tables that surround a water fountain and grand piano. Sometimes a man in a tuxedo sits at the piano and plays while shoppers dine. The man in the tuxedo is not here today and Dixie and Melody eat their nachos next to the fountain and listen to the water splash.

Two boys sit at the table next to them. They are eating Chinese food with chopsticks. One is wearing headphones attached to his cassette player. He bobs his head rhythmically as he eats. The other boy wears an earphone attached to his Sony Watchman. He is watching the Lakers game. His shoulders feint and weave along with the players' moves. When the boys are done eating, they both walk off together and disappear up the escalator, still bopping, still feigning. Dixie never saw them exchange one word.

'This was a good idea,' Melody says. She scrapes her finger along the bottom of the empty plate for what's left of the black beans. She licks it off her finger. 'I feel better.'

'I'm glad.'

'He's still a fucking rat bastard.'

Dixie finds it hard to be too critical of young Toby. She is old enough now to know that boys don't always mean to be cruel, they just aren't used to the demands of their dicks. As a woman matures, she knows better what to expect, not to judge too harshly. Not to take everything so personally.

'I guess I was asking for it,' Melody says. She grins. 'I was blinded by the glamour, red condoms and such.'

They both laugh. People are standing around the perimeter of the dining area with trays in their hands waiting for empty tables. The one flaw in this grand design is that there are never enough tables for the diners and they are forced to walk in circles with their trays loaded with steaming food searching out someone who is almost ready to abandon his table. Then everyone dashes for it. Dixie finds this practice a little humiliating for everyone. 'Let's go,' she says and they stand up.

Immediately several tray-carrying diners break for their little table, weaving around the other tables, soup and beverage slopping over onto their trays. A middle-aged woman and her lanky blond daughter cut off a couple of other women in tennis clothes and slide into the chairs.

As Dixie and Melody head for the escalator, Joseph Little steps in front of them. He smiles, strokes Dixie's arm. 'Jesus, am I lucky or what?'

'Hey, Joe,' Dixie says.

'Hi.' Melody nods glumly. She is a frequent customer of his, but she obviously doesn't want him around right now. She looks at Dixie.

'I thought you said you were going off to your granny's today?' he says.

'Something came up,' Dixie says.

'Christ, if we missed a planned trip to my grandparents, they'd stroke out.'

Dixie doesn't answer. This is getting complicated. For the past couple of weeks he's been chasing her around. She's avoided him, claiming to be angry about the hickey he gave her. Captain Janeway keeps calling her in for progress reports, wants to know if she's any closer to Little's source. She tells him to be patient. Cops think it's easier to get close to high school students than to pimps or hookers or adult criminals. Maybe it used to be, but not anymore. They've seen too much TV, they've learned

221

not to trust anyone. The best way to get close to Joseph Little is to run away, let him get close to her.

'Look, you guys,' Joseph says. 'I'm trying to pick something nice out for my mom for Mother's Day. Maybe you guys could help?'

Melody gives Dixie another look to indicate she'd rather they were alone. Joseph picks up on the look.

'Hey, I'll make it worth your while.'

Melody is interested. 'Like how?'

'What do you want?' He touches his finger to the outside of his nostril, makes a little snorting sound, and grins.

'Whatever,' Melody says, smiling.

The three of them go from store to store searching through thousands of items. Dixie can tell by the way he keeps touching her that he's hot for her, not just as a conquest like before, but as something more. This is a perfect opportunity to get closer to him, gain a little more of his confidence. She wants to give Randy a call to cancel their plans, but when she feigns having to go to the bathroom, Melody insists on coming along. She's excited about getting free cocaine.

They are browsing through May Company, women's sportswear. They've been at it for almost two hours.

'What is it exactly you're looking for?' Dixie asks.

He shrugs. 'I'll know it when I find it.'

They keep searching.

'Hey, this is neat.' He holds up a blue silk dress.

'Nice,' Dixie says. 'What's her size?'

'I'm not sure. She's about your height, a little bigger all around though.'

Melody comes over holding a sweater in front of her. 'This is nice.'

Joseph shakes his head. 'She's got more sweaters than teeth. I like this dress.'

'Yeah, that's good too,' Melody says.

He studies it on the hanger, holds it up at different angles to the light, puts it in front of Dixie, frowns. 'I don't know. It's hard to tell on the hanger. Would you try it on for me so I can get a better idea how it'll look on her?'

Dixie hesitates, then shrugs. 'Sure.'

She takes the dress into the dressing room, closes the door behind her. She hangs the dress on the door and checks the price tag: $258.00. She's never owned a dress that costs that much. Dixie strips down to her panties and is about to remove the silk dress from the hanger when her dressing room door opens and Joseph steps in. He is smiling wickedly.

'Hi,' he says and steps toward her. He is staring at her small breasts, down her stomach to her panties. Her skin tingles as if his eyes were a wet tongue.

'Are you nuts?' she whispers.

'Find out for yourself.' He is right against her now, holding her, kissing her ear, her cheek, her mouth.

Dixie stands rigid. She doesn't push him away, but she doesn't respond. Timing is everything in this kind of work. You can only push the man away so long; after that you wound his pride to where he doesn't want you around anymore to remind him. Dixie senses this is that turning point. He risked sneaking in here to prove his sincerity; if she kicked him out now, she might blow any chance of him showing her his drug supplies. Officially and legally, any sexual contact taints the case, though that is not always how things actually work out. Still, she has no intention of fucking him here, now, ever, anywhere. But she must encourage him, give him hope.

'I'm sorry about the hickey before,' he whispers. 'I was just showing off. I didn't mean anything.' He kisses her lightly on the lips, tentatively, as if he's not certain whether or not she will suddenly bite his lip off.

Dixie returns his kiss. Surprised, he kisses her harder,

223

plunging his tongue into her mouth. She sucks it in. He presses tightly against her until they are up against the wall, crushing the blue silk dress. His right hand comes up and holds her breast, squeezes it briefly and immediately moves to her crotch. He cups his hand outside her panties, his fingers nudging at the fabric over her vagina. Dixie is embarrassed to feel her own panties getting wet. She can even smell her own earthy scent.

Karl was an inept and indifferent lover. Randy is more experienced and satisfying. But Dixie is not used to this kind of urgency, the jungle swamp passion, the four-wheel drive need. She feels her own body responding though she concentrates on keeping her mind detached and objective. He is grinding his hips against her. He is kissing her breasts, sucking on the nipples, tugging them with his teeth. He sticks his hand down the back of her panties, holds her butt, slides his hand around to the front and rams a finger deep inside her, practically lifting her off the floor. Dixie feels the sweat dripping down her forehead as she straddles his hand, her clitoris pressing against his palm.

He unzips his pants, pulls out his penis and guides her hand to it. His penis is hard as a hammer head, warm. He thrusts it against her hand and she squeezes it.

Joseph is trying to get her panties down. He has them over her hips to her thighs. He pushes his penis toward her, against her stomach. He lifts her a little, trying to get her in position so he can enter her. Dixie knows she cannot let this happen, that that would be crossing the imaginary line. She quickly begins to stroke him, rapidly tugging on his penis, her palm building up friction. She looks at his closed eyes and feels something for him, not passion, but an almost maternal compassion, as if she were putting a hurting child out of misery. Maybe that's the greatest part of sex anyway for women. It doesn't seem to be for Trina. *Hell, what do I know*, Dixie thinks as she keeps stroking.

Joseph moans and his warm come shoots across her hand and wrist. He collapses against her and the rest of it pumps onto her stomach. 'Jesus,' he sighs, sagging. 'God.'

Dixie looks around, finds some tissue paper used to package shirts and sweaters. She wipes her hand and stomach, then wipes the tip of Joseph's penis. He seems embarrassed by this, like a little boy whose hair has been combed. He backs away, tucks himself back into his pants. He looks as if he'd like to say something important. Finally he speaks. 'I'll meet you outside.'

'Gross,' Melody says.

'Jesus, they're ugly,' Joseph says.

They are standing in Fashion Island's only pet store. Melody wanted to see the puppies. Joseph has one arm around Dixie, the other holding the bag with the blue silk dress gift-wrapped for his mother. The three of them are standing in front of a dry aquarium filled with the yellow frogs. The frogs' skin is rubbery and their eyes are red. They don't blink or move. There is a hand-lettered sign taped to the aquarium that says, ALBINO FROGS. YES, THEY ARE *REAL*.

'Well, they don't look real,' Joseph says.

There is another sign taped to the glass. FEED THEM FOR A QUARTER. Next to the sign is a coin plunger.

'Give me a quarter,' Melody says. Her face is practically pressed against the glass. She holds her hand out to the two of them. Joseph digs into his pocket and slaps a quarter into her palm. She slides the coin into the slot and pushes the plunger. A live grasshopper drops into the aquarium on to the back of one of the frogs. The frog doesn't move, his red eyes staring blindly ahead. The grasshopper sits on his back a moment, then hops off onto a rock. None of the dozen frogs move.

'Shit, they're not real,' Joseph says. 'They're plastic or

rubber or something. This is just some gimmick to get quarters.'

Dixie watches Melody's rapt face. Melody seems mesmerized.

'They're alive,' Melody says.

'How can you tell?' Joseph asks.

'I can see them breathe.'

'Batteries,' Joseph says. 'My sister has a doll that does the same thing.'

The grasshopper jumps around the tank undisturbed for a minute.

'Look!' Melody shouts. People in the store turn to see what she's shouting about.

Several of the frogs slowly stir, like dinosaurs suddenly thawed. They shift around on their rocks bumping into each other. Their eyes beam that unnerving red. They don't seem to know where they're going, just that they should move. One frog turns, knocks into the grasshopper, but doesn't make a move for it. Another steps forward and unknowingly steps on the grasshopper, pinning it beneath its webbed foot. The grasshopper wriggles and struggles, squirming to get free. The frog ignores him for more than a minute, then shifts his head toward it, stares for almost another minute. Then he swallows the grasshopper.

'Some hunters,' Joseph laughs, squeezing Dixie closer.

'Gimmie another quarter,' Melody says.

'No way,' Joseph says. 'We can't count on one of them stepping on it this time. It could take days for them to figure out the bug's even in there. It's a wonder they don't all starve to death.'

Melody snaps her fingers. 'Come on, I'll pay you back.'

'Shit.' Joseph digs out another quarter for her. After she plunges it into the machine another grasshopper drops into the tank, he leads Dixie out of the store. 'We'll wait outside,' he calls back to Melody.

Outside the sun is bright. Dixie shades her eyes and stares out over the ocean. Two enormous sailboats glide by. She wishes she were on one of those sailboats right now instead of giving handjobs to high school drug dealers and watching her "best friend" drop bugs into a frog tank. Christ, how did she get to this place in her life? Will she ever be able to shop at the May Company again? Of course, the activity in the dressing room won't appear in her report, that's part of the unofficial training you get in undercover work. Any infraction where it's your word against one other person, don't report. Maybe the public would be shocked to know that, maybe they'd rather not know, as long as the drug dealers are cleaned out. Still, Dixie feels awful. Moving among these kids, affecting their lives as she has already makes her feel so sneaky, a parent abusing a child's trust. Yeah, it's for their own good, she knows all that. Dixie takes a deep breath, smells the moist salt from the ocean mixed with the tangy soap scent from the May Company rest room where she washed herself off after Joseph exploded on to her. She looks at him, wants to shake him and give him a lecture. He's a bright, good-looking kid from a nice family. There's no good reason to be doing what he's doing. But lectures aren't her job. She must keep her perspective. In L.A., one woman cop doing this same thing got thrown off the force for having sex with one of the students. Another male cop quit the force to marry one of the high school girls he'd started dating as a cover. Perspective is everything in this job.

'I really like you,' Joseph says to her tenderly.

'I like you too.'

He nods, looks out to the ocean. 'Kinda strange back there, huh?'

'The frogs? Yeah.'

'Not the frogs. Back there.' He hooks a thumb over his shoulder toward the May Company. 'What we did.'

227

'It was nice.'

'I just didn't want you to get the wrong idea.'

Dixie doesn't say anything. They are standing side by side, both shielding their eyes with their hands as they stare out over the ocean.

'It wasn't just sex,' he says.

'No, I didn't think so.'

'Good. I really like you. I mean, I like sex, don't get me wrong. But I like you too. For who you are.'

Three helicopters appear out over the ocean. They are too far away to hear, but they move together in a precise pattern. A flock of sea gulls follows behind them.

'I just thought we might spend some time together. Outside school.'

'We are, Joseph. Right now.'

He looks at her. 'You know what I mean.'

She watches the helicopters turn and head back in the same direction they just came from. The sea gulls turn too and chase after them. She glances over at Joseph. 'I know what you mean. I'm just not sure. You're kind of a mysterious guy. I'm not crazy about that.'

He looks uncomfortable, like he'd like to tell her more but can't. 'No big mystery.'

'You deal drugs.'

'You've bought some off me, remember? That's how we met.'

'Buying a few poppers and some coke for recreation isn't the same as dealing. I'm not sure I want to get involved with someone who's got such a dangerous job.'

'Hey, you let me worry about that.' He tries to sound tough, but it comes out melodramatically, just the way Randy sounded this morning when he was trying to be tough with Karl.

'It's not you that frightens me, Joseph,' she says. 'It's the people you deal with.'

228

He thinks that over. 'I can handle myself.'

Melody comes out of the store. 'Gimme another quarter. It's so cool the way they finally figure out there's food in there. The thing has to practically hop into their mouths. Jeez. Come on, gimme another quarter.'

'This is getting old,' Dixie says.

'Yeah? So's this,' Melody says, nodding at Joseph's hand around Dixie's waist. 'I thought you and I came here to spend some time together.'

'We did.'

'Yeah, right.'

Dixie doesn't know what to say. She doesn't want to hurt Melody's feelings, but her job is to stick with Joseph. Now she's closer than ever. With a little pressure, she should be able to get enough info out of him over the next week to figure out when he makes his routine buy. Maybe even follow him.

'Omigod, Dixie!' a voice cries out. 'What the hell are you doing in that outfit?'

Dixie feels her stomach clench as she spins around and sees Diva and Barcelona walking toward her. Jesus Christ, no!

'Your hair!' Diva laughs. 'What is this, a masquerade?'

Dixie turns to Joseph and sees the smile on his face harden.

16

That morning, before running into Dixie:

Barcelona rolls over in bed and is surprised to bump into Eric.

'Ow,' he says sleepily. 'My shoulder.'

'When did you get here?' she asks.

'An hour ago. You were asleep.'

'Oh.' She is pleased that he is here. He has his own key now. But it bothers her a little that she didn't hear him or feel him enter her home. A naked man climbed into bed next to her and she didn't notice. This makes her nervous about break-ins and she thinks about having a burglar alarm installed.

'Rub my shoulder?' he asks.

His shoulder is sore from softball. He plays on a coed team from Austin House, his home for abused women. They are last in the Social Services league. Drug Rehab is number one. Eric tries to joke about this, but she can see that being last really upsets him. He is an exceptional athlete, one of the most competitive persons she has ever known. He takes being last personally and often discusses the faults of his teammates with her. Sometimes he cuts out articles from sports magazines about how better to field a ball, or he draws stick figures showing the proper way to swing a bat. He photocopies and hands them out to his teammates at work. Barcelona has seen his team play; drawings won't help. Eric doesn't agree. He believes practice and dedication and sheer willpower will bring their batting average up. In this way, he is a lot like Dixie.

Barcelona massages his right shoulder and he hums with pleasure under her touch. He scoots his bare butt backward until it touches her leg. His clothes are arranged neatly on the wicker clothes hamper against the wall: nylon shorts, white socks, mesh T-shirt, Tiger running shoes with gel in the soles. An ankle brace crowns the pile. Barcelona wonders why it is that every guy she's dated over thirty has a chronic sports injury of some kind. Ankle, knee, elbow, finger. With very little prompting, each will recall in detail the exact moment the injury occurred, during what specific play of the basketball/football/racquetball/softball game.

'What did you tell Luna?' Barcelona asks.

'That I'm out running.'

'Anything else?'

'Like what?'

She stops rubbing. 'She called me last night. Left a message on my machine.'

Eric sits up. He tries to look casual, but she can see the panic in his eyes. 'What did she say?'

'Nothing really. She wants me to call her. Have a talk.'

Eric thinks this over, absently twisting his lips with his fingers. Barcelona remembers this habit from graduate school. There she found it cute, endearing. Here she's not so sure. 'Maybe she just wants to get together. She likes you.'

'She told you that?'

'God, yes. After that first night you met. She thought you were so smart and beautiful and sophisticated. And she loves your writing. Really.'

Barcelona feels awful. She and Eric have not really discussed their new relationship, nor have they talked much about Luna, except in informational ways. Luna is at school. Luna went to visit her sister for the night. Bulletins of Luna's whereabouts so they could better arrange their lovemaking. Barcelona feels as though she knows Luna very well, merely through her schedule of activities.

She had not really felt guilty about her rekindled relationship with Eric until this moment. She always considered Luna the interloper here, the one who took Eric from her, not the other way around. This affair is merely rebalancing nature. Except that Luna is Eric's wife. But that's not what makes her feel bad. It's that Luna likes and respects her writing. She feels as if she were betraying a fan, as if she were writing something bad, sloppy with plotting, careless with prose.

'What now?' Barcelona asks Eric.

'What now?' he repeats. 'Now I get up and take a leak, then I come back to bed and we make love. That's what now.'

Barcelona nods. 'Sounds reasonable.'

He smiles at her and they kiss. He gets out of bed and she stares at his naked body walking toward the bathroom. She is again surprised at how the sight of his bare bottom cause her heart to literally vibrate. His lean body is bumpy with long sinewy muscles. He stands over the toilet bowl and aims.

'Jesus fucking Christ!' Eric hollers and leaps back from the toilet, startled. Some of his urine squirts onto the carpet before he controls his bladder. 'Holy shit!' he shouts.

'What's the matter?' Barcelona asks, jumping out of bed. Maybe he found blood in his urine?

'That!' He points behind the toilet bowl. There behind the toilet, between the plumber's helper and the bathtub, are two dead mice. One is brownish and big as a French roll. His back is torn open and his internal organs are exposed in a red meaty soup. He looks like an anatomy exhibit for a high school biology class. The other mouse is small and gray. It has been decapitated, its head bitten off and spit out a few inches from the rest of the body.

'Goddamn it, Larry,' Barcelona says. She recognizes his style. She glances over her shoulder into the bedroom hoping to see him, but of course he is not there. She nudges Eric out of the way. 'He does this about once a week. Don't worry.'

'I'm not worried,' Eric says, a little offended. 'I was just startled. Surprised. I wasn't expecting to see a rat head first thing in the morning.'

'They're mice.'

'Mice, rats, shit. Why don't you get rid of that cat?'

Barcelona looks at him for a moment. 'I don't know. I really don't. I should, I guess.'

Eric softens. 'I don't mean have him put to sleep. I mean give him away to someone. Maybe someone on a farm who needs rats caught.'

'Mice,' she corrects, stooping over. She looks up at Eric. 'Go ahead and use the other bathroom.' He hesitates a moment, but finally he trots off down the hallway. Squatting, Barcelona tears a handful of toilet paper from the roll and uses it to pick up the big brown mouse first. The body is stiff so Larry must have done it sometime last night. Once again she has an uneasy feeling as she realizes that Larry was killing and dismembering these animals ten feet from her bed and she hadn't even known. First rodent mutilation and then a full-grown man climbs into her bed. She sleeps through all of it. Something must be wrong with her instincts.

Barcelona drops the mouse and toilet paper into the toilet. It makes a loud plop and a couple of drops of the urine water inside splashes on her arm. She tears off more toilet paper, wipes her arm, then uses it to grab the small gray mouse. The body is warm and limp, a fresh kill. It is also too small to get a good grip without crushing it. She repositions the toilet paper and picks the mouse up by the tail. She lifts it a couple of inches off the carpet when the tail detaches and the little headless body drops back to the carpet, blotting it with blood.

She sighs and makes a sour face. 'Sorry,' she says to the mouse. She tosses the toilet paper and tail into the toilet, unfurls more paper, and scoops up the body. Then the head, so small and delicate, she feels like a surgeon just picking it up. She dumps it in the toilet and flushes without looking.

She walks over to the sink and scrubs her hands and fingers and arms all the way to the elbow.

'Are we having fun yet?' Eric says upon his return to the bedroom.

They decide to make love. At first Eric is angry because he can't find his condom, though he's sure he brought one with him. Usually he leaves a box here, but he'd remembered they'd used the last one a couple of days ago. He couldn't run out of the house carrying a box of condoms, not without Luna asking questions. So he'd tucked one into the tiny pocket inside his running shorts. He stands next to the bed rifling through his clothes, even checking his ankle brace and socks. Barcelona lies in bed, head propped up on one hand. Watching him search frantically makes her think about this whole condom issue between them. All the years they were dating and then living together, they'd never used them. Now that he is married to Luna though, he always uses them. He knows she is on the Pill, so she tries to understand the ramifications of the condom. Sure, everyone is afraid of AIDS and all the other diseases, but there are subtler statements being made. Barcelona feels as if she were under suspicion for some terrible crime. As if her vagina were a secret depository for biological warfare. Slipping on a condom implies you are a slut, pumped regularly by slobering degenerates with oozing pustules. Was Eric protecting himself for himself? Because he wanted to protect Luna? Because he didn't want to get caught? Were these the adulterer's equivalent of the burglar's rubber gloves? No fingerprints, no pecker tracks?

Barcelona flops back on the pillow. God, it is complicated now. Everyone is a potential killer. How could people fall in love today under these suspicions?

'Eureka,' Eric says finally, holding up the foil packet. 'It fell out of the pocket and slipped behind the laundry hamper.'

They return to their lovemaking, though some of Barcelona's enthusiasm has waned. She scolds herself for being so silly and forces herself to become more energetic.

Afterward, she patters downstairs to make them some breakfast. She cinches her bathrobe as she walks into the kitchen and sees Larry sitting on top of the TV cleaning himself. He pauses, looks at her, returns to cleaning.

'Men,' she says to him and laughs suddenly. The sound startles him and he jumps down to the floor and runs out the cat door.

Barcelona opens the refrigerator, takes out the orange juice, the Weight Watchers margarine, and four eggs. She puts the iron skillet on the stove and turns the flame on. Then she reaches for the telephone. No point in putting it off any longer. This way, at least, she can talk and cook at the same time and once the eggs are done, she'll have an excuse to hang up.

She dials.

'Hello?' the deep, German-accented voice says.

'Hi, Mom.'

'Barcy! How are you, sweetheart?'

'Fine. How are you?'

235

'Great. Terrific.' The voice is cheerful, peppy, energetic. Her mother's trademarks. Her mother is not a complainer. Any illnesses or injuries her mother suffers, Barcelona usually only hears about once her mother has healed. Her father is just the opposite. Most of his ills and injuries are imaginary, though described with great attention to physical detail, no matter how personal.

'How's Dad?'

'You know. He's been dying for forty years. Cancer's been killing him for the last twenty, though the doctors can't find any.'

'Things never change.'

'The more things change, the more they stay the same, right? How's the weather?'

'Hot.' Barcelona doesn't really know what the weather is like outside. All her blinds are down and it has been a little overcast and cool the past couple of days. But her mother doesn't want to hear that. She wants to hear that California is just as she remembers it from their trips out here: hot, sunny, bright.

'What's it like in Pennsylvania?'

Her mother sighs, begins to speak in German. 'Rain and more rain. The basement leaked water again and we had to have some guy come and pump it out for two days. Cost us an arm and a leg. Or as your father puts it, we have to sell two hundred dozen bagels to pay for it.'

'He always knows how to put things in perspective.'

'He's your father all right.'

Barcelona wonders what that means. She doesn't ask. 'How's business?'

'Booming!' she says in English. 'Hold on a second, sweetheart.' Her mother puts down the phone and she can hear her walking away on the linoleum floor. Barcelona pictures the green and red tiles in her mind. The store is so small you can hear every sound in it. 'This all you have,' her mother is saying to a customer. 'A fifty-dollar bill for a cup of coffee and a toasted sweet roll?'

'It's all I have, Milan,' the man says. 'Unless you want me to owe you.'

'Owe me? Forget it. The way you tip I should just keep the change and you'd still owe me.'

Barcelona hears the man laugh, the ancient cash register ring, the drawer splat open, change being made.

'Bye, Tom,' her mother says.

'Bye, Milan.'

The door opens and closes.

Milan. She was named by her mother after one of the Italian cities she and her husband had visited on their honeymoon; Milan's sisters were named Florence and Roma. The tradition was continued by Milan, who honeymooned in Spain. Barcelona wondered if she too would follow the same tradition. But what would she call the kid if she did? Barstow? San Pedro? Anaheim?

'Hi, sweetheart, you still there?'

'Was that Tom Lipton?'

'Who else? Coffee and toasted sweet roll for lunch. And those damn fifties.'

'What's Dad doing?'

'Baking, natch? We have onion bagels on order, three coffee cakes, meat platters. And my waitress broke up with her stupid boyfriend so she moves around here like a zombie.'

Barcelona slices an English muffin and sticks it in the toaster. One slice doesn't quite fit so she takes it out and flattens it between her palms. Now it fits.

'So how's the writing going? What are you working on now?'

Milan Lee is sincere when she asks about Barcelona's writing. She proudly reads her daughter's books and tells all her customers to buy them. On the wall of their little

237

restaurant where the Hebrew National kosher meats poster used to be, is a display of framed covers from all of Barcelona's novels.

'I'm writing a screenplay now.'

'A screenplay!'

'Relax, Mom, it's nothing. Just a possibility.' She explains the situation.

'Lynda Kramer! My God. Will you meet her?'

'Maybe. I don't know.'

'Hold on, honey, let me get your father.' The phone clunks down and her mother runs down the wooden stairs to where Max Lee, formerly Lebowitz, bakes onion bagels, sweet rolls, coffee cakes, and the rest of the goodies they sell upstairs. The actual restaurant itself is tiny, no larger than most people's living rooms. It is built as an addition onto an old Victorian-style house constructed at the turn of the century. Her parents own the house too, which they rent out as single furnished rooms to students attending the local Methodist college. The basement of the house serves as the kitchen for the restaurant. It also is where they store their dry goods and freeze the baked goods and meats. They have four large freezers down there. Barcelona's father keeps several T-shirts in one of the freezers. When he is finished baking for the day, he dries the heavy sweat from his body and slips into one of the frozen T-shirts. She remembers watching him do that, how he always braced himself against the cold but smiled in relief as he pulled it on. Once when she was fourteen, he offered to put her bra in there for her, but she called him disgusting and stomped away. His laughter made her laugh even though she felt embarrassed.

'Barcy?' her father says into the phone. His voice too is heavily accented with the harsh German inflection, tongue beating each word into submission.

'Hi, Dad.'

238

'What's this about some screenplay?'

'It's a long shot. You know Hollywood.'

'You're not quitting teaching? You still have your college job, right?'

'Sure.' This is not the time to discuss her plans to quit. That would involve a long lecture. She changes subjects. 'How's your health?'

'Oh, the same. You know.'

Barcelona cracks two eggs into the frying pan and they sizzle as soon as they hit. Steam rises to her face, the sour smell of frying eggs and burned margarine. She winces and backs away. 'How's your throat?'

'Sore. Always sore.' She can see him stroking his throat now, even as they talk. 'Like sandpaper inside.'

'Quit smoking.'

'You always say that.'

'You always have a sore throat.'

'Quitting smoking is not so easy. You don't know, you never smoked. You know how long I've smoked?'

'More than fifty years?'

'Yes, that's right. More than fifty years,' he repeats, sounding proud. 'It's hard to quit something, anything, after fifty years. Try quitting to breathe for five minutes. That's what it is like.'

Barcy looks at the clock on the stove. She flips two of the eggs, Eric's. She spreads plum butter on half the English muffin, hers. 'How's business?'

'You know. Sometimes good, sometimes bad. I have lots of orders today. Onion bagels, meat platters, coffee cakes.'

'Look, Dad, I'll let you know what happens with the screenplay. You take care.'

'Okay. I've got to check the ovens now. The coffee cakes should be done. Here's your mother.'

'Sweetheart?' Milan's voice says.

'Hi, Mom.'

'I went into B. Dalton's last week at the mall. They were all out of your books. I made them order some.'

'Thanks, now I can make that house payment next month.'

Milan Lee laughs. 'What are mothers for?'

'You still getting those obscene calls? Dixie asked me.'

'She's the singer?'

'The cop, Mom. That's why she asked.'

'Oh, the skinny one, right. No calls for almost a month.' The first calls started about six months ago, a muffled voice, not clearly male or female. Just a low whisper. 'Funny, but the guy's changed his dialogue. At first it was all sex stuff, things he wanted to do to me, and who could blame him with my gorgeous bod at fifty-nine. Now, though, it's mostly just foul language, calling me names.' In German, she mentions a couple of the tamer words.

'Does it bother you?'

'No, why should it?' Her mother pauses. 'Sometimes.'

'I've got to go now, Mom.'

'I won't ask.'

'Good, don't.'

'Is he at least good looking?'

'Very.'

'Has a good job?'

'Mom.'

'Single?'

'You weren't going to ask, remember?'

Her mother sighs. 'I ask because you expect me to.'

'That doesn't mean I want you to.'

'Doesn't it? Don't you see me as some comic Jewish mother out of some television show, nags about career and marriage? Isn't that how you prefer to see me? Keep me in my pigeon hole?'

Barcelona's heart thumps wildly in her chest. She is

240

surprised by her mother's outburst. 'Mom, why do you say that?'

'Never mind. I didn't mean anything. We've been busy, that's all. I'm tired. Customers, sweetheart, I have to go now.'

'Bye, Mom.'

'Good-bye, Barcy.'

The eggs are overcooked when she scrapes them out of the frying pan. The toast is cold, the juice warm. She still can't get over her mother's statement. Not like her at all. Barcelona is unsettled and anxious; the chat did not go well. She doesn't know why it didn't. They are her parents, she loves them. She sees them now, her mother joking with the regular customers as she bags doughnuts and rings up the sale. Her mother, who was born Catholic but converted after marrying Max, now sounds more Jewish than Mel Brooks. She sees her father, seventy, downstairs in the hot kitchen, bent over the baking bench, rolling bagels, wrapping the dough around his hand, a dozen centerfolds from *Playboy* tacked up in front of him by his wife. He probably hasn't even noticed them for at least ten years. They are covered with a mist of flour. Barcelona remembers helping her father with the baking as a child, staring at the young naked girls who were always smiling, their skin as tight as water balloons. Standing or lying, showing breasts, legs, buttocks. Not shyly, not embarrassed. Smiling. That's what Barcelona thought growing up to be a woman would be like: always smiling, always happy.

Now she realizes the girls were only children themselves, most of them barely out of their teens.

Barcelona carries her breakfast upstairs and hands a plate to Eric. He is reading her *New York Review of Books*.

'Fascinating article in here on the new bio of Sartre.'

Barcelona puts down her own plate, throws open her robe, and strikes a centerfold pose. She smiles so widely her jaw aches.

Eric stares at her.

'Well?' she says through smiling teeth.

'Well what?'

'Do I look happy?'

The phone rings. It is Diva.

'Have some spare time today?' Diva asks.

Barcelona looks over at Eric. He is dressed, stretching out on the floor for his run home. It is ten miles, but since he took the bus here, he should be able to make it. She doesn't know what he will tell Luna about why he was gone so long. She doesn't ask.

'Sure,' Barcelona says. 'Why?'

'Can we meet for lunch?'

'Okay. Where?'

'How about the Atrium?' Diva's voice sounds funny.

'Fine. You okay?'

'Yeah, I'm fine. I just want to talk to you about something.'

'Okay. Noon?'

'See you there.' Barcelona hangs up and watches Eric lean against the wall, stretching his hamstrings.

'We saw that Japanese film down at the Balboa the other night,' he says. 'You should see it. It's very witty, very satirical.'

He has been recommending books, articles, movies, art shows, and records since they've been seeing each other again. He gives her books and records as gifts, buys her tickets to showings (two tickets, he's so open-minded). His taste is very good and she has enjoyed most of what he's recommended. Nevertheless, she resents his suggestions. She's not sure why yet. Maybe because he assumes she wouldn't read, see, or hear these things without him first recommending them.

When will I see you again? lies stillborn inside her.

'I'll call you tomorrow morning,' he says. 'Luna is in a racquetball league.'

She doesn't want to know these details, though he always insists on sharing them. As if they are spies together, he wants her to know what he risks for her sake. 'I may be out in the morning,' she says. She doesn't know why she's said this. She has no plans. Maybe so he would ask her where she might be.

He doesn't. He gives her a look, then shrugs. 'Tomorrow night then. I can probably sneak out of the house for a few minutes.'

'What do you mean "sneak"?'

'Huh?'

'Are you going to creep out of the house, crouched over like this?' She crouches and walks like a cat burglar.

'No.'

'Then you're not going to sneak out of the house. You're going to walk out under false pretenses.'

He frowns. 'I didn't realize you were heavily into semiotics and philology.'

'I am.'

He steps toward her, his voice soft, caring. 'What's the matter, hon?' He takes her into his arms and holds her. She likes the feeling and hugs him back. Her nose is against his ear and she sniffs his special smell.

'Nothing,' she says. 'Nothing's wrong.'

Diva comes running out of the Atrium Court and waves to Barcelona from the edge of the sidewalk. 'Don't park,' she shouts through cupped hands.

Barcelona sees her just as she is pulling into a tight parking space and brakes halfway in. Capturing a space so

243

close to the main building on a weekend is such a rare break, she hates to give it up. Nevertheless, she throws the gear shift on the steering column into reverse. Nothing happens. She shifts into drive then quickly back into reverse. Something metallic clunks under the hood and the Geezemobile starts to sluggishly back up.

Backing this tugboat out of the narrow space requires the concentration of a Zen archer. Slowly she coaxes the car out, aware of the danger of chrome and fiberglass and expensive paint jobs on either side. A shiny vanilla BMW waiting behind her for the parking space honks twice—long and irate blasts. In the rearview mirror, Barcelona sees the darkly tanned woman behind the wheel scowling. The BMW has two yellow BABY ON BOARD signs, one suctioned to the front windshield, another to the rear windshield. Barcelona sees no baby in the car. The woman blares the horn again for almost five loud seconds.

Barcelona shifts back into drive and chugs off down the long row of parked cars. In the mirror she sees the woman neatly tuck her BMW into the vacant space. At the end of the row, Barcelona swings around into the next aisle and pilots the car past dozens of shoppers hurrying to and from the stores. It doesn't seem to matter if they are coming or going; all scamper with intent expressions as if late for the lab results on their tumor biopsy.

Barcelona pulls up next to the sidewalk and Diva climbs in.

'I forgot to stop at my bank for cash,' Diva says. 'It's just a few blocks away.'

'I can buy lunch.'

'Fine with me. But I still need some cash.'

'Then you buy lunch.' Barcelona looks over her shoulder, waiting for a chance to ease back into the flow of traffic.

'What was that woman honking about?' Diva asks.

244

'I don't know. I guess I wasn't moving fast enough.'

They see the BMW woman walking across the parking lot. She is wearing a short blue tennis skirt that wraps snugly around her narrow hips. Each stride exposes her matching ruffled blue tennis panties. She is very tan. She walks briskly and carries a large Robinson's bag. Her back is stiff, her gaze purposeful. The look of someone returning faulty merchandise.

'Bitch,' Barcelona mutters softly.

'Asshole,' Diva says a little louder.

Barcelona grins. 'Shithead,' she says, even louder. A couple of teenage boys passing by smirk.

'*Cuuunt!*' Diva hollers at the top of her voice. Several nearby shoppers as well as the BMW woman stop to look at them. Diva flips her the finger. Barcelona laughs and quickly nudges the car into the traffic and drives away.

'That felt good,' Diva says.

'I hope she didn't get my license number,' Barcelona says. 'She looks like the type to hunt you down.'

Diva laughs and shrugs. 'Fuck her if she can't take a joke.'

Barcelona is surprised at Diva. This is not at all the type of behavior Diva has ever demonstrated before. This is something Trina might have done.

Diva suddenly looks very serious. 'You're right, though. It's best not to say anything to people like that. I read something scary the other day, really shook me up.'

Barcelona follows the unicorn on Diva's pointing finger around a corner.

'This kid,' Diva says, 'just seventeen. He's riding along the freeway in the passenger seat of his girlfriend's new Jetta. She just got the car for graduation. I think her dad was some kind of tax lawyer or something. Anyway, these two kids are heading north on the San Diego Freeway, in the fast lane, driving toward Magic Mountain to meet some friends from school. She swears they were traveling at sixty-five miles per hour. Suddenly this yellow Toyota or Datsun, I can't remember which, comes roaring up behind them, practically smacking their bumper. He starts honking and flashing his lights, trying to get them to pull out of the fast lane so he could pass them. Turn here.'

Barcelona steers the Geezemobile around another corner. She waits for Diva to continue her story, but Diva doesn't. She is staring straight ahead. 'So the yellow car wants to pass them . . .' Barcelona prompts.

'So he wants to pass them, but the girl gets so pissed at the guy's obnoxious behavior, she deliberately slows down to fifty-five. The Toyota or whatever swerves out into the right lane, pulls up alongside them, rolls down his window, and shoots the boyfriend twice in the neck. Kid dies immediately.'

'Jesus.'

Diva points to the building she wants. 'There. Pull up there.' She starts rummaging through her purse for her wallet. 'Later the girl tells the police that when the guy rolled his window down she could hear the Beach Boys' "Surfin' USA" on his stereo. How can you murder someone while listening to the Beach Boys?'

Barcelona pulls up in front of the Wells Fargo Bank. Three other people are standing in line in front of the automated teller. They look hot and irritable in the sun. One woman is uselessly fanning herself with her bank card. Barcelona looks at Diva. 'Is that true? Where'd you read that?'

'Some magazine.'

'You always say that. Can't you ever remember the names of the magazines you read all this stuff in?'

'What difference does it make?'

Barcelona loses interest in the discussion and leans back against the hard seat.

Diva opens her wallet and flips through the plastic windows past photographs, credit cards, a blood donor card, driver's license, to her list of phone numbers. 'My accounts have been closed at so many different banks for bouncing checks, I can never remember what my current ATM number is.'

'You shouldn't write it down. Someone steals your wallet, they can clean out your account.'

'I write it down as part of a phony telephone number under a bogus name. Here, see? Otto Teller.'

'Clever.'

Diva gets out of the car and looks down at Barcelona with a serious expression. 'I'm not dumb.'

'Of course not,' Barcelona says, but Diva's already walking away. What is wrong with everyone today? First her mother acts wacky on the phone, now Diva flips the bird at some strange woman then announces she's not dumb. Christ. Is there a full moon? Are they both having some new virulent form of super period?

Barcelona keeps the motor running. She doesn't want to take any chances that the engine won't start. The Geezemobile legacy includes an electrical system that occasionally dies for no reason. No one has been able to figure out what the problem is, let alone fix it.

Lately, Barcelona has taken to visiting new car lots. She wanders among the new models, sits in them, plays with the air conditioner, sometimes just smells the interiors. The Geezemobile smells too much of lilacs, her grandmother's perfume. It's even in the vents and comes blasting into her face whenever she turns the fan on. She can't bring herself to sell the car, though. Not just yet.

'All set,' Diva says, stuffing two twenties into her purse as she slides into the car. 'Let's eat. I'm starving.'

They drive back to the Atrium Court and park a few acres away. Inside, they try to decide what kind of food to eat. Neither is very hungry. Barcelona stops at the baked potato stand and gets one filled with broccoli and cheese. Diva order a burrito from the Mexican food stand. Rather than stand around like vultures waiting for a table to open up, they take their food outside, sitting on the steps of the courtyard, where there are sometimes noon concerts. Not today, though. Today there is just a little boy chasing a sea gull.

'What's the matter?' Diva asks.

'What?' The question catches Barcelona by surprise. They are here to discuss Diva, not her.

'You seem distracted. You okay?'

Barcelona is tempted to tell her about Eric. She hates keeping secrets, even her own. She hasn't yet been able to sort out her feelings from her thoughts, to think things through. She doesn't want to fall into the same traps as before, make the same mistakes. Sometimes at night, when Eric isn't there, she thinks of this whole thing as one of those cheesy in-love-with-a-married-man TV movies. But most of the time she doesn't really think of Eric as married. Maybe that's just convenient thinking, but it makes sense at the time. Still, she doesn't think Diva is who she would like to share her doubts with. She likes Diva, but sharing confidences has never been a part of their relationship. There is a pecking order of shared intimacies among the four of them. Diva shares with Barcelona. Dixie shares with Trina and Barcelona. Trina shares with all of them. Barcelona shares with Trina, sometimes. Now that she thinks about it, though, she doesn't really tell very much, mostly she keeps things to herself. Why then did she always have the feeling that she told Trina everything?

'I thought we came to talk about you,' Barcelona says.

Diva takes a big bite of her burrito. Some rust-colored juice runs down her chin and she wipes it with a napkin. She sips her Diet Coke. 'Just beans and salsa in here. And some sour cream and guacamole. No meat. I'm still a vegetarian.'

'Great. I admire your dedication.'

'I don't really miss it much. I actually think not eating meat has made my voice better. People say my singing's improved.'

They both sit in silence while Diva eats her burrito and Barcelona picks disinterestedly at her baked potato. Barcelona watches the little boy chase the sea gull across the courtyard. When the gull finally flies away, the little boy tries to jump in the air after him. He jumps several times, perplexed that he is unable to fly with the bird. Finally in frustration he jumps so hard that he falls down and bangs his knee. He starts crying. Barcelona and Diva watch him cry for almost a minute before a woman younger than both of them runs up to the boy, picks him up, and kisses him on the cheek. She carries him away.

Barcelona waits for Diva to speak. She senses that Diva is uncomfortable about something.

'I was reading this article,' Diva says. 'About Borneo. They've got this bug there that bites you on the face, sucks out your blood, then when it's full, takes a dump next to the puncture. When you scratch the itch, you end up rubbing the bug shit into the wound. It takes anywheres from one to twenty years, but eventually you start to die from it. At first the symptoms are like malaria, but later on they're like AIDS. Can you imagine, dying twenty years later from a little bug bite?'

Barcelona mashes some stray broccoli chunks into her potato.

Diva continues. 'There's another one, another bug mentioned in the same article. This human botfly, whose larvae bore into your skin and eat little bits of you for forty days. After that they pop out as inch-long maggots. Like in *Aliens* or something.'

Barcelona pushes her potato away. 'Why are you telling me this?'

'I know, I know. It grossed me out too. But here's the one that really got me. In the Amazon, if a man walks into the river naked and takes a piss, they have this tiny fish, a candiru, that smells the urine and thinks you're a big fish. It swims right up the stream of piss, right up into the guy's urethra, burrows in, holding itself in place with some spiny barbs. They say the pain gets so bad he has to be rushed immediately to the hospital before his bladder bursts. Once there, he has to ask the doctor to cut his penis off.'

'Where do you read this stuff?'

'Magazines. I read lots of magazines. Wild, huh?'

Barcelona watches Diva finish the burrito. She eats mechanically, chewing, wiping her mouth whether or not it needs it, sipping her drink through a straw, then starting the routine over again. Bite, chew, wipe, sip. Her sandals scrape nervously against the steps.

'What's the matter?' Barcelona asks. 'You sounded desperate on the phone.'

Diva puts the stump of the burrito down. She looks straight at Barcelona. 'I need to borrow money.'

'How much?'

'I'm changing the whole focus of my career, Barcy. I've decided that it's not enough anymore to sing. I've got to have the right material. My own trademark.'

'You want to buy some songs?'

'I want to *write* some songs. My own songs. Then record them, make a demo. I need the money to make a demo.'

'How much?'

'About two thousand dollars.'

Barcelona stabs her plastic fork into the baked potato. She keeps stabbing it, thinking. Every few months someone comes to her to borrow money. Usually it's a teacher from school. They all think she has thousands stashed away from her novels. They don't realize she lives from month to month just like they do. But for some reason she has always managed to lend them the couple of hundred they've asked for, even it it meant living lean for the rest of the month herself. But two thousand dollars! She doesn't have that kind of money. She still hadn't been paid the script money from that producer, Roger Carlyle. Apparently there were some legal details to the contract he and Grief were arguing over. To get the two grand, she would have to borrow from the teachers' credit union.

'Okay,' she says. 'Take me a couple days to get it.'

'Really?' Diva says. She smiles, tears surround her eyes. 'God, I didn't think you'd do it. I mean, I thought you'd think this was just another fucked up idea of mine, another dumb way to blow money.'

That's exactly what Barcelona thinks. But she wouldn't say that. She knows the record business is enough like the publishing business to put the odds of Diva ever selling her demo to a record company as very remote. According to statistics, she is more likely to be killed by terrorists, or marry happily.

'I'm taking every bit of cash I have,' Diva continues, 'and then I'm charging up my credit cards to their limits. I'm going to take all that, plus your loan, and make the best demo around. I've got lots of friends in the business who'll play for me cheap.'

'Have you written your song yet?'

'I'm working on it. It's kinda country, kinda rock. I haven't decided which angle to emphasize yet. But I feel good about it, I really do.'

Barcelona forces a smile. Diva is setting herself up for a long, hard fall. When that happens how will she react? Shrug it off as another valuable life experience? Go back to singing directions to car lots? Barcelona sighs. Diva is a fried zucchini waiting to happen. Or even a maraschino cherry. 'Let's walk,' Barcelona suggests, feeling the need to move.

They throw their paper plates and plastic silverware into the garbage. A couple of gray sea gulls perch on the nearby lamp, watching. As soon as the women walk away, they swoop down to inspect.

'Let's stop by the music store,' Diva says. 'I need a new capo for my guitar.'

On the way to the store, they chat about nothing special. The day is sunny and clear and they can see Catalina Island from Buffum's. Suddenly Diva swerves away toward a pack of high school kids.

'Omigod, Dixie!' Diva cries out. 'What the hell are you doing in that outfit?'

The three kids turn around. One of them is indeed Dixie, her hair combed straight down, her eyes heavily lined with mascara, her whole posture uncharacteristically slouched.

'Your hair!' Diva laughs. 'What is this, a masquerade?'

Barcelona sees the panic in Dixie's eyes and realizes that Dixie is working. The girl next to her is wobbly, bleary-eyed, maybe a little drunk or doped. The boy is clear-eyed and handsome. He is staring at Dixie with uncertainty.

'Dixie,' Barcelona says, quickly walking up to them. 'I can't imagine your mother knows you're out here dressed like that.'

A shimmer of gratitude flickers in Dixie's eyes. 'No, Mrs. Lee, she doesn't.'

'And your hair, young lady.' Barcelona shakes her head. 'You have such beautiful hair. Why not use it to your advantage?'

Diva stars at Barcelona a moment, then catches on. 'Yes, Dixie, we know she's bought you nicer clothing than that.'

252

'Come on, Mrs. Klosterman, it's the weekend.'

'People still see you, even on a weekend,' Barcelona says.

'Je-sus,' the girl with Dixie says and starts walking away.

'I think you ladies are absolutely right,' the handsome boy says. 'I try to get her to take more pride in her appearance, but what can you do? Every teen's a rebel these days. Until you take their credit cards away.' He laughs charmingly. 'Joseph Little,' he says, extending his hand toward Barcelona. 'Dixie's friend.'

Barcelona looks at Dixie but gets no response. She shakes Joseph Little's hand. 'Barcelona Lee. Friend of Dixie's mother.' She turns to Diva. 'We'd better hurry or we'll be late.'

'Yes,' Diva says. 'Yes, we'd better hurry.'

'Nice meeting you,' Joseph Little says with a big smile.

'Bye,' Barcelona says. 'Bye, Dixie.'

Barcelona locks arms with Diva and they hurry away. They don't stop trotting until they are in the parking lot.

'God, Barcy, what have I done?'

'It's okay. I don't think they noticed anything.'

Diva is trembling. 'I didn't know. I didn't expect to see her here on a Saturday being undercover. I mean, it's the goddamn weekend.'

Barcelona pats Diva's arm. 'Don't worry. We covered up pretty well. If anything, we may even have helped. Now they've had her identity confirmed by a couple outsiders.'

'You think?'

Barcelona nods, though she is not at all sure. The boy seemed nice enough, but there is no way to tell for sure. 'Where are you parked?'

Diva points. 'Other side of the building. I guess I shouldn't have walked over here, huh?'

'I'll give you a lift.'

They walk across the lot, weaving between parked cars.

253

'Feels funny to be leaving this place without carrying a couple packages,' Barcelona says.

'Speak for yourself. I'm leaving with two thousand dollars.' She laughs. 'Don't worry, when I make it big you'll have front row tickets to all my concerts.'

'What about backstage passes?'

'I'm saving those for my groupies.'

Barcelona walks between two cars and discovers a cement garden of some green spiny plant like mistletoe. These little patches are all over the lot. She tries to squeeze by, but she accidentally brushes against one of the overhanging leaves and it cuts her scabbed ankle.

'Damn it!' she says. 'This ankle's never going to heal.'

Diva wends her way over, looks at the ankle. 'Nasty. The plant do all that?'

'I had a scab from before.'

Diva toes the plant. 'Prickly pear. They plant a lot of this down on Balboa. Keeps the dogs from urinating wherever they're planted. Apparently they can cut their little dicks on the leaves.'

Barcelona laughs. 'I don't even want to know where you got that.'

Diva grins. 'Some magazine.'

A gray Volvo stops next to them. The driver is a heavy man with a thin mustache and bad skin. The woman next to him is young and thin and exceptionally attractive. 'You leaving?' he asks Barcelona.

'Yes,' she says. 'But we're parked two more aisles over.'

He looks around at the fender-to-fender parking lot. 'I'll follow you,' he says.

Barcelona and Diva continue to squeeze by the cars until they reach the Geezemobile. They can see the gray Volvo rolling down their aisle. He brakes ten yards away and waits for them to back out.

Once inside the car, Diva touches Barcelona's arm. She

has a very serious expression on her face. 'I know you think I'm a flake,' Diva says. 'That you won't ever see your money again. That I'm going to fall on my face.'

'Diva—'

'But I'm not stupid. I know the odds and still think I can beat them. I believe in myself, even if no one else does.'

'We believe in you, Diva. We all do.'

'I'm not stupid,' she says.

The gray Volvo honks loudly and Barcelona starts to back up. Silently, she kisses two thousand dollars good-bye.

17

'So when do I get my free coke?' Melody asks Joseph outside the Fashion Island pet store. 'Either that or give me some more quarters to feed those albino frogs. They look hungry.'

Joseph doesn't answer. Dixie can feel his sharp eyes on the back of her head as she watches Barcelona and Diva hurry away in a panicky trot. 'They're in my mom's aerobics class,' she explains casually. 'Major yuppies.'

'The fat one needs a few more classes,' Joseph says. 'But I wouldn't mind doing a few leg-lifts with the other one. Barcelona.' He lays his hand on Dixie's shoulder.

Dixie pretends to be jealous, shrugs his hand off. 'They're kinda old, for God's sake.'

'Experienced.'

'Fuck you.'

He laughs, walks up behind her and wraps his arms around her. 'Hey, I'm just kidding, Dixie. Just teasing.'

'This is so fucking lame,' Melody says, making a disgusted face at the two of them. 'Dixie and I are supposed to be shopping together, Joey. Then you come along and worm your way in. Okay, man, we helped you buy your mother a fucking dress, now give me my coke and split.' Her eyes are fierce and wet, her voice is loud enough that nearby shoppers glance at them.

Joseph grabs her by the elbow and jerks her quickly

along the sidewalk. 'Keep you goddamn voice down.'

'Ow, man, that hurts.'

Dixie runs after them. She still hopes to get home within the hour so she can have dinner with Randy and his son. She missed miniature golf, but she'd make it up with dinner and a movie, her treat. All would be forgiven. Eventually.

Joseph drags Melody around the corner behind the Brooks Brothers store and shakes her by the shoulders. 'You'd better learn when to shut up, Melody.'

'Eat shit, homo,' Melody says, pulling free.

'Hey, guys, cool it,' Dixie says. 'You wanna get us busted?'

Melody rubs her arm where Joseph had grabbed her. 'Fuck you too. You're on his side. You were supposed to be spending the day with me, remember?'

'I was supposed to be spending it with my family. I don't know why I let you talk me into coming here. I'm outta here.' Dixie swings her purse over her shoulder and marches away.

'Come on, Dix,' Joseph pleads.

Dixie keeps walking, her rubber flipflops slapping an angry rhythm.

'Hey, I'm sorry, okay?' Melody calls. 'I'm serious, Dixie. Jesus, just wait up.'

Dixie slows enough to allow them to catch up, but she keeps walking toward the parking lot. They run up on either side of her. Melody takes out her silver flask and swigs some Southern Comfort. She offers it to Dixie. Dixie pretends to drink then offers it to Joseph.

'I'm not into that shit,' he says.

'Speaking of shit,' Melody says. She lowers her voice to a hoarse whisper. 'How's about our free sample you promised.'

'I didn't say today.'

'When?'

'Maybe tomorrow.'

'Fuck, Joey, that's so fucked.' Melody stumbles over a crack in the sidewalk and Dixie catches her. 'I need something today, man.'

'Hey, I'm out. Running on empty. I've got to meet my source first. Restock the shelves.'

'When's that?' Dixie asks.

'What?'

'When you meet your source.'

He looks into her eyes. 'Why? You want to make a buy on your own? Be my competition?'

'Just curious when your shelves will be full so I can do some shopping.'

He doesn't answer. He buries his hands deep into his pockets and does a little soft shoe dance as he walks beside Dixie. He whistles 'Singin' in the Rain.'

'Oh, man, I saw that movie,' Melody says.

'Yeah,' Dixie says. 'With Gene Kelly. He was so cool.'

Melody laughs. 'Not that movie, the one with Malcolm McDowell. Remember the part where he's singing that song and kicking that old guy?'

'*A Clockwork Orange*,' Joseph says.

'I guess. Something like that.' Melody mimics Joseph's dance steps, singing the song: 'I'm singin' in the rain . . .' When she sings 'rain' she lets go with a vicious kick at the air. 'He did it like that. In the guy's gut.' She stops a moment, a little wobbly. 'That part was funny, but I was kinda mad at myself for laughing. Those guys were so *mean*.'

'Let's take her home,' Joseph says to Dixie. 'Before she passes out.'

'Let's find Toby and beat the shit out of him, the rat fuck,' Melody says. She stops, leans against the glass window of a fancy shoe store. The elderly clerk inside glares at them but Melody is rooting through her purse with an intense expression. The purse is as big as a saddlebag so there is a lot of rustling, clanging, and jingling. 'You guys gotta try this shit . . .'

Dixie is afraid she will pull out a bottle of pills or crack, but when Melody's hand finally reappears it is clutching a can of soft drink called Jolt. The logo on the can reads: 'All the sugar and twice the caffeine.'

Melody pops the can and sips. 'This stuff really sobers you up.' She offers the can to Dixie.

Dixie refuses. 'I drink diet soda.'

'I read somewhere that Nutra Sweet kills brain cells immediately upon contact. Saccharin used to cause cancer in rats, but you had to drink gallons of the stuff every day over twenty years. But this Nutra Sweet shit works right away. Goes right in and kills them.'

'All that junk is bad for you,' Joseph says. 'We did an experiment in science class once where we dropped these human teeth and nails into a glass of Coke. A couple weeks later the teeth and the nails were gone, dissolved.'

'Come on, Melody,' Dixie says. She guides her to the Mustang and helps her into the passenger seat, buckling her seat belt for her.

Melody giggles. She drinks out of the can. Some brown liquid dribbles down her chin onto her blouse. She doesn't notice.

Joseph leans against the fender and shakes his head. 'This is so low-budget.' As Dixie walks by him to get into the driver's side, he grabs her wrist. 'I'll follow you, then we can go for a drive.' His other hand cups her butt and pulls her close so she's straddling his thigh. He nudges his leg up against her crotch. 'You want to go, don't you?'

Dixie hesitates. Randy is probably already fuming that she missed miniature golf; to miss dinner too would mean he wouldn't speak to her for days. It's happened before. Divorced men are especially sensitive about time you're supposed to spend with their kids. It's some kind of test they put you through.

'Come on,' Joseph coaxes. 'You said you were worried because of what I do. I'll show you what I do and you'll see there's nothing to it. It's just a big giggle.'

Bingo. Her way in. He said he was meeting with his supplier tonight; maybe she could be there to make an ID. Then they'd have both of them, which meant tonight would be her last day in high school. Randy would just have to understand.

'Yeah, okay,' she says. 'I'll go.'

Dixie parks the vintage Mustang behind Joseph's shiny black Suzuki Samurai Jeep. He steps out and strikes a model's pose next to his car, one hand on hip, the other placed on the roll bar of the Jeep. Cool California Dude Scamming Chicks on Sunday Afternoon at Beach. She's seen guys do variations of this pose all her life and it always makes her want to laugh. Instead, Dixie smiles coyly at Joseph and he abandons his pose to open her car door.

'Thanks,' Dixie says, hopping out.

'You keep up pretty well out there.' He'd driven the twisty stretch of Pacific Coast Highway at ninety miles per hour.

'No trick to driving fast,' she says. 'Just step on the gas and it goes.'

'The trick is getting there alive.'

She smiles. 'I'm here, aren't I?'

He puts his arms around her and kisses her. His body leans into hers, his weight pinning her against the Mustang. A few cars drive by, inches from their bodies, honking horns and shouting encouragement. One girl sitting on a guy's lap squeals, 'Go for it!'

Joseph's tongue is in her mouth and she almost giggles at the feel of it. Knowing that this case is now almost over has started her withdrawal process. This is what Cinderella must have felt like when she saw the gilded coach transform back into a pumpkin, the horses to mice. What was once big is now small. Joseph Little has reverted from drug lord suitor back to high school boy. His tongue in her mouth is comically intense, his hands on her ass and on her breasts seem like a little boy's urgent gropings. She feels a twinge of sadness, though, when she realizes that after tonight, these are the last breasts he'll touch for a while. Female breasts, anyway.

She gently pushes him off her. 'You trying to get us killed?'

'Not a bad way to go.'

'Yeah, sideswiped in Laguna Beach.' She brushes dirt from the car off the back of her jeans. 'So what're we doing here?'

'Let's go down to the boardwalk.'

She shrugs. She has been unable to get any information out of him about who his connection is or when they're meeting. If she brings the subject up he makes a joke or grabs her ass. Considering the close call back at Fashion Island, she decides not to press him too much.

Dixie does not get down to Laguna Beach much, though she was twice offered a job on their police force. Both times she turned down the job, despite the promotion that would have gone with it. Laguna Beach is too fashionable, the people too good looking. It is a hybrid community made up of wealthy professionals, surfer drones, gays, artists, revisionist hippies, beach yuppies and variations combining these groups. They are smug in their good fortune, self-congratulatory. They see themselves as the children of the sun and Dixie could never get committed to risking her life for these people.

The main beach stretches out along Pacific Coast Highway in the middle of town. During the spring and summer the beach is crowded every day of the week. The three volleyball nets are in constant use by serious players. The basketball courts next to the beach attract tough players from all over the county. It is a fascinating place to be, but living here would be the same as staying undercover in high school forever.

Joseph looks a little too dressy in his pleated white pants, powder blue Italian loafers, and yellow shirt with a giant colorful cockatoo emblazoned from shoulder to waist. He holds Dixie's hand very tight as they stroll amid the crowd along the boardwalk. She wiggles her fingers to get him to loosen his grip, but he doesn't.

'Hey,' she says, 'relax. I can't feel anything in my fingers.'

He looks surprised and immediately releases her hand. 'Sorry. I didn't want to lose you in this crowd.'

Dixie kisses him on the cheek and smiles. 'You won't lose me that easy.'

He smiles and takes her hand again, this time more gently. Dixie walks beside him, staying close to keep from getting jostled by the crowd. The scent of sun screen and coconut oil sweetens the air. Most people walking by are in swimming suits or shorts. The smell of their greased flesh and the kaleidoscope of bright colors makes Dixie a little dizzy.

'I'm thirsty,' she says. 'Let's get a Coke.'

'In a minute,' he says. Joseph seems nervous and distracted, not at all his usual cool and assured self. The closer they get to the beach, the more sullen and nervous he becomes.

'You okay, Joe?' Dixie asks.

'Let's sit here.'

'Joseph?'

'I'm fine.' He looks at her and flashes a big smile. 'God, you're gorgeous.'

262

They sit on the edge of the boardwalk, feet dangling near the sand. Joseph watches the teenage volleyball players in front of him, but his eyes keep darting off around the beach, down the boardwalk, across the street. He's looking for someone, Dixie realizes. Her own adrenaline starts pumping and she can feel her muscles tense across her stomach. The buy is going to go down right here, right now.

'I've gotta go to the bathroom,' she says. She needs to find a phone, get some backup down here.

'Sure. Over there.' He points down the boardwalk.

Dixie is about to get up when suddenly a shirtless teen on a skateboard rockets down the boardwalk right toward her. People jump out of his way. The plastic wheels rumble against the warped wood boards like a stampeding buffalo. Dixie thinks she will be hit by the shirtless kid on the skateboard and leaps off the boardwalk into the sand four feet below. She lands in the sand on her hands and knees.

The kid leans back on his rolling skateboard, swivels his hips, and brings the skateboard to a stop inches from where Dixie had been sitting. He steps off, stomps the curled lip of the board. It flips up in the air and he catches it.

'Hey, Brandon, knock it off,' Joseph tells him.

Brandon laughs. 'Learn to live with it, dude.'

'You okay, Dixie?' Joseph climbs off the boardwalk to help Dixie to her feet. He brushes sand from the knees of her jeans.

Dixie looks at Brandon, who is staring at her with a smirk. He is maybe sixteen. His bare chest and arms are well muscled for his age. His shaggy hair is brown but highlighted with blond streaks from the sun. People walking by seem to instinctively avoid him. He drops his skateboard into the sand and stands on the edge of the boardwalk with his back to Dixie. He springs into the air

263

and does a perfect back flip, landing in the sand next to her. 'Ta da,' he says. 'Applause is welcome.'

Joseph is obviously angry, senses that Brandon is somehow making a fool of him. But he is just as obviously a little afraid of him too. 'Dixie, this is Brandon.'

'Hi,' Dixie says.

'Yeah, hi.' Brandon's eyes are large and gray. Looking into them is trying to peer through a thick fog.

The teenage volleyball players at the net shout crude greetings to Brandon.

'Hey, Gary,' Brandon replies to one of them, 'you play like a fag.'

'You should know,' Gary says.

'You're a fudge-packing fool,' Brandon replies and they all crack up.

Joseph glances impatiently at his watch.

Brandon turns his attention on Dixie. 'What are you anyway? Nip or gook?'

'Chink,' Dixie says.

'My dad was in the Nam.'

'Which side?' she says.

He laughs. 'You're funny.' He looks her over more carefully now, his gaze so intense she feels as if she is being strip-searched. 'What school you go to?'

'My school,' Joseph says.

Brandon nods absently, his gaze now distracted by a couple of shapely women in bikinis strolling by on the boardwalk. One of them has large breasts hanging out of the too-small top. 'Jesus fuck,' Brandon says aloud enough for them to hear. 'I'd eat a mile of her shit just to lick the hole it came from.'

The women hurry away.

Joseph makes a face. 'I didn't come down here for this crap, Brandon.'

Brandon's smile is cunning. 'Then why did you come

down here, dude?' He touches Joseph's parrot with his finger. 'Not to get tan.'

'Don't screw around with me. You know what I'm here for, same as always. You want to do business or what?'

Brandon's smile stiffens on his face, an imitation of a smile. 'Since when do you have a business partner, dude?'

Joseph puts his arm around Dixie and pulls her next to him. 'Whenever I want one.'

'One thing I learned long ago. Never mix business with pleasure.'

Dixie has a bad feeling. Things aren't going down well. Brandon is suspicious. Maybe she's just spooked, maybe he's always that way. But she doesn't want to take any chances. She doesn't have enough for an arrest, not without witnessing the transaction, but at least she's been able to identify Brandon. Let the local police chase him down. She'll bust Joseph, which will take care of most of the drug traffic at Principal Peterson's school for a while.

'Look,' she says. 'Why don't you guys just do whatever it is you want to do. I'll drive home.'

'No,' Joseph says. 'Wait.'

'I'll meet you later,' she says. 'It's okay.'

Joseph fidgets with his watch. Dixie knows what is going through his mind: He doesn't want her to know that he is intimidated by Brandon, a kid two years younger. In high school two years' difference is a whole generation. He looks at Brandon when he speaks to her. 'No. I want you to stay. This won't take long.'

Brandon grins. 'Hey, stay. No biggie. You're a lot better looking than Joseph here anyway.'

Joseph's hand tightens around Dixie's waist, a secret squeeze of triumph. She climbs back onto the boardwalk and shakes the sand off each flipflop. Joseph and Brandon climb up beside her.

'Let's go to my place,' Brandon says.

Joseph nods and takes Dixie's hand.

'I've got to go to the bathroom,' Dixie says, still hoping to get a phone call off.

'Got one at my place,' Brandon says. 'Just a few blocks.'

Dixie feels their eyes on her and she shrugs. Things are tense enough between them that she doesn't want to push it. 'Let's hurry, okay?'

Brandon laughs. 'Girls just can't hold it like guys.' He waves to the volleyball players. 'See you faggots later.'

'Eat me,' one of them yells back.

'Tastes great but less filling,' Brandon says.

They all laugh, their faces sweaty and cunning.

Joseph winks at Dixie and squeezes her hand. He thinks this is a romantic adventure the two of them are sharing. She feels sorry for Joseph, smart and basically nice, about to go down for dealing drugs. She'll be at the trial to hear the testimony of psychologists who will explain why a smart boy like him with such wonderful parents and all the opportunity in the world does such terrible things. The psychologists' explanations will sound reasonable; they will probably be true. But Joseph will still do time, because that's the way the moral pendulum has swung lately. When she is sitting on the stand describing how she bought drugs from him and witnessed him buying drugs, she will be forced to look at him. That is standard testifying procedure, to look the criminal in the eyes while testifying, to show the jury that you are in the right. She will do that, but she will feel rotten afterward.

With Brandon, however, she will sit on the stand and stare at him, point her finger in identification, and describe in detail his crimes.

'This stuff I got is great,' Brandon says as they head down the street together. He has one foot on the skateboard and pushes himself along with the other. Sometimes he glides ahead and stops to wait for them to catch up. 'You're gonna love it, dude. The crack now comes in these pills, man, like aspirin. Only they got their own brand mark. This shit's got an R stamped on it, stands for Rocket.'

'An R,' Joseph says. 'Why bother?'

'Customer loyalty, man. See, you sell some crack to this dude, he gets off on it like never before. Next time he wants to make sure he gets the same quality, but how can he be sure? Easy, he looks for the one with an R stamped on it. Like Bayer aspirin. Ask for us by name. Satisfaction guaranteed.'

Joseph nods. 'Good idea.'

'Fuck yeah. That's why this first batch is so good, they want to build brand identification. Get it? Like a promotion gimmick.'

They have walked down several streets, back away from the business section up into the foothills where the residences are. They come to a large house hidden behind lush tropical foliage. Palm trees fan out overhead, slicing the sky into wedges of light that fall at crazy angles across the lawn.

'You live here?' Dixie asks.

'Nah, out back.' He skateboards down the driveway to the white two-car garage. He unlocks the side door and enters. Dixie and Joseph follow.

The inside surprises Dixie. The room is decorated and arranged with surprising taste. The double garage door is painted a bright red with the Coca-Cola logo in white in foot-high letters. The lettering is precise so that it looks like the official logo, yet it has something more, a flair that isn't in the original. On another wall is a duplicate of the Nike logo in black and red. In fact, all the walls and doors and even the ceiling are painted in various logos: 7-Up, Michelin, Fender, Pacific Bell, Taco Bell, *Los Angeles Times*, Volvo.

'You did all this?' Dixie asks.

'Who else would do this shit?' Brandon answers.

'You want to go into art or something? Like doing commercials?'

Brandon laughs. 'Fuck, I hope not. Who wants to sit around all day doing what somebody tells you? Fuck that.'

'You're good,' Dixie says. 'These are very good.'

Brandon shrugs. He is not being modest, Dixie can see. He doesn't really care. He leans his skateboard against the wall and flops down on the bed. Next to the bed is a small refrigerator with a hot plate and electric frying pan on top. A package of Lorna Doone shortbread cookies lies open next to the hot plate. He reaches over and grabs a few. He doesn't offer any to Dixie or Joseph. 'Well?' he says to Dixie.

'What?'

'I thought you had to go to the bathroom.'

'Yeah. Where do I go? In the house?' She starts for the door.

'No. I got my own bathroom,' he says. He points to a doorway in the corner she hadn't noticed before. The doorway has no door but she can see the toilet squatting in the tiny room. 'In there,' he says. 'The Mendlesons built that on when they converted this garage into a rental unit. Jews'll put a crapper in their Caddy if it means renting it out for a few more bucks.'

'There's no door,' Dixie says.

'Don't need one. Don't worry, we've heard it all before. Plop plop, fizz fizz.'

Dixie looks at Brandon. He lies back on his bed, his fingers laced behind his head. His knees are bent so that she can look down the leg of his shorts. He isn't wearing underpants and she can see his genitals. He grins at her, knowing.

'That's it, I'm going home,' Dixie announces. She turns

to Joseph. 'Call me later if you want.' She heads for the door.

'Dixie,' Joseph calls and starts after her.

She spins around angrily. 'I'm tired of this shit. You brought me along and now you let this asshole treat me this way?'

Joseph's face reddens until it matches the shade of the cockatoo on his shirt. Even the tips of his ears are red. His lips move as if he's testing words, but no sound comes out.

'Oh, hell,' Brandon says, jumping off the bed. 'If it means that much to you.' He takes a key off a hook and hands it to Dixie. 'You can use the Mendlesons' downstairs bathroom. They let me use their shower.'

'I can't just barge into their house.'

'They're away on vacation. Canada, I think.'

Dixie takes the key and marches out, yanking the door hard behind her. Once outside she lingers out of sight near the door.

'Jesus, Joe,' Brandon says. 'She's got your nuts in her pocket.'

'Fuck you, man. You don't know anything. All your girls are thirteen.'

'Hey, bro, you gotta get 'em before they grow teeth down there.' He laughs.

'Let's just do business, okay?'

'Sure. Let me take a quick piss first. Hope you aren't too sensitive to listen. You can wait outside if you are.'

'Fuck you.'

Dixie hurriedly unlocks the Mendlesons' backdoor. This opens into the kitchen and she heads straight for the wall phone next to the refrigerator. On the refrigerator are notes held by magnetic fruit. A grocery list that includes Thomas' sourdough English muffins. Sourdough is underlined three times. Fresh squeezed orange juice. Fresh is underlined twice. Another list includes: stop the newspaper, cancel bridge game, set auto timer for lights, take Grover to vet, etc. Each item is crossed out except the last item, call Mother & Father. Either they didn't call or they didn't cross it off their list.

Dixie dials the number to her police station. 'Ed, it's Dixie. I want you to send two cars immediately, and tell them I'm still undercover. The address is 179—'

'Hang up,' Brandon says. He is standing in the doorway with a baseball bat. Joseph, his face grim and puffy, stands behind him. Brandon points at her with the bat. 'Hang it up, lady, before I do a Reggie Jackson on your skull.'

Dixie hears Ed DeMerra speaking her name, asking her for the address, pleading with her. She stares at Brandon, assessing how serious he is, what her chances are of fighting both of them off, of running. Either one alone she could handle, but both of them would be too much. She hangs up the phone.

Brandon taps the bat against his palm and grins. 'This is gonna be fun.'

18

Barcelona pushes her reading glasses higher on her nose with the back of her wrist. She is wearing only underpants and a T-shirt and her butt is stuck to the vinyl chair. Her eyes burn and her back is sore from hunching over the typewriter for the past two hours. Ordinarily she uses the typewriter now only to type envelopes. But the screenplay format is so complicated that her computer can't do some of the required notations and she has to type certain phrases on each page. Using two fingers, she types the final (MORE) under the dialogue to be continued onto the next page, yanks the sheet out of the typewriter, and inserts it in the complete script.

She hefts the script in her hand: 128 pages. A little long by usual standards, according to the books she's read. Figuring each page to equal one minute of film, the producers like to have the script no more than 100 to 110 pages. Any film that runs longer than two hours reduces the number of showings per day in each theater. That means one less paid showing and one less trip to the snack bar. Form fits function.

She takes her reading glasses off, rubs her eyes. She swivels the chair around and drags the phone across the desk. Once again she dials Dixie's number. She has been calling Dixie all afternoon. There still is no answer.

Barcelona stares at the title page of the script. The title,

Live Wires, is in bold and underlined. She tries to imagine it on the marquee, then on the movie screen. Would she be drawn into a movie with that title? She's not sure.

She peels her butt from the vinyl chair and walks over to her little Canon photocopier. She turns the machine on and waits for the green light to stop flashing. Then she begins to make two copies of the script, one for Roger Carlyle and one for Grief. As she feeds each page into the machine, she can't help but think about Lynda Kramer, imagine their first meeting, see herself on the set of the film. She begins reading the script again as she copies it. Not bad. Pretty damn good, she thinks as she feeds another page in. Lousy, she thinks as she sees the copy come out the other side.

Barcelona walks back to the phone and dials Dixie again. No answer. Not even the phone answering machine. Nothing to worry about. It is Saturday, and if Dixie had to work today she probably has to keep on working tonight.

She dials again and halfway through realizes she is dialing Eric's number. She immediately slams the phone down as if it had bitten her. She picks it up again, dials Dixie's number, gets no answer.

She goes back to the photocopier and continues to feed her script into the machine. Afterward she will have to hole-punch it and stick those little brass clasps through the holes. Then it will look just like the scripts Roger Carlyle sent her.

Saturday night. The Holy Night of dating. Harley Buss had offered to take her out to dinner and a movie, but she'd turned him down. Not that she had anything better to do, but since seeing Eric again she's been less interested in dating casually where there is no real interest. Friendly dating and friendly sex was getting a little tiring. She wanted some of that good old teeth-rattling passion. The kind where you change your outfit twelve times and your

272

hair eight before your date shows up. She has not felt that kind of passion in years. Eric is the closest she's come to that since . . . well, since pre-Luna Eric.

She stares at the phone. Eric never comes over on a Saturday night. This is when he and Luna usually go to a play. She loves little theaters, community groups, college shows, the cornier the better. Whenever he speaks of this passion of hers, he gets this stupid little grin that makes Barcelona angry, though she is careful not to show it. What are her grounds for anger?

Barcelona crosses the room and snatches up the phone. She stabs the numbers and listens to the electronic tones. The phone rings and rings. Finally the sleepy German-accented voice of Milan speaks, 'Yes, hello?'

Barcelona bunches her T-shirt over the mouthpiece and, in a throaty disguised voice, whispers a long string of obscenities.

PART THREE

Fault Lines

**In Which Romance
Takes Unexpected Turns**

19

Barcelona tries to stop the bleeding with scented toilet paper.

She tears a thumbnail-size piece from the yellow roll and pastes it against her wound. The tissue paper immediately turns limp with blood. It reminds her of time-lapse photography of a wilting flower.

'Christ,' she says.

She tears off a large hunk of toilet paper, folds it neatly in a thick square, and presses it against what is left of the scab on her ankle. The paper expands, grows heavier with the seeping blood. She can almost feel the blood soaking up into the paper, as if it were eating it layer by scented layer. She stares at the top of the wad, waiting to see the yellow paper melt into bright crimson like litmus. It's like some old black and white horror movie, waiting for the zombies to burst through the locked door.

She is sitting on the edge of the bathtub in her panties and bra. The metal runners for the shower enclosure cut sharply into her buttocks and she shifts uncomfortably. The yellow plastic Lady Bic razor is on the lid of the toilet tank next to the spread-eagled copy of Ann Beattie's *Love Always*. During her shower this morning, Barcelona had forgotten to shave her legs, so she thought a few quick swipes before dressing would be okay. Something had distracted her for a moment as she'd been carefully edging around the ankle and she'd sliced through the scab.

The toilet paper doesn't turn red. The bleeding must have stopped. She carefully peels the wad back and sees the half scab crusted next to the open hole brimming with sticky blood. She thinks it looks like the mouth of a volcano. She risks walking a few steps to the medicine cabinet for a Band-Aid and tapes one over the wound. This gives her a good excuse to wear slacks today. This is just as well because she is driving into L.A. later to have lunch with Trina and to drop her completed screenplay off at Grief's office.

Putting the Band-Aid box back in the medicine chest, Barcelona looks into the mirror for the first time that morning. 'Oh my God.' She frowns. 'What next?'

On her forehead, right above her left eyebrow, is a swollen red blemish. It looks large enough to pick up radio stations. She leans closer to the mirror to examine the monstrosity and discovers it is not a blemish, it is a flea bite. 'Larry, you son of a bitch!' she hollers. She storms into the bedroom and finds Larry sitting on the wicker clothes hamper licking his tail. He looks up as she enters the room, seems unimpressed, returns to grooming his tail.

Barcelona snatches up a pillow from the unmade bed to throw at him but changes her mind and tosses it back on the mattress. Larry looks up again and she notices he is missing yet another patch of fur on his shoulder. For a neutered, clawless cat, he gets in a lot of fights. 'Good, you little shit,' she tells him. 'I hope they scalp you bald.' He lies down on the hamper and closes his eyes.

Barcelona feels a nasty pinch on her toe and ankle and looks down at her foot. A black flea is nibbling on her toe and another is attached to her ankle near the Band-Aid. She hurries over to the toilet, lifts her foot over the bowl, and brushes them into the water. They float like poppy seeds, one kicks toward the edge of the water. She wonders who teaches them how to swim. Meantime, another flea has hopped onto her other foot. She reaches down, plucks it off, and presses it between her two thumbnails until the body pops. A tiny drop of blood squirts across her thumbnails. It makes her shiver to realize that drop of blood is her own, slurped out of her by this bug. She flicks the flattened flea into the sink and washes her hands.

Barcelona goes back into the bedroom and dials the phone. She has been calling Dixie all weekend and no one has answered. She's called Diva and Trina, but neither has heard from Dixie. Yesterday, Sunday, she drove over to Dixie's house but no one was there. So far she has avoided calling the police because she assumes Dixie must still be undercover. When Eric called last night from the neighborhood grocery store, she explained her concern about Dixie. He brushed off her worry, saying no cop goes undercover without informing other cops. They'd know where she was. Maybe he's right. But if Dixie isn't back by tonight, she will rethink that stance.

No one answers the phone this time either.

She returns the phone to the cradle, her hand still resting on the receiver. The plastic is warm. Perhaps its warmth comes from the millions of voices shooting through the wires, all that emotion condensed into electronic pulses. She thinks about calling her mother. Will Milan tell her about last night's mysterious caller?

Barcelona isn't sure why she has been making these obscene calls to her mother. Eric would certainly offer her a few choice psychological theories with nasty-sounding names. True, she didn't start them; she only picked up where the original caller left off once he stopped calling. She quickly jerks her hand away from the phone, as if her thoughts might somehow be transmitted directly to Milan.

Whatever dark reason is snorkeling through the swampy

muck of her id, this one memory comes back to her again and again when she calls:

The summer Barcelona turned eighteen. She worked that whole summer in her parents' deli, waitressing. On the Hebrew National calendar on the wall, she used a red Magic Marker to cross off the days until college started. Her cuticles were red and swollen from pickle brine, her hair smelled of smoke from fried pastrami. Her fingers were nicked from washing silverware.

The deli's customers were mostly travelers, on their way to or from somewhere, stopping off only for a quick bite and to use the tiny rest room. They were all universally poor tippers. Nevertheless, Barcelona tossed their quarters and dimes and nickels into her Styrofoam tip cup, each clink getting her closer to college and farther away from here.

While her father baked fresh goods downstairs in the basement, her mother would sit on the end stool of the small counter, smoke pack after pack of Benson & Hedges cigarettes, and do the crossword puzzle in the New York *Daily News*. The coffee cup and cigarette butts in front of her were branded with her red-brown lipstick, the color of dried blood. And so it went, day after day, the summer burning away toward fall.

Barcelona's nights weren't much more exciting. Dating local boys meant a drive-in, calloused palms groping under her blouse, beer-flavored kisses.

But one day the routine shifted.

A boy—he seemed like a man at the time—of about twenty-two came into the deli, straddled a stool, and, without looking at the menu, ordered a tuna fish salad sandwich on white bread.

'We don't carry tuna fish,' Barcelona told him.

He wore a baseball cap, which he took off and put back on again, smoothing back his hair in between. 'What kind

280

of diner doesn't have tuna fish salad?' he said with a slight drawl. He wasn't angry, just curious. He smiled at her; his teeth were straight and white, but the front one was chipped.

'We're not a diner, sir. We're a deli.'

He looked around the store as if noticing it for the first time. He saw the slabs of corned beef and pastrami in the refrigerated showcase, saw the Star of David on the menu.

'Oops,' he said. 'Tell you what, why don't you make me the best sandwich you all serve. No harm done.'

Barcelona made him a Reuben sandwich, grilling corned beef, sauerkraut, and Swiss cheese between rye bread. When he ate, some of the Russian dressing slid down his chin. She laughed and pointed. He wiped his chin with a napkin and said, 'Man overboard, huh?'

He came in every day that week for lunch. His name was Tim Beufort, from Tea Kettle, North Carolina. He had come to town to play baseball for the local farm team. He played shortstop but was angling for the first baseman's position.

The second week Tim asked Barcelona out. That evening they drove forty miles over to Lewisburg to eat dinner and see *Butch Cassidy & the Sundance Kid*. She did not return home until six the next morning. When she did, her dress was torn in three places, her nails broken, her shoes ruined. Mud was caked across her face. Blood striped her legs from knees to ankles.

Barcelona walked about the back of the house to let herself in the backdoor. Her father would already be at the store, down in the cellar baking danish and doughnuts. He drove down at 4 A.M.; Barcelona and Milan followed at 7 A.M. With any luck, she could sneak into the house and miss Milan altogether. No explanations.

But as Barcelona rounded the house, she nearly tripped over Milan on her hands and knees, weeding the flowers along the walkway. She wore huge leather pads on her knees, thick weeding gloves, and a wide-brimmed straw hat with a green visor embedded in the front brim. The hat was useless since the sun was still not up yet, but barely lit the east mountains directly behind them. Still, this was her gardening outfit and she wouldn't dream of wearing anything less than the entire ensemble.

'*Gutten morgan*,' Milan said without looking up.

'Good morning.'

'Did you have a nice time?' She yanked a weed up by the roots and threw it on the others on top of a spread piece of newspaper.

'Do I look like I had a good time?' Barcelona snapped.

For the first time, Milan looked around. Her eyes were red and tired, as if she hadn't slept well. '*Ach Got*, child. What happened?' She started to rise but Barcelona touched her shoulder, preventing the gesture.

'I'm fine. Tim's car blew a tire and we went over an embankment. The road was pretty deserted, so we had to dig ourselves out. Took most of the night. Believe me, Mom, nothing else happened. I swear, Tim was the perfect gentleman. Nothing happened.'

Milan stood up, wiped her hands on her jeans, and touched her gloved hand to Barcelona's cheek. 'Of course not, dear.' Then she gathered up the newspaper full of weeds and carried it to the garbage can.

Barcelona stood on the walkway alone. She was shaking with anger.

It had been the truth. The flat tire. Digging the car out of the dirt. Nothing else happened. No attack. No sex.

Despite the evidence to the contrary, her mother had believed her instantly. No cross-examination, no disapproving look. Ordinarily, that response would be wonderful, the envy of every teenage girl. But Barcelona knew it wasn't trust that had motivated her mother's statement;

282

the trust for a well brought-up child to do the right thing. No, when Milan had stood up and touched her cheek and said, 'Of course not, dear,' she was making a declaration, not of faith, but of destiny. The trust you have for a blind child who says he did not steal your car and drive it to the next town.

Of course not, dear. How could anything happen? You aren't capable of such spontaneous passion.

Barcelona pushes the phone away and returns to the bathroom to stare at the red bump on her forehead. She is not one who uses much makeup, but this red-eyed dinosaur needs some heavy camouflage. Trina once taught her a makeup trick that she has yet to use. But if there was ever a time for makeup magic, this was it. She runs downstairs to the kitchen, grabs a bottle of mineral water from the refrigerator, rushes back to the bathroom. She dumps some of her Revlon foundation in the palm of her hand, spills in a few drops of mineral water, dabs a little moisturizer on top. She stirs with her finger and begins applying the mixture to her face. The red bump sinks out of sight.

'There,' she says, staring at her reflection. 'Not everything needs to be a disaster today.'

Barcelona is driving to school. She keeps leaning over, checking her forehead in the rearview mirror, wondering if the flea bite has chewed through the makeup yet. She changes lanes and—

Bam!

A sudden explosion causes Barcelona to instinctively duck down in her seat and pull the steering wheel to the right. Instantly she remembers what Diva told her about the kid shot by an irate driver and wonders who she might have pissed off on the four miles from her home to here.

283

The Geezemobile rolls to the side of the road and the rest of the traffic whooshes past her without breaking rhythm. Fortunately she avoided the crammed freeway this morning and took a back road that wends through the construction sites and farm fields, so it is not too difficult to make it to the dirt shoulder. From the thumping roll of the car, Barcelona realizes now that no one has shot at her; she merely has a flat tire. The second one in her life.

She gets out of the car and walks around to the front right tire. A ragged hole the size of a baby's fist gapes at her. She takes a deep breath and her eyes widen at the lingering odor. This is the same road on which she killed the skunk, though that happened about a mile away. Still, as she walks along the edge of the shoulder, she glances down in the drainage ditch for the body. She sees a couple of squashed rabbits, flat and dry as cardboard. No skunk.

She unlocks the trunk and removes the jack and spare tire, leaning the tire against the back bumper. Her hands are black with dirt and she is careful not to wipe them on her slacks. She has an auto club card, but she doesn't want to hike to a phone, then wait the thirty more minutes or so for the truck to show up. Her class meets in half an hour and she has no intention of being late.

She positions the jack and starts wenching up the car.

'Need a hand?' a voice calls to her.

She straightens to her feet and sees two boys getting out of a beat-up Impala parked behind her car. Their skulls are shaved to the flesh on the sides, the top has a quarter inch of bristle. They are maybe eighteen. She recognizes them as marines from the El Toro base less than a mile away from here. She looks over her shoulder across the condo sites and the strawberry fields and there stands the two monstrous hangars where the helicopters are stored. The hangars are gigantic, shaped like lunch pails. She's read that clouds actually form up in the rafters.

Barcelona has often driven by the base, seen the drab concrete housing where the marine families live, the wet towels hanging off the wooden balconies, the rusted barbecues, the overturned tricycles on the patchy brown and green lawn. The marine families can often be seen in Irvine, a sharp contrast to the affluent families that make up most of the community. Marine families are seen mostly at the fast-food restaurants, sitting noisily at Wendy's or McDonald's or Carl Jr.'s, wolfing fries and burgers, the kids screaming, the father telling them to shut up, smacking sticky fingers that spill ketchup. The marine wives are always young, mostly overweight, with pasty skin and dull eyes, hair always limp and unwashed, looking like children themselves, but always with a child of their own riding a hip or clutching a hand. Sometimes in the movie theaters, she will see marines sitting together in what the locals called Marine Formation: with an empty seat between them, so as not to sit too close to another man.

Relations between the locals and the marines are not very good right now. Many local residents are annoyed by the constant noise of the helicopters, not to mention the threat of them crashing. Also, marines seem to be involved in more than their share of drunk driving accidents. Two months ago, a marine was arrested for robbing a Denny's restaurant.

'Need any help, ma'am?' one of the boys asks again. He is wearing black motorcycle boots, torn jeans, and a green T-shirt. His face is red from a bad sunburn.

'It's just a flat,' she says.

'Yes, ma'am. Me and Bundy seen flats before.' He's not being smart, he's just friendly. He smiles broadly. Bundy lags behind looking vaguely uncomfortable. Stopping was clearly not his idea. 'Wouldn't bother us to change it real quick. Wouldn't do for you to be getting all dirty over a dumb tire.'

Barcelona is torn. She is fully capable of changing the tire herself. There is nothing in the act of changing this tire that requires superior strength. As a woman, she feels some obligation to do it herself, if for no other reason than to prove to these two that she can do it. On the other hand, she is dressed in nice clothing and doesn't want to be late for class.

'Thank you,' she says. 'I wouldn't mind a hand.'

'Name's Carson,' the boy says, holding out his hand to her. 'Not related to Johnny.'

'My hand's dirty,' she warns.

'Mine will be soon enough,' he says and grasps her for a firm shake. 'Let's do it, Bundy.'

Bundy frowns and sighs but finally squats down next to Carson and they quickly go about the task of changing the tire.

'I see by your outfit that you are a teacher,' Carson says, squinting up at her.

'How'd you know?'

He laughs. 'Faculty parking permit on your back bumper. Sand Coast College, huh?'

'Yup.'

'What do you teach?'

'English. Some composition, some literature.' She feels slightly pretentious saying this to him.

'Really?' he says, looking up at her again. His face is so sunburned, Barcelona winces. 'You teach poetry?'

'Some.'

'Now that's interesting because I'm kind of a poet myself.'

'Oh?' she says.

'Yeah.' Bundy smirks. 'He's the Death Squads official poet.'

Carson elbows Bundy in a friendly way. 'Ignore him, ma'am. Bundy's brain don't kick in 'til sometime 'round noon. Only Death Squad we got is the cooks in the mess hall.'

Bundy looks up at her and grins but not in a friendly manner.

'I really dig writing poetry,' Carson continues as they switch tires. 'The rhymes are the hardest part, though, thinking up new ones all the time. I been meaning to get one of them rhyming dictionaries. Think that would help?'

'It might.'

'Damn, I wish I had some of my poems with me now. I could show 'em to you and you could tell me if they're any good.'

Barcelona goes into the car and picks through her purse. She comes back and hands him her business card with the college's address. 'Send me a couple here. I'll look them over, make a few comments, and send them back.'

Carson stands up excitedly. 'No shit? Hey, great!'

Bundy releases the jack and stores it in the trunk. He slams the trunk lid harder than necessary. 'Let's go, Shakespeare. We'll be late. Then you can start figuring what rhymes with latrine duty.'

'Marine cooty,' Carson says, grinning. He reads her card. 'Barcelona? That really your name?'

'Uh-huh.'

'That's cool. That's why I joined the marines, to meet women with names like yours.' He laughs and returns to their rusted Impala. They drive away and he waves her business card at her and smiles.

Barcelona drives to school. She enters her classroom one minute late and gives her students a pop quiz on John Milton just for the hell of it. They moan and complain. Someone asks if she had a fight with her boyfriend and everyone laughs. Barcelona laughs too. The grades are fairly high. One student fails, but he always fails.

*　　*　　*

'They sent me to talk to you,' the young woman says.

Barcelona is bending over the drinking fountain, slurping up cold water from the tiny trickle that dribbles out. The water is refrigerated and it jolts a nerve in her upper right bicuspid. She's needed root canal work on that tooth for more than a year now but has put it off. She hopes to keep putting it off despite the dentist's warnings and the little drawings of the damaged root he does every time she visits him.

'They said I should see you,' the woman repeats.

Barcelona straightens, wipes water from her mouth and chin. 'Who're they?'

'I'm Crystal Ponce,' the young woman says, ignoring Barcelona's question. 'I'm writing a novel.'

'Ah,' Barcelona says.

'Someone in my advanced comp class said I should talk to you. You've published novels.'

Crystal Ponce looks like a younger version of the rude woman in the BMW the other day. She is maybe twenty-eight and is wearing a short denim skirt, a blowsy white sweater, and flat Capezio shoes. Everything casual and inexpensive. Except for the wedding ring, a knotted tumor of raisin-size diamonds worth at least $5,000.

Crystal seems to sense Barcelona's hesitation, for she says, 'I just want to ask you a few questions. Okay?'

'Sure,' Barcelona concedes. 'Ask.'

Crystal looks around at the milling students. 'Can we talk in your office?'

Barcelona had hoped to avoid that. Once they settle comfortably into a chair, they can't be pried out in less than forty minutes. Out in the hallway, she's usually able to keep them down to ten or fifteen minutes. 'You might be better off seeing me tomorrow during my office hour. I'll have more time then.'

'This won't take long.'

Forty minutes later, Crystal Ponce has worked her way from her troubled childhood in a wealthy Rhode Island family to her current role of wife and mother in a wealthy California family. 'I'm young, I have a great husband, two terrific kids,' she says. 'My husband is a realtor, loves to surf, has the nicest ass of any man I've ever seen. Wants to screw every other night. And my kids. My kids are so loving, so sweet, it makes me cry sometimes. But I want to write, be a writer, a novelist like you.'

'Have you read any of my books?'

'No.'

'Then how do you know you want to be a novelist like me?'

Crystal stares at Barcelona. 'Have I offended you somehow?'

Barcelona immediately feels bad. The woman is serious and deserves to be taken seriously. 'I'm sorry. I just don't know what you want from me. You seem to have everything. Being a wife and mother doesn't have to exclude being a writer. You just have to learn to organize your time wisely, let your family know this is an important priority for you, tell them—'

Crystal waves her hand impatiently. 'No, no, you don't understand.' She crosses her legs, revealing lots of trim tan skin. One narrow ankle is circled provocatively by a thin gold bracelet. 'My family is not the problem. I have lots of free time.'

'What is the problem?'

'What I'm writing about. I'm not sure I'm doing it right. Can you take a look?' Without waiting for an answer, she opens her shoulder bag and pulls out a bunch of papers held together by a pink paper clip.

'I really don't have time right now, Crystal,' Barcelona explains. 'You can leave it with me and I'll try to get to it next week.'

'It'll just take a minute. It's the first chapter. I promise you, you won't be bored. I just need to know if I'm on the right track.'

Barcelona sneaks a glance at the last page number. Ten. Not too bad. She can read ten pages, make a few general comments, and be rid of Crystal Ponce. She flattens the chapter on the desktop and begins to read. The novel starts with a woman, twenty-eight, with two adorable children and a hunk husband. She is in their vacation home in Lake Tahoe; she is alone. She has come here without telling anyone. She has brought a gun. She sits in the hot tub with a glass of expensive wine recalling wonderful times with her family. Then she places the gun to her head. Haunted her whole life by a terrible affliction she can no longer live with, she has decided to kill herself. Her affliction: she's too beautiful.

Barcelona stops reading, looks up at Crystal's intent expression. The woman is serious.

Barcelona bites her cheek to keep from laughing and finishes the chapter, which ends with the woman cocking the hammer. Barcelona looks up from the chapter again and leans back in her chair. 'What happens next?'

'The rest of the novel is a flashback that shows how she's reached this point, how her beauty has driven her to this desperate dilemma.'

'Then at the end, she either pulls the trigger or not. That's the hook, right?'

'Yes. Though I haven't decided whether or not I'll show what her choice is. Maybe I should leave that up to the reader. What do you think?'

Barcelona stares at Crystal Ponce now, examining her face, her long thin nose, the tiny flat eyes, the stiff over-sprayed over-frosted hair. She is somewhat attractive, yes, but far from the mind-numbing beauty of her character.

'Do you really think this character's problem is that . . . disastrous?'

Crystal laughs bitterly. 'Take my word for it. No one takes you seriously when you're beautiful. They think you're a ball-buster, spoiled bitch, or dumb. Or all three. They all want you, sure. The women want to look like you and the men want to fuck you blind, but nobody *cares* about you. They don't take you serious. I'm not stupid.'

That last phrase startles Barcelona. It's what Diva had said on Saturday. A chill nibbles on her neck. She has a strange feeling that all the women of the world held a meeting recently without inviting her and in it they all agreed to act weird. Her mother attended, so did Diva. So did Crystal Ponce.

'I don't know what to tell you, Crystal.'

'Is it any good, my chapter?'

'The writing is smooth and clear. It's an interesting premise, though I'm not sure you've made her sympathetic enough that the average reader is going to care about her. We don't readily identify with her problem.'

'What do you mean?'

A loud knock on the glass startles Barcelona. Crystal, however, offers no reaction. She waits for an answer to her question.

Barcelona looks up and sees Harley Buss waving through the glass partition. She waves back. Harley points to his watch, flashes a questioning expression. Barcelona holds up one finger.

'I have an appointment now,' Barcelona lies. 'Why don't you keep working on it and we'll discuss it later.'

Crystal doesn't budge. 'When?'

'Next week.'

'Monday?'

Barcelona rises and opens the door, holding it open. 'Tuesday. During my scheduled office hour.'

291

Crystal gathers her chapter and walks out of the office without a word. Harley gives her an appreciative glance as she passes him and Barcelona wonders if maybe Crystal was right about her beauty after all.

'Do you think she's beautiful?' Barcelona asks Harley when he closes the door.

'Who?'

'Who? The woman who just strolled by.'

'I didn't notice.'

Barcelona laughs. 'You turned your head, you watched her ass wiggle down the corridor.'

'Reflex action. I look, but I don't always see. Was she cute?'

'Jesus.' Barcelona sits back in her chair. She opens her desk drawer and pulls out a packet of Breathsavers. She offers one to Harley, but he shakes his head and settles behind Susan Mesa's desk.

Nothing is said for almost a minute.

'You come in here for sanctuary?' Barcelona asks. Ordinarily she enjoys Harley's visits, but this morning she is in a rush to grade a few papers and hit the road. She still has to meet Trina for lunch and deliver her script to Grief.

'I'm doing the budget.'

'Uh oh.'

'But that's not why I came in.'

'Oh?'

'I came in to ask you if you gave my phone number out to one of your friends.'

Barcelona blushes fiercely. Her face is so hot she presses her palms against her cheeks. The Breathsaver suddenly tastes oily and bitter. 'Well, I, I didn't—'

Harley grins. 'Not that I mind. Actually, it's kind of flattering that you think so highly of me you'd recommend me to one of your friends.' He leans forward, his hands steepled together on top of the desk. He looks like he's praying. 'I know our friendship isn't going to develop along any other lines. Not that that's bad. Hell, I've gotten to the age where I'd rather not screw up a good friendship with romance. When you do, you usually end up losing both.' He leans back in the chair again and laces his hands behind his head. 'So what can you tell me about her?'

Barcelona doesn't know what to say. Only Trina would have the guts to call Harley this way and Barcelona is torn between admiring her courage and resenting her aggressiveness. Somehow she feels as if Trina is stealing a little bit of her life away. She knows that's silly, that she herself gave Trina Harley's name. Still. 'She's very intelligent. She's sexy. Pretty. I don't know, what do you want to know?'

'Is she rich? If this works out between us, can I retire?'

Barcelona throws a paper clip at him. He catches it with one hand. 'I didn't know you were a golddigger.'

'I can learn. Besides, when she told me she was a professional singer, I thought maybe she—'

'A singer? Who?'

'Who are we talking about. Dianne Klosterman.'

'Diva?'

'Yeah. She said that's what you called her. That's cute. How come you never made up a nickname for me?'

'I did. You just don't want to hear it.'

Harley laughs and tosses the paper clip back at her. Barcelona is too distracted to catch it and it skitters across her calendar desk pad and drops onto the floor.

Diva. Barcelona is shocked. When did Diva start to be so aggressive? She did say she was changing her life; maybe she meant all of it, not just the career part. Barcelona looks over at Harley, his sleepy sexuality, tall tanned figure, his secret passion for T.S. Eliot's poetry. She thinks of Diva, chubby beach rat, reads only dumb magazines.

293

Her philosophy of life is determined by the Top 40. There is no way they will hit it off.

'Just answer me one thing,' Harley asks.

'What?'

'She's not into anything strange, is she? Horseback riding or anything?'

'No, Harley. She likes volleyball.'

He thinks that over. 'Volleyball is okay. I can stand that.'

'Thank you, Mr. Romance.'

Harley gets up and stretches. 'No big deal. It's just dinner and a movie. Maybe a drink afterwards if we can still stand each other.'

'And if you can't stand each other?'

'Then we skip the drink and just have sex.'

Barcelona laughs.

Harley winks and leaves. Barcelona reaches for the phone and dials Dixie's number again. Still no answer. She is not in the mood to grade papers now and stuffs them into her briefcase. She is just stepping out of her office when Crystal Ponce steps up to her. 'I had a couple more chapters in the car. I thought I'd leave them with you. Okay?'

20

Trina walks into The Candidate's office that morning and finds Mary Abrahms trying to set Warren Schuller on fire. She'd heard their hollering all the way from the elevator.

When she first opens the door, Mary and Warren are sitting together on the small leather sofa shouting into each other's faces, their shrill voices a jumble of high-decibel insults. Warren's usually neat beard looks oddly chaotic this morning, as if scribbled onto his chin with a frayed Magic Marker. Mary orchestrates her verbal abuse with a lipstick-smeared cigarette bobbing up and down on the end of her lips like a conductor's baton. Smoke escorts every word from her mouth.

The Candidate is sitting behind his glass desk, watching them without expression. When Trina walks in he hikes up his pant leg and points at his ankle to show he is wearing socks. He grins.

'You don't understand what I'm saying,' Warren tells Mary. Warren is a bony stick figure of a man, emaciated to the point that he sometimes looks as if he's dying from a voodoo curse. Childhood photographs have confirmed that he always looked like that.

Mary is squat and stubby, built like a '50s jukebox. Her face is round as a pumpkin and as homely. Her eyes are pale gray as if stained by her constant smoking. Her black hair is straight and lifeless, chopped unattractively short.

'I understand every word, Warren, I just don't agree.'

'Then you don't understand,' Warren says. 'Maybe my concept is too sophisticated for you.'

'You little shit,' Mary snarls and thumbs her Bic lighter into a high flame. She brushes the flame quickly over Warren's arm. A patch of hair on his forearm shrivels and withers.

'Hey!' Warren yells, jerking his arm away. He scoots across the sofa hugging his arm as if he's just been shot by a sniper. 'That burns!'

'No shit,' Mary says.

Warren carefully touches his arm. Several crisped hairs drop off. 'That really hurt.'

Mary chuckles hoarsely.

Trina can smell the sour scent of roasted body hair. She rubs her nose and closes the office door behind her. 'I see you guys started the discussion without me.'

The Candidate nods. 'Warren and Mary were just explaining their new election strategy.'

'I'm always wary of campaigns that involve setting the candidate on fire.'

'I'm a little reluctant myself,' The Candidate says.

'We have troubles, Trina,' Warren says. 'Bad troubles.'

'Deep shit,' Mary agrees. She stubs out her cigarette but keeps the lighter clutched tightly in her hand like a grenade.

Trina sits down in the matching leather chair and sets her briefcase on the floor, a little imitation-leather wall between herself and Warren and Mary. Even when silent, their anger at each other is radioactive. Trina can't get over how much they've changed in the past six months. When this campaign first started a year ago, Warren and Mary were happily married to each other, decorating their new home in Santa Monica. Monday mornings they would come bustling into the office and tell how they drove down to Mexico over the weekend to find just the right hand-painted tiles for the bathroom. Or how they drove to Oxnard and bargained with some rude farmer for an antique grape press. Now they are separated. Trina isn't sure whether the cause of the split was the pressure of the campaign or redecorating their house. A month ago Mary moved out of their painstakingly completed house and into a flashy chrome-and-glass Marina del Rey condo with her new boyfriend, a black relief pitcher for the Dodgers. Trina suspects that Warren, who used to be a rabid Dodgers fan, hates Mary more for taking away his pleasure of rooting for the Dodgers than for her leaving him.

They have always disagreed loudly on campaign strategies, even before the separation, but lately their disagreements have escalated beyond raised voices. Two weeks ago in front of Mary's desk, Warren scissored his own precious Dodgers warm-up jacket he'd worn daily for eight years. Last week Mary threw a pen at Warren, hitting him in the back and leaving an ink mark on his expensive new Ralph Lauren jacket. Enraged, Warren picked up the pen and threw it back. Mary tried to catch it but missed. The sharp point gouged a blue hole in the palm of her hand. There was some blood. The sight of blood seems to have destroyed any civilized boundaries between them. Now, anything goes.

Their bickering has become annoying to Trina, but it is too close to Election Day to replace them. Despite their marital status, they continue to operate as partners in their political consulting firm. Besides, they're very good. Both have worked on many campaigns, most of them for underdog candidates with liberal leanings. Warren, forty-two, the only son of labor organizers, spent his early years after college helping run campaigns within labor unions. One night a couple of beefy goons warned him to quit the campaign, then broke his windshield with a Louisville

Slugger. The next day Warren quit. His father, who in his young union-organizing days had been shot twice and beaten a dozen times, has not spoken to him since. His mother and he correspond secretly.

Mary's route was more conventional. College as a political science major hoping to end the Vietnam War. Warren had been a guest lecturer at one of her classes their first week together. They smoked dope and made love every night; the second week they got married. Mary has a tiny lobster-shaped scar on the back of her neck, which she received when a cop yanked off her seashell necklace during the Chicago Democratic Convention riots in 1968. She has shown the scar to everyone in the office.

'So, how deep is this shit?' Trina asks. Her own voice surprises her, coming out so flat and cynical. As if she didn't really care. She suddenly realizes she *doesn't* really care. She doesn't really care about this campaign, about whether or not The Candidate is wearing socks, whether or not Mary sets Warren on fire. She has a whole day of this kind of crap in front of her and all she really wants to do is go home, slip into a steaming tub, and read a trashy novel.

This attitude scares her. It's not just Monday morning blues. She didn't leave the house this morning feeling this way. She rarely has dreaded her work; in fact she genuinely loves it. Her job is as much her avocation as vocation. She even likes the pressures, the competition, getting down and dirty with the best of them. She's not sure why she feels this unexpected loathing. She feels disoriented, as if she's been ambushed. Maybe it has something to do with watching Mary and Warren's marriage dissolve slowly over the months, like a snake digesting a lump that once was a rabbit. Maybe it's just rampant hormones. Whatever the reason, Trina trembles a little in her seat, senses a sharp panic worming up through her stomach. She feels hot and sweaty. Feverish. She tries to shake it off, concentrate on the business at hand. Act the professional. After all, that's what she is: Trina Bedford, Jr., The Ultimate Professional Woman. She screws her face into a serious businesslike expression and says, 'What's the problem, Mary?'

'We were doing fine in the polls,' Warren says before Mary can answer. 'Better than we'd expected last month. Inching our way up slowly, but rising, always rising. I think in another twelve days we would have been even with Bennington.' He smacks a rolled-up newspaper against his knee. 'Then this.'

'Then what?' Trina says.

Mary sighs and shows Trina a photo of Carla Bennington in this morning's *Los Angeles Times*. She is in a park wearing a headband and jogging outfit, sitting on the grass stretching her legs. The headline is 'Candidate Runs a Different Kind of Race.'

'Carla Bennington is running in that multiple sclerosis benefit marathon in a couple weeks,' Mary says. 'She'll have cameras on her for days before the race as well as during the whole thing.'

'Just the kind of sex-and-sentiment crap the media eats up,' Warren says. 'A candidate, especially an attractive woman, walking around in skimpy shorts and a tight T-shirt.'

The Candidate looks at his copy of the newspaper spread open on his desk and smiles. 'She's got the ass for it.'

'You understand what this means, Cory?' Warren says a little testily to The Candidate.

The Candidate smiles, but his eyes narrow. 'Gee, Warren, I think so. It means—and please help me out if I get stuck—that during the next two crucial campaign weeks Carla Bennington will be on a shitload of local talk shows on TV and radio supposedly publicizing the marathon. She'll probably make a big show of keeping the whole thing nonpolitical. When they ask her about the election, she'll flash that sincere-as-a-nun smile of hers and say, 'I didn't come here to talk politics. I came here to help people with multiple sclerosis.' Voters will admire her commitment to a worthwhile cause as well as her integrity at not taking political advantage of all that free air time.'

'Um, yes.' Warren looks contrite. He lowers his head and tugs his beard.

The Candidate winks at Trina.

'Let me see that,' Trina says to Mary, taking the newspaper. She studies the article on the marathon, spots a disturbing detail. 'Hmmm. Here's an ugly coincidence.'

'Yeah,' The Candidate says, leaning back in his chair. 'Ain't it.'

'What?' Mary asks.

'What?' Warren echoes.

The Candidate props his feet up on his glass desktop. A worn patch of white chewing gum is stuck to one heel. 'The race route travels through several different districts to make sure it's nonpartisan. However, coincidentally, the route cuts through a corner of Carla's own district, specifically the Capshaw area, the one where she's lowest in the polls and we're the highest.'

'Shit,' Warren says. 'I missed that.'

Trina looks at The Candidate and once again is impressed by his sharpness. Despite his casual appearance and manner, not much slips by him. She has the feeling that he could run this entire campaign without any of them.

Mary lifts her hand and thumbs her lighter into a tall flame. Warren flinches and leans away. Mary chuckles and sticks a cigarette between her lips, torching the end. 'What we need,' Mary says, then turns to Trina. 'And this is what we were discussing before you came in. What we need is something new for Cory to make a stand on. Some reason to call a press conference, focus some of those cameras on him. Steal some of the air from her sails.'

'What'd you have in mind?' Trina asks.

'We were hoping something also to do with sports,' Mary says. 'I suggested we arrange something with Cory and some guys I know from the Dodgers. A sports demonstration for disabled kids or something.'

'That's stupid,' Warren says, spit flying from his lips and dewing his beard. 'Nobody gives a shit about the goddamn Dodgers right now. They've lost their last five games.'

'So what? They're still athletes. They project a healthy, vibrant, youthful impression. That's what we need, especially considering how tough Bennington's going to seem after she's finished that goddamn marathon. Like she could eat nails and piss wine.'

'Maybe she'll dehydrate and start puking,' The Candidate says. 'We could get photos of that. Remember when Jimmy Carter swooned during a run, that picture of the Secret Service holding him up. That cost him a few votes.'

Warren and Mary think this over, nodding. 'I wouldn't count on it, Cory,' Warren says. 'She's always finished without any problems before.'

Trina shakes her head. After all this time, they still can't tell when The Candidate is kidding them.

'Well, you're my advisers,' The Candidate says. 'So advise.'

Warren unconsciously strokes his burned arm hairs while thinking. His arm rests in his lap like a pet. 'Maybe something with AIDS. Some rock benefit.'

'We've covered that issue,' Mary says, annoyed. 'Six months ago.'

'The homeless.'

'We already issued a plan for helping them,' Trina says.

'We issue a new plan,' Warren says. 'More benefits.'

301

'Forget it,' The Candidate says. 'We've beaten that one to the ground. What else you got?'

'Crime?'

'Covered,' Trina says.

'Specialized crime. Drugs.'

'Bad timing,' The Candidate says. 'They'll think we'll want to raise taxes.'

Warren looks depressed; he's rubbing his charred hairs. 'Pit bulls are hot. We suggest a bill to outlaw pit bulls. That will give TV news a chance to whip out their footage of pit bull attacks.'

'That's lame,' Mary snorts.

'Fuck you!'

'I'd rather fuck a pit bull.'

'You probably have.'

'Knock it off,' Trina says. 'What's our weakest area? Which voters are we least appealing to?'

Mary and Warren look at each other, thinking. Instantly gone is their animosity, their hate, as they silently shift back into their role of a successful business team facing a sticky challenge. Their angry outbursts are completely forgotten during these intense stares, as if they were communicating on some psychic level. Their eyes soften, their mouths go slack. Watching them during these moments is as intimate as peeping into their bedroom during sex. They were born to be a team, but *only* a business team. Trina wishes she could tell them that, but she knows it would be no use. She is the Cassandra of human relationships, destined to be right, cursed not to be believed.

'Our weakest area,' Mary says, 'are those people who vote for incumbents, no matter who is in office. They're afraid of any change, good or bad.'

'Forget them,' Trina says. 'We can't touch them. Let's stick with the undecided.'

'Well,' Warren says, 'there are also those who perceive

302

Cory as being too liberal, too sympathetic to minorities. Too soft. Our own polls have pointed that out several times.'

The Candidate laughs. 'I could burn a cross in Dodger Stadium in front of crippled kids. Cover all the bets.'

Trina opens her briefcase and rifles through her file of newspaper clippings in the folder marked District Problems. She doesn't find anything suitable and abandons that file for another one marked So. Cal. Problems. 'I've got something. Hold on . . .' She keeps flipping through them until she finds the one she wants. It's a two-inch story with a six-inch photo. She hands it to Mary, who reads it, looks at the photo, makes a disgusted face, and passes it to Warren. Warren has the same repulsed response. He hands it to The Candidate.

The Candidate reads it, looks at Trina. His face is grim. He is not joking now. 'Christ, Trina. Gutted bears?'

'Gutted bears.' Trina nods. 'These black bears are protected by the state, but they're being killed and gutted with an alarming increase, as the picture shows.' The photograph is of a dead black bear on his back, his stomach and chest sliced open, the blood-matted fur peeled back from his ribs, his internal organs jumbled like the contents of Trina's purse. She points at the clipping in The Candidate's hand. 'All these poachers want is the gall bladder.'

'The gall bladder?' Mary says, wrinkling her nose. 'What the hell for?'

'Powdered gall has been used for centuries by Orientals. It's supposed to relieve arthritis, high blood pressure, impotence, lots of stuff. They grind it into powder and sell it at three hundred forty dollars per ounce.'

'That much?' Warren says, impressed.

'That's about the same as gold,' Mary says. 'Or good Maui weed.'

'So what are you suggesting here, Trina?' The Candidate

says briskly, all business. 'We don't have any goddamn bears in this district. We don't have many Orientals either. We're mostly whites and Latinos who don't give a shit about de-galled bears.'

'That doesn't matter. We have you suggest an ordinance or something that will raise the fines for poaching bears. We call a news conference. The newspapers will print it, and it's got a kind of an amusing angle that the TV news will certainly run with some cute footage of bears romping playfully in the woods. The gall bladder stuff is a bit weird and occult, they'll love it. Believe me, I know.'

'So what do we get out of this?' Mary asks. 'Other than some cute footage.'

'Oh yes. Yes, yes, yes.' Warren is nodding, grinning. He understands. 'Jesus, Trina, that's brilliant. It's fucking brilliant.' He sits up on the sofa, leans forward excitedly, stroking his beard. 'The conservative uncommitted voters will think you're cracking down on the Orientals, which they will see as a policy of getting tough with minorities.'

'Of course!' Mary is nodding now too, smiling. 'And the liberals will see it merely as a conservationist policy, protecting wildlife and the environment.'

The Candidate shakes his head. 'All over some bear's gall bladder?'

'Politics is all illusion,' Trina says. 'You know that.'

'Campaigns are all illusion,' he says. 'Not politics.'

Trina is again surprised. Sometimes she forgets that The Candidate is serious, that he really does want to win the election, and not just to have office. He wants to do some version of good.

The meeting disbands as Mary and Warren rush out to start putting the gall bladder campaign in effect. They leave chatting excitedly, like teens on a first date. Mary holds Warren's arm. But soon, Trina realizes, within minutes, something will remind them of the other part of their relationship, the failing domestic half, and they will again begin gnawing on each other's spleens.

'Trina,' The Candidate says, gesturing for her to stay.

She walks over to his desk.

He opens one of the black wire basket drawers and pulls out the folded flyer they recently mailed out. The front displays three unflattering photos of Carla Bennington's face while she is talking. They'd hired a photographer to stalk her for weeks to get those shots that made her look like a bitching fishwife. Above the photo in one-inch letters is the line: TALK IS CHEAP. Beneath the photos of her open mouth is another line: UNLESS YOU'RE PAYING FOR IT. Inside the folder are the usual facts and figures and razzle-dazzle oatmeal of words meant to confuse the issues rather than clarify them. Trina wrote the flyer herself.

'I'm convinced that these flyers are the reason I've been coming up in the polls,' he says.

'I think you're right.'

He smiles. 'Good, I thought you might fight me on that one.'

'What for? I'm damn good at what I do.' She hears her own voice being much too loud, as if she were arguing or picking a fight. Why? For Chrissake he's complimenting you, girl. She is careful to lower it when she speaks again. 'Trust me on this bear thing. I know it sounds silly, but it will work.'

'I'm sure it will. It's just that one day when I'm president of this great country, I hate to think I rode into the White House on a bear's gall bladder.'

'Some have ridden in on worse.'

'True, true. But as much as I appreciate your brainstorm here, and I do recognize its subtle brilliance, Trina, I would still prefer something with more substance to defeat our opponent. What about Carla Bennington? Anything on those mysterious trips of hers yet? Have you connected them to city funds, illegal junkets, anything like that?'

'I'm still chasing down a couple leads.'

'The fuse is lit, Trina. It's only a matter of time before we have to start running for cover.'

'What the hell does that mean?'

'We need it soon. Very soon.'

'Immediately, O Wise and Great Pretender to the Throne of Los Angeles.' She bows formally and starts to back out of the office.

'That's more like it,' he says.

Trina sits at her desk and dials Dixie's number for the fourth time that morning. Ever since Barcelona told her what had happened with Dixie at Fashion Island over the weekend, she's been calling. The phone rings and Trina rests her head on her hand, waiting. The desktop is a mess of wrinkled papers stacked in indiscriminate piles. Three open Diet Cherry Coke cans stand together on one stack. Two of the cans are half-full, opened sometime last week. One is fresh from this morning. She straightens a few papers while listening to the tenth ring. No answer. She hangs up the phone but keeps her hand on the receiver, trying to decide if she should call Dixie's captain.

The phone rings suddenly and she pulls her hand away as if she's received an electrical shock. The phone rings again and she answers it. 'Hello?'

The voice is entirely too cheerful: 'You want it? 'Cause I got it.'

'You bragging, Howdy? Because remember, I've seen it.'

'Ho, ho. Two ho's, that's all you get. And all you're going to get if you aren't nice to me.'

Trina sighs. 'Pretend this is me being nice.'

'That's the best you can do?' Howdy White says. 'Not nice enough, not for what I've got.'

'Okay, dazzle me first, then we'll talk nice.'

'Not good enough, Trina.' His voice is still cheerful, but a serious edge has crept in. 'Remember that raise we talked about, the one when I come to work for you and Cory Meyers?'

'The one we didn't talk about.'

'I want it, Trina. In exchange for what I've got.'

'You sound like a blackmailer, Howdy, the creepy murder victim out of the old "Perry Mason" show.'

'I've always had a theatrical streak. Well?'

Trina thinks it over. 'Is this a firm something or just a maybe?'

'A firm maybe. I got it going through Lila's purse. If she ever found out she'd cut my dick off and throw it in the blender. So I'm running some risk here, sweetheart.'

'A small risk.'

'You get one ho for that.'

'Christ, Howdy, when did you become such a bastard?'

'I've always been one. You never noticed before.'

Trina takes a sip from one of the soda cans, one of last week's she realizes too late. Her mouth puckers from the flat sour taste. She presses her palm against the other two cans, chooses the one whose aluminium is a little cooler, and sips. The sweetness washes away the metallic taste in her mouth. Howdy's disloyalty to Councilman Nicastro was to be expected; that's just political survival. But betraying his own girlfriend suggested an attitude that, should he come to work for The Candidate, might eventually prove dangerous.

'You stalling, Trina?' Howdy asks.

'Okay, you get your raise,' she says. 'Only if what you give me works out to our advantage. I mean, if we chase her mystery days down to find out she's working as an aide in a nursing home, you get zip.'

'Understood.'

Trina hesitates. She's already made up her mind that no matter what happens, she will have to find a way to back out of hiring Howdy. If Nicastro and Lila can't trust him, Cory sure couldn't. 'Okay, James Bond, gimme what you got.'

He chuckles. 'There's more truth to that than you realize. Lila was in the shower while I was rummaging through her purse. You wouldn't believe the shit she keeps in there. Ticket stubs, old grocery lists, enough tampons to plug a leak in the Hoover Dam. Suddenly the shower stops and she's walking down the hall in a towel talking to me about which movie we were going to that night. I swear, I just barely got the damn purse closed by the time she enters the room. I was in a cold sweat.'

'What did you find out?' asks Trina flatly.

'Councilwoman Bennington is due for another disappearance sometime this week.'

'When and where?'

'I don't know where.'

'Do you know when?'

'At two-thirty P.M. She'll be leaving from City Hall.'

'What day?'

He chuckles again. 'Today.'

21

'Ready for lunch?' Barcelona asks.

Trina jumps out of her desk chair as if she's just had a few hundred volts wired through her. Her face looks pale and clammy. 'Is it that time already?'

'Just about.' Barcelona checks her watch. 'I'm twenty minutes early. The freeway traffic was a little light. Can you leave?'

Trina nods absently, stares at her hands, wiggles her fingers.

'You okay, Trina? You're acting kinda goofy.'

'Goofy is in. It's happening, it's now, it's sexy. It's in all the women's magazines.'

Barcelona nods at the telephone. 'You get a hold of Dixie?'

'Not yet. You?'

'Nothing. I'll try again after lunch.'

'Speaking of which.' Trina opens her desk drawer and hands Barcelona a sheet of paper. 'Here's our menu, kiddo. Lots of beef, a couple come with some serious lettuce.' She rubs her fingers together to indicate money. 'Plus one guy I thought of later, Jamison Levy. He's that reporter I told you about.'

'Ah, him.'

'I think he'd be perfect for you. Smart, sexy, talented.'

'What about for you?'

'Too smart, sexy, and talented. I like 'em dumb, homely, and klutzy. They're more grateful that way.'

Barcelona holds the menu in front of her. She's having a little trouble reading the elite typeface without her glasses. 'Diva didn't waste any time. She's already called Harley Buss and arranged a date.'

'I know. I had an early breakfast with her and gave her a copy. She called right from Coco's. I think he was still sleeping.'

Barcelona looks at the typed list of men and their vital statistics, shaking her head. 'I don't know about this. This goes beyond goofy, makes me feel sneaky, like a spy or something.'

'Shit, Barcy,' Trina snaps angrily, 'it's just for fun. We're not trying to screw with your existential dialectical bullshit. Just for fucking fun. You don't want to call, don't fucking call!'

Barcelona is startled by Trina's outburst. Obviously Trina also attended that secret meeting of the world's women, the one she wasn't invited to. She wonders if she went to Trina's house would she find a space pod under the bed. 'What's wrong with you?'

'Nothing. Nothing's wrong. You're just making a big deal out of a simple lark.'

Barcelona picks up one of the soda cans from Trina's desk. She shakes it, listening for any sound of carbonated fizz. Nothing. 'Any of these fresh?' Trina hands her a different can and Barcelona sips. 'Hey, I'm sorry. I'll lighten up if you do. Deal?'

Trina nods. 'Sure.'

The Candidate knocks at the open door and comes in. 'Mail call,' he says. He waves a handful of envelopes and hands them to Trina. 'These are yours,' He turns to Barcelona. 'Hi.'

'Hi.'

'Barcy, this is Cory Meyer, The Man Who Would Be City Councilman. Cory, my friend Barcelona Lee, the famous author of a soon-to-be-released major motion picture.'

He smiles and his lips peel back to unsheathe a magnificent set of teeth that makes Barcelona immediately promise herself to floss and brush more often. His smile is truly dazzling, almost hypnotic. A sense of well-being seems to wash over her. 'Trina has spoken of you,' he says.

'You too,' Barcelona says.

'Yes, I pay her to lie about me.'

His smile dwindles to a grin hiding those teeth and she relaxes a little. He is not at all what she expected. He is not as lifeguard handsome as in the posters, but he is far more attractive. He stands close to both of them, not guarding any personal space that men seem to protect, but neither is he hovering in a sexual way. He's just there. Barcelona has the feeling that she could say anything to him and he wouldn't be shocked. Suddenly she has an image of him in the shower with Trina, standing behind her as she described it, his hips pumping away, steamy water sluicing across their skin, his eyes closed, a low moan at the back of his throat. His hands gripping her hips tightly, pulling her back onto him.

'You okay?' he asks her.

'What?' Barcelona says.

'You look a little flushed. You feeling okay?'

Indeed, Barcelona feels heat across her cheeks and forehead. 'I'm fine,' she insists.

'Look, Barcy, I'm sorry but I have to cancel lunch. Something's come up.' Trina turns to Cory. 'A lead on Carla Bennington's lost weekends. I've got to hurry.' She starts gathering her purse and briefcase.

'Okay,' Barcelona says. 'You want to try for dinner

311

tonight?' She is supposed to see Eric, but she's concerned about Trina's strange behavior.

'Uh, not tonight. This lead may take me out of town. I'll call you. If you reach Dixie, leave a message on my machine.'

'Yeah, okay.'

Trina hustles out of her office without saying good-bye to either of them.

'Well,' The Candidate says, unleashing his smile again. 'How about I take her place for lunch? You've still got to eat, right?'

22

Diva is locked in the trunk of a 1978 Buick. Her head is resting on the spare tire and every once in a while the car drives over a bump and jostles her. Her hands are braced against the trunk lid to keep from getting too badly bruised. A tennis racket handle digs into her hip, but when she shifts away from it her other hip presses against a baseball bat.

She tries not to think about the stuffy heat and sinister darkness of the place. She has never been afraid of the dark, but this darkness is so complete, so final, she is having trouble swallowing. She smells the unmistakable odor of marijuana. She wouldn't be surprised if she rooted under the spare tire to find a Baggie or two of the stuff. The intense heat of the trunk is cooking it just enough to produce a slight scent, like brewing tea. She wishes she were smoking some of it right now.

The car hits a dip and Diva lifts off the bottom of the trunk and slams her head into the lid. She falls back down and her head bounces off the tire, her hip is gouged by the tennis racket. She is getting tired of this shit.

The car slows, turns left, stops. The motor idles. They are here.

There is some muted conversation. The guard is checking IDs. After a couple of minutes she hears the guard say okay and the Buick drives away, making a lot of sharp

313

turns before leaving paved road and rolling slowly across gravel like crunchy granola. The car stops, the motor is shut off, but no one opens the trunk. Minutes pass. Diva is starting to feel spikes of panic piercing deep into her chest. Sweat thick as glycerine rolls along her nose, down her chin, into her ears, behind her neck. Her legs are drenched, She imagines the bright sun outside, the hot rays that are hitting the metal trunk having traveled millions of miles to get here from the sun. Having come all this way just so it could turn the trunk of the Buick into a tin oven and fry her brain. She wonders if the brain literally does fry, the brain juices sizzling against the hot skull bone, steaming like clam chowder soup.

She kicks the lid of the trunk. 'This isn't funny. Let me out.'

'Sssshhhh,' Forge says, pounding the trunk. 'Lost the damn trunk key.'

She isn't sure whether he is serious or merely saying that for the benefit of a passerby who'd heard him talk to the trunk. Either way, she doesn't like it. She begins to doubt the wisdom of all this.

Finally the trunk pops open and Forge stands over her smoking one of her black cigarettes. 'Left your purse in the front seat. How can you smoke this shit?'

Diva quickly climbs out of the trunk and brushes dirt from her knees. She plucks the cigarette from his mouth, takes a drag, then throws it away. The cigarette rolls under his car. 'You hit every goddamn bump on Melrose, you dumb asshole.'

Forge shrugs. 'Melrose needs some serious work.'

She slams the trunk, grabs her purse from the front seat. She opens her compact and sees a tread mark across her cheek. Wetting her fingertips with saliva, she rubs the black tire smudges from her face. 'Let's get going,' she says, dragging Forge along the narrow sidewalks of Paramount Studios. He follows without protest.

Diva went to high school with Forge. Back then all he did was surf and smoke dope. Now he surfs, smokes dope, and builds sets. In high school she sometimes surfed with him, sometimes she smoked dope with him, occasionally she even had sex with him, usually in his converted VW dune buggy. He is only an inch taller than she is, but he has remarkably muscular arms, thick as telephone poles. He wears a faded black Iron Maiden T-shirt with the sleeves torn off to highlight his bulging biceps. On his right arm is a sloppy tattoo of a swastika on a surfboard and the words 'surf nazi' crudely printed under it. In high school Forge was arrested once for beating up some fifteen-year-old kid from Manhattan Beach who'd come down to Huntington Beach to surf. Locals didn't like outsiders stealing their waves.

As they walk, Forge is explaining his job: 'We're building these cool sets now for some sitcom pilot about this family, only they aren't really a family. There's a father, mother, teenage daughter, and teenage son. Only they aren't really related. They're all in the Witness Protection Program, given new identities because they testified against the Mob. The Mob is still looking for them too. But because of budget cuts, the Feds had to stick these four people together as one family, even though none of them knows the other and they don't like each other. Makes for some really funny gags.' He chuckles and Diva can smell the marijuana on his breath.

'Hey, Forge,' Diva says. 'Thanks for sneaking me in, I appreciate it.'

'No prob, Dianne. We done it a couple times at the drive-in, remember?'

'There's Tommy's building. I've got to go.'

'Sure. See ya. Maybe we can get together sometimes, hit the waves at Doheny.'

'Yeah. Thanks again.' Diva cuts across a couple of lawns to a white building in the back of the lot. She passes the elevator and climbs two flights of stairs because she doesn't want anybody to stop her and ask her any questions. Finally she finds the recording studio. Tommy is sitting behind a pair of SL4000-E mixing boards with hundreds of knobs, dials, switches, and lights. Directly in front of him is a plate glass window looking onto the recording room, which is empty except for half a dozen microphones. Above the glass window is a paneled wall with a dozen speakers built in.

Diva opens the door. Tommy doesn't see her or hear her. His back is turned toward her. He is hunched over the control board with earphones on. Occasionally he slides a knob or twists a dial. He hums a few notes, is silent for a few seconds, then hums another snatch of melody.

Diva pats down her wet bangs. They are stringy and matted, pasted to her forehead with sweat. She fusses with them as she walks toward him but finally gives up. She looks the way she looks. That's how it's always been.

Just as she reaches to tap him on the shoulder, he turns around and stares directly into her eyes. This sudden movement startles her and she jumps back with a gasp. 'Tommy!'

He hasn't seen her in over six months, but he doesn't seem especially surprised to see her now. 'Hi, luv.' Tommy speaks in a fake cockney accent, though he is from Akron, Ohio. He spent his junior year of Kent State in London. That was sixteen years ago, but the accent seems to get stronger with each year. His hairline has receded back to the middle of his head, but what is left is long and heavily waxed, pulled straight back into a black samurai knot. He also spent a year in Japan playing lounge shows with his

316

rock band, Fully Lined. For the past five years he's been dubbing sound tracks to movies.

'How'd you get on the studio?' he asks.

'I snuck on.'

He nods, not pleased. 'Security here has been going downhill. None of us is safe. Some writer last month had his show canceled and he charged into some exec's office during a pitch meeting and urinated on the guy's desk. All over his scripts and everything. In front of everyone.'

Diva laughs. 'Maybe he'll get a rewrite credit on the scripts.'

Tommy doesn't laugh. 'It's getting scary.'

Diva tries to look serious. A year ago Tommy would have told this story with a grin and laughed heartily at the end. He would have said pissed instead of urinated. The fired writer would have been the hero of the story.

'Listen, Tommy, I need a favor,' Diva says.

Tommy sighs and nods grimly as if he's come to expect those words. They've known each other for six years. He used to mix some of the commercials Diva sang on. They became friendly. They went out a few times. He banged her in the men's room at a Gordon Lightfoot concert. She straddled him while he sat on the toilet. People who heard him moaning must have thought he was passing a gallstone. That's how she got the job singing a mock-Bette Midler rendition of 'Do You Want Some Plants' for that chain of florists. Tommy got her the job. It was never stated that she had to screw him to get the job, but she knew, even if he didn't.

Tommy removes his headphones. 'What favor?'

'I'm writing a song. It's almost done. It just needs some polishing, sweetening really. Can you tinker with it for me?'

He looks her over, his heavy-lidded eyes checking her out from tits to toes and back, deciding what's in it for

317

him, whether he even wants it from her again. If he does, Diva will give it. Not because of what he can do for her, but because in some strange way she is flattered that her body, puffed and flabby as it is, still can wield some power.

'I'm busy now, but I might take a look at it if you come over tonight, luv.'

She remembers her date with Harley Buss, the department chairman at Barcy's school. He had such a nice voice on the phone, charming and funny. 'How about tomorrow night?' she offers.

'Busy. Stuff to do tomorrow.' He reaches back and smooths his Japanese ponytail. He looks at his watch. 'We could look it over now, I suppose. We don't have much time.' He reaches over and strokes her bare thigh

'Sure,' she says. 'Whatever.'

Walking out of the lot, she thinks she sees Tom Cruise. He is walking across the lawn with a young woman executive-type who is at least six inches taller, four of the inches from her black patent high heels. She is doing most of the talking and he nods and sometimes laughs, says a few words, then listens intently. At one point he stoops and picks something off the sidewalk, a coin it looks like, shows it to the woman, then pockets it. Later she shows him a piece of paper, appears to read it aloud to him. Afterward, she leans over and kisses his forehead playfully. He laughs and looks embarrassed.

Diva starts to follow them, but they turn a corner and disappear behind some shrubbery.

She walks the two blocks to her '71 VW van with the imitation Peter Max psychedelic flowers painted all over it. She bought the van from some ex-hippie folk singer who'd moved to L.A. to become the next Donovan and made ends meet by playing backup on radio commercials. He was very proud of the fact that he'd once spent ten days in a Boston jail for wearing a patch of the American flag on the butt of his jeans. He ended up selling everything he owned to open a little health food restaurant with a girl he met in a movie line in Westwood. Now they own a trendy chain of restaurants throughout the Valley.

Once inside, she immediately lights up a black cigarette to burn the taste of Tommy's come out of her mouth. He was the saltiest semen she's ever tasted, like anchovies rolled in salt or something. The cigarette helps.

She takes a deep drag and blows it against the windshield. The smoke curls back on itself like a horizontal atomic cloud. She reaches into her purse and takes her song out. Tommy scribbled a few unintelligible notes in the margins of the lyrics, suggested a few chord progressions, but otherwise wasn't much help. She knew he wouldn't be. But Tommy has always fancied himself a deep-thinking songwriter, especially after his trips to Europe and Japan. His songs suck and everybody knows it except Tommy. However, Diva knew that by asking him to help, she had him hooked. He would try, fail, and then like a man who has just gone limp during sex, try to make it up some other way. And that's what Diva had actually come for. She needed a sound engineer, and that's what Tommy was exceptionally good at. He promised to help her mix her song when she was ready to record, maybe even get her a break on some studio time from a friend of his.

Diva pulled the van into traffic. With Barcy's loan and a few more favors, she should be able to cut a demo by the end of the month. Maybe sooner if she could finish the damn song.

Freeway traffic isn't too bad and she gets back to Balboa in a little more than an hour. As soon as she enters her apartment she dials Dixie's number again. Still no answer.

Even Dixie's phone answering machine isn't on. Diva calls Barcy at school, but she's gone. She calls Trina at work, but Trina has left already too. She calls the police station that Dixie works out of and asks for her, but of course she isn't there. That was dumb. Even if Dixie is okay, she would still be undercover at that high school. And she certainly wouldn't be using her real name. Diva considers driving over to the school and looking around, but that's what started the trouble in the first place. Finally she pushes the phone away and goes to the bathroom thinking about her date. She checks her face in the mirror for any pimples or blackheads.

23

'I never use urinals. Never,' The Candidate says. He takes another sip of his gumbo soup while Barcelona laughs.

'Then how do you pee?' she asks.

'Same as you. I sit. Men's bathrooms are never as crowded as women's, never a line. Guys go to the bathroom, they're in a hurry to get out again. They walk in, step up to the urinal, don't look to the right or left, do their business, and rush out.'

'Like sex,' Barcelona says.

'There's a distinct similarity. More like a grocery store express line. However, unlike after sex, I've noticed here men rarely even bother to wash their hands.'

Barcelona pulls a French roll in half and butters one side. 'Sounds very efficient.'

'Scary is what it is for most guys. The men's room can be traumatic. Guys are afraid that if they take too long, other guys will think they like it in there, and why would they like it in there unless they were homosexual. The big H. A lot of guys think it's something you can catch, like cancer, only worse. An alien force, not of this world.'

'But you're not afraid?'

'Terrified. Not of catching it, but certainly I don't want to be labeled as one. It would ruin my political career on the spot.'

'I had no idea male bowel movements were so

321

traumatic.' Barcelona shakes her head, grinning. 'I don't usually talk about urinals at lunch. How did we get on this subject anyway?'

'Your fault. You asked how voters can be certain I'm honest. And I told you, I never use urinals. I don't piss standing up.'

'Maybe I'm a little slow today, but I don't get the connection.'

The Candidate takes the other half of her French roll and runs it around the bottom of his empty soup bowl. 'Okay, my reasons for urinating the way I do are purely practical. First, when you stand and pee into a toilet bowel, the urine sometimes hits the water with such force, it splashes out of the bowel on your shins or trousers. Same with a urinal, it hits that hard porcelain and bounces right back at you. Second, when you're done peeing, there's always a few more drops that keep dripping out. You have to shake the thing a couple of times, and sometimes you get those drops on yourself. Both of these problems are eliminated by sitting.'

'That's very interesting,' Barcelona says. 'But how does that make you an honest politician?'

'In prison, the toughest and meanest convicts force the weakest inmates into becoming their sex slaves. They treat them like women, make them dress up like women, act like women, even got to the bathroom like women. They're forced to sit to pee. So if I went to prison and they saw me sitting to pee on my own, they'd be all over me. That's why I have to remain an honest politician. I can't afford to go to jail.'

Barcelona laughs. They have been chatting for almost an hour, during the walk to the restaurant, while waiting to order. He asked her a lot about herself, her writing and teaching, seemed impressed by both. He never looked for an opening to talk about his own achievements. He waited until she asked and even then made a joke of the whole thing. Cory Meyers is as charming as Trina had described him. Smart, witty, and attractive. She doesn't trust anyone that together.

'You want me to lose, don't you?' he says suddenly.

Barcelona is about to make a joke, but she sees by his expression that he is serious. 'Why would you think that?'

The waiter arrives with their orders. Australian lobster tail for Barcelona and soft shell crabs for The Candidate. Both are drinking iced tea.

Once the waiter has finished fussing about, clearing plates and sweeping bread crumbs, wishing a hearty appetite and complimenting Barcelona on the loveliness of her silk blouse, he leaves and they are alone together. This time there is an awkward intimacy to their meal. Like a long-married couple on the verge of a fight.

'You haven't answered me,' Barcelona says. 'Why would you think I want you to lose?'

'That's not a denial.'

'That's not an answer.'

He waves his napkin in surrender. 'That wasn't fair of me,' he says. 'Forget it.'

'Don't pull that "forget it" crap.'

He chuckles. 'You sound like Trina now.'

Being compared with Trina right now is somehow annoying. Usually she'd be flattered by the comparison, but not now. 'Maybe she sounds like me?'

'Okay, okay. Here's my two-bit, pocket guide to psychological analysis.' He leans back in his chair and wipes his mouth with his napkin. 'There are two reasons you want me to lose. First, you want me to lose because I'm a man running against a woman. A woman who is attractive and single like yourself. Highly accomplished, like yourself.'

'So far I like your description, if not your reasoning.'

'Who's roughly in the same age range.'

'Careful.'

He laughs. 'Give or take a decade. Also, Carla Bennington has done a good job in office.'

'You make a pretty good case for her.'

'She's a good person, as far as we know.'

'Ah, the dirt that Trina's trying to dig up. The fuel of politics. Considering what you just said about her, why should I vote for you, if I were in your district?'

'I think I can do a better job.'

'Because you're smarter, younger, manlier?'

'Because I'm more ambitious. Everyone knows I have ambitions beyond this city, maybe even beyond this state. People like to have friends on the rise because they may need a powerful friend later down the road. That makes them a lot more yielding today to proposals I may have, more willing to compromise. And for me to have a shot at higher office, I need to really prove myself in this office. I need results. People know I'll work my butt off to get those results.'

Barcelona has hardly touched her lobster tail. She stabs her fork into it, twists thoughtfully. 'Say you're right about the first reason. Maybe I would prefer to see a woman in there, even if you are more ambitious and therefore a little more effective. What's the other reason?'

He looks straight into her eyes and Barcelona recoils as if he's struck her across the cheek. 'Because you know I made love to Trina.'

Barcelona looks away from him, concentrates on her lobster tail, digging out the meat with an eye surgeon's precision. She can feel his gaze on her, waiting. She doesn't like the way this lunch is going anymore. She speaks without looking up. 'I'm not a moralizer, Mr. Meyers. Trina's a big girl.'

But Barcelona realizes The Candidate is right. Despite his charm and intelligence, she has been disapproving of him, partially for the first reason he mentioned. Going after a woman in a position in which there are already too few women saddened her, made her feel vulnerable. But mostly she disapproves for the second reason: fucking Trina in the shower from behind when he's got a wife at home. She recognizes her own hypocrisy in this matter. She's been humping with Eric while his young wife waits at home for him to finish his run so they can go grocery shopping. But she's not running for public office, she reminds herself. She sighs at her own shallow rationalizing. 'I'm not a moralizer,' Barcelona says again.

'All of us are moralizers. Some of us would rather not be, but we are nevertheless. Judging people is what we do best. I'm not going to make any excuses. Really it's none of your business except that Trina told you and for some reason I haven't figured out yet your opinion of me seems to matter. It shouldn't. You're not even from my district.'

'I-I don't . . .' She trails off, not certain what she was going to say. She shrugs, looks up at his face. He smiles at her, a low-wattage smile that only shows the tips of his teeth.

'Morality is such a slippery thing,' he says. 'Like trying to grab a handful of wiggling eels.'

'You getting folksy on me, old-timer?'

He laughs. It sounds melodic, as if he were humming a tune while laughing. 'We'll keep it mathematical. Let's take two guys, one looks like Warren Beatty . . .'

'Too old.'

'Rob Lowe.'

'A baby.'

'Mel Gibson.'

'Perfect.'

He takes a deep breath and continues. 'All right. One guy looks like Mel Gibson, the other looks like Dom DeLuise. Now, our Mel lookalike has committed adultery twice, but our Dom clone never has. Who's less moral? Numerically speaking?'

'You really want me to answer?'

'Yes. It's a test.'

'I know it's a trick, but for the sake of your test, I'll say Mel.'

'Okay. Mel is less moral because he slept with two women and Dom hasn't slept with any. But suppose Mel, charismatic animal that he is, has had a hundred offers, gorgeous women with shapely legs, firm asses, Ph.D.s, M.D.s, BVDs, every kind of sexy woman you can imagine. They come on to him constantly. They hand him their panties with their room keys taped to the crotch. He's turned down ninety-eight of them, each requiring extraordinary willpower. Now Dom, nice guy that he may be, has only had one offer from a matronly sort with false teeth and gin breath. He turned her down easily. Mel's fidelity has been tested a hundred times and he's passed ninety-eight times. Dom has been tested only once and he passed once. Who's the more moral?'

Barcelona chews her lobster tail and shakes her head. 'You're a lawyer, right?'

'Yes. Is that another prejudice you have?'

'Yes.'

'Rise above it. Come on, what's your answer? Who is more moral? The man who has proven it ninety-eight times, or the man who has proven it only once?'

'Who's the murderer?' Barcelona says. 'The man who is angry enough to kill a hundred times and on the hundred and first time does, or the man who gest angry once and does nothing? The first guy resisted a hundred times. But there's still a dead body.'

The Candidate grins. 'Very good.'

'Not really. It's a little truth with a lot of bullshit, just like yours. But, okay, I see the truth in what you say.

326

Logically, you're right. But sometimes logic is cold comfort to those who get hurt. Mel's wife isn't going to clap him on the back like a hockey goalie and say, "Way to go, honey. Great goal-keeping. Only two scored." She's going to cry herself to sleep for weeks.'

The Candidate looks around, then lowers his voice. 'That's not my situation at all, as I'm sure Trina explained.'

'Look, it's really none of my business. Really.'

Barcelona shovels some rice pilaf onto her fork and eats. She is conscious of each bite, her teeth crushing each rice kernel, mashing them all together with her saliva until they form a starchy lump. She doesn't want to swallow but can see no graceful way to spit the mess out. She swallows.

Damn, everything had been so light and amusing at first; why did it suddenly turn serious? Why did he feel it was necessary to justify himself? Especially to her. She hasn't exactly been Mother Theresa. Yet, she did act superior, let him squirm unnecessarily.

What was going on lately? All her women friends were acting like maniacs. Like sun-crazed survivors of a plane crash who've wandered through the scorched desert for days without food or water. Trina was remote and brusque; Dixie's disappeared; Diva's charging at windmills. And Barcelona's screwing her ex-boyfriend, her *married* ex-boyfriend.

The waiter glides up to the table with a big silver tray filled with pastries. He smiles hugely and bows, offering the tray. 'Dessert?' he asks. 'Everything is guaranteed nonfattening.' Then he laughs and laughs until Barcelona can hear the loose tip change jingling in his pockets.

'There's an epidemic of trench mouth among editors in New York,' Grief tells Barcelona. 'I heard this last week from another agent there.'

'Trench mouth?'

327

'It's an infection soldiers in the trenches in World War One used to get. I don't know much about it except they've all got bad breath.' She chuckles. 'They're all going around to these power meetings talking movie rights and sucking Breathsavers.'

Grief is sitting behind her desk nibbling on Mrs. Fields cookies. She reaches into the little red and white bag, breaks off a corner of cookie, and eats it with tiny bird bites. When she finishes with one piece, she breaks off a new piece. She never takes a whole cookie out of the bag.

Barcelona's finished screenplay sits on Grief's desk. With the hand that isn't breaking off chunks of white chocolate cookies, Grief leafs through the manuscript. 'Looks good, Barcy. Very professional.'

'Let's hope it reads as well as it looks.'

She waves her hand. 'It will, it will.' Grief is not a worrier, that much Barcelona knows. When they first met years ago, Grief had told Barcelona that her motto in life was the same as Alfred E. Neuman's in *Mad* magazine: 'What, me worry?' She'd had a lifetime of chest-pounding and hair-pulling from her father, an activist lawyer who'd worked on Ethel and Julius Rosenberg's defense right up to their execution at Sing Sing prison. Taking the defeat very hard, he'd moved his family—wife and three daughters, Mary, Laura, and Susan—to a Vermont commune long before hippies began doing it. He legally changed the daughters' names to Felicity, Hope, and Grief, what he considered the cornerstones of a balanced life. After a couple of years of this his wife gave him an ultimatum: either they moved back to New York together or she and the children moved back without him. They moved back together and he began defending writers against Joseph McCarthy's accusations of Communist party affiliations. Which is how Grief came to know so many writers when she decided to become a literary agent. Her sisters changed their names back to Mary and Laura. But Grief liked the attention her name brought her.

Grief brushes cookie crumbs from her desk and reaches for the phone. She flips through the Rolodex, dials, asks for Roger Carlyle. 'Roger? Grief. Barcelona Lee has delivered the screenplay of *Live Wires* . . . I just finished reading it. It's terrific. Tell you the truth, I'm sorry we made an agreement with you before she wrote it. This thing is worth a helluva lot more.' Grief listens, laughs, rolls her eyes for Barcelona's sake. 'Fine . . . Uh-huh . . . Good-bye.' She hangs up.

'So?' Barcelona asks.

'He's sending a messenger over for it. He'll read it tonight, take it over to Lynda Kramer's people tomorrow.'

'What if he doesn't like it?'

Grief's smile is sharp, almost cruel. 'Listen, honey, chances are he won't even read the whole thing before he gives it to them. He'll read just enough to know what the hell we're talking about. Even if he did read it all he wouldn't know if it were any good or not. All he knows is Lynda Kramer is interested. Even if he hated it he'd take it to her. So relax. His opinion isn't worth shit.'

Barcelona looks under Grief's desk and sees the stocking-covered bunion poking out of her agent's foot. A pair of discarded and very expensive beige pumps lie on their sides next to the afflicted foot. She is fascinated by the growth, wants to ask questions, get down on her hands and knees and jab at the thing as if it were a strange reptile, see what it will do. Crazy. But she feels a little crazy after her lunch with Cory Meyers, The Candidate. Everything had been going so smoothly, the height of sophistication. Witty banter, casual flirting, attentive waiter, everything like in a Cary Grant movie. She was Ingrid Bergman, of course. Then he got serious and ruined it all. After that, there was a silent dessert and a stilted, awkward walk back to his campaign headquarters. Why couldn't he have stuck to the script?

'When do you think we'll hear from Lynda Kramer?' Barcelona asks.

Grief shrugs, rubs her bunion against the carpet. 'Never know. Maybe tomorrow, maybe not for six weeks. Depends.'

'Depends. That covers a multitude of sins.'

Grief reaches into her Mrs. Fields bag but finds no more cookies. She crumbles the bag and drops it in her wastebasket. She seems antsy and Barcelona rises to leave. 'I should be going. Don't want to hit the freeway rush hour.'

Grief nods. 'Relax, lamb. We'll hear when we hear. I feel very good about this, very good. I have psychic abilities, did I ever tell you?'

'No.'

'Well I do. Hunches, feelings, they're almost always right. I have a feeling now. About this script.'

'Maybe it's gas.'

Grief smiles. 'I'll call soon as I hear.'

Barcelona gets on the freeway heading south. Traffic is starting to knot up. A few miles later cars have slowed to a crawl and she sees why. An accident. A green Yugo is crushed against the steel railing that divides the north- and southbound freeways. The front end of the car is flattened back to the windshield. The driver is lying by the side of the road. Paramedics have a neck brace on him and are bandaging his head. Both his pant legs are shredded as if he'd been attacked by a tiger. Blood soaks both legs. Barcelona thinks she sees a small hole in the driver's window and she wonders if this is another freeway shooting.

She turns on the radio and listens to the Zombies' 'Tell Her No.' A few yards past the accident, traffic speed picks up and soon she is zipping back toward Orange County and home. The news comes on the radio and the announcer says that the Department of Defense Maintenance Award has been given to Marine Heavy Helicopter Squadron 466, which services 16 CH-53E Super Stallion helicopters. The general making the award reaffirmed his dedication to the helicopters despite the crashes that have plagued them. Also, David Bowie may be getting married again.

The rest of the drive home Barcelona wonders what she will write next. Now that the script is done she should jump right into something new, maybe another script. She has lots of ideas tacked up on her bulletin board. She considers each one in detail as she whisks past the exit signs.

It is early in the afternoon when Barcelona pulls into her garage. She sees Eric's car parked on the curb near the mailboxes. She's pleased. This day has been unsettling and all she wants to do now is crawl into bed with Eric and be held.

As she hurries out of the garage lugging her briefcase, she runs into Dave walking his Lhasa apso, Foxy. He's carrying a brown lunch bag that looks pretty full.

'Hi,' Dave says. He has a strained look on his face, as if he can't remember her name, knows it's something odd, wants to say something like Berlin or Budapest, but just settles for hi.

'Hi, Dave.' She bends over and pets Foxy's moppy head. Foxy licks her hand. His tongue is rough and slimy.

'Just finishing up our little walk, eh Foxy?' Dave says. He reaches into his pocket and pulls out the garage door opener. The big wooden door swings open with a groan. 'How's it going with you?' he asks but keeps walking toward the garage. Barcelona is forced to walk with him or seem rude.

'Fine. You?'

331

He nods, shrugs. 'Foxy and I manage.' He smiles. He sets the lunch bag containing Foxy's shit down on the floor, and pries the lid off a huge plastic garbage can. Inside the can are dozens of similar lunch bags. The smell hits Barcelona like a bat across the skull. She winces and cups her hand around her nose. Dave dumps the new bag inside and closes the lid.

'Strong stuff, eh?' he says with a grin.

'Potent.'

He stoops down and scratches Foxy's ears. 'This fella eats pretty healthy. Don't ya, boy?' Foxy flops onto the garage floor and rolls onto his back. Dave scratches his stomach.

Having done her neighborly duty, Barcelona turns to leave when she sees something leaning against the wall at the back of Dave's garage that startles her. She walks toward it. 'Jesus,' she says. 'Where'd you get this?'

He follows her. 'Something, isn't it? Must've taken her three years to complete. Everything had to be just right. Everything's to scale, you know.'

Barcelona stands in front of it. 'Jesus.'

'It's in sections now,' he says, gesturing at the different parts leaning against the walls. 'But when it was all together, the thing measured twelve by twenty-five feet. It was a son of a bitch to lug around, I'm telling you. But it's accurate. Totally to scale and looks just like Elvis's real Graceland.'

Foxy sniffs at a pile of boards and a tiny mouse runs out. Foxy watches it without chasing.

Barcelona reaches down and touches the miniature fence that guards the entrance to this miniature Graceland. Woven into the wire design is an outline of Elvis strumming a guitar, surrounded by musical notes. 'It's fantastic,' Barcelona says.

'Over here's the mansion.' He pulls out another board

with tiny trees and fake grass surrounding a huge mansion with white columns. 'Darlene spent all her spare time working on this. You'd be surprised how hard it is to find a model of just the right Cadillac that fits into the scale.' He points to one of the red Cadillacs glued to the painted driveway.

'I never knew she did this.'

'She didn't like to brag.'

Barcelona looks at Dave, but he is not smiling. That wasn't a joke.

'She was planning to start in on Elvis's childhood home in Tupelo, Mississippi next. Before she hung herself.' He stoops next to the mansion and strokes out one of the white columns. Foxy comes over and sniffs at his shoes. 'She did it on Elvis's birthday. I like to think that was some comfort to her.'

Barcelona thanks him for showing her the models and says goodbye. She walks briskly along the sidewalk, her heels echoing in the greenbelt. Larry the cat sticks his head out of a neighbor's bush, sees it's her, and ducks back in. Barcelona hurries into the apartment, anxious to see Eric. She hopes he will be waiting by the door.

He isn't.

She opens the door and finds Luna sitting on the couch reading the newspaper. When she sees Barcelona she looks up with a friendly smile and says, 'Hi. I hope you don't mind, I let myself in with Eric's key.'

24

'Can you squeeze me in?' Trina asks, leaning over the counter.

Marlene sits at the desk behind the counter and runs her white and orange striped fingernail along the appointment book grid. Neatly printed names fill every fifteen-minute slot. Marlene frowns. 'May take a few minutes of juggling.'

'I appreciate it. Whoa, Marlene, that's some nail polish.'

Marlene wiggles her fingernails. 'Leopard stripes. Matches my underwear. Whatever pattern my panties are, that's how I do my nails, that way Gary always knows. I read about it in *Working Woman* or something. It's supposed to keep the passion fires alive in a marriage.'

'Does it?'

Marlene shrugs. 'Sure. Especially when we're out with other couples. All through dinner Gary keeps staring at my fingernails. It drives him nuts, as if I were sitting there in front of everybody in nothing but my panties. Makes him hot as a toaster. You should try it.'

Trina shows her own ragged, chipped nails. 'These already reflect the condition of my underwear.'

Marlene laughs. She leans forward and lowers her voice to a conspiratory whisper. 'I'm glad you dropped in, Trina. Doctor could use the break. These kids this morning are a particularly bratty bunch.'

'I'll try to act my age then,' Trina smiles.

Marlene chuckles and rolls across the cubicle on her customized office chair. She's been running this office for the five years it's been open and Trina has yet to see her get up out of that chair.

Trina sits in one of the waiting room chairs, Swedish modern design, blond wood and bright red cushions. She doesn't want to think about why she is here so she passes the time studying her fellow patients and their parents. One redheaded girl about seven has a gauze patch the size of a folded washcloth taped to her cheek. A brownish stain has seeped through. She is sitting quietly next to her mother looking miserable. The mother holds her hand and whispers cheerfully to her. Another little girl closer to ten or eleven is chattering away to her father. She wants to know if she'll have to go back to school after the doctor's done or if they can go out to lunch and maybe shopping. The father has his leather brief-case balanced across his knees and reminds her that if she is too sick to go to school, she's too sick to go shopping. Then he leans over and kisses her on the fore-head.

Trina gets up and walks to the magazines spread out on the big circular blond wood table. *Highlights* seem to be the most popular, followed by *Sesame Street* and *Life*. She grabs one of the tattered *Highlights* and returns to her chair. She leafs through it until she finds her favorite puzzle, the drawing crammed with hidden objects you have to find. She locates the stove, the baseball glove, the cow, then loses interest.

She walks back to the counter. 'Marlene, can I use your phone?'

'Sure, Trina. Come on through.'

The door buzzes and Trina walks through. Marlene slides the black telephone across the desk. 'Leave your quarter on the desk,' she kids and rolls away on her chair to file some folders.

Trina dials Rob's office.

'Rob Barre,' he answers. Brisk and businesslike.

'Rob, it's me.'

Cold silence. She can hear the clacking of his computer as he continues to type. Rob is a partner in one of Orange County's fastest-growing advertising agencies. He's the one who came up with the 'Wouldn't you like to sleep with a cold Fisch tonight?' campaign for Fisch air conditioners. After the divorce he claimed he got the idea from sleeping with her. Finally he speaks, sounding like a recording. 'Trina, I'm working.'

'I know, I'm sorry to disturb you—'

'Uh oh, you want something.' The computer clacking stops.

'I'd like you to take Karyn for the evening. I have to go out of town. It's all very sudden.'

'Everything all right?' His voice lowers with concern. She feels that familiar stab of loss in her stomach.

'Yes,' she says. 'It's just business.'

'This is only the second time you've ever asked me to take Karyn when it wasn't my turn. The first time your mother had surgery.'

Trina uncurls a backward kink in the coiled telephone wire. She wouldn't be giving Karyn to Rob now if she didn't think she had to track down this Carla Bennington mystery. Not for The Candidate's sake or anything so noble, but for her own piece of mind. She's been acting like such a flake lately she needs to prove her old reporter's instincts, her old do-or-die professionalism is still there. That she isn't yet ready for menopause and bridge clubs. 'Really, it's just business. Unexpected. If you can't do it—'

'I can do it. Don't overplay your hand. Want me to pick her up from school?'

'Yes. Tell her I'll pick her up tomorrow from school. Don't let her fake a bellyache in the morning and stay home.'

'Don't worry,' Rob says. 'I can take care of my own daughter.'

'Right, sorry. I appreciate this, Rob.'

'You can owe me.' He chuckles. 'Anything else?'

'No. Thanks again.'

'Bye.' He hangs up.

Trina clears the line and gets another dial tone. She dials Dixie's home again and still gets no answer. Again she considers calling the police but decides against it.

Marlene rolls up to Trina's feet. 'Doctor said to hide you out in number five. She doesn't want anybody to see you. Kids don't like it if they know their pediatrician is treating an adult.' She winks. 'Giving comfort to the enemy.'

Trina wonders when and how Marlene spoke with the doctor. She hasn't left this little reception area and Trina hadn't heard her even speak. 'I know the way, thanks,' Trina says and walks down the hall. She passes one tiny blue room where one of the doctor's young female assistants is helping a little boy up on the examining table. The little boy holds a rubber sea gull and is pulling at its wings. The wings stretch and snap back in place. The boy has a small scrape on the side of his cheek. 'Looks like you had a nasty fall, Peter,' the assistant says. Peter nods and stretches the gull's wings.

Trina passes another examination room, this one yellow, and sees another teenage assistant weighing a skinny little girl about nine.

'This is wrong!' the little girl says adamantly. 'I don't weigh this much.'

'The scale is the best there is, Lisa,' the teen assistant says sweetly.

337

'Nuh uh. The one we have home is better. It has a digital display that lights up in red letters. Not stupid weights you gotta slide around. This is stupid.'

The assistant is wearing a pink blouse and blue skirt, the same cheerful uniform as the other assistant and Marlene. She pats the girl's blond head and smiles patiently. 'This is a very good scale, Lisa.'

'It says I weigh too much. I don't weigh this much. It's off three pounds.'

The teen assistant suddenly sees Trina and comes over to the open door. She looks embarrassed, as if she's been caught mistreating the child. She whispers, 'We see this all the time. Parents with little girls sometimes set their scales back a few pounds.' Then she smiles. 'But then, so do I.' She giggles and shuts the door.

Trina continues on to room #5. This room is white with purple stripes. She puts her purse on the examining table and looks out the fourth-story window to the rest of Fashion Island below. She stares between two tall buildings made of white stone like sand and blue glass to reflect the Pacific Ocean half a mile away. The ocean is calm this morning. Spring fog blurs the horizon; she can barely make out a dark shadow in the fog that is Catalina Island. She leans her forehead against the window glass and looks down. Her eyes rake the sidewalks and parking lots, hoping she'll spot Dixie still wandering around. But this is the medical section of Fashion Island. This is where the damaged shoppers gather to be repaired.

Suddenly the door bursts open and Dr. Whitney Hempel-Oakes rushes in. Her right hand grapples in her white jacket pocket for a pack of cigarettes, sticks one in her mouth, and lights it. She sucks in a deep breath and blows it out slowly. 'Fuck,' she says. 'That's good.'

Trina grins. 'Still trying to hide your smoking from parents, huh?'

338

'First it was my parents, now it's my patients' parents.'

'I think you get off on having something to hide. I always longed to have some dark secret.'

'You and me don't know shit about secrets,' Dr. Whitney Hempel-Oakes says bitterly. She reaches into her other deep pocket and takes out a wire coat hanger that's been pretzeled into a strange squiggly shape. She throws it on the examining table next to Trina's purse. Then she sits down on a metal stool and leans back against the wall. 'Guess where I got that?'

'You lock yourself out of your car?'

'I just examined a twelve-year-old girl who sneaked it in under her sweater. She wanted me to show her how to use it.'

Trina makes a face. 'Jesus, you're kidding.'

'I wish. Turns out she jacked off some boy her age in his folks' swimming pool. Some of his come floated up and touched her face. She's been terrified ever since that she's pregnant. Hasn't eaten or slept for two weeks. Mother thought she had mono or something.'

'I thought the schools taught them about stuff like that now.'

Whitney sucks hard on the cigarette and shakes her head. Smoke leaks out her nostrils and mouth. 'Conservative backlash.'

'More like backwash.'

'The little girl had heard something about using a coat hanger to abort, but she didn't know how to do it. She saw some cop show on TV, some guy picking a lock, so she twisted the hanger into the shape of a lock pick. Thought she'd work on herself the same way.' The doctor stubs out the cigarette on the inside of the trash can. Without getting up, she rolls her stool over to the sink and washes her hand. 'So, what's up with you?'

'You mean generally, or why did I come to see you?'

339

'Both.' She opens a drawer, removes a small sample bottle of Scope, washes some around in her mouth and spits it into the sink. 'Well?'

Trina begins to describe her symptoms. The forgetfulness. Loss of ambition. Paralysis. She tries not to exaggerate, but as she listens to herself it all sounds so lame, so wimpy. She's worried that Whitney will think she's a whiner.

But Whitney listens carefully, her attention focused on every word Trina says. She has always been that way, since they were college roommates. Trina doesn't have a regular doctor, except her gynecologist. Whenever there's any other kind of medical problem she comes directly to Whitney, despite her friend's specialty in pediatrics. Seven years ago, Whitney wasn't even a doctor. She was a socialite. A tennis-playing, party-throwing member of the elite with a B.A. in art history. She'd married right out of college, a man who was darkly handsome, sexy, and wealthy. He bought her an expensive house in Big Canyon and gave her the full-time job of hostess. They vacationed often in exotic places. In her spare time, of which there was plenty, Whiteney enrolled in the occasional art history class at the University of California at Irvine. On a lark, she took the school's aptitude test which revealed that she would make a good physician. She told her husband, suggesting it might be fun to become a doctor. He suggested it would be more fun if she slept with him and his secretary, the three of them together.

After the divorce, Whitney enrolled in medical school, became a doctor, and opened her own practice. Then she married another doctor in the same building, a neurologist who is every bit as handsome, sexy, and wealthy as her former husband. Not that she ever went looking for wealthy men. Somehow they just found her.

'I'm worried,' Trina says. 'Like maybe I have the

Epstein-Barr virus. The symptoms sound the same.'

Whitney smiles and it is as if someone opened a curtain in a dark room. A smile to rival even The Candidate's. Her blond hair is short on the top, teased up into a feathery heap. The sides are long and straight, hugging her neck to her collar. Her figure is as perfect as her face, both of which remain sexy and youthful. Her eyes and mouth are oversized, her nose undersized. The effect is wholesome, doll-like. During college she managed to earn some extra money modeling, though it was not a career she actively sought. A big-time fashion photographer on campus for a shoot spotted her kicking a broken vending machine and hired her. Early in their relationship Trina had been jealous of Whitney's spooky good luck. She'd even taken to calling her, instead of Jewish American Princess, Voodoo American Princess. There was no other explanation for her good fortune except the supernatural. But after a while Trina got used to it, realized that it wasn't anything special that Whitney did that brought on this luck. It just was. She had a magic aura, the Midas touch.

'I don't know,' Trina says. 'For a couple days I was even convinced I was pregnant.'

'Did you want to be?'

'Not really.'

Whitney raises a blond eyebrow.

'A little,' Trina admits.

'Your period normal?'

'Yes. But I've been feeling this way for more than a month now. I mean it, Whit, I'm starting to get a little scared.'

'Of what?'

'Jesus, you want me to name the possibilities? AIDS for one.'

Whitney shook her head. 'You're okay there. I ran a blood test on you the last time you were in.'

'You did? You didn't tell me.'

'No, I didn't.'

Trina looks into Whitney's large eyes. She isn't sure whether she should be angry at the invasion of privacy or relieved with the results. She settles for relief. 'What about Epstein-Barr? Do I need tests or something?'

Whitney rolls her stool over to Trina and picks at some bran muffin crumbs on Trina's beige blouse. 'You know better than to wear whites. Not with the way you eat.'

'Are you listening to me, Whitney? I'm goddamn worried here.'

Whitney rolls her stool back against the wall and leans back. She fishes out another cigarette and lights it. 'You're overreacting, Trina. It's probably just stress.'

'Stress. Shit, I could've gotten that much from my mother. I want an expert medical opinion.'

'You're getting one. I'll run a blood test if it'll make you feel better. Hell, I'll get your piss and hair analyzed while I'm at it. But it'll probably come down to the same thing. Tension, stress. You're coming to the end of a long and difficult campaign. Your body's put up with a lot of abuse from you over the past year. Now it sees the end coming and it's starting to limp toward the finish line.'

Trina frowns. This is not the kind of advice she's come for. She wanted to be told that there was a definite physical reason for her body shutting down at times; an identifiable physical ailment with a tricky Latin name they could fight with equally Latin wonder drugs. She did not want to hear that it was all due to her own weak mind, her shortcomings. 'Don't you even want to take my temperature or blood pressure? I mean, it could be Epstein-Barr, right?'

'Yuppie Flu? There are some actual cases of something that may indeed be Epstein-Barr, but it's doubtful you're one of them. Every decade has it own disease, just like its own music or slang, dude. The Fifties had iron-poor blood

342

thanks to "Ted Mack's Amateur Hour" talking about it every week to sell Geritol. Then hypoglycemia, low blood sugar, got blamed for everything. For a while after that it was thyroid conditions quickly followed by PMS. Epstein-Barr is the vogue disease now. There's a whole movement of doctors that blames candida for the problem.'

'Speak English.'

'Candida is a yeast that lives on the body's mucous membrane. The next medical witch-hunt will probably be after the human B-cell lymphotropic virus, HBLV, a member of the ever-growing, ever-fun herpes family, like Epstein-Barr.'

'Maybe I have herpes.'

'Have you had any lesions, itching, burning while you urinate?'

'No. What about myasthenia gravis?'

'Where'd you hear about that?'

'Magazine. Some soap star has it.'

'That's a neuromuscular disease. You don't have it.' Whitney smiles. 'Sorry, you're clean. You need to slow down, but I know you won't, not until the campaign is over. Meantime, delegate responsibilities to others. Don't go looking for crises. You used to get this way every semester during finals, don't you remember?'

'No, I don't. I remember studying my ass off while you barely glanced at a book.'

'I had an easier major.'

Trina shakes her head. 'What happened to the good old days when doctors always had a disease or two they were ready to pin you with. And of course a prescription to cure it.'

'I can give you tranquilizers if you want. They might take the edge off.'

'No, I need my edge to get through this.' Trina picks up the twisted wire hanger and twists it more. 'Next time,

343

though, I expect a lot more medical mumbo jumbo. Instrument trays, rubber hammers on my knees, the whole bit. You're not the only pediatrician in the book you know.'

Whitney laughs, the cigarette smoke chugging out of her mouth. 'Look in the book next year and you won't find my name either.'

'What do you mean?'

'I'm thinking of going back to school.'

'Christ, Whit, why?'

'That's what Micky asks.' Micky is her husband. Whitney drags in another lungful of smoke and blows it out while fluttering her tongue against her lips. It sounds like the rotor blades of a helicopter. 'Crash and burn, baby,' she says. She stares at the glowing tip of the cigarette. 'Okay, here's the punch line. Ready? I'm going back to become —drum roll, please—a *psychiatrist*.'

Trina hops up onto the examination table. She scoots back a little and the movement tears the white hygiene paper that runs the length of the table. 'A psychiatrist, huh?'

'You say it as if it's a moral crime.'

'I'm just surprised. I thought you liked being a pediatrician.'

'What makes you think that?' The cigarette is only half-smoked, but she stubs it out on the inside rim of the trash can. 'I hate smoking, but I still do it.'

Trina is truly surprised. She has watched Whitney with her young patients, seen her stop a sobbing toddler's tears, comfort child and parent alike. 'I'm shocked, Whit. Really. I thought you were so good at this.'

'I am good at it. Damn good. I just don't like it. The aptitude tests tell you what you'll be successful at, not what you'll enjoy.'

'Will you enjoy being a psychiatrist?'

'It beats getting puked on by a five-year-old who's just

swallowed a bunch of live grasshoppers. Besides, the malpractice insurance is cheaper.'

Trina twists the hanger some more, trying to restore it to its original shape and purpose. 'What about Micky?'

'Micky supports whatever decision I make. He's a doll, Trina. It's just hard for him to understand my ambivalence. He wanted to be a doctor from the time he was eight and examined little Marcy Gruber in the garage. He worked his way through med school bussing tables in the cafeteria. I breezed through on a generous divorce settlement, driving to classes from my condo. He borrowed up the kazoo to open his practice, worked days and nights, moonlighting in emergency rooms to buy equipment. I waltzed in with enough money to start free and clear. I've been successful here from day one. He's never said so, but I can tell he's irritated by my luck.'

'I know I am,' Trina says.

Whitney smiles. 'You're just like him. You think I owe my luck something. Neither of you understands because you both know what you like and you like doing it. I envy your passion. I'm just good at things I don't care about.' She gets up off her stool and takes the gnarled coat hanger from Trina's hands. She dumps it in the trash can. 'You know the one thing I did in my life that I really enjoyed?'

'Yeah, screwing Gordon Effrem in our dorm room while I was in the other bed pretending to be asleep.'

'Gordon thought you were, that's what counted.'

Trina laughs. 'Okay, other than that, what did you most enjoy?'

She looks overhead at the ceiling. 'I expect hidden alarms to go off when I say this, but I most enjoyed being a hausfrau. I feel like some redneck shit saying that. But I mean it, Trina. I liked staying at home, planning menus, playing tennis, discussing having children. Yeah, we were going to have kids. One anyway.'

345

'What about you and Micky?'

Whitney shrugs. 'We talk about it and talk about it, but I think the mood may have passed me. I've decided I'm more the aunt type. Like with Karyn. I love seeing her and talking to her, but I'm probably just as happy to be leaving her at your place.'

'And sometimes I wish you'd take her along.'

'You don't mean that.'

Trina nods. 'Sometimes. But not most of the time.'

Whitney opens a drawer and removes the little sample bottle of Scope. She rinses her mouth again and spits into the sink. 'Some psychiatrist I'd make, huh? A patient comes to me and I do all the complaining.'

'You're entitled.'

'I'll remind you of that when you get my bill.'

'Doesn't matter, I never pay them anyway.'

Whitney puts her arm around Trina's shoulder and squeezes. 'Listen, you take it a little easier for the next couple months and see if those symptoms don't back off.'

'And if they don't?'

'Then you come back here and I'll send you upstairs to Micky for some tests. He thinks you're pretty sexy stuff anyway and would love an excuse to get you naked.'

'Well, that insight will certainly help me relax the next time I see him.'

Whitney laughs. 'What do you think, doctors have no sex drive? When I was a resident, I had to examine a few naked men that got my pulse up to the danger zone.'

Whitney walks Trina out to her private exit. 'Remember, take it easy. You can't be everything to everybody. A career's just a job you've had for a long time. Being good at it doesn't make you a slave to it. There's more out there. Christ, there'd better be. You want children, have children. Change isn't always bad. Don't be afraid of change.' She stops suddenly and Trina can see that

Whitney's out of breath. Whitney smiles an odd, troubled smile. 'Say, who are we talking about here, anyway?'

Trina avoids the freeway because last night there was another freeway shooting. A red Gremlin was tailgating a pickup truck. The truck driver fired a .32 slug into the Gremlin's hood. The driver was not injured. She takes Wilshire Boulevard instead where the drivers are crazy but mostly unarmed.

She cruises the parking lot at City Hall until she finds Carla Bennington's space. The other City Council spaces are packed tight with their dark and shiny city-supplied Oldsmobiles. Carla's space is occupied by her own little blue Ford Pinto which she has been driving for ten years. Not accepting a car from the city because it was frivolous government spending earned her a lot of positive publicity. So did her insistence on owning a made-in-America car and her fiscal conservative attitude symbolized by driving the same car for ten years. Trina smiles at the sight of the small perfectly preserved Pinto dwarfed between the larger Oldsmobiles. By driving that car she'd managed to convey her campaign philosophy with more impact than if she'd made a dozen speeches outlining her fiscal policies.

Trina admires the woman's savvy. Carla is shrewd, but she is also vulnerable. During an economic slump, being the incumbent sometimes backfires, especially on a minority or woman. No matter how good a job that person has done, citizens become restless and dissatisfied with their lives. They want change: divorce, new jobs, fresh leaders. When the incumbent is a minority or woman, the voter figures he's done his social duty, now it's time to get back to basics. Time for a white male to set things straight. This attitude is prevalent among minorities as well. Trina's research had shown this pattern to be especially consistent in large sprawling cities like Los Angeles. Carla Bennington is ripe for an ousting this year.

Trina looks at her car clock. If Howdy's information is correct, Carla should be coming out any minute. Then all Trina has to do is follow her to the airport or train station or wherever she is going, buy a ticket to the same destination, find out what she does there, and whether she uses any of her public funds to do it. Hotel bills, theater tickets, anything like that.

Trina opens her purse and finds a couple of loose vitamins among the stamps and paper clips. She pops them into her mouth and swallows them dry. They scratch like lumps of coal all the way down her throat. She feels something strange on her tongue and pulls a long hair out of her mouth. It must have been stuck to one of the vitamins. She rolls open her window and tries to shake it loose from her fingers. No use. Finally she just plasters it against the car door.

A loud gaggle of voices draws Trina's attention back to the building and she sees Carla Bennington hurrying out of the building. She is closely followed by a camera crew headed by local TV anchorman, Griffin Foley. Foley towers over everyone else; he has to stoop a little so the makeup woman can dab at his forehead. Walking beside Carla is Benjamin Logan, her campaign manager. Benjamin is close to seventy and looks and dresses like Spencer Tracy in *Inherit the Wind*. His face is brown and craggy with sailing, his sole passion outside of politics. His hair is buzz cut, white as bleached bones. He wears a belt and suspenders but is always hitching his pants up as if he didn't trust either the suspenders or belt. When Foley approaches, Benjamin steps back in the shadows with a satisfied smile on his lined face. Trina doesn't blame him for smiling. The marathon angle is a sweet one, undoubtedly what they're interviewing her about today.

Even among all those bustling people, Carla Bennington stands out with a certain elegant serenity. Her clothes are hopelessly mismatched, but that only adds to her casual dignity, as if she didn't concern herself with such mundane things while there is a populace to be served. She pushes her long black hair back from her forehead and the two-inch wide streak of gray that ribbons through it gleams like metal in the sun. She still has her bifocals on and Benjamin reaches over and snatches them off her face just as the cameraman sets his position.

Trina watches Griffin Foley ask a few questions which Carla answers briefly and pleasantly. Everyone looks relaxed and friendly. No hard-hitting questions today, just fluff. They must be doing some special feature on sex and politics, otherwise Foley wouldn't be out here in person. The only time he comes out from behind the anchor desk is during ratings sweeps, and even then only if the feature has the word sex in it. Afterward, the cameraman shoots over Carla's shoulder to show Foley nodding. This will later be edited into the interview as if he were listening intently to Carla's answers. Foley looks pleased with himself.

Carla kisses Benjamin on the cheek and walks quickly toward her Pinto. She seems excited. Benjamin's face looks concerned as he watches her climb into the car. Maybe he doesn't know where she's going either, Trina thinks. The newspeople load the TV equipment into their van. Griffin Foley pulls out a thick cigar from inside his jacket and lights up. Benjamin scowls at Foley and fans the smoke away from his face. Carla waves to Benjamin as she drives past him and out of the parking lot.

Trina follows. She keeps a row of cars between herself and Benjamin Logan as she parallels Carla's car through the lot then pulls out behind her into traffic. She stays a couple of cars behind. Her stomach flutters with

349

excitement at the adventurous nature of what she's doing: following an L.A. City Council member to some unknown destination. The intrigue is thrilling. She flashes back on her old reporter days. She was a hell of a news hen back then, back before Karyn was born. A sudden sadness clamps onto her chest and she heaves a great sigh to dislodge it. She conjures up images of Karyn running home from school with gossip about her friends and teachers, the two of them lying in bed Sunday morning watching TV together, or leafing through the same magazine while sharing a bowl of strawberries and ice cream. The sadness is mostly gone now so she refocuses her attention on Carla Bennington's blue Pinto.

After half an hour, Trina realizes that Carla is not heading for the airport or the train station or even home. They drive north on the Hollywood Freeway up into San Fernando Valley. Traffic is sparse so they move along at a fast speed. The speedometer needle floats past 80 mph. The sense of drama at secretly following someone quickly wears off and Trina gets bored as they approach the Grapevine. She turns on the radio, switches around from station to station but finds nothing she wants to hear. She feels squirmy and restless. She opens the glove compartment and pulls out a handful of tapes: *Love Songs of Jim Croce*, Peter Gabriel's *So*, Genesis. She tosses them aside and reaches back into the glove compartment. She finds her Learn Spanish E-Z tapes. There are ten tapes and she's listened to the first six. She sticks number seven in the cassette player. A man's deep voice begins to converse slowly in Spanish. He has a slight lisp, or maybe that's just proper pronunciation. He speaks a phrase, translates it into English, then asks the listener to repeat after him.

'*El omnibus esta veinte minutos tarde,*' he intones. 'The bus is twenty minutes late.' Trina says the sentence with him.

Spanish is the first on her list of self-improvement projects. Next comes French, then Japanese. Also she intends to take piano lessons with Karyn.

Six months ago she started on her self-improvement kick. She determined that no day would go by in which she didn't learn something new about the world that she hadn't known when she'd awakened that day. She read more magazines, biographies, even encyclopedias. She was thinking about taking calligraphy, fencing, maybe tap dancing through extension courses. She hadn't told Barcy or the others about it because she didn't want them to keep asking how things were going when she'd hardly done anything yet but listen to six tapes. She still couldn't remember most of what she heard.

'*Estas zapatos me pinchan los pies,*' he says. 'These shoes pinch my feet.' He says 'pinch' with a whine as if his feet really hurt. Everyone's an actor.

Someone honks a horn and she looks around with a start. She realizes she'd stopped watching the Pinto while she'd been thinking. She looks all around, can't find it anywhere. She pulls into the next lane where she can see better and spots Carla Bennington's Pinto gliding over to the right lane to exit. Trina has to nudge into a small space between a postal truck and a station wagon to be able to make the exit. The man in the station wagon glares at her. She follows the Pinto down the ramp but gets trapped by other exiting cars in the turn-right-only lane while the Pinto turns left. The lights turn red and she has to wait while the Pinto sprints into a Union 76 station.

'*El padre te puede ayudar con tu problema.* The priest can help you with your problem.'

'Not this time he can't,' she says and ejects the tape. She quickly lowers her window and waves at the kid in the idling car next to her. He is fat and smeared with grease, wearing a mechanic's uniform. He is drinking from a Dr.

Pepper can, rapping the can against the steering wheel while he bobs his head to some music. She motions for him to roll down his passenger window. He does and she can hear Prince's 'Purple Rain' blaring between them. He makes an inquisitive face.

'Can you let me in?' Trina shouts. 'I'm in the wrong lane.'

'Huh?' He leans closer but doesn't turn down his stereo.

Trina expects the cars behind her to start honking because she isn't turning right on the red light, but they are all uncharacteristically patient.

Trina repeats her request and the kid nods. 'Sure. Just don't shoot out my windshield, okay?' He laughs and toasts her with his Dr Pepper can.

The traffic light changes and Trina swerves over in front of him. She passes the service station where Carla is pumping gas into her Pinto. Carla is no longer wearing a skirt, panty hose, and pumps. She must have changed them all during the drive, for now she's wearing shorts and sandals. Only the white sleeveless sweater remains from her previous outfit.

Trina pulls into the Chevron station next door and pumps five gallons of unleaded into her car before Carla finishes and climbs back into the Pinto. Trina quickly pays the attendant and jumps into her car. She gets ready to turn left to follow Carla back onto the freeway, but Carla doesn't go to the freeway; she turns right and drives west toward the ocean. Trina follows her to Pacific Coast Highway where they head north again. Trina tries to imagine various scenarios of where the councilwoman is going, who she is going to meet. A young lover, maybe someone on her staff, a beefy married man with a pregnant wife. A daughter she'd had secretly when she was sixteen who was born retarded when the umbilical cord choked her during birth. Trina toys with possibilities as they drive along the scenic highway, the Pacific Ocean spanking the shore.

In San Luis Obispo, Carla Bennington drives the Pinto into the parking lot of an Alpha Beta supermarket. Trina follows her into the store. Carla steers a rickety cart around while Trina trails with a red plastic basket. Occasionally Trina puts a can of something in the basket, olives, cat food, bamboo shoots. Carla, however, knows exactly what she wants. She wheels past the fresh fruits and vegetables to the frozen foods aisle. She opens one of the frosted doors and rummages inside, rearranging cartons, apparently looking for something specific. When she emerges she's holding a quart of ice cream. Next stop is the cookie aisle where she tosses in a bag of peanut butter cookies which Trina recognizes as a brand she buys too. Potato chips are next, then soft drinks, Diet Slice Mandarin Orange. She stops among the magazines and paperbacks and looks them over, picking up a couple of books, reading the back covers, putting them back. Finally she decides on two magazines and a romance novel. Trina can't make out the title, but she can see the woman on the cover in a turbulent red dress held from behind by a man nibbling at her neck. Now there's a secret to topple governments: Councilwoman Bennington Reads Trashy Bodice-Rippers. Except that Trina used to read them too, three a week, until her recent plan for self-improvement. Since then she has given up on novels of any kind in favor of nonfiction. Just the facts, ma'am. Illusion is useless out here, but knowledge could save your life. *El vestido tiene muchos butones*; the dress has many buttons. Never know when that will save your life.

Carla pilots the cart around the corner and heads for the liquor department. She expertly examines several bottles before choosing a bottle of rum.

Aha, Trina thinks. One lost weekend coming up.

Carla wheels through the express line and pays in cash.

Trina sets her red basket down next to the cereal and leaves the store. Carla drives a couple of blocks to a video rental store. Trina waits outside in the car. When Carla comes out with three tapes, she follows her through town to a quaint Victorian bed and board house. Carla parks in front and carries her groceries and tapes inside. Trina parks across the street and watches the door for a while. Maybe whoever she's meeting is already inside, in his own room. Maybe he's one of the half a dozen men who's gone in since Carla checked in. How would Trina know? She shakes her head. God, this is weird. Trina shoves her tape back in the cassette: *El coche por poco me atropella.* The car just missed running over me.

Carla reappears. She stands in front of the house, shades her eyes from the setting sun, squints down the street, and starts walking. Her hair's wet and pulled back into a ponytail. She's changed out of that terrible sleeveless sweater into a T-shirt with an airbrushed giraffe on it, but she still looks disheveled, as if she dresses without ever checking the mirror.

Trina gets out of the car, thumbs a couple of quarters into the meter, and follows Carla on the opposite side of the street. Carla enters Favio's Pizza My Heart. She sits near the window. A teenage waitress sulks by with a hostile glare that could only mean she is family of the owner. A minute later she sets a glass of wine in front of Carla. Carla sips the wine, puts on her bifocals, and begins reading her romance book.

This doesn't make sense, Trina thinks. Where's the hunk? She drives all the way up here, four hours on the road, just to have wine and pizza at Favio's? Must be a hell of a pizza. Maybe he's late, tied up in traffic, making excuses to his sick wife, visiting hours at the home where she abandoned her retarded love child are over for the day. Trina stops speculating and just watches Carla. She eats the pizza with small bites but chews with her mouth a little open. Sometimes she'll seem especially involved in a page and stop in mid-chew while she reads. Her glasses slip down on her nose and she raises a finger to push them back but sees the pizza grease all over it and uses her wrist instead. She finishes her wine and orders another glass.

Trina is standing on the street, pretending to browse in the window of a hardware store. She tries to show interest in the beach chairs, Smashball paddles, ice chests, and sun visors, but after a while it loses its magnetism.

'Hi,' the voice behind her says. Carla Bennington's voice.

Trina's heart bolts out of its mooring and tries to escape up her throat. She swallows just in time to send it back down into her chest. But it cowers there, trembling. Trina turns around and faces Carla Bennington. 'Hello.'

'We met at City Hall, remember? Howdy White introduced us.'

'Yes. How are you?' Trina pumps confident energy into her voice, offers her hand.

They shake.

Carla smiles without saying anything. She has a cardboard pizza box under her arm. 'How was the drive?'

'The drive?'

'The drive here. I tried not to lose you. Almost did at the off ramp though. You must have been distracted.'

Trina doesn't know what to say. Denying it would only add stupidity to incompetence. Her skin shrivels with embarrassment, but she tries not to show anything. 'I was involved in my language tapes. Trying to learn Spanish.'

'*Sentirse pequeño o insignificante.*'

'I'm not that far along. What's that mean?'

'To feel small.' Her gaze is steady, amusement in her blue eyes. Trina nods. 'Yeah, that's the feeling all right.'

Carla hands her the pizza box. 'Here, this is for you.

355

I'm going back to my room for the rest of the evening. If you intend to watch my room you're going to get hungry.'

Flabbergasted, Trina accepts the box.

'Say hi to Cory for me. Tell him better luck next time.' She walks away.

'It wasn't his idea. It was mine.'

Carla stops, looks back at Trina. Looks her over from head to toe. 'You must feel pretty clammy in that suit after a hot day like this. Even James Bond takes an occasional break. Come on.'

'Where?'

'My room. You can look it over, check under the bed, in the closet. Then you can either drive back home and get a good night's sleep, or you can camp outside my room all night waiting for the secret lover who isn't coming. I'll introduce you to Lily, she owns the place. She'll show you my bills and my charge slip on my personal American Express card. No public funds are misused. Any other scenarios you had in mind?'

'A long-abandoned illegitimate child, retarded from birth when the umbilical cord choked off her air.'

'Right. Stashed in a home under an assumed name.'

'Something like that.'

Carla laughs. 'Sorry, no such luck.'

Trina shrugs. 'Desperation.'

'You don't need anything else. I saw that new mailer. Talk Is Cheap. That was very clever. Your idea?'

'Yes.'

'You've run a hell of a campaign. I think Cory has a good shot at my job.' Carla starts walking back toward the bed and board house.

Trina falls into step beside her, still carrying the pizza box. She reaches under the lid, tears off a piece of pizza and eats. 'You don't seem too nervous about our chances.'

'I'm realistic. It'll be a photo finish. Cory is a good man, key word here being man. As enlightened as we all like to think we are these days, all other qualifications being equal, a man still has the edge in politics. We prefer the father to the mother in such matters.'

Trina feels creepy and guilty, like the hangman walking the condemned to the gallows, chatting about his newborn baby. She keeps munching the pizza to keep from having to talk and feel worse. They arrive at the house and Carla opens the door for Trina, but Trina doesn't go in.

'I'm not going to search your room,' Trina says. 'I already feel like an ass, no need to feel like a shit too. I think I'll just head back home.'

'Okay.'

'Listen, I'm sorry about all this. I used to be a reporter. I think I just got caught up in the Watergate syndrome.'

Carla smiles. Her smile can't touch The Candidate's. His is life-giving, a small sun radiating warmth and light. Hers crinkles her eyes so the lines bunch up at the corners. The teeth are small and even except for one on the bottom that is crowded a little forward. She looks like a little girl who's just walked into a surprise party. When the smile fades her face rearranges to that of an attractive woman with brains and humor. The contrast of expressions surprises Trina.

Carla reaches into her purse and pulls out a tissue. She steps toward Trina and wipes her cheek. 'I don't know how you managed to get pizza sauce all the way over there.' She shows Trina the red smudge on the tissue.

'Red badge of carnivore. I'm going to devour the rest of this pizza on the ride home. It won't be a pretty sight.'

Carla laughs and wipes tomato sauce from Trina's lapel. 'If the police stop you they'll search the car for a body.'

Trina nods and starts to walk away. She waves good-bye, stifles a yawn. She turns back to Carla, who is just entering the house. 'Listen, maybe this is against the Geneva

Convention or something, but I wonder if you'd let me take a quick shower. I don't think I can stay awake for the four-hour drive back.'

'Five or six hours,' Carla says. 'Rush-hour traffic.'

'Great.'

Carla crooks her head for Trina to follow. They go inside the house and up the winding stairway to the second floor. The banister is highly polished. The hallway walls have dark wainscoting and thick salmon wallpaper.

'This place is gorgeous,' Trina says.

'Isn't it? I've been coming here for years. Actually, since my divorce. Right afterwards I needed to get away from lawyers and my husband and daughters. They were all being terrific, there was no hostility or anything, I just needed to be alone.'

Trina nods. 'I went to San Diego after my divorce. Took my daughter to the zoo every day for three days. Finally she begged me not to take her the fourth day. I don't know, there was just something about the place that made me relax.'

'The caged animals?' Carla kids.

'The anonymity. The crowds of people looking at all those animals, reading signs about how they behave, no one caring about other humans for a couple hours. Fuck the starving masses, refugees from political torture, screw the plight of the farmer. And the hell with your divorce too. You know what I mean?'

Carla unlocks her room door and they enter. 'The bathroom's over there. Don't be shy about the towels, there are plenty.'

'Thanks. Nice digs, Councilwoman.'

'Fuck the homeless,' she says.

Trina laughs and so does Carla, both looking a little naughty, as if they'd just scrawled something nasty on the stall in the girls' lavatory.

358

Trina goes into the bathroom and closes the door. She strips off her wine-colored jacket, its double-breasted rows of gold buttons gleaming in the mirror. She steps out of the pleated skirt and hangs both on the hook behind the door. The panty hose are next, then the bra. She turns on the shower, but the water is cold. She holds her hand in the stream and feels it slowly turn warm, but far from hot. While waiting for the water to heat up, she stares at herself in the mirror over the sink. Thick billows of steam from the shower curl around behind her like angel wings. The image makes her laugh. St. Trina on a heavenly mission to expose corrupt politician's umbilical-strangled retarded child, hostage to ambitious career. Jesus Christ, Trina, she thinks, shaking her head. She picks up the red toothbrush from next to the sink and stares at it a moment before replacing it. She nudges it a few times to make sure it is exactly where it was. There is nothing else personal in the bathroom. Nothing to spy on.

Trina looks at her breasts' reflection. They are so big they look unreal. The stretch marks are etched in acid. The nipples are circled by tiny bumps that look like pimples. Perfectly normal, but guys always seem to recoil a little when they first see them in the light. This body has no right to be investigating the body of a woman who can run marathons.

She steps into the shower and lets the hot water punish her skin. The magazines warn against hot water, especially against the face. Water ages skin. Trina sticks her face into the shower stream. She soaps herself, underarms, neck, pubic area. She remembers The Candidate in the shower, clamped behind her, his penis crammed deep inside her. And Jamison Levy, the journalist, blow-drying his sheets. She laughs and water from the shower rains into her mouth. She spits it out. Nice men. All the men she's slept with are nice. Some wanted to marry her. Some didn't.

They all seemed to expect something from her and she didn't know what it was. Some seemed to find it with her, others seemed disappointed when they didn't. It was all very intuitive, no one could articulate it, find words to match the feelings. She doubted these men even consciously knew it. Rob had found it with her but later accused her of changing, taking it away from him. She never knew what he meant. Trina couldn't imagine marrying again until she discovered what it was they found in her or didn't find.

Trina shuts the water off, sweeps aside the plastic curtain, and climbs out of the shower-tub. She is thankful the mirror is steamed over. She's had quite enough of her body for a while. She wraps a towel around her body and uses a second towel to dry her legs and arms. When she is done she puts her skirt and jacket back on. She balls up the textured cranberry panty hose and stuffs them into her pocket. The pocket bulges like that of an inept shoplifter. She steps into her pumps.

Trina opens the door and walks into the bedroom. Carla Bennington is sitting on the sofa with her legs curled under her, eating a bowl of ice cream. Three peanut butter cookies stick out of the ice cream. The television is on and a magazine is open on her lap. 'So that's your big secret, huh?'

'I couldn't hide it any longer,' Carla says. 'Junk food, junk magazines, junk book, junk TV. I'm a junkie.'

Trina smiles. 'What flavor?'

'Almond praline.'

'The magazines?'

'*People, US, Cosmopolitan.*'

'The videos?'

'*The Magnificent Seven, From Russia With Love, Private Benjamin.*'

Trina walks over next to the sofa and sees Steve

McQueen talking with Yul Brynner on the TV. 'This is the kind of information that can ruin you, you know?'

'I was counting on the kindness of strangers. That and a bribe.' She points her spoon at the mini-refrigerator next to the dresser.

Trina opens the refrigerator and pulls out the carton of ice cream. She uses the plastic spoon on top to scrape some into the paper bowl. She also grabs a handful of peanut butter cookies. 'I don't come cheap.' She sits on the sofa next to Carla and they watch the movie in silence, eating ice cream, crunching cookies. This is as relaxed as Trina has felt in a long time.

'I don't usually come up here during the week,' Carla says as Charles Bronson chops wood in exchange for breakfast. 'But I campaigned all weekend on the rubber chicken circuit, and then the photo session for the marathon, I just had to get away for one night. At home I feel compelled to answer the phone. Here I don't.'

Trina spoons ice cream into her mouth and squashes it against the roof of her mouth with her tongue. The cold dripping down her throat feels good. 'I feel funny.'

Carla looks alarmed. 'You mean sick?'

'No, I mean funny creepy. Coming up here like some dime-store spy going through your underwear or something. Then you're so nice.'

'I feel a testimonial coming on. I hope this comes with a watch.'

Trina laughs. 'Christ, you are tough, aren't you?'

'Yes, I am. It's no act, no I-am-woman-hear-me-roar crap. I was three. My mother raised seven kids, five of her own and two of her sister's when she and her husband were killed in a car crash. Even today I'm closer to my cousins than to my own brothers and sisters. Maybe I empathized more with their being orphans. I always wanted to be an orphan.'

361

'My parents wanted me to be an orphan too. Except they didn't want to die, so we were at a standoff.'

Carla pushes the magazines off her lap, sets her bowl on the arm of the sofa, and gets up. 'A tough woman is like a mutant breed in most people's eyes. Like a five-legged dog, three-eyed cat. The extra appendage is unusual, even fascinating, but basically unnecessary. A freak of nature.' She laughs. 'Sometimes I even agree.'

'So you come up here to mellow out.'

Carla stoops beside the bed and opens the night table cupboard door. 'The council meets three days a week. Two days a week I spend on district work. I have two district offices I have to watch over. I'm on the Planning and Environment Committee which is trying to rezone two hundred thousand parcels of land. Our meetings sometimes go on for six hours at a time. Fridays is zoo day, when we honor the local citizens with awards of merit. Each one wants a photo of them with the council. Saturday is walk day, during which I walk my district to hand out campaign literature.' She stands up and holds up the bottle of rum Trina saw her buy. It hasn't been opened yet. 'Talk about mellowing out.'

'What about all those rich glamorous guys you date?' Trina tries to keep the envy out of her voice. 'Don't they help mellow you a little?'

Carla grins. 'Sometimes we mellow a little together.'

'Don't you want someone to mellow with permanently?'

'Don't you?'

Trina shrugs. 'Sure. I've just gotten pickier as I've gotten older. I have a mental list of what they can and cannot do. Every year my list of Can'ts grows longer and pickier. Can't use double negatives. Can't like movies with subtitles.'

'Can't brush their teeth right after sex.'

'Can't use the phrase "woman's perspective."'

362

'Yes!' Carla says. 'That's on my list. Can't have a large dog.'

'Can't have season tickets to the Dodgers.'

Carla laughs. 'We should type these up and compare with other women. We could have a checklist to hand out to prospective dates.'

'I don't know,' Trina says. 'A lot of my friends' lists of Can'ts are getting smaller. It's like when you're in college, there aren't any can'ts. Except you can't be hideous or carry a slide rule in your pocket. Then you go out in the world, you're young and sexy and in demand, so you can afford to start your list of Can'ts. Then you get older, married, divorced, have kids, your butt looks like a quilt, you can't afford to have much of a list of Can'ts anymore.'

Carla opens the refrigerator and takes the carton of ice cream out. She brings it and the rum back to the sofa and sits down. She pours a little rum over the ice cream. 'Try this,' she says and pours some over Trina's ice cream.

'Hey, you got some on the cookies.'

'You'll like it. Trust me.'

Trina scoops a spoonful of ice cream and rum and eats it. 'Whoa!'

'Good, huh?'

'Yeah, I think.' She eats another spoonful.

'I always hated booze,' Carla says. 'Which made it tough when you're growing up trying to appear sophisticated and worldly. You tell your date you don't drink and they think you're a goddamn Quaker. Naturally they equate drinking with sex.'

'"Doesn't drink" equals "doesn't put out." The mathematics of dating.'

'Exactly. But I found I could tolerate rum and Coke, so that became my standard drink. After a while, I even got to really like it. A guy I used to date. some state senator,

363

really took his booze seriously. He introduced me to a flip.'

'Sounds painful.'

Carla pours a little more rum on her ice cream. Trina takes the bottle and pours more on hers too. She stirs her peanut butter cookie in the mix and eats it.

'A flip is a drink from back in the seventeen hundreds. It's a combination of rum, ale, and whipped egg whites that was seared with a red-hot poker.'

'Yikes.' Trina laughs.

'Back then American rum was shipped to Africa and traded for slaves. The slaves were then shipped to the Caribbean where they were traded for molasses, which was shipped to New England to be distilled into rum.'

'So we're eating a piece of history here,' Trina says.

'Damn right. Most of today's rum comes from Puerto Rico.' She holds up the rum bottle. 'Bacardi Silver Label. This stuff. But there are some exceptional rums. Dark rums aged in Limousin oak casks. Great stuff.'

Trina finishes the ice cream and cookies and stares at James Coburn shooting a man off a horse from half a mile away. 'Great shot,' Trina says.

'I was aiming at the horse,' James Coburn complains.

Carla and Trina laugh.

They talk through the rest of the film. When the movie ends, they stick in another cassette, *From Russia with Love*, though they talk through that too. During their conversation, they pass the rum bottle back and forth.

'Don't worry,' Trina says, handing Carla the bottle, 'these sores on my mouth are almost gone.'

Carla laughs, tries to drink, laughs again, finally takes a swig, almost choking on it as she breaks out laughing again. A few drops of rum spray onto Trina's skirt.

'Hey,' Trina says, 'I already showered.'

'In ice cream it looks like.' Carla licks the end of a paper napkin and scrubs the dried ice cream spots fron Trina's skirt.

'Someday I'm going to have to learn to eat neater.'

'Or wear rubber pants.'

'I've already been made that offer by one guy.'

Carla laughs again. Her long hair falls forward, the silvery gray streak covering one eye. She laughs so hard that she drops the napkin, which rolls down Trina's skirt and lands on the floor. Trina and Carla both lean over to retrieve the napkin and bonk their heads together with a thunk. Both stagger back from the impact.

'Shit,' Trina says. 'That hurt.'

Carla rubs her forehead. 'I hope it doesn't bruise. That'll be a tough one to explain to reporters. Tipsy Candidate Knocks Heads With Rival Campaign Manager.'

'Actually, I'm just PR. Mary and Warren are the campaign managers.' Trina brushes Carla's hair from her forehead and pushes her hand away. 'It's a little red, but it won't bruise.'

'My God,' Carla says, looking at Trina. 'You've got an egg.' Trina gingerly touches her forehead and feels the lump. 'Doesn't feel too sore.'

'That's because you're drunk.'

'I'm not drunk.'

'You're drunk,' Carla insists. 'I should know.'

'Why?'

''Cause I'm drunk.'

'Oh,' Trina says.

Carla goes to the ice bucket and brings back a few cubes. Water drips between her fingers onto the carpet and sofa. She presses one against the lump. Carla's other hand is cupped behind Trina's head, to hold it steady while she applies the ice. She is so close Trina can feel her breath against her cheek. Trina closes her eyes and lets Carla rub the ice around the bruise. As the cube melts, cold water drips down her brow and eyes and cheek. The drops collect at the corner of her mouth and she licks them.

Suddenly she feels lips pressed against her lips. She opens her eyes and Carla is staring into her eyes, her lips still kissing Trina. Trina doesn't know what to do. Carla is still holding the ice cube to her forehead, the other hand behind her neck. The lips feel soft and wet. They aren't grinding against her, there is no tongue prying them apart. Just lips. Full soft lips a little like Karyn's.

Carla pulls away. She looks flustered. 'I've never done that before.'

They don't say anything. The ice in Carla's hand has melted. She walks over to get more, brings the bucket back. 'That's not entirely true. When I was eight the girl next door tried to teach me how to kiss boys. She was nine.'

Trina doesn't know what to say or do. She can't move. She wipes some of the melted water from her face and is surprised at how hot her skin feels. She looks at the TV. Sean Connery is kissing a woman on a train. Robert Shaw bursts in and tries to kill him. Love is dangerous.

'This is weird,' Carla says, shaking her head as if coming out of a long coma.

'I guess you were right. We are drunk.'

'That's what I said.' Carla hands her an ice cube from the bucket. Trina holds it against her lump. Carla pulls her own hair back from her face and clutches it in a severe ponytail. She stares at the TV too.

'God, he was sexy,' Trina says as Sean Connery slams Robert Shaw against the wall.

'I think he's sexier now, bald and all.'

Trina can still taste Carla's lips on her own, feel the imprint. She picks up the rum bottle and takes a swig. It is almost empty. 'Hair of the dog,' she says.

366

Carla nods, her eyes fixed on the TV.

Trina puts the bottle down, tosses the ice into the bucket. She leans over and kisses Carla. Carla doesn't move. She closes her eyes and then Trina does too. The kiss is the same kind as before. Chaste. Lips snuggled against lips. Soft and yielding. Trina leans away and they are both breathing faster.

'What do you expect me to do?' Carla asks.

'I don't know. Maybe we should yell fag or something. Maybe that would sober us up.'

'You want to go further?'

Trina shakes her head. 'I don't think so. You?'

'No. This is what I imagined it would feel like to try heroin or something. The guilt and danger pumping my heart.'

Trina is angry. 'I didn't bring photographers if that's what you're thinking.'

'I didn't mean that. Calm down.'

They sit there not looking at each other. The film ends and Carla sticks in *Private Benjamin*. 'I saw this at a benefit screening with Goldie Hawn. I can't remember what we were benefiting, isn't that terrible?'

'Criminal.'

They look at each other and somehow they are kissing again. Trina doesn't really feel as if she is the one sitting there kissing another woman. She feels like a spy witnessing the whole thing from her hiding place in the rafters. Mentally she snaps photos with her miniature spy camera made to look like a cigarette lighter. She will study them later, figure out how two such nice people could have fallen to such depraved depths. She knows that it is not really her sitting here on the sofa hugging this woman, pressing lips together, feeling some tongue now, accepting it into her mouth. She knows it's not her because she would feel worse than she does. Trina would be horrified. Gay rights is fine in general principle, but the act itself is disgusting. Yet she is not disgusted.

While Goldie Hawn marches in circles in the rain, they make their way to the bed. They strip each other naked. Carla's body is much firmer than Trina's and she feels a little embarrassed as Carla unfastens Trina's bra and those huge boulders plop out. Trina is not aroused by the sight of Carla's naked body; she is more curious. Like a child at a petting zoo. The soft touch of Carla's hand on her hip, the fingers on her cheek, the lips against her neck. They touch something that quickens Trina's heart.

Neither touches the other's breasts or pubic area. They stroke each other's back and legs and buttocks. They cling to each other and kiss. Trina feels Carla's smaller, firmer breasts squash against her own. She thinks hers might actually swallow Carla's like giant sponges. Carla's hand is holding firm to Trina's hip, not moving up or down.

After a while they break apart and look at each other. They both laugh.

'I feel like a clumsy kid in a crystal shop,' Carla says.

'You touch it, you bought it,' Trina agrees.

'Silly.'

'We've come this far, I guess we might as well go the rest of the way.'

Trina nods. It's funny to be talking so casually to someone you're having sex with. Not that she wasn't casual with Rob when they were married or with the other men she's slept with. But the casualness seemed a little forced, like they were both trying to prove that sex was no big deal. No commitment. No contest.

She feels Carla's lips on her breast, the tongue lapping the nipple. She watches Carla lick her. Carla looks up and smiles with Trina's nipple between her teeth.

She closes her eyes as Carla moves to the other breast. What does this all mean? That she's a lesbian? She read

368

an article somewhere that psychiatrists had a convention and agreed that one homosexual episode after you're an adult means you're gay. But if she were gay, why didn't she ever lust after any other women? Maybe she should discuss this with Whitney. If she is gay, how will she explain that to Karyn?

Carla drags her tongue down Trina's stomach. Trina peeps at her and sees Carla looking at her spread apart legs. She is studying her vagina like a first-time swimmer told to dive into the pool. Slowly she lowers her head and Trina feels the tongue gently stroking. Carla's hand presses against Trina's pubic hairs. The tongue flicks over the clitoris and Trina's hips spasm suddenly. The intensity of her reaction surprises her. Carla continues and Trina's breathing becomes rapid and shallow. She looks down at Carla and sees her looking back, her chin slicked and shiny. Then both close their eyes.

Trina feels it coming like a locomotive rushing up each leg heading for a collision at her crotch. Carla is using no special technique. The difference is that Trina doesn't have to think about when to say 'slower' or 'gentler' or 'faster' or 'here' or 'there.' Carla just does it and Trina can lie back and feel the locomotives chuffing at 200 mph along her inner thighs, roaring toward each other with whistles screaming, neither willing to give an inch, until finally Trina bucks up at the impact. Twisted hot steel flying everywhere. Steam billowing. Trina crying out like a wounded survivor.

Then it was Carla's turn.

Trina wakes when the toilet flushes. She sits up and sees Carla coming out of the bathroom wearing her running clothes. 'What time is it?'

'Five in the morning.'

Trina rubs her eyes. 'What's going on?'

'Training. I have a marathon coming up. I need the publicity if I'm going to beat your Cory Meyers.'

Trina nods. 'Right. Cory.'

'Besides, I have to get back to L.A. Today's one of my district days. Glad-handing local merchants. Tell them how I'm going to get more customers into their stores.'

Trina looks around the rooms. She sees her clothes neatly arranged on the sofa. The rum bottle is gone, the ice cream debris is gone. Everything is neat and tidy. It is almost as if last night didn't happen. 'We aren't going to talk about it?' Trina asks.

'If you want to.'

'I don't know. I feel funny. Like I should rush right out and seek counseling or something.'

'Before it spreads.'

Trina laughs. 'Something like that. How do you feel?'

Carla lifts her leg onto the back of the sofa and stretches her hands out to touch her toes. She holds this position while she talks. 'Guilty. I never thought anything like that would ever happen to me. I mean, I'm not gay.'

'Yeah, that's what I feel.'

'Still, we did it. So what does that make us?'

'Maybe we shouldn't worry about what that makes us and wonder what we got out of it.'

'Sex.'

'Sure. Anything else?'

Carla smiles. 'You're not going to send me flowers and promise you'll call next week, are you?'

Trina frowns. 'You don't want to talk. Go ahead and run.'

'What's there to talk about? Do you want me to jump in bed and start in again?'

Trina thinks that over. 'No. Not that I'd mind, I guess. I didn't last night. But I think what I really want right now

370

is for us to have breakfast together and talk, not about this. Just talk. Like last night.'

Carla frowns. 'I have to train.' She goes to the door and opens it. She looks back with a grim expression. 'By the way, I told you I was tough. If you intend to use this episode to help Cory, I have some photos of you and he leaving the Travel Lodge together. And a few telescopic shots of you after your water sports. Grainy, but clear enough.'

Trina stares at her. 'You are tough, Carla.'

Carla's eyes lower a second, then return Trina's stare. 'I told you that.' She leaves, closing the door behind her.

Trina sighs. 'The miniseries of my life.'

25

The pain is exquisite.

Like a syringe needle jabbing into the bottom of her foot. Her mouth snaps open so wide her ears pop. The second burning jolt hits her so quickly, so unexpectedly, she's not sure whether she is feeling pain or pleasure. It is like standing knee-deep in the surf with your back to the ocean and suddenly being attacked by a wave. There's a thrilling rush of excitement at impact, a moment when the pleasure of the cool water enveloping you is flash-burned away by the fear that the wave may also pick you up, flip you over, and smash you headfirst into packed sand, leaving you with a fused spine and a lifetime in a squeaking wheelchair. Diva is surprised that she has time to think such thoughts as she falls. She drops to the ground, landing hard on her butt. Sand grinds into the lip of pink skin that protrudes from the bottom of her swimming suit. Her ankle is already swollen grotesquely. The mutant blue skin puffs like an inflatable pillow. The pain is a steady throb now, the syringe needle has been replaced by a rusty corkscrew being cranked into her ankle.

'Fuck, man,' Coma says. He stoops down beside her, the volleyball tucked under his arm. 'You okay?'

'It's sprained,' Diva says.

Coma nods at the information. Sand from his hair sprinkles across Diva's thighs. He presses a finger against the swelling, leaving a white moon imprint that quickly evaporates. He stands up and offers her his hand. She takes it and he yanks her to her feet with a powerful jerk that almost sends her flying past him. She hops on one foot off the volleyball court over to her beach chair and collapses in it. The two guys on the other side of the net haven't moved. Coma is also still standing on the court. They watch her hop to her beach chair, open Coma's cooler, remove some of his ice, and press it against her ankle.

'You okay?' Coma repeats.

'Yeah, I'm fine. Go ahead.'

Coma looks down the beach at the other net. A game is going on there between Cliff and Bart and two guys whose names Diva can't remember. 'Hey, Bart,' Coma shouts. 'I need a partner.'

Bart is about to receive a high serve. When he hears Coma's voice, he catches the ball and drops it onto the sand. Immediately he runs over to this net and stands beside Coma. The three guys at the other net grab some surfer kid who was watching them play to fill in for Bart. They aren't mad at Bart, Diva knows, because it's an honor to play with Coma.

Diva sighs as the ice melts around her ankle. Just her luck, spraining her ankle before her first date with Harley Buss. She grabs more ice from the ice chest and clumps it against her skin. The swelling shrinks back a little. The game continues in front of her. Bart is a harder hitter than she is, but he isn't as steady. His passes and sets are a little sloppy. Coma gets frustrated with him even though the other team has yet to score any points. 'Put me on the net, goddamn it,' Coma scolds Bart.

Diva reaches over to check her watch which is strapped to the handle of her beach bag. 'Shit,' she says, reading it. She has just enough time to go home and shower and

373

change before Harley Buss arrives. She's been nervous about this date all day. She'd only come down here to play a couple of games and work off that nervousness, maybe sweat off a couple of extra pounds before he saw her. Now she is going to limp her way through this date like Piper Laurie in *The Hustler*.

Diva slowly manages to stand, her bad foot cocked back like a flamingo's. She gathers her bag and beach chair and starts hobbling clumsily back to her apartment.

Coma, about to serve the ball, looks at her. 'You okay?'

'Just a sprain,' she assures him.

He nods and serves the ball.

'Hi,' Harley Buss says.

Diva greets him at the door wearing her lucky sand dollar earrings, though she can't remember why she considers them lucky. She is also wearing black silk pants that hide her pouchy belly under a billow of pleats, a beige silk blouse with a Nehru collar, and red pumps for a hint of passion. Her panty hose are also black to hide the elastic ankle brace. She feels dressed for deception, hiding more than she is revealing. He is wearing a beige sports jacket, a cobalt blue polo shirt, and khaki pants. He is carrying flowers.

'Flowers,' she says, taking them. 'I haven't gotten flowers on a date since the prom.'

'I'm very traditional,' Harley says. 'My mother's waiting in the car to drive us.'

Diva laughs. 'Come on.' She steps out of the way to allow him to enter. She follows him into the living room, taking small steps and trying not to limp. Her ankle aches as if a bear trap is clamped onto it, shredding flesh with each step. She forces a smile and tries not to yelp in pain. He is better looking than she had expected. That makes her even more nervous.

He sits on the sofa and looks around the apartment, studying it like a cop. The poster from *Gandhi* catches his interest. 'Good movie,' he says.

'I never saw it,' she says. 'I just hang the poster as a dieting aid.'

He doesn't laugh, even though she meant it as a joke. *Great, now he thinks I'm dumb and fat.* His eyes scan her bookshelves, where a few lonely volumes sit, most of them popular novels, gifts still unread. He frowns as if he's looked straight into her brain, saw some serious dust bunnies, and now wants to scrub his hands and brush his teeth. He seems to be avoiding looking at her. She's been on blind dates before and recognizes this sympton. It's not good.

'Look,' she says, still holding the flowers. 'I've never been on a blind date before. I don't know how I got the nerve to call you in the first place. But we don't have to do this.'

Harley looks at her directly for the first time but doesn't say anything.

Diva continues, 'What I mean is, if you're disappointed, we don't have to go through with this.' She imagines the svelte stick figures he usually goes out with, young slim students, brilliant teachers like Barcy, executive women with appointment books and no tan lines. 'I'm probably not what you expected.'

Harley nods. 'No, you're not.'

The organs inside Diva jumble to switch places like a Chinese fire drill. Her heart is where her stomach was, her intestines are strangling her lungs. She clutches the flowers to her stomach. 'Well, like I said, we don't have to do this.'

'Okay,' Harley says. He gets up from the sofa and walks down the hallway to the door. 'Nice meeting you.' He walks out and closes the door behind him.

Diva is stunned. She limps to the kitchenette and finds a drinking glass big enough for the flowers. The flowers are a mixed bunch, brightly colored petals with sturdy stems. She can't name them, though. One looks like a marigold, but she's not sure. She fills the glass from the tap, sticks the stems in the water. She thinks about getting an aspirin for the water, but she doesn't want to drag her bad ankle to the bathroom. Besides, she doesn't want these damn flowers to last any longer than they have to. In fact, she doesn't want them around at all. She snatches them out of the glass, water dripping from the steps all over the counter and floor, and throws them into the trash can under the sink. They don't fit so she has to mash them down a little to keep them from spilling out.

'Those were expensive,' Harley says.

Diva looks up and he is standing next to the refrigerator. He shows her the receipt from Conroy's Florists. 'I keep the receipt to everything now. I got audited a couple years ago. That IRS woman told me I kept the worst records, everything from the last twelve years in an old suitcase. She said by the time she got to the bottom of that suitcase she was afraid she'd find Jimmy Hoffa.'

'What are you doing here?'

Harley shrugs. 'We have a date.'

'You left.'

'You got what you deserved,' he says. He goes over to the sofa and sits down exactly where he was before. 'What kind of way is that to start a date? "I'm not what you expected. We don't have to do this." Christ.'

Diva limps to the sofa and sits down next to Harley. 'I'm not what you expected, am I?'

'No.'

'You expected someone prettier, right?'

'Yes.'

376

'And with a better body?'

Harley nods.

Diva stares at him. 'I hate honesty.' She leans back and lifts her ankle up. 'I sprained my ankle today.'

'How?'

'Volleyball. You play?'

He shakes his head. 'Tennis.'

She lowers her foot back to the floor but continues to stare at it. 'This evening isn't going how I'd hoped.'

Harley gets up, stands directly in front of her. 'I've got an ulcer, hemorrhoids, and herpes. Some of my pubic hairs are gray. My chest hairs are all gray. Sometimes when I play tennis, I cheat; I call balls that hit the line as out. I'm lousy at finances, which is why I live from check to check.' He sits back down next to her. 'There. Feel better?'

'A little.' She looks him up and down. 'Except what am I doing going out with a loser like you?'

'I've never seen gray pubic hairs before,' Diva says.

Harley lifts the sheet and stares at his crotch. 'Distinctive, huh? Looks like Peter Lawford.'

Diva doesn't know who Peter Lawford is. She leans back against the headboard while Harley relights the joint they'd been smoking earlier. He takes a drag and hands it to her. She sucks in a small amount, holds her breath, and looks around his bedroom. There are bookshelves covering an entire wall. The books are hardbound and thick. Many are biographies of writers. She recognizes Poe, Melville, Faulkner, Hemingway. Some names she doesn't recognize —Trollope, Carlyle, Goldsmith—but assumes they must be writers too. On both bedside tables are stacks of books and magazines. The magazines aren't like the ones she reads. They are smaller and plain looking, with names like *Georgia Review, American Scholar, Prairie Schooner*. They

377

have torn snips of paper in them to mark pages.

Diva offers him the joint back, but he refuses. He didn't really smoke much of it earlier either, though he was the one who'd suggested it and brought it out.

'Why don't you have any pictures up?' Diva asks, gesturing with the smoking joint at the bare walls. 'Paintings or posters or something.'

'I haven't found the right ones yet. I have to find the exact right one before I'm willing to put a hole in my wall.'

'How long have you lived here?'

'Three years.'

Three years! Diva sees such pickiness as a bad sign. If he's that finicky about a little hole in the wall, imagine how he must be about a girlfriend. Still, she likes him a lot. Dinner was fun. He took her to a new restaurant that served flowers as entrées. 'I'm determined to give you flowers tonight,' he'd said, 'one way or the other.' She was apprehensive at first, even for a vegetarian, but she ate a salad of hibiscus, day lilies, pansies, fuchsias, nasturtium, and lettuce in a raspberry-hazelnut vinaigrette. Diva had read about such restaurants and people who regularly dined on flowers. She'd read about one new bride whose bridal bouquet was made of edible flowers. After the ceremony she'd tossed the bouquet into the salad.

Suddenly Harley whips the covers off both of them. 'I can't stand it any longer,' he announced loudly. 'I'm starving. Pansies just don't stick to ribs.' He jumps out of bed. 'You care to join me?'

'I did that, remember?'

He grins. 'For food, madam. Real food.'

Diva pinches out the joint and climbs out of bed. She looks around for something to put on. She doesn't like the idea of walking around naked in good lighting in front of him. How long can she stand around sucking in her stomach?

'Come on,' he says and takes her hand.

She hobbles beside him, her only clothing the elastic bandage on her ankle. He puts his arm around her waist to give her support. His fingertips lay against her pouch, which was much less prominent while she was on her back in bed. With her arm around his waist, she can feel his flat hairy stomach.

The kitchen is immaculate. No dirty dishes, no counter stains, no crumbs on the floor. No brown ring around the sink drain. 'Boy, you can clean my house anytime,' she says.

'I have a cleaning lady who comes in once a week. During the week I eat most of my meals out, and those that I eat here I eat off paper plates or standing over the sink. This is the cleanest room in the house.' He opens the refrigerator and takes out a lump wrapped in aluminum foil. He peels it open to reveal chopped meat. He sniffs it, pauses, sniffs again. 'I think it's okay. You game?'

'I'm a vegetarian.'

'Oh, right.' He opens the refrigerator, roots through the drawers, comes out with a zucchini and a suspicious-looking tomato. She frowns at them. 'I can make you some soup,' he says.

She looks at the red meat piled on the foil. Her stomach grumbles with desire. But she is determined to keep control of her life now that she's made some major decisions. She can't ease off anywhere or all the rest of it might crumble in on her. 'Toast would be nice.'

'An English muffin.' He opens a drawer with a built-in bread box, removes two English muffins, pries one apart, and stuffs it into the toaster. The other one he sticks in the toaster oven. 'Sit,' he says, pulling out a chair from the kitchen table. 'I'll take care of everything.'

Diva sits and watches him slap the hamburger meat back and forth between his palms until it is flat. He tosses it in an iron skillet and it smokes and sizzles. While it fries, he sidles up behind Diva and puts his arms around her shoulders. His arms rest just above her breasts. She feels warmed by the gesture. He kisses the back of her neck and she crooks her head to offer him more. 'You'll burn your buns,' she says.

'Bragging?' he says. He takes the muffins out of the toaster and the toaster oven. 'Jam?'

Diva hesitates. Jam suggests she's a pig, gives cause to her lumpishness. Plain, no butter, dry as dust. That's how a skinny person eats. 'Nothing, thanks.'

'Yuk,' he says. He takes a paper plate from the drawer and hands her the muffin on the plate.

'I need to use your phone a second,' Diva says.

'Sure. This one, or if you want privacy, there's one in the bedroom.'

'This is fine.' She dials Dixie's number. There is no answer. Anxiety and guilt squelch any appetite she had. She hangs up the phone.

'No one home?' he asks, lifting the charred burger out of the pan with a spatula.

Diva shakes her head.

'What's the matter? Suddenly you look sad.'

'Worried about a friend. I haven't been able to reach her for a couple days.'

Harley sits down at the kitchen table and begins eating his hamburger. He's poured Catalina salad dressing over it. He nods as he chews. 'Good,' he says, chomping happily away. He offers it to her. She shakes her head again.

They sit silently for a while. Harley stares at Diva, smiling. He looks enormously pleased.

'What?' she asks. 'What are you staring at?'

'You.'

'Didn't we go through this earlier? I already know I'm not what you expected.'

'No one is ever what the other expects. Maybe expects is the wrong word here. Hopes is the right one. You didn't look like I'd hoped you'd look.'

'How'd you hope I'd look?'

'Like Kim Basinger. That's how I hope every woman will look. That's what fantasies are all about. I'm sure I didn't look like you'd hoped.'

She tears off a piece of English muffin and eats it. 'Actually, you looked better than I'd hoped.'

Harley looks surprised. 'Really? Who were you expecting, Charles Laughton?'

'Who's that?'

'*Hunchback of Notre Dame*, Captain Bligh opposite Clark Gable.'

'Yeah. He had a wart on his nose or something, looked like a bulldog.'

'That's him.'

Diva nods. 'That's what I was expecting.' She laughs. 'I'm kidding.' She tears off another piece of muffin. 'I just wanted someone nice looking, but not so nice looking that he made me look ugly. There's nothing worse than seeing a real knockout guy walking down a movie aisle with a fat homely woman. Everyone in the audience wonders what they're doing together. They assume she has money or some kind of sick hold over him.'

'That hasn't happened to you, has it?'

'No, I'm the one in the audience who always assumes the fat chick is loaded.'

Harley chuckles. 'I'd like to hear you sing sometime.'

'You already have.'

'When?'

'On your car radio.' She sings to the tune of 'Bali Ha'i': '*Ed Landers' Ford is calling you/Four-oh-five free-way/ Harbor Boulevard ex-it/Right away, right away. Landers' Ford, Landers' Ford, Landers' Fooooord.*'

381

'I've heard that,' Harley says, laughing. 'That's you?'

Diva nods. 'That's me.'

'You have a terrific voice.'

'Well, I do requests. Wanna hear "Hold the Pickle, Hold the Lettuce"? Or how about oldies but goodies: "And flush those troubles down the drain. Roto-Rooter!"'

Harley puts his hamburger down. 'Do I hear a note of irony in your melody?'

She picks up his hamburger and takes a huge bite. At first the meat tastes funny, unfamiliar, almost exotic. Then her taste buds remember and she feels the need for more hamburger, fries with ketchup, a strawberry milkshake. She stops chewing and goes over the the sink and spits the bite out.

He stands up and helps her hobble back to her chair. He reaches down and lifts her sprained ankle to his lap. Then he sits back and asks her questions about her singing, her career, where she is going, what she wants. His sleepy blue eyes stay fixed on hers the whole time, as if he were trying to memorize each word. The intensity of his attention is unusual for Diva, but she finds she likes it. Somehow he even coaxes her into singing what she had written so far of 'Cocktail Waitress.' When she's done, he applauds.

'It's not finished,' she says, both embarrassed and pleased by his reaction.

'You'll finish it. You don't know your own strength.' He get up, arranges her foot gently on his chair, and leaves the room. Diva feels funny sitting at his kitchen table nude, her sprained ankle up on a chair. She is about to go back to the bedroom to get dressed when Harley comes running back into the kitchen with a silver picture frame the size of a record album. She can't see what it is in the frame though. 'I used to write too,' Harley says. 'All through high school and college.'

'What'd you write?'

'Poetry mostly. Some stories.' He holds out the frame to her. 'This is my only publication.'

Diva takes it with reverence, like a sacred text. It is one glossy magazine page mounted on royal red paper. The glass is dusty, the silver frame a little tarnished. 'Is this a story?' she asks.

'Read it.'

Diva begins to read aloud: '"Dear Penthouse . . ."' She stops and looks up at him. 'You're kidding?'

He grins. 'Read on.'

'"Dear Penthouse, I never believed any of your letters could be true until this happened to me. I was sitting alone in my dorm room studying for my physics midterm the next day when my roommate's girlfriend, Linda, came in with two of her foxy friends. I told Linda that Biff was out, but she just winked at her friends and they all giggled. They'd just come from cheerleading practice so they were all covered with sweat. I could see the drops beaded on their slender thighs. For some reason, sweaty girls have always turned me on. Then Linda locked the door."' Diva skims ahead silently as the girls all take off their clothes and seduce the studious physics student.

Harley is leaning over her shoulder now. 'There.' He points at a paragraph near the end. 'That's my favorite line.'

Diva reads it aloud. '"After fucking her two friends until they'd passed out from pleasure, I was ready to come."' Diva looks up at Harley. They both laugh.

'That's me: Name and Address Withheld By Request. My first byline.'

'Sweaty girls turn you on?'

'That's just a character I created. Although I do like a certain amount of sweat on a woman at certain times.'

383

She hands him back the silver-framed letter. 'What about your stories and poetry?'

'Dreadful stuff, really. My writing lacked one ingredient to be successful.'

'Encouragement?'

'Talent. I didn't have any.'

'I don't believe in talent,' Diva says. 'I believe in hard work. You work at something hard enough, they'll eventually call it talent. Nobody can agree on what's good and what isn't, so how are they going to agree on who's talented and who isn't?'

'Barcy's talented.'

Diva's scalp tingles with jealousy. 'She's worked at writing a long time. She deserves her success.' Her voice sounds like a public service announcement. She hopes Harley doesn't notice the pettiness in it.

'I had a student a couple years ago,' Harley says. 'He was a double major, English and computer science. He wanted to program a computer that would be able to judge whether a sample of writing was good or bad. He wanted my advice as to what writers to include as the data base for great writing. His idea was that when he was finished, a writer, instead of agonizing whether or not what they'd written was any good, could just stick the chapter or poem or whatever in the computer scanner. It would read the work, compare it against the samples of great writing, then evaluate it as either good or bad.'

'That sounds awful.'

'Not really. It takes the guesswork out of art. Eventually we could do that with paintings and music. Then we'd only like what was good.'

Diva makes a face. 'You don't believe that, do you?'

'It's a tempting idea. Then writers like me have a chance.'

'You're too hard on yourself. That was a hell of a letter

384

to *Penthouse*. I'm sure you had teenagers across America whacking off in bathrooms everywhere.'

'See, that's the same idea as that kid's computer. You know when you've written good porn because the guy gets a boner. Like a lie detector. No question, no doubts.'

Diva tears off another piece of English muffin and rolls it into a ball between her thumb and index finger. 'So you've stopped writing?'

'Just for the past twenty-one years. I'm waiting to be inspired again.'

Diva tosses the wad of English muffin at him. He opens his mouth and catches it, chews, and swallows. 'You're pretty fast for a guy with a gray crotch.'

On the drive back to her apartment, Harley coaxes Diva to sing her song again. He suggests a couple of changes, a few additional lines. Diva agrees they improve the song. When they reach her door, she invites him in, but she is happy he refuses. They've both had too good a time together to risk anything going wrong now. He leaves and she stays up late writing down the changes in her song.

26

'Don't look so nervous,' Luna says, putting her magazine aside. 'I didn't come here to fight.' The magazine is the *Journal of the American Medical Association*. Since Barcelona doesn't subscribe, she assumes Luna brought it with her. For some reason the magazine makes her even more uncomfortable. She finds it intimidating, implying the reader is one who cares about people and healing them. Only to be read by the pure at heart. No husband-fuckers allowed.

'I'm not nervous,' Barcelona says. 'I'm surprised to see someone in my house who hasn't been invited.'

Luna smiles and her thick pouty lips part to reveal a slight overbite that makes her look like Carly Simon. She is wearing a plain gray sweatshirt and tight Lycra exercise pants that stop at mid-calf. The pants are black with bright blue and yellow slashes diagonally across the thighs. She is also wearing thick white socks rolled down over the tops of her high-top athletic shoes. Her black frizzy hair is held back by two yellow banana clips. The overall effect is of someone extremely gorgeous, energetic, and intelligent. This depresses Barcelona until she remembers that despite all that, Eric still prefers her over Luna.

'Mind if I get some water?' Luna asks. 'I'm dying of thirst.' She holds up her palms. They look stained with blue ink, until Barcelona realizes those blue stains are bruises. 'I taught four aerobics classes today for a sick friend. I haven't done that in six months. My hands couldn't take all that clapping.'

'You want a soft drink or some iced tea?'

'Water's fine.'

Barcelona leads her out to the kitchen, scoops some ice into a glass, and fills it with tap water. The silence between them is damp and warm, like the air before summer lightning. What's there to say? Barcelona wonders. L: Leave Eric alone. B: That's his choice. L: He's my husband. B: He's my lover. She shakes her head at the imaginary conversation. Surely real people don't say those things.

Luna guzzles the whole glass of water at once. She refills it herself at the sink. She drinks again. Some of the water spills down her chin and neck, soaking into the collar of the gray sweatshirt. Luna doesn't seem to mind. When she's finished she unleashes another Carly Simon smile, rinses off the glass, and turns it upside down on the drain board. 'I reread *Live Wires* last week because Eric said it was going to be made into a movie.'

'Well, not necessarily. Right now it's just a script.'

'I understand. Still, it's a terrific book. The women are so cool. How's that for a literary term?' She laughs and the sound is so charming it makes Barcelona smile. 'What I mean is, the reader feels for their dilemma, their need to find some way to give love in a futuristic society that only allows them to receive love. That restricts by law, by pain of execution, any overt expression of love. Yet they are forced to allow themselves to be loved and lauded. All poetry, music, art must have women as the subject. Sex is forbidden except under the most worshipful ceremony.' She shakes her head with admiration. 'It left me wrung out, really.'

Barcelona doesn't know what to say. Is Luna's praise

genuine, or is she mocking? When in doubt, be polite, Milan would say. 'Thank you,' she says.

She doesn't offer Luna a chair, she doesn't want her to stay. But Luna wanders back to the living room and sits down on the big white sofa. Barcelona follows, stands between the stairs and the front door, waiting for something to happen. Luna doesn't look violent, but one can never tell whose glove compartment holds a pistol. Barcelona dreads this, she hates confrontation.

'My family is cursed,' Luna says suddenly. 'Truly. My full name is Luna Tituba Sewall. You familiar with those names?'

'No.'

Luna shrugs. 'Not many people are. But back between May and October of 1692, Tituba and Sewall were famous names.'

Barcelona feels a flicker of recognition. 'Tituba was the West Indian slave who went around telling all those voodoo stories that started all that witch hysteria.'

'I'm impressed. Not many people know that. Poor little Tituba got people so scared that a group of young girls claimed they were possessed by the devil and as a result three Salem women were put on trial. Three men were chosen as judges, John Hawthorne, William Stoughton, and Samuel Sewall. People went nuts accusing each other. Eventually public opinion turned against the trials and the legislature adopted a resolution for repentance, including setting aside a special fast day. It was on that day, January 14, 1697, that Samuel Sewall publically admitted the injustice of the trials. Of course, that was after nineteen men and women had already been hanged. Family gossip has it that we're descended from that Samuel Sewall. Some legacy, huh?'

Barcelona is fascinated despite the circumstances of Luna's visit. 'And so your parents named you after the slave girl?'

388

Luna reaches back and lifts a hunk of her frizzy hair. 'There's also some family gossip that there's some Negro blood in the line. Maybe Tituba incarnating within our family.'

'What do your parents say about all this?'

'They get off on it. My dad thinks it's neat to have this mysterious background, even though we're not sure we're even related to that same Judge Sewall. My mom thinks it's all very romantic. It was her idea to name me Tituba, to break any curse that might be on us in case Tituba really was a witch.'

'Jesus.' Barcelona laughs.

'Hey, a little melodrama never hurt anyone. They feel special and now they don't have to shoot anybody on the freeway to feel that way, right?'

Barcelona sits on the gray-carpeted stairs. 'Why are you here, Luna?'

'Because Eric comes here so much.'

'And you want to know why?'

'I already know why,' Luna says.

I wish I did, Barcelona thinks, staring at the beautiful young girl on the sofa. Luna is smart, sexy, and lively. And young. Why would Eric not want to rush home to her every night?

Barcelona sighs and rubs her face in her hands. 'I'm not up to this today. I'm really not. Can you come by tomorrow and we'll play this scene out.'

Luna stands up and walks over to Barcelona. She hovers like an older sister. 'I didn't come here to make a scene, Barcy. I didn't bring a scarlet letter to staple to your chest. God, I don't blame Eric for being attracted to you. You're terrific. Beautiful, sophisticated. talented. What I don't understand is why you'd want Eric back.'

Barcelona is confused. The conversation isn't going the

389

way she'd expected. She has no reference point from which to determine what she should say. No novel or play or movie with lines she can borrow.

The telephone rings and Barcelona hurries to the kitchen to answer it. She can see Luna from the kitchen. Luna is sitting on the stairs in the same place and position that Barcelona just left. That and the witch stuff Luna told her makes Barcelona feel a little spooked as she picks up the phone. She half expects to hear a heavy breather, violent obscenities.

'Barcelona?' the voice says.

'Yes?'

'It's Cory Meyers.'

The Candidate. Barcelona is relieved that it is someone normal. It gives her a chance to assess what is going on in the living room with Luna, to imagine several scenarios, to write some good lines for herself. But nothing comes to mind. Cory Meyers's voice interrupts.

'I'm down here in the netherworld.'

'Hell?'

'Close. Orange County.' He laughs. 'I've been hobnobbing with some environmentalist group that is headquartered in Newport Beach. They have some wealthy yuppie members in my district in L.A. who might want to make a campaign contribution.'

'The sum also rises, huh?'

He laughs again. 'I have a gnawing suspicion that you're too smart for me.'

'Is your wife?' Barcelona says this with an edge she didn't mean. She can't believe her own gall. She has the wife of the man she's been sleeping with out in her living room and she splashes cold moral superiority in Cory Meyers's face.

His voice is a little brittle when he answers. 'I thought I explained all that to you.'

'You did. I'm sorry. My mouth has a short circuit somewhere. I'll get it fixed.'

'I like your mouth,' he says softly.

She looks through the kitchen door. Luna is leaning back on the stairs reading her medical magazine. She has an intense expression, as if she not only understands it, but also is moved by what it all means to humanity. This makes Barcelona feel even more like the evil stepmother with a hooked nose and long warted chin. 'I can't talk now,' Barcelona tells Cory Meyers.

'Okay. The reason I'm calling is, I have a house in Corona del Mar.'

'A house in L.A. and one in Corona. I didn't know you were rich.'

'I'm not. The house is a family home. My parents are both dead. I keep meaning to empty it and rent it out, but I haven't gotten around to it. Anyway, sometimes I stay there overnight when I'm down here for business. I thought I'd stay tonight, maybe talk you into dinner.'

'Eating it or being it.'

'Have I insulted you somehow?' he asks sternly.

'No, no. I'm sorry, I'm just beat, that's all.'

'When you're tired you turn into Jerry Falwell?'

'Oral Roberts. You got any blindness you want healed, a bum knee?'

'Actually, I do have a torn rotator cuff in my shoulder. Tore it playing touch football a few weeks ago.'

'Sports injury. Figures.'

'What'd I say now?'

'I can't talk, Cory.'

'Then let's talk at dinner.'

'Can't. Maybe some other time.'

'Did I do something disgusting at lunch? Pick my teeth, blow my nose? Blow your nose?'

391

Barcelona laughs. 'No, lunch was fine. You give great lunch, okay?'

'So, do you want to eat again? Together.'

Without thinking, Barcelona says yes. Then she stops to think about it and realizes that she really would. 'Yes,' she repeats. 'But not tonight.'

'Okay,' he says. 'I'll call you.'

Barcelona hangs up and returns to the living room.

'This is amazing,' Luna says, holding up the magazine. 'They've discovered a way to create a noise that cancels out other noise and results in what sounds like silence. They match peaks to valleys in the decibel readings. The human ear then hears silence. They've already tested the benefits on reducing stress in the average working place. Amazing. Maybe you could use something like that in your next book?'

'Maybe,' Barcelona says. She sits on the sofa where Luna had been sitting before. She takes a deep breath; it's time to get this over with. 'Look, Luna, I appreciate your coming over here like this. It must have taken a lot of courage. But I really don't know what to say to you. If you want Eric to stop, you should probably be talking to him about this, not me.'

'I didn't say anything about wanting you two to stop.' Luna closes the magazine and balances it across her knees. 'That wouldn't solve the problem. Eric's problem.'

'What problem?'

'He's afraid of me. You're a comfortable memory he can relax around.'

Barcelona's neck burns with anger. 'I think I understand Eric a little better than you do.'

'In some ways I'm sure that's true. But not in this way. Surely you must have asked yourself why he's come back to you after all this time. Especially since he's with a younger woman who is also attractive and intelligent. Plus a little less sexually inhibited.' She says all this without malice, just like a lawyer citing the facts of the case.

'Less sexually inhibited.'

'Well, he mentioned there were a couple things you didn't like to do.'

'Christ.' Barcelona is so angry at Eric right now her vision blurs. She had sucked, licked, and fucked in just about every position he could come up with over the years, and even a few new ones since they'd started seeing each other again. She had drawn the line at adding another woman and at jerking him off in the movie theater. She wonders if Luna, being less sexually inhibited, has fulfilled those needs.

'Don't get mad,' Luna says. 'It's not easy for a guy Eric's age to be married to a younger woman. You think it's every guy's fantasy and so you resent me. But lots of time it's better as a fantasy than as a reality. To Eric I'm unpredictable. He's so scared I'll leave him for a younger guy, someone my own age, he's had some trouble keeping it up lately.'

'I haven't noticed any such trouble,' Barcelona says, hoping it hurts Luna as much as she hurts.

Luna shrugs undaunted. 'Of course, not with you. You're safe. His own age, emotionally unattached. He can relax, be his old self again. See, the problem with Eric is that he's finally met the girl of his dreams and doesn't know how to handle it.'

'Jesus, I admire your balls,' Barcelona says. 'Maybe he's met the girl of his dreams and now it's time to wake up. Dreams aren't always so wonderful in the light of day.'

Luna tucks her knees up against her chin. She looks sad. 'I didn't come here to hurt you, though I see that's what I've done. I thought you'd understand.'

'Understand what?'

'Eric can't come back to you. Nothing can come of it any more than it could before. You two didn't split up because you were bored or restless or anything like that. You split up because there was a part of you that Eric could never be part of. He tried to influence every other aspect of your life, right? What you read, saw, listened to. He's very competitive.'

Barcelona nods. 'Lots of men are.'

'But you had that one thing he couldn't understand. You had your art, your writing.'

'Oh, shit, you've been reading too many women's books.'

Luna smiles. 'When you wrote, you excluded him, made him feel unimportant. It wasn't a big conscious thing on his part. That's just his competitive nature. The more you wrote, the bigger your success, the more diminished he felt. That's really what separated you guys, and why you'll never be able to get back together again. He was too much in awe of you.'

'Don't you think you're a little young to be lecturing so much?' Barcelona says.

Luna doesn't answer. She unties her shoelace and reties it.

'Eric was my biggest supporter,' Barcelona says. 'When I got rejection after rejection, he comforted me.'

'That's Eric too. He loved you and didn't want to see you hurt. I'm not taking that away from him. Hell, that's one of the things I love about him. But then I'm not an artist. I can't write, draw, play a musical instrument, or sing. I can study and get A's. I can do four hours of aerobics. I can apply theories, but I can't think of any on my own. That's why I'm so perfect for Eric. He's the same way. Even his thesis is based on someone else's theory. His professor suggested it to him.'

'Really? He never told me that.'

'See what I mean? He didn't want you to think he wasn't creative too. The dissertation is first-rate research, but he would never have been able to think up the idea on his own.'

Barcelona thinks this information over. Why would Eric tell Luna all this and not her? She sighs at Luna. 'After knowing what he's been doing here with me, why do you still want him?'

Luna's smile is without sadness or irony. 'He may not be the best man in the world, but he's the best man in *my* world.'

Barcelona leans back into the sofa. She picks some of Larry's hair off a cushion then glances at Luna. 'Now what?'

'Nothing. I didn't come here to break things up. I just thought we should talk. I don't want you to get hurt.'

'Me? Doesn't it bother you knowing he's been sneaking over here to sleep with me?'

'I'm disturbed that he feels so vulnerable around me right now that he has to retreat into his past. But after a while he'll see that I'm with him to stay and all that anxiety will pass. Then he'll be back.'

'Our having sex doesn't hurt you?'

Luna smiles at the notion. 'Why should I be hurt just because he sticks a fleshy part of his anatomy into a slippery part of yours and rubs it until it squirts?'

Barcelona presses her finger against the refrigerated glass. 'Gimme a pound of the chicken salad.'

'Yes, ma'am,' the blond boy in the white apron says. His hair is slicked back and shiny in the *GQ* style that Barcelona detests. It makes men look like predators, gigolos with insincere smiles. Maybe that's the way men feel today. The numbers were finally on their side.

The blond boy slaps the plastic container on the top of the showcase. 'Anything else, ma'am?'

'A pound of red potato salad.'

'Yes, ma'am.' He slides open the door and begins ladling the potato salad into another plastic container. He weighs it, pastes a computerized sticker on the lid that tells the date, the weight, the price. He stacks it on top of the chicken salad. 'Anything else, ma'am?'

'No, thank you.' Barcelona came to the market for cat food. She was out and Larry was starting to stalk her. He didn't cry or make any sound, he just followed her around, sitting near her, staring, as if he were waiting for her to fall asleep so he could eat her face. This market didn't carry the 9 Lives brand that Larry preferred, but Barcelona was not about to fight the early evening crowds lined up behind their overflowing carts at each check stand at the supermarket. This little market was in and out. Chicken and potato salads for her dinner. Kal Kan for Larry's.

Luna. What to make of her? Barcelona waits at the checkout stand and watches the tall skinny woman checker ring up her total. The woman's hair has been frosted so often it looks brittle enough to crackle in a breeze. Barcelona tries not to stare as the woman bags the cat food and salads.

'Thank you, ma'am,' the woman says and immediately waves to a man in the other checkout line. 'I can help you over here, sir.' He looks at her hair and hesitates.

Barcelona had intended to cook that night. A curried eggplant dish from a vegetarian cookbook that Diva had suggested. It nettles her somewhat to think that Diva is strong enough to become a vegetarian and she isn't. After all, Diva has never been known for her self-discipline. But maybe that's just because her body looks like it lacks discipline. Fuck it, Barcelona thinks, climbing into the Geezemobile. Tonight she will eat the flesh of chickens while Larry eats the minced flesh of cows. They will have a carnivores' party. The climax will be when they eat each other.

When Barcelona enters her home she is surprised to find no one waiting. The house is empty except for Larry who immediately runs in through the cat door and hops up on top of the TV. She turns it on hoping the radiation will quicken his demise. A movie with Charles Bronson is on. A couple of guys are machine-gunning Bronson's crop of watermelons. Actually, that looks like fun.

She empties a can into Larry's bowl. He watches but doesn't move. Not until Barcelona is seated at the kitchen table does Larry jump down and begin eating his dinner.

Barcelona has four containers in front of her. She opens each: a plastic vat of chicken salad, a plastic vat of red potato salad, a jar of chunky peanut butter, a box of Waverly crackers. Some of the crackers she smears with peanut butter, some she uses to shovel up chicken salad. She uses a fork to eat the potato salad. Charles Bronson searches for the men who killed his melons.

It is during a Toyota truck commercial that Barcelona decides not to see Eric again. At least as lovers. She thinks sadly of the lost sex, the kissing, his warm breath in her hair. She will miss the laughing when they both try to take a bath together in her tiny tub. She will miss skipping any conversation and heading straight for the bed because they both just wanted to get naked and slide across each other's bodies.

She will not miss the books he brings for her to read, the records to listen to. The pressure to improve.

Luna was right about Eric. Barcelona had felt that even as she had shaken her head while Luna spoke. There had even been a moment, a flashbulb microsecond, when she had felt closer to Luna because of the truth they shared than she ever had with Eric. Maybe Luna was indeed part witch.

Whatever. The truth remained, Eric was hiding out in Barcelona's bed, hiding under the covers from the woman he really wanted to be with but couldn't handle the way he could Barcelona. And Barcelona knew she was as much to blame for this as Eric was. She had allowed herself to fall back into that same comfortable bed because she had romanticized their former relationship out of proportion.

Barcelona smears a cracker with peanut butter and plops some chicken salad on top. She eats it while Charles Bronson fires a shotgun from the back of a pickup truck. That too looks like fun. Shooting watermelons and firing shotguns from the bed of a pickup truck is much more fun than thinking about relationships, certainly more fun than having them.

She is full but continues to stuff herself with crackers, peanut butter, chicken salad, and red potato salad. It is easier than getting up, switching channels, putting the containers away, rinsing off the fork.

The doorbell rings and Barcelona is confused. There aren't any doorbells in the bed of a pickup truck. Larry, who has climbed back on top of the TV, looks up. That is how Barcelona knows it is her doorbell chiming. She isn't expecting anyone, but she suspects it is Eric. He must've missed his key, figured out what Luna's done, and come here to talk. He will want to sit on the sofa, not within intimate range, just close enough to reach over and touch each other in a comforting way, close enough to look thoughtfully into each other's eyes. Somewhere along the line one or both of them would shed tears. Afterward there would be tender sex, sleeping wrapped in his arms.

Right now that sounds pretty good and as she walks toward the front door, she does not feel the same strong resolve to end their relationship just yet.

She peeks through the peephole. 'Christ.' She opens the door.

'Hi,' Cory Meyers says.

'Hi. Let me guess, there's a save-the-warthog group in this neighborhood that you're soliciting for campaign contributions. So you dropped by.'

'Actually they're a nuke-the-warthog group. But I'm flexible.' He looks over her shoulder into the living room. 'Nice place.'

She smiles, steps aside to let him in. 'I know a hint when I hear one.'

He enters and looks around. 'Still a nice place.' He looks at the two prints on the walls. They are by different artists, but they are both desert landscapes. One is chalky white and pink, the other brightly colored. 'They match the color scheme of the carpeting,' he points out. 'And the furniture.'

'Something wrong with that?'

'No. It's just interesting.' He follows her out to the kitchen and watches her put the containers of food away. 'Have you eaten?'

'Yes.'

'Are you hungry?'

'No.'

He nods, looks around, scratches Larry's head. '*Mr. Majestyk*,' he says.

'His name's Larry.'

'No, the movie.' He points at the TV screen. 'I've seen this one. I like when they shoot his watermelons.'

'This isn't a good time to visit,' Barcelona says, leaning against the refrigerator door. 'I've been feeling crabby all day and it's just getting worse.'

'I can take it. Let's go out to dinner. Take your mind off whatever's troubling you.'

'If I ate another bite I'd puke.'

He shuts the TV off. 'We'll find a restaurant where no one will notice. One with sawdust on the floor.'

Barcelona knows that sooner or later tonight Eric will call or come over to have an intense talk. She does not want anything intense right now. 'Okay,' she tells Cory. 'Let's go.'

'Still no answer,' Barcelona says, returning to the table.

'Maybe she's still undercover.'

'God, I hope so.' She sits down and sips her wine. 'I feel responsible.'

'You didn't do anything. In fact, you probably salvaged the situation for Dixie.'

Barcelona shrugs, unconvinced.

Cory Meyers reaches across the table and touches her hand. 'You want me to call? I have a few cop friends who might be able to find something out, even down here in Orange County.'

She smiles. 'I don't know. Let's see what happens tonight.'

'Okay.' He removes his hand from hers, but her skin retains his warmth. She looks at it as if she expects to see the imprint still there from his hand. 'Why'd you come over tonight after I told you not to?'

'I don't know.' He shakes his head, stabs his blueberry pie with his fork. 'It's not like me.'

'I'm not sure about that.'

'You're still pissed at me because Trina and I had sex a few weeks ago. You can be very self-righteous sometimes. Give Trina some credit; she wasn't being seduced. It was her idea.'

Barcelona drinks her coffee. She'd been too full to eat, but she'd had three cups of coffee while watching Cory polish off a club sandwich, fries, and his pie. They are sitting in a coffee shop in Corona del Mar, a cozy little coastal city where the livin' is easy but the rents are high. Fashion Island looms on the ridge above the city.

Cory and Barcelona sit in silence for a couple of minutes. Barcelona feels like a saboteur, planting verbal mines for Cory to hit as he pilots through the conversation. He hits one, it explodes, stuns him momentarily, but he pushes on. She likes that about him. She hates herself for being so mean to him, but she can't stop herself.

'Trina is not as tough as she acts,' Barcelona says.

'I know that,' Cory says. 'Neither am I.'

'Oh? Strong but tender. Sounds like a campaign promise.'

Cory Meyers sighs, leans back in the booth, and looks away. Barcelona steals a glance at him, sees his jaw tense. He looks back at her and she looks down into her coffee. 'Look, you want to go home, you only have to ask.'

'Let's go.' Barcelona starts to slide out of the booth. She stops, looks at him. His face is grim. 'I'm sorry. I know I've said that before to you. I don't know why I'm acting this way. Stop me before I insult again.' She points at what's left of his blueberry pie. 'Go ahead, throw it in my face. I deserve it.'

Cory picks the plate up and Barcelona is shocked to think he might actually throw it at her. She flinches. He sets the plate down and laughs. 'I'd have been within my constitutional rights to let it rip, you know?'

'I know.'

'But I'm too civilized.'

'I appreciate it.'

He hands her the bill. 'Here, your treat. It certainly hasn't been mine.'

She grins and takes the check. She lays a twenty-dollar bill on top of it. The waitress, a young redhead with a Band-Aid tattooed on her thigh, scoops up the check and the twenty and rushes off.

'What do you think the tattoo means?' Cory asks.

'She breaks easily?'

He looks over at her standing at the cash register ringing up the bill. Her body and face are lean as a greyhound's. 'I don't think she breaks easily.' He looks at Barcelona with a funny expression that she can't read.

'I always wanted a tattoo,' he says, unlocking the front door of his house. 'In college my best buddy and I decided to get our heads shaved and our scalps tattooed. That way when our hair grew back no one would know about the tattoos.'

'Then what's the point of getting them?'

'Our little secret. Like having a secret identity. During the day, mild-mannered students at a major metropolitan university. But at night, party animals with tattooed skulls and super libidos.'

'I never wanted a tattoo, even after Cher got hers.' Barcelona walks into the house.

Cory follows, flicking the light switch. 'It's a little musty,' he says. 'I haven't been down here in a couple months.' He goes over to the window and, after a couple of unsuccessful tugs, yanks it open.

'This is nice,' Barcelona says. 'Quaint.'

'A dump. Two tiny bedrooms and one bathroom. But we're only two blocks from the beach so it's valuable. Actually, I find it hard to believe that my parents managed to raise me in such a little gingerbread house. It didn't seem all that small when I was growing up. Except when I sneaked a girl into my room.'

'It was her idea no doubt,' she says.

He looks at her, sees she is kidding this time, and nods. 'Women can't keep their hands off me.'

Barcelona walks around the living room. It is paneled in white wood, the tan carpeting is worn and stained.

The pictures on the wall are bland landscapes probably purchased at garage sales.

'Pretty dreadful stuff, huh?' Cory says, gesturing to the paintings. 'If it wasn't for bad taste, my folks wouldn't have had any taste.'

'Did you like them?'

'Sure. My dad won the sand castle-building contest three years in a row when I was a kid. He could really make those towers. That was before they brought in all these professional architects with molds and shit. Back then all you were allowed was a pail and a shovel. Period.'

'What about your mom?'

'No, you couldn't use your mom, just a pail and a shovel.'

Barcelona laughs. 'You're too weird to be in politics.'

'Too weird to win, maybe, but just weird enough to try. Sit.'

There was no sofa, just two white rattan chairs. They each sat in one. 'My mom worked part time as a private nurse for terminal patients. I always liked it when her patients died because then she spent more time at home. I didn't realize how grizzly that thought was until later. Once she came home earlier than expected and I said something like, "Oh, good, Mr. Monroe died." She looked at me horrified for a moment, like I was some ghastly bug she'd never seen before. I thought she was going to squash me right then and there. But suddenly she just grabbed me and gave me a big hug. I never said anything like that again.'

'But you thought it.'

He smiles. 'My secret.'

Barcelona moves her head and her earring snags the collar of her blouse. 'Shit.' She fiddles with it, but her neck is crooked at such an awkward angle she has trouble unhooking it.

403

'Here, let me,' Cory offers, coming over. 'I've had some small experience at doing this.' He kneels beside her and gently works the earring free. 'You'll live.'

She looks into his eyes and there is a moment when they are close enough to hear each other breathing. Barcelona feels silly at such moments, clumsy and uncertain. She wants him to kiss her, wants to kiss him. After all these years the rules still aren't clear. It's one thing to believe it's okay to make the first move; it's another to actually do it.

But then he leans over her, his mouth on hers, lips magnetized, pulling against each other. His hands, bigger than she remembers them, hold her shoulders. Her shoulders feel small and delicate in his grasp. She feels each bone shift under the pressure of his fingers. Her breasts brush against his chest and she feels a rush of adrenaline that shoots up to her lips like a shot from the dentist. The effect is so powerful the eyes behind her closed lids ache. She pulls back, breaking contact. He leans further forward, kisses her cheek, her neck. She cups her hands behind his head. She kisses him. Her tongue slides over his.

'I want to ask you a question,' she says, their faces inches apart. 'Truth is optional.'

'Ask,' he says.

'Don't take this wrong. This isn't me being Billy Graham. It's just that I'm coming out of a screwy relationship and I don't want to get into another one.'

'Define screwy.'

'Married.'

He nods. 'Oh.'

She pulls back into her rattan chair and he sits down on the floor next to her. 'Maybe I'm making more of this than I should. It's just a kiss.'

'Not just a kiss,' he says softly.

She leans her head on the back of the chair and looks up at the speckled ceiling. 'This is the hard part. They should have preprinted relationship cards distributed along with condoms to every kid at puberty. The dialogue is pre-written so all you have to do is hand the card to the guy or girl of your choice and they can check the boxes.'

'I don't have any diseases that I know about. I haven't had the mumps though.'

'That's not what I'm getting at.'

He pulls off his deck shoes and rearranges himself so he's sitting cross-legged. Then he pulls off her shoes and squeezes her big toe. 'My wife?'

Barcelona nods. 'Are you sure this isn't just a temporary thing you two are going through? A spat. A dry period. You get over those things.'

'I'm sure.'

She waits for him to go on. When he doesn't she says, 'Well, I'm glad that's cleared up. I feel better.'

He looks at her with a serious expression. 'Can't you just take my word?'

'You're a politician,' she says, smiling.

Slowly he smiles back. 'I see your point.' He strips off his sports jacket and flings it across the other chair. 'Women always want a lot of words.'

'They want to share. They want men to be open.'

'Do they?' he says mysteriously. He shifts around so he's facing her, sitting cross-legged at her feet. 'My wife is a beautiful woman. She got straights As at Stanford in physics. Now she teaches at UCLA. We get along wonderfully, care about each other very much.'

Barcelona's heart stalls. She's waiting for the 'but.'

'But,' he says, 'we have reached an impasse.'

'About what?'

'Sex.'

'Sex?'

405

'She doesn't want any.'

Barcelona shrugs. 'You mean she doesn't make love as often as you'd like?'

'I mean she doesn't make love at all. Period. No sex. After a couple years of us trying to work it out, scheduling sex, trying different techniques, more foreplay, less foreplay, different positions, different rooms, props, she finally came up to me and said she'd decided that she just didn't want to have sex anymore, ever. Not that she begrudged me my wanting to, she just didn't like it. It saddened her to do it and she'd come to the irrevocable decision to forswear it for the rest of her life. I suggested she seek therapy, but she smiled and said that she didn't feel bad about not wanting sex, only in that it hurt me. She still loved me and we could remain married, I could have affairs whenever the urge was upon me.'

'My God, how did you feel?'

Cory smiles. 'You won't believe this, but I felt good. Not for our marriage, but for Dayna. I could tell that she felt better than she had in a long time. Her decision had freed her in a way. I was proud that she was able to reach her decision.' He leans back on his elbows. 'Of course, I didn't think we should stay married. I'm still trying to get her to seek some therapy, but she says she's the happiest now that she's ever been.'

'Maybe she's gay?'

'She says she isn't. She claims that sex with either man or woman is equally repulsive.'

Barcelona fidgets with the earring that had snagged her blouse earlier. She takes it off, then puts it back on. 'Weren't there any signs when you first were dating?'

'No. We screwed like rabbits. She says she liked it then but somewhere along the line just lost it. Makes you wonder what I did wrong, huh?'

In fact, that's exactly what Barcelona was wondering.

He must have done something weird to turn her off from sex so radically. 'No, of course it wasn't anything you did.'

He stares at her with glowering intensity. 'Now you know why men don't talk much,' he says angrily. 'Women want men to be open, but only if they say what women want to hear. They don't really want to hear the truths in a man's mind. Men sense that and keep quiet.'

'That's ridiculous,' Barcelona says. But she wishes she hadn't heard the truth.

He stands up, slips into his shoes. 'Getting kinda late. Ready to go?'

She is ready to go. She wants to go. The complexities of talking to Luna, then to Cory, of still not being able to reach Dixie have wrung her out. But now she feels insensitive and cruel. She draws painful confessions from a man, then backs off from him afterward. Somehow she knows Luna would have handled this better.

She had made up her mind to sleep with Cory tonight. He is attractive, fun, and very sexy anyway. Besides, she owes him some comfort, she needs to prove she's not affected by his revelation. She wants to blame the problem on his wife, things like that happen to people. She gets up and kisses him. He is surprised at first, but then responds.

'Pity kiss?' he says.

'You complaining?'

'I'm just curious how far you'll take pity.'

'You're too sensitive,' she says. 'Where's the bathroom?'

He points down the hall. 'You can't miss it.'

Barcelona goes into the bathroom, drops her pants and panties, and pulls the tampon out. It is barely pink since she is at the end of her period. She sits down and pees, looking around for a magazine or something to read. There is nothing. She takes the Tampax box out of her purse and reads that: For Light to Medium Flow. 10 Slender Regular. Made of rayon fiber, rayon nonwoven overwrap, cotton cord, and cotton thread. Associated with Toxic Shock Syndrome (TSS). TSS is a rare but serious disease that may cause death.

When she is finished peeing she dabs herself with toilet paper. She decides against inserting another tampon. She expects that she and Cory will soon end up in bed and there was no need to waste a tampon now. She buttons up her pants, flushes, and checks her face in the mirror. The ugly yellow wallpaper surrounding her casts a jaundiced shade on her skin. She passes a brush through her hair twice and lets it go at that. But as she's leaving the bathroom, she notices the toilet is starting to burp and bubble. Yellow water is regurgitated back up the bowl along with her pink spongy tampon. The toilet bowl is almost full and still rising. The tampon is swirling around the bowl.

Panicked, she hits the handle again, but nothing happens. 'Oh God,' she says. 'Oh, God!'

Yellow water is brimming and starting to overflow onto the floor.

'Cory!' she hollers. 'Cory!'

She hears him running down the hall. He twists the doorknob, but she'd forgotten to unlock the door. Water stained with her piss is spilling onto the floor. She unlocks the door.

Cory looks at the toilet and lifts the seat. Barcelona's pink tampon gushes over the plastic toilet seat onto the floor. She cringes with embarrassment. He tiptoes in his socks to the cupboard under the sink and removes a plunger. He shoves the plunger into the toilet, spilling even more water onto the floor. A couple of plunges and water begins to gurgle down the drain. He tosses the plunger in the corner.

'This is so embarrassing,' she says as he leads her out of the bathroom.

'Now we're even.'

408

'I hope I didn't break anything. They're supposed to be flushable.'

'Plumbing is ancient. It's done that before. Don't worry. Sit down.'

Barcelona returns to her chair, leaving wet footprints on the carpet. Cory returns with a blue bath towel. He kneels in front of her and dries her feet. He stops, hoists up her pant legs, and rolls off her knee-high stockings. Then he returns to drying, even getting between each toe. When he's finishes he says, 'Ready to go home now?'

She grins at him, kisses him on the cheek. 'Yes.'

He drives down the dark roads and they hardly speak. He reaches out to touch her hand; she slides closer to him. She leans her head against his shoulder. He squeezes her thigh.

'I like sex,' she says, staring out the window.

'I figured you did.'

They drive past the university. Over the freeway. Even at this hour the freeway traffic whooshes by.

He pulls up to the curb and shuts off the motor. He kisses her, his hand chastely holding her waist. She presses herself into his body so her breasts flatten against his chest. His tongue licks across her teeth.

'I'll walk you in,' he says.

'No, it's only around the corner.' She kisses him quickly and jumps out of the car.

'I'll call you tomorrow and we'll try again.'

'Your plumbing or mine?' she says.

He drives away laughing, waving his hand out the window. Barcelona walks to her door. She feels happy about Cory Meyers, though she also feels guilty about Eric. She is cheating on him. She recognizes the absurdity of that thought, yet it is real nevertheless. She returns to her resolve not to see Eric again as lovers. Knowing that this resolve is made easier by Cory's interest does not make her feel especially noble.

Larry is waiting at the front door even though he could have entered through his cat door. In the lamplight by her door, Barcelona can see the glint of blood on his scalp. 'What have you done now, you little jerk,' she says, but feels compassion for him anyway. She picks him up, which he rarely lets her do without a fight, and carries him to the upstairs bathroom. She dabs his wound with peroxide. He hisses at her and nips her finger with his teeth.

'You little shit,' she says, but holds him tight. She sprays the wound with Bactine and lets him run.

She goes down to the kitchen to check her messages on the answering machine. There are only two. The first is from Grief: *'Sorry, honey, but the script deal is off. Complications. We're out of it altogether. Call me tomorrow and I'll explain.'*

The second is from Trina. Her voice is uncharacteristically shrill with panic: *'Barcy, Jesus! Call my service immediately. They'll page me and I'll let you know where I am. Jesus.'* Pause. *'Call me. Dixie's husband has been arrested for murder. I can't . . .'* Pause. *'Just call me, I'll tell you the rest.'*

Barcy pulls up a chair and begins dialing Trina's answering service. She misdials twice before getting the right number.

27

Dixie can hardly breathe. She is facedown on Brandon's bed. Her arms and legs are spread-eagled and tied to the separate feet of the bed. The rope is bright yellow and very rough. The skin on her wrists and ankles is already rubbed raw.

Brandon and Joseph stand next to the bed, staring down at her as if she were some modern art exhibit at a museum.

'What do we do now?' Joseph asks. Dixie can hear the panic in his voice.

'I don't know. I haven't decided.' Brandon's voice is oddly calm, somehow more assured than before. But there is a strange edge in it too, like that of a jumper balanced on a twelfth-story ledge toying with the idea of leaping, wanting to savor it all first, imagining the free fall over and over before actually stepping into the abyss. Brandon sounds as if he is looking over the ledge now and this scares Dixie more than anything else.

'Don't do anything stupid here,' Dixie says forcefully. 'I'm a cop, for God's sake. So far all you've done is deal a little dope. No big deal. I haven't even see a buy, so I can't testify to that. That puts you in the clear, Brandon. And Joe, you know my testimony against you has been compromised anyway because of our physical contact. I've got nothing on either of you. If you let me go right now.'

'She's right, man,' Joseph says. 'She didn't see anything go down between us.'

Brandon opens the drawer of his dresser and pulls out a T-shirt and puts it on. It has the logo of Puma sporting goods on it, the name and a leaping cat. Dixie sees the same logo painted on the wall next to the refrigerator.

'We let her go,' Joseph says, 'she's got nothing.'

'What about us tying her up. She could get us for assault, or maybe even kidnapping, unlawful imprisonment. Cops can always get you for something, dude.'

Dixie twists her head around to look directly at him. 'You think I want everyone to know I let a couple teenagers tie me up? Christ, just out of personal pride I'd let this case drop.'

'She makes sense,' Joseph pleads.

Brandon doesn't say anything. He walks over to the bed and sits down, his back to Dixie. She can smell coconut oil from his suntan lotion. 'I don't know,' he says and leans back so his head is resting on her butt. 'I've got to figure this out.'

'There's nothing to figure out,' Joseph says. His voice is angry now. Apparently, despite Dixie's betrayal, he still sees her as his date. Anything Brandon does to her reflects badly on him.

'There's plenty to figure out,' Brandon says, bouncing his head a little on Dixie's butt. 'This mama's harder than a couple granite rocks. Loosen 'em up a bit, babe, I don't like no rocky pillows.' When Dixie doesn't relax her buttocks he suddenly twists around and swats her hard with his hand. Her skin burns. 'I said loosen those buns.'

'Fuck, man,' Joseph says. 'Knock it off. We're trying to negotiate our way out of this, not make things worse.'

'I like things the way they are.' Brandon grins and nestles his head against Dixie's butt. 'Ah, that's better.'

'We've got to let her go.'

'Do we?'

'What else can we do?'

Brandon chuckles. 'Keep her. Like a pet.'

Dixie can't see Joseph as he paces out of her line of vision. She tries to control her breathing, conscious that Brandon can feel any shift in her pattern from his position on her backside. She doesn't want him to know how scared she is. Her only hope is Joseph.

'You're fucking crazy, you know that?' Joseph says. 'We can't keep her.'

'Who's gonna stop us?'

'The cops, that's who. They know she's undercover, she must've told them about me. I'm the first one they'll come after.'

'Just stay cool. Without her they've got nothing on you. You came down to the beach, watched the surf, had an ice cream, and went your separate ways.'

'That won't wash,' Dixie says. 'They'll be all over him until he talks. You two have been seen together, they'll find out and haul both your asses to jail and keep him there until they find me.'

Brandon rolls off her and kneels next to the bed. He lays his head on the bed six inches from her face. 'What if they don't find you?'

'Why take any chances?' Joseph says. 'Just let her go.'

Brandon stands up. 'I've always wanted a slave. I may never get a chance like this again.' He claps Joseph on the back. 'Lighten up, dude. I'll protect us.'

Joseph backs away from him. 'You're nuts, Brandon. I'm not getting involved in anything like this.'

'You don't have any choice, Joey. You buy your shit from me, but I buy direct from some very tense guys who wouldn't want to see their interests threatened. I tell them you're a loose cannon and they'll come over to your house and stomp the shit out of you and your folks, then you'll fuck your dog for dessert.'

Joseph doesn't say anything. He paces back into Dixie's view. She twists her wrists against the rope, but the knots are too tight. She feels the skin on her wrist scrape away. She tries to make a mental list of her options, but she can't think of any. Only Joseph.

'You dumb bitch,' Joseph yells at her. She can see the fear and anger in his eyes. 'How old are you?'

'Thirty-three,' Dixie says.

'Fuck,' Joseph says.

'Twice as old as me,' Brandon laughs. He reaches down and rubs her butt. 'But she's got the tight ass of a thirteen-year-old. We could have some real fun with it.' He bends over and bites her left butt cheek through the jeans. He chomps down hard enough to bring tears to her eyes, but she doesn't cry out. He stands up and laughs. '"Yummy, yummy, yummy, I got love in my tunny." You know that oldie? It's from your generation.'

'Jesus, man, this isn't the time for that shit,' Joseph says.

'You're getting on my nerves, dude.' Brandon sits on the bed and gently rubs the spot he just bit. The flesh is so tender that Dixie winces under his touch. 'Oops, a little sore?' His hands slip down between her legs and he presses his finger against her crotch. 'That better?'

'That's enough,' Joseph says. He kneels down next to the bed and starts untying the rope. 'We're letting her go.'

Dixie expects Brandon to say something, start arguing, but when she looks back at him he is calmly watching Joseph untie her left hand. His face is oddly serene in its concentration, as if he were seeing a knot being untied for the first time. When Joseph frees the left hand, he runs around the bed, kneels, and begins untying the right. Dixie purposely says nothing, not wanting to tip the balance of power or rattle Joseph's resolve.

'I'll drop her off at her car,' Joseph prattles to no one in particular. Sweat pearls are lined above his lip. He avoids looking at Dixie. 'She can holler to the cops or anyone after that, it won't matter. She's got nothing.'

The rope drops away from her wrist and she rubs circulation back into the skin, avoiding the raw sores. One wrist has a flap of skin turn loose by the rope. She yanks it off and tosses it on the floor. Joseph is at her right foot now, loosening the rope.

Suddenly Dixie feels a shift of weight on the bed. She turns just as Brandon grabs the baseball bat from against the dresser and swings it at Joseph. Dixie yells 'No!' at the same instant the bat connects with Joseph's head, just above the right ear. The sound at impact is like breaking a board over your knee. Joseph wobbles sideways a moment, his eyes fluttering white. He moans, tries to rise from his knees, staggers against the bed.

Brandon wallops him again.

This time the sound of the bat connecting with the skull is eerie. Instead of a solid thud, it sounds mushy, like jumping with both feet into thick mud.

'Joseph!' Dixie cries out as he slumps across the backs of her legs.

Brandon walks around the bed, cautiously pokes Joseph's jaw with the bat. Warm blood is spilling out of his cracked skull and soaking through the thighs of her jeans. Brandon pokes him in the ribs and jumps back when the body begins to slide off the edge of the bed. Joseph crumbles onto the floor.

Brandon kneels over him, checking for a pulse. 'Well,' he says, looking up at Dixie with a shrug. 'That's that.'

The rest of Saturday was spent tied facedown on Brandon's bed while he played CDs, listened to the radio, or watched TV from a huge overstuffed chair as big as a sofa. For about an hour he tried to learn to play 'Hotel California' on his guitar, following the chords in a guitar book, playing them over and over again. Around midnight, he munched on peanut butter and Ritz crackers. About four in the morning, while watching *Teacher's Pet* with Clark Gable and Doris Day on the Atlanta Superstation, he decided to paint the logo from the Ritz cracker box just below his Perrier and above Miller Lite.

For most of the night, Joseph's body was hunched into a fetal position next to the bed and enclosed in two large black trash bags. One was pulled over his head and torso, the other was pulled up over his legs and hips. Then the two overlapping ends were neatly stapled together. Brandon had gone about the whole thing very methodically.

Dixie feels Joseph's dried blood on the backs of the legs of her jeans. The blood stiffened the denim and it chafes her skin. If she twists her neck around until a sharp pain needles the muscle, she can see Joseph lumped up into the trash bags like a month's worth of newspapers. Surprisingly, the smell isn't bad.

But by Sunday morning, after Brandon has finished his Ritz logo, he drags the body into the bathroom.

'It wasn't as bad as I thought,' he says to Dixie, wiping the yellow and blue paint from his hands with a turpentine-soaked rag. 'But not as good neither. Murder. The big M. I thought it would feel different.'

'Different?' she says, trying to keep him talking.

'I don't know how, just different than it was. More thrilling, I guess.'

'Maybe if you eat his heart,' she says. 'Some tribes do that to give them the strength of their enemy.'

'Nah, too messy. Besides, all I've got is a hot plate anyway.' He sits on the edge of the bed. This is the first he's talked to her since yesterday when he'd killed Joseph.

The scent of turpentine from his rag stings Dixie's nose, but she's happy for the stimulation. Her body aches from being strapped down and unable to move. She concentrates on making her voice calm, nonthreatening. That remark about eating the heart was wrong, provocative. She needs to defuse the situation, try to bring some rationality, convince Brandon there's a way out. 'Look, Brandon, you're only sixteen. Even with Joseph's death, chances are a good lawyer can convince a jury that you were the junior partner to him, that he was the drug kingpin. You were his unwilling accomplice.'

'Yeah,' he says. 'But I still killed him.'

'Involuntary manslaughter. An argument over drugs. He wanted you to keep dealing, you wanted out, you'd come to realize drugs were wrong, blah, blah, blah. A half-decent lawyer can make that work.'

'Except you'd testify otherwise.'

'Without any additional physical evidence, I don't much like the state's chances of winning the case, do you? I figure you'll walk, worse case a suspended sentence or a couple months in juvy.'

Brandon nods. 'You're probably right.' He gets up, unties her left foot, walks around the bed, unties her right foot.

Dixie tries not to show her anxiousness. She moves her legs a little, though they are asleep and it feels as if she is trying to drag two redwoods up a hill. She waits for him to untie her hands, but he stands behind her, not moving.

She is surprised to suddenly feel his hands on her waist, lifting her hips up as he reaches around to unbutton her jeans. She twists against him, struggling to squirm out of his grip, but he straddles her from behind and begins to roughly yank her pants down. He gets the jeans over her butt when he starts to laugh.

'Red panties,' he says. 'Nice.' He pulls them down too

and pokes her cheek where he bit her. She tenses her muscles so she can't feel his touch. 'Fuck, where'd you get those muscles?'

'You don't want to do this, Brandon,' Dixie says calmly. 'You do this and even a smart lawyer won't be able to help you. There won't be any innocent dupe defense. Your age won't matter.'

He leans over so his face is in her hair, his mouth against her ear. 'Who cares?'

He tugs her pants and panties off over her feet and reties her ankles to the bed. He sits on the bed and runs his fingertips along the crevice of her buttocks. 'See, I've figured it out. I just made my buy for the month, so I'm flush with goodies, lots of product to sell, if not around here then somewhere else. This place is getting pretty lame anyway. I'm bored doing the same shit, seeing the same assholes every day, fucking the same tired pussies. My folks begging me to come back home. I'm ready for a change of scenery. All I gotta do is sell some of my shit and then take off for parts unknown.'

'Where can you go? Cops everywhere will be looking for you.'

He shrugs. 'They can look, but they can't touch. Shit, cops aren't that smart. I've been dealing for three years and they never busted me once.' He slaps her ass soundly.

Dixie isn't sure what tactic to use now. Reason hasn't worked and isn't likely to, mostly because he's right. With a few bucks in his pocket he could disappear and probably never be found again. He is smart, cunning, and completely without a conscience. She feels the black hood of despair slipping over her head. He intends to rape her, of that she is certain. The question now is will he kill her afterward?

She relaxes her bladder and begins to urinate.

'Jesus fuck!' he says, jerking his hand off her butt.

The warm urine soaks into the blankets and bed sheets.

418

Her massive consumption of vitamins gives the urine an especially pungent odor.

Brandon laughs. 'I didn't know I scared you so much.'

That's what Dixie wants him to think. She hopes he will untie her to change the sheets, hopes that somewhere during her being untied she will have an opportunity to jump him, crush his skull with a baseball bat, drag his brains out of his skull, and stomp them into the floor with her feet.

He unties her legs but not her hands. He pulls the blanket and sheets off under her like a clumsy magician yanking a tablecloth out from under a set of fine China. The blanket burns her stomach as it is jerked out from under her. Then he reties her ankles back to their separate posts. 'You piss again, you can lie in it. Don't matter to me.'

She looks around at him just as he is stepping out of his shorts. His penis is already hard and pointing straight up. It is long and thin, pinker than a man's. The hair is finer. He takes a running start and leaps onto the bed landing with his feet astride her hips. He jumps up and down a few times as if on a trampoline, slapping his hands against the rafter overhead. The mattress bounces hard against Dixie's face. It smells of coconut oil, turpentine, and urine. Brandon drops to his knees, one on either side of her hips. He strokes the skin of her ass and says, 'Eeenie, meenie, minie, moe.'

'Can I have some water?' she asks.

'Sure.' He gets a plastic glass from the orange crate next to the refrigerator and goes into the bathroom. She hears the faucet running. He comes back and stands next to her head. 'Nearly tripped on ole Joey. Tilt your head back.'

She does and he puts the glass against her lips and slowly

419

pours. Most spills down her chin and onto the mattress, but she manages to swallow some.

She is completely naked now. He's cut her blouse and T-shirt off with scissors. There is a nasty bruise around her left nipple where he bit her. The ragged teeth marks look like the outline of an eye with the nipple as the pupil.

In the past three hours he has raped her five times, twice anally, twice vaginally, and once orally. He had trouble getting into her anally so he'd spit on her and rubbed the saliva on her anus. She thinks that was the worst part of the whole ordeal, feeling this sixteen-year-old killer's spit splatting against her skin. She can still feel each spot on her skin where his spit had hit. She's convinced that there are actual physical marks there, like the blisters acid might cause.

She is so tired now she just wants to sleep.

She closes her eyes. She is pretty sure he intends to kill her. Afterward, he'll probably climb on her for one more ride, see if it's better than Space Mountain. Somewhere outside she hears the putter of helicopters and imagines a rescue squad of marines coming after her. The rotor blades sound like a baseball card stuck in the bicycle spoke she fashioned as a child. Thwacka-thwacka-thwacka. The rhythm rocks her to sleep.

The hiss of carbonation fizzing wakes her. Brandon stands next to her drinking a Miller Lite beer. 'You're starting to smell a little,' he says and pours some of the beer on her ass. The shock of cold causes Dixie to jerk, but as the liquid runs down between her legs it actually soothes her a little.

Her mouth is so bitter and dry she has trouble speaking. Her head hurts from the turpentine fumes. 'Stop now,' she says so quietly she can hardly hear herself.

'Can't hear you, lady. Jesus, you're a fucking mess. Smell like a pig.' He laughs. 'Well, hang on, babe. I've got a few more calls to make, some shit to sell, maybe even line you up with a couple dates. Dudes who'd pay extra when I tell them you're a cop. They may play a little rough though.' He heads for the door. 'Be right back.'

He leaves, carrying the key to the Mendlesons' house and a black address book.

The moment the door closes Dixie begins struggling against the rope. She feels weak and dizzy, though, and stops struggling after less than a minute. She starts to cry and her own tears surprise her. She does not cry easily. The tears make her angry. She turns her head and bites her own upper arm. Hard. The pain sizzles through her brain and she feels a rush of adrenaline spasming through her body. She stares at the rope on each wrist. She has not lifted all those thousands of pounds of weights all these years just to lie helpless now, strapped to the bed of a sixteen-year-old while his friends pay to rape her.

She pulls against the rope, at first trying to break it. But that is a Hollywood fantasy. She changes tactics. She wiggles and squirms her wrist against the rope, trying to loosen it enough so she can slip one hand free. No use.

Another tactic. She tries to stretch her head close enough to the rope to get her teeth on it. She'd chew through the rope. But strain as she does, her teeth fall short by three inches. Now she is trying to decide whether she has the courage to chew through her own wrist to get free. Knowing he is going to kill her anyway, wouldn't it be better to sacrifice one hand?

She will try one other tactic first. She flexes her leg muscles. This is the same position she'd be in if she were at the gym about to do calf raises on the weight bench. She had raised over two hundred pounds once. How strong could the legs of this rickety bed be compared to her legs?

She begins to raise them, bend the legs at the knee, curl them backward. The rope goes taut. She tightens her stomach muscles and concentrates all her energy on those legs, imagines them as huge mechanical winches lifting a crashed car out of the river, water pouring out of the smashed windshield, the dead bodies flopping forward, held tight by shoulder harnesses.

The bed shifts suddenly, the bottom half lowers a fraction. The metal legs of the bed are bending. She grits her teeth and flexes her legs again. The bed's legs bend a little more. Her legs spasm with exhaustion and flop against the mattress. She tries to raise them again, but they don't respond.

Dixie thrusts her face toward the rope at her right wrist. Her front teeth barely touch. She had hoped to use her stronger back teeth, but right now she is thrilled to have any chance at all. She begins gnawing at the rope. The fibers are stiff and sharp as boars' hair. Several times the fibers stab her lips and gums. She can taste the blood in her mouth. Still, she keeps chewing. She tries not to think about Brandon or how long his phone calls will take. She just bites into the rope and yanks her head back and forth until the rope slips out of her teeth, then repeats the action. Each fiber has to be severed separately. Two of her front teeth are loose and sore. The pain shoots straight through the roof of her mouth into her eyeballs. She clamps her teeth on the rope again and shakes her head, her teeth sawing through the stubborn fibers.

She is halfway through the rope when one of her front teeth flies out of her mouth. Blood pours out over her lip. She ignores it, using her other teeth to grab hold again.

Then the rope breaks.

Within two minutes she has untied herself. She staggers to her feet, slips on shorts and a T-shirt from a pile on the dresser, and rushes for the door.

Just as Brandon enters.

His hair is wet and slicked back and there is still some soap in his ear. He has taken a shower while he was in the house. He looks at her with surprise at first, then he grins when he sees her raw and bleeding mouth, the gap.

'I guess I know what you'll want for Christmas,' he says. He starts toward her.

Dixie feels light-headed. She knows there are things she learned to do in such situations, things from the Academy, from experience. But she can barely remember the Academy. If pressed, she wouldn't be able to name one police officer she works with. She doesn't even remember the boy's name.

But she does remember she wants to live. She charges at him and as his hands reach out to grab her, she steps sharply into them and swings her elbow into his throat. His hands fly to his neck as he gasps for air. She drives the same elbow into his nose and hears it pop, blood shooting out each nostril. He drops to his knees. She brings her knee straight up into his chin and his head snaps back. He falls over, grabbing her ankle as he falls. She stomps on his wrist with her other foot and the bone crunches at impact.

She runs out the door.

She doesn't look back. Her bare feet whack pavement. Sharp pebbles gouge her soles, but she doesn't stop. She runs as fast as she can. She doesn't have to look to know he is running behind her. She dodges down an alley, across a yard, through a parking lot. She should stop, she knows, ask for help. But he may be armed now. He may have a gun, aiming the sights on her back even as she runs.

Finally out of breath, panting from exhaustion, legs too wobbly to run, she stops at a public phone and dials, punching in her Calling Card number in lieu of any change.

'Hello?' the voice says.

She is surprised. It is not the police station. 'Karl?' she says to her ex-husband.

Karl picks her up within fifteen minutes. He lives in Irvine, ordinarily a twenty-minute drive, which for Karl would translate into thirty or forty minutes. Not this time. When he sees her sitting on the curb in front of the phone, he double-parks the car and leaps out, leaving his door open. Cars honk at him and drivers shout at him. He ignores them. He kneels in front of Dixie. 'My God, are you okay?'

She hadn't told him anything on the phone. Just that she needed him, it was an emergency. She didn't know why she had dialed his number in the first place, and having done so, why didn't she just hang up and dial her cop friends? Or even the local cops? She wondered about that while she'd sat on the curb waiting for him. She wasn't sure. Maybe she needed to see someone she knew was on her side. Cops would be on her side, sure. They don't like it when one of their own is mauled. But they were still men. They'd be sympathetic, but they'd know she'd been raped; they'd look at her wondering, picturing her naked and spread open and she'd have to relive it every time she looked in their eyes. She'd be able to do that eventually. But not with the first face she sees. Maybe that made her a bad cop. Right now she didn't much care.

'I'm taking you to a hospital,' Karl says, lifting her gently to her feet. 'Don't worry, Dixie, I'll take care of you.'

Yesterday those words would have annoyed her. Right now they were just what she wanted to hear.

He helps her into the car. When other drivers see her they stop honking and yelling at him. They just gawk. She slides into the car and he closes the door behind her.

'I was raped,' she tells him when he gets in.

He doesn't say anything. He switches on the turn signal,

checks the traffic, and pulls over into the next lane. 'Everything will be fine, Dixie. You're in shock.'

That struck her as funny. She felt tired, sure, but not in shock, not a zombie. To prove to him that she wasn't in shock, she told him what happened, described it, told him the address. He listened with grim concentration on his driving. When she was finished he asked her if she'd call the police to have Brandon picked up. She said she hadn't, she'd forgotten.

He instantly swings the car over in the left lane, cutting someone off. They honk repeatedly. Karl makes a left turn and shoots up the small Laguna street, navigating the car until they are back on the same street where Brandon lives. She is surprised to see Brandon running along the sidewalk. He is dressed in jeans and a leather jacket and has a backpack over one shoulder. She guesses the backpack contains the rest of his drugs and the twenty-five dollars he got from the brothers.

'That's him,' she says calmly.

Karl, who has never had a single scratch on any car he's ever owned, who methodically washes the car every Sunday, yanks the steering wheel and sends the car hopping the curb, over the sidewalk, and across someone's freshly cut lawn. He brakes twenty feet in front of Brandon.

Brandon sees Dixie. There is no cocky grin now. His nose is crooked with blood crusted around each nostril. A dark bruise curls around his lower jaw. He sees the car door opening and Karl lunging out toward him and he turns and runs in the opposite direction. Karl has never been in a fight in his life, but he chases Brandon as if he has done this all his life. Dixie remains in the car watching. Looking at it through the frame of the windshield makes it seem a little like a movie.

Karl tackles Brandon. They both sprawl across the sidewalk, but Brandon is on the bottom and his face scrapes along the cement. Karl straddles the boy and begins to clumsily pummel him, fists pounding down with unerring rhythm. He reminds Dixie of the guy on those slave ships who pounds out the rowing boat on a huge drum. Finally exhausted, Karl stops, slumps a moment to catch his breath, then gets up.

Dixie leaves the car and goes over to join him. She bends over and presses her fingertips against Brandon's neck. No pulse. 'Well,' she says to Karl. 'That's that.'

PART FOUR

One Size
Fits All

In Which Dixie's Rape
Has Unexpected Effects
on Each Woman's Life

28

Barcelona closes her office door and says, 'You surprise me. You really do.'

'Surprise you?'

Barcelona walks back to her desk and sits down. She lifts the fifty-eight typewritten pages in one hand and hefts them up and down. The edges flap like a sluggish moth. 'I can't believe this is the same book you brought in here a month ago. It's amazing.'

Crystal Ponce seems confused by Barcelona's enthusiasm. 'It's the same book,' she says. 'Except for the changes.'

'That's my point, the changes are phenomenal. Very impressive.'

Crystal frowns as if annoyed at the compliment. 'It's still the same story. I just touched it up a bit, that's all.'

Barcelona leans back in her chair, still holding the fifty-eight pages. Finally she understands. Crystal resents any implication that the changes Barcelona suggested might have improved the book. She wants the book to be all her own, not share any credit.

'I just wrote, that's all,' Crystal says. 'I don't try to intellectualize everything.'

Barcelona sniffs the air. Crystal's perfume is too strong, Opium, she thinks, or Poison. At least it smothers the charred odor that's been hanging in the air the last three

429

days. Brush fires in the foothills of Riverside and Santa Ana Mountains have made the air greasy with smoke. While driving on the freeways she can see dark gray clouds blossom on the horizons like exploded atomic bombs. Barcelona has taken to washing her hands and face several times a day, each time scrubbing away layers of soot and smudge. Her throat is always dry and scratchy. She drinks Diet Cokes constantly to soothe the rough membrane.

Crystal digs through her purse. Her hand emerges with a stick of sugarless gum which she carefully unwraps, folds in half, and sticks in her mouth. While she chews, she folds the silver foil into a little square and stores that back into her purse.

Crystal Ponse is one of the most infuriating women Barcelona has ever met. When she'd first entered Barcelona's office four weeks ago with those dreadful ten pages about the woman whose life had been ruined by her exceptional beauty, Barcelona had wanted to shove her face into a toilet bowl and keep flushing until her expensively frosted hair lost some of its moussed stiffness. Aside from being as cold and humorless as a gutted cod, her novel had been trite, boring, and unintentionally laughable. Why Barcelona let herself be bullied into reading more pages of the awful thing she doesn't know. The first chapter was truly nauseating, but the next chapter was even worse. Endless whining about the burdens of growing up wealthy, having to endure other children's jealousy. And of course the dreaded Face. Too gorgeous for most mortals to behold. Other little girls went screaming to their mothers, crying over why they couldn't be as beautiful. Little boys feared her perfect face, scattering from playgrounds at the sight of it as if it were a visitation from the gods. It all sounded so turgid, like Ayn Rand with cramps.

Barcelona hefts the revised pages in her hand again. For the first time they feel substantial. The beginnings of a real book. Once a week for the past month she's met in this office with Crystal, endured the younger woman's patronizing attitude of a wealthy matriarch listening to a maid explain why the vacuum broke down.

But something happened during those meetings. However vacant or argumentative Crystal acted whenever Barcelona suggested changes, she actually began making some: fixing only grammar at first, then eliminating some of the more obvious clichés. Then she seemed to get into the spirit and made more and more changes, polishing, cutting, creating new, richer characters, until these pages were so well written they were scary. Harley had once asked Barcelona if she'd ever had a student she thought might be a better writer than she was. Not yet, she'd said at the time, confident that she never would, not at this level. There were many students of exceptional ability and keen insight, many whom she had encouraged and advised and even helped get published. Crystal wasn't nearly as smart or educated as they were, nor was she as talented. But of all the writers Barcelona ever had in her classes, she was shocked to think that this woman, *whom she didn't even like*, would be the one who would put it all together in just the right combination. What Barcelona couldn't understand was how such a rich book could come out of such a shallow mind. True, she had worked closely with Crystal, but she couldn't take credit for the raw power in the style, the energy hunkering behind each word. Yet how could a woman with no insight, no self-knowledge write it? It's like having a priest as a pimp.

'I want you to know, Crystal, I think so highly of your rewrite I've talked to my own agent about it. She's willing to take a look and waive her usual reading fee.'

Crystal shrugs. 'Sure. I guess that'd be okay.'

Barcelona knows better than to expect enthusiasm or gratitude. But that doesn't matter. What matters now is the book. Even though Crystal is a shit, her novel isn't. The book deserves to be finished and published and people deserve to read and enjoy it. 'I've written down the address. When you write your cover letter, be sure to remind her that I recommended you.'

Crystal takes the paper from Barcelona and studies it with a frown. 'I'm not under any obligation to her, am I?'

'What?'

'If I don't think she's getting me high enough offers I can dump her, right?' Barcelona stares dumbfounded. 'Besides,' Crystal continues, 'wouldn't I be better off with a New York agent? I hear they can get you more money because they have lunch with these editors all the time. Can't you get me a New York agent?'

Breast cancer. Barcelona concentrates on those two words, on the image of rabid cells clumped into a carnivorous tumor in Crystal's breast. The surgeon's scalpel slicing into the breast as if scooping out the meat of a grapefruit. Only conjuring up such a vile image keeps her from laughing in Crystal's rigid face. There is no point in getting angry. Crystal would not understand such a reaction. But Barcelona must remember exactly what Crystal says so she can tell the others at dinner tonight. This will be their first dinner together since Dixie's release from the hospital three weeks ago. They'll all be a little tense. This should give them something to laugh about.

'I've read all about the Literary Brat Pack,' Crystal says. 'And they all have New York agents.'

'I don't know a lot of New York agents,' she tells Crystal. 'But you can write query letters to a few of the better known ones and see if they're interested.'

Crystal reaches across Barcelona's desk and picks up the fifty-eight pages, tucking them neatly into her leather notebook. She takes Grief's address and begins folding the paper into a smaller and smaller stamp, like the gum foil.

'Maybe I'll do that. I'll have to think about it first. Maybe I'll let your agent take a look. I don't know.'

'Gee, I hate to leave her dangling on a hook like this,' Barcelona says, knowing that Crystal either doesn't understand sarcasm, or chooses not to hear it.

'I just want to be sure. I've put so much of myself in this, I don't want it to end up as just some little paperback. Like your books.'

Barcelona laughs. 'No, I don't blame you. Don't let what happened to me happen to you. Let my life serve as a warning to others.'

Crystal fixes her with that flat stare. 'I'm easy to make fun of. I know. I'm too blunt and aggressive sometimes. Women don't like that in another woman.' She stands up and walks to the door, stops and turns around just as her hand touches the knob. 'But maybe if you'd have been blunter and more aggressive back when you were starting out, you'd have done better.'

Barcelona stares at Crystal's flat eyes, the over-frosted hair whipped into a bad imitation of something vaguely European. She can imagine Crystal with a page torn out of *Vogue* with some Parisian model flouncing near a fountain, Crystal handing the page to her hairdresser saying, 'Make me look just like that.' Crystal turns the knob and opens the office door. The gaudy cluster of diamonds on her wedding ring sparks fluorescent light from the overhead bulbs. Something softens in Crystal's eyes. 'You look tired lately.' It was the first statement of personal concern she'd ever made. 'Your eyes are red, your skin isn't the right color. You should soften your eyes by dotting eyeliner close to the lashes instead of drawing a solid line.'

Is this her way of paying me back for critiquing her manuscript all these weeks? Barcelona wonders. Beauty tips.

'We can't all be beautiful,' Barcelona says.

433

'I don't take any credit for the way I look. I know it's mostly just lucky genes.'

Barcelona can see the too-thick foundation coating Crystal's cheeks like latex paint. The blush is too bright and clownlike. Her lipstick is too dark for her face. Barcelona wants to start circling the flaws with her red pen as if Crystal's face were a sloppy manuscript. 'I just haven't been sleeping well lately,' she says. Which is true. For three weeks now she's spent most nights wrestling with her pillow. 'But thanks for your concern.'

Crystal nods solemnly and leaves without another word.

'Gawwwd,' Barcelona says aloud and reaches for her Diet Coke. Her hand brushes the Elvis bank on her desk, spinning it around so he's facing the wall. The bank is a black plastic box with a plastic figure of Elvis on top, holding a guitar. This is pre-blubber Elvis, in jeans and open shirt, collar up, one leg cocked off the ground, one hand raised above the guitar in mid-strum. You get the feeling the next strum would be so powerful it would launch him into space. Between his feet was a coin slot. When you put a coin in, the arm came down in a mock-strum, the hips swiveled back and forth once, and the coin was swallowed into the black box. The bank had been a gift last week from her neighbor Dave. Darlene's husband.

Dave had been standing next to the bushes that lined Barcelona's garage. He'd been kneeling over scooping Foxy's shit into a brown lunch bag. Foxy sat in the grass nearby looking appropriately contrite. Barcelona had just come home from school and was leaving her garage, one hand clutching her briefcase, the other balancing thirty-five student essays on Chaucer's *Canterbury Tales*. Dave's garage door was open and five or six women were rummaging about, picking up Elvis items and showing them to each other and discussing them, then packing them into cardboard boxes. They were young women, Barcelona's age and younger. They wore shorts and tennis outfits and jogging pants and makeup. Four of them were blonde and they were all mildly attractive.

'What's going on, Dave?' Barcelona asked as Dave twisted the neck of his lunch bag.

'Oh, that's Darlene's Bible study group. They used to get together once a week. They're having a rummage sale and I said they could help themselves.'

'I didn't know Darlene belonged to a Bible study group.'

'Just for a couple months. She was lonely during the day, just her and Foxy. She wasn't very athletic, so she couldn't join the tennis club. She was lousy at cards, so she couldn't join the bridge club.'

'What about a job?'

He shrugged. 'Yeah, well, she did some volunteer work at the hospital. She didn't want a real job just yet.'

'That left the Bible.'

'I don't think she ever actually read the Bible before. But then, who has?'

Foxy started barking at the sky, running back and forth, yanking on the leash. Barcelona and Dave looked up and watched a plane with a fat square body fly overhead.

'That's a C-138,' Dave said, shading his eyes. 'Air tanker. They're using them to fight the fires.'

It was the first time Barcelona considered the fires a personal threat. 'Are we safe?'

'Oh, sure. They'll have them snuffed before they get here.'

Foxy stopped barking, squatted, peed.

'Too much excitement, eh Foxy?' Dave said, laughing.

Barcelona started to walk away. 'See ya, Dave.'

'No, wait.' He reached out and touched her arm. 'Wait. I want you to have something.' He started toward his open garage with Foxy trotting spritely at his side.

Barcelona glanced toward the refuge of her home.

Through her own kitchen window she could see the African violets on the sill and beyond them the nineteen-inch TV which she'd hoped to plant herself in front of for a few minutes while she drank a glass of wine.

Dave stopped at the entrance of his garage, turned, smiled. 'Come on,' he said, waving the brown bag.

She followed him into the garage. Dave did not introduce the pretty women who were busily filling cardboard boxes with Darlene's Elvis memorabilia. The women smiled politely at Barcelona but didn't talk to her. A couple of them were discussing how to transport Darlene's miniature Graceland.

'We could cut it in half,' one of them said.

'Put hinges on it. My Jim could do that. He's handy with tools.'

Another woman mumbled something and they all laughed.

'I *wish*,' the woman married to Jim said.

'Here,' Dave said, handing Barcelona the Elvis bank. 'This was one of Darlene's favorites. We drove all the way to Phoenix to buy this. The owner was a pharmacist.'

Barcelona stepped back without taking the bank. 'I couldn't, Dave. It's too precious. I'm not even a big Elvis fan.'

'Me neither,' he said. 'I mean I like a few of his songs. I like "Don't Be Cruel" and "Teddy Bear," but that's about it. Tell you the truth, Darlene wasn't that big of a fan of his music either. She hardly played his records. She just liked him. Go ahead, take it. I know she'd want you to have it. She thought highly of you.'

'Me?' Barcelona said, surprised.

'Oh yes. She always told me whenever she ran into you while walking Foxy. She thought you were so together. So modern, she used to say. A writer and teacher, all that.

436

An Eighties woman. Like Elvis was a Fifties man. She admired you. She read all your books.'

Stunned, Barcelona accepted the bank. Then, as quickly as she was able, retreated to her home while Foxy yapped at the women packing boxes.

Now the Elvis bank sits on her desk and Barcelona thinks about Darlene. *What connection had Darlene imagined between Elvis and me?* Barcelona wonders.

Barcelona finishes the rest of her Diet Coke and drops the can into her wastebasket. Her eyes are a little watery from the smoke-laden air.

Barcelona has a few minutes of her office hour left before she can go home, shower and change, and meet the other women. She has mixed feelings about dinner. Sure, she is anxious to see her friends, but she senses a certain drifting away among them since Dixie's rape. It's been weeks since any of them have seen each other. She promised Trina she'd meet her early so they could talk. The last time she saw Trina in the flesh was in Dixie's hospital room. Since then everyone's been so busy. Finally they all managed to schedule tonight's dinner, an inauguration of sorts welcoming Dixie back. Barcelona had tried to see Dixie several times, arrange for lunch or a shopping outing, but Dixie was always busy.

Barcelona has been busy too. Having been so abruptly dumped on her ass by Roger Carlyle, Lynda Kramer, and Hollywood in general, she decided to return to what she knew best, writing novels of the future. Imagining the world as it will become, a hoary reflection of the way it is now. Casting the bones, reading the entrails, figuring the odds and probabilities. The modern math of soothsaying. Cassandra of paperbacks. She started her current novel last week after receiving the Elvis bank from Dave. In a way, Darlene was responsible.

She has devoted herself to this novel like none of her

others. She works on it every spare moment, polishing every word with an artisan's compulsiveness. Her fussiness is more than artistic exactitude; she feels Crystal Ponce's spearmint-scented breath on her neck, the clicking of her stiffened hair like iced branches in a winter breeze.

Devoting herself to this new novel has also allowed her some distance from her personal life, to put that in better perspective too. Everything in that department is finally under control. Eric is definitely a thing of the past, filed under Old Boyfriends. They have talked a couple of times on the phone, but he has not been satisfied with her explanation of why she won't see him again. She has avoided seeing him in person. She feels good about her decision, though she misses him.

Cory is another matter altogether. After flooding his toilet with a tampon, she needed a little time to get over the embarrassment of seeing him again. He calls every day and they've had lunch together twice but have not ventured near his Corona del Mar home or her house. She wants to see him only on neutral grounds. With only two weeks until the election, his campaign has demanded most of his time, especially now that the polls have him surprisingly but firmly leading Carla Bennington.

She doesn't know what to think of Cory. She enjoys being with him but isn't sure whether he thinks of her as just a diversion from his high-pressure election, or whether there's something else going on there. Maybe she'd ask Trina tonight, see if he's talked to her about them.

Barcelona looks at the big clock on the wall and decides to cut her office hour short by five minutes. She begins tucking papers into her briefcase.

The phone rings. She and her office mate share one phone so she has to reach across both desks to grab the receiver.

'Hello?' she answers.

438

'Barcelona Lee?' the woman's voice says. 'The writer?'

'Yes.'

'Oh, good. I tried you at home first, so ignore my message on your machine.'

'Who is this?'

'Oh, God.' She laughs. The laugh, oddly familiar, sounds like the first few notes of the Beatles' 'Across the Universe.' 'I'm sorry,' she says. 'There's something strange about calling a professor. I'm having these prickly flashbacks about my own college days. I'm afraid I wasn't a very good student.'

'Who is this?' Barcelona repeats.

'Sorry, I'm doing it again. This is Lynda Kramer. Hi.'

What do you say to an international star of stage and screen? Barcelona wonders. 'Hi.'

'I just took a chance that you'd be in,' Lynda Kramer says. 'I know when I was in college my professors were never in their offices. Maybe that's just Princeton though.'

'Maybe.' Barcelona doesn't feel part of this conversation. She answers only when Lynda Kramer cues her to.

'Well, I'm glad you're conscientious, or we could have kept missing each other for days.'

'I didn't know we were looking for each other.'

'That's what I'm calling about. To explain.'

Rapid knocking vibrates the office door. The sound is angry, urgent.

'Excuse me a moment,' Barcelona says to Lynda Kramer.

'Sure. It'll give me a chance to untangle my daughter's head from the telephone cord.'

Barcelona is silent, pretending to be gone, but listening. She hears: 'Come here, Sarah. Let mommy have the cord. Come on, sweetie.'

The knocking continues. Barcelona puts the telephone

439

down and walks to the door. She is about to open it when Eric charges into her office.

'What the hell's going on?' he demands. 'Why won't you talk to me, Barcy?' He is wearing a denim shirt with snaps for buttons. It is new, but it looks just like the one he wore in graduate school. So do the jeans, so do the suede hiking shoes.

'Hiking shoes,' she says sharply. 'Just where the fuck are you planning to hike this afternoon, Eric?'

Eric is stunned by her response. His anger ebbs a little in the face of hers. He stands in the middle of the office and looks down at his shoes. 'What are you talking about?'

'Never mind. Just wait outside until I'm through on the phone.'

'We have to talk,' he insists. 'Clear this up.'

'This is my job, Eric. Not the appropriate place.'

'You won't return my calls.' A vague whine has entered his voice. 'I love you, Barcy. I know you love me.'

'Wait outside,' she says like a teacher to a student. It has always been the other way around.

He looks at her sadly and the white scar that cleaves his eyebrow seems to pulse with its own life. The smooth phosphorescent white reminds her of his selfless act on behalf of that woman. How he had stood up for her, protected her against her bully of a husband. Barcelona feels she owes him something for that abused woman's sake, if not her own. 'Please, Eric,' she says softly. 'Let me finish this call. We'll talk afterwards.'

He nods and leaves. She can see him through the wired glass sitting on the sofa in the waiting area. He is sitting next to a Vietnamese girl who is reading *People* magazine. Eric reaches into his back pocket and pulls out a paperback book. Barcelona can't make out the title, but she knows what it is from the familiar shapes on the cover: *The Doctor and the Soul: from Psychotherapy to Logotherapy* by Viktor E.

Frankl. It's one of his favorite read-in-public books.

Barcelona sits down behind her desk, takes a deep breath, and picks up the phone. 'Hello?'

'Sounds like I caught you at a bad time,' Lynda Kramer says.

'Just some unfinished business.'

'I know whereof you speak. I always think of that poem by Stephen Crane. Where he says love is like a burnt match skating in a urinal.'

'Hart Crane,' Barcelona corrects, but she is impressed by the quote nevertheless.

'Oh, right. I don't know why I get those two mixed up. Hart as in heart as in love. I took a memory course once because I always had trouble remembering my lines.'

'Do they work? I've always thought about taking one myself.'

'Why? You don't have to remember lines.'

'No, just to remember things, I don't know, dates and such.'

'You can't remember when you've got a date?'

'I mean dates of writers, historical movements, that sort of thing. Teacher stuff.' Actually, now that she's had to explain it, it does sound kind of silly. Barcelona is dying to know why Lynda Kramer is calling, but she's afraid to be too direct fearing there might be some mistake. She feels a little childish to be so thrilled at talking to a movie star. She sees Eric staring in at her through the glass and she shifts her head away from his gaze so he won't know how giddy she is.

'First, I owe you an apology,' Lynda Kramer says.

'Oh?'

'About that script you wrote. We never even read it. To tell you the truth, my agent advised against it. Not because of the script, he never read it either. It was because of Roger Carlyle.'

441

Barcelona fishes the Diet Coke can out of the trash and begins slowly bending the tap up and down.

'After we talked with him the first time we agreed to take a look at the script he said he had. Then he said there was a delay because you were doing a rewrite.'

'Actually, I hadn't even written it yet.'

'I'm not surprised. He wasn't all that interested in your script anyway. He was trying to parlay his loose association with us into a studio job in production. He went around saying he had a deal with us. When we found out about it, we had to cut off any association with him. Unfortunately, that included you too.'

Barcelona twists the tab to the left then the right. 'So he was never interested in my novel or script except as a means to a job.'

'Mostly. Though there was also a chance your script might sell.'

'So why are you calling?' she asks. 'Are you interested in my book?'

'Well, unfortunately, Roger Carlyle optioned your book for a year with an option to renew another year. That effectively ties it up for two years. I can't wait that long to get started on my next project.'

The tab snapped off in Barcelona's fingers. She dropped it into the can. 'You must have hundreds of projects coming at you all the time.'

'True. But I'm anxious to move in a new direction, expand a little. To tell you the truth, I'm a little tired of playing neurotic, hothouse orchids with foreign accents and a Dark Past to hide. I'd like to prove I can do genre work too. But I want something classy and sophisticated, not schlock.'

Barcelona's heart was thumping solidly in her chest. 'Where do I come in?'

'I read *Live Wires* and a couple of your other novels.

442

There's something about them that really touches me. I'm no big sci-fi fan, understand. Can't usually get past all the technical jargon. But yours are so rich with people, that's what captures my attention. I think you can do a fine script.'

'A script from which book?'

'Well, that's the thing. I haven't read them all and, to be honest, there's not much of a chance I'll get to them either. What I'd like is for us to have a cozy little lunch and hear you pitch the story lines of each book. See where we can go from there.'

Lunch with Lynda Kramer! Barcelona wants to go to the door and wave Eric back in, have him listen to the conversation. She wishes there was a way she could hook this into the public address system.

And yet. Barcelona is very involved with her new novel. She has never been happier writing, more involved with her characters. She's not sure she's ready to risk losing this sense of fulfillment for another iffy project. She explains that to Lynda Kramer.

Lynda Kramer pauses. 'Tell me about your new book. What's it called?'

'*Feasts*.'

'*Feasts*? Just *Feasts*?'

'Just *Feasts*.'

'Sounds a little spooky, like something from Stephen King. There aren't any space creatures in it, are there? I'm not interested in bumping heads with Sigourney Weaver. Nothing with aliens.'

'No, there aren't any aliens. It's about a woman living a hundred years from now. Only in a hundred years they will have discovered a drug, a medicine that will prolong life. Actually double life expectancy. The problem is that the drug only works on men. Has to do with their chromosome makeup.'

'So the men live twice as long as the women?'

'Right. You can see the social problems, especially when it comes to love and marriage and raising families.'

'Yeah. What does a guy do with his wife when she's old and he still has another seventy years to live?'

'Exactly.'

Lynda Kramer sighs. 'Okay, I'm hooked. Tell me.'

'The society has evolved a very sophisticated approach. Women kill themselves when they reach the age of sixty to allow the husband to seek another wife and even raise new children. The "feasts" in the title refers to the ritualized meals the women prepare, their last meal laced with a painless poison. The entire family gathers to watch her eat it and stay with her until she dies. It's all very loving.'

'Sounds faintly Japanese.'

'Yes,' Barcelona agrees. 'It's meant to.'

'What about the heroine?'

'She's a scientist whose mother is a week from her sixtieth birthday. In the week it takes her mother to prepare her final feast, our heroine attempts to find some way into the pharmaceutical lab where the life-prolonging formula is kept. She believes there's a conspiracy by the men who own the company to keep the drug from women, that the formula can be revised to include them.'

Lynda Kramer laughs happily. 'I like it. Suspense, conspiracy. I hope there's romance.'

Barcelona says, 'There's always romance. This time with another scientist who's trying to help her.'

'And they uncover the conspiracy?'

'No. They discover that there is no conspiracy. That the formula really only works on men and that they haven't been able to find one that works on women, though they have tried.'

Lynda Kramer says nothing for a while. Then, 'I don't

understand the point. That's kind of anticlimactic, isn't it?' There is a faint hint of disappointment in her voice.

'Not really. The point isn't whether or not there was a conspiracy. That doesn't even matter. The *real* conspiracy is that the men took the serum even knowing that there was none for women, that the women they loved would die. That they adopted ritualized suicide as an okay social event rather than forgo the drug until they had one for everybody. That's the point.'

Again, Lynda Kramer doesn't speak. Barcelona can hear a baby's gurgling, a pen tapping against plastic. Through the glass strip she sees Eric talking with the Vietnamese girl. His home for abused women had started to see more and more Vietnamese women, Westernized enough to decide beatings were not a natural part of the marriage routine. To help them better, Eric had begun studying Vietnamese and now spoke with remarkable fluency. The girl outside the office is laughing and when she looks at Eric, Barcelona recognizes an infatuational glint in her eyes. Barcelona feels a surge of affection for Eric and suddenly wonders if she hasn't made a mistake with him.

Lynda Kramer says: 'If it's okay with you, I'll have my lawyer contact your agent and see what agreement we can reach for me to purchase the film rights for *Feasts*. Naturally I want you to write the script, the first draft anyway.'

'What kind of money are we talking about?'

Lynda Kramer laughs. 'That's for our agents to decide.'

'Ballpark,' Barcelona said.

'I shouldn't be saying anything. My agent, lawyer, and accountant would take turns strangling me.'

'I need to know.'

Lynda Kramer pops her lips a few times as she thinks. 'I'd say $50,000 for the film rights and another $50,000 for the first draft of the script. More if the film actually gets made.'

Barcelona presses her palm against her stapler and squeezes out a couple of crumpled staples. She sweeps them off her desk onto the floor. A hundred thousand dollars. Eat shit, Crystal Ponce.

They say good-bye with Lynda Kramer expressing how excited she is about the project and that they would talk again soon.

After hanging up, Barcelona sits at her desk and stares across the office at Susan Mesa's desk. It isn't as tidy as Barcelona's. She has photographs of her family on it. There's a large rock the size of a turtle. The rock is painted with Apache symbols that her twelve-year-old daughter learned about at summer camp. There are three books open on the desk, each a critical study of *The Great Gatsby*, which Susan will teach this afternoon. Susan has no ideas of her own about the literature she teaches. She acts pretty much as a researcher, looking up various interpretations of the works she teaches, then explaining those interpretations to her students. Barcelona had teased her about that once and Susan, unashamed, had said, 'I never could figure out what my professors were rattling on about with these books. I just liked the stories. But I was hell on wheels in the library. Come class time, I could spout literary bullshit with the best of them.'

Barcelona tries to imagine a hundred thousand dollars in her bank account. She pictures the numerals written neatly in her checkbook where it says current balance. She is torn between redecorating her office and quitting her job. She wants to drive over to South Coast Plaza and buy clothing, any clothing. She can't believe her luck. This is the kind of good fortune that never happens to her. Everything she's ever gotten has been through steady plodding, long-range planning. She prefers dumb luck.

She needs to share the news, tell someone. She remembers Eric waiting, but when she peers through the glass he's not on the couch. She gets up and opens the door. The Vietnames girl is still reading *People* magazine. Eric is gone.

Barcelona pulls a sheet of blank paper from her desk and writes on it with a red marker. On her way out, she tacks the paper to the door. It says: GONE HOLLY-WOOD.

29

Trina bites into her hot dog and ketchup squirts out the other end of the bun and globs onto her blouse. She looks down just as the crowd of parents on the bleachers screams and applauds and leaps to its feet. She looks up and sees Karyn running for a ball spitting across center field. Karyn runs toward the ball on her skinny legs, glove positioned on the ground, ready to scoop the ball up. The ball rolls quickly, hopping and hiccuping along the bumpy ground like an escaping rodent. Karyn closes in on the ball, her glove less than a foot away. She swoops toward it. The ball hits something unseen in the grass and hops over her glove and rolls away from her. Her teammates are yelling at her to get the ball.

'Go, go, go!' Tommy the pitcher yells.

The catcher stands on home plate awaiting the arrival of the runner from second base. He keeps socking an anxious fist into his mitt.

The batter is a slow runner, but she's closing in on second base anyway.

'Get the ball! Get the ball!' Coach Lyle hollers from the bench. He is chewing gum furiously, waving with both hands.

The coach from the visiting team is shouting for the batter to keep going to third.

And Karyn is running after the ball now, trotting behind

it as it continues to skitter and wobble just out of reach. Finally she hurls herself on it, trapping it under her body. She grabs it, stands, throws to the shortstop, Bill Leader, who's followed her into the field.

By the time the ball makes it to the catcher, a chubby kid Trina thinks is named Axel, the runner has scored and the batter is on third.

Karyn sulks in center field, her face red with exertion and embarrassment. She slaps her glove against her leg. That was the first ball in four innings hit anywhere near him. Trina can almost hear Karyn's muttering as she scolds herself, questions the Fates, and curses the stupid bumpy ground. Karyn is a mutterer, wandering the house in times of emotional stress emitting low-decibel grumbling accompanied by exaggerated face-making. Sometimes Trina tries to secretly follow her when she's doing that just to catch her in one of her strange faces, her eyes wide, her nose scrunched, her mouth twisted into a scowl. Eventually, Karyn always talks herself out of these moods. She's not a moper.

Trina dips the corner of the napkin she had around her hot dog in her 7-Up and scrubs the stain off her flannel blouse. The stain rests on her left breast and the scrubbing causes the breast to shake. Out of the corner of her eye she sees a couple of men on the bleachers watching her progress. She smiles at their furtive stares and tries to figure out what's so sexy about a swollen clump of fatty tissues jiggling under a blouse. Why is it you can have an ass that's too fat, legs that are too fat, but men never think tits are too fat?

She has had her hands and lips on Carla's breasts, felt the soft swell, kissed the plucky nipples. But she has never felt lust for them. Actually, she's had her hands and lips everywhere on Carla's body and has not ever felt lust. She has felt affection, strong caring, but never the dripping,

449

sticky, rip-my-panties-off desire she's felt for men. Yet, and this is the incredible part, the actual sex isn't really much different from that with men, even men she'd thought were gods, men she'd loved, men who'd loved her. That surprises her.

'You okay?' Rob asks. He is sitting next to her on the bleacher, his hot dog gnawed neatly to a nub. His has ketchup, mustard, and relish on it and not a drop of any of them has spilled.

'You know me,' Trina says, nodding at her protruding chest. 'The Continental Breakfast Shelf.'

'They catch better than Karyn.' He grins.

They both laugh. He hands her his spare napkin. He always remembers to ask for a second; Trina never does. There was a time when he used to just automatically reach over and swab barbecue sauce from her face, brush bread crumbs from her lap, dab salad dressing from her blouse. There was something especially intimate about that, gestures of love and affection. Now he hands her his spare napkin, gesture of polite friendship.

Trina has come to the last six Little League games in a row. She used to just alternate games with Rob, but since she's been seeing Carla, her guilt quotient has skyrocketed. She sees herself as a perverse role model for Karyn. She worries that Rob will find out and begin court proceedings to have Karyn taken away. The word lesbian will be used a lot. It's a funny-sounding word and Trina doesn't know how she will react to having it used in connection with her.

When Trina had gone into the office the day after she had followed Carla up the coast, The Candidate had walked into her office cheerfully whistling 'The Jet Song' from *West Side Story*. 'So,' he said. 'What'd you find out?'

'Easy, Action. Your turf is safe. No need to rumble.'

He laughed and sat on the edge of her desk. 'Talk or I fart and scatter these papers all over the room.'

Trina slapped hands on two separate piles of papers. 'I'll talk, boss.' She leaned back in her chair and stared into his eyes, looking for something in them she wasn't sure was there. She'd have to find out the hard way. 'I found out she's tough.'

'We already know that.'

'She's also smart, and very savvy.'

'Cut to the chase, Trina.'

Trina sighed. 'What if I told you she was having an affair?'

The Candidate paused, shifted on the desk. 'Does it involve misuse of any city funds?'

'It involves a chicken, a goat, and long flashlight.'

He laughed. 'I'd say she's more fun than I thought.'

'Really, what would you say, Cory?'

'I'd say that's her business. As long as it doesn't involve abuse of her position.'

Trina stood up and placed a hand on his cheek. 'You really are a nice guy, aren't you?'

'You're surprised?'

Trina kissed his cheek and sat back down. 'I'm always surprised.'

'You're a jaded romantic.' He got up and swaggered toward the door, snapping his fingers. 'Tell Tony to meet me at the gym. And walk tall.'

'We always walk tall,' she said, playing along. 'We're Jets, the greatest.'

He turned and winked. 'When you're a Jet you're a Jet all the way.'

Trina bites into her hot dog again. She watches Karyn adjust her hat. Adjusting hats is what her team does best. Playing baseball is what they do worst. They are in last place without much hope of ever getting out. Karyn has been talking about quitting the team. During soccer season she is one of the stars on a first-place team. She doesn't

451

buy Trina's speech about losing being character building. Trina doesn't buy it either.

Karyn's team makes a double play and Rob waves his arms. His leather jacket squeaks with each movement. Karyn told her that Rob has a bunch of hair transplant pamphlets in his bathroom. Trina glances over at him and tries to imagine him with those terrible connect-the-dot patches on his scalp. She wants to tell him he looks just fine, maybe even a little better with those deep bays cutting into his hairline. But it is no longer her place to make those kinds of statements. Too easy to take it the wrong way: Is she saying that because she doesn't want me to look good for other women? Is she saying that even more hair won't make me attractive? Is she coming on to me? Etc., etc.

Actually, Trina has been getting along quite well with Rob lately. They are cordial, friendly, sometimes even tender. More important, her physical ailments are gone. No memory loss, no disorientation, no hot flashes about wanting to get pregnant. Miraculously, The Candidate has pulled ahead of Carla in the polls. Everything's been just great the past three weeks.

Almost perfect.

That first week after spending the night with Carla, though, that had been awful. Dixie being raped and tortured. Trina's own guilt over Carla had chewed her stomach into wormy confetti. And there was still a campaign to work.

That first week, just returning from the hospital after visiting Dixie, Calvin the office gopher holding one hand over the phone, said, 'Line three for you, Trina.'

'Who is it?'

He shrugged his pointy nineteen-year-old shoulders. 'Some guy.'

'What guy? Always get a name.'

452

Right.' He nodded but didn't do anything.

Trina marched into her office, still trying to shake the image of Dixie lying in the white hospital bed, wincing with pain when she tried to shift her hips. Trina tried not to imagine the damage hidden under those crisp sheets.

'Hello?' she said into the phone. 'This is Trina Bedford.'

'One moment, please,' the man said. There was some clicking as the call was transferred.

'Hi,' Carla Bennington said. They hadn't spoken or seen each other since that night five days before.

'Hi,' Trina said. She kept her voice cool, businesslike. Her skin tingled, like when she was a kid stealing a quarter from her father's pants. That tingle was like an invisible skin sensing danger, warning her that she was about to get caught. Trina flashed on a possibility that the conversation might be recorded, that it might somehow be used against The Candidate. She shrugged that off as absurd.

'Surprised?' Carla said.

'Yes.'

Carla laughed. 'Not as surprised as I.'

Trina said nothing.

'Sorry for the spy stuff. I had an aide call in case someone there might recognize my voice. I don't want to put you on the spot.'

There was a long pause. Neither spoke. The only sound was their breath whipping across the mouthpiece.

Finally, Carla spoke. 'I'd like to see you again, Trina.'

'I don't think that would be a good idea.'

'I'm not talking garter belts and push-up bras. Just lunch or something.'

'I feel uncomfortable. I have a young daughter.'

'Just lunch, Trina.'

'Okay.'

They ate in Long Beach, away from anyone who might recognize them. They talked about their lives. The polls

453

that morning had shown The Candidate nipping at her heels. They had joked about it. Carla had seemed unconcerned. Even later, after Cory had pulled ahead, Carla only praised Trina's work, lamented that she hadn't hired Trina first. Trina feels bad for Carla, but also good for herself. Her own success keeps her on an equal level with Carla, dulls the competitive edge that always hovers between them. They both like that edge.

Two days ago they slept together again for the first time since that night in the hotel. Karyn was at an Angels game with Rob. Trina and Carla rented a room at a motel in Seal Beach, south of the city. They undressed, made love. The whole time Trina felt like a scientist on a secret mission, pretending to be someone else, exploring the differences between making love with a man and a woman. She imagined a diary or notebook in which she jotted down her scientific observations: Smell and feel completely different. Soft, enveloping, meshing as opposed to hard muscles bouncing off each other. Lying in man's arms, safe, protective. Woman's arms, open, honest, no secrets. Talking afterward, no subtext, no hidden meanings.

'Are we dikes?' Carla asked afterward, her arm across Trina's bare stomach.

'I don't know. Technically, I guess.'

'I don't feel like one.'

'How does one feel?'

Carla rolled over and stared at the ceiling. 'I don't know, I've never done this before.'

'Never?'

'Just that time I told you about when I was eight and that neighbor girl tried to teach me to kiss. That's the extent of my dikishness. Dikehood. Whatever. Mostly we giggled.'

'I miss giggling,' Trina said.

The baseball game ends. Karyn's team loses 15-1. Karyn

454

struck out once, walked once, and was thrown out at first. She shuffles over to Trina and Rob but doesn't look at them. Rob congratulates her for playing hard, tells her that having fun is more important than winning, kisses her on the cheek, and leaves. Karyn never looks at him.

On the drive home, Karyn sits staring out the side window, muttering. Trina tries to talk her out of her mood, but nothing works.

'You'll get them next time, kiddo,' Trina says.

'No we won't. We'll never get them. They're better. All the teams are better.'

This is true and hard to respond positively to. 'Even better teams can be beaten. They get cocky and a smart team can use that against them.'

Karyn turns in her seat and glares angrily at Trina. 'That's crap. Maybe if they all were handcuffed together, maybe then we could beat them. But that's all.'

'You can't give up.'

'What do you know about sports? You didn't play when you were a kid. All you did was ballet.' She says 'ballet' as if it were a disfiguring disease.

'Hey, don't knock ballet, kiddo. You try prancing around on your toes for an hour and see how you feel.'

'Why would I want to? That's stupid. What good is standing on your toes?'

Trina doesn't feel like going into it. When Trina was Karyn's age, ballet ruled. Every little girl wanted to go on toe, lift a leg so gracefully that everyone would swoon in envy. Trina had been good, one of the prize students at the Kirkland School. From three until twelve she glided, flowed, twirled, and leapt through childhood, performing little impromptu snatches during recess or for her parents' friends. Then disaster. At twelve her breasts inflated as suddenly and dramatically as a sea vest. The other girls made jokes. Trina slouched, no longer opened her arms

455

with gleeful abandon. Her movements became cramped, stopped flowing as she tried to hide her bulging chest. Finally, she stopped taking classes. She became a cheerleader instead, where big tits were an asset.

'And guys always act like they're doing you a favor letting you play,' Karyn says as they climb out of the car. 'Like they coulda won if only they didn't have dumb girls on their team.'

'The other team had girls,' Trina says.

'Mom, that's not the point.' Karyn huffs into the house, exasperated at Trina's ignorance. Trina follows, smiling and shaking her head.

Trina goes straight into the kitchen and plays back the phone machine while looking through the refrigerator for some possible combination of foods that might make a dinner for Karyn.

Beep. *'Hi, Trina. Can I catch a ride home with you after dinner tonight? Harley's dropping me off at the restaurant. Please, please, please. I'll paint your portrait on my fingernails.'* Diva. No other messages.

Thinking about dinner with everyone tonight makes her a little nervous. She reaches into the refrigerator and grabs a yellow plastic pitcher with about an inch of sugar-free Wyler's Tropical Punch. She tilts the pitcher and drinks out of the spout. Some of the punch sluices down her chin and drips onto her blouse. She finishes the punch and sets the pitcher on the counter. She wonders how to act around Dixie, what to say, what not to say.

'I'm making dinner,' Trina hollers, 'so hurry up and take your shower.' Karyn doesn't answer, but Trina knows she heard.

She slices some cucumbers, tomato, and an avocado, drapes a few rings of red onion over the top. Salad.

She heats up the iron skillet and dumps the plastic bag of chicken fajitas in. She stir-fries the chicken, bell peppers,

456

onions, whatever else is in there. They come premixed at the Irvine Ranch Market. While they're cooking she lays three flour tortillas between wet paper towels and nukes them in the microwave. Entrée.

A car screeches outside, the brakes wail in a loud primal scream.

'Jesus,' Trina says, stopping to listen for a crash. None comes. The car continues on. Trina wonders about dessert. There's hardly enough time to make anything and still get changed for dinner with the others. Still, guilt pecks at her and she feels compelled to prove herself as Mother of the Year. All this could be used later in court on her behalf.

She laughs at that thought. She is peering into the freezer, relieved to find some Dole blueberry fruit bars that will serve nicely for dessert, when another scream of tortured car brakes shoots adrenaline through her system. She closes the door to listen, hears shouting. A man. And Karyn's voice.

'Oh, God,' Trina gasps, running for the front door.

The street outside hovers in twilight, the street lamps fighting back the night. In the street in front of their house, a blue Lincoln is parked at an angle in the middle of the street. Heavy black tire marks jut out behind the car for three or four feet. A bald man in a business suit is yelling at Karyn. Karyn listens without saying anything. Trina's heart calms a little to see her daughter alive, but there is a deeper horror just under the skin: *How did she leave the house without my knowing*?

'Karyn,' Trina calls as she walks briskly toward them. 'Karyn, what happened?'

'This your daughter?' the man says. His face is red from yelling.

'Yes. What happened?'

'Some piece of work you've got, lady. Some fucking piece of work.'

457

'Don't talk to my daughter that way, buster, or you'll be walking with a hitch in your getalong.'

He glowers at Trina, but when she doesn't back down he just snorts and starts toward his car. 'Maybe the cops would like to get in on this conversation.'

Trina's neck heats with fear. She looks at Karyn, but her daughter doesn't return her gaze. She is no longer dressed in her baseball uniform, but wears shorts and a sweatshirt. Trina follows the man to his car.

The man walks around the front of the car. Lying pinned under his wheel is a dummy made of Karyn's baseball uniform stuffed with sheets and pillowcases, clothing Trina recognizes from the dirty laundry hamper. The head is a small pink pillow from Karyn's room, stapled to the collar of her baseball jersey. 'Your daughter crouched behind that car there'—he points back at a neighbor's car parked on the street—'and when I drove close, she tossed it in front of my car. Naturally I thought it was a child and I slammed on my brakes. Nearly had a fucking heart attack. When I hit it, I thought I . . .' He shakes his head and sags against the fender of his car. He looks terribly shaken.

'Are you okay?' Trina asks him. She purposely avoids looking at Karyn until her anger is under control. 'Can I get you some water or something?'

'No, I, I guess I'm just relieved I didn't kill anyone. I don't know if I could live with that.'

'No, no, of course.' She puts her hand on his shoulder. He is near fifty, overweight. She can smell the sour stench of fear pouring from him. Her touch seems to calm him a little.

'I didn't mean to swear at her like that. It's wrong. I just . . .' He sighs. Trina has the feeling he'd like to cry with relief.

'My fault entirely. I should have listened to you first. Didn't mean to snap like that. Mother's instinct, I guess.'

458

'Sure. You have a right.'

'Don't worry. I'll take care of this. I'll make sure it never happens again.'

'Yes, please,' he says. There is pleading in his tone.

He gets in his car and slowly pulls forward, unpinning the dummy. Trina drags it out from under his car and he drives away, lighting up a cigarette with shaky fingers.

Trina carries the dummy back to where Karyn is and shoves it into her arms. 'First, you're off the baseball team, young lady.'

'Big deal,' Karyn says. 'I'm off a last-place team. I'll deal with it.'

'Good, because you can deal with this too: You're grounded for a month. Straight to school and straight home again afterwards. No playing with Angela, no movies, no TV. And the same will be true when you see your father. Understand?'

Karyn turns away and starts walking toward the house.

Trina is on her in three steps and grabs her arm, spinning her around. 'Answer me, Karyn. Do you understand?'

'Yes, I understand. Big fucking deal.' She throws the dummy down, a black tire pattern across its pink head, and races for the front door.

Trina runs after her, through the front door, down the hallway, and into her room.

'Get out of my room!' Karyn screams. 'This is my room!'

Trina grips both of Karyn's arms and yanks her down on the bed. 'Stop that! You will not yell at your mother.'

Karyn struggles to twist away, shaking her head. Her hair lashes against Trina's face, but she holds tight.

'Stop this!' Trina says.

'Shut up,' Karyn snaps back.

Trina wrestles down the urge to slap Karyn. She is determined to settle this without hitting. 'Don't you see what you did out there was very wrong? That man could

459

have been killed. He might have swerved and hit another car. He might even have hit you. You both could have been killed.'

'I was just doing it for fun.'

'Scaring someone like that, maybe causing someone else harm, that's not fun, Karyn. That's stupid.' Blah, blah, blah, Trina thinks. *I wouldn't listen to me either if I weren't the one talking.*

'You think everything is stupid.' Karyn hollers this as loud as she can for some reason.

'I certainly do not.'

'You do. You think everything is stupid. You and Daddy. You think I care about baseball? I don't care. You don't want me to do what I want to do.'

'What do you want to do?'

Karyn says nothing. Tears start to flood her eyes. Big tears, the size of dimes. Her cheeks are a steady stream. Great sobs hunch her over. 'Daddy thinks I can't play. I did lousy today. You guys aren't proud of me at all.'

Trina finally understands. Kid logic is hard to follow sometimes; the words aren't always good clues. They can be misleading. Karyn thinks Rob is ashamed of her because of the game. Now Trina understands the relentless practicing in soccer and baseball, why Karyn studies so hard for a sixth-grader. Part of her thinks that if she excelled at everything, school and sports, Trina and Rob would be so proud of her they'd get back together again.

'It's just that we're a lousy team,' Karyn says. 'I could be better with another team. I'd make you proud.'

Trina's own eyes tear, her mouth quivers. She fights it. She wants to comfort Karyn, not cry with her. But she can't help herself. The tears bounce off her cheeks, splash into her mouth. She pulls Karyn close and they sob into each other's arms. Trina stops crying after a minute, but Karyn continues on, sometimes with loud sobs, sometimes

460

with just a low humming sound. Trina's blouse is soaked through. She can feel Karyn's heart patter against her own. Slowly, Karyn's crying stops and she drifts into sleep.

This was nothing really, no more than a spat like a hundred before and a hundred to come. But Trina thinks this is the happiest she has ever been in her life.

30

Barcelona asks the waitress what time it is. The waitress has three bright Swatches on her wrist, each a different color and face design. 'Six-fifteen,' the waitress says. 'I can tell you the time in Tokyo too. Or Sri Lanka.'

'Six-fifteen?' Barcelona repeats, checking her own watch, which says six-twenty.

'Seven more months of waiting tables and I'll have saved enough to go to Tokyo. Japan and Sri Lanka, those are the places I've always wanted to visit.'

The waitress beams at Barcelona. She is about nineteen, with short blond hair except for the back which is red and feathers down her neck past her collar. Like all the other waitresses in Forty Carrots, she wears a white blouse and black pants. Her pants are so tight the V at her crotch hugs her pubic mound in revealing definition. 'I heard that Japanese men worship blondes,' she says. 'Is that true?'

Barcelona wonders when she reached the age where she looked like she'd know the answers to obscure questions like that. 'Yes, it's true. They are obsessed with blondes. Especially tall ones.'

'I'm five six.'

'To them that's tall.'

'Great! From waitress to goddess. Only in America, right?'

'And Japan.'

'Oh, right.' She giggles. 'You want to wait for your friend before you order?'

Barcelona checks her watch again. Trina is twenty minutes late. 'Bring me another glass of white wine while I wait.'

'Sure thing.' The waitress rushes off as if late for her plane. Barcelona's table is outside the restaurant, in a section of mall made to look like an outdoor café, with a fence and plants corralling in the patrons. But there is still something funny and uncomfortable about sitting at a table in the middle of an enclosed mall while shoppers laden with packages trudge back and forth next to you, staring at your food or drink with greedy eyes.

This is not the restaurant where they will be having dinner, but this is where Trina agreed to meet Barcelona so they could chat a little, catch up on each other's lives before the dinner with the others. The dinner restaurant is a ten-minute drive, plus the five-minute walk to her car. That doesn't give her much time with Trina, which makes her angry because she had such great news to share. A phone call from Lynda Kramer, for Christ's sake. She'd actually been *hired* by a famous movie star. Her first thought, absurdly, was how this would look at her twentieth high school reunion just a few years away. Sitting by the phone afterward she'd had a sudden vision as white-hot as grease rags bursting spontaneously into flames: she and Lynda Kramer walking into the Muncy High School gym together, standing there amid the spiraling crepe paper and mirrored ball while her old classmates gaped and cooed and wept with envy. Until now the only thing her hometown is famous for is once having spawned the national poster child for the muscular dystrophy campaign. Jerry Lewis sang a song to the kid on the telethon.

Barcelona has already told her parents. Naturally they were thrilled, proud of her. She and Grief had discussed

463

it too, but that was on a strictly professional level, not personal. Grief knew only what it meant to her career, not her self-esteem. She'd tried to call Cory, but he'd been out all day on the campaign trail. Here she was bursting with important news and no one close to tell it to.

Except Eric.

He'd been waiting for her at her home when she'd left school. She drove down the shared driveway between all the garages and saw his car blocking her garage door. He sat behind the wheel reading a book. She honked at him. She saw his head shift slightly to glance in his rearview mirror. At first he didn't move. She honked again. Finally he started the engine and backed it away just enough for her automatic garage door opener to swing the wooden door open. She drove in, parked, and left by the side entrance. He was waiting there for her.

'We have to settle this, Barcy,' he said.

'It's settled, Eric. Really, it's settled.'

'Why are you doing this to me? What did I do?'

She stopped and looked into his face with sympathy. 'You didn't do anything. It's me. I just don't feel right with you anymore.'

He snorted. 'What's that supposed to mean? You feel guilty about Luna?'

'Yes, I do. Some.'

'So that's what this is about. You want me to leave Luna.'

She unlocked the front door but didn't open it. She turned and stood in front of the door, blocking it, making it clear the conversation would not be continued inside. 'I don't want you to leave Luna. She loves you very much. You love her very much.'

'Yeah, I love you, you love me, she loves me, I love her. How come if there's so much love floating around here, we're all so miserable?'

I'm not miserable, she wanted to tell him. *Lynda Kramer called me today and my life is almost perfect. I'm having dinner with my closest friends, I'm seeing a man who is handsome, smart, and sexy. Everything is finally coming together in my life. Don't slop your misery around me.*

She said, 'I have to go, Eric. Think about what I said and we'll talk later.'

Eric stepped back a few feet and looked at her. The afternoon sun was lodged behind the condos near the community pool, shooting just enough bright beams across the grass belt to case a shimmering aura around Eric. For a second he seemed frozen in time, looking just as he had that first time she saw him on campus, standing near the entrance of Sproul Hall arguing with another shaggy student about whether or not Freud was homosexual. His finger had jabbed the air in front of the other boy in such a graceful yet forceful way you had the impression that through this sudden gesture he was conjuring some dark forbidden powers, that any moment black lightning would crackle from his finger and crisp the other boy on the spot.

Standing there on the sidewalk outside her condo, Eric pointed that same finger at her now and began jabbing the air again. 'This is not you. You're not this fucked.' He said it with such assurance that Barcelona wondered for a moment if he was right.

He turned and walked away, his hiking boots scuffing against the sidewalk.

The mall is crowded, but the restaurant isn't. Barcelona listens to an older couple at the next table. They are discussing Kitty Kelley's unauthorized biography of Frank Sinatra. 'Pret-ty Kit-ty Kel-ley,' the man says with disdain. 'I heard she wrote the book because Sinatra wouldn't sleep with her.' The woman dips her fingertips in her water glass and dabs the drops in her eyes. 'Damn smoke,' she says to him. Barcelona thinks she means the smoke in the air from the forest fires, but the woman turns sharply and looks at the two young women at a nearby table who are smoking cigarettes. Even though this is the nonsmoking section, the older woman and her companion pick up their water glasses and move to another table. When they sit down, the man says, 'Frank Sinatra was ruined by women. Yes he was.'

Barcelona watches Trina walking down the mall toward her. There are dozens of other people walking beside, in front of, behind her. Their shoes all clack against the hard floor in a confusion of sound. But Trina's shoes clack louder than anyone else's. She sounds like a metronome keeping time for everyone else, clacking out the right rhythm for the rest of the crowd to follow. Maybe it's Barcelona's imagination, but she thinks that the people surrounding Trina begin to alter their walking rhythm to fit hers. Without interrupting their conversations, shoppers begin to match Trina's stride, legs scissoring in unison, arms swinging with hers. People look like they are marching next to her, like happy troops escorting her to her destination. Trina doesn't seem to notice. She sees Barcelona and waves cheerfully.

'Jesus, look at the packages,' Trina says, sitting. Trina pokes through the cluster of shopping bags under the table, spoils of Barcelona's celebration spree. 'I hope there's something in there for me. A small token of your esteem. Diamond earrings are nice.'

As always, Barcelona's irritation evaporates in Trina's presence. 'Oooh, this is gorgeous,' Trina says. She pulls out a marled cotton knit turtleneck. 'Eighty-five bucks! That's not like you to spend real money on yourself.'

'A new, improved me. I have heard The Word and The Word is Retail. Now put it back before you spill something on it.'

Trina shoves it back into the bag.

The waitress with the three watches stops in front of the table. 'Ready to order?'

'White wine,' Trina says. 'And a dish of frozen yogurt. Vanilla.'

'We're going to have dinner soon,' Barcelona reminds her.

'Gee, Mom, really?' She nods at the waitress, who hurries off. 'You see how tight that girl's pants are? A yeast infection waiting to happen.'

Barcelona is anxious to tell her the good news. But she doesn't want to just blurt it out. She wants to savor it a little. Telling Trina will somehow legitimize the whole thing, make it real. But before she can start the words, Trina leans forward with a serious expression. Bracelona notices for the first time that her friend's eyes are red and a little swollen. She's been crying. 'What?' Barcelona says, a little frightened.

Trina sighs, looks away. 'I'm not sure I can.'

'Can what?'

'Tell you.'

'Oh, Christ, Trina, don't do this. Tell me what?'

Trina stares at the passers by. Barcelona follows Trina's gaze, staring at the shoppers. Their eyes are glazed from seeing too much merchandise. Some look manic, anxious to get home with their purchases; some look vaguely disappointed, uncertain about the wisdom of what they bought. Most look tired. They walk stiffly like witnesses to a horrible accident.

'I'm going to tell you something,' Trina says. 'It's going to shock you. Hell, it shocks me.'

'What, for Christ's sake?'

Trina begins speaking, her head leaning across the table, her shoulders hunched protectively. The waitress comes, delivers the wine, and runs off again. Barcelona listens to Trina's words, concentrating on each one because the whole gist is somehow getting lost. Words pile up like tax receipts. Something about following Carla Bennington, sleeping with her, still seeing her. Suddenly Trina stops talking, leans back, and sips her wine. She stares expectantly at Barcelona. 'Well?'

Barcelona feels dizzy, disoriented. She takes a deep breath, but the air is scratchy with smoke. She tastes ashes at the back of her throat. 'I don't know what to say.'

'You're angry. Jesus, you're angry.'

'I am not angry.'

'Look at you. Your face is clenched, your ears are red. You're fucking pissed at me, aren't you?'

Barcelona thinks about it a moment and realizes that she is indeed angry at Trina. Trina has taken what should have been a perfect moment at a perfect time in Barcelona's life, and screwed it up with some twisted confession about sex with another woman. Barcelona feels as though she should be somehow supportive, understanding of Trina's emotional turmoil. But she isn't. She wants to reach across the table and smack Trina across the face.

'You think I became a lesbian to make you mad?' Trina asks.

'You're not a lesbian,' Barcelona says quickly. 'You don't just become one, like transferring buses or converting to Catholicism. Homosexuality is an inclination, something you're born with, not a conscious decision. Read the fucking literature before you join the club, okay?'

'You act as if I did this to be in vogue, Barcy.'

'Didn't you?'

'I thought you knew me better than that.'

Barcelona doesn't know what to say to that. Anger is replaced by hurt and she decides to hurt back. 'Guess not,' she says.

Trina rolls the stem of the wineglass between thumb and forefinger. The yellowish wine swirls in the glass. It reminds Barcelona of a toilet flushing and she thinks of that quote from Hart Crane that Lynda Kramer used: 'Love is like a burnt match skating in a urinal.'

'I'm surprised,' Trina says quietly. 'I didn't think you'd act this way at all. I thought you'd be more understanding. On my side.'

'Sorry I wasn't so predictable. But I do have a mind of my own.'

The older woman and her male companion at the nearby table look toward them. The woman is eating potato-cheese soup, the spoon is full and halfway to her mouth.

Barcelona lowers her voice. 'Do you really think you're a lesbian?'

Trina laughs. 'What an odd question. I wish I had an answer. I don't think I am, not in the implied meaning. I don't want to leap across the table and stick my tongue in your mouth.'

Barcelona frowns and looks away.

'I do care for Carla. I do have sex with her. The caring is a lot like how I feel for you. Like friends. Mostly we talk, mostly with our clothes on.'

'Don't make fun of me, okay? I don't deserve that.'

Trina sighs, looks across the mall corridor to the toy store opposite the restaurant. Again, Barcelona follows her gaze. A giant gorilla doll sits in the window with a tiny stuffed kitten in its lap. A stack of picture books are displayed around the gorilla. The book is *Koko's Kitten*.

'I'm nervous,' Trina says, looking back at Barcelona. 'I feel guilty and scared about Karyn. I keep expecting to come home and find Karyn gone and Rob's lawyers pelting me with subpoenas.'

'It could happen,' Barcelona says.

'Thanks for cheering me up.'

Barcelona feels rotten. She isn't handling this well. Not as well as Eric would have handled it. Eric would have put his arm around Trina, made her laugh, calmed her fears. Even Luna could have done that much. Trina is her best friend and she's only making her more miserable.

'Let's go meet the others,' Trina says, looking at her watch. Her voice is cold.

'Wait,' Barcelona says. She finishes her wine, taking her time draining the glass, thinking what to say. 'I don't mean to be angry. Maybe I'm just jealous.'

Trina's smile is as cold as her voice. 'You've already seen me naked. You had your chance.'

'You know what I mean. Your friendship with Carla Bennington. I was your best friend, now somehow she is.'

Trina doesn't deny it. 'You wouldn't be jealous if it were a man.'

'Sure I would.'

'Not as much.'

Barcelona nods. 'Not as much. Because sex was never an issue between us. And friendship with a man can't ever be the same as with another woman. I don't want to wonder if we would have been better friends if we'd had sex. That we're no longer best friends just because we didn't sleep together.'

'You're obsessed with the sex. Believe me, it's such a small part of Carla's and my relationship. We've only done anything twice. It was nice, that's all, more like a massage than a fuck.'

'And that's enough for you?'

Trina shrugs. 'For now. I have a close friend I share my life with and I get off occasionally.'

'I don't know, I just feel like you've given up just because you haven't found the right man yet.'

Trina laughs loudly and several customers turn to look. Even passing shoppers look. 'Jesus, Barcy. You idealize your relationships too much, even ours. I have a feeling when we're not around you make up snappy dialogue for us. Real people must be something of a disappointment to you.'

'I know what I want.'

'Do you? I used to, now I don't. Lately I think all I really want is for someone to occasionally pat me on the head and say, "There there, Trina. There there."'

'There are men who will do that. You have to be patient.'

Trina makes a face. 'I'm so sick of all of us bitching and whining about the Perfect Relationship. That's a fucking unicorn. Love is where you find it, right? That's a song, I think. I found someone who I care about and who cares about me. Period. No mystery to it. I don't desire other women and I haven't given up my lust for men. A tight-assed hunk still gets me wet, okay? I'm just not sitting around with that hungry look anymore. And I'm happier than I've been in a long, long time. And if you can't live with it, then I'll have to live without you.' Trina stands up, tosses three dollar bills on the table and walks away.

Barcelona pays the rest of the bill, calculates fifteen percent toward the waitress's Japan Goddess Fund, and leaves the restaurant. She walks among the crowd of shoppers, but no one follows her cadence.

Lesbian.

Such a strange word. It reminds her of something out of a high school science textbook about microscopic organisms: 'The lesbians swim furiously in the pond water unseen by the naked eye.'

Dixie is sitting alone at the table drinking red wine. Barcelona sees her from the entrance and waves. Dixie waves back enthusiastically. Barcelona is surprised by Dixie's appearance. She looks gorgeous. The bruises are all gone from her face and she is wearing clothes that are more stylish than usual. She's actually wearing a coordinating outfit: wool cardigan sweater that stops at the waist

471

over an ivory silk broadcloth blouse with ruffled lace collar, and lambsuede circle skirt with lace trim at the hem. She looks like a model.

'Wow,' Barcelona says, sitting across from her. 'That's some outfit. Where'd you get it?'

'Nordstrom. I met with one of their personal shoppers who helps you select matching outfits.' She opens the sweater more to show off the blouse. 'This is for the trial. I'm testing it out on you guys first.'

'Looks terrific.'

'But does it look virginal? Karl's lawyer wants me to look virginal.'

'It looks good. You look good.'

'Yeah, I feel good.'

Barcelona smiles and tries to study Dixie's face without seeming to. She's so happy, so positive, looks so radiant. Almost like a bride. This is not at all the way Barcelona expected to find her. She expected brave smiles through trembling lips, pale skin, watery eyes, gnawed fingernails, occasional lapses of attention as she relives her horrible ordeal. The woman had been beaten, raped, and sodomized. Barcelona looks for the darkness in the eyes, the hint at Dixie's inner turmoil. She doesn't find any. 'You look good,' she says again. 'The outfit, the hair. Everything.'

Dixie nods. 'Thanks.'

Trina arrives like a whirlwind. 'My God, Dixie! Look at you. Are you undercover again, as a woman with taste in clothing?'

'At least I can keep mine clean.' Dixie laughs.

Trina sits and waves and looks around for a waitress. 'I'm dying of thirst.'

'It's the fires,' Barcelona says. 'Dries out the throat.'

Trina ignores Barcelona, doesn't even look at her. 'So, Dixie cup, how're you feeling? Back to pumping iron yet?'

472

'Some. Not much.'

'How's Karl?'

Dixie smiles. 'Hanging in there. He's tougher than I thought. We made bail by putting up my house, but he's not moping around or anything. We meet with the lawyers a lot. The rest of the time I'm at work.'

'You're not back on the job already, are you?' Barcelona asks.

'At a desk. Paper Shuffling R Us.'

From across the room, Diva's voice: 'Hey, guys.'

They all look around and see Diva walking toward them with Harley at her side. Barcelona knows from Harley that they've been seeing each other every day since their first date. Harley seems entirely smitten, which Barcelona has trouble understanding. He's dated smarter, prettier, sexier, wittier women. But he acts as if he sincerely loves Diva.

'Oh, you tramp,' Diva says to Dixie, laughing. 'Look how great you look. I come here after having lost fifteen pounds, dying to show off my new body, and you upstage me. I hate you.' Diva leans over behind Dixie's chair and hugs her. Dixie kisses Diva's cheek.

It is true, Diva has lost weight. Her cheeks are a little more defined, her stomach doesn't bulge as much. The improvements are slight, but she does look better.

'Don't worry,' Diva tells them, 'Harley isn't staying. He just dropped me off. That is, as long as Trina can give me a lift home.'

'Trina's shuttle bus at your service,' Trina says.

They all look at Harley. A long silence follows.

'This reminds me of Butch Cassidy and the Sundance Kid,' Harley says. 'Remember that scene where Redford is called a cheater? Newman tries to get him out of the saloon before there's a gunfight, but Redford says he won't go until they ask him to stay.'

'Would you like to stay, Harley?' Dixie says.

'Thanks.' He grins. 'Can't.' He walks over to where Barcelona is sitting and rests his hands on her shoulder. 'I just wanted to come in and congratulate Barcy.'

Barcelona looks up at him, surprised.

'What for?' Dixie asks.

'She hasn't told you?'

'Told us what?'

Diva claps her hands. 'Lynda Kramer called her today, wants Barcy to write a script for her. For real this time.'

'Lynda Kramer called *you*?' Dixie says.

Trina doesn't say anything, looks at the menu. Barcelona wants to reach over and grab her hand, squeeze it, hug her, cry on her shoulder and tell Trina their fight was a stupid mistake, everything will be okay. She doesn't. 'How did you find out?' she asks Harley.

'Evelyn overheard some of it through your office door.' Evelyn Logue is the department secretary. Her breasts are slightly larger than the jets on a 747 and she's known among the faculty, men and women alike, as 'Heavy Evy.' She also has a reputation for snooping, though usually people hear her coming because her industrial strength bra squeaks with each step. Her desk is right outside Barcelona's office door. Harley bends over and kisses Barcelona on top of the head. 'Congratulations, Barcy. Long time coming.'

He says good-bye to everyone and leaves.

'This is so exciting!' Diva says, sitting. 'Dixie looks like a million bucks. Trina's candidate is ahead in the polls. Barcy's got herself hooked up with a superstar. And me'—she smiles broadly, holding out her left hand to show her gold ring—'I got myself married.'

There are general cries of surprise.

'Do you wish for a drink before ordering?' the tiny

Japanese waitress asks. Barcelona didn't even see her approach.

'Wine?' Dixie asks the others.

'You know what I feel like?' Diva says. 'Beer. Let's hoist a few in celebration.'

They order a round of Japanese beer.

'Beer is actually better for you than wine,' Diva says. 'There are sulfites in wine. I read where several people have died from that. People our age.'

'Jesus, Diva,' Trina says. 'We're celebrating, okay?'

'Married,' Dixie says, patting Diva's hand. 'When did all this happen?'

'Last week. We haven't told anyone except my parents and his mom. We were waiting.'

'For what?' Trina asks.

'To hear about our song, "Cocktail Waitress." We finished it two weeks ago and sent it off. Yesterday we heard from the record company that they're interested in it for Rod Stewart.' She crossed her fingers.

'Rod Stewart,' Dixie says. 'Fantastic.'

Diva's smile fades; she looks thoughtful. 'We've all been so lucky these past few weeks. It's almost spooky.'

'Lucky?' Barcelona says. 'After all the years we've worked, the odds were in our favor. It's physics. Universal laws of odds.'

Trina shakes her head. 'I don't know. All of us at once. That's more than physics.'

'Maybe the moon's in the seventh house and Jupiter's aligned with Mars,' Barcelona says. 'Come on. We're just hardworking women with stained dress shields to prove it. Finally our hard work is paying off and you want to pass the credit on.'

'Maybe Barcy's right,' Diva says. 'After all, we aren't all lucky. Dixie sure wasn't.'

'Me?' Dixie says, smiling. 'I'm better than you think. I

475

know you kind of expected me to come here drooling or hearing voices, but I really am okay. Which reminds me . . .' She reaches into her purse and pulls out a hardcover book by a rabbi, *When Bad Things Happen to Good People*. 'I swear I've gotten five copies of this book so far from friends. Anybody want one?' She tosses it in the middle of the table.

Diva picks it up and begins leafing through it. 'I read about this somewhere.'

Dixie continues, 'My life really has gotten better. I don't mean just better than that day, but it's better than it was before the rape. I'm not suggesting rape as a form of therapy, understand, but it hasn't destroyed me. True, I wish this might have happened ten years ago when rape was trendier to the general public. Back when it would have made a good Movie of the Week. Now it's just a cliché. I was raped. It's like saying I caught the flu or admitting I'm clumsy.'

'Hell,' Trina says. 'Every personal crisis is a cliché now. Elizabeth Montgomery has played them all out on TV.'

The waitress returns with four Kirin beers and distributes them. She takes the dinner orders and leaves.

No one speaks. They wait for Dixie.

'I'll tell you how I feel,' Dixie begins. She looks each of them in the eye and smiles. 'I was molested as a child. Nothing big, no intercourse. Just some serious touching. A doctor friend of my dad's, also Chinese. I was seven. He was supposed to be examining me, but I knew even then this was more than an exam. I could tell from the look on his face, his fast breathing, his smell. It happened just that once.'

'Did you tell your dad?' Barcelona asks.

Dixie shakes her head. 'No point. He wouldn't have believed me. It didn't scar my whole life or anything. To tell you the truth, I hadn't really thought much about it since then. Until the past few weeks. I think back on all my training, all those hours of lifting weights, toning my body, getting as strong as I could. And still when I was tied down to that sixteen-year-old kid's bed, I was as helpless as I had been when I was seven.'

'There was nothing you could do,' Diva says.

'Oh, I know that. I don't blame myself. In fact, this may shock you some, in a way I feel relieved. I imagine what a young prizefighter must feel like getting into the ring with some bone-crushing champ, how his knees must be shaking, his stomach churning, circling, bobbing, but all the time waiting for that legendary punch. When he finally gets hit, even if it knocks him to the canvas, the punch is never as bad as he imagined it. It must be kind of a relief saying to himself, "That's all?" I guess that's how I feel, like I've been in training all my life. If that's the worst punch they can throw and I'm still standing, then fuck 'em. I don't have to be afraid anymore.'

Barcelona pours her beer into the glass. She likes the way the beer foams energetically. Barcelona would like to toast Dixie for her courage, but that would only embarrass Dixie. Plus, she's a little resentful at how well Dixie's adjusted. It makes her feel somehow inadequate.

'Now what?' Trina asks Dixie.

'Now I help Karl with his trial. You have no idea how much work is involved. I've always come at it from the other side, prosecuting. Suddenly my law classes are a hell of a lot more interesting.'

'And Randy?'

'He couldn't handle all this.' She doesn't elaborate.

Trina shakes her head. 'What about that principal who was interested in you? Peterson was it?'

'Kevin Peterson.' Dixie stares into her glass of beer. She looks more Oriental now that she ever has before, though that could be the makeup. 'He's called, sent flowers. He even visited me at the hospital. He's nice.'

Diva says, 'I talked to him at the hospital once. He was sweet.'

'He's in the National Guard. His unit was called up a couple days ago to fight the forest fires. I think he's up in the San Bernardino Mountains right now.'

'And when he gets back?' Trina asks.

'Right now, Karl needs me. I think I owe him a little loyalty during this time. Besides, I couldn't ask another guy to hang around while I'm constantly busy with my ex-husband's court case. Not the most romantic circumstances. Right now my main concern is Karl.'

'And after the trial?' Barcelona asks.

Dixie shrugs. 'First things first.'

Silence descends as they slurp their soup. Spoons clack against porcelain.

'I want to know something,' Trina says loudly, pushing her empty bowl away. 'I want to know right now if we're going to keep up these dinners now that this extraordinary luck has blown our way. Love seems to have touched most of us . . .' She glances at Barcelona. '. . . in some form or other. I'd hate to have that break us apart. I mean, was being single the only reason we hung out together, like some kind of nerd club?'

'Hell no,' Dixie says. 'I just did it for the gossip.'

'I'll keep coming,' Diva says. 'Though you may have trouble recognizing me. Harley's taking me out on a major shopping binge this week. New clothes, new hairstyle, everything. An entire makeover for my act.'

'What act?' Trina says.

She smiles brightly and rubs her hands together. 'I'm putting a lounge act together. Get a backup group, sing at local restaurants and such. Maybe Vegas.'

Barcelona is pleased at Diva's enthusiasm, but a little

478

irked to hear about the shopping binge. Especially with the $2,000 still owed which Diva has not mentioned since receiving the check almost a month ago.

The food arrives. The waitress quietly and gracefully distributes the large plates of tempura or black boxes of sushi. Rice bowls are placed next to each woman. 'Enjoy,' the waitress says and bows slightly before hurrying off.

Diva clumsily scissors her chopsticks around a chunk of sushi. 'At first Harley tried talking me out of this whole vegetarian thing. He says it doesn't matter what we eat, it's all part of the chain of life, something like that.'

Trina says, 'That's what I told you when you first started this veggie kick.'

'We shouldn't think of ourselves as individuals eating another individual,' Diva continues, ignoring Trina. 'More like a group of kids within the same family trading baseball cards. One kid only owns the card a short time before it gets traded to another and another. And they all stay in the same drawer anyway. He wants me to read some book by Robert Heinlein. You know him, Barcy?'

'I've read him, yes. He's very good.'

'Yeah, that's what Harley said. *Stranger in a Strange Land*. He says it's about the beauty of cannibalism. Is that right?'

'Partly,' Barcelona says.

'God, *Stranger in a Strange Land*,' Trina sighs nostalgically. 'We read that in high school. All my friends passed it back and forth, we had grok groups.'

'Crock?' Dixie says.

'Grok. That's what they did in the book when they were really talking from the heart. Like an alien rap session. Boy, I hadn't thought about that in years.'

Diva seems to sense the conversation slipping away from her. She raises her voice a little and speaks rapidly. 'Well, I'll read it then, but I'm staying a vegetarian. Look what

479

it's done for me. And I feel great too. And you know what?' She leans forward and whispers. 'My pussy smells different too. Sweeter. I'm serious.'

Trina says, 'Yeah, if you like the smell of brussels sprouts.'

Dixie laughs.

'Go ahead and laugh,' Diva says. 'But I read this article that proves that we pick who we love by smell.'

'God,' Barcelona says, rolling her eyes.

'It's true. We've got smell molecules called pheromones and the part of your brain which registers smell feeds into the part involving emotion and memory. See, what we're smelling is the genetic code of each person.'

'How does she remember this junk?' Trina says.

'These scientists ran these tests with mice. Given a choice, the mice select other mice with an opposite genetic code so their offspring will be stronger.'

'I think I read something about that in the hospital,' Dixie says.

'Maybe that's where I read it,' Dixie says. 'Visiting you.'

'Yeah, that article said that studies show couples who mate with similar genes have a high rate of spontaneous abortions.'

Barcelona picks up a piece of tempura shrimp and dips it in brown sauce. 'So we don't really pick who we love, we just respond to their smells.'

'That's what the article says,' Diva replies.

'I guess it depends on where they smell,' Trina says and Dixie and Diva laugh.

Barcelona imagines the shrimp in her hand sniffing out its mate and puts it back on her plate. She has lost her appetite. Also, she's a little annoyed but she's not sure why.

'Speaking of weird,' Diva says, lowering her voice and

grinning. 'Harley's got this giant collection of pornography in his garage.'

Barcelona is surprised. She has known Harley for years, slept with him, stayed at his house, but she didn't know that. She feels a twinge of jealousy at Diva, similar to the way she felt when Trina told her about Carla. 'He's got half a dozen cardboard boxes full of the shit. His ex-wife collected it in some campaign she was running to get dirty magazines out of the liquor stores in Irvine. She used to haul the stuff out at city council meetings and dump them on the tables. Apparently she was quite a character. She campaigned for bike trails and against smut.'

'What's he do with the stuff?' Dixie asks.

'That's what I asked him. He said nothing.'

'Oh, right. He keeps it for sentimental reasons.'

'Well.' Diva grins coyly. 'He did tell me his ex-girlfriend used to read the letters aloud to him to get them both hot.'

Barcelona is again amazed and annoyed. Amazed at the revelation and annoyed at the shared intimacy Harley has with Diva that he never had with her.

'He told me he still masturbates to them sometimes. I asked him why. He said, "What do you mean? To get off, that's why."'

Trina laughs. 'Good answer.'

'I said, "Yeah, but why do they get you off? You know these letters are all made up by some scummy guy with acne scars and yellow teeth and underpants with skid marks sitting in a smoky room that smells like dog puke." He said, "Yeah, I know." So I said, "Is that what gets you off, knowing that?" He said no.' Diva shakes her head. 'I told him I didn't understand. You know what he said?'

Trina nods. 'He said, "And you never will."'

'Yes!' Diva says, amazed. 'How'd you know?'

'That's what they always say.'

* * *

481

After dinner Trina suggests they hit a couple of bars to celebrate Dixie's recuperation and everyone else's good fortune. Everyone agrees. Barcelona follows Dixie's Mustang down the street though she isn't much in the mood anymore. She hopes some of their high spirits will rub off on her.

This is not at all how she expected to feel tonight. She thought she'd meet with Trina, share the good news about Lynda Kramer, and they would both be overjoyed and giggle like teenagers. She thought Dixie would be withdrawn and she was prepared to spend all evening coaxing her into a good mood. She thought Diva would come in smoking black cigarettes and complaining about her weight/career/love life. Nothing is as planned.

Dixie follows Trina's car into a parking lot next to an old rundown movie theater in the old part of Costa Mesa. Barcelona pulls into the slot next to them. There aren't many cars in the lot. As they get out of their cars, she notices the dark shadow of smoke in the distance, vague flickerings of light from the Saddleback fires. The others don't even look.

Barcelona had never before noticed the bar behind the theater. The building is dark and squat with black windows and a pink neon sign that says THE USUAL SUSPECTS.

'Great place,' Dixie says sarcastically, looking the building over. 'Where's the delousing shower?'

'This place is great,' Diva says. 'I used to come here all the time back with Crawler.'

'Which one was Crawler?' Barcelona asks.

'You know, the one with the eye patch. Thought he was Dr. Hook. Even wore it during sex. Only time he didn't wear it was when he was sitting on the toilet. Then he'd flip it up so he could read better.'

They all laugh, including Barcelona. It's working. She's starting to feel better. She will make a point of pulling

Trina aside and apologizing. Drive up to L.A. and have lunch with her like old times. Whatever it takes. This is going to be fun. She's not even sure why she was so mad before.

Inside the room is long and narrow like a trailer and smells of spilled beer, some small tables are scattered about with neon beer signs for light. The left side of the room has a traditional bar with three faceless customers hunched quietly over drinks. They are not together. Opposite the main bar is a piano bar. A fat woman in her mid-forties sits behind the piano and plays while singing. She is wearing a pink chiffon dress and a pearl necklace. Her hair is a lacquered beehive. She looks as if she was stood up for the prom twenty-five years ago and has been sitting here playing melancholy music ever since.

'*You are the sunshine of my life,*' she sings, '*that's why I'll always be around.*'

'She's good,' Barcelona says, surprised.

'Yeah,' Diva says. 'Jo used to sing radio commercials with me. But her daughter got sick, some rare disease that paralyzes you for a few years. She has to be home during the day to take care of her.'

Jo sings, '*You are the apple of my eye,*' and nods recognition at Diva.

Diva and Trina sit at the piano bar facing Jo. Dixie sits next to Trina and Barcelona sits next to Diva. At the far end of the bar is a woman in her late fifties smoking an unfiltered Camel cigarette and drinking a dark-colored drink. She shakes her glass and watches the ice cubes shift around. She doesn't seem to be aware of the four women, of Jo, of the music. When she finishes her drink, she orders another by shouting over at the bartender. While waiting, she reapplies her lipstick, a bright pink bubblegum color.

Jo finishes her song, reaches over, and shakes a Camel out of the woman's pack. The woman pushes the Bic lighter at her and Jo takes a deep drag. They never exchange words.

'So, Diva, these the friends you're always telling me about?' Jo says.

Diva introduces everyone. Jo nods at all of them without much interest. 'Voice sounds good,' Diva says.

Jo shrugs, 'you wanna take over while I hit the john?'

'No, thanks. I'm resting my voice for the Hollywood Bowl.'

Jo snorts smoke out her nose. She gets up and walks to the back and enters the room marked Women.

'Gee, Diva,' Trina says, 'you know the nicest places.'

'Hey, this joint is a little offbeat, but it's fun.'

Barcelona likes the place. The three men at the bar never seem to move. There are a few couples at the tiny spool tables, but overall the place has the feel of someplace you'd go to start an affair or end one.

Diva goes over to the bar and brings back their drinks, setting each one before the proper person. 'Full service tonight, girls,' she says. 'Tipping permitted.'

'Someone should make a toast,' Dixie says. 'Barcy, you're the wordsmith.'

'And the oldest,' Diva adds with a laugh.

Barcelona holds up her rum and Coke. 'From my lofty years, looking back on when I was your tender age, I remember something my father used to say in times like this . . .'

'Jesus.' Dixie laughs.

'He would turn to me with that sad but knowing look in his eye, perhaps a lone tear clinging like hope to the rim of his eye, and he'd say, "Barcy," with a tremble in his voice. "Barcy," he's say. "Smoke 'em if you got 'em."' Barcelona raises her glass higher.

'Here, here,' Dixie says.

They all drink. Barcelona looks at Trina who is drinking but avoiding her gaze.

'I want to add something,' Diva says. 'I think we should drink to Luck. I mean, it's kind of spooky how great everything's been going for everybody the past few weeks, I mean since . . .' She hesitates. 'Since Dixie got out of the hospital.'

Barcelona puts her drink down. 'That's nuts, Diva.'

'What's nuts? It's true.'

'You know what you're suggesting?'

'I'm not suggesting anything. I'm just observing.'

'You're being an idiot.' Barcelona feels her whole neck aflame. Her eyes are dry and sticky in her sockets. Her throat is tight as a guitar string. 'You're acting as if what happened to Dixie was some kind of catalyst, that we all benefited from it.'

'She didn't say that,' Trina says.

'Didn't she?'

'Well, it is kind of true,' Dixie says. 'From the day I was raped we've all had some pretty terrific changes. Even me.'

'That's disgusting,' Barcelona says. 'The things that happened to us were long overdue. We're talented, intelligent women who've been busting our asses for years and it's finally paying off.'

'No one's suggesting voodoo here, Barcy,' Trina says. 'We're just saying it's an odd coincidence.'

Dixie nods. 'It is odd.'

Barcelona wants to holler at them, but Jo returns from the bathroom and slides behind the piano. She is so close, to continue the discussion now would be like invading her privacy.

'Gimme that thing,' the woman at the end says, gesturing with her hand.

Jo hands her the microphone. 'You gonna tell me or what, Lila?'

Lila stubs out her cigarette and grins. 'You'll pick it up.' She puts the microphone to her mouth and begins to sing: '*The night we met I knew I needed you so . . .*'

Jo comes in with the piano, smiling and bobbing her head in time.

Lila continues, both hands gripped around the microphone: '*And if I had the chance, I'd never let you go . . .*'

'This is a great song,' Diva says excitedly.

Barcelona looks at Dixie and Trina. They too are caught up in Lila's singing. The three of them are smiling, swaying with the familiar song. Lila's voice is every bit as good as Jo's. For some reason, Barcelona finds this astounding. What is all this talent doing here in the tar pits?

'*So won't you say you love me,*' Lila sings. '*I'll make you so proud of me . . .*'

Jo plays with the cigarette in her mouth. When the ash gets too long, she continues to play with one hand, flicks the ash into the ashtray, sticks the cigarette back into her mouth, and plays again with both hands.

'*Be my, be my baby,*' Lila sings. '*My one and only baby . . .*'

Lila sings another verse and when she's done the four women applaud. Barcelona can't get over how well she sang, or how well Jo sang either. They aren't just good party singers, there was training, technique, style in their voices.

'What's her story?' Barcelona asks Diva.

'What story?'

'Her voice. She's so good.'

'Yeah.'

'So what's her story? Did she sing professionally? What happened?'

486

'Nothing happened,' Diva says and turns toward Jo. 'Hey, give us that mike, Jo. My buds and me are gonna sing for you.'

'Oh, no,' Dixie says. 'I don't even sing in the shower; my voice rusts the pipes.'

'I'll do the lead, you guys back me up,' Diva insists. 'It'll be fun.'

'Diva Klosterman and the Supremes,' Trina says. 'It does have a certain ring.'

Diva begins to sing and Jo quickly comes in with the right chords:

> 'When I'm with my guy and he watches
> all the pretty girls go by.
> And I feel so hurt deep inside
> I wish that I could die.
> Not a word do I say
> I just look the other way . . .'

Diva points at the others and Dixie, Trina, and Barcelona join in on the lines, '*Cause that's the way boys are. That's the way booyyys are.*'

They sing other songs, old party songs that they remember from junior high school. Lila joins in on a few. After singing 'Angel Baby,' Barcelona slides a twenty-dollar bill over to Diva and says she has to leave. She decides that this should be more fun than it actually is. Dixie and Diva try to talk her into staying while Trina remains silent, tearing the edges off her cocktail napkin and staring straight ahead.

'I've gotta go, really,' Barcelona says and walks down the narrow path toward the door. She can feel their eyes on her back, even the eyes of the other patrons, the men hunched at the bar, the couples hiding in the dim light of the neon bar signs. The good-byes were brusque, forced, a little cool. She has managed to alienate her three closest friends in one evening. So much for their theory of good luck.

31

Barcelona sits at the kitchen table making a list. She has a yellow legal pad with the words Fuck You Women neatly printed at the top and underlined twice. She stares at the three words a moment and then underlines them again. Then she adds an exclamation point.

It has been three days since the disastrous dinner at Fuji-Kan and the bizarre singalong at The Usual Suspects. She hasn't spoken to any of them since. Dixie called once and left a message on the machine to call her back, but Barcelona hasn't. She promised herself on the drive home that night that she would call Trina and patch things up. She hasn't done that either.

At school today, she ran into Harley in the mimeograph room. He is growing a beard. He scratches his face constantly and his teeth look whiter contrasted against his dark stubble. For some reason she couldn't name, the beard annoyed her. She wanted to ask him why he never told her about his pornography collection, but she didn't want him to know Diva had mentioned it to them. She found it hard to be civil to him.

Grief called yesterday and said that Lynda Kramer had authorized $50,000 to be paid up front and another $50,000 to be paid when the script was done. There were other escalators involved in rewrite steps, but Barcelona didn't pay attention to them. This is more money than she has made in all her books combined. Grief was very excited. Barcelona was now the hot new writer in her agency. Grief was preparing a whole campaign, lunch with producers, studio executives, directors. 'We have to make the deals now,' she'd said, 'while you're still the flavor of the week.'

At school, Foster Malone and Hester Hoffman, who had worked so diligently to keep Barcelona from teaching any writing courses, approached her yesterday with an offer to teach Introduction to Creative Writing the next semester. Foster smiled in what he doubtlessly thought was a charming expression, stroked his reddish beard, and said with an exaggerated brogue, 'Will there be any chance, darlin', of bringin' the lovely Lynda Kramer down here for the students to meet?' Hester added, 'We might even have a dollar or two in the faculty kitty for some sort of reception for her.' Barcelona said she didn't know about Lynda Kramer and she wasn't sure about teaching the class, indeed whether she'd be back next semester at all.

This morning Lynda Kramer called. Her baby cried through most of the conversation so they kept it short. Barcelona imagined her sitting there all in white cotton, bouncing her baby in her arm, a cup of steaming herbal tea next to the phone, a vase of exotic cut flowers on the desk. The furniture would all be rattan, the food would all be pastel colored. Barcelona was surprised to find herself not all that excited this time to be talking to Lynda Kramer. She wasn't even excited by the money, which was still weeks away from actually being paid. The only new thing they discussed was Barcelona's changing the title of the script. '*Feasts* just sounds too spooky, like a vampire movie or something. We don't want to confuse the audience.' Joking, Barcelona suggested they change the title to *The Usual Suspects*. Lynda Kramer loved it: 'It's got wit, yet hints at suspense. The *Casablanca* reference is perfect.

God, this is going to be great. I knew I picked the right person in you.'

Barcelona sits at the kitchen table and draws a hyphen between Fuck and You. The W of Women is round at the bottom of each dip and looks either like buttocks or breasts. She draws nipples in to make them breasts. She just now came up with this idea, the list of Fuck-You Women. Women with that special look, that aura, that way of sitting down, crossing their legs, laughing, sipping coffee, some single aspect of the person that embodies their whole attitude, that says 'Fuck You, Jack' to anyone who doesn't take them seriously. She writes Sigourney Weaver at the top of the list. She has Fuck-You lips, sharply defined and eager to speak. Next she writes Susan Sontag. She has Fuck-You hair, long and black and thick as her intellect.

Barcelona looks at the clock in the stove. Almost ten. Cory will be here any minute. He had a late dinner with some boys' athletic group in Los Angeles, but he said he really wanted to see her tonight. They talk every day on the phone. Since the infamous Night of the Tampon, they managed to have sex once at his Corona del Mar house. It was during the afternoon and both had to rush right off afterward so it was hard to gauge anything more from it than it felt good. Very good. Certainly nothing about it to explain why his wife Dayna had decided to give up sex forever. She suspects that they will have sex again tonight and has therefore changed the sheets and put on new panties.

Joni Mitchell is singing 'Blue' on the compact disk player. '*Blue*,' she sings, '*songs are like tattoos . . .*' Barcelona writes Joni Mitchell on the list. Her lyrics say Fuck You.

She tries to think of other names. Gloria Steinem? No, looks too pampered. Dianne Feinsten? Not really. Jane

491

Fonda? Nope. She writes Lynda Kramer, stares at the name, then crosses it off.

She writes her mother's name: Milan Lee. She underlines it. Yeah, Milan's got it. The way one scythelike eyebrow lifts in a high arc over the eye when she listens to you talk makes you feel like a suspect hooked up to a lie detector. The eyebrow bobs and rears with each answer, etching a graph of your obvious lies that are recorded in the wrinkles of her forehead. Many of Barcelona's breathless explanations for youthful misdeeds from skipping school when she was fifteen to revealing her abortion when she was twenty-two met with this same test, followed by a brisk nod and the deadly words: 'I see. Well, we'd better not tell your father.' Barcelona can remember a dozen such instances, mostly minor infractions of obscure rules, each somehow uncovered by Milan and requiring an explanation. Each sealed with the incantation, 'I see. Well, we'd better not tell your father.' The result was a pact, one Barcelona didn't want, a secret society of the two of them, sharing secrets, secrets she didn't really care if her father discovered. But to tell him after her mother's pronouncement would be worse, an act of betrayal.

Barcelona writes Trina's name on the list. She stares at the name awhile. Her throat starts to itch. The fires in the mountains are all out now, but smoke still lingers. The air is gritty. She gets up and goes to the refrigerator and opens the door. The bitter smell of rotten food rushes her face. 'Jesus,' she says, squinting and holding her breath. She opens the vegetable drawer and finds a plastic bag of zucchini that has melted into a greenish-white slop. She tosses it into the garbage can. Then she takes the garbage bag out of the can, chokes it with a twist-tie and places it outside the backdoor on her patio. By morning the slugs and snails will be crawling all over it, but she's not in the mood to take it out to the garage right now.

492

She grabs a Diet Coke and returns to the list. She writes her own name on the list, stares at it, tilts her head to the left, to the right. She underlines it. She crosses it out with three heavy lines.

The doorbell rings.

She glances at the clock. Cory is earlier than expected. She pads barefoot across the gray carpet to the front door and peaks through the peephole. Her chest tightens.

'Hi,' she says, opening the door.

Diva and Harley walk in.

'*Angel baby,*' Diva sings. '*My angel baby.*' She does a funky little dance while Harley looks on with amusement and scratches his stubbly beard. 'God, Barcy, it's fan-fucking-tastic!'

'What is?'

'We sold it. We goddamn sold it. The song. "Cocktail Waitress" is going to be recorded on Rod Stewart's next album!'

Barcelona hugs Diva. She feels tremendous warmth for her right then. 'I'm so happy for you, Diva. For both of you.'

Diva squirms like a child, fluttering around the living room with manic energy. 'Jesus, Jesus, Jesus. I can't believe it. I have to tell you, I never really thought they'd buy it, never in a million years. That kind of luck never happens to me. Never. It's like we're all charmed.'

Barcelona hugs Harley. His jacket smells earthy but nice. His beard scratches her cheek. 'That's some cheese grater you've got there, Harley,' she says rubbing her cheek.

'Isn't it?' Diva says. 'He's about scraped all my skin off, and not just on my face.' She laughs heartily and kisses his cheek. Harley smiles and scratches his neck. 'Oh, shit,' Diva says suddenly. 'Almost forgot why we came here.' She opens her purse and dips her fingers in. Her fingernails are green with miniature musical instruments painted on each one. The thumbs have guitars, the index fingers trumpets, followed by french horns, crossed drumsticks, and tiny cymbals on the pinkies. She pinches a folded check between the guitar and trumpet and hands it to Barcelona. 'I can't tell you how much this meant to me.'

Barcelona reads the amount: $2,200. 'I didn't want interest, Diva. This was a loan between friends.'

'I told her,' Harley says.

'I know that,' Diva says. 'But I used it to make a hell of a lot more money. You came through when no one else would or could. I want you to know how I feel about that. Like you invested in a winner for once.'

Barcelona nods understanding. She feels guilty about her previous uncomplimentary thoughts about Diva being a deadbeat. She decides to use the extra $200 to buy them a wedding gift.

'Well, we're off.' Diva hugs Barcelona quickly and opens the door. 'The record company wants to see some more songs so me and John Lennon here are heading back to the drawing board. We bought this neat synthesizer that makes every damn sound but a buffalo farting. We can practically make our own demo with it.'

'This is just the beginning for you guys. I can feel it.' Barcelona stands next to the open door.

'See you at school,' Harley says, walking out into the night. Sprinklers are hissing across the greenbelt. Some of the spray brushes his pants legs and he steps out of the way.

Diva runs out. She is wearing a denim miniskirt and the sprinklers soak her knees and shins. 'Ooooh.' She laughs. 'Feels good.'

They run off toward their car through the gauntlet of sprinklers. '*Cocktail waitress ain't got an easy life*,' Diva sings loudly in the dark. *'Gotta talk like the devil and listen like a wife.'*

A couple of dogs start barking furiously and Diva's laughter drifts back to Barcelona's open door.

'This is nice,' Cory says.

Barcelona nods.

'Isn't it?' he asks.

'I nodded yes.'

'Oh.'

They are lying on top of the bed watching TV, the last few minutes of a remake of *D.O.A.* in which the hero is poisoned and tries to discover the killer before he dies. They are both dressed. Cory has removed only his shoes and jacket. He still wears his tie. His arm is draped across her bare thigh. The pant leg of her shorts is hiked up so that the white material of the pocket peeks out. Barcelona keeps expecting his hand to creep up her thigh and slip under her pant leg. She would be happy if it did, but she has to admit that she is equally happy lying here with him just watching TV. She can tell that they will make love later and she kind of likes the anticipation.

She looks over at him and catches him staring at her with a dopey grin on his face.

'What?' she asks.

'What?' he says.

'What's wrong?'

'Nothing.'

'You're staring.'

'I like the way you look,' he says.

'Oh?' she says.

A minute passes.

'How would you describe my look?' she asks.

He makes a serious face, works his lips around in concentration. 'I don't know.'

495

'Would you say I have a Fuck-You Look?'

He laughs. 'Jesus.'

'Would you?'

'Not exactly. More like a John Henry look.'

She brushes his hand off her thigh. 'Wrong answer, Toad Lips.'

He kisses her neck and she laughs. 'You know, like in the folk song: "John Henry was a steel-driving man." Remember?'

'Hmm. So I look like a large black steel-driving man?'

'You're going to make this tough, aren't you?'

'Yup.' She smiles.

He takes a deep breath. 'What I mean was, John Henry had to prove something, prove he could drive railroad spikes better than a steam drill. Of course, it's impossible, but he challenged the steam drill to a contest to see who could drive more rails faster.'

'I know the song. Where do I fit in?'

'Well, he beat the steam drill and became a hero. But he broke his heart doing it, and died.'

Barcelona frowns. 'I don't think I like this analysis.'

'What I meant was, you don't have a Fuck-You Look, you have an I'll-Show-You Look. Big difference.' He leans over and kisses her on the lips. His hand slides up her thigh and teases at the edge of her shorts. He leans back, his hand withdraws. 'Okay?'

'I'll think it over,' she says.

'That's the trouble with women,' Cory says. 'No compliment is ever enough.'

'Oh, is this one of those male truisms?'

'Observations. One of many that men share among themselves.'

'Really? Like what else?'

'Don't you get the newsletter?'

She pokes him playfully in the ribs. 'Come on, what else?'

'Like don't ever sleep with a woman who has more problems than you do.'

'That's no problem, there aren't any women with more problems than men. Besides, once a man's in the mood, he doesn't care if she's axed half the city, as long as she doesn't ax him 'til he's done.'

He reaches over and pulls her toward him. They kiss. She reaches down and squeezes his penis. It is hard and straining at his pants. 'I didn't argue the point,' he says.

'I hate that guys say things about women,' she says.

'Why? Women say things about men, don't they?'

'Sure, but we're accurate. Guys mostly talk about young girls, firm tits, thighs that don't touch when she walks. It's all so childish, trying to recapture their youth, which probably wasn't so hot anyway.'

'That's not it at all.' Cory shifts to look her in the face. His expression is serious. 'Men aren't trying to recapture youth. They're thinking back to the time they traveled in packs, like wolves, roaming the playgrounds and parking lots with their friends. Back when the air was thick and potential, when adventure wasn't just possible, it was inevitable. Maybe because they were all together like that, even the smallest action, walking on railroad tracks, took on mythic status. Big screen proportions.'

Barcelona watches his face, fascinated by the intensity in his eyes.

'Someone might say, "Hey, let's beat up someone," and you'd all say, "Yeah, okay," and maybe you'd beat up some kid you happened on or maybe you'd lose interest looking. Didn't matter. "Let's beat up someone" or "Let's find some girls" had the same meaning. The day was filled with unpredictability.' He leaned over and kissed her hair.

497

'But once you throw women into the formula, it all goes bad.'

She pushes him away. 'Fuck you, John Henry.'

'Girls were organized. Clean. Terrified of dirt. Dirt is the fuel of adventure, the currency of boys. With girls around, "Let's go walk the railroad tracks" would meet with "It's too dirty." That's okay because guys eventually trade adventure for women. But at some point a man misses that. It's not youth exactly, it's not the midlife crazies or any of that shit. He misses the feeling of the pack, the smell of dirt. Not soil, as in mowing lawns and mulching. Dirt. The unpredictable. Somehow Sunday afternoon at the mall doesn't fill that need.'

'We like adventure too,' Barcelona says. 'We're not just house slaves.'

'I know. It's just different. No point in talking about it; every time one side brings up the differences the other side gets defensive.'

Barcelona did feel defensive. Somehow he'd made her feel like some kind of spoilsport, the evil mother calling Johnny in from play to eat his overcooked vegetables and smelly fish sticks. That is not how she saw herself.

The movie ends sometime during their conversation and the eleven o'clock news is on. Cory sits up straight and stares at the TV. 'I want to see this,' he says.

'Why?' she asks. 'You announce your candidacy for president today?'

'Sshh.'

They watch the headline stories: another random free-way shooting, no one injured; a cute side story about a company manufacturing bumper stickers that say 'Don't shoot, I'm only changing lanes,' and 'Don't shoot, I'm going as fast as I can.'

Larry the cat skulks into the room, his head low in a predatory stance. Cory pats the bed, encouraging him to

498

join them, but he just stares a moment, then wanders into the bathroom. After a minute they can hear him drinking from the toilet bowl.

The news does a couple of stories on the fires, showing blackened ground, charred homes, bodies being hauled off in bags. Twenty-four of California's fifty-eight counties have been declared in a state of emergency by the governor. They show old clips of the special fire retardant being prepared for the bombers and helicopters to drop. Ammonia sulfate powder is mixed with water and a pink dye to create a slush that looks like melted strawberry ice cream. The dye allows them to see from the air how accurate the drop was. The ammonia sulfate is a fertilizer. Another story shows how the 22,000 firefighters were fed in those remote areas. The news team interviewed one of the twenty-five caterers hired to serve these men the eight thousand calories a day required by the U.S. Forest Service. There is film of a man making huge cauldrons of mashed potatoes by mixing them with a power drill. There is film of three women cracking eggs into a giant hydraulically assisted tilt skillet that can cook seven hundred eggs at once.

'For this I'm missing reruns of "Taxi"?' she teases him.

'*A surprising announcement today from City Council candidate Cory Meyers,*' the anchorwoman suddenly says.

Barcelona sits up. Film of Cory at a news conference fills the screen. Dayna is standing next to him, smiling.

Candidate Meyers told reporters that he and his wife of ten years, the former Dayna Churchton, have separated in preparation for divorce.'

'Jesus, Cory,' Barcelona says.

'*Mr. Meyers was asked why he chose to make this announcement now, just ten days before the election.*' The camera cuts to a closeup of Cory in front of a gnarled cactus of microphones. '*This is an amiable separation. I wanted the voters to know everything before they voted for me.'* Cut to closeup of Dayna Meyers, her flawlessly beautiful face smiling with confidence. Anchorman's voice-over: *'Mrs. Meyers said she still supported her estranged husband's candidacy and will continue to work on his campaign. They were still best of friends and would remain so regardless of the election or divorce.'*

Barcelona looks at Cory, shocked. 'Why'd you do it?'

'What if I told you I did it for us?'

'I'd say that scares me. I'd say we don't know each other that well yet. That if you lost the election because you pulled a stunt like this for me, I'd feel like shit.'

'Okay,' he says with a grin. 'I didn't do it for us.'

She touches his face with her fingertips, strokes his jaw. 'I mean it, Cory. I like you. There may even be something more going on between us. Something that could be something. Jesus, where are the words when you need them?' She takes a deep breath. 'But we don't know each other that well.'

'Now we can, without hiding all the time. I wanted you to know how much I value this relationship.'

'What relationship?' she says. 'We've talked a lot on the phone, had a couple meals, and made love once.'

'That can be remedied,' he says, reaching for her. His good humor annoys her.

She holds him off. 'I'm trying to tell you that it scares me a little that you care about me enough to risk so much without knowing me better. This is not the action of a stable personality, a man in control of himself.'

'I didn't ask you to marry me, Barcy. I only announced my separation. Now you know this isn't just about a fling. Besides, I'm glad I came clean before the election. I feel better.'

'How's Trina taking it?'

'Something's going on between you two, isn't it?'

'Why?'

'She acts funny when I mention your name. Puts on a show of being unconcerned.'

'We had a disagreement. We'll work it out.'

Cory shrugs. 'Okay. In any event, she wasn't pleased. She even tried to talk me out of it. Ten days can't make any difference, she kept saying.' He laughs. 'She really wants me to win.'

'So do I.'

'So do I,' he says. He rolls toward her and gathers her in his arms. He kisses her and she likes the feel of his lips on hers, his hand cupped under her right buttock, his tongue ricocheting around her mouth. The TV drones on about sports. In baseball, lots of home runs were hit and there's more controversy about why.

They quickly undress. His clothes are stubborn, lots of buttons. She manages to yank his shirt off and pull his pants down. He tugs hers over her hips, pants and panties together, and stares at her body. He kisses her pubic hairs once, then they shed the rest of their clothes.

His hands are gentle but firm, grabbing hunks of her here and there, a thigh, a breast, a buttock. His penis pokes into her stomach and she reaches down to hold it. She likes the feel of it, large and heavy. Its skin is hot against her palm. She squeezes it and he gives a sigh of pleasure. Men are so easy to please, she thinks, but so hard to satisfy.

He lowers his head to her belly button and stabs his tongue into it. She jerks and laughs. 'That tickles.'

'Good,' he says, but he stops. He drags his tongue down between her legs and burrows in there.

Barcelona glances down, watching Cory's head bob and twist, each movement squirting hot lava into her stomach. He knows what he's doing. But he isn't mechanical about it the way Harley used to be: insert tongue A into slot B

501

and rotate a quarter turn. Cory's movements seem to give him as much pleasure as he gives. She grasps his head with both hands and rocks against his mouth. Her eyes roll shut and she sees vast forests on fire, smoke thick as fog choking off the sunlight. She breathes fast, in gasps, gulping air as the smoke grows darker and thicker. She comes in a small spasm, then a bigger one, then one more that causes her to grind her teeth.

Cory climbs on top of her and eases his penis into her. The sensation is something like sliding down a banister, if the banister were inside you. He doesn't move a lot right then, gives her time to catch her breath. He lies on top of her, supporting his weight with his arms, just enjoying being inside. Barcelona's eyes snap open suddenly and she thinks she may have passed out for a moment, lost consciousness. He is still on top of her, his penis is still inside, swollen and hard, so if she did pass out, she didn't miss anything. He starts to move slowly. In and out. In and out. She pulls her legs up to her chest to feel him better. She gasps with each thrust. His hips smack against her ass with a thump. His penis is punching a button that goes directly to her brain, where it honks the horn and flashes the lights, then pulls back and she feels like her guts are being sucked out her vagina each time he retracts a little.

Finally he picks up his pace, hammering at her. She curls her fingers into his back, encouraging him. She wants him to come. He does. His lips slam into her and he grits his teeth. 'Oh, fuck,' she thinks he wants to get inside her even farther, though this is impossible. He sags, panting, finished. Then he starts to laugh. A big hearty laugh, with head thrown back and teeth and gums glistening with saliva.

'What's so funny?' she asks.

He rolls off her and she lowers her legs. Her skin stings

502

from the sudden rush of air against her sweaty chest. He is still chuckling.

She smiles at him. 'Why are you laughing?'

'No reason. It just felt good. Sometimes I laugh when I'm happy.'

'That's strange.'

'Stranger things are yet to come.' He nuzzles her neck.

They watch TV awhile then make love again. Afterward both fall asleep. Sometime later Barcelona wakes with a start. The TV is still on. She stares at it without comprehension, finally recognizing a rerun of 'Rockford Files.' She glances at the clock/radio next to the bed: 12.37 A.M. Her heart is pounding terribly and she wonders if she is having a heart attack. She can see the thumping under the skin. She thinks about waking Cory, but she doesn't. She read somewhere that caffeine was good for a heart attack. She gets out of bed, her head spinning dizzily, and stands on wobbly knees. She falls back to the bed. Cory doesn't stir.

'God,' she says and gets up again. This time she can stand. She makes her way downstairs by bracing herself against the walls as she walks. She opens the refrigerator and that same rancid smell whacks her face. She grabs a Diet Coke, pops the tab, and drinks. She sits naked on the wood floor in front of the open refrigerator door and lets the cool air pucker her skin. She feels better. No heart attack.

She walks back upstairs and stands over the bed. Cory is muttering in his sleep, though she can't make out any words. He's smiling and that's a good sign. He's kicked the covers off and she stands there a minute admiring his body. It is trim and toned with only a slight hint of looseness at the waist. He is a good, responsive lover. He is warm and wise. He is honorable. He likes her enough to pull a crazy stunt like separating from his wife before the election.

Her heart starts thumping again and she has trouble

503

breathing. She goes into the bathroom and flicks on the light. Larry is curled up inside the sink sleeping. He looks up when she opens the medicine cabinet. Barcelona studies the row after row of medicines and remedies, but she sees nothing appropriate. Meantime, Larry has roused himself and is poking his head into the cabinet, licking the tube of Ben-Gay. He is very intent, biting the cap, pulling it out. He drops it on the counter and starts to dance around it. He falls to his back and twists and turns as if he were possessed. This is more animated than she's ever seen him. He jumps up again and attacks the Ben-Gay tube, gnawing at the cap in desperation. Barcelona wonders if there's some kind of catnip in the ointment. She pulls it away from Larry and puts it back in the medicine cabinet and closes the door. Larry continues to dance around the counter, knocking over her makeup bottles and scattering her Q-tips. Barcelona picks him up to make sure he's okay, but he writhes and squirms with such ferocity that he leaps free of her arms and falls to the floor. His senses impaired by the Ben-Gay fumes, he lands on his hip with a squawk, then gets up and limps away.

For an instant, Barcelona knows how Larry feels clawing at the damn tube: blood thumping behind the eyeballs, choking off light, yet still scratching away in blindness. That gnawing unspecific need drilling deeper into the stomach sending gusher after gusher of corrosive acid splashing against tender membrances. The temptation to cry out, not for help or comfort or out of desire, just to hear the sound of your own confusion before the fumes crush the larynx, choking off air. And all the time scratching at the tube, trying to get at the source, knowing when you release the cap, what is inside may kill you.

Barcelona leaves the room and wanders down the hall to her study. The room is painted bright red to keep her attentive during her work. Overstuffed bookshelves scale each wall. The overflow is stacked in neat piles on the floor. Barcelona sits behind her computer and stares at the dark screen. She is astounded at her own good fortune. Before tonight everything was wonderful: money, impending fame, Grief's hot new writer, celebrity at school. All she needed for it to be perfect was for Cory to be unattached. Now he was. Now everything was perfect.

She was charmed.

Yet she didn't feel charmed. She felt as if she'd just been driven home in a police cruiser by two large and silent police officers. As if her clothes were tattered, unrepairable, and her body smelled of dried blood and hospital disinfectant. She could feel the scratches on her face and thighs, where ragged fingernails clawed for purchase. But that wasn't her, was it?

She turns on the computer, punches up the last pages of the script for *The Usual Suspects*, and rereads what she's writing. She picks right up and starts typing a new scene. The cadence of her typing seems to calm the thumping of her heart. It slows back to normal. When she is finished writing the scene, she copies the disk, shuts off the computer, goes back to the bedroom.

While Cory sleeps, Barcelona quietly dresses, packs a few things, gets into her car, and drives all night to Las Vegas.

32

The dealer wears clear fingernail polish. He shuffles the cards gracefully and deals seven card stud. His glossy nails flicker under the bright casino lights. 'It keeps my nails from splitting,' he tells Barcelona, though she didn't ask. The other players ignore his monologue and study their cards. 'All this shuffling, the dry desert air, handling dirty money. Cracks the nails.' He taps his perfect fingernails on the green felt in front of an old woman with a deuce of clubs showing. 'Deuce opens, sweetheart. Deuces never loses.'

The old woman throws in two quarters. Barcelona folds. Others see the bet or fold. The dealer tosses out another card to each player. 'Some people look at the polish,' the dealer says to Barcelona, 'and they think I'm a fag. Just because I wear polish they think I'm a fag. I'm not a fag.' He winks at her. 'At least not yet.'

Barcelona has been playing seven card stud for four straight hours. This is a one-dollar and three-dollar table, minimum bet is one dollar, maximum bet is three dollars. She is ahead eighty-seven dollars. Her car and overnight bag are in the casino parking lot. She hasn't even checked into a hotel yet. She drove all night through the cool desert air in the Geezemobile, stopping once for gas and a Snickers bar from the vending machine. During the entire drive, she listened only to the all-news station on the radio, even though they kept repeating the same stories over and over. This was unusual because she always plays either her tapes or the oldies stations on her radio. But she told herself this was not a pleasure trip, she was on a sort of mission. She needed constant cold splashes of reality to keep her mind focused, help her concentrate on the task at hand. She needed news, facts.

The radio played one science story that Barcelona can't get out of her mind. It was about how the long-horned beetle bites through the poisonous veins of the milkweed leaf before eating the plant. Like a burglar snipping the wires to an alarm. This causes the toxic fluids to drain off and not poison him while he dines. This also allows the woolly bear caterpillar and the army worm, normally not milkweed eaters, to also eat the plant now that the toxins are gone. Of course, the beetle does ingest some of the creamy poison in the process of severing the veins, but not enough to kill him. Barcelona thinks of Dixie. Even the insect world has its charm.

'Where's the nearest pay phone?' she asks the dealer.

He points. 'By the hologram.'

She walks away, leaving her chips on the table. She wends her way through the maze of slot machines to the giant hologram of a leprechaun sitting in a pot of gold that has poured out of a slot machine. It's a fuzzy hologram, hard to see. It's not clear whether the leprechaun is rolling on his back joyously throwing the gold coins in the air, or if the gold coins are raining down on him and have knocked him onto his back.

She finds the phone, calls Orange County information, memorizes the number, and dials her neighbor. He isn't home so she leaves a message on his answering machine: 'Hi, Dave, it's Barcelona. I wonder if you'd do me a big favor and feed Larry tonight and tomorrow. I was called out of town unexpectedly and I'm not sure when I'll be back. I'll phone you later with details. The spare key is outside my garage under the first flagstone. If there's an emergency, you can reach me at Caesar's Palace in Las Vegas. Thanks, neighbor.' She hangs up and returns to the poker table. She imagines Dave's chubby face as he listens to the message, the leash in one hand, the brown paper bag in the other.

Barcelona sits down and discovers a new player sitting in the chair next to her. He is short and rotund, triple chins accordioned at his neck. He is wearing a plastic name tag with the printed words HELLO, MY NAME IS followed by his typed name: Dr. Earl Downey.

'So, Doc,' the dealer says, throwing cards around the table, 'you with the convention?'

'Yes, I am.'

'So what kind of doctor are you? Gynecologist?' The dealer grins and taps his polished fingernails on the felt in front of Barcelona's up card, four of hearts. 'Low card must open, ma'am. What's your bet?'

Barcelona throws in two quarters.

'Fifty cents,' the dealer announces. 'Major wager.'

Barcelona peeks at her cards underneath, a five and another four. Not enough to bet up, but enough to stick around for another card. Her next card is a six. Someone else with a pair of jacks showing bets two dollars; she calls. She ends up with a straight to the eight and wins another twenty-four dollars. She tips the dealer fifty cents.

'Thank you, thank you,' he says. He taps the coins against the metal edge of the coin tray before sticking the money in his shirt pocket. This is done after every tip to signal that they are not stealing casino money. Above each table, the ceiling is a glittery crazy-quilt design of bright lights and mirrors. Behind the one-way mirrors are cameras watching each game all over the casino. Barcelona looks up and stares at the hidden camera. The bright lights reflect off the mirrors into her eyes, blurring her vision. She strains to see the camera behind the mirror, but all she sees is her own reflection which resembles, with her blurred vision, that fuzzy hologram of the leprechaun.

Barcelona sits naked on the bed eating Kentucky Fried Chicken, extra crispy. The bucket sits between her crossed legs and she hunches over it while she eats so the crumbs fall back into the bucket. A few crumbs sometimes miss and drop into her lap, snagged in the thicket of pubic hairs. To her right a *USA Today* lies spread open to the state-by-state news summary. To her left is what remains of a six-pack of Diet Coke. Three full cans are still looped into the plastic holder. Two empty ones lay on the bedspread, one has rolled down and leans against her left buttock. One is still half-filled and she occasionally sips from it, setting it back on the bedspread where it tilts precariously.

The TV is showing a local talk show.

On the dresser is a stack of her winnings: $376.

She reads the newspaper with her reading glasses, intermittently glancing up to watch a few seconds of TV while taking a bite of chicken and a swig of Diet Coke, and then back to reading the newspaper. Her throat is still a little sore, Vegas Throat they call it, an irritation caused by the constant blasting of icy casino air-conditioning combined with the smoke from millions of free cigarettes streaming hourly into the air.

A psychologist is on the talk show. He is sitting on a cushy chair facing the host. The psychologist looks remarkably familiar. Jesus, Barcelona thinks in mid-bite, he looks like that dealer with the clear polish. The show's host is a shapely woman in her mid-thirties with frosted hair and a nose that Barcelona is positive has been fixed. The psychologist is promoting his new book about relationships, *Intimate Inmates: How to Break Out of Confining Relationships*. The cover photo shows a man and a woman bursting through a brick wall of a jail.

'*How, Dr. Novinger?*' the hostess Vicki asks, squinting intently. '*How can we break out, or even know that we want to?*'

'*First thing one needs to do is recognize that the relationship is indeed confining.*' His voice startles Barcelona; it too sounds exactly like the dealer's. She leans closer to the TV, her breasts dipping into the bucket of chicken. '*It's not always easy to see that a relationship we're in is really a prison of our own construction.*'

'*Ah,*' Vicki says, nodding.

'*For example, the clothes women wear often make them coconspirators in their own imprisonment. High heels are designed to alter the natural shape of the leg to a more sexy angle, but at what price? Strained muscles, chronically sore legs, twisted ankles. The concept is much like the Oriental custom of binding a woman's feet. Much of women's clothing is designed to hinder their movements, like the leg irons on a prisoner. Tight short skirts allow only small steps, as do the high heels just mentioned.*'

'*But men seem to like the way they look,*' Vicki points out.

'*Yes,*' Dr. Novinger agrees, '*as long as he doesn't have to walk with her, drag her behind him. See, that's the point. The clothes are meant to enhance a woman's looks, not her functioning ability. This makes her an object. How many times have you worn panty hose on a hot mucky day when you didn't want to?*'

'*You sound like a man who's tried them on.*' She laughs, poking him in the ribs.

Dr. Novinger smiles good-naturedly. '*Why are panty hose preferable to men than the bare leg? Because the panty hose shapes the leg more, hides the flaws, makes them more*

*attractive to look at. Even more destructive than clothing is
the cultural pressure for women to shave their bodies.'*

*'Come, now, Dr. Novinger, you're not suggesting hairy
legs and unsightly armpits? Men shave their faces, don't
they? You do.'*

*'There is a difference. Men shave for reasons of comfort
and sanitation. Women shave for aesthetic reasons. We have
told them that it is better to shave their bodies so they look
like little girls than let their hair grow and look like an adult
of their species. Everything we do as a culture is to reduce
women to the confines of adolescence, the restricting clothing, the shaved bodies. Make them look like children so
they can be controlled like children.'*

Vicki looks offstage. *'Our phones are ringing. Dr. Novinger will be answering questions from our home viewers.'*

Dr. Novinger raises his hand to adjust his glasses and
his fingernails flicker under the bright studio lights.

'I saw a guy who looks just like you,' Barcelona tells the
dealer when she returns to the table.

The dealer tosses cards to the players. 'Richard Gere
must be back in town.'

'Not exactly. A psychologist on TV. Looked just like
you, except he wore glasses.'

The dealer taps his glossy nail under his eye. 'Contacts.'

'Two bucks,' a man with a pipe says. He throws in two
chips.

'Two dollars,' the dealer echoes. 'Two dollars to peek
under the fat lady's dress.'

Barcelona sits down at the five-dollar blackjack table.
She is the only one at the table. 'Kinda slow today,' she
says to the woman dealer.

'Kinda.' The woman nods and gathers up the decks
of cards. She shuffles them one stack at a time, hands

511

Barcelona a red plastic card to stick in the deck. Barcelona does so and the dealer cuts the cards and stuffs them into a black shoe. 'Place your bet, ma'am,' she says with a drawl. She has bleached blond hair as stiff as the cards.

Barcelona has won over four hundred dollars at poker. She takes twenty five-dollar chips out of her purse and stacks them on the felt table. She places one chip in the square in front of her. The dealer tosses out the cards faceup for Barcelona and one up, one down for the dealer. Barcelona has a nine and king. She stays. The dealer has an eight showing. She flips over a ten and pays Barcelona.

Barcelona is not discouraged. She places another chip in the square. She wins again. She tries not to lose hope.

'Hi, Evelyn?' Barcelona says into the phone. 'This is Barcelona. I want you to post my class today, I won't be coming in . . . No, nothing too serious.' Evelyn Logue, the department secretary, persists in asking for details, symptoms. Barcelona refuses to give any. 'You can get Ben Lawrence to substitute for me, he knows how I run the class. Thanks.'

She hangs up the phone and walks to the cashier's cage, feeling guilty about canceling her class. She has never done that before except for severe illness. Still, she had to.

She dumps her stack of chips on the counter and pushes them under the window bars. The kid behind the counter starts stacking them and counting.

'Five hundred and sixty-five dollars,' he says. 'How do you want it?'

'Big,' she says.

He counts out five hundred-dollar bills, a fifty, a ten, and a five.

'Thank you,' she says. 'Where's the luncheon buffet?'

He points. 'Past the hologram to the left.'

Barcelona follows his directions until she's walking down

a hallway behind a couple of beefy college-age boys in USC Trojan sweatshirts.

'Have you eaten at the buffet before?' one of them asks the other.

'You mean the *barf*-et.'

They both laugh.

The buffet is served in the showroom where their top entertainers perform at night. Joan Rivers and the Smothers Brothers are billed for tonight. Barcelona hopes it looks more glamorous at night because right now it looks pretty cheesy.

Barcelona browses past the bins, piling food onto her plate: roast beef, turkey, salads, rolls, gelatin molds, fruit, mashed potatoes. She sits in a booth by herself and eats ravenously, finishing everything on her plate. The food tastes bland, but she has never been so hungry. She goes back for seconds and eats that too.

A black girl wearing a short skirt and high heels asks Barcelona if she wants to play $50,000 keno. Barcelona shakes her head and the girl hurries to pick up the keno sheets from other diners.

Keno is not part of Barcelona's plan; the odds are too crazy. Winning or losing at keno won't prove anything. She has worked it all out very carefully. It is crucial to play each game to win, not take stupid chances and buck the odds. The only way any of this will make any sense is if she plays the games she knows with as much skill as possible. The longer she plays, the better the odds fall in the casino's favor. It is inevitable then that they will win. According to all known laws of probability, she will lose all her money. Once she has, she will have proven her point beyond all doubt.

Barcelona tears her bagel in half to mop up some of the tasteless gravy left on her plate. The bagel is dry, not nearly as good as her father makes in his bakery. She

513

remembers the hot Saturdays downstairs in the kitchen, when she was twelve, helping Dad make the bagels. The bagels were the last thing baked and when they were done she was allowed to go off to the movies for the matinee. Her favorite part was squeezing the yeast for the dough. Eight ounces of Fleishmann's yeast in half a pan of warm water. She had to submerge her hand in the water and keep squeezing the sticky clump of yeast until it melted into a tan soup. Sometimes the warm water made her have to go to the bathroom and she'd squirm and dance until she finished and then run off to pee. When she was done, the melted yeast was poured into the huge robot-sized dough mixer with twenty-three and a half pounds of flour. There were eggs and oil and salt and sugar. Then her father would switch on the mixer and the giant metal arm would stir through the gunk. Her father would stand beside the machine, studying the mixture as it spun, adding water at mysterious intervals until it somehow became dough.

Then, after the dough rose, her father would roll it out, cut it into small squares in another machine, and stand next to his wooden bake bench for hours rolling the dough into fat snakes, wrapping one around his hand, then rolling it closed and flopping it on a tray. When the tray was full, the bagels would rise and then be boiled in water and baked. When the first tray was taken out of the oven, Barcelona had her pick. She ate her bagel hot, often burning her mouth, but nothing was ever more delicious, just as nothing was ever quite as sensual as squeezing that yeast in the warm water.

Upstairs in the store, her mother would be waiting on customers, bagging baked goods, pouring coffee, slicing corned beef, smoking cigarettes. Men especially liked Milan, found her deep voice sexy, her easy laughter flattering. Whenever Barcelona carried a tray of Danish up to the store, her mother would be sitting at the end of the counter,

514

smoking a cigarette, laughing with someone, usually a man. Barcelona and her father had a secret joke about Milan. Whenever Barcelona would return to the basement kitchen with the empty tray, her father would say, 'What's your mother doing?' Then he would make an exaggerated face, as if puffing an enormous cigarette the way Milan did, and they would both laugh.

The thing Barcelona remembers most about her parents' store is the door that separated the upstairs from the downstairs. Upstairs was all light and life, with its brightly lit showcases filled with fresh baked goods and delicatessen meats and four tables and Formica counter with six wobbly stools and lively customers. Downstairs was the basement where the freezers and storerooms and kitchen were, where the actual baking was done, the salads made, the platters arranged. Immediately at the bottom of the stairs was the tiny rest room. The door leading downstairs was short and a customer had to bend and hunch to go down the four steps that led to the bathroom. Above the short door was a big sign hand-lettered by Milan, the black letters looking vaguely European. It said: WATCH YOUR HEAD!!! Even so, Milan or Father or Barcelona knew to add a verbal warning whenever a customer was going up or down those stairs. Nevertheless, not a day went by without someone cracking his head on that overhanging beam and stagger around a full minute rubbing his skull, cursing and wincing. Occasionally there'd be blood.

Barcelona thinks of that sign now, of all the people, herself included, who smacked their heads on that beam on their way to and from the bathroom. WATCH YOUR HEAD! she thinks and finishes eating the stale bagel.

Four hours later she is $824 ahead. Sometimes she loses hands, but soon after she wins it all back plus more. She changes seats to avoid the occasional fluke deck that continuously lays winning hands at one seat. Finally she changes tables too. She keeps winning. The cigarette smoke is so bad she lights one up in self-defense.

She decides the problem is that she isn't risking enough. She is betting too small. She needs to put more money on the line. Much more. Her puny bets aren't a mathematical challenge.

She moves up to a higher stakes poker game. Minimum bet is forty dollars, maximum is eighty dollars.

'Fresh blood,' one of the players says to her. He wears his long brown hair in a ponytail and dresses like a Western outlaw, complete with leather vest and boots. He hasn't shaved for a few days.

'Welcome,' the woman dealer says. She is painfully thin with cheekbones as sharp as a pickax. Her eyes are sunk so deep it's hard to tell what color they are. 'I take it you're familiar with the game, ma'am?'

'Yes,' Barcelona says. She's played poker since she was old enough to distinguish the difference between the cards. Her parents are both avid poker players with a weekly game at the house every Friday night. Her father is a steady odds player, Milan is more the reckless intuitive type.

Barcelona stacks her chips in front of her. Compared to the tremendous stacks of the other players, her pile of chips is embarrassingly small.

'That's what I call confidence,' another player says. He's an old man in his seventies. The cheaper tables are filled with old men and women, but there are few at these stakes. Las Vegas casinos seem overrun with old people shuffling around with their bucket of change or single fistful of chips. It's as if they were at a giant amusement park especially constructed for the retired and dying.

There are eight players at the table, including Barcelona and excluding the dealer. The room chatters with the

516

constant clacking of chips being stacked, unstacked, re-stacked, mostly from the players fidgeting.

'Deal 'em, dealer,' the ponytail says.

She does. Cards fly and land in front of each player. Bets are made. Barcelona loses eighty dollars before dropping out of the hand. An Oriental woman in her late twenties wins the hand. She is wearing a blue jogging suit and a ring on each finger. Barcelona guesses the rings' worth to total over $300,000. When she goes to the bathroom, someone says she's married to some ambassador and that she once lost half a million dollars in one night shooting craps. Her husband hasn't allowed her to play craps since.

Barcelona folds early in the next hand. After the fourth card, the only two left in the pot are the old man and the ponytail. The old man throws in eighty dollars. 'Get outta my pot,' he scowls. Ponytail raises eighty dollars. The old man raises another eighty dollars and repeats, 'Get outta my pot.'

The Oriental woman returns, lights a cigarette, and holds it straight up between finger and thumb as if it were a candle. She looks off toward the crap table.

The old man finally drops out of the pot and ponytail rakes it in. 'My pot now, Jim,' he says. The old man shrugs.

Four hours later, Barcelona is $2,785 ahead. She is playing well, but no better than the others. She decides she still isn't risking enough. So far she's been playing only with her winnings. She needs to bet big, *really* big. So big that she can't afford to lose.

At the cashier's cage she is taken to see a credit manager. They are in a private office. He is young, maybe twenty-four, but wearing a fabulous suit. He is also extremely handsome with a large mole on his upper lip. Actually, the mole enhances his looks. He is very polite and respectful to

517

Barcelona, but there is a slight feeling of pity or contempt in his look. Most of the people who work in Las Vegas have that look, as if they can't help but think of you as a born sucker.

He jots down all the pertinent information on a pad, stands, and says, 'I'll be right back, Ms. Lee. Naturally we have to check it through some computers, make a few calls. Then I have to get it approved by my supervisor.'

'Of course,' she says.

'A hundred thousand dollars, right?'

'Yes.'

'Make yourself comfortable, this may take a few minutes.'

'I'm comfortable,' she replies.

He leaves. She picks up a copy of *Esquire* from the table and leafs through it. She gave the young man Grief's home number to verify the deal with Lynda Kramer, and of course she did have good credit, equity in her condo, a salary, and some royalty income.

Half an hour later he returns. He stands behind his desk and says, 'Fifty thousand is the best we can do.'

'I'll take it,' she said. But it's not enough. Not nearly.

'Hello?' the sleepy voice whispers. 'Hello?'

Barcelona listens to her mother's tired voice squeeze through the telephone. She is calling home to ask for money, a loan against the money she will be earning for the script. She has never borrowed from them before, not even for college. They could wire her the cash in the morning. She needs another fifty thousand dollars to make her total of one hundred thousand dollars. Playing with a hundred thousand dollars will settle this issue once and for all. Then the stakes will be high enough.

'Hello?' her mother says again. 'Who's there? It's late.'

Barcelona can't talk. Her lips are stuck shut. Finally she

pulls her sweater lapel over the mouthpiece and is about to whisper an obscenity when she hears a soft sobbing. Her mother is crying. 'It's all right,' her mother says through the sobs. 'It's all right, really.'

In that instant she realizes her mother knows it is her, that her mother has known all along it's been her making the calls.

Barcelona immediately hangs up the phone. Her hands are trembling.

Barcelona sits in the cocktail lounge and sips a dark beer. On the small stage behind her identical twin sisters in matching cowgirl outfits sing 'Desperado.'

The most noticeable aspect of people in Las Vegas, Barcelona decides, is the hair. There are many different styles, all seem carefully constructed, with lots of angles, dips, bumps, then solidified with so much grease, mousse, and spray that they resemble hood ornaments on old cars. The twins' platinum hair is freeze-dried to resemble Patsy Cline's.

'Hello,' a nervous voice behind her says.

She turns and sees the short stout man who'd been playing poker at her table earlier. The doctor with the convention. He is sitting at the next table. She smiles politely.

'They're pretty good,' he says, gesturing with his drink at the twins on stage.

'Yes, they are.'

He gets up and brings his drink to her table. 'I'm Dr. Earl Downey,' he says, sitting next to her. 'We played poker.'

'I remember.'

'Actually, you played poker, I made a donation.' He chuckled.

'My favorite charity,' she says. 'Give 'til it hurts.'

'Are you still winning?' he asks.

'I'm ahead a couple bucks.'

'I'm way down.' He says it in a bragging manner, as if losing were admirable as long as you lost big. 'But that's why I come here.'

'To lose?'

'To gamble. Take chances.' He looks at Barcelona to see if she caught the suggestiveness in that last phrase. She stares back innocently. He stares at the stage while he speaks. 'You here alone?'

'Why?'

He shifts uncomfortably. 'Curious. A beautiful woman like you all alone in Las Vegas. Must make you nervous.'

'Why should it?'

He shrugs. 'No reason I guess.'

'Oh, I get it. You think I might be mistaken for a hooker. Is that it?'

He is clearly shaken by her directness. He looks over his shoulder longingly at his old table. 'N-No, not necessarily.'

'It's all right. I'm sure you meant that as a compliment.'

'Well, of course, I . . . I didn't mean to offend.'

Barcelona finishes her beer. 'Have you ever been with a prostitute?'

He bristles at the implication. 'No, of course not.'

Barcelona looks at her watch. It is past midnight. She didn't sleep last night and she doesn't plan on sleeping tonight. Sleep would ruin the experiment, screw up the equation. She must do this without sleep, keep playing the games without closing her eyes. Stamina is part of this too, physical prowess. But she needs more money. Cash. She has already received cash advances from her MasterCard and Visa that took them to the limit. She cashed a check that wiped out her bank account, and now she has a credit line with the casino for $50,000. Still, it isn't enough, it

520

doesn't risk enough. She needs more money. Only a hundred thousand will do.

Dr. Earl Downey sips his drink, avoiding Barcelona's gaze. He looks over at the twin cowgirls who are singing 'Candy Man.' He taps in time on the edge of the table.

'Still,' Barcelona says, 'I wonder how much a hooker makes around here, don't you?'

He tries to kiss her in the elevator. She has to bend over to meet his lips. They are thick and rubbery and taste of bitter cigars and cheap scotch. He tries to poke his tongue in her mouth, but she pulls away. They are on their way to his room and he is very excited. He has his arm around her waist and he lets it slide down so he can feel the curve of her hip under his pudgy fingers. She lets him.

Barcelona feels a little dizzy as the elevator rushes skyward. Dr. Earl Downey is under the impression that Barcelona is going to have sex with him in exchange for money. Two hundred dollars was mentioned in an oblique way. Barcelona hasn't decided yet what she will do when the elevator door opens. She needs more money to prove her point. She is in the middle of a great chemistry experiment and she's run out of one of the main ingredients, cash. Also, there is something proper about getting the money this way, from Dr. Earl Downey in exchange for a quick jump. Somehow it adds unity and dimension, universality to the experiment.

Dr. Earl Downey kisses her again, pressing his lumpy body up against hers. He tries to force his tongue between her teeth again, but she keeps them clamped together. Meanwhile, he rubs up against her, his crotch thumping against her thigh. He rubs so fast and furiously the denim on her jeans is heating up. Suddenly he makes a high-pitched moan and jumps away from her. His body spasms and she thinks he is having a heart attack. But it is only his hips that are spasming. They both look down at his crotch and she can see the wet stain soaking through the material around the zipper.

'Oh, God, no,' he says, staring.

'Oops,' she says.

The elevator door opens and Dr. Earl Downey runs out without her, one hand groping in his pocket for his room key, the other hand clamped over his crotch. Barcelona presses the Lobby button and the doors close and the car descends. She wonders if the restaurant is still serving.

Barcelona is standing in the shower when she hears the knocking on her door. 'Just a minute,' she hollers. She shuts off the faucet and wraps a towel around her body.

The knocking continues. Firm but not impatient.

'Just a minute, I'm coming.' She quickly towels off and climbs into her panties, jeans, and a sweatshirt. They smell of cigarette smoke, but she only packed a change of underwear. She walks over to the door toweling her hair. 'Who is it?'

'Autrey St. James,' he says.

Barcelona opens the door. 'You're early.'

'I like to be punctual,' he says, entering.

'Twenty minutes early isn't punctual, it's pushy.'

'Sorry,' he says, though there is nothing in his voice to indicate sincerity. He is about twenty-five, the same age as the young man from the casino who gave her the credit line. Autrey St. James is in the same business, extending credit, but without a casino to back him. He is strictly a private entrepreneur. He has a cocky walk, stiff but purposeful, a half march as if he's capturing the room. His clothes are a little too hip: white linen jacket with the sleeves rolled up to his elbows, peach-colored shirt unbuttoned to his sternum. His watch is worth more than her car. So are his shoes. He sits on the edge of the bed and smiles at her. 'So, down to business, okay?'

'Okay,' she says. She lifts her room service tray off the desk chair and sits down.

'You must've been hungry,' he says, nodding at the stack of empty plates.

'Cards make me hungry,' she says. She had eaten a stack of buttermilk pancakes and a three-egg Denver omelette, including juice, toast, and coffee. There was little else to do all night but watch TV, read newspapers, and eat. She refuses to gamble another dime until she has her entire amount, one hundred thousand dollars. Since the casino would give her only fifty thousand dollars in credit, she still needs another fifty thousand dollars. A few chats with several well-tipped bellboys got her a phone number.

'I've done some checking on you, Ms. Lee.' Autrey St. James smiles but his face seems to resent the exercise. 'You're not un-well known.'

'Un-well known?' She smiles at the word.

His face stiffens. He is not sure how, but he senses an insult. 'You're not exactly famous either. But I gather from my sources, you do have some readers. I only mention this because I want you to feel at ease. I have many famous clients, names you wouldn't believe me if I told you. Top TV stars, singers, movie stars. I conduct business with a lot of celebrities.'

'You lend them money?'

'Sure, money. Whatever they want.'

Barcelona watches him. Everything about him is studied and rehearsed, even his smile and the pout of his lips. Every gesture is calculated for effect. He reminds her of all the young goal-oriented executives at large corporations, grooming themselves for their eventual seat on the Board of Directors.

523

He crosses his legs and tugs the wrinkles out of the knee of his trousers. 'Fifty thousand is a lot of money.'

'You wouldn't be here if you didn't know I can make it good.'

His smile widens. His teeth flicker in the lamplight like the dealer's fingernails. 'Yes, you can make good. But I also know you received a similar line of credit from the casino. If you lose both, you'll be ruined. I know all about your screenplay for Lynda Kramer, but after your agent's cut and taxes, you won't see much of that money, maybe half. You'll lose your house for starters. The casino has legal means to collect. I do not. You understand?'

Barcelona yawns. 'Sorry.'

His face tightens into a grim mask. 'I'm not boring you, am I?'

'No, I'm sorry. Not enough sleep.'

He relaxes. 'You do understand, don't you? I won't make any loan until the client is fully aware of his obligations to me and how serious I am about those obligations. With responsibility, we're no better than animals. Our obligations make us civilized.'

Barcelona finds it amusing that she's sitting here doing business with a man who is basically threatening her life, promising bodily harm if she does not pay, just like in the movies. Barcelona is not really concerned, she has more important things on her mind. Actually, the threats are good because they raise the stakes considerably for her. Make the contest more real. Now she will have her full one hundred thousand dollars to gamble with and if she loses, she loses everything. That's what must be at stake for this to work.

Everything.

'Do you have the money here?' Barcelona asks.

'Not so fast. Do we understand each other concerning the terms?'

'Yes, I understand the interest rates and payment schedule. I also understand the penalties for late payments.'

He smiles approval. 'You're very smart.'

'That's what I'm here to find out.'

He reaches into his jacket pocket and pulls out a stack of envelopes. 'These are stamped and addressed. This is what you mail your payments in. The dates due are written on the inside flap for your convenience. Send a money order, no check, made out to the name on the paper inside each envelope. It's a different name each time.'

'Very efficient,' she says.

'I've been doing this awhile.'

'You're so young.'

'I'm also so rich.'

She unwraps the towel from her wet hair. 'Do you have the money here?'

He leans back on the bed, propping himself on his elbows. He is smiling again, trying to look suave and sophisticated. He manages sharkish. 'You're a writer, so you probably have some ideas about how I do business. You probably imagine I'll send a couple goons around to rough you up and give you another chance. Or maybe that you'll come home and find your cat hanging in your closet, his throat cut.'

Barcelona's skin chills at the mention of Larry. That Autrey St. James knows about him is an intimacy she didn't expect. She told him about her finances, but nothing personal.

'But that's Hollywood talking,' he says. 'I'm much more practical. I don't come around and I don't send anyone around. You miss a payment.' He holds up a finger. 'Just one. You miss one and the next thing you know you will be driving down the street and suddenly in a major car accident. A lawyer defending the victim, my associate, will be suing you and your insurance company for a lot of

525

money because, believe me, the accident will be your fault. Witnesses will testify to that. That's easy to arrange. The tricky part is controlling the injuries during the accident, that's guesswork. Either way, I get paid.'

Barcelona stands up, snatches a stray bite of cold pancake from the room service tray and eats it. 'Do you have the money here?'

He laughs. 'I like a woman who knows what she wants.' He stands up and unzips his fly. 'As long as she knows what I want.'

Barcelona eyes his zipper without expression.

Autrey St. James reaches into his fly and pulls out a roll of cash secured with a red rubber band. He reaches back in and pulls out a second roll. 'Crowded in there,' he says, grinning. He zips his pants back up.

Suddenly someone knocks on the door and says, 'Barcy? You in there?'

Barcelona doesn't answer.

'Come on,' Cory says. 'The maid said you were in.'

Autrey St. James's eyes look feverish as he glances at the door. He snatches up the two rolls of hundred dollar bills and quickly stuffs them in his jacket pocket. 'This better not be a rip-off,' he warns through clenched teeth.

'My boyfriend,' she explains, knowing she sounds like a teenager caught necking with a boy from a rival school. But she doesn't want a man like this to know Cory's name.

Barcelona opens the door and Cory enters. He looks at Autrey St. James who is again leaning back on the bed, grinning with sexual innuendo. 'You okay?' Cory asks her.

'Of course. How'd you find out I was here?'

'Your neighbor with the dog. I was still at your place when he came over to feed Larry. I'd been on the fucking phone all morning trying to find you. What's going on?'

'What's it look like, pal?' Autrey St. James says.

Cory ignores him. 'You okay?'

'I told you, I'm fine. This is just business.'

'What kind of business?'

'Research. I'm gathering material for a book.'

Cory turns to Autrey St. James. 'Thanks for dropping by. Ms. Lee will contact you later.'

'Ms. Lee's already *contacted* me,' he says with a lewd grin.

'Then that must conclude her research into microdicked morons who masturbate until they lose all their manners and taste in clothing.'

Autrey St. James stands slowly. His eyes don't blink, don't waver. His voice is lower, throatier, as if filtered through a bucket of water. 'Why don't we just ask the lady who she wants to stay?'

They both turn to Barcelona. 'Christ,' she sighs. 'Cory, can you wait downstairs for me?'

Autrey St. James leans his face close to Cory's and grins. 'Bye bye, baby.'

Cory throws his fist into Autrey St. James's stomach, doubling him over. Autrey St. James drops to his knees clutching his stomach, coughing. 'Son of a bitch,' he gasps. 'Fucking faggot.'

'Jesus, Cory,' Barcelona says, running over to help up Autrey St. James. 'I know what I'm doing. I don't need protection.'

Autrey St. James pulls out a six-inch switchblade and clicks it open. He slowly rises from his knees, pointing the knife at Cory. He doesn't say anything, make threats, growl insults, curse. He just concentrates on his knife like a pool shark about to make a difficult shot.

Cory is backing up, looking nervous. 'Hey, okay, you made your point,' Cory says. 'Now put the knife away.'

But Autrey St. James doesn't answer. He stalks.

Barcelona picks up a nearby plate from the room service tray and throws it at him like a Frisbee. It clips his shoulder

527

and he grunts in pain and spins around to face him. 'Cunt!' he says.

That's when Cory jumps him. Both Cory's hands grip Autrey St. James's wrist, trying to shake loose the knife. Barcelona also grabs the wrist, her hands wrapped around Cory's hands. Suddenly Autrey St. James punches her in the side of the head with his free hand and she tumbles backward over a chair and sprawls on the floor. Her head throbs. Getting punched hurts more than she imagined.

Cory manages to shake the knife loose and kick it under the bed. Autrey St. James punches Cory in the jaw and knocks him into the wall. A painting of a serene Alpine village drops to the floor. Cory rubs his jaw. 'That should about make us even. Right?'

Autrey St. James glares at him, fists held high in front of him. But Cory makes no threatening move, he just stands against the wall, waiting. Barcelona is impressed that Cory doesn't appear scared. Autrey St. James stands in his boxer's crouch for a long time, just staring at Cory. Finally he takes a deep breath, brushes the wrinkles out of his jacket, and walks to the door. 'I'm a businessman, not a thug. I won't do business this way.'

He walks out of the room.

'You okay?' Cory asks Barcelona as she rises from the floor.

'How many times you going to ask me that?'

''Til I get an answer I believe.'

She walks over and touches his bruised jaw. 'That hurt?'

He winces. 'Yes.'

'Good. That's what you get for poking your face into my business.'

Cory goes into the bathroom and soaks a washcloth in cold water. When he returns he presses the folded washcloth against Barcelona's forehead where she'd been punched. It feels good. Not just the coolness of the nubbled cloth, but the warmth of his caring. She leans against him and feels his arms enclose her. She closes her eyes and smells the jet fuel fumes in his shirt. It's nice. 'You've ruined everything, you know,' she says softly. 'I needed the money.'

'If you needed money you could have asked me. I'd make you a loan.'

She chuckles into his chest. 'Fifty thousand dollars?'

He pauses. 'If that's what you want.'

She considers it but shakes her head. 'No, that wouldn't work. If I lost it and didn't pay you back, you'd just let me get away with it. You wouldn't sue me or arrange an accident.'

'Jesus, Barcy, what are you talking about? What accident?'

'I'm talking about my work, my life. I'm talking about who deserves what. Something like that.'

'You're not making sense.'

'Not to you.' She yawns.

'You need sleep.'

She pushes away from him. 'That would be cheating. Invalidate the whole experiment.'

'What experiment?' he asks in frustration.

She starts pacing the room. It's impossible to explain to him, he wouldn't understand. He takes his good luck for granted. 'I need money.'

'I told you, I'll lend it to you.'

'I told you, it wouldn't count.'

He looks at her with sad eyes. 'You want it to count? We'll make it count.'

Barcelona walks up to the one-hundred-dollar blackjack table. No one is sitting at the table, most gamblers are at the five-dollar tables. The dealer is a tall redheaded woman with pale skin and a small Band-Aid over one nostril. Her arms are crossed across her chest. The cards are spread out on the table in several fans.

'You open?' Barcelona asks.

'Yes, ma'am,' she says, uncrossing her arms. She gathers up the cards and starts shuffling.

'Not too busy yet.'

The dealer, whose name tag says Billie Jo, looks around the casino. 'Still early. In another hour this place will be shoulder to shoulder. You could have five meaningful relationships just walking across the room and never meet one of them.'

Barcelona laughs. She is in good spirits, excited and jittery, but somehow calm inside. Like one of those Mexican high-cliff divers poised on the edge of the cliff looking down. Once you've made the resolve to dive, the rest is easy.

She empties her purse on the felt table. One hundred fifty chips spill out. Each chip is worth a thousand dollars.

Billie Jo glances over at the chips but shows no reaction. She continues to shuffle the cards. 'Not a good idea to be walking around with that much in your purse.'

'I thought the Mob scared all the muggers out of Vegas.'

Billie Jo laughs. 'Yeah, that's what a lot of people think. Only it ain't so.'

'Don't worry,' Barcelona says. 'I'll either be walking away with twice this amount or none of it.'

Billie Jo glances up into Barcelona's face. Barcelona detects that same look of pity and contempt. 'Good luck, ma'am,' she says.

Barcelona begins stacking the chips. It took all day, but Cory managed to raise another one hundred thousand dollars. They went to several banks, he made several more phone calls from her room. He borrowed against some personal stock, against his house, against things he didn't tell her about. But he raised it. During the whole day he didn't try to talk her out of what she was doing. They didn't eat a single meal, they didn't make love, didn't even touch. When he finally handed her the money he touched her arm and said, 'Is this what you want?'

'Yes,' she said. 'It's important.'

'The stakes should be high enough now. If you lose, I'll lose everything. There'll be press inquiries and it will eventually come out that I was in Las Vegas when I did all this. The public will draw its own conclusions.'

'I didn't ask you to do this. I can make my own arrangements.'

He kissed her cheek. 'I don't want to watch,' he said. 'Call me afterwards if you want.' And he walked out of her room.

She didn't stop him.

Barcelona stacks twenty-five chips in the square in front of her. She'll start with a twenty-five thousand dollar bet, just to get her feet wet. To tease.

'Five thousand dollar maximum,' Billie Jo says.

'I could play all six slots,' Barcelona says. 'But I don't want to have to move.'

Billie Jo turns and says something to the man in the suit standing behind her. The pit boss. He is in his fifties with curly brown hair that refuses to be tamed by whatever grease he is using. Various strands poke wildly from his scalp like broken springs in a mattress. He lifts his glasses up to his forehead and looks at Barcelona, sizing her up while Billie Jo whispers to him. When she's finished, he nods approval.

'Okay,' Billie Jo says. She hands Barcelona the red card to cut the shuffled decks. Barcelona sticks it in the middle and Billie Jo cuts and stuffs the cards into the shoe.

A small crowd gathers, attracted by the stack of chips in front of Barcelona. They mutter and fret among themselves.

Barcelona watches the first card float down to the felt in front of her. A three.

The dealer has an eight showing.

Barcelona's next card is a seven.

The dealer's card is down.

Billie Jo waits. 'Take your time,' she says. 'You have ten.'

Barcelona is touched by the kindness in Billie Jo's voice. That kindness gives her confidence. 'Double down,' she says. The crowd buzzes and fusses as she stacks another twenty-five chips next to the first pile. She has bet fifty thousand dollars on the next card.

Billie Jo deals.

Seven.

Billie Jo flips her card: jack.

Barcelona loses.

She smiles. The odds are catching up. Her heart is compressed in her chest to the size of a pea. But she has enough strength to push another twenty-five chips out.

Billie Jo deals: six and two to Barcelona, a six to herself. Barcelona doubles down again, pushing in another twenty-five thousand dollars. Billie Jo flips over her hole card and reveals a five. Eleven. She takes another card. A four. That gives her fifteen. The next card is a seven. Twenty-two.

'Bust,' Billie Jo says, almost relieved. She counts out fifty chips and stacks them next to Barcelona's two piles.

Barcelona stares at the four stacks. She has lost one hand and won one. The next deal would be the tie-breaker. Proof positive of something, though she's lost the train of her former reasoning. She's suddenly not sure anymore exactly what she's trying to prove. Still, she's here, she's gone this far.

She pushes in all of her chips.

The crowd flutters and bumps into each other.

The pit boss wanders over, raises his glasses again, and stares at Barcelona. A stubborn curl on his forehead points at her.

Billie Jo starts stacking the chips into neat piles. Three stacks of fifty thousand dollars each. She glances up and Barcelona sees a warning look, but it's so brief she thinks she may have imagined it.

'The bet's a hundred fifty thousand dollars,' Billie Jo says.

'I'd like new decks,' Barcelona says.

Billie Jo looks at the pit boss. He nods. She brings out four new decks, breaks the wrappers, fans them out faceup, and counts the number in each deck. Then she messes them all in together and starts shuffling.

The crowd has grown even larger. Barcelona doesn't look at them; she resents their marginal participation in her battle. A Greek chorus of bystanders, cattle looking through a fence at life on the other side. They can't possibly understand. And now neither can Barcelona. All that's left now is instinct.

'Would you like a cocktail?' Billie Jo asks. A cocktail waitress stands next Barcelona waiting.

'Gotta talk like the devil and listen like a wife, don't you?' Barcelona asks her.

'You know it, honey,' the cocktail waitress says.

'Nothing, thanks,' Barcelona says but drops a dollar tip on her tray anyway.

'Thanks,' the waitress says and moves away to the next table. She isn't concerned about the outcome of the next hand, Barcelona realizes, but about the next tip.

Billie Jo hands Barcelona the red card.

Barcelona shoves it in the middle of the deck, cuts the cards, and lays the deck into the shoe.

For the first time, the crowd falls silent.

*　　*　　*

Barcelona sleeps.

She wakes up, looks around. The heavy curtains are drawn so she doesn't know whether it is day or night. She goes back to sleep, not caring.

Barcelona sleeps.

She wakes up, looks around. A tray with orange juice and pastries sits on the floor next to the bed. She doesn't remember ordering this, doesn't know how it got here. She drinks the orange juice and goes back to sleep.

Barcelona sleeps.

She does not dream. She does not replay the past few days.

She wakes up, looks around. On the floor next to the bed is an ice bucket. Inside are three cans of Diet Coke. The ice is almost completely melted. She fishes a can out of the bucket, pops it, drinks. Some spills down her chin onto the sheets. She goes back to sleep.

'Do you remember?' he asks.

She sits up in the bed and rubs her eyes. 'Yes.'

Mostly she remembers watching Billie Jo's hands as they shuffled the cards, cut the deck, laid the decks into the shoe as carefully as if she were handling a newborn infant.

She remembers reaching over to her chips neatly stacked on the felt betting square, her hand cupping the upright towers, and pulling them gently toward her without spilling one. She remembers saying, 'I've changed my mind.'

She remembers the crowd making loud grunts of protest, enraged at her choice. She remembers the look of relief on Billie Jo's face. The pit boss lowered his glasses without changing expression and wandered away to watch another table.

Barcelona remembers walking away from the table with

her purse full of chips, remembers the man in the crowd who grabbed her arm as she passed by, pulling her close and kissing her hard on the lips. She remembers kissing him back, recognizing the taste, the texture of his skin, the piney smell, the pressure of his arms around her without having to look. Afterward, him saying, 'Can I have my money back now?'

Barcelona grabs another pillow and sticks it behind her back. 'I remember everything. How long have I been asleep?'

'Two days,' Cory says.

She nods at this information, thinks about it. 'Am I crazy?'

'Only if you don't hang on to a great guy like me.'

'Oh, really? What if I told you all those orgasms I had with you, I faked them.'

'That's okay. So did I.'

She laughs and and hits him with a pillow. 'Okay, I didn't fake them. But I could have. And you would have risked your whole campaign on a lie. A misperception.'

'To me the truth wasn't in how you felt about me, but in how *I* felt about you. That's what I based my decision on. And that was no misperception.'

She thinks about that a moment. He sits on the side of the bed and lays his hand on the sheet covering her leg. She feels the warmth of his flesh through the stiff sheet.

She leans forward and kisses him. She closes her eyes and relaxes in his arms. In the darkness of her closed eyes she drifts into a place that may be sleep or a dream, though she can still feel the anchor of his arms keeping her from drifting forever. In this place she sees her parents' store, the door leading downstairs to the basement, the kitchen, the bathroom. And the sign over the door, hand-printed, the letters vaguely European, the sinister warning: WATCH YOUR HEAD!

'How was Vegas?' Diva asks.

'Vegas was Vegas. Noisy, smoky, you know.' Barcelona digs her fork into her cheesecake.

'Did you win?' Dixie asks.

'Broke even.'

'Broke is the key word when I go to Vegas,' Diva says.

The three of them are sitting in the Garden Café eating dessert. This is not one of their regularly scheduled dinners. Just a spontaneous lunch to celebrate Diva's song being picked up by Rod Stewart. Trina told Dixie she would try to join them if she could get away, but the crunch of the last few days before the election demands most of her time. This may be an excuse, though. Barcelona still has not spoken to Trina since coming back from Las Vegas. She called twice and left messages, but Trina has not called back.

Barcelona spent last night with Cory in his Corona del Mar house. After they made love he waltzed around the room singing songs from various musicals. He knew all the songs from *Man of La Mancha*, *West Side Story*, *Camelot*, *Oklahoma*, and a few she never even heard of. He had a terrible voice but was so enthusiastic that she loved watching him perform anyway. Plus, he seemed totally convinced his voice was just fine.

They never spoke of Vegas, of the money, of why she

went, what she was trying to prove. She only vaguely understood it herself. It had seemed so clear, such an epiphany when she'd been in the manic state on the drive down, the sleepless days that followed. Now it was just something that happened a long, long time ago in a galaxy far, far away. She wasn't sorry, nor did she feel foolish. Just distant, as if it had all happened to a great-great aunt and the story had been passed down generation after generation until it became more myth than truth.

While she was gone, Larry got into the medicine cabinet and dragged out the Ben-Gay. He bit through the tube and ate some of the ointment. Dave took Larry to the vet and the bill was $74.50. Larry welcomed Barcelona home by stepping in his food dish and tracking gravy across the kitchen floor.

'We're going to Hawaii,' Diva announces, chewing her apple cobbler. 'A little surf and sand will give us a chance to come up with some new song ideas.'

'Sounds great,' Barcelona says.

'Yeah, we haven't exactly been reeling them off here. I think all the excitement and everything, plus us still getting to know each other. I mean, we just got married on top of everything else. I think that may be inhibiting us a little.'

'Get away,' Dixie advises. 'That's what I'm going to do when this damn trial is over. Take a river raft trip down the Colorado, something exciting like that.'

'With Karl?' Barcelona asks.

Dixie digs out another piece of carrot cake, avoiding eye contact. 'We'll see.'

Barcelona finishes her last bite of cheesecake and gets up. 'I'm going to the rest room. Could you beg our waitress to give me some more coffee?'

In the bathroom, Barcelona sits on the toilet even though she doesn't have to go. The seat is wobbly and uncomfortable. She is enjoying the lunch, but she misses Trina. Trina was her other half at these meetings. Not just at these meetings, at everything. She reads the graffiti on the stall door. MEN SUCK is scratched into the paint. Underneath is scratched a reply: IF THEY DID, THEY WOULDN'T NEED US. Barcelona stands up and opens the door.

Trina is standing by the sink. 'Don't forget to wash your hands,' she says.

Barcelona stares. 'When did you get here?'

'A couple minutes ago. I saw you come in here and followed you.'

The door opens and two women walk in talking about work. 'The guy's a jerk,' the taller woman says. 'And his secretary is worse. She thinks she's Nixon's secretary, whatshername, the one who erased the tape.'

'Rose something,' the other woman says.

'Whatever. They're both going to get caught if Phillips finds out the way they're operating the department.' The taller one goes into a stall and pees while the shorter one washes her hands and applies makeup. The three of them can hear the tinkle of the tall woman's urine against water. The short one tries to cover for her friend by washing her hands again. The two women give Trina and Barcelona odd looks as they leave.

'Well,' Trina says, 'there goes your reputation.'

'You get my calls?'

Trina nods. She takes out her lipstick and starts applying it. They stare at each other's reflections in the mirror. Barcelona sees her own face and notices how well the makeup covered the bruise on her forehead from Autrey St. James's punch.

'I see Cory's still ahead in the polls,' Barcelona says.

'He's going to win.'

'What's Carla going to do?'

'There are other offices to run for, she may even teach at UCLA. What about you? Quit your job yet?'

538

Barcelona leans against the stall. 'Not yet. Probably never.'

'Good. These kids need you.'

Barcelona shakes her head. 'No they don't. I need them.'

Trina packs her lipstick away and turns to face Barcelona. 'Are you still worried about everyone's good luck since Dixie's rape?'

'Maybe it wasn't as good as it first seemed. Diva's sold her song, but she and Harley haven't been able to write one since. An obscure cut on an aging rocker's album isn't exactly a state of grace.'

Trina nods and starts to walk toward the door. Barcelona walks toward the door too and somehow they intersect, bump into each other. The bump suddenly becomes an embrace. Barcelona feels Trina's fuller body against her own and wonders what it must be like for Trina and Carla when they hug to feel another woman's body, but to also share that other intimacy. She is still jealous of Carla, but she loves Trina. She smells Trina's neck and hair, shampoo and perfume and something stronger, like wet sand at the beach. 'There there,' she says. 'How's that?'

'About a four on the sincerity meter,' Trina says.

They both laugh, still leaning against each other.

The rest room door opens and Dixie and Diva walk in.

'What the hell are you two doing in here?' Diva asks. 'Dancing?'

'When did you get here?' Dixie asks.

'A couple minutes ago.'

Dixie points at Barcelona. 'We came in to check on Barcy, she's been in here so long.'

'We thought you were sick,' Diva adds.

'I'm fine. We were just talking.'

'Four women in a toilet,' Diva says, looking around. 'There's got to be a hit song in this.'

Barcelona laughs, closing her eyes. Behind closed eyes,

539

she sees the camera pull back and up, rising high above them, and we look straight down and see the four women talking and laughing, getting smaller and smaller until they are indistinguishable, the room shrinking out of sight, starting to spin faster and faster until it bursts into flames and becomes another twinkling star in some undiscovered galaxy. Barcelona feels the warmth on her face from the tiny star. It is comforting to be a star among this constellation, among this universe. Among four women in a spinning white room watching their heads. She looks around at her friends and marvels at them, their beautiful eyes flickering under the bright bathroom lights, like the dealer's polished nails, Autrey St. James's knife, helicopter rotor blades, Eric's scar. Like stars.

Four women in a toilet. Laughing.

Fade out.

WICKED WOMEN

PART ONE

How to Have a Near-Death Experience

1

When I finally arrived at the police station, Wren was standing on the front steps under a bright light, a pair of blue panties balled up in her right fist. She was waving her fist around like she was about to do some sort of magic trick with her panties, turn them into a dove or something. At the same time, her flushed face was leaning into some young uniformed cop's pale face, yelling at him. The top to my Rabbit was down, so I could hear each word as crisp as snapping carrots.

'This is total bullshit!' Wren hollered.

The skinny young cop was leaning as far back as he could without flipping backward over the railing. His eyes were wide and unfocused, as if he'd just been told he was the offspring of incest. Like most men who've come face-to-face with Wren's temper, he looked both a little murderous and a little in love.

I quickly swung the Rabbit to the curb and honked twice.

Wren didn't take her fierce eyes off the young cop. She continued to glare at him as she backed down the steps toward my car without actually looking where she was going. As if she were guided by some psychic homing device. Anyone else I'd have been worried would trip and fall. But not Wren. She had never done one ungraceful thing in her entire life. She'd probably pirouetted out of her mother's womb and done the Maypole dance with the umbilical cord. Finally, Wren turned toward me. This is when I noticed the huge tan bandage the size of a business card angled across her forehead, partially covering her left eyebrow. A moist rusty spot soaked through the center of the bandage. Three drops of blood formed a teardrop constellation on her white T-shirt.

Wren had only descended two steps when she stopped abruptly and pivoted back around toward the cop. Her tennis shoes squealed against the smooth cement. The startled young cop flinched. His hand dropped to his gun.

'And you are an asshole!' Wren proclaimed, pointing her panties at him. 'You hear what I'm saying, Officer? Do you?'

She marched toward my car, climbed in, and slammed the door. 'Let's get the fuck out of here before I kill someone else.'

*   *   *   *   *

'Stop that,' Wren said, slapping my hand.

I have this nasty habit when I'm nervous of reaching inside my collar and rubbing my thumbnails back and forth against my bra strap. I do it in class, I do it at work, I do it before and after sex. During sex I rub them along the seam of the mattress edge. Both my thumbnails have deep ugly groves in them as if they'd been crushed under very thin bicycle tires. Fingernail polish only makes them look worse. A student once asked if I'd had them amputated and sewn back on again. I usually try to hide them in public.

'Loony, goddamn it,' she said, slapping my hand again, harder.

'Ow,' I said, slapping her hand back. But I stopped.

She lifted her butt off the seat and pulled out some papers she'd been sitting on. 'What's this?'

'A petition. Sign it.'

She picked up the pen that had been rolling annoyingly across the dashboard and signed the line under my name. 'What's this for?'

4

'A new law.'

'Oh.' She opened the glove compartment and stuffed the petition inside. She smiled and picked up my purse tucked next to her seat. 'Got anything interesting in here?' She started digging through it looking for a joint. She wasn't going to find one. I'd given up on that stuff after I split up with Robby two months ago. He was the one who liked to get high anyway. I never really did, not really. Not in my teens, not in my twenties, and especially after I turned thirty last year. Marijuana seemed like such a sixties thing to do, a nostalgic act, like teatime for American Anglophiles. But I'd been in diapers for a lot of the sixties and felt no nostalgia for its return. I was relieved now I didn't have to fake being hip anymore. The only good part of smoking dope was that when Robby got the munchies afterward, he'd cook us a ten-course gourmet meal. His dad was a real chef in a fancy Beverly Hills restaurant. At home, his dad had dozens of black-framed photographs on the wall of himself in his white chef's hat and white tunic that buttons up one side like a military uniform. In these photos, Robby's dad is leaning over the table between some celebrity and his or her dining companion, smiling directly at the camera. His arm is usually resting on the celebrity's shoulder. My favourite is of Jay Leno, who has a straw up his nose and is pretending to snort the freshly grated Parmesan cheese from his plate. He signed it: 'I could eat your food by the kilo.' I loved watching Robby putter around the kitchenette, naked except for his dad's white chef's apron framing his boxy buns.

'You going to tell me what happened?' I asked Wren, taking one hand off the steering wheel to tug at her tattered panties. Wren only wore one kind of panty, plain cotton, no lacy designs, cut French style, high on the hips with only a small pouch to cover the crotch and skinny string up the behind. What I called her 'butt-floss panties'.

'These old things?' Wren unfurled the panties and stretched them out between her two hands. They had a

5

hundred tear marks in them, like some hungry dog had been chewing them.

'Jesus, Wren,' I said. 'What happened?'

Wren tossed the panties up into the night air. The draft around us sucked them into the dark. She craned around to see where they landed. 'Tomorrow some bicycle-seat-sniffing brat will find them and be in horndog heaven.'

'It must be gratifying to know you've done your part to relieve his adolescent anxiety and clear up his skin to boot.'

'What can I say, I'm a humanitarian.'

'Meantime, Dr. Schweitzer, you mind telling me what the hell happened with the cops?'

Wren returned to my purse, digging until she found a lone rat-gnawed cigarette at the bottom. Smoking is another habit I no longer had since I no longer had Robby, all part of my new purification program. Like my volunteering to gather signatures for Amnesty International petitions. I said, 'So what crime did you commit?'

Wren stuck the cigarette in her mouth, punched the car lighter, and waited. I knew she wouldn't answer until the cigarette was lit. She was very theatrical that way.

'Wren, it's after midnight,' I reminded her. 'I just got home from the library twenty minutes ago after twelve butt-numbing hours studying a dozen of the ninety some doctoral dissertations that have been written about Thomas Pynchon. I got your message on my machine. I'm here. I haven't eaten since breakfast and I'm close to killing you for the food stuck between your teeth. So just tell me what the hell happened.'

'Pull over! Pull over!' She gestured frantically.

'What?'

'Pull over.' Wren grabbed the steering wheel and jerked. The Rabbit squealed across two lanes and I braked to a stop in the bicycle lane in front of the A&W fast-food place. They were closed. Even though Langston, Oregon, was a small university town, almost everything in

6

it closed down at six o'clock. It was as if the residents didn't want to admit that most of their livelihood depended on the students who comprised half the town's population. Luckily, there was no traffic after six either.

'Jesus, Wren,' I said, clutching my pounding chest.

But Wren wasn't listening. She tossed her just-lit cigarette into the gutter and started ransacking my glove compartment. 'Paper,' she demanded. 'Paper, paper!' Then she mauled my purse again. She found an envelope and started scribbling on the back.

'Not that,' I protested, reaching for it. 'That's the letter from Robby's lawyer about our divorce.'

'I'm writing on the envelope, not the fucking letter.'

'But the letter's inside. I have to, you know, file it or something.'

Wren yanked the letter from the envelope and shoved it at me. 'Here. File it.' Then she returned to her scribbling. It was pointless to interrupt her now.

I unfolded the letter and looked at it again. Brief. Polite. Two paragraphs. Divorce proceedings were in effect. Blah, blah. No fault. Blah, blah. Sincerely yours. Blah.

The law firm's name was longer than the letter.

I looked over at Wren writing furiously in the dim glow of the streetlight. Her shoulders were hunched, her eyes squinted in concentration less than eight inches from the envelope. She appeared to be conjuring dark forces.

'Let me pull up to the streetlight,' I said. 'You could ruin your eyes.'

'Hmmm,' she muttered to herself. 'Yes, yes.'

Like a woman enjoying sex.

I refolded my letter and placed it on the dashboard. Down the street, a couple of rugged boys from the university came out of the 7-Eleven convenience store. They laughed in that raunchy way males laugh when they've just said something derogatory about women or the other guy's penis.

I yawned until I could feel my ears pop and the bones in my jaw click. I took off my glasses and rubbed my tired

7

eyes. I'd been reading small print on the fourth floor of the library for twelve hours. At some point while I was reading about Pynchon's *V.* I nodded off and dreamed I was in hell. I was surprised to discover hell was a lot like Dante described it, complete with various rings depending on the nature of the condemned's sins, only the rings were marked by round cardboard fences like at a circus. There was no fire, it wasn't even particularly warm. I had this big heavy sword I could hardly drag behind me and for some reason I was expected to battle all these hellish demons that kept rising up out of the ground. The demons had the thick scaly bodies of sea serpents and two heads. The heads had the faces of Willie Nelson and Julio Iglesias.

'Let's just pull up to that 7-Eleven,' I said to Wren. 'There's more light for you and more food for me. I'm starving.'

'Shush,' she responded.

I shushed. I didn't know what she was writing. It could be anything. She wrote poetry, plays, stories, screenplays, scholarly articles on literature, art, sculpture, philosophy. She already had masters' degrees in art history, philosophy, and English literature.

Wren was a genius. This had been documented by test scores since she was a toddler. She was also stunningly beautiful. This could be documented by observing men pretzel their necks to watch her walk by. I was neither a genius nor a beauty. I was a worker bee. Everything I did required strenuous work and long hours. In high school, I had been a B+ student who had earned As by doing extra-credit reports on Guatemala (major exports: coffee, sugar, bananas, corn). My look was milk-fed wholesome, poster girl for the Council of American Churches. For Wren, gathering knowledge and boyfriends was like walking through an apple orchard where all the ripe apples are within easy reach. She merely needed to stretch out and pluck them. In my orchard, all the branches were high, out of reach. I had to jump up and down, whack at them

8

with a stick. By the time I actually got an apple, there was nothing left but pulp.

I'd been slaving over my master's degree for four years; Wren earned hers in eighteen months. Her dissertation was already finished, two months ahead of the due date. It was a comparison of the metaphysics in the lyrics of Paul Simon and the poetry of William Blake. Some New Age publisher in New York bought the thesis last week and intended to bring it out in time for Christmas. Last Christmas the same publisher had a bestseller with *Mother Knows Best: Mother Theresa's Teaching Applied to MBA Strategies*.

My stomach gurgled. I reached across Wren and rooted through the glove compartment. I found half a roll of wintermint Breathsavers. I popped all of them into my mouth.

'Loony!' she said, annoyed. 'Sit still.'

I spit a wet Breathsaver at her. It plopped onto the envelope she was writing on. Without looking up, she picked the white ring up and sucked it into her mouth. She kept writing.

My name is Luna. It means moon. My father was a physicist with NASA since it was established way back in 1958, the year before I was born. Actually I was born exactly nine months after he started at NASA, so I imagine he and Mom had quite a celebration the night he found out he got the job. After I was born, Dad had some security clearance trouble over my name because the Soviets had a whole bunch of space shots called the Luna series. Luna 3 was the first space vehicle to photograph the far side of the moon in 1959. Anyway, they grilled poor Dad for months about the significance of naming his daughter after the Soviet lunar space program. They interviewed his college sweetheart and asked her if Dad had ever read Karl Marx to her. I suppose I was lucky to be named Luna; Mom tells me Dad's first choice was a combination name, Abby Baker, after the two monkeys, Abel and Baker, they sent 300 miles up into space in 1959.

Suddenly Wren looked up from her writing. She was smiling. 'So I'm sitting in my cell. There are two other women in there with me.'

'Hookers?'

'No, not hookers. You watch too much television.'

This was true. I never used to watch, but then Robby bought his homemade decoder box from one of his students so we wouldn't have to pay the cable company. He made it sound like screwing the cable company was a political act, but mostly I think he got off on the prankishness of it. So he hooks the box up and something in the TV explodes so that the only channel we got clearly after that was ESPN. At first, we couldn't afford to fix the TV; then Robby left me. By then I'd gotten in the habit of watching sports. Sometimes I'd breakfast over a billiard game or grade papers during a rugby match. Once I set my alarm for two A.M. so I could watch a rodeo. I'm not sure what it is I like, maybe the variety of rules and terminology. In trapshooting if they launch the target before the shooter's call, that's a 'no bird'. A face-off in field hockey is called a 'bully'. It's a little like traveling to a foreign country, only cheaper.

'So the three of us are in this cell,' Wren continued. 'This one girl is young, maybe twenty. A business major. She and her boyfriend had been stealing typewriters and computers from the secretaries' offices. They've been putting themselves through school for two years doing this. Campus cops caught her tonight but her boyfriend managed to get away.'

'So, what about her?'

'Her? Nothing about her. I was just giving you the general ambiance.'

The two boys coming down the street from the 7-Eleven were drinking beer from paper bags, punching each other in the shoulder, laughing.

I looked over at Wren. 'So what happened? What are you writing that was worth almost getting us killed?'

'I'm sitting in this prison, mentally listing famous people

10

who have also done time. Thoreau, Cervantes, Joan Baez—'

'Wren, a couple hours in a local jail is not having "done time".'

'—Gandhi, the Berrigan brothers, Galileo, Robert Mitchum—'

'Hitler,' I added.

The boys were getting closer. I could make out their features now. We were all sharing the same umbrella of weary light from the same dim street lamp. One of the boys noticed Wren. He couldn't take his eyes off of her.

'—Martin Sheen, Martin Luther, Martin Luther King—'

'Uncle Martin from *My Favorite Martian*. Wren, get to the point.'

That's when Wren lunged across the seat at me and began to tickle me. Her strong fingers teased my underarms, my waist, my neck. She plowed my pelvic bones, weeded my rib cage. She was relentless. I flailed my arms, laughing and choking, pushing at her. My glasses fell off. My elbow cracked her forehead. The rusty spot on her bandage turned bright red with fresh bleeding. She didn't seem to care.

'Stop it,' I cackled. 'Stop. I'm going to wet myself.'

Wren stopped, leaned back in her seat. 'Okay, now tickle yourself.'

I gasped for air, retrieved my glasses from my lap. 'Okay, now fuck yourself.'

'I'm serious, Loon. Tickle yourself.'

'You can't tickle yourself.'

'Try.'

I tried. I fluttered my fingers in the same spots, but nothing happened. 'Goochy goochy goo. Satisfied?'

'Did you know that the ancient Chinese used to tickle people to death? Thousands of years ago, they used it as a form of torture.'

'Hey, girls,' one of the boys said with a smirk. They stood a few feet from the car. 'Looks like fun.'

11

'Need any help?' the other boy asked. This was the one who couldn't stop staring at Wren. They were both big, athletic-looking. Teammates.

'Let's go, Loony,' Wren said. She wasn't afraid, only annoyed.

I, however, was afraid. I quickly started the car.

'Come on, girls. Don't be that way.' Wren's boy came up and leaned on Wren's side of the car. He had blond hair mildly spiked. He looked a lot like Tom Cruise and seemed to be aware of the resemblance. His friend didn't look like anybody. Tom C. smiled at Wren and winked. 'I could get interested.'

Wren laughed. 'Yeah? Well, come back when you can get interesting.'

'Oh, I'm pretty interesting right now. Once you get to know me.' He put some extra English on 'know me'.

Wren turned toward him, smiling now in an interested way. 'You mean "know" in the biblical sense?'

'Sure. Whatever.'

'Lady,' the other boy said, 'if dicks could talk, his would spout poetry.'

Both of them laughed at that. So did Wren. I twisted the flexible wire earpiece of my glasses, not looking directly at them.

'Really?' Wren said. 'Poetry?'

'With some encouragement,' Wren's boy said.

'Okay,' Wren said. 'Whip it on out.'

'What?'

'Whip your dick out and come here. I'm a poetry lover.'

'What?'

'I'm going to suck you off.'

'Really?'

'That's what you want, isn't it?'

'Well, sure. Yeah. I guess.'

'Okay. Just flop it right here on the car door.' She patted the ledge of the door. 'Careful of the paint job.'

The boys frowned. 'Here?' her boy said.

12

'Sure.' She pointed at the other boy. 'You too, Jack. I want both of you at once.'

'Both of us?' Wren's boy made a face.

'Don't worry, you'll fit.' She opened her mouth wide. 'See? Lots of room.'

'What about her?' Pointing at me.

'She likes to watch.'

I put my glasses back on and wheezed at them. 'Asthma.'

'Let's go, man,' Tom C.'s pal said, pulling his arm. 'She's just yanking your chain.'

Wren laughed. 'Maybe you two boys should go home and yank each other's chains.'

Wren's boy, seriously angry now, massive shoulders bunched, remembering all the tough guys he's mowed down on all those muddy football fields across the state, clamped his huge hands on the car door and leaned menacingly toward Wren. The car tilted toward him. 'I could fuck you right now, sweetheart. Fuck you in the mouth, in the ass, any place I fucking want.'

'Then fuck this,' Wren said and stabbed my pen into the back of his hand. He hollered and jumped back, holding his hand and staring at the welling blood. Wren turned calmly toward me. 'Drive.'

I pulled the car away from the curb and drove off.

'Fucking bitches!' the boy who didn't look like anybody hollered. He threw his beer can at us and it bounced off my rear bumper and clattered across the pavement.

'Lesbos,' they shouted. 'Fucking dikes!'

'Fuzz bumpers to you, boys,' Wren shouted back.

My heart was thumping from the confrontation. I slipped my thumb under my bra strap and felt relief when the strap snuggled into the groove of my thumbnail. I swallowed, took a couple deep breaths, pretended to be as calm as Wren.

'So, the point is,' Wren said, resuming our former conversation as if nothing had happened, 'you can't tickle yourself. We know that. Yet, we can be tickled by others,

tickled until we hurt, even die. But if we can't tickle ourselves, then tickling is obviously not merely a physical
reaction.'

'Freud already said all that.'

'Exactly. It has psychosexual overtones, a manifestation
of repressed emotions.'

'How many people in this car are bored? Raise your
hands.' I raised my hand.

Wren ignored me. 'So those ancient Chinese, when they
tickled a man to death, were basically helping a person
kill himself. I wonder if the suicidal implications of tickling have been researched. The *thanatos* aspects. Suicidal
tendencies as displayed by ticklishness. If we could map
the tickle zones and see which repressions they represent,
then gauge the intensities, we could recognize people who
were predisposed toward suicide. I think there might be
an article in this.' I knew that by the end of the week,
Wren would be showing me such an article. By the end of
the month some psychology journal will have sent her a
check for it. She would use the check to take me out to
dinner and I would have to act thrilled for her. It was an
annoying cycle.

'Wren, that's all very interesting,' I said, my voice suddenly tight. 'But why were you in the goddamn jail and
why were you waving your goddamn panties around and
what happened to your goddamn forehead? That's all I
want to know.'

'Byron,' she said with a sigh.

I waited. Byron Caldwell was her husband. The details
are a little sketchy because Wren didn't like to talk about
him. When she did talk about him, it was the only time I
ever saw her act uncertain, clumsy. Like he was kryp-
tonite, sapping her strength. Then she could have tripped
over anything. This much I knew: Byron and Wren were
still married, although she had walked out on him one
week after the wedding for some unspecified reason;
Wren hadn't seen Byron in almost two years; Byron was
in a federal prison somewhere.

Wren twisted the radio knob. 'Crying' came on.

'Is that Roy Orbison or Don McClean?' she asked, like it was a quiz.

'Roy Orbison,' I said. 'Wren, what about Bryon.'

'Okay, so I'm out to dinner with Geoffrey. We drive all the way into Portland to celebrate, which in his crummy car is—'

'Whoa. Slow down. Celebrate what?'

'Oh, right, I haven't told you yet. I've got a job interview at *Orange Coast Today*. They called this morning. Want me to fly down to California in two weeks.'

'Really? An interview? To be what, a reporter?'

'It's a magazine, Loony, not a newspaper. One of those thick glitzy regionals with lots of health club and plastic surgery ads. But, yeah, I'd do some writing, some editing. Mostly I want to learn the business end. You know, the technical side of running a magazine. I'm not talking First Amendment, I'm talking layout and payroll and whose palm to grease and ass to kiss to make deadline. Nuts and bolts shit.'

'You didn't tell me you were applying to magazines.'

She shrugged. 'No big secret. I didn't want to get my hopes up.'

'Wren, that's great. Really great.' A long, rickety sigh whooshed from deep inside of me, like escaping locusts knocking into each other in midflight. 'Did I sound sincere?'

'Not very.'

'Good.'

'Don't be petty.'

'Petty is my main character trait. Without petty, I might not have any personality at all.' I drove without looking at her. Sure, I felt happy about Wren's good fortune, but mostly I felt jealous. Wren had sent out only five résumés, this was her third interview. As of yesterday, I had sent out 116 résumés to various universities, colleges, high schools, and military schools and had so far been offered one lousy interview. Somewhere in Kansas. A city with

15

the word wheat in it. Wheatfield. Wheatvale. Wheatville.

Wren's dream was to study as many different disciplines as interested her and then start her own magazine, a kind of up-scale down-to-earth women's magazine that featured articles combing the esoteric and the everyday. Articles like: 'Sartre in the Workplace', 'Dating the Compulsive-Obsessive Anal Retentive Executive', 'How Would Emily Dickinson Throw that Baby Shower?' Stuff like that. Okay, maybe I was being petty again. Here's how she described it to me: 'You know what the nineties woman needs? Something that doesn't pander to her vanity or ignore her social responsibility. Something that shows her how to incorporate art and philosophy and psychology into everyday living. *Vanity Fair* without the gossip and perfume inserts; *Whole Earth Catalogue* without the granola; *Mother Jones* without knee-jerk Latin American politics; *Ms*, without the simplistic slogans. Can you see what I'm saying, Loony?'

Kind of. Well, Wren had the degrees, she had the publications. All she needed now was some hands-on magazine experience, which is why she'd applied for this job. The differences between us often discouraged me. Wren wanted to write, to create, to fill a cultural void in the lives of women all over the country. I just wanted a nice cozy teaching job somewhere where I could expose the thrills of English composition to sleepy freshmen and have a good dental plan.

My thumbnail was skating back and forth under my bra strap again. As if I were trying to generate some enthusiasm for my life.

'So, we went to dinner,' Wren said.

'What?'

'Dinner. Geoffrey and I. To celebrate.'

'Oh, yeah.' I'd forgotten about the story, about the arrest, the tattered blue panties. I realized I no longer cared. I just wanted to go home and watch television, it didn't matter what was on.

But Wren continued: 'We drive to Portland to eat.

Geoffrey's going on and on about some gorgeous guy he met at a tennis tournament.'

'Another gorgeous guy?'

'He's lonely.'

Geoffrey's real name is Jeffrey, but he had it legally changed so it would be the same as Chaucer's. I'm not sure why, since he didn't seem to have any particular affinity with or affection for the dead poet. Also, Geoffrey is gay. He confided this to Wren and me in very hushed tones one afternoon after his short story had been shredded by our Fiction Workshop. He thinks his gayness is a secret, even though all of the characters in all of his stories are gay. Nevertheless, we swore ourselves to secrecy. 'I don't want any homophobic bias to affect the others' critiquing of my work,' he'd explained seriously. 'I want their complete honesty.'

Fat chance.

Wren grabbed my hand and pulled it away from my bra strap. 'Stop that, you little mutant.'

'I'm listening.'

'Anyway, we're having dinner and Geoffrey is going on about—'

'Cut to the chase, Wren. How does Byron fit in?'

Wren reached over and started honking the horn, shouting out the car with each honk, 'PMS alert! PMS alert!' A big orange cat dove under a parked car.

I stopped the car in the middle of the street. We were still the only traffic on the street. Wren was laughing, her head back, her mouth open. Her teeth were large, something like Carly Simon's. Here's the thing: she had just returned from some sleazy adventure involving arrest, jail, a convict husband, and tattered blue panties. And she was laughing. I had done nothing more adventurous all day than turn pages and I was the emotional wreck.

I couldn't help but stare at her. I tried to see her the way men see her. As a woman who could change their lives around. That was what they all saw. I'd heard men say this about her. They confided this to me. God, they'd say, Wren is the kind of woman who can change my whole life around. At thirty, I still looked pretty much the same as I did in high school: straight wheat-blond hair that without the miracle of perms would always look like the matted hairs on the hind leg of an English sheepdog; thin body with arms and legs straight as toilet-paper tubes; thick glasses because I was allergic to contact lenses; a semi-pretty face that was often referred to by adults as lovely and by my peers as sweet. I didn't turn men's lives around. I adorned their lives, enhanced them somewhat, like Sweet'n'Low in bitter coffee. But I didn't actually change anything.

'I'm going home,' I said quietly. 'I'll drop you off.' I shifted into first and began driving.

Wren leaned back in her seat and wedged her knees up against the dashboard. 'After dinner we came back to Geoffrey's apartment. He invited me to take a dip in the Jacuzzi with him, but I didn't have my bathing suit so I just went along to sit with him. There were a few other people already soaking, so we all sat around and talked and drank a few beers. Geoffrey left to call his tennis friend. I stayed. Well, I got tired of sitting at the side and watching everybody else enjoying the water, so I took off my skirt and T-shirt and climbed in. It's not like I was nude or anything. I had my bra and panties on. But some asshole in one of the apartments called the cops and they came over.'

'And they arrested you for that?'

'Not exactly. One of the guys in the Jacuzzi, big brawny type from Sweden, grad student in comp lit, started to give the cop a hard time. He was a little buzzed from the beer and hot water, so I admit he did use a few harsh terms. So the cop runs my name through his computer and comes up with Byron's name, which is excuse enough to start hassling me, asking questions, you know, being a cop. Then the Swede jumps in to protect me and there's some shoving. I get knocked to the ground and scrape my

18

head on the lip of the Jacuzzi. The Swede knocks the cop into the hot water. Next thing I know we're both arrested.'

'You could have talked your way out of that, Wren. No one's better at that than you.'

'I could have,' she said. But she didn't continue.

'What about the panties?'

'Yeah. The smart-ass cop makes me give them over when they throw me in jail. Says he doesn't want me to hang myself with them. They gave them back when they released me, only they're all shredded. He and his pals were probably gnawing on them for dinner.'

'Christ, you could sue them.'

'Probably.' She studied her notes on tickling, no longer interested in the incident.

I drove in silence for a couple miles until we were at her apartment complex. I hit the turn signal.

'I don't want to go home yet,' Wren said, sitting up with sudden fidgety energy.

'Then don't,' I said. 'But I'm dropping you off. I'm tired.'

'One more stop,' she said. 'Come on. There'll be food there, I swear.'

'Where?' But I already knew.

'BeeGee's.'

'Damn it, Wren, it's late.'

'Come on, don't be such a rag.'

'Right now I'd eat a rag.'

'BeeGee always has food, you know that.'

I turned the car around and headed for BeeGee's house. BeeGee was Wren's abbreviation for Bat-Faced Girl.

It was after midnight and we were on our way to see the Bat-Faced Girl.

*   *   *   *   *

19

The Bat-Faced Girl was cleaning her gun.

'Smith & Wesson Shofield .45,' she said. 'Like the one Jessie James used.' She thumbed a cartridge into the dark chamber. 'The same one my dad used to blow his brains out. Hungry? Help yourself.'

We were standing in the kitchen. The Bat-Faced Girl sat at the table polishing the black gun barrel with some sweet-smelling oil. The refrigerator door was wide open, but the refrigerator was empty except for the television set on the metal rack. *The David Letterman Show* was on. It was disconcerting to see David Letterman's head where a head of cabbage should be, but I was almost used to it by now. If I'd opened the oven door, I'd have found her stereo system. The records and compact discs were stored in the dishwasher.

BeeGee, real name Esther, worried about thieves.

She even had a letter she wrote to herself from the County Health Department on official-looking stationery she designed on her computer. The letter was sad to inform her that her test results reveal that she has AIDS. She kept this letter in her car and when she left the car, she displayed it openly on the driver's seat. She hoped this would scare away car thieves.

'Don't you think that gun is clean enough by now?' Wren said.

'It's an antique,' BeeGee said. 'I clean it twice a week, just like my father did. I don't want someone breaking in here in the middle of the night and have the thing misfire.'

'You really think you could use that on someone?' I asked.

'A thief gets what he deserves,' she said.

Wren opened the cupboard under the sink. A mini-refrigerator squatted there next to the garbage disposal pipes. 'What do you want, Loony?' She leaned over, poked through the shelves.

'What are my choices?'

'We've got your standard two slices of Domino's pepperoni pizza, the traditional half a breast of Kentucky fried fat, a tub of macaroni salad, three Chicken McNuggets, a strawberry yogurt, and unsweetened applesauce.'

'Yogurt,' I said.

'Check the date,' BeeGee warned.

Wren looked at the bottom of the container. 'Just under the wire.' She tossed it to me. I grabbed a spoon out of the drawer and sat at the wooden table across from BeeGee. David Letterman had dozens of Ping-Pong paddles fastened to his body, up and down each leg, across his chest and back. He was wearing a motorcycle helmet with a paddle stuck to the top like an alien antenna. He gave the signal and Paul Shaffer turned on a machine that fired Ping-Pong balls at David. They bounced off at crazy angles. They played the whole thing back in slow motion.

'There's plenty of food in the cupboards,' BeeGee said.

BeeGee favored those freeze-dried meals in a pouch that Dick Cavett touted on television. You microwaved them and they were supposed to taste like a regular TV dinner. But I couldn't eat them because they reminded me too much of disaster food, the kind of stuff you store for an emergency, a nuclear war or something. I thought of the bomb shelter my dad had built in our backyard when I was a child. We spent Labor Day weekend in it once as a test of endurance and family strength. Mom beat Dad about a hundred times in gin rummy and we never did that again. Occasionally I saw them sneak down there together, giggling, and come out disheveled and flushed. When we sold the house, the new owners thought it was a marvelous place for a wine cellar.

BeeGee snapped open the pistol's cylinder and thumbed another cartridge into the chamber. I saw this out of the corner of my eye as I watched Ping-Pong balls pummel David Letterman.

Wren hopped up onto the counter across from me and began spooning applesauce into her mouth. She sat cross-legged, her denim skirt stretched tight against her thighs. With her short skirt and no panties, she was pretty well exposed.

21

'You mind?' I said, pointing with my spoon. 'I'm trying to eat.'

Wren laughed and flicked her tongue in a lewd way.

I laughed too.

BeeGee thumbed another cartridge into the chamber.

'What'd your new doctors say?' I asked BeeGee.

BeeGee shrugged. 'The usual crap. Mine is the most unusual case they've ever seen. They practically played patty cake at the thought of the medical papers they would write about me. They gave me more benzodiazepines and talked about stimulus control procedures. Same old bullshit.'

BeeGee had insomnia. Not just stay-awake-late-cranky-in-the-morning insomnia, but never-sleeps-a-goddamn-wink insomnia. She did not sleep. Ever. Hence the nickname Bat Girl. Which Wren changed into Bat-Faced Girl because that's a phrase from a Paul Simon song.

BeeGee, by the way, did not look like a bat. She had a round, but pretty face, though the features did seem a little squished together. The overall effect was that of a small pumpkin carved by a talented but untutored artist.

Because she never slept, BeeGee made her house available to grad students from all disciplines. Twenty-four hours a day you would find biochemistry lab rats drinking beer with lawbots. Psych nerds watching TV while journalism scabs waited for the campus newspaper to be delivered. Even a few professors dropped by to relive their old college days by pretending they didn't need sleep. BeeGee always had plenty of food and drink, though it was not unusual for a group of students to arrive with half a dozen bags of groceries to show gratitude.

I looked over at BeeGee. 'What's stimulus, uh . . '

'Stimulus control procedures. That's when they give you a set of rules to make the bedroom associated with only good feelings of sleep. For example, if I get into bed and can't fall asleep within ten minutes, I have to leave the bedroom and return only when I'm sleepy enough to

22

go to sleep. I've been through that stuff before with the other doctors. It doesn't work.' She looked at me very intently. 'I miss the dreaming, Luna. I never get to dream.'

I thought about my dream earlier at the library, the circles of hell, the horrible two-headed demons with the faces of Willie Nelson and Julio Iglesias. Not much to miss there.

Wren hopped down from the counter and tossed the empty applesauce jar into the trash. She went to another cupboard and grabbed a jar of unsalted peanuts, funneling them into her mouth with her hand. 'I had this idea about tickling,' Wren said to BeeGee while munching. 'I want to run it by you.'

'Hypergargalesthesia,' BeeGee said. 'That's extreme sensitivity to tickling.'

Wren smiled. She had come to the right person. Running it by me had been okay for a start, the way a businessman might practice his speech in front of his dog before trying it out on a colleague. I didn't blame Wren. BeeGee was the only other person around who knew as much as she. Of course, BeeGee had the unfair advantage of never sleeping. David Letterman was her one weakness. The rest of the time she read. When she wasn't home reading, she worked at the campus library. She knew something about everything. The difference between her and Wren was that though BeeGee knew more information, had more facts stored in her brain, Wren knew how to use information, how to make connections between things and translate all that into articles that anyone could understand.

Wren and BeeGee discussed Wren's theory of tickling. BeeGee cited scientific research in the area. I watched them out of the corner of my eye because I didn't want them to feel as if they had to include me in the conversation, which would have only made me feel dumber. I'd done a pretty fair job as a teaching assistant this year, goading students into cranking out literate essays. I

23

thought I'd probably make a good teacher somewhere. But a few minutes with these two made me feel criminally incompetent, an underachiever.

David Letterman turned on his bubble maker and everyone applauded.

BeeGee's calico cat jumped onto my lap. Her left hindquarters were shaved down to the skin. Three red scabs pocked the skin.

'Hey, Sphinx,' I said. 'What happened to you?'

'Cat fight,' BeeGee said. 'Cost me $174.' She held out her arms and I handed Sphinx to her. 'I have to give her antibiotics twice a day. Make her swallow these pills, same as me.' BeeGee began picking at the cat's biggest scab. Part of the crust broke away from the skin. She dug out the rest of it.

'Yeech,' I said, making a face. 'What are you doing?'

'You have to keep the wound open,' Wren explained. 'So it doesn't get infected.'

I took off my wire-rimmed glasses and cleaned them with the tail of my Oxford shirt. One of the wire earpieces was all chewed up. Last week I'd been studying outside the library, actually leaning up against a tree the way you see in college catalogues, my glasses lying in my lap while I rested my eyes, when some gnarled black mutt with a red bandanna tied around his neck comes running by, snatching my glasses up in his yellow teeth, and loping off across the quad. I climbed on my bike and chased after him, but by the time I caught up and wrestled the glasses away from him, the end of the earpiece was gnawed off. The stump that was left was all jagged, which I tried to bury under a hundred layers of clear fingernail polish, but which wore away leaving the jagged metal to rub against the top of my ear. I could even feel a callus starting to form up there. I put my glasses back on and turned back to watch David Letterman. 'I have to get home pretty soon, Wren,' I said. I didn't want BeeGee to think it was because I was sleepy, so I added, 'I have a lot of studying to do.'

'Right,' Wren said. 'A few minutes more.'

'Excuse me,' BeeGee said. She laid the gun down on the wooden table. It thumped heavily, like a bowling ball. She stood up and walked into the bathroom, closing the door behind her.

Wren and I exchanged grins. I clamped my hand to my mouth to smother a laugh.

Finally, we heard it. The low hum of the vibrator.

BeeGee was well known for her habit of getting up suddenly in the middle of a conversation and disappearing into the bathroom to use her vibrator. I think it was therapeutic more than sexual. A woman who could never sleep tended not to attract men. It made men nervous to think of her awake, walking about while they slept. One guy who had dated her briefly told me it got so he couldn't sleep either. 'How can I sleep, knowing she's in the next room doing things.' What things, I'd asked. I don't know, he'd said, *things*.

BeeGee returned a few minutes later, her face as expressionless as when she'd left. Her cheeks were a little redder. 'So, what'd I miss?'

Wren pointed at me. 'Loony wants to know the best brand of vibrator. She's in the market.'

'Well,' BeeGee said with a serious expression. 'It depends upon what kind of features you're interested in.' And she began a discussion of the merits of various types, styles, attachments, voltage. She sounded like a professor discussing species of plankton.

Wren grinned at me from over BeeGee's shoulder.

'You can go in and try mine, if you like,' BeeGee offered.

'A test drive,' Wren said.

'Thanks,' I said to BeeGee. 'Some other time.'

BeeGee shrugged, picked up her gun, and took a rag to the walnut grips. Sphinx curled up on the tabletop next to her.

'We should go,' Wren said, standing.

BeeGee nodded.

I stood up.

BeeGee cocked the hammer of her gun, placed the tip of the barrel against Sphinx's head, and pulled the trigger. The explosion made me jump. Sphinx's limp body flew off the table. A bloody clump of fur stuck to my cheek.

'Jesus, BeeG—' I screamed.

She turned the gun toward me and fired. The explosion and bullet hit me at the same time. A hot wind pulled at my face. My legs went numb and I collapsed against the table, knocking over a chair. My chest burned. I was afraid to look, afraid I'd see a hole straight into my heart. See the bullet stuck in it. Funny, when I thought about it, I didn't imagine a real heart, a fist-sized muscle, I saw one of those Valentine Day hearts, plump and red.

I saw BeeGee cock the hammer again, the gun aimed at my face.

Wren leapt at her like some hero cop on television. BeeGee didn't flinch, she calmly swung the gun around and fired into Wren's chest. Wren dropped to the kitchen floor.

I tried to crawl toward Wren, but nothing worked. The only thing moving was my heart pumping gurgling blood through the hole in my chest.

BeeGee spoke to no one in particular. 'The mistake many people make is putting the gun to their head. It is too easy to miss the vital parts of the brain, which often results in leaving the victim paralyzed, not dead. This is the proper method of disposal.' BeeGee opened her mouth, slowly lowered her head over the barrel, and pulled the trigger.

2

'I need to urinate,' I said.

'Go right ahead,' she said.

'But I'm in bed.' My eyes were closed. I had the feeling that I could open them if I really wanted, but I wasn't confident enough to test my theory. What if I was wrong? I decided instead to impress everyone with my patience.

'Go right ahead and pee, dear,' she said.

I did. I didn't feel the urine, just the relaxing of my bladder, like a fist gone slack. The sheets around me stayed dry. Stiff and dry.

'Who are you?' I asked.

'Your mother.'

'My mother is dead.'

'Sorry to hear that,' she said.

*　　*　　*　　*　　*

'How is Wren?' I asked.

This was sometime later, after one of my naps. I still didn't open my eyes. After all, what if she really was my mother. I had thought my mother was dead. Killed in an auto wreck when I was eighteen. They'd used the jaws of life to cut her out. I read that in the newspaper account. The jaws of life. Silly phrase. An oxymoron. I'd pictured a fat shark chomping open the station-wagon door. I thought I'd attended Mother's funeral, wearing a new black dress because I hadn't owned anything black. I'd settled on a velvet dress because it was summer and it was the only black dress I could find that didn't have huge white polka dots. My shoes were navy blue but no one seemed to notice. Dad gave me Mom's pearls to wear. They broke in the limo on the drive to the cemetery. I'd been rubbing my thumbnail against them. We were on our knees gathering the pearls into his linen handkerchief. He twisted the corners and tied them in a knot. For a moment he looked like a little kid holding a prized bag of marbles. That was the only time I ever remember Dad looking young. They buried Mom in the morning, the grass still wet from the lawn sprinklers.

Or maybe they didn't bury her. Maybe I dreamed all that in some etherized haze. If she were alive it must have hurt her deeply for me to pronounce her dead. Some Freudian slip, she must wonder, wishful thinking? I didn't want to see the hurt in her eyes. I kept my eyes pressed closed. 'Is Wren okay?'

'Who, dear?'

'Wren Caldwell. She was shot too.'

'I don't know her. Pretty name, though. Wren.'

My chest hurt. As if a starving rodent had gnawed through the skin and muscle and now was crunching through the bones of my rib cage. Each breath felt like another bite.

'Can you check on Wren, please?'

'Sure, dear. Now get some sleep.'

'Is it okay if I urinate again?'

'Of course, dear. Fire away.'

*   *   *   *   *

'What day is it?'

'Saturday.'

'Thank you.' I counted days. Three. Three days since the Bat-Faced Girl shot her cat and Wren and me. I was

28

unaccountably cheerful. 'Saturday. I've always relied on the kindness of Saturdays.'

'That's very funny,' she said.

Encouraged, I opened my eyes. They worked. I couldn't remember why I'd thought I'd be better off with them closed. I looked at the woman standing next to my bed. 'You're not my mother.'

'Of course I'm not. You said your mother was dead.'

'You said *you* were my mother.'

'Glover,' she said. 'Nurse Glover.'

Your mother. Nurse Glover. They did sound similar.

I stared up at her as she made the empty bed next to mine. She was a chubby woman in a rumpled white uniform. She wore a nubby blue sweater over her uniform. She had clumsily bleached hair and the vacant look of someone who'd graduated at the bottom percentage of her nursing class. But she moved around that bed like a pool hustler lining up a money shot.

'I'm sorry about the misunderstanding,' I said.

'It's the drugs, dear. You had a lot of drugs. You'll snap out of it.'

'How's Wren? Did you check?'

Her face snapped taut as the fitted sheet she was smoothing. 'I'm not allowed to discuss other patients.'

I sighed with relief. 'If she's a patient, then she's okay.'

'I can neither confirm nor deny that.'

'That doesn't make any sense. She's my friend.'

'This is a hospital,' she said by way of explanation. She turned her back and fluffed a pillow. The back of her sweater was matted with long white cat hair.

'Who can tell me about Wren?' I asked.

'You'll have to speak to your doctor. Dr. Granger.'

'Where is he?'

'She. Dr. Jennifer Granger.'

'Goddamn it, Wren's my best friend.' I tried to sit up. The hungry rodent bit into my plump heart. Sparks sizzled

29

in my brain. I dropped back onto my pillow. 'Just tell me if she's alive.'

'I'm sorry,' she said and hurried out of the room.

* * * * *

'Hello, Mrs. Devon, I'm Officer Simmons.'

I opened my eyes. 'You're the one Wren yelled at the other night. At the police station.'

He grinned and nodded. His cheeks flushed. 'She was quite a woman.'

'Was?'

His baby face drained white. 'Well, I mean, she's uh, dead.'

My body sort of collapsed in on itself. Like time-lapse photography of a rotting grape shriveling into a raisin. 'No,' I said, the calmness of my voice surprising me. It was my teacher voice. 'There is obviously a mistake. Wren couldn't be dead. You must have looked at the wrong charts or something.' Isn't that what people on TV always said?

'No mistake, Mrs. Devon. I was at the scene that night.'

He cut himself off but I could tell he'd been about to relate convincing details to me about the size of the hole in her chest, the amount of blood, how he had closed her vacant eyes. He didn't understand. Those things didn't matter with Wren. She couldn't die.

'I need to ask you a few questions,' he said.

'Esther shot her cat,' I said. 'How's the cat?'

'Dead.'

I nodded. My sinuses filled with fluid and stung my nose and eyes. I wanted to cry but somehow I couldn't. Crying seemed too easy, a melodramatic cliché. Wren deserved better.

'Miss Kleinman is dead also,' Officer Simmons reported.

'Yes. Of course.' I sat up. My chest clenched in protest, but I ignored it. 'This is what happened. Wren and I went over to see BeeGee—'

'Who?' He stopped writing.

'Esther Kleinman. We ate, watched David Letterman in her refrigerator, Esther shot the cat, then me, then Wren, then herself. End story.'

'Why did she do it?'

'What do you mean?' I asked.

'Well, she was your friend. Why would she shoot you?' He tried to look innocent and boyish, but his eyes were tense and suspicious.

'I don't know. Maybe because she was a severe insomniac and had gone nuts from not being able to sleep. Maybe because she couldn't dream.'

'Drugs were found on the premises.'

'Shouldn't a detective be asking me these questions, Officer? Aren't you supposed to advise me of my rights?'

He looked hurt. 'We are a very small department, Mrs. Devon. As to your rights, I'm just asking a few questions. However, if you wish to have an attorney present, that is your right.'

'Listen, you found what, a couple joints?'

'I can't confirm or deny what we found, Mrs. Devon.'

'You find a couple joints and you think you've walked into the Colombian Connection? You think this was a drug deal gone bad, that BeeGee was running a crack house?'

'I'm just investigating all possibilities.'

'Then why'd she shoot the cat, Kojak?'

'Pardon?'

'If this was about drugs, why shoot the cat? He short changed her on a delivery of cocaine?'

'I can neither confirm nor deny anything to do with the investigation, Mrs. Devon.'

'Bullshit,' I said. 'Do you hear what I'm saying, Officer? Do you?'

He leaned backward, the way he had that night, and for an instant, in his startled face, Wren was still alive.

I closed my eyes and went back to sleep.

* * * * *

The doctor drew a picture of my left breast. She made it look larger than it was. I wondered if that was meant to cheer me up.

'This is your breast,' she said.

'Before or after the implant?' I said.

She smiled, but she didn't look up. She drew a small circle on the breast and scribbled it in with her pen. 'This is where you were shot.'

I wondered why we didn't just use my real breast, since it was already naked and I could see exactly where I'd been shot. A white gauze pad covered the hole, but I'd seen the hole too. Dark moist crater, like a tar pit hiding the tiny bones of extinct species.

She dotted the paper breast a few times. 'These are the powder burns.'

I looked at my breast, saw the tiny scabs on my skin where the powder had burned through my skin where my blouse had been unbuttoned. A V-shaped pattern. Ducks flying south toward my navel.

'Actually,' the doctor continued, 'it's good that you were so close. The bullet punched right through your chest and out your back. The police call it a "through and through". In one hole and out the back door. Less damage. The bullet doesn't have a chance to expand or fragment. If you were farther away, the same bullet might have killed you.'

'Like Wren.'

'Yes, like Ms. Caldwell.'

Dr. Jennifer Granger was at most twenty-seven. Naturally I hated her. Three years younger and she was diagramming my personal organs as if she'd known them all her life. I thought of snatching up her pen and drawing her face: short no-nonsense hair, brown as a melted candy bar, snub nose the size of a nipple; thin lips that if it weren't for lipstick you wouldn't even know were there. Here's the part I liked, she had a small rash of acne splashed across her chin. You could tell she'd tried to cover it with makeup, but clumsily, so she only managed to call more attention to it.

'This is your heart, Luna,' she said. She drew a heart under the breast. It looked very official. A real heart, like in cancer commercials. It looked like my father's knotted handkerchief swollen with my mother's loose pearls. 'This is where the bullet nicked you. The left ventricle.' She drew an arrow that pierced the heart Cupid-like. 'This is the bullet's trajectory. Shaved a little of the papillary muscle, but missed the arteries and valves. You were very lucky.'

'I keep hearing that.'

She clicked her ballpoint pen, retracting the ink cartridge. She looked up at me, an expression of concern wrinkling her features. That is how she would look fifteen years from now. 'Depression in these circumstances is to be expected, Luna. An act like this, so violent so—' she looked around the room as if searching for the right word —'random. So random. It shakes our sense of stability. Rattles primordial fears. That's to be expected.' She placed a hand on my bare shoulder. Her flesh was cool and soft. 'If you'd like, I can have a therapist talk with you. Your insurance will cover it, so don't worry about the cost.'

I didn't want to see a shrink or a wannabe shrink. I had papers to write and a class to teach. My thesis on the reclusive Thomas Pynchon still wasn't finished.

'When can I get out of here,' I asked.

'What about the therapist?' she asked.

'I'll think it over.'

She shook her head and rubbed the bridge of her nose the way people who wear glasses do, though she wore contacts. Old habits die hard. I rubbed my thumbnail along the seam of the hospital mattress.

'When can I get out?' I repeated.

She gathered up her clipboard and pen and started for the door. 'I'll see what I can do. No promises, though.' Like she was my lawyer negotiating a plea bargain. 'And think about the therapist. There's no stigma in asking for help.'

'Help me get out of here,' I said, pulling my gown back on. 'There, I asked.'

She chuckled and walked out of the room.

*   *   *   *   *

'Don't open your eyes,' he said.

I didn't.

'Hold out your hand.'

I did.

'Keep your eyes closed. Don't cheat now, keep them closed.'

'They're closed,' I said.

'Okay, don't move. Don't move. Do. Not. Move.'

My open palm filled with an unmistakable and familiar presence. My fingers curled around it.

'Can I open my eyes now?'

'Open, Sesame.'

I opened my eyes. I looked right at it and laughed. Laughing twanged the stitches in my chest. My left boob ached as if someone were tightening long brass screws through my nipple directly into my heart. But I kept laughing anyway. I couldn't help it.

Robby's penis was laying in my hand like a small flashlight. It was only semi-erect, but that was plenty large enough. On the head, he'd drawn eyes with a black mask around them, and red liner around the pee hole made it look like a mouth. He even had a tiny cowboy hat strapped to it with a rubber band. The entire shaft of the penis was drawn with a web of fish scales all around it. 'Return with us now,' he intoned in his deep radio announcer's voice, 'to those exciting days of yesteryear and the Lone Flounder.' He wagged his dick against my palm as if it were swimming. 'Great idea for a TV series, huh? The Lone Flounder swims up into the toilets of evildoers and bites them on the ass. He'll have a girlfriend known only as His Koi Mistress. What do you think? Am I a fuckin' genius or what?'

'I think you'd better put it away before a nurse walks in.'

'It'll give her a thrill. You wanna bet?' He skipped around the room wagging his dick and humming the *1812 Overture*. 'Da dum da dum da dum dum dum. Hi Ho, Scrotum.'

I laughed again. 'You're going to get Thumper thrown out of here.'

His penis was Thumper. My vagina was Bambi. At first, in those early lustful years, we'd called his penis Godzilla because of that short film 'Godzilla Meets Bambi'. The one where Bambi is playing sweetly in the woods and suddenly a huge prehistoric foot stomps her into a tortilla. We saw that film on one of our first dates back in college, so giving our sexual organs names seemed pretty funny at the time. But I didn't like calling his dick Godzilla because he'd sometimes call it God for short. At first, that was funny too. 'Come and worship your God, Luna.' Or 'God requires another sacrifice, Luna.' That kind of joking. It cracked us up quite a bit. But after a while, it just made me uncomfortable. Not that I'm religious, which I'm not. It's just that I felt like we were ridiculing other people and I didn't want every time we made love to be an act of ridicule. So I changed its name to Thumper.

Robby removed the tiny cowboy hat and stuffed the Lone Flounder back into his pants. He sat on the edge of the bed and squeezed my thigh through the blanket. His eyes turned watery and I thought he might cry. 'Jesus, Loon. Jesus.'

'I know. Weird, huh?'

He just shook his head in wonderment.

'Wren's dead,' I said.

'I know. I can't believe it. I thought she was too tough to die.'

Did he ever think if I was too tough to die? Or was he surprised that I was alive instead of Wren? Was my being alive proof of a naturalistic world without moral order? Wren's death proof that the good die young? Robby had had a crush on Wren since I first brought her home. He couldn't take his eyes off her, stop talking to her. I never held that against him since it seemed that every guy felt that way about her. He never did anything about it, probably because he knew Wren would tell me.

'Robby likes you,' I'd told Wren once. We shared the same tiny office on the top floor of the English Department, where all teaching assistants were sentenced to serve their time. We were grading freshman compositions at our respective gray metal desks. The walls were a faded lime-green, which gave the whole building the drab air of an abandoned post office.

'You hear me?' I asked.

She looked up from the composition, her drugstore reading glasses resting on the tip of her nose. 'What?'

'My husband, Robby, who is my husband, likes you. Did I mention that he was my husband?' I expected her to say something like well, I like him too, pretending that she didn't know what I meant.

'Yes, I know,' she said, returning to her grading.

'How do you know?'

She slapped her pen down and frowned at me. 'Give me a break here, Loony.'

'I'm serious. How the hell do you know?'

'How the hell do *you* know?'

'I'm his goddamn wife. He talks about you in that way men have, you know, when they're so infatuated they need to talk about a woman, but they couch it in seemingly innocent observations. "Doesn't that Wren have an

interesting insight into Martin Heidegger's philosophy?"
When what they mean is "Doesn't Wren have an ass to
die for?"'

Wren laughed. 'Don't worry, he hasn't touched my ass.'

'And if he did?'

'Would you want to know?'

I hesitated. 'Yes.'

'Then I'd tell you.'

'Would you turn him down?'

She picked up her pen and tapped it absently against
the composition on her desk. I wondered how the student
would interpret those pock marks.

'I can't answer that,' she said. 'I don't know what I'd
do.'

That night I'd told Robby about my conversation with
Wren about him and he'd stormed around the apartment
waving his copy of Virginia Woolf's *To the Lighthouse*,
which he'd been reading in the bathtub. He had a towel
knotted around his waist but he was dripping all over the
carpet. He protested that he had no sexual interest in
Wren, merely intellectual appreciation. He did not want
to sleep with her. He was very disappointed in me for even
suggesting such a thing. Then he went on to list her faults,
punctuating each flaw with a slap to the cover of Virginia
Woolf's novel. Wren was self-centred. Wren was pushy.
Wren was a snob. Wren laughed too easily. Wren smoked
too much. Wren used too much biographical background
in interpreting literature. Wren's hair was too frizzy.

As the list went on, I realized I'd only instigated another disguised declaration of love. Standing there listening to him was like having your husband rehearse his
seduction speech for another woman. When I mentioned
this to him, his face grew red and he slammed his book on
the table and said, 'Women don't know shit about men!'

Now in the hospital, he seemed concerned about me
but somehow remote. A few months ago he would have
been camped out in my room, spending all his time with
me, grading his papers, doing his Ph.D. work, watching

37

television with me. He'd be talking about how he would take care of me once we got home. Make soup with oyster crackers, bring me *People* magazine. But now his backpack was leaning against the wall, ready to be grabbed on the way out. This was just a visit, an obligation. Lending support to the soon-to-be-ex. Doing the Decent Thing.

'You made the television news,' he said. 'Local anyway.'

'I saw. They weren't very kind to Esther.'

He shrugged. 'She doesn't care anymore.'

'They all carried the same photo of Wren. That one she did as a joke, where she looks like she's posing for the cover of *Cosmo*.'

'I saw.'

'It's like no event is really a tragedy unless someone pretty dies.'

'This stuff is starting to itch.' Robby scratched his crotch.

'What?'

'This body paint on my dick. It's starting to itch.'

I gestured to the bathroom. 'Go wash it off.'

He went in and ran the water. While he was there he took a leak. He left the door open so he could keep talking to me. I listened to the drumming of his urine against water.

'How's class?' I asked.

'We're finished with poetry. They're writing short stories now.'

'Are they any good?'

'One girl shows some potential. The others are all into the twist-ending syndrome. You know, someone wakes up at the end and it's all been a bad dream. Shit like that.'

'How's it going at the station?'

'Bunch of assholes. Nobody wants me to play jazz anymore. It's rock 'n' roll or nothing. Radio is dead.' He was scrubbing his penis with soap.

'How's the novel coming?'

'Novels are dead. I'm doing something different. A

38

non-novel. It's like a time-warp thing where all these yuppies are on this Love Boat cruise and the ship sinks. A small group of them wash up on this island where all these famous people from history keep appearing through this rip in time. Like Socrates and Shakespeare and Teddy Roosevelt. It's so cool, you get this tight-assed stock-broker type face-to-face with Mussolini and they end up discussing their daughters' braces. Fascism on Elm Street.'

Robby was in his last quarter of finishing his Ph.D. in English. When we were both undergraduates together ten years ago, he was one of the star writers in the department. His teachers expected great things from him. He'd published a few poems and stories in prestigious literary magazines. After graduation, he went right into graduate school for his master's and I went to work at an employment placement service, headhunting for executives. I had been an English major too, but I didn't write. My poems were sappy and my stories were about people who woke up at the end and the whole thing was a dream.

One of Robby's professors helped him get a New York agent and for about a year we were giddy with anticipation that Robby's first novel would be bought for big bucks, like those other young writers we kept hearing about. Then we would go to Hollywood so he could write the screenplay for even bigger bucks, only we wouldn't get corrupted like everyone else. But it never happened. Editors liked his style but lamented a lack of plot. Robby's second novel didn't fare much better.

After receiving his master's, Robby decided he didn't care about writing that much and preferred to have a family. He was very excited about this new direction we were going to take. He got a steady job at a radio station playing jazz records that I couldn't bear listening to. We worked at getting me pregnant, which was a peculiar feeling after the years of elaborate precautions and silent tension if my period was even a few days late. Finally I became pregnant and we celebrated as jubilantly as if he'd

39

sold his novel. A month later I miscarried and the expression of relief on Robby's face was so plain that without even discussing it we returned to our cautious sex. Robby applied to return to graduate school for his doctorate.

I applied too, not out of any dedication to a new career, but mostly, I think, because I didn't want Robby to start looking at me with the same contempt he sometimes looked at his students. I didn't want to live through those after-movie sessions where he would patiently explain some literary allusion to me. It wasn't that he was snobby, it's just that he had a great mind and a true love of literature and couldn't understand why everyone else wasn't as obsessed as he.

Robby came out of the bathroom with a smoking joint between his lips. He inhaled deeply and offered it to me.

'This is a hospital,' I said brusquely. I don't know why I said that, I didn't care that he was smoking.

'Right, a hospital. You holding out for bigger and better drugs?'

'Robby, don't be an asshole.'

'You called me an asshole. That must mean you're feeling better.'

'I'm not feeling anything.'

He pinched out the tip of the joint and stuck it back in his pocket. He sat back on the edge of the bed. 'You don't mean physically, that you're paralyzed or anything.'

'No, Robby, I'm not paralyzed. I'm just . . . tired, I guess.'

Robby looked at me and for a moment it was the old look, the look of genuine love and concern. His long blond hair curled in a hundred directions at once. I wanted to reach out and touch his hair. Seeing his hair made me miss him more than holding his penis.

His eyes flickered, just a little, and I could tell he'd just remembered who we were now. He looked over at his backpack near the door. When he looked back at me I could see what was in his mind: his classes, his non-novel,

40

his new woman. He was dating Dr. Helen Jaspers, the Dean of the English Department, eight years older but still trim and energetic. She was an expert on Milton.

'Tell me, Luna,' he said, his voice rich with sincerity, but his eyes blank as Milton's, 'tell me how you feel.'

He reached out and held my hand, his fingers in their natural grooves just like my thumbnail in my bra strap. There was a time, back in the Thumper and Bambi days, when that look, that hand wrapped around mine, that radio announcer's voice, would have made me pour out everything inside of me. But I wasn't sure if there was anything inside of me. I felt the bulky bandage on my back where the bullet had exited. It was as if that bullet hole had allowed whatever I felt about anything to leak out. Like there was no more of me left inside. Just the empty husk of Luna.

'Robby,' I said, squeezing his hand. 'I hate jazz.'

*   *   *   *   *

My father phoned the day I was being released. Nurse Glover had just handed me the plastic bag with my hospital toothbrush, shampoo, soap, and dental floss. You get to keep those.

'Hello?' I said into the phone.

'Luna, my God, I just heard. How are you, honey?'

'Fine, Dad. They're just releasing me today.'

'I'd been following the Tijamuchi River. I just heard.'

I'd called Dad the first day I was able to open my eyes. His phone machine in Houston had a recorded message informing the caller that Ben Masters was out of the country and wouldn't be back for four months, leave a message and maybe, if he had the time, he'd call you back.

'God, Luna, I just got back to a city with telephones. I called in for my messages. I couldn't believe it. Jesus, shot. How are you? What the hell happened?'

'I'm fine, Dad. Where are you?'

41

'Bolivia. La Paz. Incredible discoveries, sweetheart. I spent three months with a tribe that speaks nothing but original Altiplano. They've managed to avoid any contact with the mainstream population by moving up and down the river. They believe that the river itself is God. Women menstruate in the water. Pregnant women sit in the shallow bank to give birth. The elderly and the sick drown themselves so they may return the water in their bodies to God, who in turn returns it to the tribe. Incredible stuff.'

'Sounds fascinating.'

He cleared his throat uncomfortably, as if realizing this wasn't the time or circumstances to be going on about Bolivian women's placentas floating downstream. 'Well, you know me, sweetheart,' he said quietly. 'I get carried away sometimes.'

Dad had quit NASA the day after Neil Armstrong stepped onto the moon. I think he was disappointed by what they'd found there, which was pretty much what they'd expected to find. The predictable in people or in nature irritated him. NASA tried to keep him, offering him more money and a significant promotion. Alan Shepherd and John Glenn both called, asking him to reconsider. But he refused. Dad was looking for something special and he suddenly realized he wouldn't find it in outer space.

One day he gathered Mom and me into the kitchen. On the kitchen table was my old metal globe, the one with the dent in Spain where I threw my shoe when I got grounded back in third grade for beating up Kathy Hodges, the wimpy little bitch from next door. Dad reached over and spun the globe. It squeaked and wobbled and I remember wondering if the planet squeaked and wobbled that much when it turned. Maybe that's what thunder was. I got very excited thinking I may have discovered some new scientific theory, but then Dad started talking and I forgot my idea.

'This is my new job, ladies,' he said.

'Repairing globes?' Mom said with a smile.

42

Dad grinned back. He was in an exceptionally good mood and that made me happy too. Since I didn't really have a clue to what he did at NASA, the fact that he'd quit didn't really mean much to me. Mom didn't give any indication that she was worried either, so I looked at this whole thing as if Dad were just changing schools.

'This is the plan,' Dad said. 'I've decided to become an anthropologist.' He looked at me with a big smile. 'That means I study people, Luna. People from all over the world.'

'Not that again, Ben,' Mom said, not really annoyed.

'You know I've always been interested. The timing is perfect.'

Mom gave the globe a little spin. 'Anybody going to pay you to do this?'

Dad winked at me. 'As a matter of fact . . .'

Somehow Dad had gotten an assignment to go to someplace in Africa where a warrior tribe from the mountains was working on a crude pair of wings made from water buffalo hide stretched over elephant bones, hoping to use them to swoop down and kill their enemy across the river. Some magazine thought it would be ironic to have Dad go there and give his space-age perspective. He went and the article was successful. Other assignments followed. Dad studied on his own, reading Darwin to Thomas Henry, Huxley to Ashley Montagu, always with a book in his hand and an amazed expression on his face.

He became his own astronaut, launching himself into the remote corners of the planet, doing his own moonwalk along the Amazon. I think Mom played along because she thought he would burn himself out after a short while. Or maybe she really thought it was a good idea and was as excited as he was about changing our lives. I was only ten at the time and the only real difference to my life was that now Daddy went off to work in jungles and deserts instead of Houston. When he'd worked for NASA he'd taken a lot of trips, so it wasn't as if he was really gone any longer than before. But now when he returned he was tanned and his presents were something carved out of foul-smelling roots by barefoot natives instead of something with batteries bought in an airport gift shop.

That was twenty years ago. He'd been an anthropologist longer than he'd been a rocket scientist, but I still thought of him as the space physicist on a leave of absence, like a defrocked priest or something.

'What does the doctor say?' he asked.

'That I still have a heart.'

'Then you're going to be fine?'

'Yes, Dad. Good as new.'

'Robby knows what to do, right? How to take care of you?'

Nurse Glover steered a wheelchair through the door and parked it next to me. I made a face at it. She mouthed, *regulations*. I nodded.

'Dad,' I said, 'Robby and I are getting a divorce.'

'Because of this? That son of a bitch!'

'No, Dad, not because of this. We've been working out the details for a few months now.'

'Jesus, Luna.' He was silent for a while. 'You want me to come there, honey? I could be there by tonight or tomorrow morning.'

He would come if I asked. But I didn't want to have to ask. And, to be fair, I didn't know what I'd do with him if he did come. We were neither close nor distant, more like people who'd survived some great natural disaster who hold annual reunions.

'I'm okay, Dad. I just want to get back into the swing of things. Get back to teaching. Finish my degree.'

'How goes the hunt for the elusive job?' he asked.

'The job has gone from elusive to endangered. I'm sending out another fifty résumés before I declare it extinct.'

'Don't give up, honey. You can't give up.'

Sure, I can, I wanted to say. It's easy. Just ask the Bat-Faced Girl.

'Um, sweetheart,' he said, his voice hesitant. 'One thing.'

'What?'

'Uh, well, this isn't the best time, but it never is, we talk so seldom.'

'What, Dad?'

'I got married.'

'What?' Dad never talked about women, never seemed to be interested in them after Mom died. Widows and divorcees called for him incessantly. On occasion I'd even tried to arrange a date for him. But he always refused. This had to be one hell of a woman. 'Jesus, Dad, married.'

'Yeah, I know. I want you to meet her.'

'Sure. Is she in Houston?'

'No. She's down here with me.'

Great, another globe-spinning anthropologist putting a microscope to the natives. 'When are you two coming back so I can meet dear ole stepmum?'

'I'm not sure, honey.'

Pause.

'You see, I still have to teach her English.'

Throat clearing.

'I'm the first white man she's ever seen.'

'Jesus, Dad.'

'She has a very important job in her tribe. Very important.' His voice became animated again, the voice of Thomas Edison when the damn light bulb finally worked. Or Wren when she made me pull over that last night. 'The tribal elders believe that a little viper venom mixed with the semen of the tayra—that's a huge, extremely vicious weasel—produces a potion that keeps them forever virile. It's her job to milk the semen from the weasel and the venom from the viper. Extraordinary stuff, really.'

'Excuse me, Dad, you mean she jacks off weasels to make a sperm milkshake for these old farts so they can keep their withered peckers up?'

'In essence. Of course, it's easy to make fun from the comfort of the land where everyone thinks what the Nielsen families think. These people take this very seriously.

45

Hers is a very important position in the tribe. Very respected. She has three servants of her own.'

'Hey, I'm not making fun. At least she has a job, that's more than I have. I can't wait to see the home movies of stepmum hard at work.'

Nurse Glover tapped her watch in a friendly way and nodded at the wheelchair. I held up a finger to indicate one minute. I didn't really have anything more to say anyway. I was just goading him now and there wasn't really any satisfaction in it. Dad was being as predictable as the moon. Before Mom had died we'd been a fairly close family, even with Dad gone for months at a time. When he was home, we did everything together. Mom's exuberance held us together. When she died, he stayed with me for a year, but we hardly spoke. Finally he left me with his sister, Aunt Lydia. After that, he was gone for longer and longer periods of time. What did I expect from him now? To jet home to be by my side, watch TV with me at night while I graded freshman compositions on the pros and cons of the death penalty? Dad was looking for answers as far away as he could get from his own past.

'Actually,' Dad explained, 'I'm not permitted to photograph her until she goes through the Ceremony of the River next month. After that, it will be okay because her soul will be known by the river and can no longer be stolen by the camera.'

'Ceremony of the River? Sounds impressive. She becomes chief of the tribe or something?'

'No, it's the same ceremony all tribal men and women go through.' More throat clearing. 'When they turn fifteen.'

3

'Come in. Come in. Come in. Come in.'

I entered his office. 'Relax, Theo, I'm in already.'

'Sit, sit, sitsitsitsit.' Theo gestured grandly at the red leather wingback chair across from his desk. The brass studs lining the chair glinted in the fluorescent light like an airport runway at night. I shuffled toward the chair. Even after a week out of the hospital, a samba shuffle was the best I could manage.

'It's you,' he said with a boisterous tone. 'Really you.' He paced behind his desk until I had gingerly lowered myself into the chair. He watched me with barely concealed alarm, tugging at his gray, manicured beard. When I was finally seated, he dropped into his own chair. 'For God's sake, Luna, sit back and relax. Relax already.'

'Actually, Theo, I can't sit back. I have a bullet hole in my back.'

'My God, really?' He bounced forward in his chair, yanking on his beard so frantically I thought he might tear chunks out. 'I'd heard it was just the one wound.' He touched his own chest. 'How insensitive. I'm frightfully sorry. Sit any way you want, Luna. I'm serious. Relax however suits you.'

'You relax, Theo. I'm fine. Really. In fact, if I stand naked in a stiff breeze, the hole through my chest can whistle a perfect C sharp.'

Theo shook his head. 'How do you do it, Luna? How do you? How?'

'Just keep turning until the wind hits the opening like a Coke bottle.'

'You know what I mean. How do you keep your spirits up like this? You're so brave. Most women—hell, most men—would have curled up into a quivering ball of phlegm.'

'Phlegm, Theo?' I laughed.

'You know what I mean. I mean, I would have expected this kind of bravado from Wren, she was . . .' He gestured, indicating Wren was something unexplainable. 'But you, you're so . . . My God, how do you do it?'

'Drugs help.'

He forced a laugh. 'I know you're kidding, Luna. But around here, a university and all, we have to be careful about even joking about drugs. Even the offhand remark, the casual bon mot, can be misunderstood, misinterpreted.' He webbed his fingers together and wiggled them back and forth, I think to show how remarks get misinterpreted.

'I'm talking about prescription drugs, Theo.'

'Of course you are. I understand that. But someone passing by, a young student maybe, they overhear a fragment, they don't know the whole story. They tell their parents. Pretty soon I'm ass-deep in religious fundamentalists and undercover narcs.'

Theo wasn't just being paranoid. Three tenured members of the faculty had been arrested this year for drug possession. Two of them had been turned in by their own students. The third drove his car through his ex-wife's backyard Halloween party. The publicity had hurt campus enrollment.

'I'm sorry, Theo.'

He nodded relief. He stood up and paced around his office as if to measure what he had to lose in the event of a narcotics bust: hundreds of books about composition (one of which he wrote and we were required to use in all the composition courses), a facsimile edition of T. S.

Eliot's *The Wasteland* with notes by Ezra Pound, etchings by Balding Grien, a brass-studded red leather chair.

Dr. Theodore Bentley, fifty-eight, had been Dean of Instruction for the English Department Composition Program for eighteen years. He was a fussy little man who seemed to agonize over everything. He ran the thirty-three sections of freshman composition, all taught by graduate students, with efficiency if not imagination. To him, the teaching of composition was merely a matter of following routine, similar to filling in a crossword puzzle. Although he was born in Sioux City, Iowa, he had cultivated a sophisticated European look, dark suits and vests, cuff links, even affecting a slight British accent at times. When he got drunk or flustered, he quoted T. S. Eliot a lot. Thursday through Sunday evenings he moonlighted as a head waiter at a fancy French restaurant. He claimed it relaxed him and helped keep his ego in perspective. Plus, he made more money than as a full professor. His wife, Casey, was a boxy little woman with giant breasts who worked for campus security. She wore a snappy uniform and drove one of those golf carts, handing out parking tickets.

I watched Theo pace and tried to imagine him making love to his wife. I pictured him in his waiter's tuxedo, her in her starched blue uniform. That's as far as I could get without laughing.

He sat back down and looked at me. His gray eyes drifted to my breast. Beneath my sweater, I was wearing a regular bra with a hole scissored in as not to rub against the bandage. Still, everyone who knew about the shooting couldn't help but stare at my wounded breast the way people are compelled to pat a pregnant woman's belly. Perhaps they thought my breast should be smaller, as if part of it had been shot away. It made me self-conscious.

'They're still there, Theo,' I said.

'What?' He looked up. 'What? Of course they are. Of course.' He shuffled some papers on his desk, absently transferred a few file folders from basket to basket. 'Of course they are. I didn't mean anything. Was I staring? I didn't mean to stare.'

'I know you didn't, Theo.' I shifted in the chair. It was very uncomfortable to sit this straight. 'Look, I just dropped by to let you know I'm ready to pick up my class again.'

'So soon?'

'The sooner the better. I just want to get back to my class, finish the semester out. The doctor says I can start back on Monday.'

'Monday?' He frowned.

'Sure, what's wrong with Monday?'

'Monday.' He stood up and paced again, twisting a hunk of beard into a point.

'What's the problem, Theo? It is my class. I've only missed two weeks. Christ, my students miss more than that during ski season.'

'Monday,' he said, straightening an etching on the wall. 'I don't know. Monday.'

'Yes, Monday.'

He stopped pacing and sat back down in his chair. The walk seemed to have exhausted him. His face was gray and stern, like a head waiter's. 'Can't do it, Luna. I'm sorry.'

'What are you talking about? It's my class.'

'Well, technically, it's the university's class. You are assigned to teach it. Now we have someone else teaching it. I can't see that the students would benefit any to have their classroom dynamics disrupted again. We're almost at the end of the semester anyway.'

'What are you talking about?' My breathing became labored. Each inhaled breath felt as if the air were leaking out of my bullet holes before it had a chance to reach my heart. I tried to breathe deeper.

'Are you all right, Luna?' Theo asked.

'Yes, I'm fine. Just tell me what the hell is going on?'

'Of course, you will be encouraged to complete your

50

degree. If you need an extension of time to complete your thesis, I've been assured there will be no problem in getting one. And don't worry about the money. You will remain on the payroll as a teaching assistant until the end of the semester. So money is no problem.'

'I want to teach, Theo. That's what I do. That's what I'm applying to do after I leave here. It's why I came here.' The last part wasn't strictly true, but I didn't care about truth anymore.

'And you'll make a wonderful teacher, Luna. Wonderful.' He leaned back in his chair with a sigh. His face lapsed. His head waiter's expression was gone. Now he looked like an old man with financial worries. 'Luna, the circumstances of your accident are such that the university has to weather a whole new storm of controversy. A university employee shoots two university students, who are also employees. You can imagine the public-relations nightmare. If you were a parent, would you risk sending your child here?'

'I'm the victim here, Theo, not the criminal.'

'I know, I know. But just your appearance in the classroom is unnerving to some. And we know that drugs were found on the premises.'

'A couple joints, Theo. And I wasn't smoking any. Ask the cops, they did tests.'

'I know you weren't. But you were there. We're talking about appearances. The university has to appear as if they are taking things under control. Bottom line, we think it's better if you stay away from the classroom, except as a student.'

I wondered how Wren would have handled this. Because I knew that by the time Wren left this office she would not only have gotten her class back, she would have Theo apologizing. She would have used logic, she would have used emotion, she would have used threats. I could do that. But it wasn't just what she would have said, it was how. It was how she did things. That's what made her Wren.

51

'Relax, Luna. Go home and rest. Concentrate on completing your degree.'

I slowly stood. My lower back hurt from sitting so upright. My butt was numb. My breast ached as if I were nursing a sharp-toothed ferret. I probably looked like an old lady walking stiffly toward the door. I could see the pity on Theo's face and that made me even sadder.

'T.S. said something once,' Theo said. 'T.S. said: "Teach us to care and not to care/Teach us to sit still." Remember that, Luna.'

Now I was angry. I wished I could make my head spin like the little girl in *The Exorcist* and say what she said: 'Your mother sucks cocks in hell.' But I merely straightened myself into an erect pose of indignant pride and marched out of his office. I hoped I looked impressive, because inside, inside where Esther's bullet had tunneled through my organs, somewhere inside there I was curling up into a quivering ball of phlegm.

4

I poured a second helping of Cheerios and my wedding ring tumbled out of the box along with the toasted Os and clanked into the bowl. I poured milk over the cereal and the ring was lifted afloat by the Cheerios like tiny brown inner tubes. The ring was just a band of gold. No inscription. No family heirloom. The only distinguishing mark was a deep scratch from the time Robby had tried to teach me to skateboard on a steep hill and I fell, scraping all the skin off my palms and gouging the ring.

I ate around the ring.

I was standing at the ironing board, eating cereal for lunch while scissoring another bra. I'd had cereal for breakfast too, and it looked like I had just enough to get through dinner if I didn't get sloppy with the milk. I'd outlined the prospective hole in the bra cup with a black pen, then started cutting. The bra I'd been wearing for the past few days had bloodstains around the edges of the cutout. All the frayed threads were red and it looked like somebody's bleeding scalp hanging from my boob. There was nothing medically wrong, my doctor assured me, spot bleeding was perfectly normal. But it unnerved me to see blood on my bra.

The television was on and I listened to *Green Acres*. Occasionally, when the laugh track swelled, I'd look up from my surgical procedure to see what was so funny, but by then I'd missed it and all I'd see was Eddie Arnold looking perplexed at Eva Gabor in a nightgown.

I was wearing neon-green shorts but nothing else. My

53

bare breasts had enormous goose bumps from the fan on the table and the way they were all bunched together in a circle around my nipple kind of reminded me of the Bolivian natives my father was studying. I imagined them all gathered around to worship at the sacred altar of the Great River Nipple. I searched through the crowd of goose bumps for Dad's wife, but I couldn't find one that looked like a fourteen-year-old girl jerking off a weasel.

I did find one that looked a little like Eva Gabor, though.

The bandage on my breast was smaller now, the size of four postage stamps, but there was a yellowish crust on the gauze that the doctor explained meant it was healing. Perfectly normal. The wound on my back itched like crazy. At times I would back up to the refrigerator door and scratch it on the handle like a dog.

The doorbell chimed.

I spooned up another glob of cereal, careful not to touch the wedding ring. The Cheerios were starting to get soggy.

Robby had given me the ring ten years ago. We'd been living together off campus then. I'd come home late one night from my waitressing job at the Haus of Pies. We'd been pushing rhubarb all night because Mr. Braun, the owner, had gotten a good deal on rhubarb and made three times as many pies as usual. He and Mrs. Braun snapped at each other all evening in German because no one wanted rhubarb. Finally Mr. Braun blasted his wife with a tirade of German gargling and stormed out, leaving us shorthanded to clean up. Mrs. Braun, in tears, gave Tina and me each a rhubarb pie to take home.

Robby met me at the door, naked except for his father's white apron. He'd had a scraggly little beard then that made him look like a failed poet with Marxist sympathies. We hugged and my hand slid down the small of his back to that crevice at the top of his buttocks, which, as always, was a little moist from sweat. With a courtly flourish, he'd guided me to the kitchen where he announced, 'Dinner is served.' I expected another one of his gourmet feasts, delicate sauces over tender slices of exotically spiced fowl. Certainly our tiny table was set for something special: white tablecloth that used to be one of our bedsheets, fancy silverware he'd borrowed from a neighbour, candles stuck in beer bottles.

He seated me, snapped open a cloth napkin (once our pillowcase), and fluttered it onto my lap.

He handed me the box of Trix.

'What's this?' I said.

'Dinner, madam. Enjoy.'

I laughed, playing along. As long as it wasn't rhubarb. The box was new, so I tore open the top flap and poured the cereal. The colored balls clattered festively into the bowl. Then the clunk of the ring. The gold winked candle-light.

Robby proposed a toast: 'Let's get married and fuck until we can't walk and then get good jobs that make money but show a social conscience and then have children and raise them to be perfect and then buy a house that will become a gathering place for all the best and brightest of our generation who will sit in our living room and discuss theories of art while we're in the kitchen doing some gourmet fucking on the countertop making the world safe for democracy and prose poetry.'

'Why not?' I said, slipping on the ring.

So for the past two months, every time I opened a new box of cereal I tossed my wedding ring back inside, shook the box, and waited to discover it again and again. Like the precious prize it had been that first time. Back when I'd thought of the ring as a round key to a thick hand-carved door behind which was our bright and shining future.

Sometimes I'd thought of it as a homing device, if I ever got lost somewhere or even felt a little lost inside, I could show my ring and say, 'Look, this is where I belong. Take me there. I'm expected there.'

Not now. Now I belonged in front of a wobbly ironing

board, wolfing Cheerios and cutting up bras. I hoped the repetition of this ring-in-the-box ritual would eventually de-romanticize Robby's gesture and help me miss him less. So far it hadn't worked.

My friends all gave me mathematical formulas for when I'd feel better. Wren had said it took one month per each year that you were together. Esther had put it at one year for every six years you were together. Others had more elaborate equations, factoring in causes for the split up or averaging the age of the couple, how much stuff you had accumulated, were there pets, venereal diseases, pension funds. *Cosmo* said falling in love again immediately reduced 'down time' significantly. *Self* said to take up low-impact aerobics or dog breeding. The physicists of heartbreak. I imagined the experts in their white lab coats, scribbling twenty-digit numbers on a blackboard, trying to figure out why my stomach always felt as if I'd swallowed a cocktail of Drāno and thumbtacks. And tell me, Professor, why do I still smell Robby on my skin?

The doorbell chimed again, followed by heavy knocking.

I chewed another mouthful of soggy cereal and continued cutting the perfect hole in my bra. I hadn't noticed before, but I was making scalloped edges. I wondered if this was how Fredrick's of Hollywood got started.

Wren had discovered my wedding-ring ceremony once when she'd come over after an all-night paper-writing session and ate the whole damn box of cereal, nearly chipping a tooth on my ring. I'd expected some sort of big-sister speech, some condemning look. A lecture about sisterhood or womanhood or wimphood. About standing on our own feet, codependent no more. Instead she'd just shuffleboarded the ring across the kitchen table to me and sighed, 'With love, dear Luna, whatever works.'

I ate the cereal around the ring until the Cheerios were all gone. The ring lay at the bottom of the bowl in a shallow puddle of milk. I spooned the ring up and put it in my mouth. I had never done that before. It had no flavor.

That surprised me. I'd expected some metallic taste, like blood or pennies. I thought about swallowing it, letting it travel through my colon for a couple days to see the sights and pop out the other end. That should de-romanticize the little fucker forever.

The doorbell rang in an impatient code. 'Ms. Devon? Hey, Ms. Devon.'

I plucked the ring from my mouth and tossed it back into the Cheerios box. I shook the box and stashed it in the cupboard next to the potato chips. My movements were slow and deliberate, as if I had all day to do the simplest task. I wasn't in shock or any physical pain, it was just that my life had been reduced to only one goal now: to finish my Thomas Pynchon paper thereby securing my master's degree. I had plenty of free time now. I had no composition class to teach, so I had no papers to grade, no office to go to. I'd returned my petitions to Amnesty International with only two signatures, mine and Nurse Glover's. There were no more teaching jobs to apply for, all I could do now was sit back and wait to see where my life would go, like shooting down churning rapids holding onto a sponge.

The two people I knew best were Wren and Esther, so I wasn't burdened with a lot of friends coming by trying to cheer me up. Robby and I had been pretty much a self-contained unit. We'd spent most of our free time alone. Occasionally we would double date with another couple, but that would be the last I'd see of them until the next time Robby arranged another outing. I didn't mind this lack of socializing; I didn't really want people to know how much harder than everyone else I had to work just to keep up. My thesis on Thomas Pynchon was taking longer than it should, most of the other students were almost finished. Why had I picked a reclusive cult writer who never appeared in public and who some thought didn't even really exist? Still, there were over ninety doctoral dissertations and thirty books about the guy. *They* did exist, so did the novels, so did my deadline. Standing there now, I couldn't remember one literary thing about the man. What were his themes, his world vision? All I could remember was a rumor about the day Norman Mailer had somehow bullied Pynchon's secret address from someone and gone over to visit the hermit writer. The story has it that Pynchon saw Mailer coming down the street and leapt out of a two-story window and ran away rather than meet his fellow author.

'Come on, Ms. Devon,' the voice outside my door called. 'I know you're in there. It's me. It's Mark, Ms. Devon.'

Since the shooting, I'd followed the strict regimen of a novitiate. I attended my three graduate classes, took notes, and read thick novels no one but students read anymore. My classmates kept a cheerful remoteness, as if they feared my bad luck might rub off on them, maybe affect their grades. Robby called sometimes, but usually our words were out of sync with our feelings, like badly dubbed kung fu movies. Once he brought by a bag of groceries. We smoked a joint and discussed Emily Brontë. He kissed me on the cheek and left. All the air in the room seemed to leave with him.

'I'm not going away, Ms. Devon,' the voice outside my door continued.

Having no second-story window to leap from, I slipped into my customized bra and pulled on a baggy gray sweatshirt. There was no witty saying or clever drawing on my sweatshirt. All my sweatshirts and T-shirts were blank.

More thumping on the door. 'I'm totally serious. I'm not leaving till you see me, Ms. Devon.'

I opened the door. 'I see you, Mark. Happy?'

Mark smiled and leaned his bicycle against the building. He looked down at my bare legs. 'I've never seen you in shorts before.'

'I don't usually wear them to teach.'

'You should. It would motivate us more. The guys, anyway.'

He edged past me into my apartment. I stayed in the

doorway, holding the door open. He was wearing some kind of pine-scented cologne that stung my eyes. As he passed, I sniffed the sweet scent of breath mints too. His curly black hair was damp from biking. 'I've been knocking here for twenty minutes. Did that shooting affect your hearing or something?'

'What'd you say?'

He snorted. 'Very funny.'

I didn't mind seeing Mark. He was the smartest student in my comp class. Smart enough not to need me and cocky enough to know it. I had a feeling most teachers would feel that way about Mark. College was a formality for someone like him, a place to pick up a diploma for what he already knew or would learn on his own. He reminded me of Wren. Also, I think a part of me was glad he was here. I wanted him to do a Good-bye, Ms. Chips routine that would bring me back some of my lost enthusiasm. If anyone could, it would be a perfect student like Mark.

'This is nice,' he said, looking around. He walked about the living room, touching things briefly. He had a worn leather backpack slung over one shoulder. A silver bicycle clip pinned the right cuff of his jeans. 'It's not how I pictured your place, though. I figured you more for, I don't know, a cactus in every corner and Navaho blankets on the walls. That whole Southwest thing.'

'Why are you here, Mark?'

'To bring you your mail.' He reached into his backpack and handed me three envelopes. One was another bill from the Modern Language Association that I'd only joined to get their job list, two were from schools I had applied to for a teaching position. 'I saw them in your mailbox at school and thought I'd save you a trip.'

'Thanks,' I said. I put the envelopes behind my back. I didn't want him here when I opened them.

'Go ahead, open them,' he said, smoothing down a cowlick at the crown of his head.

'It can wait,' I said.

He picked up the glass unicorn Robby gave me when

59

I'd acted in *The Glass Menagerie* in our junior year. Robby had stolen it from the set after the last performance. Mark pointed the unicorn's horn at my letters. 'Open them. I know you're dying to.'

'Fine,' I said. I went through my usual ritual, hefting the envelopes, trying to figure out if an acceptance weighed more than a rejection. As if they used more words, more ink, thicker paper. While Mark wandered about stroking my furniture, I tore open the envelopes.

Dear Ms. Devon . . . Thank you . . . impressive application . . . sorry to say . . . keep on file . . . sincerely.

They read very much like my divorce letter.

'I could've told you,' Mark said, plopping down on the sofa. 'They don't write when they're interested. They call.'

'I know that,' I said. I did, too, but I figured that maybe they tried to call but somehow couldn't reach me, so they sent a letter. That could happen.

'My dad's a dean,' Mark said. 'Chemistry Department back in Ohio. He sends out a lot of those letters.'

I looked over at Mark. He was staring at my legs again.

'What do you want, Mark? I have to get ready for class soon.'

'No, you don't,' he said with annoying confidence. 'Your Brit Lit class isn't until three. And your Conrad class and the Fiction Workshop meet tomorrow.'

'Quite the little spy, aren't you?'

'You got anything to drink? I'm dying.'

I went into the kitchen and brought back a can of Diet Dr Pepper. I handed it to him and he smiled up at me. He was a charming kid, eighteen going on forty. His body was as lanky and hard as knotted rope. His face was angular, reminding me of home plate in a baseball diamond. In about ten years, when he had grown into his features, he would be quite handsome. Women would talk about him longingly.

I ignored his flirting. I didn't have the energy to deal with the moral and physical complexities of hopping into

60

bed with him. He had a hard-on bulging at the crotch of his jeans, which he tried to cover by tugging his leather jacket down. Back when I was still living with Robby, I'd had an erotic dream about Mark, I can't remember what. I'd awakened slick with sweat and discovered I'd been rubbing myself against Robby's leg. I'd looked up at him and was embarrassed to see he was awake, watching. He rolled me onto my back and we made love. That was the last time we did it. Since the split-up, I'd stopped having erotic dreams the same way I stopped having periods when I went on the pill. Now I could hardly remember why I'd liked sex so much before.

'You think my bike's okay out there?' Mark asked.

'No,' I said.

He laughed. 'You're funny, Ms. Devon.'

'I crack me up. Now, what can I do for you?'

He wedged the Dr Pepper can between his thighs. He leaned forward, screwing his face into a serious expression. 'When you coming back, Ms. Devon?'

'I'm not, Mark. I'm convalescing. Didn't your new teacher tell you that?'

He shrugged, as if nothing the new teacher said could be trusted. 'How's your wound?'

'Better.'

He stared at my breasts as if he could see through my sweatshirt and bandage and was staring at the crusted hole itself. 'Can I see it? I've never seen a gunshot wound.'

I laughed. 'I don't think so, Mark. You'll just have to wait until you're old enough for a gunshot wound of your own.'

He nodded and sat back, pressing into the sofa. 'I've seen knife wounds,' he said. 'They don't look like much. Some guy at AA had one. Right here, across the gut.'

'You're in AA, Mark?'

'Sure. Me, my dad, my stepmom. It's a family affair. Even my little sister. She's fifteen. At least she's smart enough to get drunk on the cheap stuff. I guess we all got that boozer's gene.'

'I didn't know about that. About your family.'

'You don't know shit, Ms. Devon.' This was the first time Mark had ever said anything harsh to me. He hunched over a little and looked away from me.

I didn't know what to say, so I didn't say anything. My back wound was itching. I rubbed it against the back of the chair.

Mark picked up the heavy glass stein from the end table. My name was engraved across the glass. I had won the stein in a twelfth grade tri-state track meet. For three years my fiercest rivalry had been with Stephanie Cutter. She'd beat me in the long jump at every meet. She always took first place, I always took second place. Finally, at the last meet of our final season, she got sick fifteen minutes before the jump. We watched her on hands and knees in the middle of the field puking some foul goop. Turned out she had food poisoning. I won easily. I didn't keep the trophy around as a reminder of my triumph, but rather to remember that the only time I ever took first place in anything was because someone else forfeited. These life lessons help you keep a healthy perspective.

After a minute Mark put the engraved stein back and looked at me with a sly smile. 'I'm writing this paper,' he said, 'for Mr. Conner's Shakespeare class. He's such a fucking weasel, this paper's gonna blow his weasel brain away.'

Jack Conner was a fucking weasel. He was up for tenure this year and had begun a shameless campaign of glad-handing, party-throwing, and all around ass-kissing. He also spied on members of the tenure committee. Once I saw him in the faculty mail room, sneaking peeks at Dr. Loeb's mail. Sitting here now in my cutaway bra, the taste of Cheerios and sour milk in my mouth, it was hard to imagine that I'd been part of that department. It seemed as remote as my old summer camp days. I tried to remember what my shabby office looked like, the view through the grimy window. I couldn't.

'Listen, Ms. Devon,' Mark said with his usual enthusiasm. 'Listen to this. This is what I'm doing my paper on, you'll flip out. You know Guam, right? The island.'

'I've heard of it.'

He swigged his Dr Pepper. 'Well, just a few years ago there were six endemic species of bird in Guam. Endemic means these birds are found only on Guam.'

'I know what endemic means, Mark.'

'Right, sorry. Anyway, now the bridled white-eye and the Guam broadbill are extinct. Probably so is the rufous-fronted fantail. That leaves only three species left.'

'This all has something to do with Shakespeare?'

'Yeah, we're doing *King Lear*.'

'The rufous-fronted fantail plays Lear?'

'Trust me, this will all make sense. Meanwhile, back on Guam: these other three species are hanging on to existence by the tip of their beaks. Everyone's walking around scratching their heads, but nobody could figure out why this sudden decline in the bird population. Then in 1982, this graduate student named Julie Savidge goes there and finds the answer.' He clapped his hands together, startling me. '*Boiga irregularis*.'

'Sounds like jungle constipation.'

'It's a snake. She cut a bunch of them open and kept finding birds and birds' eggs. Thing is, this snake is not native to Guam. They figure it arrived on the island during World War II, probably imported to eat rodents. For a long time they called it the "Philippine rat snake", which made people think it was benevolent. But it's not a rat snake, it's a bird-eating tree snake and it's practically wiped out the whole fucking bird population.'

I was losing concentration, still trying to conjure the view from my office window. Was it the student bookstore that I stared at every day or the infirmary? How many mountains sliced the western horizon of Oregon? Didn't Wren and I used to feed sunflower seeds to pigeons on that sooty window ledge?

'Ms. Devon?'

63

I refocused on Mark. 'What do birds and snakes have to do with *King Lear*?'

'I'm getting to it.' Mark finished the rest of his Dr Pepper and balanced the can on the sofa arm. 'This snake was introduced into an environment where it had no natural predators and in which its prey had never learned to defend itself against it. I mean, the livin' was easy, man. Birds were jumpin' and the cotton was high. Fat City for the *boiga irregularis*.'

'God, you can be annoying, Mark. Did you know that? Are you aware of this irritating trait?'

'Yeah.' He smiled and I had to smile too. I suppose it was kind of flattering that of all the truly brilliant people around the department he could be telling this stuff to, he chose me instead. It was working, I was starting to feel something again, a positive attitude toward my career. Sure, why not me.

'I'm listening,' I said.

'They got something like three million of these snakes on this tiny island. They get in the electrical wiring and cause outages all the time. Anyway, they started this program to airlift the birds somewhere else, raise them, then bring them back when they've lowered the snake population.'

'Sounds like a lot of trouble,' I said. But I was encouraged to know that people somewhere were willing to bother. I probably wouldn't have.

'Thing is, Ms. Devon. Even if they succeed, they still lose. Islands are where species become extinct. That's why all those evolutionary biologist guys like Darwin and Wallace and Dammerman all go to these dinky islands to study life. Listen to this, I got this great quote.' He dug into his leather backpack, rifling the papers and notebooks, finally pulling out a book called *The Flight of the Iguana*. He opened it to a marked page and began reading: '"Small islands especially are the black holes to oblivion. Speciation proceeds more rapidly . . . The luckiest of the pioneers adapt to their new habitats. They colonize.

They specialize. They succeed. They become more sedentary than they were when they arrived—because the most restless individuals among them are constantly taking their genes elsewhere, flying off to escape or else to die trying. The others stay and stay."' He closed the book with a thump and whacked it against his thigh. 'Get it?'

I didn't get it. What's more, I suddenly realized I didn't care. I didn't care about Mark's paper, about King Lear or the fair Cordelia. Worst of all, I didn't care about teaching. I'd been moping around for days because of my lost class, but right now it was clear to me that I didn't really care if I ever went back into another classroom again. I tried to remember the faces of the students in my class, picture them all staring up at me as I explained how to write a footnote. Nothing came. I closed my eyes. I tried to picture Mark's face. I couldn't.

My chest started to ache and churn, as if there were something foreign inside. I knew the bullet had passed through me, but for that moment I swore I could feel it inside, feel its smooth head twisting toward the surface. There was thick scab beneath the bandage, but it seemed to be disintegrating now. It felt as if it would erupt and spew out the bullet. I tried to imagine the look on Mark's face when the bloody bullet spit through my sweatshirt and plopped onto the carpet. Work that into your next paper, buddy boy, I'd say with a wink.

'You okay, Ms. Devon?' Mark asked, leaning forward with a look of concern. 'You need some medicine or something?'

'I'm fine, Mark,' I said. 'Go on, go on. Tell me how Sheriff Lear cleans up Guam City.'

'It's that whole tragedy thing. The tragic hero striving to become godlike by avoiding his fate. That's King Lear's arrogance. But it's the same with us and those birds. We try to save them, only to return them to an island. It's the island that dooms them to extinction, just as we are all living on this planet, an island in space. And just as we are all doomed to extinction. But we strive to fight it anyway,

65

despite knowing it is futile. Those birds will become extinct eventually, why not now? That's what I'm getting at. You see?'

I stood up. The activity in my chest seemed to have calmed down. I didn't feel the phantom bullet anymore. I walked toward the front door and opened it. 'Thanks for dropping by to cheer me up.'

'I know it's still a little rough,' he said, also standing. 'But what do you think of the thesis, the general concept?'

'It's good. Write it. I'm sure you'll get an A.'

He shook his head impatiently. 'I *know* I'll get an A. That's not what I'm asking.'

I looked over at the TV. *People's Court* was on. An old woman stood at the defendant's table gripping a walker. She had a green and red parrot perched on the walker. Judge Wopner asked her peevishly why she brought the bird to court. She snapped right back at him that the lady who called her to be on the show told her to bring the bird, that's why. I turned back to Mark. 'I don't know what you want to hear, Mark. Just do it. It sounds good to me. Very insightful.'

'Yeah.' He made a face and I could see he was disappointed. 'Hey, you see my new tattoo yet?'

'Jesus, Mark, not a tattoo.'

He took off his leather jacket and pushed up his T-shirt sleeve. He flexed his arm muscle. High up near his shoulder was a blue outline of a little girl, barefoot, peeking into a dark window. She had an old-fashioned dress on and a flower in her hair. The flower was colored with red ink. Above this picture are the words, in red ink. VIOLENT FEMMES, arched over the girl like a rainbow. Beneath the picture are the words, in quotes: 'Words all fail the magic prize . . .'

'Very nice,' I said. 'I can see why you'd want that permanently carved into your body.'

'You don't get it, Ms. Devon. You ever listen to the Violent Femmes? "Let me go on like I blister in the sun . . ." You know that song?'

Suddenly I knew how Esther must have felt, people coming by, spilling their lives on her kitchen table, then taking off again. Leaving the residue of their plans and hopes and triumphs and defeats to hang in the air, cling to dust particles there. And Esther sitting there, waiting for sleep, her valuables hidden in the appliances, camouflaged against burglars. Yet, she was being invaded hourly by people who stole her sleep. Well, she was sleeping now. Slice open the belly of the *Boiga irregularis* and you'd find Esther there, softly snoring, dreaming.

'I don't know the group, Mark.'

'See? That's the point. You probably thought you were cool once, back when you were my age. Smoking dope and listening to the Rolling Stones. You probably thought you had it all figured out. I guess young people always think that. But then something happens, right? Somewhere along the line they slip into comas or something. Not me. I got this tattoo of their CD jacket so I'd never forget my values, what's really important. If I ever start to dweeb out, I just look at this . . .' He held up his arm closer to me. 'Then I remember what it's all about. Who I am.'

'Gee, Mark, you're right. If only I'd gotten that tattoo of Glenn Campbell's *Rhinestone Cowboy* album jacket when I had the chance.'

Mark's face tightened into anger. I had seen him tense and frustrated in class before, but never this angry countenance. He stepped toward me and I felt a twinge of fear. 'I read something else in this book, Ms. Devon. Something very interesting about rape.'

I took a step backward. 'You'd better go now, Mark. I'm tired.'

'Not yet,' he said. 'I want to tell you about bedbugs. How they fuck. It's very interesting.'

I looked around the room for a convenient weapon. Something, if need be, to bludgeon my best student's head into a bloody pulp. Funny how different your possessions look when you're judging them for their value as a weapon. Beauty loses its impact, everything is heft. Pynchon's thick novel, *V.*, was lying on the coffee table. A couple sharp raps across the temple with that might be enough to curb his sexual appetite. I took a step toward it, he cut me off.

'Here's how it works,' Mark said. 'This particular type of bedbug has a penis shaped like a dagger. He doesn't insert it into any vaginal opening. Instead, he just stabs her in the abdomen with it. I mean that literally. He punctures her with his dick. That's how they have sex. In fact, sometimes when one male is fucking another female like that, his dick stuck in her gut, another male will come up and stab the male doing the humping. Then his sperm replaces the first guy's and he can impregnate the female. Interesting, huh?'

'You should go, Mark.'

'They call it traumatic insemination. Neat phrase. Traumatic insemination. It's like the weirdest fucking thing I've ever heard of. I'm trying to work it into my Lear paper, but I don't know. They think the whole thing came about because the males used to secrete some kind of glue from their dicks after sex. They'd use this glue to seal up the female's vagina so no other guys could screw her after him. Like one of those, you know, chastity belts. Ground squirrels still do that, glue their females' twats shut. Anyway, that's why they figure the bedbugs evolved their dagger dicks.'

I didn't say anything. He stared at my face, looking for something. I guess he found it, because he smiled and backed away from me, satisfied.

He slipped into his jacket and backpack as he walked out the front door. I followed him. He straddled his bike and looked at me. I realized then that I would probably never see him again, that this might be the last time I ever saw someone who was my student.

'I'm glad you came by, Mark,' I said. 'Take care with—'

'Did you believe me?' he interrupted. He looked at me with a morose expression.

'What?'

'Did you believe me? Before.'

'When? About the bedbugs?'

'About being in AA. That stuff I told you about my family. My little sister and stuff.'

'Yes, I believed you. Of course I believed you.'

He shook his head sadly. 'You really don't know shit, Ms. Devon. From now on you'd better be real careful.'

He swung his bike around and pedaled off. He turned as he jumped the curb and waved, a big smile on his face. Like we were best friends.

I closed the door and walked to the bathroom for some Tylenol. I wrestled the cap off and swallowed three little tablets, washing them down with warm water from the faucet. I was still bent over drinking from the faucet when another knock at the door startled me. I jerked a little, banging my lip against the faucet. I tasted blood.

The doorbell rang this time.

'Fuck you, Mark,' I growled. 'Fuck you and fuck King Lear and fuck dagger-dicked bedbugs.' The mirror over the sink revealed a little nick out of my lip, a tiny flap of skin bent upward. I pressed the washcloth against it and the bleeding stopped immediately.

I marched back to the front door, the washcloth still pressed to my lip. It tasted faintly of soap and mildew. I yanked open the door ready to blast Mark. But, of course, it wasn't Mark.

'Ms. Devon?' the elegant woman asked. Her manners were as impeccable as her makeup. Her clothes were expensive but not exclusive. Her white gold bracelet would have supported me for six months. The only crack in this perfect picture was the redness of her eyes and the faint smell of brandy on her breath.

'Yes—' I nodded—'I'm Ms. Devon.'

She smiled with such relief in her eyes, as if admitting who I was had been a great act of human kindness. She held out her small pale hand. 'I'm Kate Lansing. Wren's mother. Have I come at a bad time?'

5

'You two are goddamn lucky. I'm serious. You don't know, you were this close to being arrested!' The manager shook her finger at us, wheezing as she entered the front door of Wren's apartment. She was a short woman with a thin face and skinny swizzle-stick legs, but carrying about 200 steel-belted pounds around her chest, stomach, and hips. A big brass ring of keys jangled in her hand.

'Hi, Mrs. Naughton,' I said. 'We're just cleaning up a little.'

Wren's mother and I were standing at the sink of the kitchenette in Wren's apartment washing the dishes from Wren's last meal so we could pack them. I was washing, Wren's mother was drying. Even though there were only a few dishes, Wren's mother had a dish towel tucked into her skirt as an apron. It made her look somehow scientific, like an archaeologist or a coroner.

From the crusted remains on the pot, the single blue ceramic bowl, the small salad plate, and the soup spoon, fork, and knife, I guessed Wren's final meal at home had been her favorite: tomato soup, grilled-cheese-with-tomatoes sandwich, and barbecue potato chips. For a moment, I felt like a clever detective having this knowledge, being able to piece together this information from the few crumbs that were left behind. Then I realized these were useless clues, they told us nothing valuable. Nothing we really needed to know.

'I'm telling you, I was about to call the goddamn cops,' Mrs. Naughton continued. 'I hear something up here, I

71

know nobody's home, I figure, Sally, don't be an idiot, call the goddamn cops, that's what you pay taxes for. I had the phone in my hand and I was actually dialing.' She cupped her left hand as if it held a phone. 'I'd punched nine and then one before I hung up and decided to come up here first, have a look-see. Lucky for you two I did. I mean, who knows what a nervous cop with a loaded gun might do. Jesus.' She held her hand to her ample bosom as if stilling a wildly thwacking heart. 'Of course, what would I have done if you'd really been burglars? I shoulda called the goddamn cops, not taken any chances. That's what they're paid for, right? Sometimes I'm so goddamn stupid.' She laughed and the sound caught me by surprise. It was so young and delicate coming out of that hefty middle-aged body.

'I should have told you we were coming, Mrs. Naughton,' I said, rinsing the last dish, a chipped soup bowl. 'I should've called. I'm sorry.'

Mrs. Naughton walked deeper into the apartment and looked around, shaking her head sadly. 'Best unit in the whole complex. Lots of sunlight. You could grow a goddamn jungle in here.' She yanked open the drapes and sunlight flashbulbed into the room to prove her point. 'I wish I had a hundred like her. My life would be perfect then.'

I wasn't sure if she was talking about Wren or the unit.

'Mrs. Naughton, this is Wren's mother, Mrs. Lansing.' I didn't know whether Kate wanted to be called Mrs. or Ms., but this didn't seem like the right time to wave any flags.

'Kate,' Wren's mom said, putting down the dish towel to shake Mrs. Naughton's hand.

'Kate? That's my name too. Well, my second middle name. Sally Mary Kate Naughton. Not Katherine, mind you, just Kate. My mother insisted on it. You a Katherine?'

'Caitlin, actually,' Kate said. 'Somewhere along the line it just became Kate.'

72

'I like Caitlin,' I said, mostly to be saying something. We were standing in Wren's apartment chattering away like scared kids in a graveyard. The more mundane the conversation, the better we should feel.

Wren's apartment. I had been here a couple hundred times. I'd slept over on occasion, chopped vegetables, scoured the toilet, studied Chaucer, listened to Wren play Paul Simon's *Graceland* over and over and over while she took elaborate notes on the lyrics for her thesis. I'd fed her grilled cheese and soup last month for two days when she had the flu. I had my own key, just as Wren had one to my place. I looked over at the white sofa and winced, remembering that bizarre night last month. I felt a flush spreading across my face just thinking about it and I turned away so Kate and Mrs. Naughton couldn't see my embarrassment.

I'd been separated from Robby for six weeks then, still in a near comatose depression, bitching about how I'd probably never have sex again, how I didn't even remember how to have sex, what sex felt like. Wren comforted me without babying me. We played gin rummy, listened to more Paul Simon (until Wren threw an M&M at the CD player and said: 'For Christ's sake, Paul, go to fucking Graceland already'), ate frozen pizza and chunky applesauce. She made me stay the night. I slept in her bed, she'd insisted on taking the sofa. In the middle of the night, something woke me. Faint sounds. Like Saran Wrap being unrolled. I looked at the clock, almost three in the morning. I zombied out to the living room to check on Wren, thinking maybe she'd fallen asleep with the TV on.

And there she was. Naked.

She was standing, bent over at the waist, her hands gripping the arm of the white sofa like the handlebars of a motorcycle. Behind her was some guy, his face a scribbled blotch of black hair and dark shadow. I couldn't see his face and I didn't recognize his body. His hands were folded around her hips, pulling and pushing, the two of them hammering into each other like it was bull wrestling at the rodeo. I watched his buttocks flex and lapse, flex and lapse, as he pummeled her. At one point, he jerked back and forth so frantically that his penis slipped out of her. They both groaned with disappointment. He quickly readjusted his condom, pulling it tighter the way a woman tugs her panty hose, then worked his semi-erect penis back into Wren. She reached down between her legs and cupped his balls in her hand. Oh yeah, he said, oh yeah oh yeah. He attacked her with renewed vigor. Watching their bodies grind, listening to the slap of his hips against her buttocks, smelling their thick aroma all made me a little weak. I felt like saying something rude to them, something like 'Is that sofa Scotchguarded?' But the way they were going they wouldn't have stopped for me or anything, then I would be there watching and they would know it and it would all be too perverse. Right now it was just an accident, an erotic accident. I shouldn't have kept watching, I guess, but I did, rubbing my grooved thumbnails against the hem of my T-shirt. Wren came first, Oh God, God, God yes. Then he came, Jesus, please, please, fuck yes.

When he pulled out of Wren, I saw his oily sweat dripping down her buttocks and the backs of her legs. Dozens of droplets sparkled up and down her legs and I thought of Paul Simon's 'Diamonds on the Soles of Her Shoes'. The man dropped to his knees and started licking the sweat from the backs of her thighs, moving higher. She laughed and wiggled her butt playfully.

I ducked back into the bedroom and quietly climbed into bed, trying not to disturb a single bed spring. I wanted very much to masturbate then, even slipping my fingers inside my panties and touching my clitoris tentatively. But I was afraid of making the bed squeak, then they would know what I was doing. I pulled my hand out of my panties and tucked it under my pillow. After a few minutes I heard the front door close and my bedroom door open. Wren walked into the bedroom. I pretended

74

to be asleep, my eyes pressed closed. She ignored my pretence and sat on the edge of the bed. I could smell the scent of sweat and semen and vaginal juices. This is how I imagined the Amazon jungle to smell after a tropical storm has uprooted a few trees.

'You said you forgot how to do it, forgot how it feels,' she said. 'Well, that's how to do it. And' —she paused and I knew she was smiling—'it feels *good*.' She stood up and walked out.

We never spoke about it. The next morning we had breakfast and talked more about her plans to start her own magazine. She slurped coffee and ate two English muffins smeared with jam.

But a few days later when Aaron Franzen asked me again to go to the poetry reading put on by the English Department every Wednesday at noon, I accepted. Nothing much came of it, a couple movies, some sloppy kissing, a little massaging of my breasts under my blouse but over my bra, and long talks afterwards about his thesis on Philip Roth's use of Israel as a symbol for the eros part of the libido. Still, it was a step in the right direction, thanks to Wren's unorthodox teaching methods. Hell, now she was even a better teacher than I.

'This place is so clean,' Mrs. Naughton marveled, clapping her hands together. 'If my daughter were half this clean I'd consider God's work on earth done.'

Kate smiled and nodded. That's pretty much all she'd been doing since she'd arrived at my apartment. Smiling and nodding. It was getting on my nerves. I kept waiting for some burst of emotion, accusation even. None came. She'd flown in this morning from Omaha to claim the body. She didn't like to fly, she'd told me. Her husband loved to fly, so had Wren. She'd already been by the morgue to identify Wren for the record. The body was being shipped back to Omaha. Now she wanted to pack up her daughter's belongings and ship them back too.

'Where's your husband?' I asked on the drive over.

'Oh, Jim couldn't come.'

75

'He couldn't come?'

'No. Something came up.'

Wren had rarely spoken of her parents, but when she had it had been with affection. Unlike the other students in the department, Wren scorned what she referred to as 'trips down Evil Parent Lane'. In the Fiction Workshop we both attended (I was only in it because it was required), the stories were mostly about an alienated son or daughter fighting against the awful life they have because of a parent's incompetent or malevolent style of parenting. The ending was usually some melodramatic confrontation in which said child faces up to said parent and verbally rakes them over the coals. Something symbolic always happens after the big cathartic scene, like the cat leaps off the garage roof and breaks a leg or the kid walks off into the blinding snow, dropping a mitten that is quickly buried by the falling snow. To which Wren would shake her head and say, 'Another "Fuck You, Daddy" story.' Professor O'Keefe always laughed at that.

Mrs. Naughton shoved her hands into the jacket of her sweatsuit. Her keys jangled. She looked at Kate with sad eyes. 'It's a tragedy, Kate. No other way to look at it. The worst kind of tragedy.'

'Thank you,' Kate said, folding Wren's fisherman's sweater. I'd given it to Wren for her birthday. It had been hanging over the dining-room chair, waiting for Wren to grab it on her way out the door, late to meet somebody smart, somewhere nice, about something important.

'Tragedy, tragedy, all is tragedy,' Mrs. Naughton mumbled to herself, her eyes staring at nothing now, as if she were thinking about her own daugther, the possibilities for tragedy that awaited her.

I couldn't decide whether she'd deliberately misquoted the Bible or she was just being clever. Either way, the word tragedy struck me as funny, maybe because of Mark's recent lecture on *King Lear*. I thought of Lear now, seeing his dead daughter brought on stage. I thought of the birds of Guam being gobbled up by those intruder

76

snakes. Bedbug erections. Esther the Bat-Faced Girl hiding her television set in the refrigerator. Tragedy. What's that?

On the way here, Kate and I had stopped by a discount office supply warehouse and bought a bunch of cardboard boxes you have to assemble yourself. Somehow driving behind supermarkets and pirating their old orange boxes seemed disrespectful to Wren. Kate would have unpacked those clothes later in Omaha and Wren's memory would smell of sweetly rotten oranges. *That's* tragedy.

'Well, hell,' Mrs. Naughton said, eyeing the pile of unassembled boxes, 'if it's packing you want, I can pack with the best of 'em. I've moved so often that I can pack a three-bedroom house faster than a box boy bags a cart of groceries.' She pushed up her sleeves and grabbed the top hunk of cardboard and had the thing folded and tucked and looking like a serious box in about ten seconds.

I picked up a couple of Mrs. Naughton's folded boxes and went into Wren's bathroom to pack. I thought maybe this room would be especially painful for Kate. The things we keep in the bathroom are morbidly intimate. This is where we watch the toilet for signs of blood in our stool, examine the darkening moles, the falling hair, the receding gums, the hidden lumps. Tylenol, toothpaste, and tampons, all the things we use to shore up our mortality while we cozy up to the idea of death. It's also a pretty good place to take a pee, which I did as quickly as possible. Somehow it seemed impolite to come over and whiz in Wren's bathroom, so I tried to flush the toilet quietly.

Although Wren was meticulously neat in every other room, in the bathroom she was a slob. Clumps of blue toothpaste sculpture pocked the sink. The mirror was spotted and smeared. Fingernail clippings crouched in the corners of the countertop. Strands of dental floss draped the edge of the wastebasket and curled on the carpet where Wren had carelessly tossed them after use. They looked like long white hairs, as if Edgar Winter had spent a few bad nights on the floor here.

I picked up Wren's wire hairbrush and started pulling out the hairs that were packed into it. I imagined Kate unpacking the brush in her Omaha kitchen, seeing Wren's hairs and starting to sob, collapsing against the immaculate countertop. As I plucked the clumps of hair from between the bristles of the brush, I thought of Robby, how when we kissed a few wild strands of my long hair would always somehow end up in our mouths. We'd still be kissing as I pulled them out and we could feel each hair slicing across out lips and tongues like thin wires and we'd go right on mashing our faces together as if nothing could be more important to our lives, our continued existence, than the endless kiss.

'How's it going?' Kate asked, startling me.

'Fine.' I tossed the hairbrush into the box and started stacking the Kleenex box and tissue roll.

'I could really use some aspirin,' Kate said.

I opened the medicine cabinet and handed her Wren's Tylenol. She tapped a couple out and swallowed them dry.

I stooped down and opened the cupboard under the sink. I'd never looked there before. An ancient curling iron I'd never seen Wren use was wrapped in its cord. The rest of the stuff was scattered about: an empty box with a disposable douche, spilled Q-Tips, three bars of strawberry-scented glycerin soap. A silver chain bracelet. A pewter earring shaped like a panda bear. And way in the back corner past the pipes and the Comet and the petrified sponge, a box of some kind of denture adhesive. I pulled it out and read the label. I must have been staring at it for a while, because Kate finally touched me on the shoulder.

'She didn't tell you?'

'What? Tell me what?'

Kate sat on the toilet lid. 'That girl, she loved to have secrets.'

78

'What secrets?'

'Wren wore dentures. Up here.' Kate curled back her upper lip and tapped her front teeth. 'Just a partial. Four teeth.'

I stared at the package. DenturKleen. 'Wren never told me.'

'I'm not surprised,' Kate said. 'She never told anyone anything important.'

'I don't understand,' I said slowly, stupidly. 'Her teeth came out? All the way out of her mouth?'

'Just those four. Had them knocked right out of her mouth. She almost choked on one of them. Lodged down her throat.' She picked up a stiff washcloth from the floor and began neatly folding it.

'How'd it happen?' I asked. 'A car accident?'

'That husband of hers.' Kate shook her head. 'The things he got her into.'

I expected her to say more, but she didn't. She just shook her head again, as if remembering Wren's mysterious husband, the questionable things he got her into. Oddly, she didn't seem angry at him. I was about to ask for details, when Mrs. Naughton appeared, an empty box in each hand and one under each arm.

'We move the party in here?' she asked.

'I was looking for aspirin,' Kate explained. 'I'm afraid I had one too many drinks on the airplane. I hope you don't mind, but I feel a little drunk.'

'Damn right I mind,' Mrs. Naughton said, dropping her load of boxes right there in the hallway. 'A little drunk is no good. You need to feel a lot drunk. Now that's something I do even better than folding boxes.' And she took off, kicking aside the boxes on her way out of the apartment.

I picked up two of the boxes and Kate grabbed the other two. We went into Wren's bedroom. This room was more like an office with a bed. Most of the room was dominated by the desk, four-drawer filing cabinet, the Apple computer, the bookshelves crammed with thick

79

volumes. Wherever there was floor space against a wall, a stack of books grew three feet high like a well-tended garden.

On top of Wren's desk was a large open book. It was one of Wren's many art books and the page was open to a photograph of a bronze sculpture. Small yellow Post-It notes were stuck to the page all around the photo, almost obscuring it. Each note was crammed with Wren's tiny erratic handwriting that if you squinted looked like barbed wire. I peeled a few sticky notes away to better see the photo. The sculpture was of a nude seated woman, she looked old, with saggy breasts and a thick waist. Her head was bent down at an awkward angle, as if she were ashamed, yet her one arm is behind her back as if she weren't ashamed at all. It was hard to tell because of the angle of the photo, but it looked as if she might even be smiling. The sculpture was by Auguste Rodin and was entitled, 'She Who Was the Helmet-Maker's Beautiful Wife.' The sticky yellow note beside her breast said 'see The Gates of Hell.' I closed the book and tossed it on the bed.

I pulled open the top drawer of the file cabinet, grabbed a handful of hanging files, and laid them into one of the boxes. Each file folder was neatly labeled. She had one for each course she had ever taken, all the handouts for the course, her papers, her notes.

'You know,' Kate said, opening Wren's underwear drawer, 'I didn't plan on roping you into this. I thought I could do it myself. Come here, pack everything.'

'Don't be silly, Kate. I'm glad to help.'

'Wren had spoken of you often.'

'You too,' I lied. When Wren did speak of her parents, it was in positive terms, but now that I thought of it, she rarely spoke of them as individuals, always as 'my parents', never as 'my mom' or 'my dad'.

'Jim would have been here,' Kate said. 'If he could have.'

'Of course he would,' I said. But I couldn't help but

wonder what kind of creep would let his wife do this heart-wrenching duty alone. I emptied another file drawer. This one contained bills to be paid, receipts, bank statements. The last two drawers were filled with essays and articles Wren had written about anything that popped into her head. Some had been published and there were copies of the magazines or tearsheets with the printed article. But most of the articles were in red folders with tabs that designated them as being for her magazine, the one she planned to start in a couple of years. She'd been stockpiling articles the way enemy nations hoard weapons. I packed them neatly into the cardboard box, thinking what a shame it was no one would ever read them. They were to be entombed in a dark attic in Omaha. Maybe in a few months or a year I'd write to Kate and suggest she send the articles out. Maybe knowing her daughter's words and thoughts still lived would comfort her. Maybe it would sadden her more. I probably wouldn't write anyway.

Kate made a noise, like a stifled whimper.

'Kate?' I asked, turning toward her. 'You okay?'

She was staring at the bedstand that held the alarm clock/radio, the reading lamp, a glass of water with air bubbles in it from sitting there for a few days, and the combination telephone/answering machine. The red light on the answering machine was blinking.

'Should I play it?' she asked. I was the only other person in the room, but she didn't seem to be talking to me. So I didn't say anything.

She sat on the edge of the bed, absently pushing the Rodin book aside. She stabbed one of the buttons. A faint whir sounded as the tape rewound. I'd heard Wren play her messages often enough to know that this machine didn't play the prerecorded message, so I was grateful we weren't going to hear Wren's chipper voice announcing, 'If you don't know what this is or what to do, I don't want to talk to you anyway. Bye.'

The first voice caught me by surprise. It was mine.

'Wren, it's Luna. I got your message about being in jail. I hope this is a joke because I'm too damn tired to fuck around tonight. Wren? Pick up, damn it.' Then I heard myself sigh. 'Okay, I'm going over to the police station. You'd better be there.'

I was embarrassed. I shrugged at Kate, 'I don't know if you heard about that, I mean, it was all a misunderstanding—'

Beep.

Kate waved me to silence.

The next voice was an unfamiliar woman with a very business-like but friendly tone: 'Ms. Caldwell, this is Linda Marley at *Orange County Today*. I just want to confirm your interview appointment with the magazine for next week. We have all read your sample articles and are most impressed. Please call me back at area code 714-555-4200, extension 356. Airline reservations have already been made in your name. I look forward to hearing from you and especially to meeting you. Good-bye.'

'She had a job offer?' Kate asked.

'Well, an interview.'

'It sounded like they'd already made up their minds.' Kate stood up with renewed energy, as if she expected Wren to come walking into the room and we would all go out for lunch and celebrate the new job. She picked up a pair of Wren's butt-floss panties and folded them twice like a doily.

I kept emptying the file drawers, packing folders against folders. There was more output in these folders than I imagined possible for one person. Wren had already accomplished more than I ever would in my whole life. She had a family and friends and a job interview. Even dead her future looked brighter than mine.

I realized my jealousy was irrational, so I tried to focus on some other aspect of Wren. I visualized her without her front teeth. When she spoke, her tongue would flap helplessly against her gum making her sound like Elmer Fudd. This visualization was a technique I'd learned from

one of those self-help books. Okay, I know that they're
ridiculous and that people who read them are pathetic and
deserve both our pity and contempt and maybe a sharp
rap against the skull with a brick. Yet, for a while after
Robby and I broke up, I couldn't read enough of them.
They're addictive. As long as you're reading one, you
have this overwhelming sense of power, as if you really
can overcome billions of years of cosmic determinism and
change your life. They made you feel powerful, like you
could crush a lump of coal into a diamond. My first book
was, of course, on breaking up. It had the sensitive title
of *Splitsville: A Bad Place to Visit, How Not to Live
There*. Some of the advice was pretty standard, like
don't listen to sad songs about people being dumped
on. Until my divorce I never realized how many songs
there were about splitting up. It's weird how lyrics that
used to sound so unbearably cornball suddenly seem
keenly insightful. Here's another helpful hint from the
book: change the color of your toilet paper, the brand
of your toothpaste, even the flavor of ice cream you
buy. These are emotional time bombs constructed from
shrapnel of selective memories of good times that will
explode and shred you into weeping, writhing depression. After I finished all the breaking-up books I
could find, I started in on self-esteem. Eventually I was
reading books on problems I didn't have, male menopause, manic-depression, personal hygiene disorders,
fear of the number 3. They were all filled with such
hope that they made me hopeful too.

I stuffed another batch of folders into the box. Kate was
folding skimpy panties, one at a time. I wondered if anyone was over at Esther's place, washing her dishes, folding
her underwear.

'Kate,' I said, 'what happened with Wren's husband?'

'What do you mean?'

'You know, him being in jail and all. Did it have something to do with Wren losing her teeth? Is that what happened?'

83

'Now that's a story.'

'It is?' I encouraged her.

'Byron.' She shook her head again. 'That Byron.'

I leaned forward anxiously. 'What about Byron?'

'Okay, ladies,' Mrs. Naughton shouted as she huffed down the hallway. 'Prepare for some serious guzzling.' She held up two bottles of white wine by their necks, one in each hand like a proud hunter who'd just bagged an especially elusive prey. 'As my daughter says, let's party till we puke. Follow me. I got a nose for this kind of thing.'

I was more interested in hearing about Wren's mysterious husband and her missing teeth. But Kate closed the dresser drawer with a polite smile and followed Mrs. Naughton down the hall. I sat on the edge of Wren's bed, just where she'd sat that night she'd put on the sex show for me. Where did she ever come up with ideas like that? Where did she get the guts to do them?

Compared to Wren what had I done with my life? I'd married a man I'd loved, then spent the next ten years imitating his life. He'd gone to graduate school, so I went. He studied English, so did I. He taught, so would I. Sometimes I'd take a class that Robby had already taken and the professor would ask about Robby. I'd feel like I was a little sister following her big brother through high school. Robby had never pushed me into any of these decisions, I'd made them freely. It's just that I'd never been as self-motivated as Robby. When I'd see how excited he was about what he did, I figured maybe if I did it too I'd get excited about doing something. Maybe it had worked too, it was hard to judge sitting here with a bullet tunnel through my chest, on the bed of my dead best friend, her mother and her landlady getting smashed in the next room.

*　　*　　*　　*　　*

84

Mrs. Naughton was mixing Black Russians when I entered the living room. She wasn't using any kind of measuring glass. 'Here you go, Kate,' she said, pouring vodka with one hand and Kahlúa with the other. She swirled the mixture with her finger and handed it to Kate. 'Pardon the ham hocks.'

We each had four of those Black Russians. Kate didn't seem any the worse for them, though she spoke a little more slowly. Mrs. Naughton kept up a never-ending stream of chatter about the tenants from the various buildings she'd managed, their sexual perversions, the criminal activities. She'd been writing a book, an autobiography about all these places. 'I talked to Wren once about it, shot some ideas past her. I tried to get her to help me write it but, hell, she had so much work to do. She did give me some pointers though, you know, on how to structure the story and stuff.' She gulped down the rest of her drink. 'I'm calling the book, *Roomers Flying*. Get it? Like that old saying about rumors flying, only I have the rumors spelled like a room in a house, you know, roomers. What do you think? Catchy or what?'

'I'd buy it,' Kate said.

'Me too,' I said. My tongue tingled as if it were asleep and it hurt to talk, to have my tongue touch my teeth. A practical reason to be able to take out your front teeth. I curled my lip over my top teeth to simulate having no teeth.

'You lushes could use some music,' Mrs. Naughton said. 'Luna, why don't you do the honors.'

'Sure.' I walked over to Wren's CD player and pressed the Play button. Wren always had something on the player. I expected Paul Simon's music to start, but that's not what she had on. A woman's voice twanged out 'Walkin' After Midnight'.

'Oh, I know her,' Kate said. 'I can't remember her name.'

'Patsy Cline,' Mrs. Naughton said.

'Yes. Yes. I saw that movie about her.'

'*Sweet Dreams*,' I said.

'That's right,' Kate said. 'With that girl, that blond girl from *King Kong*. What's her name?'

Now, I knew the actress's name as well as I knew my own, I'd seen every movie she'd ever been in. But for some reason I couldn't remember it either. I pictured her face on the screen, trying to see the credits.

'Damn it,' Mrs. Naughton said, tearing the seal from a fresh bottle of vodka. 'I know her name. She was in *Tootsie*, remember?'

'And *Francis*,' I said. 'It's Jessica. Jessica something.'

'That's it,' Kate said. 'Jessica.'

'Jessica what?'

'Goddamn it,' Mrs. Naughton spat. 'Not remembering is driving me crazy. I mean, I probably know more about her than I do my own daughter. She's the one married to that Shepherd guy.'

'The playwright,' I added.

'The hunk,' Mrs. Naughton said. 'You see him in *The Right Stuff*. Jesus, I rent that movie every so often, then just fast forward to the parts he's in. Even those crooked teeth get me going.'

'Jessica. Jessica.' Kate sipped her drink and concentrated. 'Jessica something.'

'Hahn?' Mrs. Naughton said.

'No,' I said. 'That's the girl Jim Bakker seduced. The one who got her breasts enlarged and stayed at the Playboy mansion.'

'Jessica Savage?' Kate said.

I shook my head. 'Anchor woman who took cocaine and drowned in a car accident.'

'I can't think of any more Jessicas,' Kate said.

'Jessica Walters,' Mrs. Naughton said, but immediately dismissed it. 'Nah, she's the one who comes after Clint Eastwood in *Play Misty for Me*.' Mrs. Naughton slapped herself briskly. 'Goddamn it, she was also in that Nazi thing, *The Music Box*.'

I went over to the CD player and picked up the empty plastic case. It wasn't the soundtrack. The cover photo was of Patsy Cline, a round-faced woman with short permed hair wearing a blue scarf tied around her neck cowgirl style. She wore a cowgirl outfit, black with long yellow fringes and what seemed like embroidered roses on either lapel. She looked like somebody's mother all dressed up for the weekly square dance.

'Doesn't say anything about the movie,' I said.

'Let me see that,' Mrs. Naughton said.

I carried the case over to her. She stared at it awhile. 'The thing about the movie, the thing that got me,' she said. She stopped, just staring at the photo of Patsy Cline. I thought she would wither, slap herself again, or start crying.

'What about the movie?' I asked. 'What got you?'

Mrs. Naughton looked up. 'Well, just look at this photo, I mean the way Patsy Cline really looked. Now listen to her songs.' She paused so we could listen to a few lines from 'I Fall to Pieces'. 'I mean, these are all songs about getting dumped, right? And you look at this photo and you know this woman knows a lot about getting dumped. She's pleasant enough, but that hair alone, Jesus. But in the movie, that woman who played Patsy, that Jessica something. Can you imagine any guy leaving her. I mean, she's the one you'd leave Patsy Cline *for*. You see my point? I'm watching this movie thinking, give me a fucking break here. She was a good actress and all, this Jessica woman, but I don't buy this little twerpy Ed Harris guy leaving her. I think he'd kiss her ass every night, happy to have her. See what I'm saying?'

'Lange,' Kate said. 'Her name's Jessica Lange.'

'Yes!' I said, feeling a sudden relief. 'Jessica Lange.'

'Bless you, woman.' Mrs. Naughton took Kate's glass. 'You just won yourself another Black Russian.'

'I think I've had enough. I still have a flight to catch this afternoon. We have so much to do yet.'

Mrs. Naughton ignored Kate's protest and handed her the drink. 'First thing we need to do is kick Patsy's sad ass out of this room.' She stood up and marched to the CD player, fingered through the CDs, found one, ejected Patsy, and injected her selection. She cranked up the volume knob. The speakers boomed with a chorus of women's voices. Mrs. Naughton threw her hands up into the air and did a dance-shuffle across the carpet that looked like Topol singing 'If I Were a Rich Man' in *Fiddler on the Roof*. 'It's Melanie,' she said. 'You remember Melanie, don't you?'

I recognized the song. Something about 'candles in the rain'. Melanie was one of those folk-rock singers with a trembling urgency in her voice as if she had to get this song out with her last ounce of life, after which she would throw herself off a cliff. This song was very upbeat, though, about people coming together to love each other and fight the darkness. I asked, 'Is this about the Kent State shootings or the Chicago Democratic Convention?'

'Woodstock,' Mrs. Naughton said.

'You sure?'

'I was there.' She smiled. 'Yeah, I know it's hard to believe. I wasn't always me, you know.'

That struck me as a funny thing to say. *I wasn't always me, you know*. I looked at her, trying to imagine her at Woodstock. Maybe she was one of those naked women with painted peace symbols on her breasts and buttocks. Maybe she looked like that Rodin statue.

Suddenly Mrs. Naughton started to sing along with the song and do her *Fiddler* dance again. She made us sing along too. When the song was over she played it again and she stood in front of us like a conductor and we sang along again.

If this had been a movie or something, this part would come at the end, the part where we all bonded together, one of those Women Across Generations things, Sisters Under the Skin. But that's not how it really felt. There was no real camaraderie here, no sisterhood. It was just three lonely women getting drunk, singing off-key, each locked in a bubble with their own desperate thoughts.

When we were done singing, we heard a knock at the open front door. A skinny boy about twenty slouched nervously in the doorway. 'Excuse me, Mrs. Naughton,' he said. 'I need to sign out the vacuum cleaner. They said you had the key.'

She tossed him the big brass ring of keys. He stuck his hand out to catch them, but when he saw how many there were and how fast they were flying at him, he pulled his hand away and let the keys fall at his feet. He stooped over and picked them up. 'Thanks, Mrs. Naughton.' He looked at each of us as if he'd just interrupted a witch's coven, then left.

'Good kid,' Mrs. Naughton said. 'Wish I had a hundred just like him.'

Kate stood up and brushed the lap of her skirt. 'I think I'd better be going now,' she said. 'I don't want to miss my flight. What's the address here so I can call a taxi?'

'What about . . .' I didn't know what to call it. Wren's stuff? Wren's belongings? Wren's life? 'What do you want to do about all this?' I gestured around the room.

She smiled. 'You were such good friends, Luna. You should keep it. I know that's what Wren would have liked.'

'No, I couldn't. I mean it, Kate.' I did mean it too. I didn't want these mementoes of my own failure. The thought of her leaving it with me made me physically ill.

Kate walked over to me and cupped my hands between hers. The sweet scent of Black Russians cloyed the air between us. I felt somehow imprisoned and wanted to pull away from her.

'Luna,' Kate said. 'The reason my husband didn't come with me is because he's in the hospital. Nothing too serious, not a heart attack. Something with his nerves. It happened the day we heard about Wren. We were just getting out of bed when the police called. I was in the shower so Jim took the call. When I got out of the shower he was sitting on the bed weeping. He told me about Wren. We both cried together. Then I stopped crying. Jim didn't. He cried all day. He couldn't stop. I don't mean he couldn't stop feeling the pain or even having tears, I'm talking about huge chest-wrenching sobs. *He could not stop crying.*' She took a deep breath and calmed herself. 'He cracked three ribs just from crying. I had to admit him into the hospital.'

Mrs. Naughton shook her head. 'Poor man. Tragedy.'

'Yes,' Kate said, looking at Mrs. Naughton, then back at me again, her face leaning even closer. 'So you see, despite my devastation at Wren's death, I still have Jim to take care of. I have to think about him now. Looking around this apartment, I see Wren everywhere and it's breaking my heart. Right now, I don't think that's what Jim needs to see. I didn't realize that until now, until standing in these rooms myself.' She released my hands. My knuckles, all the joints hurt. She hadn't held me that tight, yet still each joint ached, as if she'd transferred some bad karma or something. 'That's why I want you to keep everything that's here. I've made arrangements with her bank and insurance company, but other than that everything here has nothing to do with the Wren that Jim and I shared.'

I didn't know what to say to that. What point was there in arguing? 'If that's what you want, Kate,' I said. 'I appreciate the gesture.'

She turned away as if she hadn't heard me and picked up her purse. 'I need to call a taxi.'

'No, of course you won't,' I said. 'I'll drive you to the airport. It's not that far.'

Mrs. Naughton rose from her chair and elbowed me aside. 'Don't be stupid, girl. You're too damn drunk to drive. I'm not.'

She was right about me being drunk. I felt hot and

wobbly, my mouth seemed sticky, like I'd been licking stamps for a few hours. Mrs. Naughton looked as fresh as if she'd been drinking nothing but Kool-Aid for the past two hours.

'One quick piss and we're outta here,' she said, trotting off to the bathroom.

Kate and I hardly spoke while we waited for Mrs. Naughton's return. I felt too drunk, too burdened by the legacy of Wren's possessions. I tried to think of some gracious way to give it all back. But I couldn't.

When Kate and Mrs. Naughton left I went into the bedroom and laid down on the bed. I crossed my hands across my chest in the pose of a corpse ready for viewing. This was a very relaxing position, wasted on the dead. I looked around the room and saw all of the things I'd just inherited, clothes, computer, furniture. A lot of loot. I watched the front door for about twenty minutes, half expecting Wren to walk in, explain how she pulled this hoax off.

When she didn't come in, I opened the Rodin book and looked at the same photograph of 'She Who Was the Helmet-Maker's Beautiful Wife'. I wasn't good at interpreting art, that was Wren's specialty. To me it just looked like a somewhat grotesque woman, maybe something they'd find in the attic of a beautiful dead woman, her personal version of *The Picture of Dorian Gray*.

I closed the book and closed my eyes. I thought about the birds of Guam being airlifted away from home so they could avoid extinction. I must have nodded off because when I opened my eyes, an hour had passed. But my mind was remarkably clear. Without thinking, I reached over, punched the button on the answering machine, and listened to Wren's two messages again. When they were over, I dialed the phone.

'Extension 356,' I said to the receptionist. I listened to the recording of Tracy Chapman's 'Fast Car' while waiting. When Linda Marley announced herself, I said, 'Ms.

Marley, this is Wren Caldwell. I'm so looking forward to interviewing with you. When exactly is my airline reservation?'

6

I was on my first date since taking over Wren's name and so far it wasn't going too well. We were standing in the All-Nite Mini-Mart and my date, Ethan, was arguing with the Asian kid behind the counter.

'Just check in the back, man,' Ethan said.

'There is no need to check in the back, sir.' The kid was straining to be polite. He had dark skin and a slight accent, but I couldn't decide what it was, Korean or Vietnamese, something exotic like that. At the first sound of conflict, I'd drifted to the back of the store, behind the metal greeting-card rack, positioned like an accomplice in a robbery. A fat teenage girl all in denim stood behind me, smoking a cigarette and playing a video game.

'Just check, okay?' Ethan insisted. He showed the kid his little pocket camera. 'I need the two-hundred-speed film. It's dark out, the flash on these cheapies isn't worth shit.'

'Sir, we are out. Look, the hook is empty.'

The boy pointed at the silver hook sticking out of the blue pegboard behind him. All around that empty hook were other hooks that had little yellow boxes of film. But not the kind Ethan wanted. He wanted special film so he could take snapshots of our date, though he hadn't told me yet where we were going.

I immersed myself in the dusty greeting cards, pretending I was here on important business, a last-minute card for a terminally sick friend. Slowly I turned the

wobbly rack, studying each colorful drawing, each senti-
ment or joke. Anything to isolate myself from the turmoil
up front. Perhaps I could find a nice card for my new stepmom, though Hallmark seemed woefully lacking anything
that started, 'On the occasion of your becoming tribal
weasel whacker . . .'

'Look, man, just check for me, okay?' Ethan slid a
five-dollar bill across the counter. 'Okay?'

The boy frowned at the bill with contempt. His thin face
tightened, somehow got thinner. 'Sir, there is no film in
the back. Please try another store.'

'That's bullshit, man. Okay? I used to work in one
of these stores. We kept lots of stuff in the back. All
kinds of shit. You're just too fucking lazy, man.' Ethan
crumpled his five dollars in his fist and I flashed on
Wren's blue panties in her fist. The fat girl behind me
looked around from her video game at the fuss, lighting
a fresh cigarette, sizing the situation up like a veteran
street cop. 'Asshole,' she muttered and returned to the
game.

The Asian boy kept a stiff but serene stare. He said
nothing. I admired his composure in the face of Ethan's
older, much larger presence. Ethan had to be at least
twenty-eight, six feet two inches, and 190 pounds. The
kid was six inches shorter and half the weight. Maybe his
serenity came from generations of zen devotees. Maybe
he had his hand on a shotgun under the counter. Double-
barreled zen.

Ethan wouldn't accept the kid's attitude. 'So, what're
you saying, man?' You're not even going to look, to fucking look, for chrissake?'

'No, sir, there is nothing to look for.'

'You dumb fuck. You lazy dumb fuck.'

'Fuck you too, sir,' the kid said.

*　　*　　*　　*　　*

94

In the car, Ethan was in a good mood. He seemed to admire the kid too, held no grudge. 'Kid had a mouth on him, didn't he?'

'Yours wasn't exactly idle.'

He chuckled. 'Yeah, well, that's my job. Occupational hazard.'

Ethan was a comedian, a stand-up comic who worked the local clubs, sometimes traveled to Los Angeles or San Francisco to do his act. I found all this out the first half hour I met him, which was two days ago when I'd moved into my new apartment. He lived in the apartment above me and had offered to help me unload the U-Haul trailer that contained all of Wren's stuff. Since then he'd dropped by a few times to help me arrange furniture, hang prints, draw maps to grocery stores. He talked a lot and didn't seem to mind that I didn't, which made him pretty good company at times.

'Wren,' he said. 'Hey, Wren.'

I looked over at him and he snapped my picture. The tiny flash made me blink. I rubbed my eyes. He wedged the wallet-sized camera next to the handbrake between us. 'Something to show our grandkids,' he chuckled.

It's much easier than you think becoming someone else. First of all, you get used to the name right away. It's not like in the movies or on TV when someone is undercover or pretending to be someone else and a guy calls them by their pretend name and they don't answer at first because they forgot that's who they now are. Someone calls me Wren, I respond immediately. Maybe even faster than I did when people used to call me Luna.

The mundane details of life swapping were pretty simple. I found Wren's birth certificate when I was packing up her files. I took it down to the DMV, told them I'd lost my driver's license, and had them reissue a new one, this one with Wren's name and my photo. After that I was able to get a passport, credit cards, and anything else I needed. Once I saw how easy it was, I was surprised more people, when their lives got too complex or disappointing, didn't just up and become someone else.

In the movies when someone wants to disappear, they fake their deaths in a flaming car crash or something. I didn't have to go that far. As far as I could tell, I'd disappeared the day Robby and I split up. Now all I had to do was fake my life.

A couple weeks ago, I'd flown down to Orange County for the job interview. Wren's mother was right, it was just a formality. They'd already made up their minds they wanted to hire Wren. They took me to lunch and dinner and put me up at the fancy Ritz-Carlton Hotel. They told me the magazine had a rich new owner and he had great plans for *Orange Coast Today*. He wanted a whole new look, a whole new tone. He'd fired half of the old staff the day after he bought it. Apparently I was the first personnel step in achieving this new image, though what the new look and image were to be was never explained to me. The day I interviewed, the new owner, Jonathan Krieg, still hadn't moved from New York, so I never did meet him. Everyone spoke about him with a certain fearful reverence, as if they weren't sure what he was up to, how to please him. No one there had actually met him yet, though we'd all read about him before in newspapers and magazines. I tried to look interested, though I didn't much care about any of that. I cared that my starting salary was $35,000, eight grand more than I would have made as a teacher, even if I'd been able to be hired as one.

'Did I embarrass you back there?' Ethan asked.

'I don't know. A little.' My palms were still sweating. I had the inky tattoo of a cartoon Snoopy across my fingers where I'd clutched a birthday card too tightly.

'Sorry. That's one of my pet peeves. No one seems to want to do their jobs anymore. The whole world has turned into one big self-service pump. There's no pride. That's why we're getting fucked by the Japanese. It's not just the lower wages, it's pride in what they do. They just make better quality stuff. Everybody over there, no matter how shitty the job, does it like his life depended on it. I saw this thing on *60 Minutes* about how expensive everything was in Japan. You ever been to Japan?'

'No.'

'Me neither, but coffee costs like five bucks a cup. Anyway, they interview this one guy who owns a little sushi bar or something on some prime real estate in Tokyo. The place is like as big as my kitchen, seats maybe eight people if two of them are amputees. The guy barely scrapes by. They offer the poor schlub a couple million bucks to sell his location. What do you think happens? The guy turns them down. He's like the seventh generation of sushi makers in his family and he likes what he does. He'd rather slice squid than ride around in a limo yakking on his cellular phone. That's what I'm talking about. Pride.'

Ethan was a very handsome man. He was trim and his face was both boyish and rugged. He had a gunslinger's mustache, which didn't go with his face. It made him look as if he were playing grown-up. The blond hairs hung over his upper lip and I felt an overpowering urge to trim them back. Even though he acted like a jerk with that kid, I liked that he didn't stay mad. His cheerfulness made me feel optimistic. I couldn't decide whether or not I was attracted to him.

'So, Wren,' he said, 'what exactly do you do at the magazine?'

'I haven't started yet,' I told him. 'I start tomorrow.'

'Are you nervous?'

'No. I figure there's plenty of time for a breakdown once they tell me what my duties are.' I really wasn't nervous. I had dozens of articles already written by Wren. I figured I could feed some of them to the magazine until I learned how to do the job properly.

'I always wanted to write,' he confessed. 'I mean, I write now, all my own material, my act. But I'd like to write, you know, something bigger.'

'A novel?'

He shrugged. 'Yeah. Or a screenplay.'

97

'With you as the star, right?'

He looked over at me and grinned. 'Sure. Why the hell not? Who else?'

I didn't say anything. I watched the traffic slow for the red light. The driver of the car in front of us tossed a cigarette out his window. It bounced off the fender of the car beside him. The other driver honked angrily, but the guy who'd thrown the cigarette just rolled up his window and ignored him.

Ethan began fidgeting during the silence. Quiet seemed to upset him. 'What will you be doing when you aren't working at the magazine?'

'You mean like hobbies?'

'Hobbies, sports, extra-curricular activities. Saving the whales, preventing fluoridation, assassinating a major political figure, stuff like that.'

I had to think for a moment. Should I tell him my interests or Wren's? Just how far in-character should I go? Wren liked to ski, I'd never been skiing in my life. Wren knew how to make pottery, work a loom, had parachuted from an airplane. I knew how to shop for bargains, how to love Robby.

'Jeez, I didn't mean to ask such a toughie. Would the contestant like another minute to think over her answer.' He started humming the theme to the *Jeopardy* game show.

'I'm sorry. I'm still a little disoriented from moving.'

'Believe me, whatever you enjoyed doing up in Oregon, you'll enjoy it even more down here. This is a great place.'

'I like it so far.'

'You'll like it even more after tonight.'

He didn't say it in a suggestive way, but suddenly I realized that he thought we might have sex tonight. Not that he expected it, but he hoped. That meant at some point tonight he would make his move. Except for one brief infidelity five years ago, I hadn't had sex with anyone but Robby in ten years. My dating sensors were weak, but now they started kicking in, beeping at certain phrases, looks. Later, he would try to kiss me, then he would want to go from there. I had no idea yet what I would say or do.

He pulled into a parking lot and I saw the place we were going: The Laff Stop. A comedy nightclub.

'I thought you might enjoy some laughs. They have three comics each show. I've played here a few times.'

The parking lot was full so we parked on the street. The nearby residences were a little run-down, the yards brown and patchy, the windows protected by black bars. This looked like a high-crime area.

We stood in line at the ticket booth outside. I expected to hear large dogs barking in the distance, but all I heard was traffic whooshing by and some kind of bird half crying, half whistling. Its call was very regular, like a heartbeat.

'I did a gig with one of the guys we're seeing tonight. He's funny.' He said this in a grudging way that suggested he was so-so funny, not as funny as Ethan.

I was trying to figure out what kind of bird would make that kind of sound when Ethan spun around and flashed another photo. My eyes bled white and I blinked furiously.

'Just one more, Zsa Zsa, please,' Ethan joked. The people in line behind us laughed.

My blinking slowed down until I was now blinking in rhythm with that bird's cries. I tried to break the rhythm but it was hard to do. I got the feeling that the bird was mimicking me now, purposely crying out whenever I blinked. Ethan said something but I was still concentrating on stopping myself from blinking in time with the bird's piercing shrieks. Finally the bird stopped and I felt an enormous relief.

I clutched Ethan's arm. 'You promise not to take any more photos and I promise not to chew your face off. Deal?'

'Deal, Monty.' He grinned and pocketed his camera. 'I'm out of film anyway.'

So this is dating, I thought.

*　　*　　*　　*　　*

'You want to come in?' I asked after unlocking my apartment door.

'Sure,' he said, following me inside.

The apartment was larger than I needed. It had two master bedrooms, one of which I would have to rent out within the month if I was going to be able to keep paying the rent. I'd looked for a one-bedroom place, but the rents in Orange County were so high that I would have had to live someplace where everyone parked their cars on the lawn and the street lamps were always shot out. Linda Marley, the associate editor at the magazine, suggested I find a roommate, that's what a lot of young divorced women did. There were roommate services or I could just advertise in the paper, she'd said. After calculating my monthly budget, I saw the wisdom of her advice. But the idea bothered me, to be thirty years old and still living with a nonromantic roommate. It seemed too much like I was backsliding into adolescence rather than evolving into adulthood where one was supposed to be in charge of one's life.

'What do you do, Ethan?' I called from the kitchen while I poured a couple glasses of wine.

He followed me into the kitchen. 'You mean hobbies?'

'No, I mean occupation. Job security, dental insurance, that sort of thing.'

He gave me a hurt look. 'Oh, you mean what do I do in *real* life.'

I hadn't meant to insult him, but I couldn't imagine him making enough money doing his comedy act to support himself. 'Look, I don't know much about the comedy business. I didn't mean anything.'

'I buy textbooks.'

I handed him a glass of white wine. 'Sounds interesting.'

'Does it? Does it sound interesting to travel around to all the colleges and universities and buy back all the textbooks from snooty teachers who got the books free from the publisher anyway. A lot of them order every free copy they can so they can sell them to me at the end of the

100

semester. Does it really sound all that fucking interesting?'

'You do make it sound pretty glamorous.'

He laughed. 'Hey, it pays the rent. That's what a job's supposed to do, right? Plus, I make some pretty good change from doing my act. That's where my future is, the real money. That's my career.'

He had performed some of his act for me that first night. His specialty was impressions of famous rock stars. He'd go up on stage with his guitar and sing their songs, only he'd substitute his own verses. Like, he did the Rolling Stones' 'Sympathy for the Devil', only his version was 'Sympathy for the Yentl'. He had a nice voice and he was moderately funny.

'I'm obsessed,' he said, finishing his wine quickly. 'I'm obsessed with Johnny Carson.'

I poured more wine into his glass. He didn't seem drunk, although along with the cover charge at the Laff Stop, they enforced a two-drink minimum. I was feeling a little light-headed myself. 'Obsessed with Johnny Carson,' I said. 'Sounds like a headline in the *National Enquirer*.'

'My whole life sounds like a headline in the *National Enquirer*. "One-Headed Boy Graduates College, With C Average! Gets Lousy Job! Parents Say: 'We Told Him So.'" But Johnny Carson, man. I watch his show every night, even the reruns. I tape them and watch them again. I'm determined to get on his show. That's all I need, all it would take. One shot. You know how frustrating it is to see guys who aren't nearly as funny get all that exposure. I mean, Johnny Carson is the ticket. He's the end of the rainbow.'

I didn't know how to respond. I said, 'There's always David Letterman.'

'No, no, no.' He shook his head vigorously, like a dog just out of water. 'David Letterman dominates his show too much. Even if you are funny people think it's because of Dave. He steps on your lines, then gets all the credit for any laughs. With Johnny, you're out there on your own. If you're funny there, man, he gives you that okay sign, then you know you're on your way.' He circled his thumb and finger into an okay sign.

'Do you have an agent or something? Can't you get an audition?'

'You don't audition for Johnny Carson. His scouts find you. They go out to all the clubs and look for talent to book. They're like talent ninjas, man. That's why I keep playing all the local joints. I figure one day they'll be there on the same night I am.'

I didn't ask the obvious: what if they already had been?

'I've changed my act so many times. I used to do the straight kind, you know, where you go up and talk about your crummy childhood and what well-meaning jerks your folks were. I mean, Jay Leno made a fortune doing that kinda crap. But then it seemed like all the hot acts were doing some crazy persona, screaming at the audience and shit like Sam Kennison, so I switched and did that for a while. I must've scrapped my act a dozen times. I mean, I follow the trends and when something is hot, I do it. And I'm just as funny as the other guys. I just don't understand what I'm doing wrong.'

A fragile silence enveloped us. The intimacy of his frustration made me uncomfortable. I had no answers.

'Just be yourself,' I advised.

*   *   *   *   *

We were naked. I'm not sure how it happened. The usual way, I guess, a button here, a kiss, another button. All along I was thinking that this wasn't such a wise decision.

I tasted the wine on his lips. He licked my teeth.

Where had this started? That first kiss, the one in the kitchen. I'd gone back for another bottle of wine but there wasn't one. He said he had some in his apartment. That's when I remembered that the wine we'd just finished had been his too. He'd brought it up that first day after we'd moved everything in. I guess I felt guilty for forgetting, so when he leaned across the counter to kiss me, I let him.

'Excuse me,' I'd said after the kiss.

'Too much tongue?' he joked.

I smiled. 'No, it was fine. I just have to go to the bathroom.'

'My kisses often have that effect on women.'

'I'll be right back.' I hurried off into my bedroom and closed the door. I grabbed the phone and carried it into the bathroom. Seeing the toilet, I realized I really did have to go after all, so I pulled up my skirt and pulled down my panties and peed while I dialed.

'Hello?' A woman's voice, throaty with a hint of Louisiana bayou still clinging to the vowels.

'Hi, Dr. Jaspers, this is Luna.' This was the first time I'd actually talked to her since Robby moved in with her. I wasn't sure what to call her. The last time I'd seen her she had been my professor, and unlike some of the other faculty, she preferred her full title. Still, it seemed ludicrous to call a woman who shared your husband's penis Dr. Jaspers.

'Hello, Luna, how are you?' She sounded honestly concerned.

'Fine.'

'Your health back to normal?'

'Just a couple scars. I've had to postpone swimming the English Channel this year, but otherwise I'm fine.'

'Good.' She said it in a solid, final way, like she meant to say 'Good for you, Luna, we're all proud of you.' I could see her small face pinched with concentration. She was barely five feet tall with thick kinky black hair that hung past her shoulders and made her look more like an Israeli freedom fighter than a professor.

'Is Robby there?' I sounded like I was in high school

103

talking to someone's mother. Can Robby come out and play?

'Hang on,' she said, 'I'll get him.'

Why was I calling him? What would I say? I wanted to hang up, but it was too late. I had to try to save as much face as possible. At least he didn't know where I was. I'd turned in forwarding address cards to the post office for both Wren's mail and mine. Then I'd phoned Robby and given him my dad's address in Dallas so he could send me the final divorce papers. I never did finish my Thomas Pynchon thesis, never did collect my master's degree. That was okay, because now I had Wren's three master's degrees.

The last thing I did as Luna Devon was to visit Esther's grave. I'd heard that her mother had been too ill with cancer to travel, so one of her brothers, an architect from Phoenix, had flown in, buried her, and put the house up for sale. Her headstone was small but somehow loving. Her name was at the top, under which was the date of her birth and the date of her death. Then there was a long passage in Hebrew, which I couldn't read. I kneeled down and touched the elaborate grooved letters, ran my fingertips along the rough crevices. I liked the way they felt.

'Hey, Luna, where are you?' Robby asked. He sounded sleepy, as if he'd just woken up. I looked at my watch. 11:37 P.M. Not that late for a Saturday night.

'Did I wake you?'

'No, I was just reading Tom Robbins's new novel.'

'I thought the novel was dead.'

'This one's driving the final nail in the coffin.'

I blew a loud raspberry into the phone. That's what I always did when he made those superior pronouncements about things.

He laughed. 'I've always appreciated your articulateness.'

I didn't know what else to say. I didn't want to tell him what I was up to, how I'd taken over Wren's life. I didn't want to tell him there was a man in the next room waiting to jam his tongue into my mouth. I didn't want advice or absolution, I was listening for something in his tone, the way I imagined a medicine man would look to the wind for signs. I too was looking for some sign. I just didn't know what it was. If this were junior high school, I'd have played a sentimental song over the phone for him, something like the Eagles' 'I Can't Tell You Why'. Then, when the song was over, I'd hang up and wait for him to call me back and say sweet things.

'You in Dallas?' he asked.

'Yes. Visiting Dad.'

'How's he doing?'

I told him about stepmom.

'Jesus,' he said, laughing. 'And to think I've been doing it all these years for free.'

I heard Dr. Jasper's husky voice in the background. 'She sounded worried, Robby. Ask her if she's okay.'

'You okay, Luna?' Robby asked.

I realized there was more concern in Dr. Jasper's whispered voice than in Robby's. It was too humiliating to have your ex-husband's new lover be so caring.

'Gotta go,' I said quickly, choking up.

'No, wait, Luna. Wait.'

'Gotta go . . .' I hung up.

There was no fucking sign. Just me being pathetic. I swallowed whatever emotion had bubbled up, washed my face with cold water, and returned to the living room and Ethan.

Which led to more kissing, unbuttoning, the lights off, and the two of us naked in my bed.

'Ow!' I hollered.

'Jesus!' he hollered back.

He lunged over and snapped on the lamp.

Until now he'd been doing all his foreplay on my right breast, the usual massaging and nipple pinching. Then when we were naked he'd started to suck on my left breast and his nose hit my bullet wound. I don't know how, but I'd forgotten about it. Until his nose probe.

'What happened here?' he asked, looking at my wounded breast, trying not to look too shocked. 'What the hell happened?'

'Hunting accident.'

'You hunt?'

'It was my first time.'

Now that he knew it was a bullet wound, he seemed less repulsed and more fascinated. He leaned closer, touched the edges. 'Does that hurt?'

'No.' It didn't. Actually, it hadn't hurt that much when he'd nosed it, I was more surprised than anything. I'd forgotten about it and now I was naked with some man who would see it. For the first time it occurred to me that every man I ever slept with would see this and ask what happened.

The wound didn't look too bad, just a small crater in the skin and some shiny scar tissue like a glob of melted plastic. Ethan switched off the lamp and lowered his lips to my wound. He kissed the skin all around it, then he kissed the scar. I suppose he was trying to be nice but his actions seemed so studied, like this was something he saw in a movie. Hero slobbers on poor girl's scar.

'Wren,' he whispered. 'Wren.'

'What?' I said.

'Nothing. I just like saying your name. It's poetic.'

That's the kind of guy he was. And maybe he was being sincere. I probably wasn't in a moral position to be judging anyone's honesty.

He kissed a trail down across my ribs and stomach into my thicket of pubic hairs. He nudged my thighs apart. Suddenly he stopped and looked up at me.

'When's the last time you had sex, Wren?'

'Jesus,' I said. 'What kind of question is that?'

He nodded sagely. 'That long, huh?'

I clamped my legs shut. 'Well, if I've waited this long I can wait a little longer.'

He laughed. 'I didn't mean anything by that. It's just that you're so preoccupied, like your head is somewhere else, doing your taxes, cleaning the hair out of your drains. You act like I'm a cop who picked you up for questioning. Relax.' He straightened his back. Looming over me in the dark this way I couldn't see his face clearly. I thought of that man I'd seen with Wren, the two of them hunched over the sofa, his hands clasped to her hips, pushing and pulling. Ethan's hand touched my cheek. 'I mean, if you want me to stop, I'll stop.'

Now I wasn't so sure I wanted to go through with this. He lived in the apartment above me. No matter how things went tonight, location would force us to see a lot of each other. I didn't want to have to start peeking out of my curtain every day to make sure he wasn't around before making a crazy dash for my car.

He leaned over and kissed my lips. His hand slid across my thigh. He whispered, 'Just tell me what you want. Tell me.'

* * * * *

The next morning I peeked through the curtains, didn't see Ethan. I made a crazy dash for my car.

107

7

I'd had my eye on the rearview mirror, looking for the car that had been following me all morning. That's how I thumped into the truck in front of me.

'I just hope you've got insurance, lady,' the man barked, climbing out of his pickup truck and slamming the door.

'I don't think there's any damage,' I said.

Six lanes of cars whooshed by us less than three feet away.

The man tugged his Dodgers cap low on his forehead as if he thought I might try to snatch it. He wore his hat backward, with the bill shading his neck and the little plastic adjustment strip puckering a swatch of skin on his forehead. He walked toward me muttering, 'I need this shit' under his breath. His red hair was long and his bushy beard completely hid his mouth, except for the cigarette that bobbed when he spoke. He wore heavy work boots with rawhide laces and mud caked around the soles. His jeans were faded at the knees, thighs, and crotch. His white T-shirt looked new, though the sleeves had been torn off. Underneath the shrubbery of facial hair, he looked to be about twenty-seven, but there was a rigidness and hostility in his walk that announced to the world that this was how he would be for the rest of his life, take it or leave it.

He ran his hand along the metal rim of the side of the truck bed as he walked toward me. The blue truck was a dented, rusting heap, but that's how it had been long before I'd bumped into it.

'Could be all kinds of damage you can't see,' he said. 'Tension damage to the axle, the frame might be bent. Could be anything.'

This was my first day of work and I was already twenty minutes late. I'd turned the wrong way on Harbor Blvd. and passed a mile's worth of No U-turn signs before being able to swing around again in the right direction. That's when I got distracted by the car in my rearview mirror, the one that had been following me all morning. It had also U-turned. Right now, I couldn't see it anywhere.

'I don't think it could be that serious,' I said. 'it was just a tap.'

'Do you have insurance or not, lady?'

I reached into my purse and pulled out my wallet. I removed the insurance card, which was in Wren's name. 'Right here.'

He reached for it but I stepped back. 'I showed you mine, now you show me yours.'

He gave me a sharp look. I held out my hand palm up, waiting. He plucked his cigarette from his mouth and for a moment I thought he was going to stub it out in my hand. Instead he threw it hard against the pavement. Red sparks bounced up. He didn't step on the butt, just left it lying there, bitter smoke curling up between us.

'You rear-ended *me* lady. That makes the accident your fault. I don't have to show you squat.' He pointed at my Oregon plates. 'In California, the person who caused the accident has to have insurance.'

'Actually, that's not true. Both parties must have insurance and must show their cards. Now, we can exchange this information on our own, or we can call the police and get a legal ruling.' I looked at his muddy plates. 'Your choice, Mr. 2HJY761.'

He gave me a slow-crawl look, his eyes starting at my ankles and slithering up my thighs to my chest and finally my face. This ritual seemed to relax him. He'd checked me out, figured me for just another tight-assed, sexless bitch in a suit who, even if he did somehow get into bed, wouldn't do what he wanted anyway. Now that he could dismiss me as a possible sexual partner, he got down to business. He kneeled down and studied the rear bumper of his car. The only visible mark was a three-inch line where I'd scraped off a little rust. Right next to the scratch was a partially shredded bumper sticker that said: SSDD (Same Shit. Different Day). He straightened up and used his baseball cap to swat the road dust off the knees of his jeans. 'Doesn't look like anything too serious. Guess I could fix it myself.'

I smiled. I never won these kind of arguments with men in pickup trucks or tool belts, so I felt a little cocky. I remembered those two university boys who'd tossed their beer cans at Wren and me, called us lesbos. How nervous I'd been. Now I was standing here with a man who, as a fashion statement, had deliberately torn the sleeves off his T-shirt. And I wasn't nervous at all. Was this how Wren had always felt?

Two young men on bicycles pedaled toward us. Our cars were hugging the right curb, blocking their paths. They were clean-cut, with short hair, white shirts, skinny black ties, dark trousers, and dark shoes. They passed us single file. One of them said, 'Good morning' as they coasted by.

The bearded man shook his head in disgust. 'Fucking Mormons.'

'Jehovah's Witnesses,' I said.

He shot me a dirty look. 'Same difference.' He re-adjusted his baseball cap and climbed back into his truck. He slammed the door and drove away.

I got in my Rabbit and started the engine. I took out some lipstick and pretended to be applying it while I checked my rearview mirror for any signs of the car that had been following me. So far I'd seen it three times this morning, a white Subaru with a bent radio antenna. The first time, it had pulled out of the apartment complex behind me and I only noticed it because it was clean and reminded me I should get my car washed soon. The second time I saw the car was when it exited off the freeway with me. Coincidence, I'd thought. But then, following me down Harbor Blvd. and making the same U-turn, that couldn't be coincidence.

Could it?

In my rearview mirror I watched a red Accord U-turn at the same intersection. A black Nissan did the same. Were they following me too? I looked all around, but still no sign of the white Subaru.

I shook my head. 'Duhhhh,' I said to myself and drove off.

Okay, maybe becoming Wren had made me a little skittish. No one around here knew who I really was, and if they did, they would just bust me, not follow me around. There was no international intrigue here, no mystery. As Wren had often said, I watched too much television.

Could be I was still a little shaken after last night's sexual interlude with Ethan. I even thought that it might be him in the white Subaru, so intoxicated with passion for me that even following me from several car lengths was better than not seeing me at all. Not that I wanted that. Mostly I wanted to forget last night.

'Candles,' Ethan had asked. 'Got any candles?'

'Why?'

'Candlelight would be neat.' He'd sat up in bed, grinning. 'Candles and maybe some music. Very romantic. You got something against romance?'

'My stereo isn't hooked up yet,' I told him.

He frowned. I was frustrating his timing. The stage wasn't properly set for sex.

'You got cable?'

'Cable?'

'Cable TV. You've got cable, right?'

I gestured at the decoder box on top of the TV on my dresser.

'Great!' He leapt out of bed and padded to the TV. His

111

butt was muscular, fuller than Robby's. Hairier too. He turned on the TV, flipped through the stations. 'MTV,' he said, looking smug. 'A little music for me lady.'

The video was old and grainy, Jim Morrison singing 'Don't You Love Her Madly'. Jim's eyes were squinting but expressionless; as if he were thinking about lunch, not love.

'This guy is so cool,' Ethan said, then started singing, '"don't you love her as she's walking out the door . . ."' Suddenly he jumped onto the bed catapulting me a few inches into the air. The covers fell away revealing me in my naked splendor. He shook his head and grinned. 'And me without my camera.'

By now I'd pretty-much lost interest in Ethan but still was intent on the sex part. Somehow it seemed like a good initiation into my new life. Not that I wanted a new life of serial meaningless casual affairs. But it was nice to know that I could if I wanted. That my memories of sex wouldn't always be limited to picturing Robby. Besides, I hadn't had sex in so long, I'd invested too much importance in the act. I didn't want to be one of these bruised women who hoards her sexuality like a precious prize, a jewel to offer up to Mr. Right. When I did meet a guy I really liked, I didn't want to ruin it by putting too much expectation into the sex. I folded my glasses and placed them on Wren's clock/radio.

Ethan was a good lover. He did a variety of things and he did them well. But it all felt too rehearsed, like he was going down a checklist: let's see, we nibbled on the nipple, now let's give her a little finger action. As if this were his comedy act and he had to remember the right order of actions the way he'd remember the order of jokes. The goal for him wasn't to have sex with me, but for me to admire his sexual technique. I was less an object of desire than an audience with a convenient vagina. To him, my moans were applause, my orgasm a standing ovation.

I was surprised by his body. All evening I'd imagined us being the same physical size, even though I knew he was bigger. But in bed, I felt his shoulders, his hips, his legs. They made me feel smaller. He was gentle, but the thought kept coming back to me, He could hurt me. If he wanted to, he could hurt me. I'd never had that thought with Robby.

After Ethan ejaculated, he pushed himself up and grinned at me. 'That was soooo good. I thought I was going to pass out.' Then he laughed. 'Something else to tell our grandkids.'

I closed my eyes and pulled the pillow against my face.

'Wren?'

'Hmmm.'

'What're you thinking?'

'I don't know. Nothing.'

'Me too.'

I opened my eyes and lifted my head from the pillow. He was staring at me with doe eyes. I could tell he was about to say something mushy.

I excused myself and went to the bathroom again.

He called after me, 'Some guys make women weak in the knees, I make them weak in the bladder.'

I sat on the edge of the tub and laid my head on my knees.

I am not a mushy person. Declarations of love or friendship usually come from me couched in a joke or said in such ambiguous terms that I might be referring to something else entirely, the bean dip or a cold front from Canada. I know all the psychobabble buzzwords about such behavior, the unconscious fears of rejection and all that crap that college guys who want to go to bed with you use. And it isn't as if I didn't like hearing a little gushing directed towards me, I'd sop it up like most people. It's just that I don't think people know what they're saying sometimes. They think of words as disposable diapers, once used better not to be examined again. As if words were ethereal, airborne spores that can't be seen and therefore demand no allegiance. They don't understand how mere words can embed themselves so deeply. I mean,

how was it possible for Robby to assure he loved me every
day for ten years, to have said things like 'I want to live
my whole life with you' or 'I'd die without you' or 'I'm
happy only when I'm with you' and then dump me for a
midget Milton scholar who tawks lawk thayat? One day
he's gallantly telling me how if we were shipwrecked with
a limited supply of food and water, he'd gladly drown himself to save my life, the next day he's waving farewell from
someone else's bed. On Monday he'd have sacrificed his
life for mine. On Tuesday, it's Hey, babe, you're on your
own. Good luck.

What had changed? How had the atoms of our lives
come to realign themselves?

This was Robby's explanation: 'It's not that I love her
more than you, Luna, it's just different. It's like . . . it's
like those fish, those anglerfish. In one species the male is
about an inch and a half long, the female is ten inches.
The male attaches himself to the female's body and hangs
on until eventually his internal organs disintegrate and her
system replaces his. He literally can't live without her. He
never swims away because his body and hers are one, the
tissue is fused. She can even cause him to discharge sperm
when she wants. I'm not saying that's what happened with
us. Sometimes I think I'm attached to you, sometimes
you're attached to me. But I don't think we should be
"attached" at all.' Here he wiggled his hands in front of
him like two fish swimming parallel. 'Two people should
be separate, swimming side by side perhaps. But not
attached.'

8

When I pulled into the parking lot there was no sign of a white Subaru with a bent antenna. But I was still a nervous wreck. I hated being late for anything and I was thirty-five minutes late on the very first day of my new job. My stomach churned noisily as I ran into the building, heels popping against the floor like a cap gun. Apparently my Wren-like calm states were only temporary.

'Hi,' I puffed to the receptionist. 'I'm late.'

'Oh, hi.' She stood up and shook my hand. We'd met when I'd interviewed but I couldn't remember her name. 'I guess I'm your official welcoming party.'

'I'm sorry, I don't remember your name.'

'Billie. Billie Meyers.' Her hair was short and combed straight down, like the early Beatles. Her skin was pale, her lipstick radioactively bright. She wore black jersey pants and a white pirate blouse with ornate silver buttons, none of which were the same size or pattern. She also wore red suspenders, but backward, so the part where they usually cross at the back now crossed across her chest, separating her breasts. She was twenty-one, tops.

'Hi, Billie, I'm Wren.' I looked around the office. All the cubicles were empty. A couple Styrofoam cups of coffee sat half-full at desks. Suit jackets were draped around desk chairs. It looked spooky, like a science fiction movie where the population is wiped out and the survivors get to go through the shopping mall and take anything they want for free. 'Where is everybody?'

'Meeting Mr. Krieg.'

115

'He's here?'

'Just arrived this morning. Caught everyone by surprise. You should have seen their faces.' She laughed.

'Of all the days to be late.'

'Don't worry. People from out of town are always late the first few times. They can't figure out our weird traffic.'

I felt a little relieved. 'I couldn't make a U-turn on Harbor Blvd.'

The phone rang and Billie snatched it up. '*Orange Coast Today*. May I help you?'

She sounded like a cheery waitress: Welcome to Arby's, may I take your order. I liked that about her. When she hung up, she turned back to me with a big smile. 'I'm so glad you're working here. I read some of those articles you submitted. You're so smart. I'm totally jealous.'

I looked away, embarrassed. 'Thanks. Did they want me to join them in the meeting or what?'

'Linda said you should go see Debra in personnel, get the paperwork out of the way.'

'Where's that?'

'Down the hall. Suite 308.'

A sudden rumble of muffled laughter sounded. It came from the conference room at the back of the office. The door to the room was closed.

'Sounds like they're having a good time,' I said.

The phone rang again and Billie answered it. '*Orange Coast Today*. May I help you?' She winked at me for no reason I could think of. 'She's in a meeting. May I take a message?'

I started down the hall.

*   *   *   *   *

'You skipped one,' she said.

'Where?' I leaned closer to her desk.

'Here. Married or single.' Debra slid the form back across the desk and handed me her pen. 'Most people

116

skip weight. I remember one time, not here but the last place I worked, this woman argued and ranted, saying how this whole form was unconstitutional, an invasion of privacy. Like I really gave a flying fudge how much she weighed. I told her, hey, it's just for insurance purposes, but she was livid. Finally she scribbled in 120 pounds: I'm talking about a broad who tipped in at 185 after a two-week fast.'

My pen hovered over the two tiny boxes. Married. Single. Which should I check? How much had Wren told them about her past when she'd applied. Linda Marley hadn't asked about my husband, or maybe Wren hadn't mentioned Byron.

I checked single.

Debra looked at my checkmark and sighed. 'Good luck,' she said without enthusiasm. She looked to be a few years older than I and wore no wedding ring. She also had a heavy hand with the blush. Her cheeks were an unusual shade; if it were a shoe polish it would be called ox blood. She dressed a little young, as if she were trying to look like Billie the receptionist, despite their fifteen-year and twenty-pound difference.

'What happened there?' Debra asked, pointing a paper clip at my grooved thumbnail.

'Nothing. Nervous habit.'

She nodded. 'Me, I gnaw the cuticles. Look.' She held out her hands. They were perfectly manicured, but the skin around the nails looked raw and sore. I could see the various layers of skin peeled back. 'We all have our little flaws, I guess. I went out with this psychologist for a while, his office is up on twenty-eight.' She pointed toward the ceiling. 'He said chewing nails is a sign of self-loathing, that I wanted to consume myself.' She shrugged. 'I almost married him. Talk about self-loathing.'

I signed the bottom of the form and slid it back to her.

'Welcome, welcome,' Debra said, smiling as she handed me a large manila envelope. 'These are your benefits. Medical, dental, et cetera. We have an excellent plan here. You bust it, we cover it.'

117

'I'll try not to bust anything.'

'That's good too.'

The door behind me opened and Linda Marley, my new boss, stuck her head in. 'There you are. Hurry, we've got something for you.' To Debra. 'She can finish up here later. Okay, Deb?'

'She's done now,' Debra said.

'Great.' Linda opened the door for me and I went out into the hall with her. She set a brisk pace down the hall back toward the editorial offices. Our heels chattered chaotically, then mine seem to fall into rhythm with hers with no effort from me. It was like that bird last night, the one cawing in time with my blinking. 'Not much time to explain, Wren. Something happened this morning, Mr. Krieg wants you on it right away.'

'Me? I don't even know where the bathrooms are yet.'

'He thinks you're the only one who can handle it.' The coolness in her voice indicated she disagreed with Mr. Krieg.

'Look, Linda, I'm still a virgin around here. I don't want to get caught in any crossfire on my first day. What's going on?'

She stopped our forced march and looked at me. The frustration that had hardened her face eased a little and she smiled slightly. 'It's nothing, Wren. Really. Mr. Krieg has some new ideas, new directions he wants this magazine to go in. I have to get used to it, that's all. He's the one worth a few hundred million dollars; I'm the one with $438.45 in her checking account. He must know something, right?'

I opened the glass door for her. She entered, I followed. Linda Marley was about forty, I guessed from the fine lines around her eyes and mouth. She didn't bother covering them with makeup, which I admired. She wore a blue pin-striped pantsuit with wide lapels. A bronze woman swimmer frozen in midcrawl was pinned to her lapel. Her hair was blonder than mine and pulled tight into a Swedish braid that made her look businesslike but not manly. I suspected that when her hair was down, she looked like Faye Dunaway.

'What's Jonathan Krieg like?' I asked. 'Anything like the newspapers say?'

'He's just a man.'

I recoiled in mock horror. 'Not one of *those*.' Linda smiled and I said, 'What kind of man?'

'The worst kind. Rich. Powerful. A man who demands to get what he wants, even when he doesn't know what he wants.'

I screwed up my face. 'I don't follow, but it sounds damn profound.'

Linda laughed. 'I don't know what I mean either. It's easier to be profound that way.' She stopped at a wooden door with no name on it, knocked. 'Hello?' she said to the closed door.

'Yez, comb in, pleez,' the accented voice inside said.

I knew from television and *People* magazine that Jonathan Krieg was New York City born and raised, friends with movie stars and rock musicians, snappy dresser and dashing playboy who once dated Maria Shriver and Caroline Kennedy. He did not speak with an accent.

'Comb in, comb in,' the voice insisted.

I gave a puzzled look at Linda.

She smiled. 'Beware the Jabberwock, my son.'

She pushed open the door.

The man behind the desk was dressed in a rumpled black suit and plain black hat. His craggy face was consumed by a long black beard with two gray stripes. His sideburns were long springy curls. He smiled at us like Santa Claus. 'Shalom,' he said, waving us into the room. 'Shalom, ladeez.'

'Shalom,' Linda said.

'Sit, pleez,' he said. He gestured at the leather chairs across from the desk.

'Thanks, but I've got to run,' Linda said. She nudged me forward and said to the bearded man, 'You take care of my girl, okay. She's gonna be a star around here.'

119

He nodded enthusiastically. 'Of courz.'

'Uh, Linda,' I said.

'You'll be fine,' she said. She left, closing the door behind her.

The office was huge, the size of an airline lobby. The desk was an unpolished slab of dark gray stone the size of a door balanced on two stone pillars. The only things on the slab were a black telephone, some typed pages clipped together, and a worn blue book with gold Hebrew lettering on the cover. The Hebrew lettering reminded me of Esther's gravestone. I recognized the typed pages as one of Wren's articles. They seemed to glow unnaturally white against the cold gray stone. Suddenly the whole desk reminded me of a gravestone, as if the stone had been unearthed at some archaeological site, the lid of some dead pharaoh's sarcophagus.

'Hello,' I said to the elderly man, 'I'm Wren Caldwell.'

'Ya,' he said. 'Nize meeting you.'

'That's Rabbi Weiss,' the voice behind me said.

I turned. The Jonathan Krieg from *People* magazine came out of the bathroom drying his hands on a towel. He dried each hand separately, like wineglasses. His black hair was slicked back. He wore a black shirt buttoned to the throat and a thick white cable-knit cardigan sweater with pockets, which made him look natty and much younger than the fiftyish that I'd read he was. He was trim, his gaunt face making him look like he was leaning toward you all the time, ready to pounce. He reminded me of a corporate Dennis Hopper. He held out his hand to me. 'Hi, Wren, I'm Jonathan.'

'Hello,' I said, shaking his hand. The skin was warm despite the recent washing. 'I understand I have you to thank for my job.'

'Yes, you do.'

'Well then . . . thanks.'

He didn't seem to hear me. He crossed the room and stood behind the old rabbi, resting his hands on the older man's shoulders. 'Rabbi Weiss is from Israel. He lives on a kibbutz outside Tel Aviv. He walks with a limp because a terrorist grenade shattered his right knee. Show her your tattoo, Rabbi.'

Rabbi Weiss held up his hands in protest. 'Jonathan, pleez.'

'It's okay, Rabbi. She is an educated woman. This is also part of her education. She's a journalist now.'

Rabbi Weiss sighed as if indulging a favorite grandson, though the rabbi was probably only ten years older than Jonathan. He pushed up his sleeve and revealed a faded tattooed number on his forearm. The seven had a line through it in European fashion.

'Dachau,' Jonathan said. 'He was just a boy.'

'That was a long time ago,' Rabbi Weiss said, tugging his sleeve back down.

'His father was killed in the camps, not by Nazis, but by a fellow Jew who tried to rape his mother. The other man choked his father to death and then raped his mother anyway. How does that make you feel, Wren?'

My mouth was dry. The way he was looking at me I thought he was about to present evidence that it was one of my relatives who'd done it. I remembered something about being told my father's mother was half Jewish, though she'd never practiced the faith that I know of.

'How does it make you feel?' he repeated firmly.

'I don't know. Guilty, mostly. Also outraged.'

'Exactly!' He clapped his hands together and chuckled. 'That's exactly what we're looking for in the new *Orange Coast Today*. A new tone of outrage tempered with a hopeful sense of renewed purpose. We make our readers feel a little guilty, then tell them how to feel better. See what I'm getting at?'

'Not exactly.'

'Okay.' He thrust his hands into the pockets of his cardigan sweater and paced behind the rabbi. 'Rabbi, tell Wren why I flew you here from Israel. Why I am putting you up at the Four Seasons for the next three months. Why we are meeting every afternoon.'

121

Rabbi Weiss smiled. 'Bar mitzvah.'

'Oh, how nice,' I said. 'Whose?'

'Mine,' Jonathan Krieg said.

'I thought that happened when you were thirteen.'

'Traditionally, yes. But I was too busy when I was thirteen, too busy hustling a buck. I worked in a newsroom for a guy, a reporter name of Mannheim. Taught me a lot. He went on to Hollywood, burned out after three mediocre screenplays. Ended up doing celebrity interviews for one of the tabloids. Meantime, I bought the newspaper, sold it, bought a computer software company, sold it, bought a few more companies, sold them. I made my fortune, just like in the movies, just like the insipid movies Mannheim used to write. Sit, Wren, sit.'

I sat in the leather chair across from his desk. I had no idea what he was talking about. Rabbi Weiss didn't seem to follow either, or at least wasn't interested, because he opened the book in front of him and began to read. His lips moved, though he made no sound, and his body rocked slightly in a rhythm with his reading.

'Maybe this will help,' Jonathan Krieg said, coming around the desk and standing next to me. 'Feel this.' He crooked his arm to make a muscle.

I looked over at the rabbi, but he was lost in his silent chanting.

'Go ahead,' Jonathan urged. 'Don't be shy. Squeeze it.'

I squeezed it. It didn't feel too solid, not like Robby's.

'Well?' he asked.

'I'm not very good at this,' I hedged. 'I'm not much of a bodybuilder.'

'Honestly, tell me what you think. Is that one hell of a muscle or what?'

I thought of saying something half-hearted like, For your age . . . But that seemed an even worse insult. Wren would know what to say. I tried to imagine her here, answering. She'd make some joke, something like, That's not the muscle that counts, and everyone would laugh and forget the original point because she'd be on to something

122

else, something she read about a recent study concerning muscle memory and a group of track and field athletes at some midwestern college.

'I don't know, Jonathan,' I said. 'Feels a little soft to me.'

'Exactly!' he said triumphantly. 'I'm in my fifties and I'm way out of shape. I look fit, but I'm not. That's why I hired personal fitness trainers. A husband-and-wife team, they moonlight as stunt people in the movies. Starting tomorrow, they will come over every day and beat me into shape. You know what else? I never finished college. Took two semesters and that's it. Hell, you want to know the truth, I didn't even finish high school. So I enrolled in Pacific West University, to whom I donated a medical wing last year. They're letting me finish my degree by doing independent studies. I hired a couple tutors to help me through my first semester. See what I'm getting at here?'

'Jonathan,' the rabbi said, tapping his watch crystal. '*Mach schnell.*'

'Yes, Rabbi.' Jonathan Krieg sat on the edge of the stone desk, facing me. 'It's never too late, Wren. That's my point. I can still go through my bar mitzvah. I can still get into good physical shape. I can still earn my degree. Human potential is limitless. It's never too late for people to become who they want to be. But a lot of people don't know what they want to be. That's where we come in. What we're going to be doing here at the magazine is helping them see what kind of people they want to become.'

I exhaled a deep breath that I didn't even know I'd inhaled. 'That's a tall order for a little regional magazine.'

'That's why I bought it. I could have purchased a more popular magazine, or even a daily newspaper. I could have gone to Los Angeles, Miami, stayed in New York. But this place'—he spread his arms out and turned slowly, like Julie Andrews in *The Sound of Music*—'this place is perfect. Orange County is one of the most expensive places in the country to live. Median house prices are over $200,000. You have desperately poor areas, openly gay

123

communities, conspicuous wealth, Robert Schuller's Crystal Cathedral, one of the largest concentrations of Vietnamese refugees. We're going to double our circulation in less than a year. I guarantee it.'

'That's great,' I said. The force of his personality was so overwhelming, instead of being nervous, I felt good to be in his presence. He seemed so sure of himself, so clear about the nature of the world and his ability to make it do what he wanted, I was suddenly very relaxed.

I crossed my legs and my skirt slid up a few inches above my knee. The rabbi looked up from his reading and glanced at my legs. He smiled appreciatively and returned to his reading. I tugged my hem down over my knees.

Jonathan looked at his watch. 'We don't have much time. I have an assignment for you, part of the new direction of the magazine.'

'Yes?'

'You ever hear of Season Dougherty?'

'The name's familiar.'

'She accused her ex-husband of sexually molesting their daughter during his custody, so she sent the kid into hiding with her sister.'

'Right, I remember. The judge ordered her to produce the child but she wouldn't, so he jailed her. She's been in prison for the past few months.'

'Eight months,' Jonathan corrected. 'She got out yesterday after the state legislature passed that special bill limiting jail time in these cases. Same as that Washington, D.C. case.'

'That's good.'

'Except that I just got a call from a friend of mine at City Hall that she's been arrested again. Half an hour ago they found her ex-husband dead of a shotgun blast.'

The rabbi looked up and shook his head. 'Terrible thing.' Then he glanced at my legs and returned to his book.

'Are they sure she did it?' I asked.

'She confessed.'

I no longer felt that warm basking feeling. My stomach started to tighten. I had to pin my hand under my thigh to keep it from rubbing my bra strap. 'I don't see where I fit in here.'

'We have a window of opportunity here. I've arranged for you to visit the crime scene and then to have access to interview Season. You'll have a goddamn exclusive.'

'Me?'

'Yes.'

'I don't have any experience with this kind of thing. This is crime. You want a reporter. I do think pieces.' I opened my purse and pulled out a sheaf of papers. I'd come prepared with one of Wren's recent articles I'd printed out from her floppy disk. I thrust the papers toward him. 'This is what I write.'

Jonathan held up his hands and retreated behind his desk, behind the rabbi. 'I understand this is a little different for you. But so what? I hired you because I could see something special in your writing, a certain tone, an eye for just the right detail. Let's face it, our readership is eighty-seven per cent women. You have the voice of the contemporary woman. You are the nineties woman. You see the right slant on things, the slant that our readers want to see.'

'I just write about issues, Mr. Krieg.'

He shook his head dismissively. 'It's not about issues anymore, Wren. There is no more Women's Lib. Now it's just Women's Glib, the same issues but with a snappy, more ironic attitude. Right now we have a reputation as a glossy rag for pampered housewives. Our articles are puff pieces mostly designed to keep the ads apart. I want to change all that. Make this *the* magazine for the contemporary woman in Orange County. To do that I need to have someone who can talk to them, knows what they are thinking. Knows their language, the language of their hearts and souls.' He tapped his own chest over his heart. 'That's you, Wren.'

I squirmed in my chair. That's Wren, not me.

'You know what a sob sister is, Wren?'

'It's a newspaper term. Used to have something to do with women reporters or something.' I couldn't think. My chest was constricting around my bullet hole.

'In the old days, it referred to a reporter, usually a woman, who wrote sentimental feature stories, you know, children orphaned by train wreck, that sort of thing. Well, we're going to be doing a variation of that. You're going to be a New Age sob sister.'

I stood up, anxious to leave. 'I appreciate your confidence in me, but I don't see how this murder ties in to that whole improve-their-lives attitude you just told me about. This just sounds like old-fashioned sensationalism.'

'It's part of the harsh reality of the way things work. Remember, we're striving for impact here.' He slammed his hand on the slab desk. The rabbi didn't even look up. 'Outrage! Guilt! Outrage at what was done to this poor woman and her child, that we as a community let it come to this. Guilt that we didn't help her.' He softened his voice. 'Then healing as we explain how things got this bad, how to prevent them in your own homes and families. See?'

'No, sir, I don't see.' I waved my papers at him. 'Just read this. Did you know it's the Year of the Horse in Korea?' He started to say something but I kept talking. 'When the Buddha knew he was about to die, he invited all the animals to attend. Only a few showed up and out of gratitude he named a year after each animal. Many people think that a person receives some of the characteristics of the animal into whose year he or she is born.'

The rabbi lifted his head, his finger marking where he'd stopped reading. He watched me with interest.

'The problem in Korea this year is that women who are born during the year of the horse are considered skittish, a little wild. They are not considered good marriage material, therefore they are often shunned by the men. And now, with modern medical techniques, the parents can know what the child's sex is within a few months. The

126

thing is, because it's the Year of the Horse, many Korean women, if they find out they are pregnant with a girl, are having their babies aborted. Can you imagine the implications? This policy has caused a severe shortage of women. There are half a million men within a certain age group who have no hope of marrying. That's what this article is all about. This has everything you wanted: Outrage! Guilt! Healing!' My cheeks were hot with passion. For a moment, I felt as if I actually had written this article my-self. 'This is the same kind of New Age sob sister stuff that you want. The voice of the nineties woman.'

'Perfect,' Jonathan said, applauding. 'I love it. Really. It's great.'

'So sad,' the rabbi said, shaking his head.

I sat back down, exhausted.

'Trouble is, Wren,' Jonathan said, 'that's in Korea, half a world away. Season Dougherty is right here in Orange County in the Irvine jail. Her husband's body is in a Turtle Rock house right here in Orange County. And the name of our magazine is *Orange Coast Today*. You see a pattern?' He pushed up the sleeves of his sweater. 'I've managed to use a little leverage with an old friend to make sure you're the first journalist on the scene of the crime and the first with access to Mrs. Dougherty.' He tapped his watch the same way the rabbi had earlier. 'And our window of opportunity is slowly closing on our collective fingers.'

'*Ein ziemliches Mädchen,*' the rabbi said to Jonathan.

'He says you're a pretty woman.'

'Very pretty,' the rabbi nodded.

I stood up. 'Thank you.'

'Linda has the background information you need. But you'd better hurry.'

'What about this article?' I said, brandishing the pages.

'Maybe you can work it into the Dougherty piece. Better yet, use it when we do something about the violence at abortion clinics in Orange County. That'll work.'

127

I held my hand out to the rabbi. He shook it and said, 'Shalom.'

'Shalom,' I said.

'Good luck, Wren,' Jonathan said. 'This is the start of great things for both of us. It's great to be back in the swing of publishing again. Makes me feel like a kid still running around that newsroom.'

Was that what all this was about? I was hired so Jonathan Krieg could relive his youth. I was just part of the package, the team of human time machines gathered to help him recapture the youth he squandered amassing his fortune. The rabbi, the tutors, the husband-wife stunt team. And now me.

I closed the door behind me and stood, gathering my thoughts. What did I have to be angry about? I had a good job, the respect of my coworkers, even of my boss. Maybe it wasn't anger at all. Just fear. I didn't know how to interview a murderer. The only crime scene I'd been at was the one where I was the victim. I didn't want to get that close to other people's problems, didn't want to become intimate with their despair.

Through the door I heard the rabbi begin to sing in Hebrew. He stopped and Jonathan Krieg sang the same refrain, but haltingly, stumbling over the words. Then the rabbi sang again, even more beautifully than before. It was somehow mournful and cheerful at the same time. Jonathan tried again, his voice a monotone of determination.

'Wren?' Billie the receptionist called. 'Telephone. Line three.'

I walked to my desk, passing a few of my fellow journalists. Each stopped what they were doing to look up and say hello or welcome. I remembered a couple names but not most. Everyone was extremely friendly, but there was something in their voices, a tone they all shared, of grudging good humor and nagging jealousy. It's not my fault, I wanted to shout, I didn't ask Jonathan Krieg to make me the New Age sob sister.

My office was in a cubicle surrounded by those low temporary partitions that are covered with mauve cloth. The desk itself was a standard gray metal, not unlike the one in my office at school. Except this one had rubber bumpers trimming the edges. Also, the desktop was some sort of phony wood veneer. A flat ivory telephone with a row of clear plastic buttons sat next to a cluster of tape dispenser, stapler, and electric pencil sharpener. The button marked #3 was flashing.

In the middle of the desk was a blue file folder with a typed label on the tab: DOUGHERTY, SEASON. A typed note was clipped to the front with two addresses, Lester Dougherty's and the Irvine Police Department's. Detailed directions to each location were included. At the bottom, in florid handwriting: *Happy motoring, Billie.*

I sat down and pushed the folder aside.

Attached to the desk was a floating platform on which was bolted a Macintosh SE computer. I could see my face in the dark screen. My hair was down, which I had hoped would make me look a little more glamorous, like Rosalind Russell in *His Girl Friday*. My glasses reflected pinpoints of light. I took them off and placed them on the file folder. The right earpiece was still chewed off.

I picked up the phone and pushed #3. 'Hello, this is Wren Caldwell.'

'Thank God, thank God,' the man said. 'We've been looking for you everywhere.'

'Who is this?'

'Phil Sanchez over at Valley College. I've been trying to reach you for a week. Why didn't you tell us you'd moved here already?'

I felt panicky. Who was this guy? He seemed to know Wren, but how much did he know? An old friend/lover/colleague whom she'd contacted when she applied for this job? Would he come rushing over now and expose me to everyone?

'Uh, I'm sorry'—Phil or Mr. Sanchez? How close were

they?—'everything was so hectic with the move and everything.'

'I understand,' he said, but his voice was stern, a little put out. What had Wren done to him? 'However, you made a commitment to teach that course and classes start Monday. I called your old number up in Oregon but it had been disconnected. Information says your local number is unlisted.'

That was deliberate. I didn't want any of Wren's old friends leafing through the phone book to accidentally come across her name.

'I'd have replaced you, but the other person who teaches art history got a grant from the NEA and she took off for Mazatlan to paint. We really need you to live up to your commitment, Ms. Caldwell.'

Wren had applied to teach art history?

'You got the section you asked for, Monday nights six to ten P.M. Your class meets in Art 110. The textbook is in the bookstore, they'll give you a free copy. Your section is packed, so don't take any petitioners. Drop by the administration building and fill out the paperwork. You'll have a mailbox there in the Adjunct Faculty section.' There was a pause. 'You sound funny.'

Damn, he'd spoken to her before. 'Funny?'

'Different. I don't know, it's been a month. It's just, I don't know, I remembered your voice as being very . . . Hell, stop me before I make a complete ass of myself.' He laughed.

I laughed as best I could. I watched myself laugh in the computer screen. I looked like someone choking.

'Any questions?' he asked.

'Nope. Monday sounds good.'

'Okay then, if you have any problems, give me a call or drop in my office. Drop in anyway, I'd like to meet you. Your résumé impressed the hell out of all of us.'

'Thanks.'

'Well, good luck.' He hung up.

I hung up too. My hand was trembling. I picked up my

file folder on Season Dougherty, put my glasses back on, strapped my purse on, and wandered toward the exit. I had to go to a crime scene to view a corpse, then to jail to interview a murderer, then home to prepare to teach an art history course, about which I knew nothing. I could have backed out of the teaching, but Phil Sanchez seemed angry enough that he'd call the university in Oregon to complain about Wren Caldwell. I didn't want that.

'Good luck,' Billie said cheerfully as I left.

Around the corner was the floor's elevator foyer. I pressed the button and waited. I looked out the window at the parking lot below. There was my Rabbit, still needing a wash.

And there, parked next to my car, was a white Subaru with a bent antenna.

I jabbed the elevator button repeatedly. This time I was going to catch the son of a bitch. The elevator doors yawned open and I jumped in and punched my floor button. I watched the lighted floor numbers above the door flicker by like a countdown at NASA. My stomach was tight with excitement. Was this how my father felt waiting for his rockets to blast off. When we hit the ground floor, I ran out before the doors had completely opened, bumping my shoulder hard on the door. I pushed ahead of an elderly man to beat him through the glass door leading to the parking lot. I ran along the rows of parked cars until I found my Rabbit.

The white Subaru was gone.

9

'It ain't like the movies,' Detective Diesel said, snapping on a pair of surgical gloves. 'First of all, we don't stand around over the body and trade wisecracks.'

He squatted next to the body and stared at it for a couple of minutes. The body was dressed in gray jogging pants and a T-shirt that said Nike, Just Do It. It was sitting on the dining-room floor, back slumped against the wall, legs splayed apart like a wishbone. Someone had draped a red-checkered dish towel over the head. Dark blood had soaked through the cloth forming some strange Rorschach pattern that reminded me of sumo wrestlers colliding. Detective Diesel looked over the entire body head to toe without touching anything, as if he were about to give an estimate for the cost of hauling the corpse to the dump. He stopped to stare at the man's crotch. The shotgun blast had shredded the cloth and skin and muscle, leaving the lap nothing more than a chunky stew. The left leg's thigh bone was exposed, sticking straight up like a pink and white twig. The detective shook his head and looked up at me. My pen was poised for his insight into this kind of violence. 'If anything,' he said, 'television has ruined more cops. Especially the young ones. They all think they have to act like *Miami Vice*.'

I wrote that down in my notebook.

Detective Diesel reached for the dish towel covering the head. 'You sure you want to see this? I can always give you a peek at the police photographs later.'

'I'm fine,' I said. Actually, I really was fine. Maybe it

was morbid, but I felt somehow comfortable, more at ease right then than I'd felt since my own shooting. From the moment I'd regained consciousness in the hospital, way before I'd decided to slip into Wren's life, nothing around me seemed familiar. Everywhere I went, whoever I spoke to, I felt like an imposter, someone masquerading as a living person. I didn't even belong in Luna's body. Her skin didn't fit me, like I was walking around in a pair of too-big shoes. Every step further blistered me. Maybe that's what made it so easy to become Wren.

But here, walking around this fresh dead body, amid the sour smell of sweat and urine and faeces, I could relax. Be myself. I felt like a mini support group for the poor guy: Don't worry, pal, being dead's not so bad. I could tell him.

'Okay then,' Detective Diesel said. 'Let's see what we got here . . .' He pinched the two bottom corners of the dish towel and hesitated, like a magician about to snap a tablecloth out from under a fancy dinner setting. Then he delicately peeled back the dish towel. As Detective Diesel exposed more and more of the head, his own craggy, middle-aged face began to smooth out, the deep lines disappear. His jaw tightened, causing his small ears to flatten against his skull. He tossed the sticky towel aside.

The corpse had no face. It looked like lumpy chili or boiling tomato soup. A fat black fly landed on the face, about where a nose used to be. Detective Diesel brushed it away with the back of his hand.

The youngest uniformed cop walked up and wagged a finger at the corpse. 'See, I told you not to pick your zits.' He chuckled and winked at me.

'Donaldson!' Detective Diesel snapped.

'Yes, sir,' the officer said with some fear.

'Get me the fingerprinting gear. And keep your asinine comments to yourself. You understand me, son?'

'Yes, sir.' Officer Donaldson looked sheepishly at me, then back at Detective Diesel.

'Then move, goddamn it!'

'Yes, sir.' He ran off.

Detective Diesel shrugged at me. 'What can you do?'

'*Miami Vice*,' I nodded.

'Exactly.'

I took a couple steps closer to the body, stared at the damage. All that had happened here was that a load of pellets had collided with flesh and bone. On a molecular level it was just particles bumping into other particles, jostled electrons, atoms spinning into new orbits. Nothing had been destroyed. Only the configuration was altered, little more than a subatomic rearrangement of furniture. In the cosmic picture, what then had really changed?

'Have you done this a lot?' Detective Diesel asked.

'First time.'

He arched an eyebrow. 'You handle it well.'

'Thank you.' I was in a surprisingly good mood. The closer I got to the body, the happier I felt. I almost started humming. It was like coming out of a freezing snowstorm and huddling up to a warm fire. When I leaned over the corpse's face, my own bullet scar twinged. Maybe it was some sort of sympathetic vibration, I don't know, but my heart seemed suddenly closer to the surface now. If I scratched away the scar-tissue plug, I'd look straight down that dark tunnel and see my slippery heart fussing and squirming like a new baby. I rubbed the scar on my breast and one of the uniformed cops going through the hall closet nudged his partner and grinned at me.

Officer Donaldson returned with the fingerprinting equipment. Detective Diesel took the corpse's right index finger, rolled it across the ink pad, then rolled the inky fingertip onto a piece of cardboard.

'Is this necessary?' I asked. 'You already know who it is.'

'We *think* we know.' He held up the middle finger of the dead hand, offering it to me. 'You wanna try?'

'Sure.' I tucked my notebook and pen into my purse and knelt down next to him. 'What do I do?'

'Grasp it firmly. It's starting to stiffen up.'

One of the officers snickered and mumbled to another cop. They laughed. Detective Diesel's face flushed a deep red. 'I mean, you know, rigor mortis.'

'I know.' I prised the middle finger apart from the rest of his hand and dipped it against the pad that Detective Diesel held for me.

'Roll it from side to side. We want the whole print.'

I rolled the dead finger from side to side. Detective Diesel put down the pad and pushed the cardboard across the carpet close to my knees.

'Now do the same thing you did on the pad, roll it from one side to the other side. Firmly, but not too hard.'

I did so. The fingerprint appeared like a stenciled design. It was kind of pretty. Not unlike the art my friends with children have hanging on their refrigerators.

'Good job, Ms. Caldwell. You're a natural.'

'Thanks.' I stood up. A small smudge of ink marked the back of my hand. 'Is there really any reason to doubt that this is Philip Dougherty?'

'He fits the same physical description. We found his wallet with ID in his pocket. This is his house. We have a confession from the murderer who says this is Philip Dougherty. But with no face, it could be anybody.'

'You mean like on TV, whenever they find a body with no face, it's never who the cops think it is?'

'Exactly. As soon as they say, "The body's been burned beyond recognition," you know it's someone else.'

'But they always find a convenient watch or a necklace or something that indicates who they think it is.'

'Exactly,' he nodded, inking the thumb. 'Only this isn't television. Fingerprints don't lie. There are no two sets alike. Just like snowflakes.'

'Actually,' I said, 'I read recently where scientists discovered that all snowflakes aren't different. That the patterns are repeated.'

'Yeah?' He slipped a plastic bag over the corpse's hand and snapped a rubber band around the wrist to keep it in place. 'I hadn't heard that.'

'That's kind of interesting, though, isn't it? Imagine, there could be somebody out there with your fingerprints and he could be doing all kinds of nasty things that you could get blamed for.'

'It wouldn't surprise me.' Detective Diesel stood up, walked off a stiffness in his right leg. 'I guess that's why we now have DNA fingerprinting. Believe me, Ms. Caldwell, we're always one step ahead of the bad guys.'

'Just like *Miami Vice*?'

He smiled beautifully. 'Just like *Miami Vice*.'

* * * * *

'She's waiting to see Season Dougherty,' Detective Diesel said to the woman cop behind the desk. 'The chief said it was okay.'

'I gotta check with Dougherty's P.D. first, Bob,' she said.

Detective Diesel turned to me. 'P.D., that's public defender.'

'Thanks,' I said. I wrote that down in my notebook to make him feel good.

'I mean, you're getting the jump on the story, but the lady still has rights.' He seemed a little annoyed that strings had been pulled by Jonathan Krieg. 'She doesn't have to see you if she doesn't want to.'

'I understand.'

He nodded, turned back to the desk sergeant.

She hung up the phone. 'The P.D.'s in the building. We're still trying to find her.'

'Who is it?' Detective Diesel asked.

'Rebba Mallard.'

Detective Diesel nodded appreciatively. 'She's good.'

The desk sergeant shrugged. 'We're all good.' She looked him in the eye for some reaction, but Detective Diesel just nodded and turned toward me.

He guided me over to an orange molded plastic bench.

136

'You can wait here until they clear it. Meantime, I've got a living to earn. Nice working with you, Ms. Caldwell.'

'Now that we've fingerprinted a corpse together, you can call me Wren.'

'Okay, Wren. See ya around the scene of the crime sometime.' He started to walk away.

'Can I ask you a quick question?'

He smiled. 'That's what you have been doing, isn't it?'

'This has nothing to do with the murder. It's hypothetical.'

'Oh,' he nodded knowingly. 'You have a friend.'

'What?'

'That's how hypothetical questions to cops always begin. "I have this friend who . . ."'

'Okay, I have this friend who hacked up her in-laws and is going to ship parts of the bodies to Johnny Carson and Joan Rivers in an effort to make them friends again. She wants to know if she should turn herself in.'

He laughed. 'Okay, I deserved that. What's the problem?'

'What do you do if you think someone's following you?'

'Do you know him?'

'No. I don't know. I haven't seen his face. I don't even know if it is a him. Just the same car.'

'There are a lot of cars in southern California, you're bound to see some repeats.'

'This is definitely the same car.'

'You want to file a report, be on the safe side?'

I shook my head. I couldn't afford any kind of investigation into my past. 'It's probably nothing.'

'Get the license number, give me a call. I'll run a check.'

'Thank you.'

'Meantime, stay out of dark parking garages.'

'I will,' I said, shaking his hand. 'Thanks for all your help.'

He seemed embarrassed by my gratitude, lowering his

head as he walked away through the doors marked AUTH-
ORIZED PERSONNEL ONLY.

I sat on the hard orange bench and reviewed my notes.
They were neat notes, numbered and lettered the same as
if I were in a literature class. I hadn't lost the knack. Still,
I had no idea how to turn them into an actual article that
anybody but a paid professor would want to read. I could
whip up a theme paper maybe, with footnotes and a bibli-
ography. I closed my notebook and tried to think of an
opening line, one that would grab the reader. Nothing
came. Maybe I could call Robby, have him help me without telling him what it was about. I began concocting elaborate stories to convince him. That made me even more
depressed. Why, at every moment of crisis, did I still think
of Robby? Before, when Robby and I were together and
happy, some couple we knew would be splitting up and
they would weep and look desperate. I would be sympathetic. Months later I'd see one of them and he or she would
still be unhappy and ragged-looking and I'd think, Snap
out of it, get on with your life. I wanted to go back in time
and take the old, smug me and shake her by the shoulders,
tell her to have some *compassion*, damn it. Now it seemed
to me that breaking up was less an event and more like a
nasty virus that lodges in your spine and reappears at
every moment of weakness and doubt.

I noticed the ink smudge on my hand again. I licked my
fingertips and rubbed the spot off.

I tried to imagine what Season Dougherty was doing
right now. What did a woman do all day in prison? Was
it like those women-behind-bars movies that guys like so
much; did she have to fend off lesbian advances from
thick-necked women carrying broom handles? Was she in
there right now sharpening the edges of a spoon she
smuggled out of the cafeteria to fight off raging dikes? Or
was she at this moment poring over dusty law books, rubbing her weary eyes, adjusting her reading glasses in the
dim light, as she searched in vain for some legal precedent
that would win her freedom and reunite her with her

daughter? Was she a monster, a crazed bitch with a shotgun, who coldly smiled as she blasted her ex-husband's genitals into oatmeal? Or was she the self-sacrificing Ultimate Mother, willing to give up her own life to protect her innocent daughter? I tried to adopt an attitude toward her, but it was difficult. I wasn't in any position to take the moral high road here.

The glass door banged open and a little girl about seven ran into the lobby from the parking lot. She wore a denim skirt bleached almost white, white socks, sneakers, and a lime-green T-shirt. She was carrying a man's wallet in both hands and laughing giddily.

A man about thirty-five followed her into the building, holding the hand of a little boy, about eight or nine. 'Whoa, there, Judy,' he called to the little girl. 'Can I have my wallet back?'

She giggled, held up his wallet, then put it behind her back.

'Jud-ee, Jud-ee, Jud-ee,' the man said, imitating Cary Grant.

'Judy, Judy, Judy,' she repeated, imitating him.

'Okay, Nurse Judy. This is important surgery. We must save the patient. The fate of the free world rests in the balance. Scalpel.' He held out his hand, palm up.

'Scalpel,' she said, placing an imaginary instrument in his palm.

'You have to slap it in. Smack, like this.' He slapped his own palm. 'Again. Scalpel.'

'Scalpel.' She slapped his hand hard.

'Screwdriver,' he said.

'Screwdriver.' She slapped his hand again.

'Let me,' the little boy begged, twisting out of the man's grip.

The man turned to the boy with his palm open. 'Chainsaw.'

'Chainsaw,' the boy said gleefully, and slapped the hand as hard as he could.

'Wallet,' the man said to the girl.

'Wallet?' she asked.

'Sure. The patient's wallet to pay our bill.'

She laughed and slapped the wallet into his palm. He put the wallet into his back pocket.

'Good job, guys. Looks like the operation was a success. The patient has two heads so now he has someone to laugh at his knock-knock jokes. Now, wait for Daddy over there.' He pointed to the blue bench next to my orange one. They ran over and sat down. The man talked to the desk sergeant in a low voice I couldn't hear. She looked directly at me, then whispered something to him. He whispered something back. She laughed, then the man laughed too.

'Hang on,' the desk sergeant said in a friendly tone. 'I'll see what I can do.' She picked up the phone.

The man thanked her and sat down with his children. He wasn't very tall, I noticed, only a couple inches taller than I. And he was a few pounds overweight, giving his face a smooth, slightly puffy look. His blond hair was short and neat. His clothes were casual and baggy, but expensive.

The little girl took out a flat plastic case the size of a deck of cards. The case was filled with water and had a plastic frog inside. A bunch of colored little balls floated around the water. Apparently when you pressed a button, air shot into the water and swirled the balls around. The object was to have the floating balls go into the frog's mouth. After Judy played with it a minute, the little boy started to grab for it.

'You can't do it,' he said.

'Yes, I can,' she screamed. 'I can too.'

The man snatched the case from both their hands and said, 'Let's see how fast Daddy can do it. If I can get them all in Kermit in under three minutes, I'll take you guys out to lunch at Bullwinkle's.'

'That's not Kermit,' the boy said.

'Ready, set, go,' the man said and started working the game. The kids cheered and hollered, shoved at him to make him go faster. For no particular reason, I checked my watch when he started.

When he manoeuvred the final colored ball into the frog's mouth, he held up his hands and shouted, 'Time.' He looked at his watch, which was thin and gold.

'How long, Daddy,' Judy asked. 'Did you make it?'

I looked at my watch. Five and a half minutes.

'A hundred and seventy-three seconds,' he said.

'How many minutes is that?' the boy asked.

'Less than three!' he said.

'Yea!' the kids yelled. 'All right! We're going to Bull-winkle's.'

The desk sergeant put her hand over the receiver and said to the man, 'Still checking, Mr. Richard.'

'Thanks,' he smiled. His little boy whispered to him. They both stood up and walked over to me. 'I've gotta make a pit stop with Mark. You mind keeping an eye on Judy for me?'

'Well, I . . .' I guestured toward the desk sergeant to indicate I had business.

'Should be just a minute or two. We won't even wash our hands.'

I laughed. 'Please, wash your hands.'

'Thanks.' He turned back to Judy. 'Judy, come sit over here with the nice FBI lady.'

'I'm not FBI.'

'Really? You look sort of undercover sitting here.' I must have looked startled because he quickly added, 'I'm kidding. Actually, you look like a girl I used to date in high school. She broke my heart and kept my letter sweater. That wasn't you, was it?'

'Could be. Was the letter for band?'

'Ouch,' he said, wincing and clutching his heart.

I couldn't help smiling. 'Don't you have some hands to wash?'

'Right.'

Judy sat next to me on the bench. She didn't look at me, though, just kept playing with her frog game.

'Be right back, sweetheart,' he told her and led Mark down the hall to the rest rooms.

Judy and I sat on the orange bench, neither of us speaking. The silence seemed somehow heavy with accusation. I should speak to the child, but I didn't know what to say. To me, children were like the primitive natives my father studied, mysterious creatures with rituals and customs I couldn't begin to understand.

'Hi, Judy,' I said.

'Hi,' she said, without looking up. Colored balls swirling around a plastic frog mouth riveted her more than I could.

'My name is Wren.'

'Huh?'

'Wren. Like the bird.'

'What kind of bird?'

'The wren. Haven't you ever heard of a wren?'

She shrugged.

I opened my purse. Maybe I had something in there that would be of interest to a little girl. Some makeup, wallet, checkbook with temporary checks, keys. Grown-up stuff that didn't even interest me.

Then I found the earring. It was hooked through my keyring. A long gold dragonfly with one red ruby for an eyeball. I'd found it while cleaning out Wren's nightstand, sitting at the bottom of the drawer. There was no other jewelry in that drawer, just this lone earring, so I figured it might be special to her. I'd searched everywhere for the matching companion, but never found it. There was something about it, I don't know, like a talisman or something. I don't know. I decided to keep it in my purse as a good-luck charm. I'd stolen Wren's life, maybe I could have her luck too. I'd carried it with me ever since.

I held it up to Judy. 'See? A dragonfly. Neat, huh?'

She looked up, unimpressed. 'It's just a bug. Mark eats bigger bugs than that.'

'Oh.' I put the earring away.

My stomach started to cramp. I rubbed my thumb

142

against my bra strap. I should know what to say, I was a woman, a potential mother. I owned a womb, for chrissake. It was like an empty garage inside me, waiting to house a new car. What kind of mother would I be if I couldn't even talk to this child? Even if I didn't want to become a mother, it should be because I chose not to, not because I was unqualified for the job.

I realized that I hadn't much thought about that option since breaking up with Robby. I'd thought about how I would bluff my way through my job. I'd thought about, meeting men, maybe even one man I could love. But those thoughts about my future usually ended with that big passionate kiss after which he tells me for the first time, I love you. Waves might be crashing in the background, I'm not sure. But after that, what?

Motherhood?

* * * * *

This is what I remember about my mother.

'The first time I had sex,' Mom is saying, 'was very unusual.'

I am twelve. Mom is sitting on the sofa amid a group of men and women. Dad is sipping a cognac and standing by the fireplace. He is smiling. As always, Mom is the life of the party and he looks proud of that fact. I am drinking ginger ale and picking out all the cashews from the bowl of mixed nuts.

'How did we get on this subject?' Mom laughs. 'Why don't we dance instead?'

'Come on, Barbara,' people urge. Someone has turned down the stereo, which is playing 'Me and Mrs. Jones' by Billy Paul.

'Let's just say it was different.'

'And probably illegal in most states,' Dad says.

Everyone laughs. I laugh too, happy to have a mother who is so popular.

Everyone thought my mother was the most fun person in the world. She was exactly the kind of woman Korean men feared were born during the Year of the Horse. Coltish, wild, able to leap corral fences and keep running.

'His name was Buddy. Wasn't it Buddy, Roger?'

My dad nods. 'Buddy Hirsch. Remember, he said that was the Jewish version of Buddy Holly.'

Dad wasn't actually there, but he knows my mother's stories better than she does. He never seems to tire of hearing them. This is the first time I've heard this one, though. I pop a few more cashews and hope they don't notice I've finished washing the glasses they needed.

'Anyway, you remember that terrible science fiction movie *Night of the Scorpions*?' Mom curls her index fingers into scorpion tails. 'You know, radioactive waste contaminates these scorpions in the desert and they mutate.'

'Oh, yeah,' Dr. Lester says. 'They grow as big as houses and attack this little town.'

'That's the one,' Mom says. She touches her finger to her nose and points to him. He grins and looks around as if he's just won something. 'They shot that whole thing near Palm Springs, where I was staying for the summer with my aunt. Good God, Aunt Lena, I just remembered she had no left earlobe. Her little wiener dog went nuts on her one summer and bit it off.'

'Skip the violence and cut to the sex,' Marsha, Dad's secretary, says.

'Goodness you're a randy bunch. Okay, okay. Well, the film company needed extras, so my cousin Lisa and I went down and got bit parts. We played high school cheerleaders at this keg party. We're still in our little skirts, making out with the football team, when this giant scorpion crashes through the wall and stings the quarterback right in the balls.'

'Jesus,' someone says and everyone laughs again.

'So the quarterback obviously wasn't this Buddy person,' Phyllis Ryerson, our neighbor, says. 'Not in his condition.'

'No, Buddy wasn't actually in the movie. He was the writer.'

I was sitting cross-legged on the floor. From my vantage point I noticed all the debris on the floor, napkins, nuts, pretzels, chips, crackers, half a Swedish meatball. Tomorrow morning I would have to clean up all this before Mom got out of bed. Not that she expected me to. She would scold me for not waiting until she could help, then hug me for my thoughtfulness, kiss my hair, and call me Loony Tunes, like the cartoons. In truth, I only did it because any housework done with Mom's help took twice as long and was only half as clean. She was a lousy housewife, I guess, not because she didn't do all the things expected of a woman then. She cleaned and cooked and seemed to actually enjoy doing it. She just did a crummy job. Dad and I were always rewashing the dishes, recleaning the sinks and toilets, reironing clothes. We never let her know; Dad always made it a kind of secret agent game between the two of us to do these things when Mom wasn't around. She never noticed the improvement, either, which only made the game more fun.

'Poor Buddy,' Mom says, chuckling. 'He hadn't written the original movie, some old hack had. But the hack was in Italy working on a spaghetti western when the actress starring in our little epic got smacked with a giant mechanical scorpion tail and broke her leg. She was out of the film and they'd already shot half of it. They needed to change the script. So the producer brought in his nephew, Buddy, who'd wowed his family by getting a couple of his short stories published in literary magazines. Buddy was only twenty that summer. He'd never written a script, he'd never even read one. He was so nervous he couldn't keep a meal down.'

'You relaxed him, eh, Barbara?' Marsha says.

'I was still a virgin, remember. Anyway, Buddy and I met on the set. He came over to the house a couple times for dinner. I think he was homesick and even a one-eared aunt was better than that alcoholic cast and crew. Well, one night we drove over to the warehouse where all the equipment was stored. He had a little writing office there where he worked on the pages. We started acting out his new pages. I played the leader of the mutant scorpions.'

'Type casting,' Dr. Lester says.

Mom did have one household speciality. She knew every home remedy and trick there was. She studied those household tip books the way some people study law or medicine. It was almost spooky the way she pored over those books, like a witch or something dabbling in the blackest of magics. If I came home with bubble gum stuck to my jeans, she immediately rubbed peanut butter on it and, abracadabra, the gum was gone. Cut a turnip in half and rub it under your arm as a deodorant. Anything that had a dual purpose fascinated her. She was an alchemist by nature, I think.

'I was killing him,' Mom says. Here her voice gets wistful and she touches her thin bangs in a girlish way. 'I'd picked up one of the small scorpion tails they used for the models and was stinging him to death while he crawled across the floor to save a little child. This was the part for the actress who'd broken her leg. Since she had to be killed off, she'd insisted she die a heroine. Plus, she could crawl with the cast on and they could just shoot the top half of her body.

'So I was chasing him across the floor, stinging him with this fake tail while he read his lines. Somehow he turned over onto his back just as I was whacking him and I caught him right in the'—Mom laughs but with a pained expression—'the balls.'

'Life imitates art,' Dad says.

'I dropped to the fioor, and I don't know what I was thinking, I just rubbed him there the same as if it had been his shoulder or something. One thing led to another.' She shrugged, not interested in the details.

'So that's when you saw your first real scorpion tail,' Dr.

146

Lester says. Other people say stuff like that too. Everyone laughs after each remark.

Mom sips her drink. She tilts her glass and looks out over the rim and sees me. I think she's going to get mad and send me away, but she just winks. Suddenly I want to tell them a better story about Mom. The one she told me last week. Listen, I want to say, this is even better, much better.

I had come home from school almost crying because there had been talk at school about eliminating sex education classes and my friend Julia said that those classes taught girls how to have periods. Suddenly I was terrified we wouldn't get the class and I wouldn't know how to get my period. When I asked Mom about it, she smiled and said I didn't have to worry, it would come without me doing anything. I was skeptical, after all, Julia had known about French kissing causing pregnancy. Mom stubbed out her cigarette and grabbed a tangerine from the refrigerator. Using one of our many dull knives, she slit the skin about two inches. She squeezed. Thick syrupy juice beaded along the slit. 'Taste it,' she said. I was afraid; this wasn't how you were supposed to eat a tangerine. 'Go on,' she said, making it sound like a dare, an adventure. I ran my finger along the cut and licked my finger. 'Good?' she asked. I nodded. 'Sweet.' That's what happens to us, she explained, to women. We ripen and turn sweet, just like fruit. And when we are at our sweetest, we overflow a little. We're luckier than this fruit, though. We ripen every single month. She grinned as if we were sharing the most delicious secret. 'Don't boys ripen?' I asked. 'Sure,' she said, 'but then they just rot.' She laughed and poked my ribs and called me Loony Tunes.

That's the story I want them all to hear, not the stupid one about scorpion tails and stupid Buddy Hirsch.

But then there is music, the Rolling Stones' 'Tumbling Dice', and everyone is dancing. Mom drags Dad away from the mantel and they are dancing the Mashed Potato.

I return to the kitchen to wash more glasses.

Whenever I hear that Joni Mitchell song, the one with the lines, 'I want to get up and jive/Wanna wreck my stockings in some jukebox dive . . .' I think of Mom. That's how she was. For many years I'd wished I were more like her. When people were planning a party, I wanted to be the first person they thought of to invite.

But my stockings weren't meant to be wrecked in passionate abandon, they were meant to be washed out in cold water at night and draped over the shower door to dry by morning.

* * * * *

'Who's punishing whom?' he said.

'Pardon?' I said.

'Well, I'm gone two minutes and you two look like one of you stole the other's boyfriend. Judy, did this lady steal Jimmy Dolenz from you?'

Judy giggled and shook her head. 'Jimmy Dolenz is dumb.'

'You love him,' Mark taunted. 'You told me so.'

'I did not. I hate Jimmy Dolenz.'

'Whew, another week in which I don't have to worry about boys.' He wiped his forehead with the back of his hand. The gesture reminded me of Detective Diesel brushing the fly from the corpse's stewed face. 'Hey, thanks for watching her for me.'

'That's okay. No trouble.'

'Look.' He held out his hands, turned them over. 'We washed them. Show her, Mark.' Mark thrust his hands at me and flipped them back and forth.

'Very good, boys,' I said, which made me feel like a mother. Not the good kind who slits open tangerines and explains the world, but the other kind, the spoilsport who spot-checks for washed hands.

I looked over to the desk sergeant, hoping for some

word about Season Dougherty's public defender. But the desk sergeant was still on the phone.

'My name's Davis Richard,' the man said.

'He has two first names,' Mark said, as if this were a regular routine.

'We all do,' Judy added.

'Congratulations,' I told her.

'She's named after a bird, Daddy,' Judy said. 'Robin, I think.'

'Wren,' I said. I held out my hand to him. 'Wren Caldwell.'

He shook my hand. All the men I was meeting today either washed their hands before shaking mine, or put on surgical gloves shortly afterward.

'People are always getting my name confused,' he said, sitting next to me on my now crowded orange bench. 'Sometimes they call me Davis, sometimes Richard. Sometimes Dick. I'm hoping the latter is just because of the Richard.'

I looked at the children, wondering if that last comment wasn't a bit risqué for them. They just sat there playing with the water frog, not really listening to us.

'What are you doing here?' he asked. 'Bailing out your mother for too many speeding tickets?'

'My mother's dead,' I said flatly. I don't know why I did it. Yes, I do. I resented how comfortable he was with me, how funny and glib he could be, how spontaneous. I didn't like the fact that I liked him. I didn't like that the desk sergeant liked him. And I was jealous that he could speak to kids better than I could.

If I expected my news to embarrass him, it didn't work.

'So's theirs,' he said, nodding at the children. 'Died in labor with Judy. You wouldn't think that would be possible in this day and age, would you?'

My throat tightened. 'I—I'm sorry,' I said.

He shrugged. 'That's okay. I lied. We're divorced, she lives in Encino with her new husband, an orthodontist.'

I started to say something like 'You bastard' or worse,

but I swallowed it back for the kids' sake. I stood up. 'Nice to meet you, Mark and Judy.' Then to him, cold and steely, 'I have some notes to take. I need to be alone.' I started for the blue bench.

He got up and followed me. 'I know you think it was a terrible thing to say, but you deserved it. I wasn't hitting on you or anything, just talking. You tried to zap me, right?'

I turned to face him. 'Look, I'm just here doing a job. You took your son to the rest room, I watched your daughter. That concludes our business.' I sat on the bench trying to look cold as Barbara Stanwyck.

He sat next to me. 'We're going to do some fancy dining at Bullwinkle's when we're done here. Care to join us? The place is loud but at least the food's lousy.'

'I don't think so, thanks.'

'Mr. Richard?' A woman appeared from behind the AU-THORIZED PERSONNEL ONLY door. She was a homely woman with a hatchet face and a severe suit that might have fit her once when she was fifteen pounds lighter. Now the seams stretched into sutures, like long sloppy scars over her hips.

'Yes.' He quickly ushered her across the lobby, talking animatedly to her as they walked. He pulled out some papers from his jacket and handed them to her. She put on reading glasses and read them. They spoke a little more, shook hands, then split up. She came over to the desk sergeant, spoke briefly, then hurried out the glass doors into the parking lot. She was practically running.

Davis returned to the bench and took each child by the hand.

'I'm sorry, Ms. Caldwell,' the desk sergeant said. 'But Ms. Mallard left specific instructions on behalf of her client. Mrs. Dougherty will not be speaking to any reporters.'

I bolted up. 'When? When did she say this?'

'Just now. That was Rebba Mallard.' She pointed to the parking lot. I ran over to the glass doors and looked out.

150

The hatchet-faced woman was driving away in a black Isuzu.

'What the hell's going on?' I said to the desk sergeant.

'I told her who you were,' she said. 'She chose not to speak to you.'

I spun around to face Davis Richard. My anger was great, all the more so because I was afraid I'd blown my first assignment and would lose the job I'd done so much to get. 'What did you say to her?'

His children cowered a little, holding his hand tighter and snuggling up to his legs. Jesus, now I was frightening little kids.

'It's a long story,' Davis said with a smile. 'I can explain it all at dinner tonight. I promise it won't be at Bullwinkle's. Deal?'

151

10

I spoke softly into the phone so no one could overhear me:

'Here's the thing with breaking up. Forget whatever I said before. This is the real scoop, what it all comes down to. What you must never forget. When you're with some-one for a long time, your bodies change. I've read studies about women friends who, just because they spend time together, start to menstruate at the same time. Their cycles become sympathetic. That's what I'm talking about here. Only with a man, it's something else, something even stranger. You develop this special vision. As if that other person causes you to mutate, boosts you up another step on the evolutionary ladder. You get this third eye or something. With this eye you can actually glimpse the future. It's like the door to your future has been left open, just a crack, and you can peek through. In that sliver of light you can see the two of you sitting there years from now, a little grayer, a little crankier, but there's still two of you sitting on that ratty sofa watching TV sitcoms and reading movie reviews in *Newsweek*. He tosses you a pretzel from a bowl without looking, you sip from his beer without asking, you both still laugh when your cat licks her butt. God, that's a comforting glimpse. You think, I can live with that. But when you break up or div-orce, whatever, it's as if that door has suddenly been slammed in your face. You can no longer even imagine what your future will be like. Wait, I take that back, you can imagine, you start imagining, and what you imagine is horrible, like being on the Sahara set of *Lawrence of Arabia* and no one else is around, just windy desert stretching to the ends of the universe, and you close your eyes against the peppering sand and start walking in no particular direction, your footprints dusted clean as soon as you make them.'

'Wren,' Linda Marley called from across the room, 'can I see you in my office.'

I hung up the phone. 'Sure, Linda.'

I turned, saw Linda march into her office. She left the door open for me and I saw my future through the crack: You're fired, imposter!

I pushed the phone across the desk so everything was in its place. You couldn't even tell that anyone had ever actually sat at this desk. Which was true, I guess. I hadn't done any real work here, just this last phone call to my own answering machine. I thought about what I had just done: called my own machine and discussed the meaning of breaking up. Tonight I would go home and play back my messages and I'd have to hear it. If my life were a self-help book, how would what I'd just done be interpreted? Either it was an example of a proactive healing step one could take to come to grips with the addictions of one's life, or it was a pathetic symptom of a deeper neurosis. Some choice.

'So, how's the story coming?' Linda asked as I entered her office. A little thought-for-a-day calendar stood next to her phone. Today's thought was IN A FIGHT BETWEEN YOU AND THE WORLD BACK THE WORLD. KAFKA.

'I've hit a snag,' I said.

She leaned back in her chair, her expression one of concern, not gloating, which I appreciated. 'What kind of snag?'

'One named Davis Richard.'

'Christ, what's he up to now?'

'You know him?'

'Sure. One-time video whiz kid, started in the waterbed business, ended up producing some of those early celebrity exercise videos. Made a fortune by the time he was twenty-five. What's he got to do with a murder case?'

I told her what had happened at the police station. She didn't look at me while I spoke. Instead, she glanced around her office, studying the Victorian motif-flowered wallpaper, wainscoting, antique desk—as if she were contemplating a new decor. When I finished my story, she looked at me and shook her head. 'What's your next step?'

'I was hoping you would tell me.'

'It's your story, Wren. Jonathan gave it to you.'

'Yes, I understand that. But if Season Dougherty's lawyer won't let me speak to her, then what can I do? I guess I could interview everyone else involved with the case, piece a story together that way.'

'Yes, you could do that,' she said without enthusiasm.

'But that's what everybody else is doing, right?'

'Probably.'

I sighed. I felt frantic, like I was in the middle of a quiz I hadn't studied for. 'I could speak to Mr. Krieg, see if he has any other connections he might rattle.'

'Jonathan is out of town.'

'What? He can't be.'

'I drove him to John Wayne Airport myself.'

'But a couple hours ago he was outlining his daily schedule of rabbis, fitness freaks, and tutors. He came here to fulfill his dream of running a magazine. Christ, he was so evangelical about it all.'

Linda laughed. 'Yes, well, real business intruded. He has an empire to run. He got wind of a hotel up for sale and he's on his way to Miami. He took the rabbi with him, though, if that makes you feel any better.'

'He could still make a few calls, From Miami.'

Linda yanked a long strip of tape from her dispenser and wrapped it around her two fingers, sticky side out. She leaned across the desk and brushed the sleeve of my jacket. The tape clogged with lint. 'Wren, what have you got that no one else has?'

I shrugged. 'Stringy hair?'

'Concerning this story. What lead do you have?'

I thought. 'A dinner invitation.'

She pulled the tape from her fingers, wadded it up, and tossed it into her waste can. 'Well then?'

*   *   *   *   *

I climbed out of the car and stared at the sign above the door.

'I'm not going in there,' I announced.

Davis pressed a button and the door locks in his car thudded closed. It reminded me of those movies in which kidnapped heiresses are always being locked into the backs of their limousines while knockout gas seeps in through the ventilators. Except I was no heiress and this was a Ford Taurus station wagon. Although it did have a car phone, it also had coloring books and broken crayons on the floor.

'Be brave,' Davis said, taking my hand.

'I didn't much like the experience the first time around. Why would I want to do it again?'

'That's the point. This time it's just for fun. Now we don't have to be so geeky.'

I looked him over. The easy smile, the same casual clothes as earlier, only with the addition of a sports jacket with patches on the elbows. 'I can't imagine you ever felt geeky anywhere. You were born a lifetime member of every club.'

He laughed. 'That's the nicest thing you've said to me since we met. I'm encouraged.'

'Let's go in.'

The restaurant was called Prom Nite. They stamped the backs of our hands as we went in, a little red pineapple. It had been a lot of years since I'd had my hand stamped. I stared at it, flashing back on some of the places Robby and I used to go back in college that did this. Robby had

155

always balked at the process, I'd enjoyed it, as if it were some form of validation. You're Okay, move on in here with the others who are Okay. We'd formed a community of The Okay.

'Relax,' Davis said, misinterpreting my stare. 'It's just part of the ambiance. It's just food dye.' He licked the back of my hand and the pineapple was gone. 'See?'

The back of my hand tingled coolly as his saliva evaporated. A light shiver giggled up my spine. I brushed my hand against my wrist but it was already dry.

Davis held the door open for me and I entered.

The interior of the restaurant was a replica of a school gymnasium that had been decorated tackily for a prom. There were even basketball hoops strewn with twisted crepe paper and balloons. The wood floors were glossy with various painted lines for basketball and volleyball. Bleachers lined both sides of the room. A mirrored ball hung in the middle of the room, rotating slowly as red and green and yellow lights bounced off and sprayed the room with colored-light shrapnel. The waitresses wandered about dressed in sixties-style prom queen outfits, complete with crinoline slips and plastic tiaras. Music from the fifties and sixties played over a scratchy loudspeaker system for authenticity. When the Everly Brothers' 'Cathy's Clown' was over, a man's voice came over the PA system. 'Attention, students,' he said, 'there will be no meeting of the chess club next week because club president Herman Glimpshir will be in Baltimore at the science fair. Thank you.'

'What do you think?' Davis asked.

'Reminds me of *Carrie*. Minus the blood.'

A balding man in a white suit and red bow tie cut through the crowds and headed straight for us. His close-cropped beard and heavy eyebrows reminded me of John Ehrlichman, after Watergate when he was a writer. 'Davis, good to see you again.' The bald guy used both his hands to shake Davis's hand.

156

'Don, business looks good.'

Don looked around the bustling room as if noticing the people for the first time. 'Making a living, man. You know.'

They both nodded as if there were some deeper meaning. I'm not a male basher, but I hate when guys do that. One of them says something inane and they both pay respect to it with a moment of thoughtful silence accompanied by world-weary head nodding. Maybe Mom was right. Boys just rot.

'Don, this is Wren Caldwell. She's a writer with *Orange Coast Today*. Wren, this is Don Hamilton. He owns the joint.'

Don shook my hand. 'Now I'll be sure to renew my subscription.'

'Thank you,' I said.

'So, what's it like to work for Jonathan Krieg? Is he as strange as the *Wall Street Journal* says?'

'What does the *Wall Street Journal* say?'

Don looked surprised. 'You know, that he's very . . . well, strange. You know.'

'I guess I'll have to read that article,' I said.

Don looked disappointed that I hadn't revealed any juicy Jonathan Krieg anecdotes.

'What're our chances of getting a table?' Davis asked.

'Just leave it to Principal Hamilton, kids.' He escorted us to a table, whispered something to a passing waitress, and seated us. 'Enjoy, enjoy. No making out behind the bleachers and no smoking in the lavatories.'

'Thanks, Don,' Davis waved.

'Nice meeting you,' I said.

'Same here,' he said and walked away.

When Don Hamilton had disappeared, I asked, 'Have you known him long?'

'Since high school.'

'Band practice together?'

He smiled. 'Football.'

'Seems like a nice guy,' I said. 'And successful.'

157

'Couldn't get a date at his own prom. That's probably what gave him the idea for this place.'

There was something about his tone that surprised me. He wasn't saying it in a harsh or bitter way, rather in a dismissing way, as if Don's whole existence could be summed up by that one statement. It was what a popular kid might say about an unpopular kid.

'Fortunately for most of us,' I said, 'there is life after the prom.'

'I don't know about that. High school is where your potential is measured, catalogued, and put on display. After graduation it's just a matter of living up to that potential, coloring the numbers. Alfred Hitchcock used to plan out his movies, figure out every single shot before he ever got near a camera. He once said that after he'd planned it, the actual making of the film was boring. See what I mean?'

'The fun part of our lives is high school? That's a bit depressing, don't you think? Christ, if that's true I'd have nothing to look forward to but hemline checks and bad cramps.'

'Didn't you like high school? I bet you hung with the popular crowd. You have that look.'

What look? I wanted to ask. I remember mostly driving a carload of girlfriends between places. I could see me behind the wheel of my dad's Fairlane trying to collect gas money, though I hardly remembered where it was we were always going. But I didn't want to go in that direction with Davis. 'Can we talk about Season Dougherty? She hung with a pretty popular crowd too. Until this morning.'

A waitress arrived at our table. Her blonde hair was clamped down with one of those plastic tiaras, but a couple of the fake diamonds had fallen out leaving black eyeless holes. She wore a fresh corsage on her wrist. The smell of lilacs choked off my appetite. 'Mr. Hamilton says to take special care of you two,' she said. 'Can I start you off with some drinks?'

We both ordered beers. She left, her crinoline crackling like radio static.

Davis took a deep breath and laid his hands flat on the tablecloth. 'Okay, Wren, let me explain what happened today. I've been in the home video business for about eight years. I'm very good at producing videos so I've managed to make a few bucks at it.'

I pulled out my steno pad from my purse, flipped open the cover, and read from my notes. 'You've made over five million dollars so far and counting.'

'You've done your homework.'

'You're good at videos, I'm very good at homework.'

He looked across the table at me with a troubled expression. He avoided my eyes. 'What you don't know is I've been having serious tax problems.'

'How serious?'

'Well, whatever bread and butter we don't eat tonight, I'm taking home.' He smiled. 'Okay, maybe not that bad, but bad enough. When I got into this business, there was no competition to speak of. Now every kid with a Minicam is producing videos. You can't make a killing anymore, not like when I started. Also, I've never been a very good businessman, not when it comes to squeezing figures into those narrow columns.'

The waitress returned with our beers and a complimentary basket of french fries smothered in chili. Davis ordered shrimp and I ordered chicken.

'Anyway, for the past few years I've been trying to get into the legitimate end of the movie-producing business. You know, made-for-TV movies, theatrical releases, that sort of thing. Because of who I am, the fact that I've made some money in this end of the business, people in Hollywood will see me, take me to lunch, listen to my ideas, tell some jokes, and then brush me off like a poor second cousin. If I want to invest money in one of their films, then they're interested. If I want them to invest, they're not. Hollywood mathematics. So, I decided I needed

159

some hot properties that would force them to deal with me.'

'That's what this is about?' I must have spoken loudly because several nearby diners looked over at me. I lowered my voice. 'You made a *movie* deal with Season Dougherty? Jesus, she just killed her husband and you were already thinking about a goddamn movie?'

He shook his head. 'It wasn't like that. I'd signed the papers with her a month ago, while she was still in prison. I saw a good TV movie in it, something starring Bonnie Franklin maybe or Elizabeth Montgomery. For the past month I've been trying to cut a deal with the networks on her story. One of those heroic-woman-triumphs-over-the-system kind of movies, with a last scene of her and her daughter walking off together hand in hand, freeze frame on their smiling faces. No one knew she was going to go after the poor bastard with a shotgun.'

I watched his finger bat a crumb across the tablecloth as if he were playing hockey. 'Now that she has shotgunned the poor bastard, where does that put your project?'

'I closed a deal late this afternoon. The studios were bidding against each other for the project all day.' He couldn't help but smile.

'So now you're a movie mogul.'

'Well, I'm making a movie.'

'Then why not let me interview Season Dougherty. The publicity is only going to help your movie project.'

He shook his head. 'No can do, Wren. We're still hoping to get her acquitted. We don't want your magazine screwing with the outcome of this story.' His finger chased the crumb across the tablecloth to within inches of my hand. He stopped and for a moment I thought he was going to touch me. He didn't, but my skin still heated up fast as if he had. I didn't move my hand away.

'So where does that leave us?' I asked.

'Having dinner. Enjoying each other's company.'

'You could have told me all this at the police station. Or over the phone when I called you back.'

'Do you want to be here? If not, I'll take you home right now.'

I looked at him. His blue eyes glistened a little, his jaw was clenched tight. Maybe that's what sincerity looked like, maybe that was his negotiating face. I couldn't tell. 'Pass me the fries,' I said. 'I still have one unclogged artery somewhere.'

He smiled. 'So, tell me about yourself, Wren. Tell me everything that you wouldn't want the *National Enquirer* to find out.'

'I sometimes sleep in flannel pyjamas with feet on them. I guess that's my darkest secret. That and the clump of hair clogging my bathroom sink.'

This time he did reach over and touch my hand. Just briefly, a little squeeze of my knuckles and then gone. 'Really,' he said, his voice soft and low. 'I'm interested.'

Me too, I thought. But what do I tell him, Wren's life story or mine? Last night with Ethan it was easy, he wasn't all that interested in my past. And the few times he did ask about me for the sake of keeping the conversation going, I didn't mind feeding him chunks of Wren's life. After all, the entire evening was more like being in a stage play anyway.

This was different. Not that I had any genuine feelings for Davis Richard. Too early for anything like that. But something was going on. Atoms were smashing into each other, colliding all over the place like a slam dance. That produced heat. Yet, who was he attracted to, me or Wren? At that moment I didn't want to be Wren anymore, trouble was, I didn't want to be Luna either. Luna had such bad luck.

So I told him about my degrees in art and philosophy and English. I told him about my writing, my plans for a magazine. I sounded enthusiastic, the way Wren always did, the way she'd always known what she wanted.

161

'I've read some of your stuff,' he said. 'Very impressive.'

'My stuff? Where?'

'You submitted some articles when you applied over at
the magazine. A friend made copies for me and messen-
gered them over to me this afternoon, after we met.'

'A friend? You have a spy at the magazine?'

'Spy might be too romantic a word. I have a friend
who keeps an eye open for anything interesting that might
make a good movie.'

'A paid friend.'

'Those are the best kind.'

'How did you get to be such an expert in cynicism?'

'Divorce.'

'So you're one of those guys for whom divorce is an
excuse to be a bastard.'

'I didn't need an excuse.'

'Oh, really? What's next, you mash a grapefruit half in
my face?'

He held up his hands in surrender. 'Let's stop right
here. I enjoy this bantering with you, but this isn't who I
am. Maybe I'm trying too hard with you, I don't know.
But I'm not really that cynical, unless you consider someone cynical who suspects professional wrestling may not
be all on the up and up. And that politicians aren't all
altruistic. Other than that, I coach my kids' t-ball and
soccer teams. Believe me, you can't do that with a cynical
attitude.'

We ate our meals, talked about the world in general.
Davis was witty without making a point of proving it. He
was surprisingly informed about world politics, knew
which South American country was doing what and how
to pronounce all those tricky names of the leaders who
were always shaking their fists when they made speeches.

After dinner he drove me back to the office where I had
left my car.

'I'll follow you home,' he said.

'No need. I can find it.'

162

'Just to be safe.'

I thought about the white Subaru, but it was nowhere in sight. Just my Rabbit in the parking lot and his Taurus station wagon with the Teenage Ninja Mutant Turtle coloring book in the back seat and a broken burnt umber crayon. 'Okay,' I said. 'Sure.'

I drove onto the freeway and he stayed close behind me. I decided to change lanes for no particular reason, to see what he would do. He changed too. I changed lanes again. So did he. I slid into the center lane and cradled my car between two huge diesel trucks. He dropped behind the second truck. I darted into the left lane and sped up, passing half a dozen cars. He sped up and passed them too. I drifted into the far right lane behind two Asian women in an old Corvette. We crawled along. He crawled behind us. I was encouraged, almost happy.

When I pulled into my assigned parking space, Davis kept circling the lot until he found a place to park. I hadn't really counted on that. I had expected him to just pull up, say good night, and keep going.

Now he was walking toward me, hitching his pants, looking like nothing in the world bothered him, a man you couldn't insult or intimidate. He even kicked a stone across the lot and stopped to see how far it went.

'You're the weirdest driver I've ever seen,' he said, smiling.

'Thanks for seeing me home.'

'I'll walk you to the door. I'm a full-service date.'

'This isn't a date.'

He looked over his shoulder at a black Jeep that was pulling into a space across the lot. When he looked back at me some of that former confidence was strained. 'What do you want to call it?'

He leaned forward then and took both my arms in his hands. I knew he was going to kiss me and I wanted him to. For the first time since breaking up with Robby, I wanted a man to kiss me for some reason other than breaking the monotony of not being kissed.

163

We leaned into each other, I guess, because I was suddenly off-balance, kept from falling to the pavement by the weight of his body against mine. I could feel his body heat through his clothes. My skin went tropical. His hands slid to the small of my back and dug into the skin, two fingers pressing my buttocks.

His chin had a little afternoon stubble and I could feel the skin on my chin and cheek being scraped raw. It burned a little, but I didn't mind.

We broke apart and started walking up the walkway toward my front door. A few plump snails spotted the sidewalk like raisins in white bread. I looked up at Ethan's apartment above mine and saw the curtain move as if someone had just ducked back. I didn't know what I would do when we reached my door. Should I invite Davis inside? What would that lead to? I couldn't sleep with him tonight, not after having slept with Ethan last night. It didn't matter that this was different, that I really wanted this man who made celebrity exercise videotapes and who could speak to children. If I slept with him so soon after Ethan, I would feel too much like a prom-night slut. Okay, maybe that was a little outdated, but that was me. Me, not Wren.

We stopped in front of my apartment door and kissed again. He pulled me tighter to him, until I could smell the faint tang of his morning after-shave, something musky. His hand slid farther down my back and grabbed a fistful of buttock. His thigh bumped up against my pubic mound like a tree stump. I opened my legs a little and pressed closer.

Music from someone's apartment filtered out around us. *Sha la la, do be wa, dum dum dum, yup yup dum. Oh, blue angel* . . . Roy Orbison's mournful voice was perfect for this. I felt completely engulfed by Davis, the music, his cologne, the cool night.

'This is the kind of movie you should make,' I whispered. As I spoke, my lips moved against his. He nodded and kissed me harder. I ground myself against his thigh and he rubbed his crotch against my hip. We gyrated to the music. Perhaps I would ask him to stay after all.

'*Oh, blue angel, don't you cry Just because he said good-bye . . .*'

I had that same record. It used to be Robby's but he'd overlooked it when he'd taken his half of our collection. I think he'd left it because of that scratch toward the end—

'*Oh, blue ang—blue ang—blue ang—*'

I pulled my lips away from Davis just as the door to my apartment opened. Now the music blared loudly, the needle finally hopping the scratch as usual.

'Hey, Wren, you're finally home,' the strange man in the doorway said cheerfully.

Davis's hands fell away from my back, his thigh retreated from between my legs.

'You don't think that's too loud, do you?' the strange man asked, nodding at the record player.

I looked at him, my face frozen in shock. He was in his early thirties and tall, a couple inches over six feet. He was wearing only a pair of beach shorts, so I could see he was lean and muscled. His long brown hair was pulled back and tied into a ponytail with a white athletic sock. His bushy mustache hung over his upper lip like a grass awning. In his right earlobe was an earring: a gold dragonfly with a red ruby eye. The same as the one I carried in my purse.

He was smiling in a bright happy way, leaning against the doorjamb. My 1st Place Long Jump stein filled with beer was gripped in one hand a half-eaten chocolate donut in the other. 'We're a little low on groceries, hon. But we'll fix that, now that your beloved Byron is back in town.' He kissed me on the cheek and looked at Davis with a friendly grin. 'So, who's your friend?'

. . . and then the stranger was kissing me.

His hand, cold from my trophy glass, cupped the back of my neck and pulled me forward as he leaned over. I strained my head against his hand and crowbarred my elbow against his chest. But his lips swooped down and brushed against mine quick as a raindrop.

'Ow!' he hollered as if stung. His scream vibrated against my lips. I smelled the beer on his breath. He jerked away. 'Owowow, Jesus, ow!' He hopped around on one foot, accidentally splashing beer onto his shorts and down the front of my skirt. 'Damn, that hurts! Damn!'

'What hurts?' I said. My elbow is pretty bony so I guess I could've, if not bruised a rib, maybe pinched a nerve or something. Or maybe I'd bit him without knowing it. I licked my lips for blood. I tasted shrimp dinner, leftovers from Davis's kiss.

'Cramp,' Byron gasped. He took long limping strides, marching in choppy circles around Davis and me. The sidewalk was polka-dotted with brown snails that despite his apparent agony he hopscotched around. Every other step he hammered his first hard against his right thigh, as if driving in a stubborn nail. After a couple orbits around us he slowed down to steady hobbling gait. 'Jesus, that smarts. Wow.' His eyes shone with tears. He was knuckling them when he stepped blindly forward and we heard a loud crunching sound that at first I thought might be his toe cracking against the sidewalk. He lifted his bare foot.

The gooey remains of a crushed snail clung to his sole like a flattened potato chip. He put his foot back down without scraping off the snail, as if it weren't there. If it had been me, I'd have been under a steaming shower by now, wire scrub brush in one hand and pumice stone in the other. But Byron just stood there gulping beer with one hand and rubbing his tenderized thigh with the other. 'B-12,' he said. 'I've got this intestinal thing so I don't absorb vitamin B-12 right and I get these god-awful cramps.' He leaned up against the doorjamb, out of breath. He moved his glass of beer back and forth between Davis and me as if he were toasting each of us. 'So,' he said, 'you guys fucking each other or what?'

'What?' I asked, shocked.

'Hey, Wren, nature is nature, right? I've got nothing to bitch about. I've been away and you've got needs.' He winked at me. 'Boy, have you got needs.'

I started to protest, but all that came out was 'Oh, shut up' in a peevish little girlish voice I didn't even have when I was a little girl.

He sat down in the open doorway and stuck his feet straight out. With one hand he unknotted the white athletic sock that bound his ponytail. He shook his head from side to side. The ponytail disappeared in a flurry of whipping hair that now hung down to his shoulders in thick corkscrew curls. He mopped the crushed snail remains from his foot with his sock, then snapped the sock like a whip. Snail fragments flung off and scattered across the sidewalk like bits of a soft-boiled egg. The sock had a wet snail-guts stain on the sole. He pulled the sock onto his foot anyway. He dug into his pocket for the matching sock and crossed his leg to put that one on too. As he lifted his leg, I could look straight down his pant leg and see he wasn't wearing anything under his shorts. His bald penis lay curled in a nest of dark pubic hair like a baby condor they'd recently hatched at the zoo. I looked away.

'Like I said, I've been away. Whatever happened, happened. None of my business. You two could have humped

167

and pumped your way across this entire state, it don't bother me. The past is past.' He dug his fingers into his thigh muscle, massaging until the skin turned bright red. He looked up at Davis and smiled. 'Thing is, guys, now I'm back.'

The sprinklers suddenly came on, hissing water onto the thick green foliage that the Pine Stream Apartments prided itself on. The air smelled wet and tropical. The sidewalks were quickly crowded with more snails. Brown clumps like inflated mushrooms dragged themselves across the concrete leaving shiny fluorescent trails dotted behind them. Oddly, the snails didn't move in a straight line, the trails were winding like Arabic writing, even though they seemed to be merely crossing the sidewalk. For some reason, that bothered me. Even a snail must know what a straight line is. I was angry with the snails for their inefficiency. Half a dozen of them were swarming the remains of the snail Byron had crushed, munching silently on the body parts.

Byron stood up, wiggled his toes inside the socks. He lassoed the three of us with a circular finger motion. 'I guess we've got some figuring to do here, mathematically speaking. The way I see it, two into three just won't go. At the very least, it wouldn't be sanitary. One of us will always be stuck with sloppy seconds.'

What had Wren seen in this guy? I admit, he had a certain manic energy and dreamy bad-boy look. But there was a dangerous aura about him. It was like standing too close to a performance artist who has soaked himself in gasoline and is now jumping back and forth over a lighted candle.

'Did you know there were no bricks in your toilets? Don't you know there's a water shortage down here? I filled up a couple of your Baggies with flour and wedged them into the tanks until we can pick up a few bricks.'

I wanted to say something, take control right here and now. Tell him to take his snail-slimed socks and clear out, or else.

But I had secrets now. People with secrets must step carefully. I composed myself, softened my voice. 'Listen, Byron, I think we—'

'Ssshh, ssshh . . .' He turned around and lightly kicked the door open the rest of the way. The doorknob banged into the foyer wall. 'I love this song. This guy is so clever. Listen . . .'

I listened. Sometime in the past few minutes, Roy Orbison had been replaced by some guy with a low morose voice. He sang slowly, like a man with a sink full of dirty dishes and last week's *TV Guide*:

> 'I saw a stranger with your hair
> Tried to make her give it back
> So I could send it off to you
> Maybe Federal Express . . .'

Byron snorted laughter. 'Those lines always crack me up. Kid sitting next to me on the Greyhound ride down here, econ major at USC, played that on his portable CD player. Kept playing it over and over. He had his headphones on but he kept singing along with it in this horrendous voice that sounded like a lawn mower stuck in a clump of foot-high weeds. People kept giving him the evil eye, but he just read his textbook, made notes in the margins, and kept right on singing. Turns out he's just gone all the way up to Oregon to visit his high-school girlfriend, the former Miss Pine Cone Festival, and she dumped him the day he arrived. She'd fallen in love with the manager of the toy department of the local K mart. Who would guess the Pine Cone Queen could be so cruel?'

'And you stole his disk,' I said.

He looked surprised. 'Stole it? Why would I do that?'

'You mean he just gave it to you? A perfect stranger just gave you a CD because you liked a song you hadn't even heard properly?'

'He didn't give it to me, sweetcakes. I won it.'

'You won it? How did you win it?'

169

'A bet.' He didn't say anything more.

I imagined him shuffling a deck of cards he'd marked in prison, the backs a sleazy pornographic photograph, probably two women, both a little too fleshy, long flat tongues exposed like thirsty spaniels.

'I don't get it,' I said. 'Why didn't you "win" the CD player too?'

'I didn't want it. I'm not greedy, Wren. You of all people know that. Remember New Orleans?'

I moved closer to Davis, was comforted by his cologne.

Byron grinned and reached up and pinched his dragon-fly earring as if he were activating some hidden switch, secretly photographing Davis and I with our stunned and dopey expressions. I noticed for the first time that the tip of his left little finger was missing down to the first knuckle. The top of the stump was white and waxy like cake icing. The sight of it made my stomach clench. I started to reach for my bra strap for some serious nail rubbing but caught myself and clutched my purse instead. I slid my thumbnail up and down against the shoulder strap. Byron smiled at me as if I'd just done something he'd physically made me do. Even though I knew he hadn't, my face flushed with hot blood. I dropped my hand to my side.

'Hey, hey, hey, guys!' Byron clapped his hands festively. 'This isn't going to be much of a homecoming party if I'm the one doing all the talking. I've been starving for conversation with non felons. Tell Uncle Byron everything.' He nudged Davis with his elbow. 'She still do that water spout trick in the bathtub?'

Davis ignored him and stared straight at me. 'You're married, Wren?'

Byron slipped a bare arm around my shoulder, his hand with the glass of beer resting heavily on my collarbone. 'For almost two years now. Didn't she tell you?'

'Your paperwork at the magazine said you were single.'

I ducked and twisted away from Byron's arm. 'We've been separated.'

'Two years,' Byron nodded. 'But I'm out of prison now and we can start over. Make up for lost time.' He grinned at me lewdly.

'Prison?' Davis looked at Byron, acknowledging his presence for the first time. 'That sounds interesting.'

'Yeah? In what way?'

'I don't know. I guess the challenge. See if you can take it. Guys always wonder, I think.'

'Yeah, well, the challenge. There is that, I suppose. You don't look for any big meaning in the experience. You just want to do your time and get out.'

'I guess it's only interesting if you're watching it in the movies.'

'Oh, you want interesting? Prison lore. Inside information. How's this: You know what the most popular book in prison is? Guess.'

Davis looked at me, then back at Byron. 'A law book?'

'The Bible.'

'Oh, right. Everyone turns to Jesus because it looks good to the parole board. Is that it?'

Byron laughed. 'Some, sure. But that's not the reason. It's the paper, man. They use a high quality paper that's opaque and very, very thin.' Byron pinched his finger against his thumb and pretended to take a long drag on a cigarette. 'Very uplifting, very spiritual.'

Davis shook his head in amazement. 'You mean they tear out the pages and use them to roll cigarettes?'

'That interesting enough for you?'

Davis laughed, so did Byron. They seemed like old buddies.

'What were you in for?' Davis asked. 'If you don't mind my asking.'

Byron's grin cinched tighter. Gone was any sign of being buddies. Just that fast. 'I do mind, yes.'

'Sorry, I didn't mean to pry.'

'If you want to know if I got cornholed, fucked in the asshole, just ask. We're practically family here. You wanna inspect the evidence? C'mon, don't be shy. Here,

171

take a peek.' Byron dug his thumb into his waistband as if to yank down his shorts.

Davis looked at me. So did Byron. As if they expected me to say something or do something, change the course of events that suddenly seemed to be rushing toward violence.

'I have to go to the bathroom,' I said. I had no idea what to say to either of them. I didn't want Davis to think I'd been leading him on, but I couldn't afford to have Byron tell who I really was. I went inside the doorway. I needed to settle this thing with Byron, alone. 'Davis, thank you for dinner. I'll talk to you later.'

'You going to be all right?'

I looked at Byron. I searched for some sign that would answer Davis's question. But Byron was merely staring up into the night sky, his face now childlike with concentration. Would I be all right with a guy who smoked the Bible?

'Where's Orion?' Byron suddenly asked. 'I can never find Orion. I know about the belt thing, the three little stars, but I keep seeing those three stars everywhere.'

'There,' Davis said, pointing. 'That's Orion.'

The three of us looked up.

'That's the belt, there's the sword.' Davis wagged his finger as if sketching in the details, connecting the dots.

'Yeah,' Byron said. 'That's it all right. Amazing. Makes you think, doesn't it?'

'About what?' I asked, an edge to my voice.

'What do you mean?'

'What exactly does it make you think about? The vastness of the universe? The insignificance of man? The origins of superstitions? What?'

Byron nodded. 'No wonder I can never find it, I don't know what it means.'

Okay, I knew I was being a born-again bitch, but what other weapon did I have at that point? With a man like Byron, there was only so much bluffing a woman could get away with. It's like arguing with a cop, you can only

172

push so far before your eye starts dropping to the gun on his hip. Men always have the unspoken threat of physical violence. Even if the last time they threw a punch was on the playground in third grade, they still have that knowledge that they could throw another one if they had to. They possess the logic of knuckles. And Byron, with his long ragged hair and missing finger and dragonfly earring, was particularly threatening. Was I in any danger from him? I knew he'd had something to do with Wren's missing teeth. He'd just been in prison. How had he lost that knuckle? I imagined a prison fight over cigarettes in the machine shop while the paid-off guards looked the other way. Certainly keeping Wren's identity wasn't worth my life, or my teeth. I had options: I could leave. I could always go back to being Luna.

Jobless.

Homeless.

Loverless.

That Luna.

I made a face at the prospect.

Davis looked over and caught me screwing up my face. 'Are you going to be all right?' he asked again. He enunciated each word slowly, like someone from a crisis hotline. I loved his soothing voice. Byron's scratchy voice sounded like a plastic shovel repeatedly stabbed into a dune of coarse sand.

'I'll be fine,' I said.

He touched my arm briefly, just grazed the hairs of my forearm. Byron was still staring up at the stars, so I didn't think he noticed.

Suddenly Byron, without looking, reached back and took my hand. He pulled me to his side. His hand felt moist and slippery. I sniffed. His skin smelled like my obscenely expensive skin lotion, the French stuff Robby had given me last year for our anniversary and that I had doled out drop by precious drop like a youth elixir. He reeked of its herbal scent. First my trophy glass, now my lotion. I pulled my hand free. He didn't seem to notice.

Byron pointed heavenward again. 'You guys remember when they used to pronounce Uranus, Your Anus?'

'What?' Davis said.

'Who do you think decided we should change pronunciation? I don't think it was the scientists. I think they probably got a kick out of it the old way. Can't you just picture a bunch of them sitting around in white lab coats surrounded by billions of dollars of sophisticated equipment, and one of them saying, "I think we should send a probe up to Your Anus, Doctor." And all of them cracking up, doing variations. "Can we find boosters big enough to get all the way up to Your Anus?" "We have to see if there's intelligent life on Your Anus." And they're all laughing and spitting up their coffee and donuts at this. What do you guys think?'

Davis and I stared at him.

'I'll call you tomorrow,' I said to Davis.

Davis nodded, hesitated a moment, then shoved his hands into his pockets and ambled casually away as if he'd just spent an evening playing miniature golf.

Once we were inside, Byron closed the front door and locked it. 'Boy, did you think that guy would ever leave?'

'I was about to say the same thing about you.'

'Me? I'm the last person you want to be throwing out of here. I give your whole masquerade veracity.'

'Veracity? Where'd that word come from? Prison course in power vocabulary?'

He smiled. '*Chacun à son goût*. It means, "each to his own taste".'

'You speak French?'

'I wasn't born in prison.'

'Just to serve time in one.'

He sighed. '*Homo lupus homini.*'

'Stop showing off. Hitler spoke French too.' I didn't know if that was true.

'That was Latin, not French. It means, "man is a wolf to man". Get it?' He gulped down the last of the beer. 'Remember that line from *The Adventures of Robin*

Hood? Errol Flynn says something insulting to the evil prince and one of the prince's toadies bellows, "You speak treason!" And Flynn grins and says, "Fluently." That was the coolest.'

I thought of Wren's missing teeth. 'You're no Robin Hood.'

'And you're no Wren Caldwell. So fucking what?' The anger in his voice startled me; it was as if he'd just yanked barbed wire through my closed fists.

'Do you drive a white Subaru?' I demanded.

'If I had a car, why would I have taken a Greyhound down from Oregon? You ever use the rest room in one of those things?'

That surprised me. I had assumed that the person following me today had been Byron. I'd even been relieved to have that mystery finally solved. Jesus. Who else was poking around in my life? I needed to think, to get away from Byron and figure out what I would do now.

'I'm going to the bathroom,' I said, taking off down the hallway. In the bathroom I could think things through. Maybe I could sneak the phone in and call someone for advice, even Robby if I had to. This was an emergency. Robby would help.

'Careful,' Byron hollered after me. 'I've left a few of my things out.'

I didn't stop. 'You can repack them when I get back.'

As I walked into the bathroom, I reached over to flip on the light switch. But before my fingers found it, my foot stepped into gravel and started to skate out from under me. I fell backward, blindly catching myself on the sink with my elbow before hitting the floor. 'What the hell . . . ?' I stood up and groped the light on.

I was standing with one foot in a litter box.

Byron stood in the doorway. 'That's Hector's.' He walked into the bathroom and swept aside the shower curtain. A long-haired gray cat was lying in the tub, his head resting on a small sample bottle of shampoo. He opened one eye, then closed it. Byron pointed. 'That's Hector.'

175

'You're just out of prison, for God's sake. When did you have time to get a cat?'

'I won him.'

'You win a lot, don't you?'

'I'm very lucky.'

I shook green cat litter from my shoe. 'I don't care how you got him, get him out of my bathroom.'

'Well, the other bathroom didn't have a window, just that little overhead fan. Let me tell you, no matter what they advertise on TV, soiled cat litter stinks. So I switched bathrooms with you. Believe me, you're better off.'

I looked around the bathroom. My hair dryer was gone, so was my jewelry box and my soap dish in the shape of a porcelain hand. Everything was gone except the sample bottle of Prell shampoo under Hector's furry head.

'And,' Byron continued, 'since this bathroom goes with this bedroom, I switched them too.' He hooked a thumb over his shoulder. 'You're down the hall now.'

I ran into my bedroom. My covers and sheets were gone. The mattress was bare. A pair of men's torn jeans and white underpants were strewn next to the Sealy Posturepedic label. I slid open the mirrored closet door. My shoes and dresses were gone. His three white shirts and two black pants hungs pathetically in the huge double closet. On the floor was a pair of battered running shoes and a pair of new black loafers polished to a scaly gloss. I stomped over to the dresser and yanked open the top drawer. My underpants, bras, garter belt, stockings, and panty hose were gone.

'I already moved your stuff for you. Figured it's the least I could do.' He smiled at me as if waiting for thanks.

'This is my room, my dresser, my clothes, you bastard. How dare you touch my stuff!'

'Well, actually this dresser was Wren's. I know because we bought it the week after we were married. It's only fair I get some use of it now.'

'You don't really think I'm going to let you stay here, do you?'

He threw himself on the bare mattress, hands webbed behind his head. 'I don't see what choice you have.'

'I can throw you out, that's what choice I have.'

'You mean physically? You mean you're going to come over here and physically throw me out?' He smiled, but not in a threatening way. More like he was curious how I'd do it.

'Not me personally,' I said. 'That's what police are for.'

He sat up, crossing his legs Buddha style. 'I suppose so. Of course, when they ask who's making the complaint, what name will you give them?'

I thought for a moment, leaning against the empty dresser. 'Whatever name I give them, they'll still kick your ass out of here. And if you're on parole, they'll toss you right back into jail. Are you on parole?'

'Nope. I'm free and clear. More than I can say for you.'

'What's that supposed to mean?'

He shook his head. 'Never mind. I'm not your therapist. Aren't you going to call the cops?'

I sat on the opposite edge of the bed. I was exhausted, drained. 'You can't just bust into my home and blackmail me into letting you stay.'

'Who's blackmailing anybody? I'm just looking for a place to stay while I get my life in order. Isn't that what you're doing?'

'You have no right to talk about what I'm doing. You don't know anything about me. You don't have a clue to what I'm doing.'

'And I don't much care. I'll just be here long enough to take care of some business.'

'What kind of business?'

'Being lucky.'

'What about Wren?'

He gave me a cold stare, like we were passing on the cell block. 'Wren's dead.'

'Yeah. You don't act too broken up.'

'You aren't exactly anointing the room with tears,

babe.' He gestured to include the contents of the apartment. 'You made out okay.'

I stood up, walked to the window. I looked out and saw Ethan walking across the dark parking lot in his bathing suit. He had a Spuds McKenzie towel slung over his shoulder and two cans of beer he was holding by their plastic cuffs. He was heading in the direction of the Jacuzzi.

I had not cried since Wren's death. I hadn't shed a single tear. I had felt awful, devastated, wrung out, all those things people say they feel at a great personal loss. Yet, I had not cried once. What awful things did they say about me? More than anything else I'd ever done or not done in my life, I felt most guilty about that.

I changed the subject. 'How did you find me?'

'I talked to Kate. She told me about giving you Wren's things.'

I thought of Kate. She had cried. 'How is Kate?'

'Tough. One of the last of that breed. Pioneer stock.'

I nodded.

'Anyway, I wanted some of Wren's papers, letters mostly, and some photo albums. So I started tracking you down. It wasn't hard. The tricky part was figuring out why you'd purposely tried to disappear with that dead-end address in Texas. That got me curious. A few phone calls placed after Wren's death from her phone were down to this area. I checked that against where her transcripts were sent. The rest was easy.'

'For a criminal maybe. What were you in prison for?'

'Trespassing.'

'I don't want jokes, I want some straight answers.'

'Relax, you're safe. I'm not after your money or your body.'

'What happened to Wren? How did she lose her teeth?'

He smiled. 'Wren told you about her teeth? I'm surprised. She didn't want people to know.'

'What happened?'

'An accident.' He held up his left hand and wiggled the stump of his little finger. 'Accidents happen.'

The phone next to the bed rang and I jumped.

He reached for it. 'I'm expecting a call. Do you mind?'

'Yes, I mind,' I said. I marched to the phone and snatched it up. 'Hello?'

'Are you okay?' Davis asked.

'Yes, fine. How'd you get to a phone so fast?'

'Car phone.'

'Oh, right.' I looked over at Byron, who kept grinning at me, like he was my big brother about to tease me about some boy calling to ask me to the dance. I picked up the phone set and walked as far away from him as the cord would allow. I turned my back.

'Can you talk?' Davis asked.

'Sure.'

'You're not in any danger, are you?'

'No. I'm fine.'

There was a long silence and I thought we got cut off, maybe he was passing under some electrical wires or something.

'I don't know what to say,' he said. 'I like you, Wren. I just want to know what's going on.'

'It's complicated.'

'Just tell me this. Am I out of the picture?'

I hesitated. Things were complex enough right now without adding a romance. But then I remembered that kiss, how I'd wanted to drag him inside.

'Are you sure you're okay? There's something about that guy. I don't know. He's your husband, you know him better than I do. There's something about him, though.'

'Let me call you back tomorrow, Davis, okay?'

'You didn't answer my question. Am I out of the picture? What was going on between us tonight?'

I sighed. He wanted an answer. He deserved an answer. God knows, I didn't want him out of the picture. I wanted him very much in the picture. I turned around and looked Byron straight in the eyes as I spoke into the phone.

179

'You're not out of the picture, Davis. Things may be a little out of focus right now, but I can make you out just fine.'

'Good. That's good.' He sounded very happy.

The Call Waiting tone sounded.

'Hold on a second, Davis, I have another call.' I pressed the button and said hello. As always, for the first second I expected to hear Robby's voice.

'Where is he?' the brusque voice demanded.

'What?'

'You deaf or just stupid? Where the fuck is he?'

'Who do you want? Byron?'

'Yes, I want Byron. Put Byron on the line. I would very much appreciate talking to Byron.'

'I'm on the other line, he'll have to call you back.'

'I don't give a fuck about your other fucking line. Put him the fuck on or I'll wrap the other fucking line around your fucking throat, you fucking moron. One phone call and I can have you fucking killed within the hour.'

I pressed the button. 'Davis, I'll call you tomorrow. Good-bye.'

I handed the phone to Byron. 'Your father, I think.'

'Did he threaten to have you killed?'

'Yes.'

Byron took the phone. 'Hey, Grudge, what's up? . . . Right . . . How much? . . . Okay, an hour.' He hung up the phone. 'I've got to go.'

'I'll help you pack.'

'Just for a while. I'll be back.'

'Nice friends you've got. He threatened to make a phone call and have me killed within the hour. Like he was ordering a goddamn Domino's pizza or something. Can he do that?'

Byron stooped down beside the bed and pulled out a black leather attaché case. He opened it with the lid facing me so I couldn't see inside. He reached in, checked the contents, closed the lid. 'I'll be back later.'

'You can't stay here,' I said. 'I've got to rent the other

180

room out. I don't make enough to pay for this apartment.'

Byron turned his back, pulled his shorts down, and kicked them off. Naked, he grabbed his underpants from the bed and stepped into them. Then he pulled on his jeans. 'How much?'

'What?' I said.

'How much rent will you need to charge?'

'I don't know. Four hundred, I guess.'

He dug into his jeans and pulled out a thick roll of bills. He peeled off five $100 bills and handed them to me. 'First month plus utilities.'

I fanned out the bills. A large red stain blotted the corner of the top bill and got progressively smaller with each subsequent bill until the bottom hundred, which was spotless. 'What's this?' I asked. 'It looks like blood.'

He pulled on a blue Nike sweatshirt and came over and examined the bills. 'Yeah, that's blood all right.'

'What's blood doing on your money?'

'Don't worry,' he said, slipping into his loafers, grabbing his case, and running for the door. 'It's only dog blood.'

12

Two days later Byron still had not returned.

Four of the five $100 bills were sealed in a plastic Baggie and taped to the underside of my desk drawer at the office. The fifth bill I gave to Detective Diesel and asked him to do me a personal favor and have the bill tested.

He raised an eyebrow, thick as a root. 'Tested for what?'

'This.' I showed him the reddish-brown blotch.

'Looks like blood.'

'Probably animal blood,' I said. 'Dog.'

'What would dog's blood be doing on a hundred-dollar bill?'

I shrugged. 'Might be somebody mugged a blind person who had a seeing-eye dog.'

'Might be or already happened?'

'I don't know, i'm just guessing.' That was the only explanation I could come up with. That is, if it really was dog's blood. 'Believe me, as soon as I know anything definite, I'll let you know.'

'You don't strike me as the kind of irresponsible reporter who would risk letting a violent criminal go free just for a byline.'

'I'm not. I'm not even a reporter, I'm just a writer. A magazine writer.'

'I'd hate to be wrong about you. I don't like being wrong about people. Makes me nervous. You start misjudging people in this business, you'd better retire fast.'

I patted Detective Diesel's arm assuredly. 'You're not wrong. I'm no Lois Lane. This is only a personal matter.'

'This have anything to do with that car that's been following you?'

'I don't know yet.' I hadn't seen the white Subaru all day.

He waved the bill between us. 'This turns out to be human blood, you and me are gonna have a sit-down. A long one.'

'Absolutely.'

He gave me a stern look, like a man in pyjama pants and sports jacket picking up his teenage daughter from the police station after midnight. 'Do you know what you're doing, Wren?'

'Don't worry, Detective, everything's under control.' I slapped on a confident smile and held that pose for a few seconds until he nodded and walked off down the corridor toward the forensics lab. He held the $100 bill pinched between thumb and forefinger, away from his body, as if it were a poisonous multilegged insect. When he turned the corridor, I deflated my smile and walked on wobbly legs back to my car.

*   *   *   *   *

The first day after Byron left, a bunch of people at the office took me out for a welcoming lunch. I'd just arrived at the office, twenty minutes late because of my visit with Detective Diesel. I'd covered by saying that I'd made another attempt to visit Season Dougherty, but no one seemed to care that I was late anyway. Billie Meyers, the young receptionist, had organized the whole lunch, including reservations at an Indian restaurant called Sitar by the Sea.

'Don't get your hopes up,' Billie explained. 'There's no sea.' Apparently there was an original Sitar by the Sea in

Redondo Beach that did in fact have an ocean view. That was too far away. The one we were going to was in Anaheim, near Disneyland.

Linda Marley, my boss, begged out at the last minute after she got a phone call. With the receiver wedged between neck and shoulder, she peeled off her cardigan sweater and waved us on, mouthing, 'I'll catch up to you later.' I saw her slip her American Express card to Billie.

In the elevator Billie said, 'I like your hair.'

'Me?' I said. People rarely complimented me on my hair. I have that look, I don't know what you'd call it, but whenever I'm shopping in a bookstore, other customers think I work there and ask me where Jean Auel's new novel is. That look.

Billie touched my hair. Her nail polish was French style, robin's-egg blue around the base, tipped with white half moons. She stroked my hair once. 'It's so natural, like you don't have to do anything to it.'

'I've done everything to it but set it on fire.'

She nodded seriously. 'Now that you mention it, it is a little dry.'

*　　*　　*　　*　　*

When I returned from lunch there were three yellow While You Were Out messages from Davis. They all said, 'Call me!' The last one, which came in just ten minutes earlier, said: 'Don't make me stomp your snails.' Kirstie, who took the messages, wrinkled her nose and frowned when she gave them to me. 'What's that mean? Is that sexual?'

I was sitting at my desk reaching for the phone to call Davis when Linda Marley tapped me on the shoulder. I turned. 'Hey, boss.'

'Sorry I couldn't make lunch,' she said.

'That's okay. Thanks for picking up the tab.'

'Any progress on the Season Dougherty interview?'

'Some. I had dinner last night with Davis Richard.' I fanned out his three yellow messages.

She made an approving face. 'Very impressive. Did you sleep with him?'

'Is that everybody's favorite question?' I asked. If she would have asked me that yesterday I'd have been shocked and stuttered out some lame answer. But after half an hour exposure to Byron, I was battle hardened. 'No, I didn't sleep with him. I'm working a story, not a street corner.'

She touched my shoulder. 'Take it easy, Wren. I have to ask these questions.'

'Because you're worried about the ethical position of the magazine?'

'No, because I'm nosy.' She laughed so hard she started coughing.

'Yuckety yuckety yuck,' I said, deadpan.

She kept laughing. Just when she'd slow down and seem about to stop, she'd start up again, laughing louder than ever. It was like a child playing with the volume control on a radio. When she laughed, the skin around her eyes accordioned into a dozen folds. This was the first time I was conscious of her age, which someone at lunch had placed at forty-four.

Finally she stopped laughing, dabbed her eyes dry, and tugged on the back of my chair. 'Let's go,' she said.

'Go? Where?'

'Meeting. Jonathan Krieg is back in town and waiting to see you for an update on the Season Dougherty interview.'

'He's back already? He just left yesterday.'

'He finished his business. Today he's ten million dollars smarter. Now he's back, checking his list to see who's been naughty or nice.'

'Which list am I on?'

'Let's find out.' She gestured toward Jonathan's office and I followed. I had the feeling that she knew something

185

but wasn't telling me. Linda was a friendly woman, but she could be very mysterious. At lunch Clive Remick, the magazine's restaurant critic, had toasted her with: 'She's the best managing editor we've ever had. Unfortunately, we're the best fuck she's ever had.' Everyone had laughed. I didn't ask what he meant because I didn't want to get involved in any office politics. I just wanted to get by. Besides, she seemed to like me, though we weren't exactly chummy.

We walked to Jonathan Krieg's office door. Yesterday the door was bare, today his name was painted on in plain black lettering. Under his name, the single word: PUB-LISHER. I popped in a Breathsaver to kill the tandoori lamb taste in my mouth. Linda rapped on the door like a cop. 'Jonathan?'

'Uunnnnh . . .' came the muffled grunt.

Linda opened the door.

Jonathan was bent over, his hands grasping the seat of a straight-back chair. Straddling his hips was a muscular blonde woman in a two-piece workout outfit. Her black bottoms were cut high over her hips, cinched at the waist with a wide yellow belt. Thick ropy veins stemmed out from under the cloth covering her vagina. The strip of cloth was so narrow she had to have shaved her entire pubic area. Her midriff was bare, exposing square muscle platelets up and down her abdomen that reminded me of a turtle shell.

'Uuuunnnh . . .' Jonathan said. He was wearing shorts, a T-shirt, and new Reeboks. He had a starburst varicose vein at the back of one of his knees.

Standing next to the chair was the male counterpart to the woman riding Jonathan's back. He was equally blond and equally muscular, though his skin was chalk pale. A small Band-Aid covered his left nostril where it looked as if he'd had a skin cancer removed. Her muscles were crowded like a city skyline; his were great slabs like rocky mesas. His were so large the rest of the room suddenly seemed small and airless.

' . . . six . . .' he counted.

'Uuuunnnh . . .' Jonathan said, lowering his hips and raising them again. His face was slick with sweat. His varicose vein looked bloated with blood. His mouth hung open as he gulped air.

' . . . seven . . .'

The muscular woman smiled at me. 'These are called donkey raises. Want to climb on with me? What are you, a hundred and fifteen?'

'Hundred and eighteen,' I said.

'Uuuunnnh . . .' Jonathan huffed. He looked over at me with panic in his eyes.

'I think he can take it,' she encouraged.

I shook my head. 'I'm not sure I could. I just ate.'

' . . . nine . . .'

Jonathan's last effort was shaky. He lowered himself okay, but he couldn't seem to push himself up again. His arms wobbled, his legs started to buckle. Three drops of sweat slid off his nose into the carpet. He was stuck at half mast.

The muscular woman surreptitiously angled her toes downward to touch the ground, taking some of her weight off Jonathan's back. With a mighty grunt, he hoisted her the rest of the way up. She quickly dismounted, slapping his butt playfully. 'Not bad, masked man. Same time tomorrow?'

Jonathan nodded, too out of breath to speak. He collapsed into the chair.

'Remember, only the tough get buff. Maybe that should be boffed.' She laughed.

Her blond companion laughed too.

'Hi, I'm Vicky,' the muscular woman said to me, offering her hand.

Reluctantly, I extended mine. I expected a bone-crunching grip to send me to my knees. But she shook with only a moderate firmness.

'Vicky, this is Wren Caldwell,' Linda said.

'Hi, Wren. This is my husband, Karl.'

187

Karl waved as he packed their gear into a duffel bag. 'Hey,' he said.

'Hi.'

Vicky reached into the side of her shoe and pulled out a card. She handed it to me. It said: Vicky and Karl Mueller. Executive Fitness. Your Place. Your Convenience. (213) 555-4328.

I backed up a couple steps. For some reason, I felt nervous having such a muscular woman standing so close to me. I wasn't homophobic, it just made me feel inadequate, like watching Davis with his kids. 'I didn't know I looked that bad,' I joked.

'Looks are nothing,' Karl said mysteriously. I had the feeling Karl wanted to be someone's guru.

'Karl means, a person can look good on the outside, but still be weak. Everyone worries about their weight, but they should worry about their muscle tone, the fat content, that sort of thing. We do a lot of work in this building, no problem to fit you in.'

'Thanks,' I said. 'I'll think about it.'

She shrugged, looked disappointed. 'That's okay. This intensity isn't for everyone.'

I hadn't really intended to think about it, but now I felt bad, as if I'd not only hurt her feelings but proven myself to be a wimp. 'I just started here,' I explained. 'I have to wait until my schedule settles down.'

'Sure,' she said.

Jonathan Krieg came to life. 'Great idea, Vicky. A kind of corporate fitness program. I'm sure we'd get a break on rates from the insurance company, plus it would be a business write-off. What do you think, Wren?'

I nodded, forcing enthusiasm. 'Great idea.'

'Whatever,' Vicky said. She hoisted one of the duffel bags. Metal clanged against metal at the motion. The muscles across her chest wrenched. Her top was cut low enough that I could see her breasts were just nipples on the end of another slab of muscle. I was impressed.

When they left, Jonathan motioned for Linda and me

to sit. He pulled a small white towel over his face and inhaled, the towel conforming to his face like plastic wrap. I thought of Season Dougherty's husband, the dish towel over his chowdery face to keep the flies off. Jonathan sat with the towel over his face without moving for so long I feared maybe he'd passed out or had a heart attack or something. I looked at Linda but she kept her gaze on Jonathan, her expression cool and professional.

After a couple minutes had passed, Jonathan exhaled loudly and the towel billowed like a sail and fell from his face. When he spoke, it wasn't to either of us, but to an imaginary audience in general, as if he thought documentary cameras were always waiting in the wings. Recording.

'I've been around,' he said. 'I've done some things. I've learned from my mistakes. Guy gets to be my age, has had my successes, he might get a bit cocky, think he's'—here he made finger quotes—"arrived", But I have found there is no such thing as arrival.'

Linda said, 'Life is not a problem to be solved but a reality to be experienced.'

He pointed at her excitedly. 'Exactly. That's exactly what I meant.'

'Kierkegaard said it.'

He looked uncertain. 'Of course. The point is, I've never stopped experiencing. I'm the type of guy—'

I cringed. Wren and I once made up a list of the Ten Commandments of Dating. Commandment number six was 'Never shall ye date anyone who starts a sentence, "I'm the type of guy . . ."' (unless he is Dion singing 'The Wanderer': *I'm the type of guy who never settles down . . .*').

'—who lives for the climb, not the actual getting there. I don't care about sticking my flag at the top of the mountain, I care about the next ridge to climb. See what I mean?'

Neither Linda nor I said anything.

'The point is, I don't do anything half-assed. I've decided to do this magazine. I've set some goals for the kind

189

of circulation I want and the kinds of stories I think will get me that circulation.' He looked at me with a frown. 'This Season Dougherty thing. Linda tells me you haven't interviewed her as planned.'

'No, sir. I went to the jail but she wouldn't see me. She'd already signed away the rights to her story to Davis Richard.'

'Who's he?'

Linda said, 'Local entrepreneur. Did celebrity exercise videos.'

'He's looking to break into feature films with this deal,' I said.

Jonathan twirled his towel and snapped it at a nearby potted plant. A chunk of leaf flew off in shreds. 'I've already negotiated with a studio for the rights to our exclusive articles on this case. But none of that will work without an interview. That's the key.'

'I'll probably be seeing Davis later today. I'll talk to him about it.'

Jonathan twirled his towel forward, then backward, then forward again. The whole time he was twirling, he stared at me, directly at me without flinching. This continued for a full minute, maybe longer. Linda stared at him, he stared at me. I rubbed my thumbnail against the edge of the chair leg behind me.

'Wren,' he finally said, 'Linda and I have been discussing the situation. Perhaps we were overzealous in sending you out on such a complex assignment right out of the dugout, so to speak. Maybe you need some seasoning first. You need to get to know your way around town first. See who's who, what's what.'

'I can get the interview,' I said. 'I just need a little more time.'

'That's what I'm saying. Take your time. I'm blaming me here, not you. I rushed you into something without giving you enough time.'

Linda said, ' "Time is the longest distance between two places," '

190

'I hadn't heard that before,' he said.

'Tennessee Williams.'

'Oh. I like it.'

Linda didn't smile, didn't look at me. She stared straight ahead. Whose side was she on?

'Anyway, the point I'm making here is that we'll be assigning someone else to the story for now, maybe have them do the legwork and bring you in for a rewrite. Maybe you were right when you said this isn't your kind of story.'

And I'd meant it too. Then. But now something else was involved. Luna would have expected this, would have even welcomed the relief from pressure. But I was Wren now. Wren's life had gotten me the job, but after one day Luna's personality had me close to getting fired. I had a job I would have never otherwise gotten, I'd met a man like Davis, who I would otherwise never have met. Thanks to Wren's life, I had a chance to change mine. Biology is not destiny. If I failed here, midnight would strike and Cinderella would be back to her old ragged self. I had to get that interview.

I stood up. 'I can get the interview. Trust me.'

Linda turned toward me. 'Actually, Wren, Jonathan and I have been talking about another new area for the magazine to explore. Something we've never done before. I think you'd be especially suited for it. It's challenging.'

'What about the interview?'

'I'll be taking care of that personally.' She looked at Jonathan.

He rocked back in the chair and folded his towel into triangles like a small flag. He smiled at me. 'You'll thank us, Wren. Wait and see. You'll love this new assignment. It has everything the public wants. I've already set up a meeting. You have twenty minutes to get there.'

13

Twenty-five minutes later.

'Hello,' I said, offering my hand. 'I'm Wren Caldwell.'

'First things first,' he said to me. 'Did you bring the money?'

'Yes,' I said.

'Cash? This is a cash kind of business. They told you that, didn't they?'

'Yes, they told me. I brought cash.'

'When I say cash, I'm talking about, you know, the actual green stuff. Real money. Not a voucher, not a purchase order, not a check. Not like in department stores when they ask if you're paying cash or charge, you say check, they say that's the same as cash. It's not. Nothing's the same as cash. Cash is cash.'

'I understand what cash is,' I said. 'Can I sit down now?'

'Okay, sit.' He gestured to the chair across the table. I sat. The chair was ladder-backed and black, lacquered to a high gloss with a pink pillow on the seat. The table was the same black, except for the middle, which was thick turquoise tile. The luncheon menu was written with pink and turquoise chalk on a small chalkboard in front of me. There were five items, four of them fish. The place was called Sante Fe Depot and the cuisine was supposed to be southwestern, though I didn't think fish was a big southwestern specialty. 'I already ordered,' he said. 'I don't have much time.'

He was smoking a smelly cigarette, something French I think, that was black and twisted like licorice. There was no ashtray on the table so he flicked the ashes into the vase with the fresh-cut pink carnation. A few of the patrons from nearby tables were giving him hostile looks. Since he ignored them, a lot of those looks were then directed at me. I squirmed under their glares.

'Isn't this a nonsmoking section?' I asked.

He shrugged. 'I'm not smoking.'

He spread the pink linen napkin out on the table in front of him. He smoothed it, ironing it flat with the heel of his hand, then with the edge of the chalkboard menu. Slowly he lowered the burning tip of the black cigarette to the napkin, just enough to make a charred brown circle, but not enough to burn a hole or catch the napkin on fire. His concentration was intense, he never looked up at me. I could tell this was not just a pyromaniac episode, he seemed to be making some sort of pattern. But it was one I couldn't yet recognize. He spoke without looking up: 'I don't know you, you don't know me, we don't know each other. You're new at this, I know that and you know that I know. So maybe you think: "Well, the little bastard is going to try to take advantage of me." Right? You thinking that, Wren?'

'Yes,' I said. 'I'm thinking that.'

'Okay, good. Very good. I'm glad you said that. That means you're sensible. I can do business with someone sensible.' He glanced up at me and smiled, then returned to touching his cigarette to the napkin. The burn marks were beginning to cluster like brown pearls. 'The fact is, I *will* try to take advantage of you. Every single chance I get. I'm here for the money, strictly the money. As long as we both know that going in, then we can do business.'

'Then let's do business.'

He nodded, but didn't look up. He leaned closer to the napkin, his face only inches away from the tabletop. He lowered his cigarette tip so slowly it was excruciating to watch. He looked so damn intense, like he was defusing a terrorist's bomb. My stomach began to knot up with anticipation. He eased the glowing tip a molecule lower, until it didn't exactly touch the napkin, but the heat singed a few of the pink threads. The result was an unusual shade of rust-brown. Whatever he was making, it began to take on a certain beauty.

'What's your last name again?' he asked.

'Caldwell. Wren Caldwell.'

He stuck the brown cigarette between his lips and offered me his hand. 'James Smith. And that's my real name. Spelled just the way you think, no y instead of i, no e at the end.'

I shook his hand. 'Nice to meet you, James.'

James was about twenty. His face was smooth, still a few years from shaving daily. Three small blemishes clustered on his neck under his left ear.

'James,' I said, 'why doesn't one of the waiters come over and make you stop smoking? Isn't there a fire law or something?'

'Is there?' He dabbed the burning end rapidly against the napkin like a sewing machine needle. I could see now he was creating a face, a woman's profile. The rapid spotting was the hair. The effect was startlingly real, the hair seemed to thicken with texture. He cocked his head and studied his work, frowned, and shook his head with displeasure. He took a deep drag that brought the tip of the cigarette into a bright flare, and once again began dabbing the napkin. An elderly couple two tables away scowled at us. I gave them back a weak smile but that didn't seem to carry much weight with them. The man threw his credit card down on the check and waved at a waiter.

'I thought this was supposed to be a sort of clandestine meeting, James. We shouldn't draw any attention to ourselves.'

'Why? We're not doing anything wrong.'

'For starters, smoking in a nonsmoking section is illegal.'

'Illegal, but not wrong. Big difference, Wren. Besides, I'm not really smoking. I'm creating.'

I looked around at the waiters as they glided swiftly

194

around the tables. They all wore black pants, white shirts, and those corny square-dance string ties with a hunk of turquoise embedded in the silver slide. None of them even looked our way. 'I don't understand why someone doesn't come over here and tell you to stop. My God, you're burning a napkin. *Their* napkin.'

'They know me.'

'You eat here a lot?'

He shook his head. 'First time.'

'First time? And they know you?'

He looked up. 'You're not from around here, are you?'

'You mean Orange County? No, I'm from up north.'

'San Francisco?'

'Oregon.'

'Oh, you mean *really* up north.' He studied me a second, actually looking at me for the first time. His eyes were pale blue, almost white. The rest of his face was an odd mixture of nonmatching parts. None of his features went with the rest of his face, as if the nose, the lips, the ears, everything had been borrowed from various other bodies and slapped together to make his face. The resulting effect made him seem sickly. 'My dad's a producer. He makes TV movies.'

'Anything I've heard of?'

'How would I know what you've heard of?' He grinned. 'Sorry, that's my dad's line. He always says that when people ask him that question. He picked it up from some novelist buddy of his who, I think, got it from William Faulkner or Raymond Chandler, which gives you a perspective on the amount of originality around here.' He flicked an ash into the vase. 'My dad's movies all have the word confession in it or diary, as in "Confessions of a Mistress" or "Diary of a Groupie". You know.'

'And he eats here a lot. That's how they know you.'

'They know me because they know me.' He shook his head. 'Let me show you.' He gestured at a waiter, a young man in his early twenties with tinted glasses.

'Yes, sir,' the waiter said.

'Hey, man, how's your screenplay coming along?' James asked.

The waiter looked startled a moment. 'Pardon?'

'How's the script going? I heard you were almost done.'

The waiter's formal demeanor thawed slightly, his face sagging into artistic turmoil. 'Yeah, well, I'm having a little trouble with the third act. The third act is a bitch.'

'You'll crack it,' James said. 'Could we get some wine for the lady? Wine, Wren?'

'Diet Coke will be fine.'

The waiter, dazed, a little confused, nodded and left.

'See what I mean,' he said. 'I never saw that guy before in my life. In Los Angeles everyone you meet is a wannabee actor or director. But in Orange County everyone's a fucking scriptwriter. Cuts down on the commuting into the city. There aren't many producers living down here yet, so my dad is pretty well known. I can't tell you how many places I go, someone manages to slip me their script to give to my dad.'

'And do you?'

'Depends. Like I said, I'm in business to make money. They pay me a few bucks, I'll see Dad gets it.'

'What's a few bucks?'

'You have to gauge the person, figure what they can afford. No less than fifty, that's for sure. I've gotten as much as five hundred though.'

I couldn't help smiling at his wise-guy routine. 'If everyone else is an aspiring writer, what are you? An entrepreneur?'

'An artist.' He smiled and returned to barbecuing his napkin.

The waiter brought me a Diet Coke. He hesitated, staring at James, waiting for him to look up. I got the feeling that now that he'd thought about it, he was ready to pitch his script much better than before. Only James refused to look up. Finally the waiter drifted away.

'Okay, here's the thing,' James said, looking up now. 'Here's how we work it. I call you whenever I've got something, we meet, I give you what I've got. You pay me. Simple enough?'

'Depends. What have you got today?'

He reached inside his sport jacket and pulled out a folded piece of paper. I read it.

'Jesus,' I said.

'You can keep it. It's a photocopy.'

I read it again. Legal stationery, with a design that incorporated the lawyers' initials. Much more impressive than Robby's lawyers' stationery. The letter was addressed to a famous TV actor who played a surgeon-turned-private-detective who specializes in locating missing children. The attorney who wrote the letter was not one of the partners mentioned in the firm's logo. Nevertheless, he made it clear that his client was only twenty and pregnant with the actor's child. Naturally, if some financial settlement could be reached, none of this need go public.

I folded the letter and looked at James. 'How old are you?'

'Eighteen. But I seem older, right?'

'Yes, you do.'

He nodded, returned to torching the napkin. This was my new assignment. Gossip gathering in Orange County. I would be given my own column, though I would use a pseudonym, Missy Carver. Jonathan told me that was to protect the integrity of my real name, which they still had great hopes for on more legitimate articles. Afterwards, in the hallway outside Jonathan's office, Linda confided that the pseudonym was to protect the magazine: once I'd established Missy Carver as a valuable name, I couldn't hold up the magazine for more money by threatening to walk. 'The name is copyrighted,' she'd said.

'What went on in there?' I'd asked. 'With Jonathan.'

'What do you mean?'

197

'You could have backed me. You saw the messages from Davis Richard. That's a solid lead.'

Linda had looked off then, not at anything in particular unless it was the Sparklets water cooler. She looked as if she were trying to remember my name. 'My backing you would have done no good for you, he'd already made up his mind. But it would have hurt me because he would have had to overrule my suggestion, which would have given him more a sense that he would be better off running this magazine without me. He already has his doubts about you.'

'Why? There wasn't anything I could do.'

'That's not the point. He set up an exclusive interview and it didn't happen. That makes Jonathan look bad, weak. But not if he has someone to blame.'

'Me.'

'Exactly.' She turned and looked me in the eyes, smiling slightly. 'You don't trust me now, do you? You can't be sure whether what I just told you is the truth or a cover for some secret agenda of my own. Right?'

'Right.'

'Welcome to the Hotel California,' she'd said and walked off.

I laid the attorney's letter on the table between James and I. The famous actor in question had a hilltop home in Laguna and could be seen walking his wife and Doberman along the beach on weekends. Definitely Orange County gossip, the kind guaranteed to be picked up by the wire services. Missy Carver would hit the scene in a big way.

'How do you do it, James?'

'Concentration,' he said, burning an eyebrow on the portrait.

'Not your art. This stuff. The gossip.'

'Oh, that.' He leaned closer to the napkin, executing a tricky arch to the eyebrow. Satisfied, he looked up. 'Friends in low places. I operate a baby-sitting service made up of high school and junior high school kids. Be-

198

cause of my dad's contacts, I get a lot of the wealthy clientele. Once you're inside somebody's home, you're bound to find something incriminating. Hell, if I showed you some of the photographs and videotapes alone. Man, the stuff people like to tape themselves doing. I mean, why bother. It's not like you need a record, like you'd forget how or anything.'

'Why don't you sell those? The tapes and photos, I mean.'

He gave me an angry grimace. 'That wouldn't be right.'

I didn't bother arguing. I didn't want the photos or tapes anyway. I didn't even want this letter. I wanted that damn interview with Season Dougherty.

'So your baby-sitting brigade rummages through these famous people's houses until they find something juicy? Then you sell the goods to some tabloid?'

'That about covers it. Except now I'm selling it to you.'

'How did Mr. Krieg get in touch with you?'

James laughed. 'He didn't do squat, man. One of my girls baby-sat for the guy who used to own this magazine. She found out about the sale. I figured new broom and all that, this would be a good time to approach Mr. Krieg about my services. I practically doubled my price with that move.'

'Why do you do this, James? It can't just be the money, not if your father is as well off as you say.'

He grinned. 'God bless the child who's got his own, you know what I mean?'

'But don't you find this kind of sleazy?'

'Man, people who want to be famous deserve everything they get. They did it out of greed and ego in the first place. Now, are you gonna pay me or lecture me on morality? I mean, you don't have to buy my goodies if you think it's so wrong.'

I looked around, made sure no one was looking, then quickly slid an envelope with $800 across the table. I whispered, 'That's the amount Mr. Krieg agreed upon.'

He blew on the tip of the cigarette just as he dabbed it to the napkin. An eye seared into the napkin below the eyebrow. He clamped the cigarette between his teeth, took the money out of the envelope, and counted the bills.

'Isn't this supposed to be a little more secretive?' I asked.

'What for? Cash changes hands all the time around here. They'll think I'm either your dealer or your love slave.' He grinned. 'All here. The letter's yours. I'll have more for you over the weekend. That's our busiest time.' He stood up, held up the napkin like a matador cape. It was magnificent. Each feature was finely shaded, the eyes slightly frightened but steady. The lips puffy yet tense. Hair oddly permed, the owner desperate to give it some life, the way paramedics try to shock heart attack victims back to life. The profile was of a woman struggling to hold still, not to bolt for the nearest exit. The profile was of me.

'That's very good,' I said. 'Can I have it?'

'No.' He smiled. 'You can buy it.'

'Sure.' I opened my purse for a twenty.

'A hundred.'

I tossed the twenty down and took the napkin. He let me.

'Unusual medium,' I said. 'Cigarette and linen.'

'I like fire. Usually I do blowtorch and copper. Or firecrackers and papier-mâché. I'm thinking about something now, a new piece using glass and a shotgun. I like to use things that destroy to create. Nothing is ever destroyed, it just changes shape. You know what I mean?'

'Any work that means all that is worth more than twenty dollars.' I handed him another ten-dollar bill.

He looked confused a moment, then stuffed the bill in his shirt pocket.

'What happens when you become a rich and famous artist?'

'Then you can start going through my underwear

200

drawer and selling *my* secrets.' He smiled and handed me the restaurant bill. 'Meanwhile . . .'

I paid the bill.

14

I was crawling beneath the telephone tree. That's what it looked like, a stainless-steel cactus tree with three telephones branching off a metal post. Each station was separated for privacy by small squares of clear plastic the size of cafeteria trays. The phone tree was planted in concrete between the student bookstore and the snack stand among the aluminum picnic tables and benches, also sunk into the cement. Students still registering for summer school were walking back and forth, laughing and talking. Some just sat on the benches or lawn with heads tilted back toward the hot sun. Some smoked cigarettes in that careless and confident manner that made me wish I still smoked too.

Instead, I was on my knees hunting for the quarter I'd just dropped.

While I was down there among the cigarette butts and nuggets of chewing gum, a barefoot boy skateboarded up to one of the other phones and made a call. All I could see were his skinny legs, clothed in baggy shorts that hung past his knees with a Vision Street Wear patch at the hem of one knee. Both shins had scabs where it looked like he'd skidded across pavement. He stood on the skateboard and rocked side to side while he talked to someone named Durango about last night's date with Brook.

' . . . of course I went down on her, dude. I mowed box till my fucking lips went numb.' He listened. 'No way, man, never again. It was awful. Her pussy should have a

202

warning label like on those medicine bottles: Danger! If swallowed, induce vomiting.' He laughed.

I found my quarter and stood up, angling a little so the boy on the phone could see me through his plastic tray. Maybe I thought I could embarrass him or something. I don't know why I bothered. I guess because it was something Wren would have done and I was still in character. In high school when I played Laura in *The Glass Menagerie*, I'd limped around school for a week after the play was over.

The boy was bare-chested, his T-shirt tucked into his waistband and draping down over his butt. At most, sixteen. The receiver was clamped between his head and shoulder, freeing his hands to scratch at the phone with his keys. He looked over at me. Then he smiled in a flirtatious way and winked.

Suddenly I was angry. The tips of my ears were burning. I wanted to tear off the plastic tray between us and smash his face like some avenging Bionic Woman, watch him slo-mo backward over a few steel picnic tables. I didn't know why. I wasn't a raging feminist slapping on THIS EXPLOITS WOMEN stickers everywhere. And he was just a kid; he'd either grow out of his stupidity or he wouldn't. My world didn't hang in the balance. What did it matter to me? Except . . .

Except he hadn't even been embarrassed. He'd seen me glaring at him and it hadn't mattered. He'd felt no shame. If he had seen Wren, the real Wren, he'd have blushed, looked down, hung up, and skated away. I knew that. I wasn't mad because he'd insulted women, I was mad because he had insulted me. I was still a ghost of a person, as hollow as a dried bone. Children and animals could see through my charade the way they could recognize a vampire.

I removed my glasses and a strand of hair that had been pinched in the hinge was yanked out of my head. I winced and cursed my glasses for the thousandth time. They always did this. By the time I was forty, I'ld be plucked bald. The pain drowned my anger and I returned to the phone, thumbing my quarter into the slot. Ghost or not, I still had mortal pressures: a job killing me, a possible new boyfriend calling me, an ex-convict living with me, a white Subaru following me, an interview with a murderess eluding me, a teaching job haunting me.

I called the magazine. Billie answered.

'You got a message from a Detective Diesel, Irvine PD,' she reported.

'What'd he say.' I braced myself.

'He says: "Arf, arf."'

'"Arf, arf."'

'Yup. That's all. That make any sense to you?'

'Some.'

'It's not sexual, is it?'

'Photos will follow,' I said.

She laughed.

So, the blood on the money was dog blood after all. Byron had told the truth. I should have felt better, but I didn't. What was dog blood doing on the money in the first place? I started imagining some satanic ritual, pentagrams, ancient ornate daggers, scratchy wool robes. Puppies whimpering in iron cages.

'Any other messages?' I asked.

'Another one from Davis Richard. And I quote: "I took you to the prom, now it's your turn to put out. Call me." *That's* got to be sexual.'

I laughed. 'If it is, you can read about it in my column.'

'Oh, yeah, I heard you're doing a gossip column now. Congratulations. That is so neat.'

'It's something I always wanted to do. That and cure cancer.'

'I think it's a great idea.' She sounded genuinely excited. She paused, lowering her voice to a whisper. 'We've been a little too stuffy around here. Most of our articles are just puff pieces, booster crap meant not to offend any potential advertisers. But I figure, advertisers don't care what you say as long as you deliver the subscribers. Right?'

'Mr. Krieg would certainly agree.'

'He's wonderful, isn't he. Guess what he's doing this morning?'

'Skydiving from the top of the building?'

'He's putting chalkboards in all the toilet stalls. Men's and women's. He said having a bowel movement is subconsciously destructive and puts people in a destructive mood. That's why they scratch graffiti in the stalls. This way they can still do their graffiti and not destroy the stalls. Good for morale, good for maintenance costs. It's like, no detail is too small for this guy. Cool, huh? Maybe you could write an article about the chalkboards for the mag?'

'Actually, Freud said that defecating was a creative act, not destructive.'

'Well, the idea's the same, right? Keep the stalls from getting all marked up. We could have this cool photo layout of various stalls and their graffiti. That would be the "before" picture. Then we'd show how neat and clean the stalls are after the chalkboards are installed. Show how the graffiti changes, from limericks to poetry. Something like that. Think I should pitch the idea to Linda?'

'With you writing it?'

'You bet. It's my idea.' Her voice was loud now, with a bitter edge. 'I started working here so I could learn the business. I've got my degree in English, you know.'

'I didn't know.'

'Two years at a JC and two at Cal State Long Beach. I worked on the school newspaper.'

The boy next to me hung up his phone, checked the coin return for change, then skated away. His T-shirt flapped like a cape behind his butt. By tonight he'd probably be back in Brook's arms. Where would I be?

On the phone, Billie explained how she would pitch her idea to Linda. She told me about her term papers in her English classes. She got all As and Bs. All things considered, Billie was probably more qualified to be writing for the magazine than I was. She had more practical experience than I just by answering phones at the magazine. I had a little more education, but none that really was applicable here. I'd worked on the high school yearbook writing snappy captions to go with our candid photos. Like, we'd have this photo of Tom Novinger coming out of the boy's bathroom, the smoke still evident over his shoulder, and I'd add the caption: *Tommy continues to conduct private experiments to verify the Surgeon General's warning against cigarette smoking*. That was the extent of my journalistic experience. But now I wore the blessed Coat of Wren, magically transforming me into a valuable commodity.

I felt doubly guilty now for failing to get the interview. First, for damaging Wren's perfect reputation and second, for having a job Billie was working hard for but which I'd basically stolen. I had to try harder, justify my good fortune. Maybe if I could persuade Linda to give me another crack at Season Dougherty, she'd back me with Jonathan.

'Billie, transfer me to Linda's phone.'

'No can do, Wren. Linda's down at the Irvine Police Department.'

My hand tightened around the phone. 'She got the interview?'

'Not with Season Dougherty. Your prom pal Davis Richard has a stranglehold on that. Even Mr. Krieg hasn't been able to budge him yet. But she did manage to get an interview with Season's cell neighbour.'

Damn, that was a good idea. One I should have thought of. Wren would have.

I told Billie I'd be back in the office in an hour. I hung up.

'Do you have change for the phone?' a hefty girl with volleyball kneepads loose around her ankles asked me. She held out a dollar bill.

'Sorry,' I said. I dug in my change purse and found another quarter, which I offered to her.

206

'No, thanks. I'll just get a Coke from the snack stand. They'll give me change.'

I watched her walk away. Her legs were stocky with muscle already losing ground to fat. For some unknown reason I felt my sinuses flood as if I might cry. There was nothing significant about my exchange with the girl, no parallels with my life. I never played volleyball. A stranger never offered me a quarter. I'd never been hefty. But somehow everything on this campus seemed so familiar, like I was back in college again waiting at the student union building for Robby to get out of Bible as Literature so we could go up to his dorm room and screw before his roommate got back from water polo practice. If I checked my purse would I find my old diaphragm?

I quickly sat on the closest aluminum bench. Across the table a young boy wearing Walkman headphones looked over at me and nodded. 'Smog,' he said. 'Stage two alert.' Then he closed his eyes and turned his face back toward the sun.

I just sat there, concentrating on breathing. I was shivering, my mouth dry, the part of my throat that never sees light, scratchy. It's what druggies call 'thirsty'. When would this kind of thing end? You go along in your life, you're not thinking about the past, then Whack! you get nailed on the back of the head with a two-by-four of lethal memory. It's like a wormhole opens up beneath your feet and you're sucked down, like those people in the old *Invaders from Mars*. And as you fall, your chest and stomach are turned into a clothes dryer and all your organs are tumbling against each other, rearranging themselves inside you. Suddenly there's Robby. The two of you are naked on his narrow dorm bed. Cat Stevens's voice is muffled from the room next door. Robby suctions his mouth around your breasts and blows, making a wet farting sound. You both laugh hysterically, partially for the joke, but mostly because you can see how happy your lives together will always be.

I pressed my hands to my eyes. They were dry. No

207

tears. That was important. I could live without Robby, I'd already established that. I mean, hell, I was doing it. Then where did these flashes of profound heartbreak come from? A girl asks for change and I go to pieces. Where was the safety in that?

I stood up and walked into the Valley College bookstore. I needed the textbook my art history class would be using. On Monday, six short days from today, I would be teaching a subject I never even took.

*   *   *   *   *

The back room had all the textbooks arranged alphabetically by subject. Art 110 was easy to find, bottom shelf between Art 105: Art for Teachers and Art 112: Application of Color Theory. Each course had a card taped to the shelf telling who the instructor was and when and where the class met. Under Instructor's Name for my class they had neatly typed Staff. That's me.

I knelt down and examined the textbook. It was the same book that I'd found on Wren's desk the day I went to clean her apartment with her mother. The one with all the notations in the margins around that strange Rodin sculpture, 'She Who Was the Helmet-Maker's Beautiful Wife.' I was relieved. At least now I'd have Wren's notes to work from. Maybe, like everything else I'd been doing, I'd be able to fake my way through.

'Can you tell me where the diaries are?' a woman asked.

I looked up. She was asking me, that bookstore curse I have. She held a dull-eyed bowling ball of a baby straddling her hip. Her T-shirt barely contained her huge breasts. The legs that stuck out of her shorts were pale and bruised. A rash of pimples reddened her cheek. She was about twenty-three with a very enthusiastic expression.

'I'm sorry,' I said. 'I don't work here.'

208

'Oh.' She looked confused and a little hurt, as if I'd just tried to dampen her enthusiasm. 'I'm looking for diaries.'

I looked around the room. 'These are all textbooks. I would think the diaries would be in the front room.'

She nodded but didn't leave. She hiked her sliding baby higher on her hip. 'I want to get one of those nice diaries, you know, the kind that have padded covers and stuff. I'm going to write in it every day to tell my baby what it's like to be a mother. That way she'll know when she's grown up. I think that will make us closer.'

I looked at the baby. She was cramming her fist into her mouth. I thought about those diaries, stacks of padded covers with cute ducks or bunnies on them. Inside the chronicle of her mother's daily joys and sacrifices. Every diaper changed cheerfully, every burp translated into a first word, every gaseous squint tortured into a sign of profound thought. Each page of the diary would be crammed with the unbearable burden of hope. Those volumes will surely drive her daughter out of the house, with only an occasional phone call on holidays while her naked lover made obscene faces at her from the bed.

'I'd check the other room,' I pointed. 'By the cash registers.'

'Thanks,' she said and walked off humming.

15

That night Davis and I cruised Harbor Boulevard in search of a suitable motel to have sex. He took the occasion to explain how he got divorced.

'Beirut,' he said. 'That's what caused it.'

'Beirut?'

'That whole terrorist thing.'

'Terrorists caused your divorce?'

He nodded. He drove the Taurus station wagon without changing lanes. Cars sped up behind him, their headlights brightening the inside of the car like a flare. Impatient, they'd whip around him and rumble off. Usually we'd catch up to them at the light and they'd avoid looking over at us. I felt uncomfortable having all these irate emotions fired in our direction.

'Am I driving too slowly?' he asked.

'No, why?'

'You're fidgeting with your purse strap.'

'Nasty habit. It's a substitute for my old heroin habit.'

He laughed. I liked that he laughed at my jokes, especially the stupid ones. It made me want to say something nice to him. 'You drive like a man who is happy.'

'Huh?'

'Cautious, like you have something to lose.'

He smiled. 'I drive like a father.'

The radio was on, but the volume was so low I couldn't actually recognize any of the songs. Occasionally I'd make out 'baby' or 'love' or something easy. It made all the songs seem the same, interchangeable.

'Meanwhile, back in Beirut . . .' I prompted.

He sighed. 'You know how something across the world, an event that has nothing to do with you can snowball until it finally comes crashing into your life? Like Rube Goldberg contraptions.'

'Those drawings of machines where a bird pecks at a feeder and that causes a chain reaction that eventually lights a match.'

'Exactly my point. He fills the whole page with these elaborate chain reactions that take all the ingenuity and intellect of millions of years of evolution and in the end it does something simple, like light a match. It's overkill. That's what I'm talking about. It's like all the forces of nature and world politics conspired to wreck my marriage.'

He was silent while we waited at a light. Since I didn't know what to say, I kept quiet too. I wanted to tell him I understood some of his pain, tell him about this afternoon at Valley College when a girl in volleyball kneepads almost caused me to cry. But that was Luna's life, not Wren's. He wouldn't be interested in Luna.

After leaving campus, I'd returned to the office. Linda was out, still interviewing Season Dougherty's cell neighbour. Jonathan Krieg, having solved the bathroom graffiti problem, left for a celebrity fund-raiser. I'd finally reached Davis by phone and we'd arranged for another dinner, someplace without any ambience. After my lunch with James Smith and his flambeau napkin art, I wanted someplace that served hamburgers and fries and paper napkins. He took me to Bob's Big Boy. Halfway through the meal we both knew we were going to end up in the sack that night. The only question was where to find a sack. He had kids and a baby-sitter at his place. I had the looming prospect of Byron returning. As we walked through the parking lot toward his car I said, 'Let's find a motel.'

Motels whizzed past us. Capri Motel, Surf Motel, Sandy Inn. I didn't point them out because I didn't want to interrupt his story. Not because I wanted to hear about his divorce right then. Apparently, he needed to talk this through, like a man dutifully informing you of a past sexually transmitted disease. So I listened. I didn't want to be rude before sex.

I turned off the radio to indicate my interest. He looked over at me gratefully, but he didn't speak. I tried to change the subject. 'What's all this?' I asked, pointing at the stacks of newspapers in the back seat. 'Recycling?'

'Nope, they're all today's papers.'

I angled around in my seat for a better look. There were at least a dozen newspapers, all from different cities: Akron, Ohio's *Beacon Journal*; The Atlantic City *Press*; Greensboro, North Carolina's *News & Record*. 'What are you, a news junkie?'

He laughed. 'Strictly business, believe me. I just scan them for some interesting human interest story, something local, that might make a good movie. Lots of producers do this. Helps them get a jump on the studios.'

'Like with Season Dougherty?'

'Yes, like with Season Dougherty. As a crusading mother, she was of minor interest to the guys with the big bucks. That's how I was able to get her rights so easily. If I'd waited until after she shot her husband, I wouldn't even be in the bidding.'

I let the subject drop. This would be bad timing.

'Do you have a particular motel in mind?' I asked. 'An old favorite?'

'Why?'

'We've passed half a dozen already.'

He pointed out the window at a seedy motel with a raunchy tropical motif next to a bowling alley. 'Patty Hearst stayed there when she was on the run with the SLA.'

'Perhaps we can get their Che Guevara suite.'

He chuckled. 'You're very funny, you know that?'

I started to say something about how easily amused he was, but for the first time that I could remember I just

212

accepted the compliment. When you're cruising for a motel to have sex for the first time with a guy, pointing out your own flaws isn't a good idea. I smiled at my joke, laughed lightly.

He reached over and laid his hand on my thigh. High on my thigh, maybe six inches from ground zero. I liked the feel of his hand there, the weight of it on my skin.

'Those Lebanese.' He shook his head and squeezed my leg at the same time, like the two movements were related. 'Remember how Danny Thomas used to talk about being Lebanese on his old show? Let me tell you, Beirut is not filled with a bunch of Danny Thomases.'

'I never watched him. He's before my time.'

'I'm two years older than you. Remember, I read your application. I know all about you.' Davis looked over at me. 'Besides, with cable TV, nothing's before anyone's time anymore. There are 187 million televisions in this country. That's almost one television set per person. No show ever dies. Today when your old man says when I was your age we used to blah blah blah, his kids tune in and see what he's talking about.'

'Except they aren't watching what really happened, just what people idealized.'

'Isn't that what memory is anyway? Just what your subconscious has selected to remember, and even alter when it suits. There is no such thing as an accurate memory because any incident you see is corrupted by your senses, which aren't accurate recording devices. They interpret what they perceive.'

'I didn't realize you were such a philosopher.'

'I'm a producer, which makes me a media apologist.'

'Is that another phrase for bullshit artist?'

He started laughing hard, though not hard enough to take his hand from my thigh. If anything, it slid even higher up. 'Quit teasing me,' he said.

'What?'

'That whole speech I just made. I got it from you.'

'From me?'

'Come on. I had my secretary at UCLA all morning hunting down every article you ever published. Boy, you've been in some obscure publications. That whole television and memory deal I just babbled, I read it in *The Journal of Popular Culture*. Very high-brow title, Test-Pattern Babies: the New Immortality.' I'm quoting you almost directly.'

'Someone should have washed my mouth out with soap.'

He laughed. 'You're probably the smartest woman I've ever known. I couldn't understand half of what you wrote about.'

'So I'm smart because you couldn't understand it?'

'Oops.'

'And why would you think it's a compliment to say the smartest *woman*, which has a certain superior connotation, like saying I'm the tallest dwarf you've ever known.'

I don't know what prompted me to start saying all this, except that I was so unnerved by his catching me not knowing Wren's article that I decided to launch a counter-attack to keep him from wondering why I didn't remember my own opinions. Along with everything else, now I had to read the dozens of articles Wren had published. I doubted I would understand them any better than Davis.

'So, now that you've discovered my latent chauvinism, Doctor,' he said, 'can you recommend a cure?' The thing that most impressed me about him right at that moment was that despite what I'd said, he hadn't withdrawn his hand from my thigh.

'Yeah,' I said. 'Pull in there.' I pointed to a motel down the street. Quixote Inn. Two plaster Don Quixotes crossed lances over the entrance.

We waited at the light, again in silence. Only now his hand slid up against my crotch and two of his fingers began massaging my clitoris. I'm usually a slow builder but this time I felt the heat right away. My hips rocked against his fingers. By the time he pulled into the Quixote Inn, I'd

214

come in a muffled moan. My panties were wet and my thighs sticky. I flopped back against the seat. I said in a chipper voice, 'Well, I guess we can go home now.'

'And miss the best part?'

'What's the best part?'

'When I get undressed and tell you all the reasons why I'm not in better shape.'

I laughed. 'Go, get us a room with a TV. We're making imperfect memories.'

He climbed out of the car and walked into the office. I watched him talk to the man at the desk, a large Chicano man in a Hawaiian shirt and smoking a pipe. Davis filled out the form and paid cash. I could see their lips moving during the entire transaction. The Chicano man laughed heartily. Davis smiled at him and said something else and the man laughed again. Then he returned to the car. I got out when I saw him coming because the inside of the car smelled extremely musky. I flapped my skirt to circulate some air before he came around the car.

'Ready?' he asked.

'The night man didn't say something like "Nice to see you again, Mr. Jones," did he?'

'Turns out his father used to live in the same Mexican village where my family used to go camping during the summers.'

'Did he recognize you?'

'No. It just came up in conversation.'

'How does something like that come up in conversation?'

He shrugged. 'I don't know. People like me, I guess.'

*　　*　　*　　*　　*

Getting naked is the hard part.

Remaining sexy while rolling panty hose down your legs requires a certain flair. There is no dignified position. Even Kim Bassinger must look like she's in a Lucille Ball

215

skit while trying to squirm out of them. There's something about the amount of effort it takes removing panty hose that, according to Robby, makes a woman look like she has something to hide. He said that the first time he'd watched a woman (not me) take them off was like seeing a lizard shed its skin, both wondrous and repulsive.

Davis removed his clothes quickly and efficiently and was standing naked just in time to see me fling the wadded nest of panty hose from my toes. I yanked off my panties and reached around between my shoulder blades to unfasten my bra. Most of my bras fasten in the front, but Robby once told me that, though that is more practical, men liked to see a woman reach around her back. Very erotic, he'd said. We both stood up and peeled back the blankets. The sheets were bright white and stiff as we crawled in. We pulled only the top sheet over us. He reached over and turned off the light. All of our actions seemed so practical, goal-oriented.

'What happened?' he said, touching my bullet wound.

'Appendix. I had a bad doctor.'

He let it drop.

We scooted together and hugged. Davis's penis poked me in the stomach, then slid flat between our stomachs like a folding blade in a pocketknife.

'I'm sorry,' I said suddenly, sitting up. The sheets fell to my waist. Even in the dark I could see my nipples. They seemed absurdly long. I pulled the sheet up over them.

'What's the matter?'

'I'm sorry, but I have to talk business first. I should have said something earlier. I don't know why I didn't.'

He laughed. 'Business? You really are funny.'

I looked over at him. 'Not that kind of business. Season Dougherty business.'

He sat up. His chest was matted with curly blond hair.

'I need to interview Season Dougherty. What we're doing here, being naked and all, has nothing to do with her. This is going to happen no matter what you decide. But if I wait until afterward to ask you, then I will feel

216

like a whore. If you say yes, I'll feel like you paid me, and if you say no, I'll feel somehow bad, I don't know, like the sex wasn't good enough or something. There's a chance I'm not being completely rational right now, but it's important I get all this out in the open.'

'Okay. Business first.'

'Well, that may have been an unfortunate choice of words on my part.'

He smiled. 'You got heat at work, right? Jonathan Krieg turning up the burners?'

'He's stuck me on a gossip column. Two days ago I'd have been grateful for that. But now I've got something to prove, I guess.'

'I can't make multi-million-dollar decisions in a bed at a place called the Quixote Inn. Despite what you've heard, Hollywood doesn't operate like that.'

'Oh.'

'Now, if we were in a Jacuzzi, that would be different.' He laughed.

I tried to laugh too, but it came out more like a sigh.

'This is awkward,' he said.

'I shouldn't have said anything. Jesus, I'm stupid. Forget it.' I put my arm around him and tried to pull him back down.

'No, I'm glad you brought it up. I was going to say something later because I didn't want you to think this was a ploy to get you into bed. Anyway, I need someone to write the book about Season Dougherty's case. The studio thinks a book will promote movie sales. Besides, there's every reason to believe this thing will become a bestseller on its own. I've already had a few informal chats today with some publishers. With the national publicity this case has been getting, we're talking about an advance of a hundred thousand. Of course, you split that in half with me and the studio. Still, fifty grand ain't bad.'

'What makes you think I can write such a book?'

'Hey, I read all your articles, remember? You think I

217

sent my secretary to the library all morning out of lust? Well, okay, partially lust.'

I ran my thumbnail along the seam of the sheet. Ten minutes ago I was a failure, demoted on my second day of work. Now I was being offered fifty thousand dollars to write a book. I guess even dead, Wren's charmed life continued.

'There would be a conflict of interest with the magazine,' I said, 'If I did the book, I'd either have to quit my job or allow them to excerpt the book.'

'Excerpts could be arranged. For a fee.'

'Even so, Jonathan wanted to make the movie deal himself. He may just fire me anyway.'

'Fifty thousand is good severance pay. Besides, I expect to have more books coming my way. This is only the start.'

I thought about it a few minutes. A television from some other room was cranked up pretty loud and some brassy theme music that was vaguely familiar as belonging to a cop show echoed around the room. I didn't know what to do. With fifty thousand I could disappear again. Of course, first I had to write a book, something I had no idea how to do unless Thomas Pynchon figured in it somehow. What should I do?

'Can we just fuck now,' I said.

'Sure.'

We started the usual way, I guess. Stroking each other. Touching lightly here and there, then darting to some other place like fugitive fingers. Basic Foreplay 101. A couple of nights ago Ethan had performed his foreplay as if it had been something he'd read out of a manual. Like doing the Heimlich Manoeuvre or something. Davis was different. He was gentle, slightly awkward, but confident. He knew where we were going and that, sooner or later, we'd get there. He was a lot like Robby. Though there was something reserved about Robby's sex, as if everything he did he had at the back of his mind might be documented later in some scholar's biography of him, therefore he'd better not screw up posterity now. I'd not

218

ever thought of that until just then, but I knew instantly it was true.

Davis had his finger up inside me. I ground myself against his hand and he decided to slip another finger inside. That was nice too. I lay back with my eyes closed, smelling the antiseptic bleach of the dry sheets. I wished I'd had more experience so I could say that this was the best time or the second best time or something. But I'd only had sex with four men in my life, two of them during the past two days.

When Davis was ready to enter me, he was very considerate. He positioned the head of his penis against my vagina but didn't push it in. He kind of rubbed it around a little, like a drug-sniffing dog checking out a package at customs.

Dog. Blood. Money. Byron.

Could that be the explanation? Byron was involved in drugs and had killed some cop's dog eluding a dragnet. I opened my eyes. Davis smiled and thrust into me. My legs angled even farther apart to accommodate him. I reached around and grabbed his buttocks, urging him forward. He pumped harder, then stopped suddenly. I opened my eyes again and saw his eyes clenched, his teeth grit. He held perfectly still, trying not to come. I held still too. I felt like a teenager in my parents' living room hearing a noise from their bedroom.

A minute later Davis started to move again. He didn't talk. Neither did I. Robby liked to talk during sex. He said things like 'Beg me to fuck you' and 'Fuck me till my eyeballs pop.' And sometimes, in a more playful mood, he'd sing the music from Disneyland rides: 'Yo ho, yo ho, it's the pirate's life for me,' and I'd point to his penis and sing, 'It's a small world after all . . .'

Davis came before I did, but he politely continued thrusting until a few minutes later I came too.

'So,' I said, rolling over, 'now that you've had your way with me, you still want me to write the book about Season Dougherty?'

219

He kissed me. Then he lay back against the headboard and cupped his hands behind his head. 'This is the only time I wished I smoked. It gives you something to do with your hands while you talk.'

'Try origami.'

He laughed. 'God, that would make a funny scene in a movie, wouldn't it? This couple just finishes making love in some seedy dive with the neon sign sizzling outside their window.'

'Hot summer night. No air-conditioning.'

'Right. Just a fan blowing across a bowl of ice. She gets up, naked, takes one of the ice cubes and runs it along her neck and lips. Then she picks up a couple sheets of paper and hands him one and says, "Origami, Nick?"'

'And he says, "No, thanks, I'm trying to quit."'

He laughed again. When he laughed he made me feel somehow smarter and funnier than I really was.

'The American hostages in Beirut,' he said.

'What?'

'My divorce. It started when the Lebanese terrorists released one of the American hostages a couple years ago.'

'That professor.'

'Right. We're sitting at home watching the news. My wife and I. Actually she's in bed. I'd just come back from checking on Judy, who'd had a stomach-ache.' He looked at me again, his face serious. 'She had checked on her earlier, I'm not trying to make myself out as a better parent. Lila is a fine mother.'

'Lila's your wife?'

He nodded solemnly. 'Anyway, I'm climbing back into bed and Lila's watching the news. She's got the newspaper spread out in front of her and a bowl of double-fudge ice cream in her hands. She eats a bowl every night. Not that she's fat, she's thin as a broom handle. She just likes ice cream.'

'Just tell the damn story, Davis,' I said with a laugh. 'I'm not judging anyone.'

'You're right. I don't know why I do that. Apologize

for everything. Before the divorce I never did that. I think it's just that my divorce was my first failure at anything. I've always succeeded, always got what I wanted. Breaking up with Lila kind of shook my confidence.' He shook his head. 'Okay, so Lila's watching the TV all serious-looking, like there's going to be a quiz on it later. I ask her what's on the news. She shushes me and says, "Listen." I listen. One of the American hostages has just been released by the terrorists. He's been held captive for three years. He's walking toward a plane, waving at reporters, looking pale and frail, like he'd been locked up with Dracula for three years. When the segment about the hostage is done, Lila taps her spoon against an article she's reading in the newspaper. She's very animated. Ice cream drips onto the article. "You know what it says here? This expert on hostages says that they have to be retrained before they can enter society again. They have been isolated so long that they have to be taught how to speak. That's why they have to wait before letting them have a news conference. Also, they can't make decisions. They can't decide what clothes to wear, what food to eat." She's talking a mile a minute. I'm looking at her and she's got tears in her eyes and I'm thinking, What a compassionate woman to feel so much for these poor hostages. Then she says, "Davis, those are all the same symptoms I have. I have all the symptoms of a Beirut hostage." Next thing I know, we're divorced.'

Another TV show theme filters up through the motel courtyard. I laid perfectly still and didn't say anything. I was trying hard to come up with something comforting.

'Hell of a story, huh?' he said.

I opened my mouth, hoping something compassionate would spring out on its own. When it didn't, I pulled the sheet off his waist and lowered my mouth onto his penis.

16

'Shouldn't we talk?' he asked.

'About what?'

'About what just happened. Don't you watch TV? This is where we discuss, in muted voices and sensitive terms, how we feel about having had sex.'

I muted my voice. 'What would we say?'

He shrugged, looked around the Bob's Big Boy parking lot where we'd returned for my car. We were standing on a white line in the three-foot alley between his car and mine. My key was inserted in the car door, my fingers grasping it, ready to turn. He was leaning against his car, arms folded casually like he'd just stepped out of a crowded bar for a smoke and a look at the stars. He stepped up behind me and wrapped his arms around mine. My breasts squeezed together and looked bigger. I leaned back into him. He pressed his nose to my neck and breathed deeply. 'I thought I'd say something sensitive like: "You fill up my senses, like a night in the forest."'

'Ah, poetry.'

'Well, John Denver.'

I laughed, 'The classics, huh. What would I say in response?'

'Something equally sensitive. Like: "Life could be a dream . . ."'

'If you would take me up to paradise up above . . .'

'Sh-boom, sh-boom. See, men can open up just as well as women.'

I twisted around and faced him. We kissed. He smelled like Ivory soap from our motel shower.

'Baby-sitter,' I reminded him, tapping his watch crystal.

'Right.' He looked at his watch. 'Right.' He pecked me on the lips and ran around to the driver's side and jumped in. The passenger window hummed as it electronically lowered. He scrunched down so he could see me. I bent over. His face was soft and gentle, like a slept-on pillow. 'Call you tomorrow. Meantime, think about the book deal. I'm serious about it.'

'Sh-boom, sh-boom.'

'I mean it, Wren. This has nothing to do with that.' On 'that' he hooked his thumb over his shoulder in the general direction of the Quixote Inn. 'Just think about it.'

'I will.'

He drove off, waving at me into his rearview mirror. I waved back until his twin red tail-lights merged with the rest of the traffic. I was still waving after I was sure he couldn't see me. I looked at myself waving, observed the absurdity of the gesture. A hand flopping up and down. Or wiggling side to side. I tried both. A couple teenage boys honked and waved back as they drove by. I laughed and got in my car.

On the freeway drive home I remembered something important. After Davis and I had made love a second time, I'd dozed off for just a few minutes. Instantly, I'd started dreaming. I was black. I wore my hair in a modest afro like Angela Davis, the seventies radical professor. Sammy Davis, Jr, was trying to persuade me to teach Greek to Jewish kids in the ghetto for $10,000 a year. 'I can't do it for that little,' I told him. 'I'd starve.' He said, 'Do it for our people.' 'But I'm not Jewish,' I told him. 'And I don't know Greek.' He shook his head angrily, 'So? You're not black either.' When he said that I cried. He put his hand on my shoulder and said they'd throw in a condo along with the ten grand. Then I woke up. Tears were in my eyes but I'd wiped them on the pillow before Davis had noticed.

223

I arrived home a few minutes before ten o'clock. I couldn't believe it was so early, considering all that had happened today. A month ago my day would have consisted of two hours in class, two hours teaching, followed by ten hours at the library. The monotony of the days blurred them into a swampy sameness. Like the taste of oatmeal. I'd had to constantly consult a calendar to know what specific day it was. Before that, when I was with Robby, there was always something to distinguish the days, give them identity. Later, Wren did the same thing for me. This was the first time I experienced such variety of experience on my own.

But variety takes its toll. I was exhausted and dying for bed. The insides of my thighs were a little sore from where they'd gripped Davis's hips.

I followed the trail of snails up the sidewalk to my front door. For some reason, they reminded me of communism. I thought of them with those little fur hats. That made me laugh. A couple of snails were suctioned to my door. What could they hope to find on my door?

I noticed the lights weren't on inside, which I hoped meant Byron wasn't home yet. On the drive over I'd practiced my Farewell to Byron speech, in which I emphatically inform him that this living arrangement was not going to work out. He would have to find another place. I'd even help him pay for it if he was short on cash, maybe I could scrape up a couple hundred a month. Okay, that was like paying blackmail, but I was in the middle of a $50,000 deal and I couldn't afford to have him blabbering about Luna Devon.

As I unlocked my front door, I could hear Ethan upstairs strumming his guitar, working on a new gag song for his comedy routine. He kept playing the same three chords over and over from the Bee Gees' 'I Started a Joke'. Each time he'd sing a variation of the title. 'I started to poop . . .' Pause. 'I started the Pope . . .' Pause. 'I strangled the Pope . . .'

When I opened the door the stench from inside

thwacked me in the face like a thrown pie. 'Ohhh, Jeeeeesus,' I winced, cupping my hand over my nose.

I left the door open and quickly unlocked and slid open a couple of windows.

'Christ!' I pulled my blouse up over my nose like a surgical mask and began hunting for what I assumed was a dead and rotting body. 'Hector! Hector!'

As I neared the bathroom, the stench cranked up a couple notches. I flipped the light switch. The cat litter box looked as if it had been bombed by chunks of mud the size of ice cubes. Each little chunk was coated in green litter. They looked almost decorative.

A little yellow plastic shovel the same color as the litter box rested against the toilet. I grabbed it and began sifting. I flushed the bombs down the toilet. The window was barley open an inch; I flipped the lock and shoved it the rest of the way open. I stuck my head out and took a deep breath of fresh air.

Whatever satisfaction I had in disposing of the problem ended as I walked back toward the living room and was again hit by the foul smell, stronger than ever. And fresh. I heard a muffled noise. Rhythmic. I looked across the room and saw the top leaves of my fichus tree rustling. I circled the sofa, stepped over a small coffee table, and marched straight for the plant. Standing inside the sixteen-inch pot, Hector was digging the dirt, pawing it behind him to cover up several more moist nuggets.

I grabbed him by the scruff and hoisted him out of the plant. 'You little shit,' I scolded. He just hung limply, the skin at his neck pulling his eyes almost shut.

I carried him into the kitchen and dropped him on the floor. He landed on all fours, crouched defensively, looked around, then sat down and began licking his paws.

'I hate you,' I told him. 'I just wanted you to know.'

A stack of 9-Lives cat food cans sat on the counter. They had not been here this morning when I'd left. Also, next to the lidded trash pail stood a brown Lucky's grocery bag. Inside were a couple of open cat food cans and all the soda and fruit cocktail and soup cans from the trash. Byron had rooted through my trash and dumped all the cans in the bag. Written in thick black Magic Marker on the front of the bag was CANS (recycle!).

Next to the bag were two new porcelain bowls shaped like sleeping cats. One contained water, the other was empty except for a few pasty smears where the food had been.

Apparently Byron had been able to interrupt his mysterious travels long enough to pop home, feed the cat, and sort my garbage. How did he get in? I hadn't given him a key. But then again, he was an ex-con and he knew people named Grudge. So, anything was possible.

I opened a can of sliced veal and dumped it into Hector's bowl. He sauntered over, sniffed, licked at the sauce a little, then sat down and began licking his butt.

'Hey, *I* didn't buy it for you. Save the food reviews for your master.'

After I cleaned out my fichus, I started running the bathwater. I dumped in a packet of lilac bath salts hoping they would mask the heavier odor still apparent throughout the apartment. I undressed in my new bedroom, the smaller bedroom where Byron had stuck me. My panties were wet from leaking on the drive home. I tossed them into the laundry.

That's when I noticed the blinking light on my phone answering machine. I hadn't had a message on it since moving here, so I'd stopped checking it. Probably a wrong number, but I pressed the button anyway. The tape kept whirring and rewinding as if the entire tape had been used. I grabbed a pen and opened the *People* magazine to a page with a tampon ad that had a lot of white space for notes.

First message: 'Okay, man, I spoke to the rocket king like you asked. He says, and I'm reading directly from the paper he gave me, so there ain't no fuckin' screwups. Okay, he says: "7866." Got that? Seventy-eight sixty-six. He's waitin' to hear from you, man.'

Second message: 'Byron! You're out! Living proof that the judicial system doesn't work. Listen, I got this number from T-Bone. I hear you're still in the game. Anyway, if that's true, I know where there's some money if you want me to broker. I sure as shit am not leaving my name on this thing, so if you don't recognize my voice, well, then fuck you anyway. If you do, give my sister a call. She knows how to reach me.'

There were six more messages, all for Byron, all equally cryptic. No one left their name or number where they could be reached. There were a lot of hints about large sums of money, but no specifics as to how much or where this money would come from.

I sat naked on the edge of the bed. I hadn't written any of the messages down. What was I in the middle of here. The rocket king? Was this some kind of espionage thing? The Jet Propulsion Lab was nearby.

I pulled on some sweatpants and a T-shirt and cranked off the tub faucet. I popped the tape cassette out of Wren's machine, and took it to the stereo in the living room. Wren's stereo system included a high-speed tape-to-tape dubbing deck. I copied Byron's messages onto a blank tape. I needed a place to hide it until I'd decided which authorities I should send this to. FBI? CIA? Detective Diesel? There was no place in the apartment he considered private. He'd already gone through my belongings once. Hiding it at the office would be tricky. My job was already in jeopardy. I could show up one day with my desk drawers empty.

Hide in plain sight. Poe's purloined letter trick. All I needed was a tape he was sure not to listen to. I ran my finger across the plastic spines of the cassette cases trying to decide the extent of Byron's musical taste. Most of the cassettes Robby had bootlegged from friends' albums. When we'd split, he'd given them all to me, which I'd thought was a generous gesture until Wren informed me that the albums he'd been copying belonged to Dr. Helen Jaspers.

'Yes,' I said, tilting one case forward. The Carpenters. I labeled the copy of Byron's messages *Karen Carpenter Sings Songs of Love and Devotion* and tucked it into the case, back between Kate Bush and Tracy Chapman.

The original tape I tossed onto Byron's bed. After removing the label, I stuck the actual Carpenters tape back into the answering machine for future messages.

I closed and locked all the doors and windows, stripped, and climbed into my tub. The hot water burned the insides of my chafed thighs. I closed my eyes and sank down until the water touched my chin. I tried to think constructively, formulate some kind of plan of action. Take Davis's offer to write the book. Quit my job at the magazine. Kick Byron out. But every plan had holes. Could I trust Davis to deliver on the contract?

I looked down at my pubic hairs waving in the water like seaweed. Was that clump of skin, hair, and crevices the reason he was doing this. Or was it because he admired Wren's credentials? Which answer would be less insulting to me?

Now the questioning wouldn't stop. Would Jonathan Krieg be so mad that he tried to blackball me? He could probably do that if he wanted. And that might cause people to look into my past a little too closely. Was I even capable of writing such a book, did I have any of the skills necessary? Also, if I did write the book, I'd have to publish under a pseudonym. Wren's name couldn't suddenly appear nationwide without somebody figuring out the truth. Perhaps I could use Luna Devon as my pseudonym? I smiled at the thought and hot water crept up to my lips.

I sensed a presence in the room, staring at me. Thinking it was Byron, I quickly opened my eyes, ready to grab for a towel. Hector stood on the edge of the tub looking at the water. He lowered his paw tentatively until it touched the water, then he jerked it back.

'It's water,' I informed him. 'Cats hate water.'

He leaned farther over and dipped his head until he

228

could sniff the water. Then he stuck his tongue in and started drinking.

'That's hot water,' I said. 'You have fresh cold water in your bowl. God, you're stupid.'

He kept slurping away.

I watched him drink. His gray tail kept flipping back and forth, brushing my shoulder. It tickled and I had to keep scratching my shoulder. Finally, I grabbed his tail and held it a few seconds and he stopped swishing it. Instead, it drifted over the side of the tub and floated on top of the water.

'Hey, I want to wash my face in here.'

He sat back and started licking his butt again.

'You're disgusting,' I said. I kicked the drain lever with my foot and felt the water start to suck out of the tub. I laid there and let it. Hector didn't move. I thought of BeeGee's cat, Sphinx, a moment before she'd shoved the cocked gun against his chest. The blood, the clumps of wet fur stuck to my face. BeeGee had loved that cat. Once, she had taken a week of work without pay to stay home and care for him when he was sick. I remember making a joke about it at the time and Wren saying Bee-Gee was lucky because she was loving in the way people were genetically programmed to love, before romance fucked it all up. I was still with Robby at the time, so I told her she was full of shit and went back to grading compositions about why we have a drug problem in this country.

But this was the question Wren had asked: Do people have a greater need to give love or receive love? She'd said we needed more to give love. A child with his teddy bear. He makes that bear real, gives it personality, and kisses and hugs it and weeps hysterically if it rips along a seam. The bear gives no love back except that which the child imagines. 'People with pets are no different,' she'd said. 'People train the pet to respond in a way that they then interpret as love because it makes them feel all squishy inside. But it ain't really love, just the reflection of that person's need.' 'What about people loving people?' I'd asked. She'd smiled. 'Same thing. And not just in romantic relationships. Look at mothers and daughters. Same ole same ole. We don't resent others not loving us as much as we hate them for taking away our opportunity to love them. It's loving that gives us identity, not being loved. Once we come to accept that about ourselves, we'll all be a lot happier.'

The last of the water swirled down the drain. Hector and I watched it go together. I looked at him. He lowered his head as if expecting me to scratch it. 'Forget it,' I said, getting up.

I stepped over him and out of the tub, dried off, and dressed back in my sweats and T-shirt. Dressing for bed was new for me, but with Byron lurking about somewhere, I wanted to be prepared for anything.

I went to the kitchen for a ginger ale. On my way back past the front door, I peeked out between the shades down the front walk. I didn't see Byron. Just more snails. A clump of about ten of them were knotted together atop something. I could go out there right now, I thought, and bring one back and give it a name and keep it in an aquarium and feed it and put little colored rocks in with it and talk to it at night and maybe grow to love it. Seeing it every day, talking to it, watching it slither—after a while, I probably would love it. Is that the best we can do after millions of years of evolution? Love a snail.

I started to turn from the window when something gleamed out of the corner of my eye. White.

Subaru.

Across the small parking lot, parked against the red curb. A bent clothes hanger for a radio antenna.

I flung open the front door and hit the pavement running. I don't know why I had this sudden burst of courage or outrage or something. I just knew that I was pissed. My bare feet smacked the sidewalk twice before I felt the fragile crunch of snail shell under my heel. That could

230

have been the one, I thought, the one I brought in to love. Too late now, I kept running.

The driver saw me. A bearded man about forty-five. He'd been drinking coffee from a Styrofoam cup and reading the newspaper. He quickly crumpled the paper and batted it aside. He clamped the coffee cup between his teeth and started the car.

'Hey!' I hollered, racing toward him.

He shifted into first, but he must have bitten through the cup, because suddenly it dropped from his mouth except for a half moon of Styrofoam still between his teeth like a wafer. His window was up, but I could hear the muffled yowl of pain as the coffee spilled into his lap.

Behind me were heavier footsteps. I glanced over my shoulder. Ethan, barefoot and bare-chested, wearing only his Jockey shorts, ran full speed with a hammer in his hand. He reminded me of Thor. I didn't stop or say anything. I kept racing for the Subaru.

But the driver managed to screech out while I was still ten feet away. 'Hey!' I called after him. I slowed, feeling the gravel and ground snail shell digging into my foot.

Ethan kept running after the car. When it was clear he wouldn't catch it, he hurled his hammer. It somersaulted through the air and, surprising both of us, struck the Subaru's trunk before bouncing to the ground. Encouraged by his markmanship, he began shaking his fist and shouting. 'Get out of here, you fuck! You son of a bitch! I see you again, I'll rip you a new asshole! You hear me, motherfucker? I'll kill you!' When the Subaru had shot out of the apartment complex, Ethan bent over, his hands on his knees, catching his breath. Still panting, he turned and looked up at me. 'So, who the hell was that?'

17

'What's wrong with this?' Jonathan Krieg asked, smacking a folded copy of last month's *Orange Coast Today* on his desk and sliding it across to me.

Somewhere in the room an insect, a fly or mosquito or something desperate, was buzzing. It made that fussy sound, like when they batter their wings against glass, that sound like sizzling neon. I looked around the room anxiously.

'A quick scan's all you'll need,' he said.

I picked up the magazine and started reading the article circled in red ink.

'Just read the first paragraph,' he said. 'The first paragraph is plenty.'

I read. It was a book review of a novel I had never heard of let alone read. For somone holding a master's degree in English, I was surprisingly dumb about current writers. I knew some names—Ann Beattie, Yannick Murphy, Richard Ford, Frederick Barthelme—enough to fake intimacy if their names ever came up. At a party, I had once referred to Amy Hempel as a 'staggering talent', though I hadn't read a single word she'd written. My own studies, which had mostly consisted of catching up to what all my younger peers had already read, had kept me firmly rooted in pre-twentieth century writers. The only living author whose complete works I'd actually read was Thomas Pynchon. And he was a recluse; nobody knew who or where he was.

'I want your opinion,' Jonathan said, pacing behind his

desk. He had his corporate raider outfit on today: light gray double-breasted suit and red paisley power tie overlapping his belt like a crotch bib and pointing straight down at his penis as if it were a Red Tag Sale item. 'I want to know what you think of this piece of writing, Wren. Your expert opinion.' He held up a cautionary finger: 'This is important.'

The review was by our free-lance columnist, Judith Dwyer-Horowitz. She taught comparative literature at the University of California at Irvine and had once reviewed books for the prestigious *New York Review of Books*. I hadn't met her yet, but word around the office was that she had been fired from that job after a bit of a scandal. Apparently, she received free copies of books from publishers to review, but since she received many more than she could possibly read, she sold them to bookstores. This was some sort of ethical breach and and *New York Review of Books* printed an apology about her conduct when they announced they'd fired her. She rarely came to the office: her reviews arrived by fax. She had a better scam going than I.

'Just the first paragraph,' Jonathan prodded. He looked over his shoulder at the window. The buzzing was starting to get to him too.

While I read, I crossed my legs and scratched vigorously at my ankles. For some reason they itched like crazy.

Jonathan hit his intercom. 'Billie, come in here please.' He clicked it off without waiting for an answer from her.

I concentrated on the review. I could sense from Jonathan's agitation that something was up. This review thing was some kind of test. I wasn't sure what was being tested. My stomach was already being tag-team body-slammed by the rest of my internal organs because I'd made up my mind to tell Jonathan this morning all about Davis's book offer and be fired or quit. But before I'd had a chance, he'd called me in and shoved this review at me.

I had to tell him about Davis. I'd reached my personal best for sneaking around and wanted to at least have this one thing out in the open. Do one right thing today, Luna. Just one. The lines between right and wrong used to be as clear to me as black telephone wires against a blue sky; now ethics were cellular. Voices were somehow sent, somehow they arrived. There were no means, nothing to judge. Just results.

Billie entered the office looking like a rock singer posing as a nun. She was wearing a black knit skirt, matching black cardigan sweater, adobe-white blouse, and a black bow tie. Her thin legs were sheathed in textured black hose, capped with black patent leather shoes that came to a lethal point. Her expression was of nervous anticipation acid-washed by raw ambition. She'd never looked more beautiful.

'Yes, Mr. Krieg?' she said. He gestured at the chair next to mine. She sat on the edge of it, her narrow bottom perched like a gull on the railing of a boat.

'Tell Wren here what you told me this morning. About Judith's reviews. This one for example.'

Billie smiled guiltily at me. She needn't have. I admired her ambition, coming in early, ambushing Jonathan before the rabbi or bodybuilders got to him. I wanted her to succeed. I just didn't want to look like a fool in the process.

'Well, Wren,' she said, her voice deeper, more professional-sounding than she'd ever been as a receptionist. She reminded me of Robby's radio deejay voice. 'I was telling Mr. Krieg that I thought we've indulged Judith's peculiarities long enough. If the magazine is going to take a new direction, I think all aspects of it should also be redesigned.'

I nodded encouragement, having given up reading the first paragraph after a few sentences.

'Be specific,' Jonathan said. 'What's wrong with Judith? This review specifically.'

Billie shrugged as if it was all too obvious. 'Well, in the first place, her selection of books to review. She chooses novels that are too esoteric, too literary for the kind of audience we're pursuing. This isn't New York City. We're a coastal community, more leisure oriented. Very few people will go out and buy this book and even fewer will actually read it, even if she gives it a rave.'

'I've read this book,' Jonathan Krieg said. 'I loved it.'

Billie wilted a little, but the tumblers in her brain clicked into place almost instantly, inflating her posture. 'But you're not our target audience, Mr. Krieg. I am. Me and my mother.'

He smiled, pleased. 'Go on.'.

If it was the job of book reviewer she was after, I thought she'd just snagged it. She looked over at me and I smiled for her. I reached down and raked my ankles again.

'But what else is wrong with this review?' Jonathan continued, frowning now. 'Something else . . .'

'Well, the prose style is a little too dense, too many elaborate metaphors, too many references to other writers and books. On the whole, it's too academic. Mainly, our readers want to know what the book's about and whether or not to plunk down twenty bucks for it.'

'That makes sense.' He glanced back at the window. The buzzing had taken on a furious high pitch. He walked over to the window, searched it from top to bottom. Nothing. The buzzing stopped. 'Does that make sense to you, Wren?'

I looked down at the review again, rereading the first few sentences. I'd read Judith's reviews when I was studying the magazine before coming down here. I didn't like her reviews, though not for the same reasons Billie just mentioned. But I didn't want to torpedo Billie's chances by disagreeing. After all, she'd gone after her success; I'd merely stolen mine.

'Wren?' Jonathan repeated. His voice suggested he enjoyed watching these little gladiatorial confrontations.

'I haven't read this book,' I admitted. 'So maybe this isn't a fair assessment.'

'You've read Judith's other reviews. You're familiar with her style.'

'Yes.'

'Well, one needn't have read the book being reviewed to know whether or not one likes the reviewer. I mean, you don't have to see the movie to know Siskel and Ebert are dickheads. Right?'

I glanced at Billie. Her posture was erect and tense, as if expecting a spinal tap. Her hands were folded piously on her lap. She was absently picking at a cuticle on her thumb.

'I agree with Billie,' I said. 'I don't like Judith's reviews either.'

'For the same reasons as Billie?'

'Somewhat.'

'She's too academic, prose too dense? Her selections are too literary? Her attitude too New York City?'

I shrugged. 'Not exactly. I kind of like a dense prose style in the reviews. And I don't mind that she picks books that are more literary and less popular. I don't think the readers of our magazine who bother to read the reviews care about anyone's opinion about the new Danielle Steele or Robert Ludlum. They're going to read those books anyway. What they would like is a conversational knowledge of current literature so they can talk about these books without ever having to read them. Cultural literacy today is merely recognizing a name, not having any intimacy with it.'

Jonathan laughed. 'Keen insight. You sound like one of your own articles.'

This 'keen insight' came from my own experiences trying to keep up with the likes of Robby and Wren. I was the prototype of the cultural 'illidiot' (Wren's term), saved from being excluded from party conversations about post-structuralist semiotics by a quick scan of reviews in the library. I was barely able to pass for intelligent that way. I knew the names, I knew the buzz words. I guess long before I faked being Wren, I'd faked being Luna.

'Let me get this straight,' Jonathan said. 'Are you saying to keep Judith's reviews?'

Billie looked at me with a strangled expression, as if her black bow tie had suddenly tightened around her throat on its own. Cuticle flakes from all her fingers confettied her black skirt.

'No, Jonathan,' I said. 'I don't like Judith either. But for a different reason. Well, here's an example.' I stabbed my finger at one of the sentences and read aloud: '"This author has a rare intelligence and almost psychic ability to read people. How else can you explain her unerring insights into characters of every social class and age group. These characters are unflinchingly accurate."' I shook my head. 'How the hell does Judith know these are accurate portrayals? She should say that the characters are written so they are believable, that we care what happens to them. But what she says here is that because she herself is such a goddamned genius, with the ability to know what people of all ages and social statuses are thinking, she can recognize this same genius in others. That's what I don't like about her reviews. They're all about how smart Judith is.'

Jonathan's face was expressionless. He quietly sat down behind the desk. He opened a desk drawer and pulled out a white yarmulke and placed it on the back of his head. He dragged his Hebrew book across the desk and flipped it open. Then he started reading aloud in stuttering broken Hebrew, his finger running from right to left under each word.

Billie looked at me. She contorted her lips to signify her confusion. I shrugged. We sat there and waited for him to finish. I'd known Jonathan Krieg long enough now to know he never did anything without a lesson. Like a lot of successful people, he equated success with wisdom. It wasn't enough to be rich and famous, he wanted people to think he deserved it because of his higher plane of thinking. Every knucklehead with a car phone thinks he's Yoda.

The obnoxious insect must have changed locations,

237

because the timbre of its buzzing was different now, a faint sputtering, as if it were running out of gas.

When Jonathan finished a couple of minutes of tortured reading, he closed his book and looked at us with a huge smile. 'Not bad, huh? Two weeks ago I couldn't read any Hebrew.'

'That's amazing, Mr. Krieg,' Billie said.

He looked at me for a reaction.

'Two weeks?' I said. 'Only two weeks?'

He nodded modestly. 'What's amazing is that I still don't understand a word I'm reading. But to be bar mitzvahed, I don't have to. I've just got to read the words and give my speech.'

'Oh?' Billie said. She wasn't getting it. The Big Message. I wasn't getting it either, but at least I knew there was one to get. I also knew that, like most would-be teachers, he would tell us exactly what he meant, then he'd grin moronically at his own wisdom. Since, as a teacher, I never thought of myself as having any wisdom, I never fell into that trap.

'My point is, Billie,' he said, 'Wren is right. I don't have to understand what I'm saying. I'm performing a ritual to be accepted into the fold. That's all people ever do. They spend their lives performing elaborate rituals to be accepted by this group or that. Family, school, job, romance, it's all the same. From plucking your eyebrows to saving your soul. It's all ritual. Now, how does that apply here? We print book, movie, and theater reviews. Do you think we do that because our readers are hungry for the arts? No, they just want to be able to have an opinion, even if it's someone else's. Our subscribers read book reviews because they don't have the time or patience to read the book. But they still want to be accepted into the fold of the well-read, the intelligent, the best and brightest.'

'I see,' she said, uncertainly.

He took his yarmulke off and tossed it back in its drawer, probably next to his vitamins and exercise shorts. 'Billie, you are now this magazine's book reviewer.'

Billie's rump hopped in her chair. 'Thank you, Mr. Krieg.'

'I believe in rewarding ambition.' He held up a finger and wagged it like an old rabbi. 'People who only do what they're told have to be told what to do. But go-getters, they get on the go. See what I'm saying? You understand what I'm telling you here? You have the proper education and I've read a couple of your writing samples. I think you can do the job.'

'Thank you, Mr. Krieg. I really can.'

'However, until I'm sure you've got the right slant on what we're looking for, I want you to clear your book selections with Wren first. Also, Wren, you are responsible for editing Billie's work. This is going to be a team effort. Any questions?'

'No, sir,' Billie said and stood up. A few cuticles flaked to the floor. The rest stuck to her black skirt in a crazy mosaic pattern.

I stood up. This didn't seem like the best time to tell Jonathan about Davis's book contract offer. If I quit or was fired now, as part of his Samurai-art-of-war style of management, he might take back his offer to Billie. I couldn't bear to see that. Fifteen minutes ago, telling Jonathan the truth about the book contract would have been right, now doing so seemed hurtful, wrong. More cellular ethics.

Billie and I walked to the door. I wouldn't be able to hold off telling him long, maybe a day or two. If he found out about it on his own, it could be disastrous. Once my honesty was questioned, who knows what kinds of checking he might do on me.

As Billie opened the door for me I said quietly, 'Billie, I'm going to need your review by tomorrow morning.' I was about to offer some complicated explanation for such haste, but before I could she chirped in 'Okay!'

'Wren,' Jonathan called as I was exiting.

I turned. 'Yes?'

239

'When you get a chance, give that Judith what's-her-fuck a call and tell her she's fired.'

'You want *me* to tell her?'

'Yes, I do. You are now in charge of book reviews, so it follows you should weed out the old before planting the new.' He made a pulling motion, I guess representing pulling weeds though it resembled masturbation.

I knew enough about editing as a teacher to recognize the importance of the job. But I'd been hired for my writing, now I was baby-sitting someone else's. Jonathan wasn't testing me, he was punishing me for blowing the Season Dougherty interview. Ordering me to fire this woman was a way of letting me know how disposable *I* was. Sending me down to the minors to coach a young comer. But I had a secret, a fifty-grand-stick-it-up-your-ass-book-contract-offer secret.

'Yes, sir,' I said to him. 'I'll call her right away.'

He nodded.

I returned to my desk and called Davis's office. Before I got too cocky, I wanted to be sure that the book offer was still good, not just a postcoital expression of endearment, his way of saying 'that felt good'.

His secretary said he was out.

'When do you expect him back?' I asked.

'He's out of town, Ms. Caldwell.'

'What?'

'Hawaii. He flew to Maui this morning. However, he did leave a message for me to tell you that he would contact you as soon as he was able.'

'Anything else?'

'Uh'—I heard the sound of rustling paper—'no, that seems to be all.'

Suddenly I didn't feel so confident.

'And he didn't say when he'd be back? Give a time? A day?'

'No, ma'am, he didn't. This was an unexpected business trip. He called me from the airport an hour ago just as they were boarding.'

'What kind of unexpected business pops up in Maui?'

She laughed. 'This is crazy business, Ms. Caldwell. Mr. Richard can disappear for days at a time. But he gets things done.'

You know those commercials where some guy is sitting in a chair and suddenly a bunch of money (or tires or cereal boxes) erupts under him and lifts his chair straight up as high as a skyscraper. That's how I felt. Like I was teetering.

I decided to take advantage of my darkening mood. I called Judith Dwyer-Horowitz and, struggling to keep my voice from cracking, told her in the kindest terms possible that due to a change in the magazine's ownership and direction we would no longer be needing her book reviews.

'Oh,' she said, unconcerned. As if I'd just told her tomorrow would be balmy.

I wondered if maybe, in my efforts to spare her feelings, I hadn't made myself clear.

'You're fired,' I clarified.

I heard a chewing sound. 'Well, that's that then. Thanks for calling.' As she was hanging up I heard her say to someone, 'Not so much salt, you'll kill the ginger root taste.' To which a young man replied, 'I've got your root taste, right here' And they both laughed like lovers. Click.

I slowly lowered the receiver toward the cradle. My hand shook a little from the trauma of having just fired a woman. My throat was clogged with cement, my colon was spasming like poking a hot copper wire against an earthworm. As if I'd been the one fired. Meantime, Judith what's-her-fuck was cooking ginger roots and laughing seductively. I hated her.

I scooted my chair back past my partition. 'Gordon.'

Gordon Saunders, the magazine's most prolific article writer, was two-finger typing on his Macintosh. He would sometimes have two articles in the same issue, one on FBI manhunts in Orange County, the other in fingerpainting competitions among preschools.

241

'Gordon,' I repeated.

'Hmmm . . .' He didn't look over.

'Who runs UCI? The head enchilada.'

'Chancellor Cummings.'

'Thanks.' I scooted back to my desk. I stabbed Judith's number again.

'Hello?' she said pleasantly, still chewing something.

I pinched my voice into an officious whine. 'Ms. Dwyer-Horowitz?'

'Yes?'

'This is Chancellor Cummings's office. We've had a very serious complaint from a student about repeated acts of sexual harassment from you. The chancellor would like to see you in his office first thing in the morning. You may want to bring your attorney.'

'W-what?' she choked. 'What are you talking about?'

'The police will explain everything. Good day.' I hung up. After a minute or so she'd call the chancellor's office and discover my call was a prank. But for that minute she'd suffer some of the anguish I had when I'd first called her. There, I thought, staring at the phone, I'd done one good thing today after all.

The telephone rang and I jumped. Had they traced my call back to me already? 'Hello?'

'Hey, Wren. It's James.'

'James?'

'James Smith. Your pipeline to the stars.'

I refocused my thoughts. Gossip column. Oh, yeah, my job. 'What's up, James?'

'Time for more of that cash. Five hundred baby Cs.'

I laughed. 'For five hundred dollars, this gossip better be about me.'

'Give me twenty-four hours and I could dig up something on you.'

I let that drop. 'What have you got?'

'The name of a certain famous muscular movie star who is on the cover of every major magazine because he has a hot summer release.'

242

'What's he done to merit our attention?'

'Actingwise, not much. But last night he had a secret emergency visit by a prominent physician, whose daughter happens to go with a guy who works for me. Seems our muscle-bound megastar got his dick caught in a Dustbuster. Suffered some lacerations around the head, and I'm not talking about the one on top of his thick neck.'

I wanted to laugh. It was funny. But I couldn't. I couldn't help but wonder how it was I brought Wren from writing about the nature of human relationships and art and philosophy to quick blurbs about some poor shlub humping his Dustbuster.

'I need to check on something first,' I said. 'Let me call you back.'

I saw Linda push through the glass doors, say hi to Billie, and march straight back to Jonathan's office. I absently scratched my ankles.

I called the business department to find out what my budget was on gathering gossip. Unlimited, I was told. Jonathan was serious about this column. I told them I'd be by later for five hundred in cash. They said the paperwork would be done in twenty minutes.

I sat at my desk and drew a series of circles. Some of them I gave eyes, some ears, some noses, but never any combination. One I gave hair and feet, but that didn't seem to give it any advantage over the others.

And I thought about Davis in Maui. Robby in Oregon. Dad in the Amazon. Byron, who knows where. And me at my desk, drawing circles with appendages. I drew a penis on one circle.

I couldn't be sure about Davis and the book contract. In fact, I couldn't be sure that even if it was a genuine offer, I could do it properly. What if he discovered I was incapable after a chapter or two? Then he'd fire me and I'd be out the money and my job. I needed to get focused here. I had a well-paying job. I needed to rededicate myself to it. Forget pie-in-the-sky schemes of big money.

Work hard and store your nuts, that's the lesson of the ant and the grasshopper. I drew a pair of walnuts beneath the penis.

I smiled. I was sorry I'd called poor Judith with that immature prank. I drew Judith's surprised eyes on a circle. I chuckled. I felt much better now. I knew what to do, how to act. Who to be.

I reached for the telephone to set up an appointment with James Smith. Just as my fingers touched the phone, it rang. I pulled away as if stung. Then answered it. 'Hello?'

'Wren, could you step into my office a moment, please?'

'Sure, Jonathan.'

I walked down the hallway, knocked, and entered. Jonathan was standing at the other window, looking up into the corners, as if searching for that same insect. Linda sat on the sofa. One low-heeled pump was off and she was rubbing her arch.

'Hi, Linda,' I said.

She smiled stiffly.

'Wren,' Jonathan said, turning toward me. He was frowning. 'When were you going to tell us about your book deal?'

My insides freeze-dried. I looked down. 'There is no deal.'

'Davis Richard didn't offer you $50,000 to write the Season Dougherty bio?'

'He offered. I didn't take it.'

Linda stopped rubbing her foot. 'Did you turn it down?'

'Not yet.'

Jonathan came around the front of his desk and stood less than two feet from me. 'And you didn't think you owed it to us to tell us about this offer?'

'I haven't taken it.'

'But you're considering it.'

'No, I'm not. I'd decided not to take it.'

He shook his head. 'Maybe. Maybe you weren't. You

know the bastard already made the film deal? *My* goddamn film deal.'

I nodded.

'He thinks he pulled something. But I'm not done with
him. Tell your boyfriend I'm not done with him.'

'He's not my boyfriend.'

Jonathan made an exasperated face. 'Whatever.' He
walked back to his desk. 'In the meantime, you're fired.
Clear out your desk and leave.'

He turned his attention back to the window and continued his hunt for the defiant bug.

PART TWO

How to Cope with Desire, Both Natural and Unnatural

18

'That is so *flattering*!'

I shook my head.

'Really,' she said, nodding enthusiastically. '*Very* flattering.'

'You think so?' I said.

'Absolutely.'

I turned to look in the three-sided mirror. I was thin as a paper cut, with no stomach, no butt, and fist-sized breasts. What was there to be flattered? I'd picked this bland one-piece suit because it was cut high enough over my chest to hide my bullet scar. Red lightning bolts zigzagged down the shiny black material over my breasts and along my ribs until they stopped at the top of my crotch. It was like having two fingers pointing, saying, 'Look here, boys, hot snatch!'

When I gazed at my image doubtfully, the plump salesgirl pointed at a circular rack at the back of the store. 'We have some very lovely suits on sale back there. I just stocked them this morning. Thirty per cent off.'

'Thanks,' I said and retreated back into the dressing room.

I sat on the wooden stool. In the narrow dusty mirror of the tiny room I looked pale and bookish. Even my red lightning bolts didn't help. My white panties peeked out where I'd tried to tuck them up under the high French-cut hips of the swimsuit. Was anything more pathetic than cotton panties sticking out of the leg of a sexy swimsuit? I took off my round steel-rimmed glasses and knuckled my eyes. If they ever remade the movie *Carrie*, I would play the simpleton lead.

Getting fired is like having your wisdom teeth pulled. You keep rubbing your tongue over the gum where the tooth used to be. Maybe you're fascinated with such a radical change in so familiar and intimate a place as your mouth. You can't keep yourself from prodding. Once this fleshy curbside had a hefty tooth parked there; now it's just a cavernous void. Once I had a loving husband; now I have someone else's ex-convict husband. Once I had a terrific job; now I had lightning bolts pointing at my vagina. As if my crotch needed to be jump-started or something.

A few pubic hairs poked out of the elastic leg like wires to a burglar alarm hastily snipped. I hadn't shaved the area in a while, avoiding the red chicken skin look that my irritated skin takes on for a week afterward. With my fingertips, I pushed the stray hairs under the legs of the swimming suit and panties. How had I come to this place in my life, sitting in a small room arranging my pubic hairs? When I was about five, my mother and I were taking a bath when I reached out and touched her thick tuft of pubic hair. 'Does it hurt to have hairs grow there?' I'd asked. Mom had laughed, climbed out of the tub, and returned a minute later with a can of Reddi Wip whipped cream. I still can picture her shaking that red and white can as she stepped back into the tub and made me stand up. She lifted my arms and whooshed a white foam mound in each armpit and a foam donut around my belly button. 'That's what it feels like,' she'd said. We'd laughed and washed off. I wished she were here now to answer my questions. But what would I ask: 'Mom, how come I screwed up my life so badly that I've got to pretend to be my dead friend?' What answer could she possibly give me, what playful demonstration using tangerines or whipped cream?

I took off the bathing suit. The crinkling of the plastic crotch protector made me feel even worse. It seemed so

250

accusing. As if it had been put there especially for sleazy people like me, who used their dead friend's reputation to get a job, then dirtied that reputation by bungling the job. Just as I might dirty the crotch of this bathing suit if they hadn't anticipated sluts like me and taken these extreme precautions. I imagined myself in a police lineup with other women, all of us naked, lying back on gynecological examination tables, our legs up and apart, our feet strapped into the stirrups. *Number three, could you scoot forward please.*

I'd gone from Jonathan Krieg's office out the door and straight to the mall, wandering around South Coast Plaza as if I had a purpose. Trying to look like a busy executive with only twenty minutes to buy an expensive gift for the boss's dinner party that night. I'd stopped in the swimsuit store because they'd had a window display of bathing suits in a tropical setting that reminded me of Hawaii. Tanned mannequins, cardboard palm trees, gray sand, and a couple of rubber starfish. A hand-painted sign that read MAUI WOWIE SALE! It made me think of Davis. If his word was any good, I'd be writing the Season Dougherty book as soon as he returned from Maui. That book was all I had now as a career. I guess trying on swimsuits was some sort of good-faith gesture, as if I were showing Davis I trusted him. It allowed me to think of myself as hopeful rather than gullible.

In the meantime, I still had that part-time job teaching Wren's art history class. Maybe I could kill a few classes by lining up visits to museums and getting guest lecturers from local art galleries. With any luck, I'd never have to actually talk about art myself. Just to be safe, though, I needed to be getting home to make some lecture notes. Right now that class was my only sure source of income.

I lifted my foot up onto the wooden bench and scratched my itchy ankle. Tiny red bumps circled my ankle like a rash of measles. The skin was swollen and raw from my scratching all morning. A few bled. My other ankle was identically afflicted. I leaned closer to inspect.

Flea bites! Another gift from Hector. When I got home, Hector was going to adopt the identity of an outdoor cat.

But I didn't go straight home. I didn't feel up to confronting Hector or, worse, Byron and his bloodstained money. Instead, I went to a movie, a bargain matinee at the four-plex across the street from the mall. The elderly white-haired man who tore my ticket wore a faded black tuxedo and white gloves with snaps at the wrist. He called me young lady and made a grand sweeping gesture toward the theater door number four. The pimply kids who worked behind the concession stand snickered at him behind his back as they shoveled popcorn. That made me feel even sadder so I hurried into the dark theater. The film had already started. It was a comedy. The main character was a beautiful young prostitute. She'd been hired to corrupt a crusading lawyer who was running for governor. His wealthy ex-wife was running against him. The ex-wife had hired the prostitute, but the prostitute and lawyer fell in love. The prostitute wore garter belts a lot. The ex-wife carried a small poofy dog that yelped and tried to bite people. I was the only one in the theater, so I didn't feel bad about laughing a lot, even at the dumb parts. When the movie was over I bought a tub of popcorn and a Diet Coke and sat through it again.

During the second show a few more people joined me, scattered throughout the theater like spies not wanting to be recognized. A couple of giggly girls about sixteen sat two rows in front of me and started talking adoringly about a boy in their class named Todd. Then another one of their friends ran down the aisle with an excited expression. 'Kristy! Guess what?' she said, plopping down next to them. 'My cousin will take the rabbit.'

'She will!' Kristy squealed with delight. She and the new girl gave each other a high-five. 'That is so cool.'

'Yeah, she'll pick it up next week when they've finished building the cage.'

'That is so great! Oh, wow!' Kristy squirmed happily in her seat.

The theater darkened. As the previews for coming attractions ran, I couldn't get over how thrilled Kristy had been at this news. It was as if someone had told her she'd won a million dollars, or she would never die or feel pain or sadness again. But all that had happened was someone taking a rabbit off her hands.

I shook my head and stuffed my mouth with dry popcorn. What makes people happy? Can you experience the same level of joy from winning an Olympic gold medal as you can from winning a game of Monopoly? A person is starving, they find half a bag of soggy potato chips, aren't they as happy as the stockbroker who closes a big deal on his car phone on the drive home to his mansion? Perhaps the human body is just an organism that endures only so much unhappiness; it adjusts to the circumstances and must find its quota of pleasure the way it must demand a certain amount of food and sleep. If so, everybody in the world is really the same amount of happy. Mini-evolution, kind of like Emotional Darwinism. Like those South American bedbugs Mark had told me about, developing dagger penises because the vagina was plugged up. Same principle here. The organism *will be happy*, even if it means reassigning values to achieve it, even reversing values completely. I'd read in a self-help book that you could force yourself into being happy by clenching a pencil between your teeth for a few seconds, tricking the body into thinking you were smiling. But that was just first aid for the blues. This was very different, perhaps even profound. I perked up, thinking I could be on to something profound. I'd come in here depressed, but I'd laughed at the dumb movie and felt better. If the rest of my life had been better, would I have laughed at the movie? Was I just as happy now sitting jobless in a dark theater behind Kristy with rings of bleeding flea bites around my ankles as I had been married to Robby with a ring of gold around my finger?

I wriggled in my seat excitedly. This must be how Wren felt when she had one of her ideas, like when we were

253

driving along that last night and she'd forced me to pull over. What if my idea was right? What if researchers somewhere discovered that the human organism is generally always the same amount of happy. They find some scientific way to measure it, like brain waves or cholesterol level. So, it doesn't matter what you do or buy or who you marry, your brain will adjust and find other things to fill its happiness quotient. If this were true, would they even reveal the results to us? What would happen to our economy? Our whole society is built on the concept that we can be happier if we buy this or that item. Or find someone new and improved to love. Suddenly we discover that it isn't so. What would happen then? We'd stop buying clothes and makeup and let our memberships to health clubs lapse. We'd stay married to the same people. My mind sizzled and crackled as if charged with electricity. Maybe I could write this idea up myself, just as Wren would have. Maybe sell it to some magazine.

But the more I sat there watching the young prostitute in a garter belt and the ex-wife with her snarling little dog, the less I felt the idea had any merit. After a while, the idea seemed to have leaked out of my body and run down the theater's sticky concrete floor along with the spilled Cokes and flattened popcorn.

When the movie was over for the second time, I left the theater and drove back to the office. It was almost dark now. I'd left work earlier without cleaning out my desk because I'd been too dazed, too upset. Not that there was much of importance, I'd only been there a few days. But I did leave Davis's unlisted home number on a paper in my desk. Not to mention Byron's bloodstained $400 taped to the bottom of my drawer. Right now, that money might come in handy. Which reminded me, I would have to swing by Detective Diesel's office sometime and pick up the other hundred-dollar bill. Without a job, I no longer cared about evidence against Byron or the mysterious dog blood. I cared about rent.

Everyone was supposed to be gone from the office by

now, but I knew Steve Hawkins, the layout designer, often stayed late to work on his freelance jobs illustrating children's books. He had a brood of eighteen-month-old triplet girls at home, so he found it difficult to do any work there. He would let me in.

But when I arrived at the offices, Steve was gone. However, the glass door was unlocked, so I walked in. Cautiously, I sneaked across the room toward my desk. I had no idea who was still here this late. By now everyone would have known about my being fired and I didn't want to run into anyone to explain.

My desk drawers were already empty. The pens and yellow legal pads were gone. The stapler, tape dispenser, ruler. So were the notes I had taken on the phone. James Smith's phone number. My doodles of the circle people with single appendages. Everything. I had ceased to exist. Again. Well, that was their stuff, they had a right to it. But the money and Davis's phone number were mine, damn it, and I wanted them. I reached under the desk drawer and peeled off the $400. I counted the four bills twice before stuffing them into my purse. But where was Davis's phone number?

I patrolled the desktops of my colleagues like a Coast Guard cruiser searching ship wreckage for survivors. Maybe someone thought Davis's unlisted number might come in handy someday, maybe some closet screenwriter here wanted to send his completed screenplay to him. Desktops were for the most part bare. Reporters locked their Rolodexes in their desks at night, some even took theirs home. Not that we could honestly be called reporters, but some here had been at one time or fancied themselves as ones now.

Finally I made my way to Linda Marley's office. The light was on, her open briefcase was next to the desk. I quickly looked over my shoulder. She was the last person I wanted to run into here. Still, I was here, she was nowhere in sight. She owed me. I ducked into her office and started searching her desk. I could feel my pulse like snapping fingers in my throat. Sweat slicked the backs of my knees. My left eye throbbed. I fingered through the While You Were Out slips, the galleys of upcoming articles, memos from Jonathan Krieg.

'Hello, Wren,' Linda said behind me.

I turned and smiled pleasantly. 'I left a phone number in my desk. It's gone.'

She nodded sympathetically. 'Right here.' She walked past me and rummaged through some papers I hadn't yet gotten to. I smelled a strong scent of booze as she breezed by. I noticed her movements seemed awkward as she sloppily groped papers aside. She wasn't wearing shoes. 'It's here somewhere.'

Suddenly I felt too uncomfortable to stay. As if I'd walked in and caught her masturbating or something. 'I'll call you tomorrow,' I said. 'I shouldn't have come back.'

'You shouldn't have gotten fired. You shouldn't have taken Davis's deal.'

I didn't want to get into all that with her, so I just kept walking. 'I'll call you tomorrow.'

She followed me, staying right up to my shoulder, though I noticed she was wobbling a bit. 'I was counting on you, Wren. I picked you out myself, brought you to Krieg's attention. I'm good at spotting talent and you've got it. God knows we could have used some of it around here.'

'I did my best.'

'Bullshit!' The word came out kind of wet and slurred. Her saliva misted my arm.

'I don't want to talk about this now,' I said.

'I don't care what you want. We're not talking about you here, we're talking about me. I was counting on you, goddamn it.'

'Then why didn't you talk Jonathan out of firing me?'

'Talk him out?' She laughed. 'Hell, I had to *convince* him to fire you.'

I stopped and faced her, not hiding the shock on my face. 'I don't get it.'

'You don't, really?' Now she seemed surprised. She licked her lips with an uncooperative tongue. 'This is my magazine, Wren. I've worked on it since it was started. From the first fucking issue eight years ago. We had Susan Anton on the cover. Remember her? She was famous for being tall and dating Dudley Moore. And tan, she had a helluva tan.' She paused, swallowed dryly, her tongue making loud smacking sounds. 'The previous owners didn't care about the contents of the magazine. They just wanted to build advertising revenues to a certain level, then sell. That was their plan from the beginning. To make that happen they wanted fluff. I gave them fluff. I can write 5,000 words about anything from shopping for jelly to Flag Day parades. Words are like ether, you know what I mean. Evaporate faster than a fart. Poof.' She gestured with her hands to show an explosion. 'You know what I mean?'

I nodded.

'Then along comes Jonathan Krieg, self-made asshole, and he wants to play Ben fucking Bradlee for a few months, maybe a year. Run around shouting "Stop the presses!" or some goddamn thing. Use the magazine as a legit springboard into movies. Oh, yes, he wants to make movies. Everybody wants to make movies. No matter how rich they are, how much money they've made at something else, they all eventually come to Hollywood. Why? Glitz and tits. They want to be high priests at the only real religion this country has. Movies.' She stopped, took a deep breath, adjusted her tongue, which flopped along her lower lip. 'Yeah, yeah, yeah. It's an old story. I should know, I wrote it a hundred times for this magazine. You know what Jonathan will do next year or the year after? He'll dump us on someone else. But you know what? You know what?' She grabbed my forearm tightly. I felt nervous, as if I were being accosted by a bag woman. I tried to pull away, but she held tight. Her eyes were red and the stale odour of alcohol she breathed into my face made my stomach clench. 'You know what?'

'No, what?'

'I'm still here. I was here when I got remarried. I was here when I got divorced. I was here when I had a lumpectomy. And I'll still be here no matter who owns this rag or what kind of crap they want to print in it.' Her fingernails were digging into my arm and I thought I might have to hit her hand to break free. I tried to twist away, but she hung on as if this were a rodeo. 'It's like every actress over thirty ever interviewed in *People* or on *Entertainment Tonight*. You know how they describe themselves? As survivors. "I'm a survivor" they like to say to the camera. "I'm no flavor of the month. I'm a survivor." You know what I say? Fuck you, bitches. You don't know what survival is. If you're still around when you're forty or, God forbid, nearing fifty, then talk to me about your goddamn survival. But most of them marry some other actor or director who's got a hit show or movie or music video and then they can afford to be goddamn survivors. You know? You know what I mean?'

The way she glared at me, her eyes fogged over with liquor, but with a dark pinpoint of rage lasering through —I don't know, I had the uncomfortable feeling she was talking about me, that she knew who I was, what I was doing. I almost expected her to call me Luna. Her fingernails, short and blunt, sliced through my skin. But I didn't feel like pulling away anymore. I pushed the arm toward her as if it were a life preserver. She deserved it. Dig in, I thought. You're a better man than I am, Gunga Din. I wanted to tell her I understood. But words snared on the clump of barbed wire lodged in my throat. My mouth was open, but nothing came out.

'Mom,' a female voice behind us said softly.

Linda and I turned to the glass door at the front of the office. A young girl, maybe seventeen, stood there, dressed in a hooded sweatshirt, long shorts, and suede hiking boots. She was thin, as thin as I, with straight red hair. She had a kind face, with full lips that curved into a smile even when she wasn't smiling. She looked like the kind of kid who always brought home damaged birds and shivering animals and nursed them back to health or gave them elaborate funerals, the kind of kid everyone assumed would grow up to be a veterinarian or a nun.

'Hi, honey,' Linda said cheerfully. 'What are you doing here?'

'You're late. I called, but the answering service picked up. They wouldn't ring me through.'

Linda released my arm to look at her watch. 'Late?'

Linda's daughter sighed and shook her head parentally. 'Jesus, Mom. Have a heart.'

I looked at my forearm. Four bluish half-moon bruises tattooed the skin. I rubbed them.

'Hi, I'm Sara Marley.' She walked toward me, limping slightly. I noticed a long white scar curving around her knee. She held out her hand and I shook it.

'Wren Caldwell.'

Sara's face brightened. 'Oh, yes. I've heard all about you. I read a couple of your articles Mom had lying around. They were great. I didn't understand some of it, but I could tell it was smart. Deep.'

'Thanks,' I said. I looked over at Linda. ·She stood swaying slightly, her eyes unfocused. She looked frail in her stocking feet.

'Could you give me a hand?' Sara asked me.

'Sure.' I lifted my hands as if to carry something, then let them drop. 'What do you want me to do?'

'Get her downstairs to the car. I'll drive her home.'

'I'm perfectly fit to drive,' Linda announced.

'Don't fuss, Mom.'

'I don't need this shit from you, Sara Couldn't-t-Walk-Until-You-Were-Two-And-A-Half-Wetted-Your-Bed-Until-You-Were-Eight-Sucked-Your-Thumb-Until-You-Were-Twelve Marley!' Linda jerked away from us with such violence that she stumbled forward a few steps and bumped into a desk. A six-inch run in her stocking splayed upward between two toes. 'Remember who the mother is around here, okay?'

'You're the mother, Mother.'

They both looked at each other and laughed a kind of giggly mother-daughter laugh.

Sara nodded at me and we both slid arms around Linda's waist and guided her toward the door.

'I'd better lock up first,' Sara said. She went back into Linda's office and grabbed her purse, shoes, and brief-case. After digging through the purse a few seconds, she came up with a crowded key chain with a silver rape whistle attached. She locked Linda's office, then followed Linda and me out the front door and locked that too.

In the elevator, Sara and I held Linda upright.

'This isn't necessary, guys,' Linda kept saying, but she made no move to pull away. In fact, she slumped a little in our arms, as if relieved of a great burden.

'Don't worry about her,' Sara said. 'This isn't chronic. She's not an alcoholic or anything.'

'No, no,' I rushed to agree. 'Of course not.'

'She only does this when she has a new date.'

'A new date?'

'A date with someone new. She's supposed to go over to the Performing Arts Center tonight for some opera thing. I haven't met him yet. A lawyer, I think. Real estate law.'

'Did you pick up my dress from the cleaner?' Linda asked in a moment of alertness that passed as quickly as a sneeze.

'Got it, Mom. Everything's set. All we gotta do is sober you up within the next hour and a half. I think a couple laps in the pool ought to do it, don't you?'

Linda nodded.

Date. It sounded so odd. Linda Marley was at least fif-teen years older than I. With a teenage daughter. Is it still called a date then? That word doesn't seem dignified enough somehow for her age. Was this what I would be doing fifteen years from now? Getting drunk because I had to face another new man, another evening of revealed backgrounds, old regrets, war wounds? Like legless veterans slapping our stumps and describing how we felt the moment we stepped on that buried mine that pulverized our limbs into a fireworks burst of hot blood and charred bone.

'Date,' Linda said, as if reading my mind. 'Date sounds like a swear word, doesn't it?' She didn't look at either of us so we didn't answer. She made a face and started talking with a kind of Brooklyn swagger in her voice. 'Don't date with me, pal. I'll date you up bad, motherdater. Oh, yeah, well date you, buddy . . .' The rest was mumbled.

Linda lifted her head in another flash of alertness. She turned her head toward me. 'I'm going to still be running this fucking magazine when Jonathan New-Age Krieg is serving time for insider trading or whatever they finally catch him for. Believe it, Wren.'

'I believe it.' I did.

'That's why I had him fire you. Season's cell neighbour told me about your deal with Davis. I knew Jonathan would blow his colon. If I didn't suggest he fire you, eventually he'd end up blaming me for everything. After all, I was the one who'd championed hiring you. See my problem?'

'I see,' I said. 'You were saving your ass.'

'Surviving.'

The elevator door opened at the lobby and Sara and I struggled to pull Linda out. Her last speech seemed to have drained her energy and she slumped against us with all her weight. I lurched under the sudden burden.

'I can take her from here,' Sara said, limping a few steps away from me with her mother.

'I don't mind.'

'That's okay.' She seemed protective now, I guess because she knew her mom had fired me. 'We're fine. It's just that she hates the opera as much as she hates first dates. She'll be fine, though. A few laps in the pool. That always works.'

'Good luck, then. Nice meeting you.' I started to walk away. I didn't hear any footsteps behind me so I knew they weren't moving. I stopped and looked back. Sara was staring at me.

'What?' I asked.

'You're smart, Wren. My mom's smart too. But she never answers my question.'

'What question?'

'If she hates the opera and hates first dates, why does she go?'

The fact that that question had never occurred to me struck me as more depressing than any answer I could give.

* * * * *

I stopped at the 7-Eleven market on the way home and bought a large bottle of Kahlúa and two of vodka. At home I placed the three bottles on the coffee table in front of me like small pets I was about to groom. I turned on ESPN and watched beach volleyball while I got drunk on Black Russians.

Being drunk felt good. For one thing, my lips tingled. As if a line of chorus girls in spiked heels were can-canning back and forth across them. My lips became extraordinarily sensitive. Bright lights or loud noises made them wince. All my other senses seemed dimmer. I could hardly hear the TV or smell Hector. Suddenly I could feel everything through the outer membranes of my lips. Changes in temperature or movement registered there first. I had the distinct impression that if I pressed some-one's fingertips against my lips, I'd be able to distinguish individual fingerprints. Feel the bunched swirls of skin like icing that distinguishes corpses and criminals. I picked up a *TV Guide* and closed my eyes. I opened it randomly, pressed the page against my lips: 11.00 PM *Cheers*. Sam proposes to Diane for the second time.

Amazing!

I imagined myself as some comic-book heroine. Lip

Woman! It made me more decisive. I jumped up from the sofa humming loudly what I thought might be Lip Woman's brassy theme song, which sounded a lot like the theme to *Bonanza*. I grabbed Hector's cat-litter box and food and water bowls and carried them into Byron's bedroom. I also deposited Hector in there, closing the door after him. Let him spread his fleas and stench in there for a while.

After that I didn't feel much like Lip Woman anymore so I went into the kitchen and poured vinegar on my flea bites and that helped the itching some.

Having left the world better than I found it, I sat at the kitchen table and drank more Black Russians. Once I stuck my tongue into the glass and started lapping it up the way I saw Hector drink. That was fun for a while. My chin was cool from the vodka and sticky from the syrupy Kahlúa. Then I decided I should stop drinking like Hector and take more advantage of my decisive mood. I started jotting down numbers, trying to figure out how much it might cost to start my own magazine. The more I thought about the idea, the more excited I got. I'd screwed up Wren's reputation, but it was possible to salvage it again. I'd name the magazine after her, like *Lear's* or *Mirabella*, and I'd print all her articles to get started.

I had no idea if the figures I was fooling around with were even close to accurate. Mostly I guessed. I started with the $50,000 I would earn from Davis, and created a budget from that. I wrote very neatly, which made it look even more official and possible. I liked the idea of someday telling a talk-show audience that I'd worked out the details of the magazine at my kitchen table while drunk on Black Russians and holding a cat hostage in a convict's room.

The phone rang while I was sketching possible magazine names over Arsenio Hall's face on the cover of *TV Guide*, but I didn't pick up. I listened as the answering machine informed the caller that no one could come to the phone. Then the beep. Then: 'Hey, Byron, pick up the fucking phone, man,' the familiar caller said. 'It's Grudge, man.' Pause. 'Okay, here it is. I'm just passing this one along, so I got no fucking stake in it whatsoever, okay? This is all I know: McIntire told me that Landry is looking for you. Landry's fucking crazy, man. I wouldn't fuck with him if I were you. Okay, I delivered the message. You make up your own fucking mind, okay?' Click.

I sighed, sipped my Black Russian. How had a man named Grudge become part of my life? Why was his voice with threats and veiled violence allowed to fill up my kitchen like the smell of burnt toast? Ever since Byron showed up it was as if some rip in another world, an alternate dimension, had opened into my world and now gruesome creatures were worming through the hole into my life.

I went to the living room and turned off the TV. I put a Rickie Lee Jones CD on. I turned it up louder than usual because I thought the musical notes could kill the harsh notes of Grudge's voice, like antibodies or enzymes or something. I wanted to purify even the sound integrity of the apartment. Sterilize the karma. It was, after all, *my* apartment. Only the sounds I invited in should live here.

I couldn't find the song I wanted. Maybe it was on a different album. I couldn't remember the title, just that it was a love song. Her love songs always sound like threats. Love me or else.

Finally I gave up and just pressed PLAY. Rickie Lee sang,

> 'So you keep talking in many languages
> Telling us the way you feel
> Don't stop confiding in the road you're on
> Don't quit, you're walking Satellites . . .'

I had no idea what that meant, so I hauled Wren's art book to the kitchen and started making notes on the art works she'd marked. My handwriting was less precise now, barely legible, but I figured it wasn't the fault of the writing, just that my eyes were bleary from drinking; it would be more readable in the morning when I was sober.

I turned to a page that showed a greenish statue of a half-woman, half-man figure. The caption said it was made of copper alloy with semiprecious stones. Crafted in Nepal about the year 1000, it was called 'Androgynous form of Siva and Uma'. The book said this was a representation of Ardhanarisvara, The Lord Whose Half Is Woman, devised by theologians to emphasize the nonduality of the divine principle uniting masculinity and femininity. I underlined that, figuring I'd try to understand it later. The figure had four arms, though one of the male arms was broken off as was one of the male legs.

Wren's bold printing crowded the margins: *Influence of Indian Gupta art: compare with Matisse's Indian period— his search for constant light: feminine principle of Hindus: the god Siva, consort Uma.* An arrow was drawn indicating the figure's garment with the word *dhoti* at the other end of the arrow. A crooked arrow pointed at the upraised arms with Wren's note, *cosmic unity.* And angled in the narrow left margin, her handwriting slanted in a hurried scrawl: *Religious art as objects, not of worship, but of focal points to review fundamental principles. Compare with Siva dancing figure. No lesson is ever learned but must be relearned. Function of art to reteach the same moral lesson by evoking passion.*

A circle was drawn around the figure's single female breast. A line led to the margin where, in larger, more ragged handwriting than Wren's, someone had written: *38C! Cosmic Implants!*

I laughed. Who had written that? Someone Wren had sat next to in art class? I wished he or she were here sitting next to me now. How else would I understand all I needed to by Monday? I didn't see all this stuff that she'd noted and I didn't know all about Hinduism the way she did. I needed a third eye that could view the world the way Wren had. That could see what lurked behind the foliage of the obvious. I picked up my pen and drew an eye on the page, right in the middle of the forehead of the copper figure. Then I drew one on his/her single female breast. That made me laugh.

I had a great idea. I pulled off my blouse over my head, popping a button in my clumsiness. The white button skittered across the kitchen floor and pinged against the cupboard, where I left it for Hector to ingest and perhaps choke on. I unclasped and shrugged off my bra. I picked up the pen and began drawing a large eye around the bullet scar on my breast. The pen against my skin tickled and I chuckled as I outlined the eye as if I were using eyeliner. Then I drew the eyeball, using the scar tissue as the actual retina. I colored it in with blue ink.

'Suddenly Lip Woman becomes . . . *Tit Woman!*' I announced with a flourish and a few bars from *Bonanza*. 'The all-seeing, all-dancing, all-talking eye of Modern Woman.' I walked around the kitchen holding my breast with both hands, pointing the inky eye like a camera at things, saying, 'Ahhh. Yup. Everything is so much clearer now. Symbolism, hidden meaning, we laugh at your puny disguises.'

I drank another Black Russian and decided that I would use my new super vision to look through Byron's stuff. He knew all about me. Now I would know all his secrets too. I wouldn't have to be afraid of him. I ran down the hallway, still cupping my left breast, as if I were steering my body with it.

Byron's room was neat as a monk's cell. Hector was sitting on the bed licking his tail with long strokes. I went around the room opening drawers and closets, pointing my breast like a Geiger counter. Hector ignored me, concentrating on his tail. His attitude seemed very professional and it occurred to me that perhaps I'd judged him too harshly. I petted him and a flea leapt onto my wrist and then onto my super breast. I trapped the flea between my two thumbnails and squeezed until the body popped, leaving a tiny drop of blood on my thumbnail. The blood, I realized, was Hector's.

I wiped my thumbnails with the blood and minicorpse on Byron's pillow and continued my search. I hauled his battered suitcase out from under the bed and noticed for the first time that the tartan design on the cloth was the same as on Wren's luggage that I'd used to move in here. This case was part of her set. I flipped it open. It was empty except for the old photo album I'd given him that first night. When I'd first found the album in Wren's apartment, I'd been surprised to see that many of the photographs had been removed. The only ones in it were of Wren or Wren's family and friends. A couple of me and Robby. Now as I paged through the album, I saw that the missing photos had been restored. They were all photos of Wren and Byron. One showed them each wearing a dragonfly earring. Byron still had all of his fingers. In every one they were both laughing. They looked like the happiest couple in the world. In Robby's and my albums, we're usually grinning. This was the first time I noticed how different grinning and laughing really were. In one photo, Byron was bare-chested, holding a bottle of beer in one hand and shooting a squirt gun with the other. Only he was shooting right at Wren's crotch. The front of her shorts was soaked but she was bent over laughing. Some-one had written *Hemingway Goes a-Courting* at the bot-tom of the photo. It was the same handwriting as *Cosmic Implant*. Another photo showed them in bed surrounded by open cartons of Chinese food. Wren is straddling him, wearing a T-shirt and panties. She's holding up a cross formed with two chopsticks to Byron's face and threaten-ing to plunge a third chopstick through his heart. Written across the bottom: *Sylvia Plath's Honeymoon*.

I put the album back in the suitcase. My breast was not impressed.

The bathroom wasn't any more rewarding. Byron used kid's formula Aim toothpaste, the shiny red stripe swirling through the toothpaste like a candy cane. He shaved with the same brand safety razor as I; then I realized it wasn't just the same brand, it was in fact my damn razor he was shaving with. I removed the blade and scraped it along the edge of the wooden cabinet, nicking and warping the edge as much as I could. Then I replaced the razor and laid it neatly on the sink, waiting for his next shave. The rest of my search uncovered only one unusual item. Under the bathroom sink were ten rolls of Xtra-Soft toilet paper stacked so tightly that the cupboard door didn't close all the way. I started pulling each roll out, examining them for some clues. I held them up to my breast 'eye' as if consulting a Ouija board. Were these used to smuggle drugs, perhaps into or from prison? Was that what those mysterious phone calls were about? The guy named Landry who was after Byron? My breast was perplexed.

'Running low?' Byron said. 'Or just expecting the runs?'

19

I looked up from my place on the bathroom floor where I sat cross-legged, surrounded by scattered rolls of toilet paper, holding one such roll up to my naked breast like a silencer to a pistol. Byron was dressed in an expensive three-piece blue silk suit he hadn't had when he'd first moved in. His white shirt was starched and glowing like a TV screen in a dark room. The shirt was buttoned up to his throat; he wore no tie. His dark hair was slicked back and tied in a modest ponytail with a rubber band. His eyes were hidden behind sunglasses, which had a yellow Carl Jr.'s star on the fluorescent green temple frame, part of the fast-food restaurant's current promotion ($1.99 with a Western Burger and small fries).

I grabbed a damp bath towel from his shower door and draped it over my chest. I dropped the toilet paper roll on the floor with the others, not bothering to restack them. 'Close the door,' I said, looking his outfit over. 'An ill wind must be blowing.'

'That's something Wren might have said. You're getting better.'

'Help me up,' I said, holding out my hand.

'God helps those who help themselves,' he said. 'Look it up.' He leaned back against the doorjamb and crossed his arms.

'At least now I know who you think you are.'

'I yam what I yam.' He did a pretty good Popeye chuckle.

'Yeah, the God of Ass Wipes.' I threw a roll of toilet paper at him. He let it bounce off his chest.

He laughed and removed his sunglasses. His hand absently drifted up to his dragonfly earring, which he fondled while he stared at me. His half-size little finger looked fake in this light, like a rubber prop. Actually, except for his new clothing, he didn't look so hot right then. His face was sallow, with dark blue bibs under each eye. His eyes looked loose and watery, as if he'd been in a brisk unrelenting wind. Dark stubble peppered his jaw. He looked exhausted.

'You look like shit. Here, clean yourself up.' I tossed another roll of toilet paper at him. He didn't flinch this time either, like he was used to having things hurled at him. The roll grazed his shoulder and continued out into his bedroom. It bounced under his bed. Hector dove after it.

'What, you don't like my new duds?'

'So the emperor has new clothes.'

He just laughed again and offered me his hand. 'You crack me up.'

'I wish your skull could say the same thing.' I ignored his hand and grabbed the sink, pulling myself up to a sitting position on the toilet seat. From there it was fairly easy to get to my feet, though once I stood the carpet seemed to be rolling forward faster than I was walking, like one of those airport people movers. I knotted the towel around my chest and held on to the sink as I walked toward the door. Byron stepped aside for me to pass. He grabbed a roll of the toilet paper from the floor and followed me.

'Tough day at the Wren biz?' he asked, walking beside me. He kept tossing up a roll of toilet paper with one hand and catching it with the other, back and forth, like a juggler with one ball. 'By the way, who are you supposed to be now? Luna being drunk or Luna pretending to be Wren being drunk? 'Cause this isn't how Wren acted when she was drunk. Although the eyeball tattoo on your boob is a nice touch.'

'Fuck you.'

'That's more like it. More theatrical flair. That's my little Wren.' He applauded.

Slowly I navigated the hallway by keeping my hands firmly suctioned to the wall like a lizard. Byron juggled the toilet roll and kept pace beside me.

'What do you think the first thing a guy just out of prison would buy?' he asked.

'I don't know.'

'Guess.'

'A woman or two.'

'Yeah, some would. Or drugs. Booze. I've known some to blow it all on toys for their kids. Some on a gun, looking to get even with somebody or other they imagined did them wrong.' He hefted the toilet paper, bounced it off the wall and caught it. 'Me, I went straight to the grocery store and cleaned them out of toilet paper. The softest, sweetest smelling brand they had. I mean, I was squeezing and sniffing toilet paper for about an hour.' He shook his head and made a face. 'The kind they use in prison . . . man, they must make it out of ground glass and barbed wire.'

I kept walking, hand over hand along the wall. Easy does it. Avoid barfing in front of this man at all costs.

'Forget the electrified fences and snarling dogs. Just string that prison toilet paper around the place, and no one could break out.'

'Maybe it's a subtle form of rehabilitation,' I said. 'Negative stimulation. Every time you wipe your ass you'll remember why you don't want to go back to jail. Usually they work on the brain, but I guess they picked the part you guys use most to do your thinking.'

Byron didn't say anything for a minute, just followed along, not even tossing his roll now. Like he was chewing on a tough problem. Then, just as we entered the kitchen, he said, 'I think I'm starting to see why you don't like being you.'

I swung my hand at his face. He saw it coming and had

plenty of time, but he made no move to stop me or dodge the blow. He watched my hand smack his cheek and he kept walking as if nothing had happened. That made me angrier. I'd had my ineffectualness ground in my face all day. I wanted to hurt him, show him what Lip Woman and Tit Woman were capable of. Something had to get to him. Some blows had to be worth fending off. 'You get your phone message?' I asked, nodding toward the answering machine. 'Some guy Landry is hot for you in a bad way. Sounded pissed. Very pissed.'

I looked over at his face for a reaction. I was rewarded. Landry's name was like splashing onion juice in his eyes. He tried not to show any expression, let the name bounce off him like the toilet roll, like my slap, but fear squeezed his eyeballs. Fear and weariness. Now I was kind of sorry I'd sprung it on him like that. I walked into the kitchen.

'"*Stooop, in the naaame of looove . . .*" Awkk.' Standing in the middle of the kitchen was a black iron floor stand cage with a brightly colored bird over a foot tall walking erectly along a perch.

'Good God, now what?' I said.

'"*My world is empty . . . without you, babe . . .*"'

'He's an *Amazona* parrot,' Byron explained. 'His name's Motown.'

'His name's Dinner in about two minutes. That's how long it'll take me to reach the oven.'

Byron laughed, but when I started toward the oven, he stepped between me and the cage.

'I want him out,' I told him. 'I mean it.'

'"*You can't hurry love . . .*" Awk.'

'Jesus.' I shook my head. His voice sounded small and tinny, as if coming out of a cheap transistor radio. His tail was green but his chest was a brilliant red. He had a blue comb of spiked feathers on his head. These were colors unseen outside a Crayola box.

'The guy who used to own him is an ex-con named Berkshire. He has a hard-on for Diana Ross. He taught the bird all her song titles. He dances a little to "Baby

Love."' He turned to the bird. 'Mo, do "Baby Love." C'mon, "Baby love, my baby love . . ."' Byron did a dance shuffle by the way of encouragement.

'Give him back to the owner.'

'I said used to own. He's all mine now.' Pause. 'I won him.'

'You won him? Just who the hell are you gambling with that you always win such junk. Can't you at least win cash and valuable prizes like every schmuck on a game show. A goddamn Toyota maybe. On *Jeopardy* they win cash, did you know that? You come home with a fucking bird that thinks it's a Supreme.'

Byron stared at me with a hard expression, a prison-yard expression. 'You don't get it, lady. You know how long Berkshire had this bird, how many years it took him to teach it to memorize all these stupid titles? You have any idea how much he loved this clump of bird shit and feathers? I didn't just win a bird. I won a man's most valuable possession. I took what he cared about most in this whole fucking world, except maybe his pecker.'

'Congratulations. You make it sound so noble.'

'"*Touch me in the morning . . .*"'

I leaned my face against its cage. 'If you're still here then, I'll touch you all right.' I opened the silverware drawer and showed the bird a carving knife. He angled on his perch with one black eye staring at me. I tilted the steak knife so the overhead light glinted off the blade into the bird's eye. He blinked once and turned his back to me.

Byron took off his fancy blue jacket and draped it over the cage. Motown immediately was quiet. Byron sat wearily at the kitchen table and rubbed his eyes. 'Okay, forget appealing to your nobler senses. Think about this: These birds are brought up at great expense from Mexico and South America. They don't breed well in captivity, which makes them even more valuable. Vocabulary aside, you're looking at over two thousand dollars' worth of bird.'

273

'Two thousand dollars?' I whistled. 'He's growing on me.'

I opened the refrigerator and found a can of Byron's beer. I walked it over to the table and dropped it in front of him. It fell on its side and started rolling toward the edge of the table. I let it. I wondered if that meant the table was slanted or the whole apartment complex was. Byron didn't seem to notice and the can kept rolling until it plunged over the edge like a barrel shooting Niagara Falls. Barely looking, Byron reached out and lazily snagged the beer in mid-air. He pressed the cold can against his forehead and mumbled thanks to me.

'Baseball?' I asked.

'What?' He looked at me blankly.

'The way you snagged that beer can. I used to watch a lot of baseball on ESPN.'

He yawned loudly. 'I played some. College scholarship.'

I stared at him a long moment, still trying to figure him out. What had happened between him and Wren? What about the beatings? I sat in the chair across from him, determined to get some truth out of him. 'What happened to your finger?' I asked him.

'What finger?'

'C'mon.'

'She crossed her legs too fast.'

'Yeah, fine,' I said. I walked back to the refrigerator, grabbed a Diet Coke, and slammed the refrigerator door. The ketchup bottle rattled against the salad dressings.

'What? You toss me a beer and you think that's a front row ticket to five acts of my life?'

'You dumped your life on me the moment you came in here blackmailing me.'

'I'm not blackmailing you. I'm just renting a room. A stuffy, dusty room I might add.'

'And if I don't want to rent you this stuffy, dusty room?'

He shrugged. 'Life is full of choices. That would be one choice.'

274

'Then my choice is for you to take your flea-bag cat and Diana Ross here and find other accommodations.'

'And it would be my choice then to tell everyone you know that you're impersonating my dead wife and see which of them has you arrested for fraud first.'

'If that's not blackmail, what is it?'

He looked up through sleepy eyes and smiled. 'Negotiating. Getting to yes. Isn't that all life is? Everybody trying to get what they want, figuring out what they're willing to trade for it. Same thing in love or business. Like kids trading baseball cards. The only worthwhile question anymore is "how much?"'

'Gee, just what I wanted to hear right now, more prison philosophy. What were you, the jailhouse Buddha?'

'Am I wrong?'

I sat down and sipped my soda. 'What is it you want? What are you doing here?'

'That's not open for discussion.'

'Oh, right. I forgot. Big, tough mystery man. He has secrets. A Past. All you need now is a theme song and you can have your own TV series.' I hummed a little of my 'Bonanza/Lip Woman' theme for him.

Byron stood up, drawing himself upright like an athlete about to compete against his arch rival. I thought he was going to hit me. But I didn't duck or flinch. I just waited for the blow with grit teeth, just as he had done with my slap. But it didn't come. He just walked off into the living-room. When he returned he was carrying what was left of the Kahlúa and vodka. He poured some Kahlúa into my Diet Coke can.

'Any other astute observations about me you want to share?' he asked.

I shook my head. 'I think that pretty much covers it. Except you're probably the type of guy who begins sentences with "I'm the type of guy . . ." Am I right?'

He looked at the scrawled figures on the paper I'd written on earlier, then at the doodles on the *TV Guide*.

'*Wren's Nest. The Wren Report. Wren's-Eye View.* What the hell is all this?'

'Nothing!' I grabbed the *TV Guide* away, ripping Arsenio's face in half.

'Jesus,' Byron said, shaking his head. 'It's too pathetic. Now you want to start the magazine she always talked about. Jesus, lady, get a life.'

'I have a life.'

'Your *own* life.'

'Mind your own business, okay? You have no idea what I'm doing. Just butt out.'

'Right.' He slid the torn magazine across the table to me. He studied my figures for a moment before tossing them over at me too. 'Where are you going to get fifty grand?'

Like I was going to tell this ex-con compulsive gambler anything about my money. 'I dunno. Save it, I guess.'

'Save $50,000? How? You don't even have a job anymore.'

I spun around and glared at him.

'Relax,' he said. 'I wasn't spying. I just phoned you at work today to warn you about the bird and they said you weren't working there anymore. What happened? They finally ask you to write something?'

Here's the funny part: I wanted to tell him everything that had happened. There was something freeing about talking to him, I guess because he knew the truth about me. I could be me, not Wren. I didn't have to dazzle, be smart, be witty, be insightful. I could paint an eye on my boob and get drunk and it didn't matter. But then again, I had to be wary of him too. This could be part of his whole routine to get at the $50,000 he thought I had. Stay sharp, Luna, I prodded myself. Constant vigilance is the price of . . . something. Churchill said that. He smoked fat cigars. Sometimes a cigar is just a cigar. Freud said that.

What had I been thinking of again?

'Saving fifty grand,' Byron said.

'What?'

'You asked what you'd been thinking of.'

Jesus, I was speaking aloud without knowing it. I pushed the spiked Diet Coke away from me. 'Since I've lost my job, Byron, there's nothing left for you to threaten me about.'

'Sure there is. If there weren't you'd have tossed my stuff on the front lawn by now. That means the game is still afoot, as Sherlock Holmes would say. Let's see, who is left who would be interested in your little charade. Probably that bland-looking boyfriend of yours.'

'He's not my boyfriend. He's a business associate.'

'Oh? You guys were doing some fancy dry-humping business the other night.'

'Go ahead and tell him,' I bluffed. 'I don't care.'

'Okay, just as soon as he gets back from Maui.'

I slapped my palm onto the table. 'How?'

'That time I was spying.' He made a telephone sign with his outstretched thumb and little finger. 'One thing you learn in prison is how to get information by phone. Inside those walls, the telephone is a lethal weapon.'

'Is that why you're afraid of Landry? Tell me about Landry.'

He looked at me with sad eyes. 'You're not drunk enough.'

'We can fix that.'

* * * * *

Byron leaned his head back against the cement lip of the Jacuzzi and sang:

'It's the story of a dork named Brady
Who got tired of pounding his pud in the shower

277

So he married this hagged-out bitch with three
    nubile daughters
And sniffed their panties while doing the laundry.'

I made a face. 'Pounding his pud?'

'You prefer whipping his lizard? Stroking his dolphin?
Paddling his canoe?'

'None of the above.' I sipped more Kahlúa and Diet
Coke and shrugged. 'Why are guys so raunchy?'

He belched. 'Is that a rhetorical question?'

I tried to belch back, but nothing came out.

'Your turn,' he said.

'I never watched *The Brady Bunch*.'

'Bullshit. Everybody watched. It was like a satanic cult
or something. You watched, wondered if the brothers and
sisters ever tried to peek at each other naked.'

'God, you're gross.'

'I can get grosser. Unless you admit having watched the
show.'

'Okay, I watched a few times. In reruns. When I was
sick in bed and unable to change the channel. Between
news broadcasts and specials about the Middle East.'

'Yeah, right. Let's hear your verse.'

I shifted on the tile seat, letting the jet of warm water
thutta-thutta against my lower back. Thick bubbles boiled
up along my ribs tickling me a little. We'd been sitting in
the Jacuzzi for about half an hour, drinking and rearranging the words to some of our favorite TV shows. Byron
got the idea after I told him about Ethan's comedy act.
We'd already done the themes to *Gilligan's Island* and *All
in the Family*. I don't know why I was doing this with him.
I didn't even like him, and I certainly didn't trust him.
After all, he was blackmailing me and who knows what
violence he'd done to Wren to drive her away.

I looked down at my breast. A light bluish smudge
stained my skin where I had drawn my eye. 'My eye is
gone,' I said sadly. Words felt as thick and heavy as the
bubbles stumbling along my rib cage.

'Sing,' he said.

I looked at him. His face was still tired-looking, but he was smiling the way he had in those photos in Wren's album. His dragonfly earring dripped chlorinated water.

'Tell me about your earring. Wren saved the matching one, so it must have meant something to her. There's got to be a story behind them.'

'Sing.'

'What about Landry? Why are you afraid of him?'

He looked down in the lighted water and spread his fingers like a bride staring at her new wedding ring. Only he was looking at his stubby little finger. 'Sing,' he said softly without looking at me. 'Just sing.'

I tilted my head back and took a deep breath and sang:

'It's the story of a slutty lady
Whose husband died under suspicious circumstances
He was pretty young to have an insulin-induced heart
    attack
Especially since he wasn't even diabetic.
So she married a geek named Brady,
And spanked him with a wire brush almost every
    night,
And made him bark like a dog and beg for sex,
Which he was used to from his first wife
Before she ran off with a tattoo artist named
    Chowder Head.'

Byron splashed water across the Jacuzzi at me, laughing heartily. 'I feel like I just desecrated a church or something.'

'You started it.' I splashed water back at him.

I heard the sound of metal scraping against cement. Byron and I both turned and saw Ethan dragging a pool chair across the cement from the pool area to the Jacuzzi. He had a six-pack of beer dangling from one finger and a hammer gripped in his other hand. He eyed Byron with suspicion. 'What's going on?' he asked me.

'Hi, Ethan.' I tried to rub off the ink splotch from my breast by pretending to splash water around me. 'Ethan, this is Byron.'

Byron held out his hand to Ethan. But Ethan didn't move, he just stared grimly, tapping his hammer against his leg. Byron dropped his hand. 'What's the hammer for? Mosquitoes?'

'Wren here had some trouble the other night, some creep in the parking lot. Didn't she tell you?'

'No.' He looked at me. 'What happened, Wren?'

'Nothing. Some guy following me. Probably a mistake.'

'Yeah, well, we did some damage to his car with this baby, didn't we, Wren?'

I nodded.

Ethan hefted the hammer in his right hand as if he were just itching to use it again. 'The bastard took off like a Mormon at a wet T-shirt contest.'

Byron gestured at Ethan. 'Come on in and join us, Ethan. You can bring your hammer if you want.'

Ethan didn't move, he was still assessing the situation.

'Byron's renting the extra bedroom,' I explained. 'We're roommates.'

'Roomies.' Byron smiled.

'Roommates? I didn't know you were looking.'

'Sure you did. I told you I couldn't afford this place.'

'Yeah, but I thought you meant female roommate. I mean, if I'd known, I could've recommended someone.'

I could tell by the way he looked at me that he meant himself.

'My last roommate pissed in the sink,' Byron frowned. 'I hate that.'

'I'll try to cut down,' I said.

'I had a roommate that did that,' Ethan said. 'Got drunk, pissed in the kitchen sink. I pissed in his cologne bottle to get back at him.'

'Did he stop?'

'No. He just pissed in my Kool-Aid, then I pissed in his salad dressing, and he pissed in my car wax . . .'

'It's nice to know men can work out their disputes,' I said.

Byron and Ethan both looked at me, then at each other, then shrugged at the same instant. It was like watching synchronized swimming. That made them both laugh like old pals. Ethan tossed his hammer on the chair, stripped off his T-shirt, and hopped into the Jacuzzi. He offered Byron a beer, which Byron took.

'Beer, Wren?' Ethan asked.

I shook my head and showed him my Diet Coke. Another two unopened cans sat behind me, along with my bottle of Kahlúa hidden under my towel.

'What were you guys singing?' Ethan asked.

'You heard us?' I asked, embarrassed.

'Yeah, me and half the complex. The words were a little garbled, but it was definitely some species of singing.'

'You ever watch *The Brady Bunch*?' Byron asked.

'Sure. You see *A Very Brady Christmas* a couple years ago, where they brought them all back together for a reunion? That was so weird, I mean, the girls had actually had sex by then. Can you imagine them giving head? Jesus.'

With some encouragement from Ethan, Byron and I reprised our verses. Ethan joined in with a pretty funny verse or two of his own. We laughed and drank. I got a little overheated and stretched out along the edge of the Jacuzzi while Byron and Ethan had a contest who could stay underwater the longest. Ethan gave me his watch to time them because it had a stopwatch in it. They started breathing deeply, gulping air.

'Maybe we should make a little bet,' Byron said. 'Just to keep it interesting.'

'Sure,' Ethan said. 'How much.'

Byron smiled, looked at me as if to say, See how easy it is. I scowled at him, which made him laugh. 'A buck.'

'A buck? That's all? Shit.' Ethan signaled me. 'Tell us when to go.'

'Go,' I said unenthusiastically.

They both dunked their heads under the water. Ethan spread his arms and legs and did a dead man's float around the Jacuzzi. The jets pushed him around the small pool into walls, but he didn't react. Byron just sat on the underwater bench with his head tilted forward like a devout man lost in prayer.

One minute thirty seconds.

Ethan was leaking bubbles around his head, but otherwise was still floating.

Byron hadn't budged.

Two minutes twelve seconds.

Ethan was standing now, both hands clasped at the back of his neck as if he were shoving his own head underwater, drowning a stubborn puppy.

Byron hadn't budged.

Two minutes thirty-two seconds.

Ethan expelled all his air and whipped his head out of the water, gasping for air.

Byron hadn't budged.

'Shit,' Ethan said. He waded over to me and looked at his watch. 'I thought the bastard was already up. I couldn't see him underwater because of the bubbles. I thought he was already up. Shit.'

Three minutes.

Three minutes ten seconds.

'Maybe we should do something,' I said.

'Let's wait a little,' Ethan said, but I could hear the nervousness in his voice. He took a few steps toward Byron, his hands ready to yank him up.

'Three minutes thirty seconds!' I announced.

Ethan plunged his hands in and pulled Byron's head up. Byron opened his eyes. 'What?'

'That's three and a half fucking minutes, man.' Ethan couldn't hide the mixture of panic and admiration in his voice.

Byron's expression was oddly calm. I had the feeling that while he'd been under he hadn't really cared whether he came up for air again or not. If he did decide to come up, it would be because he was bored, not because he needed air.

Byron pointed at Ethan. 'You owe me a buck.'

'Absolutely. It's just that I couldn't see you. I thought you'd come up before me. I coulda stayed down longer. Next time I'll wear goggles or something.'

We drank some more, chatting on and off about nothing in particular. Once I nodded off for a few minutes. When I awoke, Ethan and Byron were discussing baseball batting averages. Ethan was very drunk but Byron didn't seem affected by his drinking.

I swatted at a fat mosquito that flicked around my leg. I noticed several red welts that hadn't been there before I'd fallen asleep. 'I'm going in. The mosquitoes are turning me into a buffet.'

'You gotta fight back,' Ethan said. He took some of my Diet Coke and poured it on the crook of his arm. 'Wait.'

We waited.

After a few minutes I said, 'What are we waiting for?'

'Be patient. This is neat.'

About five minutes later a mosquito landed on the sticky Diet Coke on his arm. It fussed there a moment until it settled in and started drinking blood. We watched it drink for a minute.

'Aren't you going to swat it away?' I asked.

'Ssshh . . .'

Suddenly Ethan flexed his arm and the mosquito exploded in a wet puff of blood and ragged body parts, like a small plane in a midair collision.

'Jesus!' I said, wincing.

Ethan looked over at Byron expectantly, like he was trying to make up for his underwater failure. 'Weird, huh?'

Byron stared without comment or expression.

'Thing is, you gotta wait until they're slurping your blood, then when you flex, you shoot so much blood into them they just pop. Like killing a vampire, right?'

I flashed on the photo in Wren's album, the one where

283

she's pretending to be Sylvia Plath driving a chopstick stake through Byron's heart. I looked at Byron, wondering if he was thinking the same thing. I couldn't tell, he had on his blank prison-yard look. 'Actually,' Byron said, 'you just killed an expectant mother.'

'Right,' Ethan chuckled. 'Like you could tell. What she have, swollen ankles and haemorrhoids?'

'What makes you think it was a she?' I asked, somehow feeling my role of defender of all female species was being usurped. As a woman, isn't this the kind of thing I should know?

'Only the females bite.'

'What do the males do?' I asked. 'Order take-out?'

'They sip nectar from flowers.'

'Jesus,' Ethan said with disgust. 'Faggots.'

Byron looked at Ethan with a cold stare. 'I don't like that word.'

Ethan froze, started to say something, thought better of it. He shrugged in some sort of apology.

Byron continued, his voice soft and professional. 'And the females only drink blood because they need protein for their eggs, which they lay in batches of about 200.'

'Great, then I just killed 201 mosquitoes with one flex.'

'More like 2,001, since they lay about ten separate batches in their lifetime.'

'What's the big deal?' Ethan said, squirming a little, as if Byron were judging him. 'They're just mosquitoes. They spread diseases and stuff. They kill hundreds of people a year.'

'Millions. That's why they're so valuable. They're responsible for the air you breathe.'

'Let me guess, they eat plants and fart oxygen.' Ethan was turning petulant, feeling picked on.

'You've heard of the rain forests, right? The ones in the Amazon, the Congo basin, Southeast Asia?' Byron looked at me.

'Make your point,' I said. 'I have another class in fifteen minutes and the prof hates it when I'm late.'

Byron laughed. 'Okay, here's the short of it: the rain forest accounts for half of the world's oxygen, yet we're cutting them down at a steady rate. Since we've been talking about it, another ten acres have been cleared. One of the main defenses against clearing them any faster are the 2,000 species of mosquitoes that attack the workers and settlers, spreading yellow fever, malaria, dengue, filariasis, and o'nyong-nyong fever. These little suckers are keeping the rest of the world alive.'

Our former mood of drunken good cheer now shattered, we sat there in mournful silence a few minutes. At least Ethan and I did. Byron cheerful as ever, hummed the theme to *Green Acres*, finally singing, '"Darlin' I love you but give me Park Avenue."'

'I'm going in,' I announced again. I gathered my Diet Coke cans and empty bottle of Kahlúa.

'Come on, guys,' Ethan said. 'Let's make up something to go with *The Partridge Family* theme.'

'I don't remember how it goes,' I said.

Neither did Ethan or Byron. We each tried to hum some of it, but no one could remember enough to trigger anything. We did *The Addams Family* instead, snapping our fingers and getting grosser and grosser in our lyrics.

'That guy who played on that show,' Ethan said. 'Uh, John Astin, he was Mr. Addams—'

'Gomez Addams,' Byron offered.

'Right. Gomez. He was married to Patty Duke in real life. Remember her?'

'"*Patty loves to rock 'n' roll/A hot dog makes her lose control . . .*"' Byron sang.

'Yeah!' Ethan laughed. 'She played identical cousins. Jesus, I had the hots for her.' Ethan shook his head at some wistful memory and popped open another beer can. He pointed his can at Byron. 'I like your earring. I had my ear pierced a few years ago, but I don't wear an earring 'cause of my job. The damn hole's grown shut now. But it looks good on you. What is it, a moth?'

'Dragonfly. It was a gift from my wife. Instead of rings,

285

during the wedding ceremony we exchanged earrings. She had one just like this.' He reached up and touched his.

'Earrings instead of wedding rings. That's very cool.' Ethan nodded enthusiastically. 'But why dragonflies? You some kind of bug expert or something? I mean, if it were my wedding, I'd of picked something more romantic, like moons or unicorns or something.'

Byron smiled. He hoisted himself up onto the lip of the Jacuzzi so only his feet and shins dangled in the water. He gestured with one hand like a magician about to cast a spell. 'Dragonflies, when they are about to mate, fly to some pond or river where the eggs will eventually be laid. The males arrive some time earlier than the females. Then they space themselves out along the banks, each holding and defending his territory while awaiting the females.'

'Shit, that sounds like a Club Med trip I took once. Every guy sitting along the pool waiting for chicks.'

'When a female dragonfly approaches the male, he sometimes does some courtship dancing and buzzing and she lets him know whether or not she likes it. Then they copulate.'

'I don't think fucking should be that complicated. I think you should just be able to walk up to someone and say, "Hey, let's fuck" and then the two of you go at it. That's what I think. And if more people were honest, they'd agree. That's what I think.'

Byron continued his story as if Ethan hadn't spoken. 'Sometimes the dragonflies start screwing while still flying, then they land and finish off. It can take a few seconds' —he looked at me—'or a couple hours. The female then goes off to lay her eggs, sometimes with the male still attached to her.'

Ethan laughed. 'Jesus. The La Bug Method of delivery. "Keep buzzing, dear, don't forget to buzz deeply now."' He laughed some more.

Byron smiled, his story apparently finished.

I stared at him. Why hadn't he told me that story when I'd asked him about his earring?

'I don't get it,' Ethan said. 'Which part inspired the dragonfly earring? The screwing for a couple hours?'

Byron shook his head. 'The flying together. When we were together, it was like we were flying. When we were apart, I felt like I was standing on the muddy bank of some swamp waiting for her.' He closed his eyes and the weariness I'd seen in his face earlier seemed to rush back all at once.

'Yeah, I know what you mean,' Ethan said. 'To me love is like handing someone else a sharp butcher knife and hoping they don't stab you with it. That's how I feel all the time when I'm in love. I don't think that's healthy, do you?'

'I'm not sure love is healthy.' Byron kicked some water at me. 'What do you think, *Wren*? What does love feel like?'

I guess I could've ignored the question, or made something up. Or used what Wren had once told me: 'When I'm in love,' she'd said, 'it's like one of those appliances that runs either on batteries or you can plug in. Like a portable cassette player. When I'm in love and away from that person, I feel like I'm running on batteries, like I can feel them draining, running lower with each movement. When I'm with that person, I'm plugged in, the current is constant, miraculous.' I could have said that. But for some reason I decided to answer straight. 'When I'm in love . . .' I rolled over onto my back and stared up into the sky. I couldn't see any stars, just a faint fingernail sliver of moon crowded out of the sky by black clouds. I thought of Robby and suddenly horses started stampeding across my stomach. Tears drowned my eyes the way Byron had submerged his head in the spa so long. 'When I'm in love I have the feeling that I'm suddenly a different person. That I can see more now, like I just took a giant leap up the evolutionary ladder. I start to think that I should go back and reread every book, resee every movie I've ever known, because I'm so different now, so much *more*, that I'd feel differently about everything I

287

experienced before. What I loved I might now hate, what I hated, I might now love.' I shook my head and tears spilled out along both sides of my eyes. 'I don't know what I'm saying.'

'Me neither,' Ethan said. He turned back to Byron. 'I like your dragonfly story better. It's weird how everybody seems to know some bizarre *Wild Kingdom* story that they relate to their own lives. My mom used to always tell me and my sister about all the different species that are monogamous, you know, mate for life. Like crows, they mate for life. But I think that was more for my dad's benefit than ours. Me, I saw this documentary once about the three-toed sloth, you know, that big bear-like thing, lives in South America I think. Anyway, what I heard was, the sloth goes up into a tree and does nothing but eat and sleep for a whole month. Then at the end of the month, he climbs down the tree and takes a shit. It's got to be a world-class shit if he waited a month to do it. Anyway, as soon as he starts laying cable, hundreds of insects that have been living in his fur come running out to lay their eggs in his shit.' Ethan stopped and drank from his beer can. His face was serious and sad. 'I mean, that's how I feel sometimes. Like Johnny Carson is the sloth and I'm some insect waiting for him to take a shit so I can jump into it and lay my eggs.' He looked confused a moment. 'I guess the eggs must be my comedy routine. But when they hatch, man, then everything will be right. I'll be okay.'

There was a long minute of silence while Byron and I stared at Ethan. Ethan stared down at the bubbling water like a man perched on a bridge deciding whether or not to jump.

'You have any animal stories, Wren?' Byron asked me. 'Any that pertain to your life?'

I thought of the dagger-dick bedbug a moment. I shook my head. 'I guess I need to watch more documentaries.'

I stood up and picked up my towel. Byron stood up too, handing me my empty cans of Diet Coke and the empty bottle of Kahlúa. 'Why didn't you tell me about your earring when I asked?' I said.

'You didn't ask for the right reasons.'

'Fuck you.' I wrapped the towel around my waist and walked back to my apartment. As I strolled along the bushes, I saw a white car pulling into the parking lot. 'Not again!' I growled. 'Get out of my life!' I stopped and hurled an empty Diet Coke can at it. The can dinked off the rear fender. I expected this to send the car screeching out of the lot as it had before; instead the car screeched to a halt and I could see now that the car wasn't a Subaru, it wasn't even white, more like a pale yellow. The driver, a young man with a shaggy mustache, jumped out of the car and started yelling at me. 'What the fuck's wrong with you? You nuts, you stupid bitch!'

I ducked around the bushes and ran into my apartment. I locked the door but kept my ear pressed against it. The bushes kept him from seeing which apartment I'd entered, but he was outside looking at all the doors. He knocked on one of my neighbour's doors.

'It's three o'clock in the morning, asshole!' someone yelled from one of the apartments.

'Fuck you,' the guy said.

'I'm calling the cops,' the voice responded.

'Good!' the guy from the yellow Jetta shouted back. But a few seconds later he stomped off, got in his car, parked it, and disappeared into his apartment.

I was shaken, my heart pounding, my legs wobbly. I was vaguely ashamed of having gotten drunk. Now that fear had sobered me up, I started to wonder about Byron, about the shiny blue suit, the bird, his insect lore, his interest in my money. I went to the kitchen and got the serrated steak knife out of the drawer and carried it back to my bedroom. I placed it under my pillow.

I went to bed. Faintly, mixing with the sound of the apartment complex's running streams, I could hear Byron and Ethan singing new lyrics to the theme from *The Facts of Life*.

I woke up sometime later, out of a dream I couldn't remember but still felt. I was thick with melancholy. The doorknob jiggled. I thought of Byron, drunk, fingering his dragonfly earring.

'Go away,' I said.

No answer.

'I've got a knife.'

Giggling. Two people, one female.

'I've got a knife,' I said louder. My hand groped under the pillow for the knife, but I couldn't find it.

'She's got a knife,' the female whispered. I swore it sounded like Wren.

'A what?' Byron said.

'A knife, A fucking knife.'

They laughed.

'Wren?' I said. I tried to climb out of bed. But I couldn't find the knife and no way was I opening the door without a knife. I closed my eyes and waited until the voices disappeared.

20

When the doorbell rang, I lifted my head from the toilet seat where I'd fallen asleep. My left cheek was numb where the curved edge of the seat had pressed against my face. I remembered it being about 5:30 A.M. when I'd stumbled out of bed, fallen to my knees with nausea, and crawled into the bathroom. I started heaving for about forty minutes. At first it gushed out like in *The Exorcist*, then it settled down to sporadic spasms. Sweat slicked my skin and pasted my hair to my face. Exhausted, I'd just laid my head on the seat and finished off the night there.

The doorbell chimed again.

I didn't move, hoping Byron would answer it and send whoever it was away. Probably Grudge or one of his mysterious gambling buddies, ready for another day of scavenging. Bottom suckers, Wren would have called them.

The doorbell rang repeatedly, an insistent Morse code.

I hugged the toilet bowl, the porcelain cool against my naked chest. The small room smelled like vinegar and coffee. Slowly I pulled myself upright, knowing now how difficult it was for an ancestral missing link to first learn how to walk. I wobbled slightly, hands grabbing at the walls for balance. As I passed the bathroom mirror, I noticed a curving indentation along my cheekbone, a line deep as a saber cut from the edge of the toilet seat. Charming. Like a movie Nazi with a dueling scar from Heidelberg. I yanked open the medicine cabinet and dry swallowed four Advil.

I pulled on running shorts and T-shirt and sang softly, '"The Brady Bunch, the Brady Bunch . . ."'

I unlocked my bedroom door and moved the chair I'd wedged against the doorknob last night, I guess to keep Byron out. Then I remembered hearing Wren's voice, and Byron's, the doorknob jiggling, their laughter. An alcohol-induced dream, I decided. On the bed, the serrated blade of the steak knife was sticking out from under a thrown-back sheet. I was lucky not to have cut myself on it in my sleep.

The doorbell was still chiming intermittently. Why hadn't Byron answered it? Had he been killed in his sleep by one of his ex-con cronies over a gambling debt? His throat slit and his money stolen? I just hoped they took the damn cat and bird too.

I staggered my way to the front door and pulled it open, shielding my eyes against the bright morning sun. An impossibly cheerful Davis stood there holding a fresh pineapple.

'Good morning, sunshine,' he said, shoving the pineapple at me. 'Maui's finest. Brought back at great expense and inconvenience. Ever try to store one of these under your airplane seat?' He kissed me on the cheek, right on my toilet seat crease. He probably thought it was from a pillowcase seam.

He grabbed the pineapple back and marched straight for the kitchen. 'Pineapple is also great for hangovers. Follow me.'

I did, shuffling after him like a frail convalescent. 'How'd you know I wouldn't be at work?' My voice sounded coarse, like it was passing through a cheese grater.

'My spies are everywhere.'

'Then how'd you know about my hangover? You got any spies in here?'

He smiled, tapped his nose, and sniffed. 'Kahlúa. I had a little problem with booze once. Nothing a couple weeks in an expensive clinic and a few hundred AA meetings hasn't cured.'

We went into the kitchen. The iron bird cage was still in the middle of the room, Byron's jacket still covering it. 'What have we got here?' Davis asked, peeling back Byron's jacket. Again I flashed on the dead body of Philip Dougherty as Detective Diesel peeled back the kitchen towel from his butchered face. The hungry fly diving in . . .

'"*Stop in the name of love . . .*"'

Davis laughed. 'Now you're talking,' he said to the bird. The bird repeated the song title a few more times, shifting its head to keep an eye on us. Davis threw the jacket back over the cage.

'Some kind of South American parrot,' I said. 'Byron won him.'

'Raffle?'

I shrugged. 'Poker, I think.'

'I play a little poker,' Davis said. 'I wonder what the stakes are. Can't be too high if they're paying off in birds.'

'You don't want to play with him,' I warned.

'Does he cheat?'

'I don't know. I just know he wins.'

'So do I.' He went through a few drawers before he found the right knife. Then he started hacking off the outer skin of the pineapple.

'Byron . . .' I said. I glanced toward his bedroom.

'He's gone. Left about five minutes before I knocked. He walked down the street and caught a bus.'

'Coincidence?' Every word cost me great energy, so I used them sparingly.

'Not really. I've been waiting outside for an hour.'

'Really? An hour?' I smiled. *That* was romantic. I looked more fondly at the pineapple, whose inedible core Davis was now carving away.

'I take it,' Davis said, concentrating on his cutting, 'that since you didn't know he was gone, you were either passed out or you sleep in separate bedrooms.'

I considered my answer. Admitting separate bedrooms was risky. Why would husband and wife sleep in separate rooms, especially when the husband is just out of jail? I massaged the toilet seat crease in my face and shrugged. What the hell. The man waited outside my apartment for an hour, brought me pineapple from Maui. 'Separate bedrooms.'

'Good. I know it's childish and sexist and probably a sign of latent something or other, but the thought of him having sex with you rode me with spurs the whole time I was gone.' He looked at me with a tender expression. 'I missed you.'

'Me too.'

He turned, knife still in hand, the blade slick with pineapple juice. I thought of Ethan's definition of love last night, like handing someone else a sharp knife and hoping they don't plunge it into your heart. I thought of the knife under my pillow. Of my mother slicing a tangerine to teach me about periods.

'If this were a movie,' he said softly, 'I'd say something clever here.'

I stepped toward him and he dropped the knife on the counter. It spun on the countertop like a compass needle. Davis opened his arms and I stepped into them. His arms tightened and we kissed. I kept my lips pressed together because my mouth tasted like coffee sludge. But he drove his tongue between my lips, parted my teeth, and swabbed the inside of my mouth. I relaxed in his arms and let it happen. Let it all happen.

His hand slipped under my T-shirt and massaged my breast, the unscarred one. He tweaked my nipple a couple times and it popped up like a jack-in-the-box. His hips fastened against mine and began to grind. I could feel his stiff penis mashing against my pubic hair. I reached down to his waistband, wedging my fingers inside. Davis sucked in his stomach a little and my hand plunged inside his pants. I found his penis, hard but bent at an awkward angle. I pulled it free like a trapped animal and it straightened along his stomach. A few drops of sticky semen glazed my fingers.

We yanked each other's pants down to our ankles. I stepped out of mine since I didn't have any shoes or underpants. Davis's pants puddled around his ankles like shed skin, his polo shirt bibbed modestly over his crotch. He gestured at the kitchen table, which I didn't understand. He turned me around so I was facing away from him and placed his hands on my hips. He walked me to the table, his steps shuffling like a chain-gang prisoner in leg irons. When we reached the table, he bent me forward so my chest was across the tabletop. A couple of stale crumbs of cereal from breakfasts gone by knuckled into my skin. Davis stepped between my legs, his hips wedging apart my thighs. Then he was in me.

One leg of the table was slightly shorter, so it wobbled when he did, but that seemed to add to the whole naughty ambience. Davis gripped my hips, his fingers biting into my skin as he thrust forward, easing as he rocked backward. I was a little worried that he might notice some of the mottled cellulite at the backs of my thighs, spotlighted by the bright morning sunlight illuminating the kitchen. But when I looked back over my shoulder, his eyes were closed tight, his tongue wedged in the corner of his mouth like a little boy concentrating on hitting his first baseball. I felt a warm tingle of tenderness for him right then, though I wasn't in a good physical position to demonstrate it. So I just moved my hips with even more enthusiasm. His hips slammed into my buttocks with a wet slapping noise as his movements became more intense. His hands gripped the tops of my shoulders, pulling me down on him as he thrust forward. He was grunting softly.

He slipped one of his hands under my hips so his finger could press my clitoris. With each thrust I felt an extra sensation as I slid along his finger shaft. Just picturing him behind me, knowing he was staring down at me now, looking at my most intimate and private parts as he slid in and out of me, heated my skin all the way to my scalp. I came, arching my hips up, then slamming them down on the table, crushing his hand. If it hurt him, he didn't let on. Maybe this was how Bryon had lost his little finger, I thought, then forced the thought away as some sort of betrayal to Davis.

When Davis came, it lasted for a long time. His hips convulsed, he rested, then another spasm as he squeezed more semen into me. Finally, he collapsed on my back, hugging me and kissing me between the shoulder blades. His lips were cool on my spine.

'Aloha,' he said. 'Ready for a big surprise?'

21

The jail was pretty modern, I guess. Bright paint everywhere and the smell of new carpet.

Season Dougherty, wearing an orange prison jumpsuit, sat on the other side of the Plexiglas partition speaking through a battered black telephone. There were deep gouges scarring the Plexiglas between us, as if someone had banged their receiver in frustration. I had my tape-recorder running, a suction cup microphone attached to my receiver. A young uniformed officer sat at a gray desk filling out a questionnaire for Scientology. We were otherwise alone.

The last and only time I'd been to a jail was when I'd picked up Wren the night we were shot. What would she think of me here, interviewing a murderer, having had sex on the kitchen table only an hour ago, sleeping with a knife under my pillow, getting drunk with her husband?

'Better get dressed,' Davis had suggested after our kitchen-table romp. 'We only have an hour until your appointment with Season.'

We'd showered together, lathering each other and laughing as our hands lingered here and there.

'Tell me about Maui,' I'd asked him while shampooing his hair.

'I ate a pig that had been buried in the ground all day.'

'Was it good?'

He made a face. 'I couldn't tell. I was too busy feeling like a grave robber.'

'Is that why you went, for the cuisine?'

297

'Ow, you got some in my eye.' He squinted his right eye.

I tilted my head under the shower and filled up my mouth with water. I spit the water in his right eye.

'Thank you, Florence Nightingale,' he said, rubbing his eye.

'Why'd you go so suddenly?' I left off the important part of the question, 'without calling me first.'

He got a serious expression on his face. 'Let me tell you a little something about the movie business. It's not like anything else you're familiar with. It doesn't run on logic. In other businesses, the product is the goal of the business. You make a product, you sell it, you make money.'

'Thank you, Karl Marx.'

He laughed. 'In Hollywood, movies are a by-product of business, like toxic waste. The goal is power, every individual trying to prove to others that they have power. Sometimes to prove that, you actually have to make a movie, which most people consider an annoyance. Think of it as a big pissing contest. Movies are merely the liquid you drink so you can piss. Pissing is the goal, not nourishment. And when you stop to drink, that means you're not pissing. Someone else is pissing in your place. But they stop to drink, that is make a movie, because once it's done, they can go about the real business again.'

'Pissing.'

'Right. Getting power.'

'To do what?'

He looked surprised. 'Nothing. It's the end in itself. Okay, here, this'll make it clear. It's like bodybuilding. These guys build up their muscles, pumping weights every day of their lives, hours at a time, dieting constantly, shaving the hair off their bodies, practicing posing routines in front of mirrors. What for? To look good. They don't do anything with their strength. In fact, strength isn't the issue, that's never measured. *Looking* strong is the point. Their muscles aren't used to do anything except make bigger muscles. It's all about flexing. Same in Hollywood.

Making a movie is how we pump up, but the muscle is basically useless, for show. See?'

'I don't think I care enough to see. Besides, what's this got to do with you going to Maui?'

'I heard about some woman over there, a lawyer, she'd just gotten a divorce and took her two young boys sailing in Maui. A whole unite-the-family recovery thing. Anyway, big storm comes up and sinks the boat. She rescues her boys who are trapped in the sinking ship. Very dramatic stuff, underwater diving, attacked by jellyfish or some such thing. I thought it might make a good MOW.'

'A what?'

'Movie of the Week. You know, true story family drama, woman in peril, lots of adventure, and a happy ending.'

'So the kids are all right?'

'They will be in the movie version. Remember, "based on a true incident" covers a multitude of sins.'

'What happened to the real kids?'

'One lost his leg, the other's in critical condition. The mother's in therapy. The ex-husband is suing to get the kids back claiming she was negligent.'

'But in your version one kid will just have a limp, the other a sunburn, and the mother will wisecrack as she walks bravely down the beach with her sons.'

Davis pointed a finger at me. 'Now you're thinking like a producer.' He shut off the shower and grabbed a towel. Quickly he began to pat me dry. 'I flew to Maui to wrap up the rights before anyone else got wind of the story. I'd like to get lucky again, like I was with Season, signing her up before she killed her husband. If I'd waited one more week, I wouldn't even have been in the top five bidders.'

'It's an ill wind that doesn't blow some good.'

He looked at me as if wondering if I was being sarcastic or not. 'You up to writing this book?'

I stepped out of the shower and stared at myself in the foggy mirror. Blurred by the mist, I looked like a ghost. Davis wiped the towel across the mirror and I could see myself more clearly. There was still a tiny spot of ink on the scar tissue on my breast. I thought about Season Dougherty, what had gone through her mind when she'd pulled the trigger and blasted her ex-husband in the crotch and face. Like some B-movie cliché of a rape victim getting revenge. I tried to see her action from a positive angle. Not as destruction, but creation. She hadn't torn a hole in the fabric of the universe by murdering a human being, she'd mended it by protecting her daughter. She had seen a need and filled it. Like an inventor. She had invented protection for her daughter.

Or maybe she was just a murderer.

* * * * *

'Where did you shoot him first? Face or genital area?'

'You get right to it, don't you?'

'I'm curious.'

'The autopsy report will tell you.'

'Yes, it will.'

She looked at me, studying my face. A faint smile curled her lips. 'You mean, did I want to punish him or kill him? If I shot him in the crotch first, then maybe I was out to punish him and killed him as some sort of afterthought. If I killed him first, the crotch shot was just a mother's sexual outrage. The former's murder, the latter is diminished capacity. Right?'

'Something like that.'

She didn't say anything for a while. We just looked at each other through the thick Plexiglas, our phones pressed to our faces. I wondered who was the last person talking into this phone and if they ever cleaned the mouthpieces. Season Dougherty had a wholesome scrubbed look to her face, pretty in an outdoorsy way. She was about forty, her dark hair straight and thin, but shiny and rich-looking. It was cut a couple inches above the shoulders but bounced whenever she moved her head. She kept it tucked behind her ears like Gloria Vanderbilt. I pictured her squatting in jeans next to a campfire, pouring coffee into a metal cup, a guy in chaps and rawhide gloves hopping off a horse and saying, 'Whattaya want me to do next, ma'am?'

Suddenly Season stood up and peered down through the glass to get a better look at me. 'Stand up,' she said. 'I want to see who I'm dealing with.'

'I don't see how that matters . . .'

'Come on, you've been checking me out since you got here.'

'That's my job. I'm writing a book about you.'

'And I'm supposed to confide in you. Why? Just because Davis sends you over?'

'I think because you signed a contract with him.'

She sat down. 'Right. I did that. You know why?'

I knew this was tricky ground. As tough and self-confident as she seemed, there was something shaky about her. I said, 'To let people know what happened to your daughter, try to keep it from happening to other little girls?'

She laughed outright at this. 'How noble I would have been. How wonderfully good.' She leaned back in her chair and looked around the room. Her eyes glistened. 'I need the money, Ms. Caldwell. I haven't worked in eight months, I haven't a single patient left. My equipment has been repossessed, my office leased to a veterinarian. You think my lawyers are working just for the publicity? Maybe if I were the first case like this. But I'm just some woman dentist from Newport Beach who denied a court order allowing my child-molesting husband visitation with the object of his perversion, my daughter. For a while I had some celebrity status. I photograph well and everyone loves a mystery. "Where is her daughter?" But now my case is as common as mud. And believe me all this costs money. It costs money for lawyers and it costs money to keep my daughter and sister in hiding. I am like a one-woman Witness Protection Program.'

'There are organizations, underground railroads to help women in your situation.'

'I'm not a woman in any fucking situation!'

The young guard looked up from his Scientology questionnaire and made a stern face. He pointed to a sign over his shoulder that said NO FOUL LANGUAGE. She shrugged at him to indicate she would be more careful.

'Look, I didn't kill Philip to make a statement for women everywhere. I killed him because I'd lost too often in the court system and that meant my daughter and sister were going to have to stay in hiding for I don't know how many more years. I knew Philip had hired detectives to find her and kidnap her. It was only a matter of time before they succeeded. What would you have done?'

'How do you know your husband was guilty? A judge acquitted him.'

'Are you a mother, Ms. Caldwell?'

'No.'

She just shrugged, as if nothing she could say to me would matter since I didn't have a child. I resented that maternal smugness. 'Your daughter's testimony was ambiguous at best, that's what the judge said.'

'It wasn't ambiguous to me. It wasn't ambiguous when my five-year-old daughter told me how her daddy took her into the shower with him and how he washed her and washed her and stuck his finger into her vagina and said, "We have to make sure every place is nice and clean, honey." But he kept his finger in her and made her soap his erection and rub it and rub it until he came on her.' She lowered the phone and for a moment I thought she would hang up, the interview was over. She looked around the room again, as if she kept forgetting where she was and had to remind herself. Her right index finger flexed several times, as if she were pulling that trigger again and again.

My own bullet wound ached with sympathy for her and her daughter. Yet, it was not my job to merely chronicle her account of events. I couldn't take her word for things.

302

I'd read the news accounts on the way over here this morning; Davis had the whole file in his car for me. Her daughter, Jamie, testified that she had taken a shower with her father, he had washed her off, but that nothing else had happened. Season Dougherty had testified that the child had come home crying and told her about the sex, but that now she was too frightened by her father to tell the truth. The judge had no choice but to dismiss the charges.

I had no doubt that Season Dougherty was convinced these events were real. But were they? A doctor's examination showed there had been physical penetration, some minor irritation, a disturbed hymen. But Philip Dougherty's doctors had testified that this could have happened a number of ways. Should a man be prosecuted because he showered with his young daughter, because he wasn't ashamed of casual nudity and didn't want his daughter to be?

'He had names for my breasts,' she said. 'Ethel and Fred. You know, like Lucy and Ricky's neighbours on *I Love Lucy*.'

'Why did you divorce?'

She sighed a deep, rattling sigh. 'Why do people divorce?'

'Other lovers.'

'We didn't have any. I know I didn't. I'm pretty sure he didn't, at least no long-term mistresses.'

'Then what?'

She shook her head. 'Erosion. I don't know. I thought I knew then. Then it was so clear. I told all my friends the reasons.' She laughed. 'Maybe you should ask them. Maybe they remember.'

Why had Robby and I split up? Okay, he'd been fucking his professor. But what led to that? What hadn't I given him what he needed, that he now had? Was it just for a change and that's all? A different accent, a different smell, a different taste, to hear different stories from the past? Nothing more?

303

'How's your daughter taking this? Does she know?'

'She knows.'

I waited for more. None came. 'Will you bring her out of hiding now?'

Season Dougherty looked distracted, like she was thinking of something else. For a moment she reminded me of Wren during one of her inspirational flashes. She sat up, leaned forward, her eyes wide with anticipation. 'What are you wearing?'

'What?'

'You're wearing makeup, aren't you?'

'Some. A little lipstick.'

'And foundation. Eyeliner. I can see it from here. What else?'

'What do you mean?'

'Stand up, let me look.' She smiled. 'What's it going to cost you?'

I stood up, turned slightly. I was wearing a drab brown skirt and a plain white blouse. I dressed more like a prisoner than she did.

'Panty hose, right!' She said it with an accusing bark.

I looked over at the guard, but he didn't look up. 'Yes, panty hose.'

'And heels. You're wearing heels.'

'Short heels. One inch at most.'

'And a tight skirt.'

'A straight skirt. It's not exactly revealing.'

'But it is, Ms. Caldwell. It's extremely revealing. It reveals the kind of mind-set women in this society have. You're a professional woman. Davis tells me you hold several master's degrees.'

I shrugged.

'You are among the élite of women, the educated professionals. Yet you still dress like a slave girl. What exactly is the function of panty hose?'

I studied her eyes, but she wasn't being crazy. Just intense. 'To make your legs look better, I guess.'

'By better you mean sexier?'

304

'I suppose so.'

'And high heels?'

'I don't know, it's expected. Like bankers wearing a tie.'

'But what's the effect of making you walk tiptoe in heels?'

I didn't want to play this game. 'What's your point?'

'Humor me, Wren. Just answer.'

'The point of heels is to make your calves bulge, I guess.'

'To make them look sexier.'

'Okay, yes. To make them look sexier.'

'Now, why would a professional woman want to make her legs look sexier? You aren't looking to fu . . .' She glanced over at the guard. 'To screw guys when you're out doing your job. Guys don't show their legs, do they? You shave your legs too, right? And your armpits.'

I nodded.

'Why? Why would shaving your body look sexier? Why would putting you in shoes and skirts that inhibit the movement make you sexier? Because it makes you more like a helpless little girl. That's the sexual fantasy we're promoting to the men in this society. We cover our facial lines, shave our bodies, and outfit ourselves in restrictive clothing, all to feed this male desire for young girls. Then when there's an epidemic of child molestation and incest, women start yelling at how this could come about. They accuse pornographers, want restrictions. Hell, we helped it come about. It's our fault for dressing like that, for buying into what we've been told is sexy. If a full-grown woman with hair on her body and wrinkles on her face isn't sexy, then what does that say about our men? You and I are responsible. We're the reason our own children are getting raped.'

'Don't you think that's overstating it a bit?'

She looked at me with a hard gaze, the same look I saw in Byron at times. As if they've seen something I can't even imagine. 'I read this article,' she said, her voice

305

quiet, but intense as a humming power line. 'There're whole parts of Africa where they perform a clitoridectomy on women. You know what that is?'

I didn't know, but my throat constricted at the word.

'They slice off the little girl's clitoris to prevent her from having sexual pleasure, therefore removing her motivation to cheat on him. Then they sew her up so she can pee and have very painful intercourse.'

'Well,' I said, shifting uncomfortably. I thought of my stepmother beating off weasels. 'Primitive tribes have strange customs . . .'

'I'm not talking about some lost tribe in the jungle. I'm talking about eighty million women that have this done. And you know who performs the surgery usually, who talks the girl into this mutilation? Her mother. Her mother and grandmother actually cut it off. You see my point now?' She leaned back in her chair. 'In fact, I can't talk to you anymore until you take off those fucking panty hose.'

'Pardon?'

'Take them off. Right now.'

'I can't do that.'

'The guard can't see you through the partition.'

'I don't care. I'm not stripping down in public.'

'Then I can't talk to you. I have to talk to someone who isn't helping get our children raped.' She got up and walked away.

The hell with her, I thought. Go on and walk, you hairy, flat-footed bitch. I don't need this crap from a shotgun-wielding dentist. I don't need fashion advice from a woman in an orange jumpsuit.

But I did need her, I needed this job. It was my last chance at making something of my life while I still had Wren's identity. If I blew this and went back to being just plain Luna Devon, I had no hope.

'Hey,' I called.

She stopped, looked back. I waved her to return. She didn't.

306

I looked around the room, no one was on this side of the partition. I reached under my skirt and quickly yanked my panty hose down as fast as I could. My shoes popped off as I pulled them over my feet. I pressed the balled-up panty hose against the Plexiglas partition.

She returned and sat down. 'And please don't wear makeup next time.'

307

22

'Tell me about the first time you had sex.'

I shook my head.

'Oh, come on. Don't be selfish. What's the big deal?'

'No big deal,' I said. 'I just . . .' I shrugged.

'Just tell me. Jump in, like swimming in the ocean.'

I laughed. 'The very first time?'

'Yes, the very first time. Your first naked penis, long may it wave.'

I thought it over.

'You have had sex, haven't you?'

'Ho, ho,' I said. 'By "first time" do you mean actual intercourse or just sex in general, like just touching it?'

She waved impatiently. 'Whichever is more interesting. Just make it good.'

I thought for a moment. Season sat on the other side of the Plexiglas fidgeting with a yellow pencil stub while waiting for my answer. The phone receiver was pinned between her shoulder and ear. A deep white scratch zagged across the Plexiglas between us as if someone had tried to claw their way through. The scratch hadn't been here yesterday. She licked her thumb and tried to rub out the scratch, but it didn't come off. Out of politeness, I did the same thing on my side of the glass. The scratch remained.

'I'm waiting,' she prodded.

'Shouldn't I be asking *you* these kind of questions?' I said. 'I'm the interviewer here. The book's about you.'

'I'm bored with me,' she said. 'My lawyers talk about me, the shrink they hired talks about me, the news media talk about me, you talk about me . . .' She shrugged. 'I've talked so much about me that I've kind of lost sense of me. I feel like I'm talking about an old friend now, someone I used to be close to but haven't seen for a long time. It's weird. This morning I woke up and couldn't remember what my favorite color was.'

'What is your favorite color?'

'Green, I think. Or blue. I guess I'll have to wait and read your book to find out who I am again.' She smiled crookedly and deep lines that I hadn't noticed before tugged at her eyes. Her body seemed slightly smaller than last time I'd seen her, slightly older. Her orange prison jumpsuit was puffed up around her like an astronaut's space suit. This was my third straight day of interviewing her, and each time we spoke, it was as if, in telling me her story, she were disappearing. As if every word she spoke were organic, a living part of her body. To speak was like tearing off tiny pieces of her flesh and tossing them into the air.

'I look awful, right?' she said suddenly. She tucked a few strands of hair behind her ear.

'No, not at all. You're beautiful.'

She made a sarcastic face. 'Yeah, beautiful in my soul, and I can cook. Shit, I don't want to date you, I just want some truth.'

'You look tired.'

'Tired? Christ, I look like I'm going through chemotherapy.' She gestured around the room. 'This place isn't so bad. They're transferring me to county soon. Now that place is supposed to be a real stalag. You may have to smuggle me in an iron chastity belt.'

'I'm not taking mine off for anyone.'

She laughed. The laughter shook some hair loose from behind her ear. She stopped abruptly to tuck it back. She studied me a few seconds. 'Come on, Wren, tell me something juicy about yourself. Something nasty. A little tit for tat here. Girl talk. Just so I don't feel so damn exposed all the time.'

'First sex, huh?'

'That's a good place to start. And feel free to embellish the truth to make it more interesting. I know I have.'

I laughed. 'Don't let Davis hear that.'

'Don't worry, Davis would be the last to care.'

That was probably true. Davis was busy riding a tidal wave of success through Hollywood. He'd made his deal for Season's story to be filmed, and now he'd closed the deal on the woman in Hawaii. A fortyish TV actress who'd once had a hit sitcom bought it for her own production company. Now Davis was in demand, lunching every day with a different studio mogul. Yesterday he'd met Bette Midler about playing Season. Everything was going his way. He claimed that I was his lucky charm, that since he'd met me, great things had happened. He was so happy that he would occasionally burst into song, usually a selection from *The King and I*. He was very proud of his Yul Brynner impression.

But while he sang 'Is a Puzzlement' and lunched at fancy restaurants in Los Angeles, the woman who was the real charm for his success sat in a prison awaiting trial. Of course, Wren, the woman who was my lucky charm, was decomposing in a coffin. Now Season was my new charm. I visited her every day and asked her endless questions about her life. How had a woman who'd accomplished so much come to lose faith in everything she'd believed in, the very values she'd taught her daughter? What brought her to her ex-husband's house with a loaded shotgun? What gave her the courage to pull the trigger? Was it a mother's self-sacrifice for an abused daughter? Or just an embittered ex with a grudge? Sometimes I even forgot I was writing a book and my questions were just the natural curiosity I felt. I was fascinated with how the mundane and the fantastic in our lives merge. How had someone as ordinary as me come to have a gunshot scar on her boob? In some ways, I was like a novitiate studying at the feet of a Zen monk, looking for some truth in the smallest details: What did she wear that day? How did she decide what to wear to her husband's execution? Did she put on her favorite underwear knowing she'd be arrested and strip-searched? Did she wear shoes she didn't mind getting blood and brain goop on?

Davis, on the other hand, rarely asked me personal questions about Season. He cared about her physical welfare, providing her with whatever comforts she was allowed to have in prison. He was like an attentive son. But he wasn't curious about her actions the way I was. He just took them for granted. When I asked him why he wasn't so curious, he said he'd find out everything when he read my book.

Season seemed open with me, answering all my clumsy queries thoughtfully, sometimes even humorously. But I could see she was starting to wane. She'd been under enormous pressure, with bail hearings, media coverage, constant questions from everyone about where her daughter was hiding. Davis coordinated the media interviews and was always present during them, riding shotgun along with Season's lawyer. Some questions, Davis warned the press, were taboo, the answers being reserved exclusively for me and my book. And the trial.

I never wore makeup or panty hose or heels when visiting Season. We debated her 'little girl' theory of fashion a couple times, but she didn't get rabid about it or anything. She explained it all very rationally and I found her uncomfortably convincing.

'Are you an active feminist?' I once asked her.

She'd laughed. 'I'm not a feminist, I'm a mother.'

'What's the difference?'

'Feminist is just a word people use to dismiss the truth. I've never marched or sued or written a political letter. All I did was pull a trigger.'

'You've lost me. I'm just trying to figure out how you expect women to live practically in this world, how can they compete in a male-dominated work force without conforming to some of those male expectations?'

'That's like me tossing a black slave some shackles and

311

saying, "Here, go lock yourself up for the night."' She'd yawned, bored. 'It doesn't matter. Women know they're wrong, that's why they argue so hard. Every time you take a razor to yourself, you're slicing off a part of who you are, the same as if you were binding your feet, the way Chinese did with their women. It crippled them, you know.' She'd paused, studied her hands. 'Like I said, I was never a political person. I'm just a mother who doesn't want her daughter to end up a prisoner, whether it's inside or outside the bars.'

I continued to shave my legs and armpits, though I always wore slacks and long-sleeved blouses so Season wouldn't know this. Maybe she was right in the long run, but I was no tragic hero willing to sacrifice myself for a cause. Besides, I liked the feel of my skin, smooth and soft. Did that make me a bad person?

The thing is, I'd grown fond of Season, even admired her. Not for killing her husband. I still considered that a little excessive. But at least she had done *something*, she had acted. Even if the action was brutal, even if it was wrong, it was still an attempt to make things right. Even if her reasons were self-delusion, she had acted on her version of reality. What would most women have done in her place? Shrugged, sent their daughters off to their husbands, and hoped for the best. Is that any less a self-delusion?

'Come on, Wren,' Season coaxed. 'Don't be a prig. Spill your guts.'

I shut off the recorder and removed the suction cup from the phone receiver. 'Okay. First sex. Here goes.' I leaned forward toward the Plexiglas. So did Season. Not that we could hear each other any better that way, we still had to speak through the phones. But I appreciated the gesture of intimacy. I hadn't told this story to anyone except Robby and Wren. I don't know why I was telling Season. I mean, I could have told her about Wren's first time with her handsome water polo champion cousin, or Mom's first time with her screenwriter on the set of the

312

giant scorpion movie. After all, what did it matter whose first time it really was I told about. Except that I felt as if I owed Season some little truth.

'I was fifteen. In the ninth grade. My school had a poetry contest—'

'And you won.'

I shook my head. 'Third place. I wrote something about the plight of illegal aliens or something. I just took a Bob Dylan song and replaced all the lyrics with my own. You could've sung my poem to "Mr. Tambourine Man."'

'How'd it go?'

'No. That's where I draw the line. Sex, okay; adolescent poetry no. Leave me some shred of dignity.'

'C'mon. I love Bob Dylan.'

I laughed. 'It went: "Hey, you *bracero*, with the mud between your toes/hardly anybody knows what you've been going through—"'

'You're not going to be this long-winded in our book, are you?'

'Lay off. I'm sharing a moment here.'

She snorted. 'Just get to the good stuff. Naked body parts.'

'Anyway, the three winners from our school got to go to some conference for junior high school poets all over the state. We stayed in a hotel and everything.'

'You boffed one of the other poets when he read his romantic poem.'

'Are you going to let me tell my story or what?'

'Go, go.'

'Right. So, Mr. Bilford, our English teacher who took us to the conference, calls me to his room.'

'Oh, shit, not the teacher.' She laughed. 'I've seen this movie.'

'He starts talking about my poetry and all that stuff, how good I am. Then, suddenly, he's kneeling on the floor with his arms wrapped around my knees telling me how much he likes me, how he's been watching me for a couple years, waiting until I was old enough to tell me his true feelings.'

'Was he cute, at least?'

'He looked like Peter Tork of the Monkees. You remember them?'

She nodded. 'Not my type. Then what?'

'I don't know. I was stunned. I didn't know what to do. Then he starts kissing me and hugging me. I was so scared I didn't know whether to run or what. I didn't kiss him back, but I didn't run either. I guess he considered that encouragement, because then he grabs my hand and places it on his crotch. I'm sitting there with a handful of my English teacher.' I laughed. 'I didn't know what he wanted me to do with it. So he unzips his pants and shoves my hand inside, he wraps my fingers around his penis and holds my hand there, and starts pumping. He came in a couple strokes. Then he gets a washcloth and wipes my fingers like I was a little girl playing in mud. Afterward he cries and begs forgiveness.'

'Christ, could you ask for anything more perfect your first time than a guy who cries and begs you to forgive him?'

'A week later he calls me at home and begs me to start up again with him, he wants to leave his wife, quit his job if he has to. Whatever it takes. I tell him no, I don't want to see him again in that way. He cries and hangs up.'

'What happened to him?'

'He and his wife moved to Florida during the summer.'

'Not bad,' Season said. 'I'll give it an 8.5. Diverting yet with a touch of pathos.'

'Thanks a heap. You got a better one?'

She tapped her front teeth. 'Today I have perfect straight teeth with not one cavity. thanks to the mass of grillwork I wore for most of my puberty. Believe me, the Wonder Years are a little less wonderful smiling through barbed wire.'

I fastened the suction cup back onto the receiver and pressed the Record button.

Season continued: 'I don't think I can blame the braces for any lack of sexual experience. After all, plenty of other girls wore braces and they were sleeping with plenty of cool guys. But I was painfully shy and dating made me physically nauseous. I actually used to throw up before every date. Puke breath doesn't exactly make you popular with the hot hormone crowd. Finally, by eleventh grade, I had a steady boyfriend, Joey Gregson, who did the 400-meter breaststroke for the swim team. We'd been dating for over a year. Mostly we'd done our petting with all our clothes on, though often fully unbuttoned. Usually we finished off these evenings with my no-pregnancy speciality, a one-minute blow job. But he was so afraid of my braces slicing his precious weeny that he made me wax them first. He even gave me something called Sex Wax, which is really for waxing surfboards, but which he'd brought back with him after he'd gone to Los Angeles for a week to visit his uncle. When he'd come back he was crazy to become a surfer, even though there's not much surfing in Flagstaff, Arizona, where we lived. So, I'd wax my braces and do it.' She made a tight circle of her mouth to indicate the act. We both laughed.

'This went on for about six months. Then, during the summer before our senior year, Joey breaks off with me because he's decided to go to L.A. and stay with his uncle for the summer and become a real surfer. He doesn't want any ties, he tells me, he just wants to concentrate on his surfing, not worry about me back here where he can't do anything about it. Here's the part I like: He flies to L.A., goes out surfing the first day, and gets his arm broken by a bunch of surf nazis because he's not a local and he's surfing their waves. He comes back to Flagstaff the next week with his arm in a twenty-pound cast. He calls me up and I end up with Sex Wax permanently embedded in my braces all summer.' She shrugged helplessly. 'Is it any wonder I became a dentist?'

I laughed. 'Why do people talk about sex so much? The

amount of talk about it is disproportionate to the amount of time actually doing it.'

'I know. It's kind of like you spend so much time fantasizing and analyzing that it's a bit of a disappointment to actually do it.' She tucked a loose lock of hair behind her ear again. 'Sex is too complicated. I mean, when do you know if you're doing it enough to satisfy your partner. Aren't you always wondering if he wants more than you're giving him? Or if he doesn't seem to want it as much, isn't it because you aren't as desirable? Or if you are doing it a lot, won't it just get boring that much faster. Like each couple has a specific number of times they can have sex before it starts to get stale. Then you start wondering if while he's pumping away on you if he's not picturing that young beauty he saw in the movie you both attended earlier that night. How are you supposed to feel knowing that he's imagining her body and face while he's gripping your hips?'

'I don't know. I guess you do your own fantasizing.'

'That just seems so pathetic, two people making love, each thinking about someone else. I mean, I know all the sex doctors tell you it's healthy and all. I don't know. I'm probably in no position to talk ethics here.' She crooked her thumb at the barred windows. 'I haven't had sex since my divorce over a year ago. I dated, I never had trouble with men asking me out. I just couldn't get enthused about it. I tried just doing it to myself for a while. I bought a huge ole vibrator with more gears than a Porsche. But that only made me feel lonelier. I kept imagining ghosts of my dead grandmothers floating around and watching me, feeling sorry for me.' I noticed tears brimming at the corners of her eyes.

I didn't know what to tell her. That I'd gone through the same thing after my marriage broke up. But all that was behind me now. Now that I'd met Davis. Wouldn't that just make matters worse for her? After all, prospects for getting out of prison within the next fifteen years didn't look promising.

'Here's the worse part, Wren,' she said. The tears were flowing freely now. Her mouth was contorting to fight the sobs that had started. There was an urgency in her voice, as if she had to tell me now before she chickened out. When she spoke, her voice was a hoarse whisper. 'I miss him, Wren. I miss Philip. I know it's crazy, but I do.' A loud gasping sob exploded from her as if she'd been punched in the stomach. The guard looked up from his reading, stared menacingly. I smiled at him to indicate all was well. He kept staring for a few seconds longer, then dipped his head back into his book like a cow returning to grazing.

'God help me, Wren. We really were happy once. Philip and I cuddled on Sunday mornings, had lazy sex, read the *Sunday Times*. Jamie would lie on the bed between us, coloring dinosaurs with her fluorescent crayons. Philip would then take us all out to brunch and a movie. I would feel sorry for the rest of the world, that they weren't as happy.' She looked directly at me, her eyes sagging from the weight of tears. 'And the craziest part, Wren, the part that makes me not care what happens to me now, that makes me know I deserve whatever punishment I get, is that I sometimes miss Philip more than I miss Jamie. How am I supposed to live with that?'

I sat there for a moment, watching her sob. She let the phone fall from her hand. I wanted to help her, touch her, comfort her somehow. But the guard was already up and marching toward us.

I turned off the tape recorder. I rewound a little way. I erased.

23

Davis picked me up outside the jail. 'Get in, babe. I'm breaking ya outta dis crummy joint.'

I got into his station wagon. Davis leaned over and kissed me. I hugged him hard, the way I'd wanted to hug Season.

'How'd it go?' he asked.

'Grim.'

He nodded, as if he already knew what Season had said. He pulled away from the curb. 'Well, forget it for a couple hours. Right now, get in the mood to celebrate.'

'Celebrate what? You sell another project?'

'No, you did.' He reached over and stroked my leg. 'Your book about Season Dougherty has been bought. I finished negotiating the deal a couple hours ago.'

'Really?' I said, excited. 'It's really going to happen then. Jesus, this book is actually going to be published.'

He smiled at my enthusiasm. 'Damn right it is. And it's going to sell a lot of copies.'

'How'd you do it? The publishers don't even know me. I mean, they don't know that I'll do a good job.'

'I sent them some of the tapes of you and Season. They like your interviewing style. Very unorthodox, they said, but effective. Season obviously likes you a hell of a lot more than she likes me.'

'She likes you,' I said.

'Don't bullshit a bullshitter. She tolerates me. I serve a purpose. That's okay.'

I changed the subject. 'You didn't send the publishers

some of my other writing, articles or something? Any of my published works?'

'Nope. Just the tapes.'

I leaned back against the car seat and sighed. That meant the publishers weren't hiring me based on Wren's writing, just my own interviews with Season. My own work.

'They liked the way the two of you interacted. They especially liked the panty hose story I told them, when she made you strip them off before she'd talk to you. Make sure that's in the book. That's the kind of stuff they like.'

Suddenly I wished I hadn't erased Season's confession about missing Philip. That would have made a dynamic passage in the book. Instantly I felt guilty for thinking that. Still, would I do it again, given the choice?

'Based on what they heard so far, they feel confident this will be a major seller.'

'It's nice they have such faith in me.'

'There are lots of writers around, but not everybody can talk to a murderer, get them to open up.'

Murderer. The word startled me. I didn't think of Season as a murderer. She had killed someone, so technically I guess she was one. I just didn't like hearing it. A splinter of anger pulsed behind my right eye.

'It sounds funny hearing you call her a murderer,' I said. 'Cold.'

He looked over at me, frowning. 'You're right. I've been spending too much time in Hollywood. Calling Season a murderer there makes her more valuable to those guys. Sorry, honey.'

It was the first time he called me honey. I liked the sound, I'd missed being called honey and sweetheart and babyface and cuddlebug. I wanted to hear it all again. Yet, I also felt oddly anxious. Season was a murderer, but I was a honey.

'Which brings me to this.' Davis reached over and opened the glove compartment. He pulled out a white legal-sized envelope and handed it to me. 'Wren Caldwell' was typed neatly on the outside. In the upper left-hand corner was a fancy embossed logo and address in red ink: DR Productions. I opened the envelope and pulled out some folded pages. The top page was titled WRITING CONTRACT BETWEEN DR PRODUCTIONS AND WREN CALDWELL. Paper-clipped to the top of the page was a check for $25,000. Made out to Wren Caldwell!

'Jesus,' I said. 'Jesus.'

'I'd have a lawyer look over that contract first. I'm not talking as DR Productions right now, so don't tell that slippery bastard Davis Richard what I'm saying. Have a good lawyer read it. If you think it's fair, sign it and cash the check. Don't cash the check until you see a lawyer, because cashing it constitutes acceptance of the contract. I only included it now because I thought you might need the money and I didn't want any delays later.'

'A lawyer.' I scanned the contract. It was very official. By the second paragraph I was lost in the whereases. 'I don't know any lawyers. You wouldn't try to cheat me, would you, buster?'

'Get a lawyer, Wren. I'm serious.' He took one hand off the steering wheel and laid it in my lap. He squeezed my thigh affectionately. 'We're into something here, you and I. Dating, lovers, a relationship, whatever we want to call it. I just don't want business to screw us up. Money can do that sometimes.'

'Okay,' I said, folding up the contract and stuffing it back into the envelope, then into my purse.

We pulled up to the curb in front of my apartment. I leaned over and kissed him. 'Thanks for the ride, the contract, the check. The new life. Meaning to the universe.' I looked at my watch. 'Now all I've got to do is get some notes together and go teach my art history class.'

'Want me to pick you up after class tonight? We can continue our celebration.'

I was feeling pretty nervous about class. Just envisioning a roomful of students made my stomach shred itself apart. I shook my head. 'I'd better just wait and see how it goes in class first.'

Davis looked over my shoulder at the apartment. 'Is your husband home?'

'I don't know,' I said. Byron hadn't been home since I got bombed three nights ago. I would come home every day after interviewing Season and find Hector had been fed and his litter box cleaned. The phone answering machine had been played, my messages neatly written with time and date. But no Byron.

'Let's check, shall we?' Davis said with a sort of little boy naughtiness. He swung his station wagon into a parking slot and followed me to the front door. A quick search of the apartment turned up a sleeping Hector but no Byron. Hector's litter box had been cleaned and he was wearing a new white flea collar that made him look a little like a priest.

'All clear,' Davis said, coming down the hall.

'The bird's gone,' I said, coming out of the kitchen.

'What?'

'The parrot. Motown. He's gone. The cage and everything.'

'Do you miss him?'

I shrugged. 'No, I guess not.'

Davis put his arms around me and kissed me hard. His fingers dug into my buttocks, lifting me onto my toes. He started unbuttoning my blouse. I nervously looked at the front door.

'I don't know . . .' I said. 'He could come in anytime.'

'He won't.' Another button popped free.

'We don't have time. I have to get ready for class.'

'A quickie. Fast and furious, like in the movies.' He grinned. 'Trust me.' He started singing in his Yul Brynner accent: '"But unless someday somebody trusts somebody/There'll be nothing left on earth excepting fishes."'

'Oh, yes, take me, bald stud. Take me now!'

We ran down the hall laughing.

Somehow we ended up in the bathroom. The tiny coun-

321

ter around the sink was covered with colorful cans and tubes and boxes. Deodorant. Toothpaste. Q-Tips. Nivea cream. Davis brushed them all aside and hoisted me up onto the counter next to the sink. The porcelain was cool on my skin and I could feel the faint crust of dried toothpaste. The strip of wall behind the sink was all mirror. But it was back so far that I couldn't comfortably lean against it so I sat there feeling like a little girl at the doctor's office sitting on the table, legs dangling and nothing to lean against.

Davis started kissing me, but he was impatient and left my mouth quickly and trailed down to my breasts, sucking and kissing them while his hand slid between my legs. I was naked except for my panties, which I've always been reluctant to shed during sex until the last possible second. He just slid his hand under the elastic leg and dug in. He bit my nipple firmly, hard enough to cause me to jerk a little, but not hard enough to want him to stop. I pulled his head harder against my breast and scooted my hips forward against his probing hand. He slipped one finger into me, then another, and finally a third. It felt good, but I felt a little like a turkey being stuffed by a hungry chef.

Maybe I just don't relax enough during sex. I think too much about what every action means, its ramifications. Sex makes me feel like the worst softball player on the playground, the last to be picked, the first to drop the game-losing catch. Wren used to tell me of her sexual escapades, the impossible positions, the household objects she used, vegetables and fruits that she and her partners incorporated into their sex. I would gape, which only delighted and encouraged her to tell me more details. Robby and I also had our moments of passion and inventiveness. He liked it when I wore my white socks and hiking boots to bed. We had a modest vibrator that we used on each other sometimes. Once he wore my underwear to bed and I wore his and we pretended to be each other and make love the way the other usually did. There was something

322

exciting about that, though mostly I felt like we were conducting a psychological experiment rather than making love.

My only real sexual experience other than with Robby was my one adulterous affair. Robby and I were going through the usual three-year doldrums that I have since read about in several self-help books. He was studying late all the time and we rarely saw each other and even more rarely had sex. No excuses, I just got lonely and scared and ended up in the sack with a guy who lived in the same apartment complex. He was a Zen Buddhist, though he'd been raised Jewish on Long Island, New York. His father was a copyright lawyer for a record company so he knew a lot of rock 'n' roll stars. He was the calmest guy I'd ever known. His apartment was filled with thick white candles, which he lit every morning at sunrise and every evening at sunset. Sometimes immediately after sex he'd sit on the edge of the bed, his legs crossed, his hands cupping each other, his eyes partially open but unfocused, meditating. He'd practice breathing out. Breathing out was the key, he said, though a lot of people thought breathing in was. You can kill somebody when they're breathing in, that's when we're most vulnerable. He told me about another Buddhist sect in which sex was a symbolic act, very spiritual, having to do with erasing the concept of duality and such. Even though he wasn't a member of that sect, sex with him always seemed kind of spiritual. Also, kind of colorless, odorless, and tasteless, like something that was good for you, though it wasn't especially enjoyable. Like talking to a phone answering machine. After a few times I got to feeling too guilty and I broke it off. He called me a cunt, threw a couple of candles at the wall, and threw me out of his apartment.

I guess that's the point, really, sex has always felt like practice for something better. I read once in a novel where the woman was making love and she felt as if the man were pulling her underwater, dragging her to the bottom of a swimming pool. Sex was never like that for me. I sort of sat on the edge of the pool and dangled my toes in the water.

And here I was again:

Davis lifted my legs up and pulled my panties off. He put his hands on my knees, pushed my legs apart, and knelt in front of me. His tongue lapped at me eagerly. I felt his hand wedge under my buttocks and crawl across my skin until he was at my anus. His fingers were already damp from penetrating me, so he just slid his index finger into me. I yelped from the sudden assault. This was not an area that had much experience. Robby was a little too fastidious perhaps to be much interested there. I tried to squirm away from Davis's finger, mostly out of embarrassment, I guess. It didn't really feel that bad, just a little uncomfortable.

Davis stood up, folded my legs over his hips, and entered me. He thrust hard, fast and furious, as promised. I leaned back until my shoulders were pressed against the mirror. He pounded into me and I wanted him to keep pounding. The skin on my shoulder blades squeaked against the mirror with each thrust like a squeegee against a windshield. He was breathing hard, panting, pumping. His breathing became labored and I opened my eyes to make sure he was all right. His eyes were pressed close with concentration, his face in a pained grimace. For a moment I was concerned he was having a heart attack. But he came and his face relaxed.

After a minute he pulled out of me and turned on the faucet. His penis dripped onto the carpet as he splashed cold water on his face. 'Do you really need to do this teaching?' he asked. 'Can't we just stay home tonight and do that a few more times?'

'They're expecting me.' I hopped down from the counter. My thighs were streaked with his come. My legs were shaky.

He pulled a handful of toilet paper off the roll and wiped my thighs. 'You don't need the money now. Plus, it could interfere with your work on the book.'

'If it does, we'll talk about it then.'

He held up his hands innocently. 'This isn't a male-female issue, Wren. I'm not trying to dominate you here, I'm just showing concern. I can do that, can't I?'

I patted his butt. 'I don't want to go tonight, believe me. But I've made a commitment and it's important that I keep it.' Besides, I didn't want an irate administrator phoning Wren's old university to complain about her and finding out the teacher they hired has been dead over a month.

I started my shower and Davis stretched out on the bed with the newspaper. He looked funny lying there, his naked body pink from exertion, like a pudgy teenager. Yet his face was so adult, concentrating on the articles, scanning for a story to option. I leaned over and kissed his white hip.

'Thanks.' he said.

'How come you're so pale,' I said. 'Where's that Maui tan?'

'I was there for business. For all the outdoors I saw, it might as well have been Kansas. When you and I go, that's when I'll get a tan.'

I walked down the hall to the shower.

The phone rang while I was shampooing my hair.

'I'll get it,' Davis called.

'No!' I shouted. I turned off the faucet, pulled my hair back to keep the soap out of my eyes, and ran to the bedroom for the phone. 'Hello?'

Silence.

'Hello?' I repeated.

Again, silence, though I could hear someone faintly breathing.

I took a wild shot. 'Byron's not here. You want to leave a message?'

'Sure, thanks,' came the pleasant voice. 'Tell him tomorrow's fine. If he's still up to it. I mean, we can postpone if he's not healed by then.'

'Healed? What do you mean?'

325

'Just tell him, okay? If he doesn't call, I'll be there with the money. Bye.' He hung up.

'Who was that?' Davis asked as I walked back into the bedroom.

'Friend of Byron's.'

'Oh.' Davis returned to his newspaper. I returned to the shower.

When I finished, I wrapped a towel around me and one around my hair. Davis was dressed, except for one shoe, which he was tying.

'That was fast,' I said.

'Fast and furious, as advertised.'

'No, I meant getting dressed.'

'I have some work I should do.'

'Find any potential movies?'

He shook his head and looked at the paper, which he'd left on the bed. 'Nothing I can sell.'

'I've got an idea,' I said. 'I got sick once and they took out my appendix because the doctor thought they had burst. Turned out they hadn't. They charged me for the operation anyway. That's when I got this idea. A doctor, maybe some guy who's lost his license because he did something good, but went against the medical establishment. Anyway, the guy hires himself out now as a medical bodyguard. People pay him to go into the operating room as their representative to make sure everything is done correctly. Like a medical gunslinger or something. People would feel a lot better with someone like that in there.'

Davis shook his head as he slipped on his cardigan sweater.

I'd just said it as a lark, not expecting anything. But I was a little disappointed to get no response at all.

'Of course, it needs fleshing out and stuff,' I said. 'But the idea, I mean, you can have him hired by some mobster who's getting a bypass. Something like that.'

Davis turned his back, pulled something out of his

pocket, and started writing. He turned back around and tore a check out of his book. He handed it to me. 'This one you can cash.'

It was for $2,000. 'What's this?'

'An option on your idea. I like it. Possible series, certainly an MOW or even a theatrical. We'll have to spice it up somehow. Something goes wrong during the operation, guy dies. Our hero tries to save him. Turns out he was assassinated and now the mobster's people are after the doc. I dunno, something like that. But I love the idea. It's great.'

I stared at the check. It amazed me how quickly money changed hands, especially for amounts that were more than I'd ever seen before.

'That's my standard option advance,' Davis said. 'I'll have a contract drawn up. If I sell the idea, you stand to make a lot more.'

'How much more?'

'A hundred grand at least.'

Davis left. I watched him drive away, still clutching the check in my hand. First a check for $25,000 and now another one for $2,000. At this rate, I could publish Wren's magazine within the year.

I taped the two checks to the back of the bathroom sink bowl, the last place I thought Byron might look. I wondered what the guy on the phone meant about Byron healing, but decided to ignore it. I scribbled the message down on a scrap of newspaper corner, tore it off, and carried it to Byron's room.

When I opened the door, I was shocked. The bed looked like it had been wrestled into place after a great struggle. The sheets were pulled out of place and tangled in ropy knots. The pillows were scattered across the floor, beaten into unconsciousness. Everything else in the room was in its usual prison neatness. But the bed. The mattress lay askew, a corner flopping off the frame. I inched closer, noticing red smears on the white sheets.

I leaned over the bed. I could smell the sexual activity that had taken place. A few beige stains confirmed that this chaos was the result of some wild coupling. The red smears were mostly lipstick, a tacky shade of reddish orange favored by college freshmen trying to look sophisticated. The other red stains were blood.

I went to his bathroom. The sink counter had a balled-up plastic bag from Thrifty's drugstore. The receipt listed the objects that were lined up next to the sink: peroxide, Band-Aids, cotton swabs. A washcloth, twisted into its wrung-out formation, lay in the sink, still damp, still a little bloody.

I rubbed the blood between my fingertips and sniffed it. As if it were a salad dressing and I were trying to figure out the ingredients. I didn't figure anything out. I had no theory. One of them had been bleeding. This could have happened either before or during sex. That they brought a bag of medical supplies suggests the wound had already occurred, otherwise he would have taken these things from her bathroom and used them. So at least the blood wasn't the result of their sex.

I walked back to my bedroom and finished dressing. Despite Season's philosophy, I applied some makeup. A little foundation, eyeliner. I fluffed my hair trying to make it look bigger. I'd read that elephants held their ears straight out from their heads when charging to make themselves look more formidable to their enemy. I hoped this would work with students.

As I ran the lipstick across my mouth, I noticed tiny spit wads of something on the mirror. The glass was smeared from where I'd rubbed against it during sex with Davis. I plucked one of the balls from the glass and inspected it. Skin. My skin. I felt like a detective at a crime scene. Blood, skin, lipstick, twisted sheets. Definitely a crime scene. All I had to do now was figure out the crime and find the victim.

I grabbed Wren's art book and my notes and drove to school. In the car I noticed I still had some blood on my fingertips. I spat on them and wiped them on the car seat. For no particular reason, I began to wonder what happened to the parrot.

24

'It doesn't make any fucking sense,' he said angrily. 'I mean, I just don't get it. He splits the arrow, right? Correct me if I'm wrong here. He shoots his bow and then his arrow splits the other guy's arrow, right?'

His friend sailed his stiffened index finger through the air like an arrow. He whistled sound effects. 'Thunk,' he said.

'Just answer yes or no, okay? He split the fucking arrow, right?'

'Smack down the middle, Perry Mason.'

'Well, that means Robin Hood put his arrow in the exact same spot as the other guy, right?'

'Technically, yeah.'

'So, technically, Robin Hood didn't really shoot any better than the first guy. So why did he win? Doesn't make any sense. His shot was exactly the same. Explain that to me.'

His friend shrugged. 'Hollywood, man.'

'Great fucking answer. Thanks for the insight, Joseph Campbell.'

'I'm serious, man. It's all part of the master plan. If Robin Hood didn't win, there couldn't have been a Big Speech scene from the evil prince, followed by the Big Capture scene, followed by the Big Chase scene during which Robin Hood escapes. That's the whole point. Everything in movies is directly related to how it affects the chase scene. Like divine intervention.'

'Christ, you make one sixteen-mm film for class and you

think you're Kubrick. My films aren't going to have any chase scenes, ever. Not one. People won't even walk fast. If you ever see me filming one, you have my permission to pound a stake through my heart.'

'Sure, but where you gonna get the heart?'

He didn't laugh. 'Eat shit.'

'Now, *that* you've got plenty of.' He curled his finger into a snail circle and peered at his friend through it as if it were a camera. 'You don't get it, man. Just because something is done a lot in the movies doesn't mean it's bad. I mean, look at sex.'

'You're a moron.'

'At least I'm not trying to be the next Woody Allen. Don't be so pretentious, dude. The chase scene is basically a cool concept. We all dream of having a chase scene in our drab little lives. One sinister moment when all the evil forces that have been secretly fucking up our lives since that first day in preschool reveal themselves for one final showdown. Only then, after years of stamp-licking, stain-removing, toilet-scrubbing existence, does our pathetic life take on any *real* meaning.'

'And you actually believe that shit or are you rehearsing a scene?'

'The chase puts our lives in focus. Finally we have a purpose in which the outcome of something we do actually makes a fucking difference. We're no longer just an average asshole with a million excuses why our life is a failure; we're the Only Hope in some cosmic conspiracy. It's a glimpse of total clarity, maybe the only time in our life when the sides are clear. That's why audiences love it, man. We all live in hope of one day experiencing a climactic chase scene.'

The first guy, who really did look like Woody Allen, made an annoyed face. 'You are hopeless, man.'

'What do you mean?'

The first guy threw up his hands and walked away. His friend followed, repeating. 'What do you mean?'

The two boys discussing Robin Hood had been standing

outside my classroom waiting for the Intermediate Free-hand Drawing class already in there to finish. Now they sat on a bench and continued their animated discussion. Overhearing their conversation made me even more nervous. I wasn't sure I had the nerve to do my Wren act in front of such a large audience. One on one I was okay, but this was the difference between playing Beach Boys tunes on the family upright piano at parties and appearing in concert at Carnegie Hall. Students could be ruthless. My hands were damp with sweat. Some of the ink on the art history textbook I was clutching rubbed off on my fingers.

Other students were beginning to gather around the door now, many of them older than the two filmmakers. Some of the men and women wore business suits and carried briefcases, having come straight from their day jobs. They sat stiffly on the benches provided, smoked cigarettes, or sipped from the Styrofoam cups they'd bought at the campus snack stand. Except for the two boys, the others didn't talk to each other except to make sure this was the right classroom. I'd forgotten that night classes drew an older crowd, one that worked during the day and therefore took their classes more seriously.

My stomach lurched suddenly and I tasted a couple of creamy drops of vomit at the back of my throat. I looked at my watch. Still eighteen minutes before class would begin. I turned and fled down the sidewalk along a row of faculty offices. If I could find a rest room, splash some cold water on my face, hang my head over a toilet, maybe take up meditation, or start smoking again . . .

I ran past an open door, caught a glimpse of a neat row of white toilets, and backtracked. I walked in, but this was definitely not the women's room. I knew a faculty office when I was in one: stacks of art books crammed into the bookshelves, posters on the wall of past student art exhibitions, a Year-at-a-Glance wall calendar with all the school holidays circled in red Magic Marker. I rubbed my nose, which burned a little from the harsh scent of turpentine and paint.

Five toilet bowls were crowded against the wall of the small room. They weren't connected to anything, no plumbing pipes. The lids were off so I walked over and peeked inside.

The inside of the bowls were painted. Not just painted, but each was covered with a replica of a famous masterpiece. I recognized a couple of them by name, the others I'd seen in books somewhere but couldn't recall details. Each toilet contained a cómpletely different artistic style, from Impressionist to Cubist to Romantic. The accuracy was remarkable. I leaned over even farther, holding on to my glasses so they wouldn't fall in.

'Don't squat,' the voice behind me said in a pleasant tone. 'A couple are still wet.'

I turned. She was barely five feet tall, with white-blonde hair that had gone too long between bleachings. The brown roots were starting to gain lost ground. She wore it combed straight down all around, including her bangs, like a vampy imitation of Cleopatra. Her jeans were straight-legged and faded to a pale blue. Her sandals were rubber flipflops, the heel of one had a small bite out of it, the outline of teeth marks still clear. Her sweatshirt said UCLA. Her hair, her jeans, her sandals, her sweatshirt, were all dotted with constellations of different colors of paint. I figured her for about forty, with the distracted look of a woman whose independent life-style has brought her to the verge of either great success, or buying that fourth cat that tips her over the edge from being a cat lover into becoming a cat woman.

She looked at the roll sheet in my hand. 'Adjunct faculty?'

I nodded. 'One course. Art 110.'

'Ohhh, so you're Wren Caldwell.' She smiled mysteriously. 'I thought you'd have bigger tits.'

I nodded. 'So did I.'

She went to her desk and rummaged among loose

papers and art magazines until she found a flat can. She opened the lid, pinched some loose tobacco between her fingers, and tucked the wad into her mouth. The skin next to her lip bulged tumorously, as if she'd just been stung by a bee. 'A tragedy in the making, I know,' she said, tossing the can back onto the desk. 'No excuses. I just like chewing it more than gum. Sue me.'

'Nice meeting you, Sue,' I said. 'Me Wren.'

She laughed. 'Christ, don't make me like you, okay? If I like you, I'll want to spend time with you, if I spend time with you we'll talk, I'll tell you my personal problems, and then you'll pity me and won't like me anymore and we won't spend time together and I'll be terribly hurt. So, just act bitchy and save me the heartache. Deal?'

'Fuck you, slutface,' I said. 'How's that?'

She laughed again and shook her head. 'Too late, I think. Come on, I'll give you the grand tour of my toilets.'

'There's an invitation hard to resist.'

She walked over to the toilet bowls. She picked up a dirty rag and wiped her paint-splattered hands. 'I heard about you from Phil Sanchez, our illustrious department chair. I'll tell you before everyone else does: Phil and I date on occasion, the occasion being when his wife is out of town on business. See, it's started. I'm telling you my personal secrets.'

'I've heard worse.' I thought of Season Dougherty weeping in jail, confessing her love for her child's rapist.

'Anyway, everyone on the Hiring Committee was very impressed with your credentials, though your disappearing act gave Phil another cluster of ulcers.'

'Circumstances beyond my control.'

She snorted. 'That's gonna be the title of my autobiography.'

I didn't say anything. I didn't want to encourage any more personal revelations. I was already overburdened with what I'd heard today from Season.

'I read your article on Ogata Kenzan and his pottery work,' she said. 'Very insightful stuff.'

334

I had no idea who Ogata Kenzan was. 'Thanks.'

'But I think you underestimate his brother's influence. It wasn't until Korin returned to Kyoto in 1709 that Kenzan really developed his own style. They formed a symbiotic relationship that inspired both of them to go beyond what they were individually capable of. Don't you think so?'

'I think you're confusing inspiration with invention.' I had even less idea what that meant, but I remember Wren saying that to someone at a party who was arguing with her about Tom Wolfe. No, wait, she'd said they were confusing imagination with invention.

'Perhaps,' she said. Apparently she was as baffled by my statement as I was. She held out her hand and we shook. 'I'm Carol Hill.' She pointed to the plastic nameplate on her desk. 'Dreadful name, I know. A young girl with the name Hill and no chest to speak of takes a lot of teasing. "Where are your Hills, Carol?" That sort of thing. I started a rock band when I was in high school. I thought it would make me more popular. I couldn't play an instrument, so I sang. Actually, I couldn't sing either, so I sang like Janis Joplin. I had a sore throat for three years. Anyway, we used to practice every day in the basement, which prompted my father to announce to every guest we ever had that "The Hills are alive with the sound of Carol."' She shook her head. 'Any wonder I'm so screwed up?'

'Did it work? Were you more popular?'

She looked off, as if picturing herself back then, amid the popular crowd. 'Oh, yes, it worked. I was very popular. Disappointing, isn't it? My first lesson in hollow victories, I guess.'

'This is amazing stuff,' I said, gesturing at the toilets.

'Yeah, well.' She pointed to the first bowl, stirring the air with her finger as if cleaning the bowl. 'This one's La Tour's "Magdalen with the Smoking Flame."'

A comely young woman sat in a plain wooden chair. Her hand rested affectionately on a human skull, while she contemplated the flame rising brightly from a jar of what looked like oil. Beside the flame were the Scriptures. A warm glow of candlelight surrounded her protectively like a full-body halo. She looked content, the dark skull of Death cradled in her hand held no fear for her, now that she'd renounced mortality and found the light.

I had seen this painting before in books and always appreciated its simple power. As far as I could tell, this was an exact replication. Subtle and powerful, even clinging to the curved throat of a toilet bowl.

The second bowl's art I also recognized. I couldn't remember the title. A woman sat, head tilted, her enormous rosy-cheeked child propped up on her lap. Impressionist school. The colors soft, muted, but the whole picture somehow bright, clean and hopeful. Again, the duplication was eerily accurate.

'Mary Cassatt,' I said. 'Right?'

'Right,' Carol said. '"Mother About to Wash Her Sleepy Child." The size of that kid scared me off from having any for years. But with my thirty-sixth birthday marching toward me, I've reconsidered. For my birthday, I've decided to give myself a pregnancy.'

I glanced at her finger for a wedding ring, saw none. That could be practical though, not wanting to get paint on it.

'No husband,' she said, fanning out her naked fingers. 'I'm still screening candidates.'

'What do you do with them?'

'The candidates? I fuck them.'

'The toilets. Do you show them in exhibits?'

She went over to the door, walked outside, and spit an enormous gob of brown juice into the lawn. She came back in grinning. 'That's the part I like best.'

'Its charm is alluring.'

She laughed again. 'No, I don't exhibit them. Copying someone else's work isn't really art to me. This is more of a craft. Like making bird houses out of Popsicle sticks.'

'What do you do with them?'

'Sell them. They've got an arts festival every year down in Laguna Beach. I work on these all year and sell them down there during the summer. I make a little more from selling toilets in the summer than I do from teaching full-time the rest of the year. It's a wonderful life, ain't it?'

I studied the toilets again. One of them was a replica of Winslow Homer's 'The Cotton Pickers'. Two young black women wander through an enormous field of cotton, both wearing large bonnets. One woman has a basket of cotton under one arm, the other has a bag of cotton slung over her shoulder. One looks forlornly at the cotton, the other looks hopelessly across the field at her wasted future.

'You pick interesting subjects,' I said.

She shrugged. 'I pick whatever I can forge easiest. It's not that simple to treat the porcelain to hold the paint, then treat the paint so that thousands of flushings don't wash it away with the rest of the shit.'

'Forging. That doesn't sound respectful enough for what you do. You're really good.'

Carol smiled. 'You're mistaking cleverness for talent. I'm a forger, pure and simple. I don't even imitate life, I imitate imitations. I copy other people's work, people who really knew what they were doing and why they were doing it. I take their greatness and magically transform them into kitsch, a curved replica staring up at urinating twats and straining assholes.'

I didn't want to leave on that graphic image. I liked her too much. 'You must have your own work tucked away somewhere.'

She went to the door, waited for a couple of students to pass, then hocked another gob of tobacco juice across the sidewalk. She wiped her chin with the back of her sleeve. When she returned, her hands were dug deep into her pocket. She looked so tiny then, like a penitent child. 'If I could, Wren, then I would. If it's original art you're looking for, talk to Phil Sanchez. He's got showings all the time. Or Tina Lipschutz. She's our performance artist. Terrific gal. Or Zack DuBois, our potter. He's probably

337

just a couple years shy of world famous. Those are true artists. But you want decorated toilets, you come to me.' She leaned over the trash can and spit out the clump of tobacco. She took a swig of Diet Coke from a can on her desk. 'Don't get me wrong, Wren. I'm not having an artistic crisis. Being an artist was never my goal. Teaching was. I love it. But if you want to buy a house and go on vacations, you need another income. That's all there is to it.'

I looked at my watch. 'Gotta go. Class.'

'Have fun. If I haven't scared you off, come see me sometime. We'll have lunch. You're buying.'

I started out of the office. As I reached the door, Carol said, 'Hey, you wouldn't be needing a nifty new toilet, would you? I can make you a deal. You pick your favorite masterpiece, I'll slap it into your toilet.'

I thought about sitting down on a toilet, having someone's face staring up at me. I doubted I'd be able to go. 'I'll think about it.'

I was already ten feet down the sidewalk when I heard her call after me, 'I do bidets too.'

By the time I walked into the classroom, all the desks were full. A few people stood around the door with green slips of paper.

'I'd like to petition,' one hefty older woman said. She wore a tilted black beret as if she thought this were some Left Bank art hangout. 'Do you accept petitioners?'

'I would also like to petition,' a man in an expensive suit and silk tie said. He had a slight British accent.

'Let me do the paperwork here first,' I said, showing them my roster. 'Then we'll see.'

I went to the podium at the front of the class. The room was large and stuffy. The windows and door were open, but that didn't help much. I had the sense that people were breathing the same cubic foot of fresh air, passing it from row to row like a relay race baton. I swallowed dryly.

My roll sheet showed the maximum of forty students had enrolled. At the university in Oregon, English classes never exceeded twenty-five. This was a bit overwhelming. All the desks were taken and there were half a dozen deskless people standing around looking defeated. One wall was all windows, looking out on the sidewalk that fed three other buildings. Students walked back and forth outside and many of my students looked out the windows at them. Keeping their attention was going to be a challenge.

'My name is Wren Caldwell,' I said. 'And this is Art 110, for those of you who have wandered into the wrong classroom.'

'One-ten?' someone said.

'Yes.'

A teen in a white T-shirt and sweatpants that said Ripcurl down the side got up and walked out of the classroom. The old woman in the beret bustled to capture his desk. She smiled triumphantly at those next to her as she sat down.

The rest was administrative stuff, taking roll, signing petition cards to match the number of students who hadn't shown up. Because I had more petitioners than available seats, I did a lottery, pulling names out of a bag. Those whose names weren't drawn were dismissed.

One man whose name had not been selected would not leave. 'I buy lottery tickets every week, the money's supposed to go to education in this state. I've never won a goddamn dime. Now I have to do a lottery to take a stupid art class. This is no way to practice education.'

'I agree completely, sir,' I said. 'However, we are limited by fire laws as to the number of students allowed in each classroom. You'll have to leave.'

'Like hell I do.' He went over to the wall next to the door and sat down on the floor. He wasn't a very big man, under six feet and not especially muscular, but he looked angry enough to start trouble. He was in his fifties, hair longish and streaked with gray. Perhaps an ex-hippy reliving the glory days of sit-ins and taking over the administration building, shaving with the dean's razor, urinating in file cabinets. Actually, I kind of admired him for what he was doing.

The two aspiring filmmakers I'd overheard outside the classroom whispered to each other and gestured at the man. They were probably thinking of ways to film this.

'You do understand, sir, that you will not receive credit for this class?' I told him.

He grumbled something and waved me off.

'Want me to get security?' the man with the British accent offered. He'd been one of the lottery winners. So had the older woman with the beret.

'No, thank you. Let's just get on with class.' I talked about the structure of the class, the number of museum trips required, a diary of all the art works they would see and their critical impressions, the papers due, the number of footnotes, etc. I rattled off due dates as if I knew exactly what I was doing. The attitude I exuded was that there would hardly be enough time in a single semester to cram even a fraction of my vast knowledge of art history into them. I was starting to feel pretty good, in control and confident.

I had them open their textbooks to an abstract work by Willem de Kooning called 'Woman'. It was one of his series on women he did in the early 1950s. I'd picked this one because Wren had tons of notes in the margins about it and I was able to dazzle them with history and interpretation, thanks to Wren's knowledge.

'Notice how the figure seems crammed into a confining space by the placement of the geometric shapes. Yet, despite the confinement, she seems capable of overcoming these limitations by sheer force of will and physical being.' I glanced down at Wren's scrawl. 'This reinforces De Kooning's preoccupation with woman as mother-goddess-fury.'

And so it went until break time. 'Take fifteen minutes,' I said, checking the wall clock.

The man who had lost the lottery didn't move. He sat

hugging his legs, scowling slightly. People filed out past him, some giggling, others ingoring him.

A student blocked my path as I went for the door. She was about twenty, very pretty, wearing bib overalls. 'Wasn't there some concern at the time,' she said, 'that De Kooning might be hurting the abstract movement with these works? I mean, abstract art was only just beginning to gain acceptance in the U.S.'

I remembered one of Wren's notes to that effect. 'That's true,' I said, hurrying past her. I walked quickly down the sidewalk away from the classroom. I felt exhilarated. The class had gone well so far. No one had stood up and denounced me as an imposter. Actual learning had taken place, students knew more now than they had before.

I was practically skipping. I'd never felt so elated. If I'd had any kind of voice I'd have burst into song. It was as if everything in my life had suddenly come together at once. I was writing a book and getting paid. I'd come up with a script idea and picked up another $2,000. I had a boyfriend who was kind, generous, and good in bed. I was teaching, actually teaching a subject I knew little about, yet doing a good job of it. I could do anything. It was as if I suddenly had the golden touch. I was lucky. The way Wren had been lucky. So this was what it was like to get what you want, to feel safe within your good fortune, not to worry about what might happen because it was usually good. I laughed aloud and a couple students passing me gave me strange looks. I was surprised they couldn't see the magic aura surrounding me, like the one around Mary Magdalen in Carol Hill's toilet.

I didn't know what to do. This kind of manic energy shouldn't be wasted prancing around campus. If Davis were here I'd have pulled him into the bushes and jumped him. It would have been the best sex either of us had ever had, I just knew it. But he wasn't here.

Still, I had to do *something*.

Which gave me an idea.

341

I rounded the corner of the building and saw Carol's office light was still on. Her radio was on and an old Beatles' tune was playing, 'Across the Universe.'

'Carol?' I said, entering.

She was bent over a toilet, spraying an aerosol can. When she heard me, she looked around. She had goggles on and a small mask over her mouth and nose. She lowered the can and pulled down the mask. 'They chase you out already?'

'We're on break. Can I use your phone?'

'Will this involve heavy breathing or the use of cutesy pet names like Bedbug or Cuddles?'

I laughed. 'Not from this end.'

'Okay, you can use it. I've got to go to the bathroom anyway. One of the side effects of chewing tobacco.' She wiped her hands with the same colorful rag and tossed it on the desk. 'Punch nine for an outside line.' She walked out.

I dialed Robby's number.

This wasn't going to be like the other times I called him or wanted to. This was totally different. I wasn't feeling lonely or desperate or bitter. I didn't need his help or assurance. I didn't need anything. I was on top of the world. I closed my eyes and I saw the room as if I were floating fifty feet above it, the way people who have had near-death experiences say they saw the world. Maybe that's what was happening. I was dead. I'd died when BeeGee shot me. Oh, they'd patched and wired me back together, but I was still dead. Or maybe I'd been dead *until* BeeGee shot me. Maybe she'd saved my life.

I opened my eyes and suddenly I was sucked back down into my body like a cartoon ghost into a vacuum cleaner. I listened anxiously as his phone rang. I rocked back and forth, tapping my hand impatiently on the desk. I noticed the paint-spattered cloth, the globs of red. I thought of Bryon's bathroom, the blood, the bandages. What new violence was he involved in? It didn't matter. I could even deal with him now, I had the power.

'Hello?' Helen's genteel drawl.

'Hi, Dr. Jaspers. It's Luna.'

'Luna, how are you?' Solemn concern. Like a shrink.

'"Top of the world, Ma. Top of the world."' I laughed.

She didn't laugh. 'How's Dallas? I have relatives there.'

'They send their love. They miss you.' I chuckled giddily. 'I'm kidding. Look, sorry to call so late. I only have a few minutes. My boyfriend just ran down to the drugstore for condoms and K-Y jelly. He'll be back any second. Can I talk to Robby?'

'Sure. Let me get him. You take care, Luna.'

She was gone. I'd passed the first test, getting past the beast that guarded the sacred cavern. I hadn't folded when she'd shown all that concern.

'Hey, Luna, what's up?' Robby said cheerfully. But it was his false cheerfulness, the one he pulled on like a ski mask when he felt nervous.

'Lotsa stuff is up,' I said. My cheerfulness was real. Could he hear it? 'What've you been up to?'

'Same ole shit. I'm doing a paper on architecture symbolism in Chaucer.'

I stifled a laugh. Big deal, I wanted to tell him, I'm interviewing a woman who shotgunned her husband who was raping their daughter. Architectural symbolism in Chaucer? Get real.

'What have you been doing?' he asked. 'How's your dad?'

'Dad's his usual self, traveling. In search of the perfect society, where wives don't die and daughters grow up perfect.'

'Has he tried Vegas?'

I laughed. So did he. I guess that's when we were the most intimate, when we laughed at the same thing together, the rhythm of our laughter falling into sync as if we were harmonizing in choir. It was uncanny. I felt that same feeling now. But I also sensed something else, a sadness in him. 'Are you okay?' I asked.

'Me? Fine.'

'No, really. Are you okay?'

'Really, I'm fine. Well, I've still got that problem of having to strap my dick to my thigh because it's so long, but otherwise . . .' He laughed.

I didn't want to fall into our old Robby and Luna Divorce Show routine where after we split up all serious personal discussions wound up with us joking instead of talking. 'Just talk to me, Robby. Are you happy?'

He sighed. 'Don't ask me those kinds of questions, Luna. What kind of answer could I possibly give?'

'I don't know? The truth, I guess. You left me for someone else, I have to assume because she makes you happier. So does she?'

There was a long silence. I heard some noises in the background coming from Robby's end. Dishes slamming? Then silence.

'Is she gone?' I asked.

'Yes.'

'Then tell me. Are you happier with her than you were with me?'

'Luna, Jesus . . .'

'Don't wuss out on me here, Robby. I'm not the same person you remember. I can take it. Just tell me the truth. You owe me that much.'

'Luna,' he said softly. There was a tone in his voice, that quiet tone he got in moments of intense honesty. Suddenly we were husband and wife again, curled up in our bed at night, talking in the dark. I could smell him through the phone, the scent of warm licorice.

'Tell me,' I said.

'It's different, Luna. My life is different now. It's not better, it's not worse. Fuck!' He was silent for a long time. I didn't rush him. 'I'm happy, but not necessarily happier than I was with you. Like I said, it's different. But then it's not that different either. Not like I thought it would be. It's weird. I mean, I didn't expect to be running around clicking my heels or anything. I don't know what I expected. It's just . . . I don't know.'

344

My heart pumped faster. 'Do you miss me?'

'Why are you doing this?'

'Do you?' I insisted.

'Yes, of course. I miss you every day. Everything I look at reminds me of you, of something we did.'

I could actually feel the blood washing through my veins like a rain-swollen stream. I looked at my arms, wondering if I'd see the skin rippling from the rush of blood. My bullet wound thumped as if it were a second heart.

'Maybe you made a mistake,' I said quietly.

'Luna, please . . .'

'Maybe you made a mistake. Maybe you could fix it.'

He was quiet for a long time. When he spoke, his voice was barely audible. 'It's not like that, Luna. I love Helen. True, it's not the same as it was with you, and yes, I do miss you. I can't tell you how much. But I miss you the way I miss high school. I'm happy, Luna. I didn't mean to imply anything else.'

'The way you miss high school?' I said. 'What the hell does that mean?'

Another long pause.

'Luna, Helen's pregnant.'

I sagged. BeeGee's bullet probably had less effect on me than Robby's announcement. 'You bastard,' I whispered.

'Luna, listen, I'm sorry.' He started to sob, his voice choked with mucus. 'Luna, Jesus, Luna—'

I hung up.

*　　*　　*　　*　　*

The class stared at me. They wanted something.

'Open your books to page forty-seven,' I said.

'What page?' someone asked.

I looked up. 'Forty-seven.'

'What'd she say?' I heard someone whisper.

My head felt hot, feverish. I touched my forehead, but

it was cool. Still, the heat inside me was building, like a dentist's drill held too long against the same tooth. I started to talk, but something doughy at the back of my throat caught all the words before they became airborne. I swallowed hard over and over, but it didn't matter. My eyes burned and I could feel tears trying to squeeze through the pinprick ducts. I blinked them back. I knew I would not cry. All my tears had been spent on my dissolved marriage. Three months of constant crying had dried me out. I hadn't cried once since then, not at being shot, not at Wren's death, not at being suspended from grad school or being fired by the magazine. And I sure as hell was not going to cry now. If nothing else, crying over this crap would be disrespectful to everything I hadn't cried over. Especially to Wren and Esther.

I stared at the David Hockney painting pictured in the book, 'Mulholland Drive: The Road to the Studio.' Wren's notes were lengthy and precise: Hockney influenced by Picasso's spontaneity. Van Gogh's textured brush strokes, Matisse's dominant colors. I could kill an hour on this painting and then assign some reading from the text and send everyone home early.

But when I tried to speak, a throttled sob burst out. I clamped my mouth down quickly to smother it, but the class had already heard me. I looked out at them, their puzzled faces frozen between concern and fear. I forced out a few hacking coughs, pretending that my sob had merely been a throat irritation. I opened my mouth to speak again, but another sob rushed up my throat and trumpeted several sad notes.

'You okay, Ms. Caldwell?' one of the filmmakers asked, the one who liked chase scenes.

I nodded. 'Swallowed down the wrong tube.'

A few people laughed nervously.

Now my eyes were blind with tears. My glasses magnified the tears and suddenly I was looking up at everyone from the bottom of a murky acquarium. Their faces were wavy and bovine, as if they couldn't decide whether or not to reach in and pull me to the surface. I coughed as hard as I could, doubling over a little so I could turn away and blink the tears out of my eyes. I felt a few splash onto my forearm.

I turned my back to the class and went to the blackboard. Maybe if I wrote a question or something on the board, kept my back to them, they wouldn't notice. I could stall until I was back under control. I picked up the yellow chalk and started writing: WHAT ARTISTS' INFLUENCES CAN YOU IDENTIFY IN HOCKNEY'S WORK. I'd ask them to write a list, maybe break into small discussion groups. That should do it.

God, what was I doing here? While my husband was living *my* life with another woman. My life had been stolen! Now I was nothing but a forger with no life of my own. At least Carol Hill had no illusions, no ambitions. I thought about Mom, her thin Polish skin smooth and pale as icing. Except for one mole on her neck, which she monitored the way SAC watches Soviet airspace. She feared that mole, certain it would turn into a fatal melanoma without her noticing. To live in fear that your own body would betray you. What would she think if she knew I was abandoning who she'd brought me up to be because I'd rather be someone else, someone better. She hadn't raised me to become someone else's child. Isn't that the worst betrayal of all to a mother? Dad, on the other hand, would find the whole thing interesting, maybe want to tag along with me through a typical day, take notes for an article. But Mom, she would have cried.

I was only halfway through the sentence on the blackboard when my shoulders started spasming and my hand began shaking. My handwriting turned spiky, like a heart monitor graph. My nose was running. Tears, unstoppable now, streamed wildly down my face. I tried to wrestle myself under control. I pressed my lips together, tightened my shoulders, I even stopped breathing, hoping that would stop the gasping sobs. But nothing worked.

By the time I finished writing this sentence, I would

have to turn around and face the class. When I did, there was no way they wouldn't know I was crying.

I wrote the last word, hooked a giant question mark at the end of the sentence, and dotted it so hard that the chalk snapped in half and bounced back against my glasses. I took the opportunity as an excuse to lift my glasses and quickly wipe my eyes with the back of my sleeve. But the tears were instantly replaced by others. My lips began shivering uncontrollably. They felt numb and rubbery. Fuck it, I finally decided, they've seen people cry before. Now I let the tears stampede down my cheeks as much as they wanted. My face felt sticky, webbed by crisscrossing streams of tears. Plump tears hung from my chin like icicles.

Fuck it, I thought. Fuck it. Fuck them. Fuck me.

I started to turn toward the class.

And suddenly all the lights went out.

25

The room was dark.

'Hey!' someone yelled.

'What the fuck?' someone else yelled.

I looked over at the doorway for the man who'd lost the lottery and had refused to leave. I couldn't really see anything, just a hazy outline of yellow against black where I remembered the door was. The dim yellow lights from outside gave it that spooky contrast. Now I recalled that the lottery man hadn't been there after our break. I started slowly for the doorway. Once outside, I could find security or maintenance.

'Everyone stay calm,' I said, my own voice suddenly calm. 'It's just a fuse or something.'

The darkness was jungle thick. I couldn't really see anyone as I groped with my hands ahead of me. A little light filtered in through the windows and I could see the other classrooms were still lighted.

'Oh, stop it, stop it, you brute,' one of the filmmakers joked in a falsetto. 'Oh, oh, baby, do me, do me!'

Several others laughed.

'This is not funny,' an older woman said.

I took a couple of experimental steps and bumped into someone. 'Please take your seat,' I said, sounding like a flight attendant. 'I'll find some help. Shouldn't take more than a few minutes to restore power.'

Cool hands came up to my face and wiped away the latest batch of tears.

'Excuse me,' I snapped, pulling back. But the hands followed. How could this person see?

'Go outside for a couple minutes,' the voice whispered. 'It's okay, I'll take over.'

I couldn't recognize the voice. Husky. The hands were rough and heavy against my face. A man's.

'Phil Sanchez?' I asked. Who else but the department head would be so bold as to take charge.

'Just step outside a few minutes to collect yourself. It's okay.'

This was ridiculous. I couldn't turn my class over to a voice in the dark. He could be a maniac with an automatic rifle slung over his shoulder and a couple of army surplus grenades in his pocket.

'It's okay,' he repeated. His hands fell from my face and I instantly felt cut loose, like an astronaut taking a space walk whose life line is severed. I reached out, but he was gone.

His voice got to me. Not just that it was soothing or sounded kind. There was something else. An understanding that wasn't just intellectual, like someone who only imagines what you're feeling and coos sympathy. It was more intimate than that, as if he had experienced my same humiliation a dozen times before. Maybe it was Phil Sanchez, maybe it was one of the other art instructors who'd wandered by and watched what was happening. I'd felt a kind of presence outside the door the whole time I was writing on the blackboard. But to turn my classroom over to him? That was a hell of a leap of faith.

I was in a leaping mood, I guess, because I said, 'Okay.' I groped my way out the classroom and I stood outside, pressed flat against the wall so I could peek in and see what was happening. My faith had a short leaping span.

Instantly the lights went back on.

'Let there be light,' Byron said. His hand was on the four light switches, the stub of his missing finger touching one of the switches.

'What the fuck?' someone said. Same guy.

350

'Must you use profanity,' the woman with the beret asked him, scowling.

'One man's profanity,' Byron said, wagging a finger at her, 'is another man's profundity.' He smiled at her and she smiled back, lapping up his charm.

I was hidden by the door so that none of the students could see me. Only Byron could, if he chose. Which he didn't. He began moving confidently around the classroom like a prosecuting attorney with a conviction in the bag.

I noticed for the first time that his face was battered and bruised. His jaw had two small Band-Aids. His nose was swollen, maybe even a little crooked under the swelling. A small cut angled down from his eyebrow. A longer cut near his ear had five or six stitches. The dragonfly earring was still there, though.

'Art, ladies and gentlemen, is illusion. *Art*-ificial. The history of art is like the history of magicians or politicians or just about anything else. In its history is revealed the technique for capturing the minds and hearts of the people, manipulating them so they see what the artist, magician, or politician wants them to see. That's the art part.'

'Where's Ms. Caldwell?' a no-nonsense man in a blue business suit asked.

'Who?'

'Our teacher.'

'What makes you think she's your teacher?'

The man looked confused by the question. 'She had the roster.'

'So every kid wearing a Superman cape can fly?' Byron picked up the roster from the podium where I'd left it. 'Besides, I have the roster now. Doesn't that make me your teacher?'

'That's ridiculous,' the man said. 'She's been teaching this class for over an hour.'

Byron pulled a rolled-up pamphlet out of his back pocket and waved it at the students. 'This schedule of

351

classes says Staff under name of instructor. Perhaps I'm the instructor and she was merely filling in for me.'

'Why?' one of the filmmakers asked.

'Because I asked her to? Because she gets paid to? Maybe I had a car accident that made me late.' He gestured at the cuts and bruises on his face. 'Lots of possibilities, aren't there?'

'This is ridiculous,' the businessman said again and stood up. He grabbed his briefcase. 'I'm going to see someone about this.'

I started to reenter the room. I didn't want to get fired, have any kind of investigation.

'Relax, sir,' Byron told him. 'Ms. Caldwell is fine. This was all part of a little demonstration she and I cooked up. Performance art, you might say, to help you understand the history of art better.' The man didn't sit down, but he didn't walk away, either. Byron swept past him and addressed the rest of the class. 'The history of art isn't just in studying works and memorizing artists. Art movements shouldn't be merely noted, like bowel movements. Art history is understanding the anguish of expression. What social and psychological forces lead to a new movement. Okay, everybody take out a blank piece of paper and draw a geometric design. Something of your own devising. Not too complex, not too simple. Come on. And don't take too long. I'm not collecting them.'

People started taking out paper and drawing. Even the businessman sat back down, removed a single sheet from his briefcase, and began drawing in earnest. His strokes were short and precise, like an accountant's.

'Hurry up,' Byron prodded. 'Just doodle, don't think. Remember, I'm not collecting them.'

I watched Byron pace around the room, looking over their shoulders, chuckling good-naturedly at some of the drawings. Receiving back a grateful smile from the student. I'd never seen this side of him before, the unleashed charm. He hadn't taught them a damn thing, yet in five minutes he was closer to them than I was after an hour of actual learning. But I knew him for what he was, a convict. With emphasis on con.

I took off my glasses. Tears had smudged the lenses, which I wiped on the hem of my blouse. I wasn't crying anymore, I wasn't shaking. I could go in and take over the class again. But I didn't. I was too fascinated watching him gleefully work the crowd, like a pickpocket in a crowded mall. I felt voyeuristic.

He clapped his hands. 'Okay, now fold the papers in half so no one else can see them.'

As they did so, he went around the room and collected them.

'Hey,' the pretty girl in the bib overalls protested. 'You said you weren't going to collect them.'

'I lied,' Byron said. 'Lesson number one. Art is lying. Whether it's a movie or a poem or a painting, it's a lie. That is, the artist uses lies as if they were colors to create something that forms a greater truth. Facts may be true, but they don't reveal the Truth. That's what an artist does. He or she doesn't paint an exact duplication of the subject because that's physically impossible. Instead, the artist presents a likeness. A likeness is what the artist sees influenced by his or her own unique memories and experiences.'

'I don't get it,' a woman said. 'We all see the same objects, no matter what our memories. A chair's a chair.'

I peeked in. She was in her early thirties and about six months pregnant.

'Come up to the blackboard and I'll show you.' He smiled encouragingly at her. 'That's what art is, right, showing not telling.'

She smiled back and stood up boldly. She went to the blackboard. 'How about you, young lady,' he said to the woman in the beret.

'Oh, no,' she said. 'I can't draw. I just like to watch.'

Byron made a leering face. 'Oh, you like to watch, do you? Already we have something in common.'

353

The class laughed. The beret woman shook her head in mock embarrassment, chuckling the whole time.

'Come on,' Byron said. 'It won't hurt a bit.'

The beret woman went to the blackboard and picked up a piece of chalk with trepidation, as if it were a loaded gun.

Byron quickly looked through the first few sketches he'd collected, selected one, and handed it to the businessman who'd threatened to leave. 'What's your name?'

'Ed Waldman.'

'Okay, Ed, this is what you do. I want you to give them verbal instructions on how to draw the design on this paper. They must follow every direction you give them. Only two stipulations: The artists can't ask questions and you can't use hand gestures, like drawing in the air. Simple enough?'

'Yes,' Ed said.

'Just be precise and clear. It's like you're going to talk down some nonpilot in an airplane after the pilot died of a heart attack.' Byron faced the blackboard. 'Artists, are you ready?' They nodded. Byron clapped his hands. 'Let the art begin.'

Ed studied the sheet. A little grin crept across his face. He looked confident that he would prove himself.

Ed gave directions. They were precise and clear. But by the time he spoke his second sentence, the pregnant woman and the beret woman was already drawing two different objects. Ed tried to guide them back with more complex directions, but that only made things worse. Boxes and triangles sprang up in a jumbled mess. Desperate, Ed started to draw in the air, which Byron quickly reminded him was against the rules. Sweat beaded along Ed's forehead as he continued explaining what was clearly hopeless.

'Okay,' Byron finally said. 'I think that's enough. Artists, thank you, you may be seated.' They returned to their desks. Byron took the sheet from Ed and went to the blackboard. With a few strokes he duplicated the drawing on the paper. Neither of the students' sketches remotely resembled either each other or Byron's sketch. Byron made a diving gesture with his hand, accompanied by an exploding sound. 'Crash and burn, Ed. Those planes are permanently grounded.'

The filmmaker who liked chase scenes laughed loudly.

Byron scratched his head. 'What the heck went wrong? Both artists heard the same instructions.'

A man with a bushy mustache raised his hand. 'They didn't hear what he was saying. They didn't follow his directions.'

'His directions weren't clear,' a woman at the back said. 'I tried to draw along and my picture doesn't match any of them.'

A few more opinions were shouted out, mixed with mumbled debate. Then Byron held up his hands. 'This is the artist's dilemma. To have something to say, but never sure the audience hears what he says, sees what he sees. Ed is the typical artist; the women at the blackboard are the typical audience. Now, all these historic art movements tried to make themselves heard using different techniqes. You'll learn all about that later. For now, it's enough that you understand the problem artists face.'

I walked back into the classroom as if we'd planned my cue. 'With that in mind, I want you to read chapters one through four for next week. I want to see a diary entry on each of the works shown in those pages.'

'Are we going to have two teachers from now on,' someone asked.

'No,' I said. 'This was a guest appearance. One night only.'

Some disappointed groans were heard as they filed out of the room. I didn't look at Byron until they were all gone.

'What happened to your face?' I asked.

'What happened to yours?'

'I asked first.'

355

He shrugged. 'I lost.'

'You lost? What the hell is it that you play, nude rugby?'

'Their season doesn't start for another month. You want tickets?'

'Do you really know anything about art or was that all bullshit and bluff?'

'Did it make sense?'

'Yeah, some,' I said. 'But then I don't know anything about art. Except for what's in Wren's notes and what I just got out of the library the past couple of days.'

'I know. I was listening. Bullshit and bluff.'

I pointed at his face. 'What really happened to your face?'

'Well, actually . . .' He touched the two Band-Aids on his jaw. 'These two are nicks from shaving. Someone must of run my razor blade through the washing machine.'

I looked away, embarrassed. 'I was drunk. I'm sorry.'

'It's okay. They have company now.'

I didn't know what else to say to him. I wasn't sure what I was feeling. Robby still perched heavily on my shoulders. 'This is weird, what you did. Turning out the lights and all. Very theatrical.' I shook my head. 'What were you doing here?'

'I was in a couple of Wren's art classes in college. That's how we met. At first, I was just meeting my general ed requirements with an easy course. After meeting Wren, though, I took more art classes just to be near her. That little blackboard exercise was one our professor used. He'd been doing it for sixteen years and it always turned out that way.' He sighed, looked around the classroom nostalgically. 'I don't know, I guess I thought seeing you impersonating Wren would remind me of her. Something sentimental like that. I was in an odd mood.'

'Did I remind you of her?'

His face stiffened a little. He seemed angry. 'Did you want to?'

'Look, Byron, I'm just trying to get by here. I don't

want to fight right now.' I backed away from him a couple of steps. 'Thank you for helping me out. Thank you for not pressing me about why I was crying. I'm fine now. I got my mind straight, boss. Won't happen again, I swear.' I gave him a Girl Scout salute.

He stared at me a long time. I couldn't read his expression, it was that prison-yard one he lapsed into every so often. Anger maybe. Or disappointment.

I didn't care. I wanted him to know I didn't care. 'I won't be home tonight,' I said. 'I'm going to see Davis.'

He nodded and walked toward the door, turning to tip an imaginary hat and say, 'Good-bye, Wren.'

Then he was gone.

26

I rang the bell twice. The chimes sounded the first few notes of 'I Whistle a Happy Tune' from *The King and I*.

Davis opened the door. He had a script folded back in one hand and his reading glasses on. His son Mark was standing next to him holding a Nintendo Gameboy. They looked oddly comic, unmistakably father and son. The mixture of bright light and loud sound of the TV emanating from behind them was warm and comforting. A place of families. More than anything else in the world, I wanted to be inside that house.

'Hi, Mark,' I said from the front stoop.

'Hi, Wren,' he said. 'You wanna play with my Gameboy?'

'You bet. But not right now, okay?'

'Okay.' He ran back inside and plopped down three feet from the giant TV screen.

'I thought you didn't want to see me tonight?' Davis said.

'I changed my mind,' I said. 'Is that allowed?'

'Is this the first Monday of a month with a full moon?'

'I have no idea.'

He smiled and kissed my cheek. 'It's allowed.'

We walked into the living room. Mark offered me a bowl of stubby pretzel sticks.

'No, thanks,' I said.

'They're filled with peanut butter. They taste great.'

I took a handful, saw his face gloom over, released half

of them back in the bowl. He smiled and pulled the bowl away before I took any more.

Davis sat on the sofa beside me. 'Mark's mother has a date tonight. Since I didn't have plans, I said I'd watch him.'

'Where's Judy?'

'Girlfriend's house.'

'I don't have any friends,' Mark said casually, his eyes on the Gameboy that he was playing with.

'Sure you do, Mark,' Davis said. 'What about Aaron Bloom?'

'He's a jerk.'

Davis shrugged at me. 'Last week they were best friends. They wanted me to show them how to become bloodbrothers. They were going to cut themselves with a fish scaling knife Aaron found in his dad's tackle box.'

'He's a jerk,' Mark repeated.

'Why is he a jerk?' I asked Mark.

Mark shrugged without looking up from his game.

I looked at Davis. He shrugged too.

I helped Davis put Mark to bed. As we were all walking up the stairs, Mark said to me, 'Mom lets me stay up later.' He wasn't complaining, merely pointing out an interesting fact, as if he had recently figured out that the world's rules weren't all the same, they changed from household to household. And if they weren't all the same, maybe they weren't automatically good rules.

Once Mark was tucked under the covers, Davis took the Gameboy. 'You need your sleep, pal. You've got soccer practice tomorrow.'

'Big deal. I stink at soccer.'

'All the more reason to practice.'

'Dad, if I practice and practice and practice, will I be the best soccer player in the world?'

'Depends how much you practice.'

'Dad, you've seen me play.'

Davis laughed. 'Okay, you won't be the best in the world, but you'll be better than you are now.'

'Well, if I'll never be the best, what's the point?'

Davis looked at me. 'Got an answer I could borrow? Preferably something wise and witty. Something he'll remember fondly years from now.'

'I'm tapped out in the wise and witty department.'

'Sorry, Mark,' Davis said. 'Guess you're just going to have to trust me on this one.'

'You always say that.'

'Have I ever been wrong?'

'About a billion trillion times.'

'Hey, anybody can make a billion trillion mistakes once in a while.'

Mark giggled. Davis kissed his cheek. I patted his chest. I didn't feel comfortable doing anything more maternal. I wasn't yet sure where I fit in the familial structure and I didn't want to confuse the boy.

Davis closed the door to Mark's bedroom. He led me to his own bedroom. I knew the way.

'We have the Gameboy!' he said, cackling like a mad scientist. 'It's all ours, they can't stop us now! Ha, ha, ha!'

Nothing stopped us. We made love with Davis behind me again. I was on my knees, rump in the air, head down on a pillow as if I were praying to Mecca. He had his fingers hooked around my hip bones as he pummeled me, our slapping skin making rude noises. At one point he took my hand and placed it on my vagina, guiding my middle finger to my clitoris. I rubbed it vigorously and we both got so excited we came together shortly thereafter.

'How did class go?' he asked, lying beside me, one leg thrown over my legs.

'Fine.'

I was lying on my back, he was lying on his side.

'Fine?' he repeated. 'Nothing unusual?'

'Nothing to make a movie out of.'

'Low blow,' he laughed. 'Of course, if you're going to blow, low is the place to do it.'

I told him a little about class, the students, the confrontation with the guy who refused to leave, Carol Hill's toilets, some of what I'd taught in class because I knew it made me seem smarter than I was. I didn't mention Robby. Or Byron. Those incidents didn't fit into the image I had created for Davis. My forgery of Wren Caldwell.

Davis reached over and pressed a button on the remote control and the TV clicked on. My head was hanging backward off the edge of the bed, so I watched the screen upside down. A male news announcer was talking about gang violence in Los Angeles. A stray bullet had killed a ten-year-old innocent bystander playing in her yard. Then the female newscaster discussed AIDS testing in local high schools. I flopped over to watch the rest. Davis began scratching my back.

'Don't you get the sports channel?' I said. He didn't answer. I pulled the fluffy down quilt around me like a nest and propped my head up on both hands. Davis's fingernails raked lazily over my back. I started to nod off. What would it be like to wake up in this bed every morning, I wondered.

'Jesus!' Davis said, sitting up in bed.

Startled, I sat up too. I forced my eyes open, but I felt groggy, disoriented. 'What? What's the matter?'

Davis didn't answer. He was watching the television screen. I turned and watched too. A newswoman was standing outside a suburban home. Her face was clenched in a serious expression. A breeze kept whipping a lock of her dark hair across her chin. In the background, yellow police tape could be seen and milling men in uniforms. The words LYDIA ROSS and LIVE flashed across the bottom of the screen.

' . . . family and friends were shocked . . .'

I looked at the clock. I thought I'd just closed my eyes but I'd been asleep for fifteen minutes.

' . . . Denver authorities say the suspect has offered a full confession.' A Denver Police Department spokesperson came on the screen. The name Sgt. Wanda Fueher was on the screen beneath her. 'We have the suspect,

Roger Clemens, in custody. He has offered a full confession in the shooting of Ms. Christine Palmer. Apparently, he'd been stalking her for six months, ever since the operation. Ms. Palmer had gone to court last week and gotten a restraining order against Roger Clemens, preventing him from coming within 1,000 yards of her.'

'Did you know her?' I asked Davis.

'Sshh.' His eyes were fixed on the screen.

A psychiatrist was being interviewed. Dr. Philip Rardin. He was balding and his forehead was knotted in three deep furrows. 'It is not unusual sometimes for a young man to become obsessed with the sister or cousin of a loved one when she dies. He feels such unbearable grief that he must transfer his passion somewhere or explode.' Cut to a reaction shot of reporter Lydia Ross, looking serious again. Back to the shrink. 'In Mr. Clemens's case his wife was killed in a car accident. They both had agreed to be donors and her heart was transplanted into Christine Palmer. Usually the recipient of such a heart would be an older person, but in this case Ms. Palmer was a young woman about the same age as the dead wife. So it was easier for him to obsess on her.'

Cut back to Lydia Ross. She was walking now, slowly strolling down the sidewalk as if, now that the event was over, we should consider it from a philosophical position. 'And obsess he did. Following his wife's funeral and Christine Palmer's release from the hospital, Roger Clemens began following Christine Palmer. He called her at home, sometimes a dozen times a day. He sent her letters, cards, gifts. He offered to take her to Jamaica for two weeks. Apparently that was where he and his wife had honeymooned. Finally, Christine, still weak as she struggled to adjust to her new heart, petitioned the court to keep her unwanted suitor at an arm's distance. Today, the arm's distance proved not to be far enough. Not when there's a gun at the end of that arm.' She arched an eyebrow as if to say, Get it?

'Thank you, Lydia,' the anchorwoman said and introduced the sportscaster.

Davis swung his legs off the bed and picked up the phone. 'I'm sorry, Wren. I have to be going. I'm terribly sorry.'

'Did you know her?'

'No. This is just business. I have to go to Denver.' He started dialing.

'Christ, Davis. You're not going after her family for their story. Jesus.'

'Not their story. His. Roger Clemens.' He held up his hand to indicate he had someone on the line. He spoke into the phone. 'What's the next flight you have to Denver . . . No, it doesn't have to be direct . . . That's too late. What about through LAX? . . . Okay, that's good.' He made a reservation, giving his Mastercard number and expiration date.

When he hung up I said, 'I've never known anyone who knew their credit card number by heart.'

'It's a gift.'

We looked at each other. I squeezed the down comforter. I would not be waking up here in the morning. The bathroom had a skylight. When you showered, the sunlight spotlighted you. I would not be showering here in the morning. The sun would not be spotlighting me.

'I have to call my sister,' he said. He dialed again. His sister agreed to watch Mark for the night and take him back to his mother in the morning. Her voice was very loud and agitated. Before hanging up, I heard her say, 'I wish we were married sometimes so I could divorce you too.'

'See you soon, sis.' Davis hung up and stared at me again. 'I'm terribly sorry. You don't know how sorry. But I have to go. It's business.' He shook his head. 'I know that sounds lame.'

'Do you really think people want to see a movie about a woman who's stalked by the widower of the woman whose heart she received in a transplant?'

'Absolutely. We'll get some too-handsome actor in a

series who's looking to break his nice-guy image and prove he has depth. I expect it will be a big hit.' He stood up and pulled on his underpants. 'The only question now is who will produce this hit, me or some other guy.'

'Doesn't it bother you, flitting from personal tragedy to personal tragedy, like a bee flying from flowers somebody stepped on, trying to suck out the last drop?'

'That's good,' he chuckled. 'Now I remember why I hired you.'

'This kind of thing isn't entertainment, it's tragedy.'

'Shakespeare wrote tragedies, right?'

'Yes, but he gave us some insight into the nature of people. These movies aren't tragedy, they're gossip.' Davis didn't respond. His jaw was clenched as he busied himself looking for shoes. He looked hurt. I felt bad. I softened my tone. 'I don't know, Davis, it all seems so ghoulish.'

'It *is* ghoulish. It's ghoulish, morbid, twisted, and a few other words we could come up with if we put our heads to it. Don't you think I know that? But I do it now so that in a couple years I can see this kind of thing on the news and send some other schmuck to Bumfuck, Egypt, in the middle of the night. Then I can go to sleep with my wife and watch my kid play soccer the next day. What's wrong with that?'

'Nothing,' I admitted. Besides, who was I to be pointing fingers. Talk about ghoulish, I stole my dead friend's identity and now was interviewing a murderer for money. If it weren't for dead people, I wouldn't have a life.

While Davis hurriedly got dressed and packed, I went into the bathroom, closed the door, and sat on the toilet. I had to pee, but sometimes right after sex it takes me a while to get the tap flowing. I picked up a magazine from the stack in the wall rack. An airline magazine. A piece of paper, an old airline ticket receipt, marked one of the articles. I opened it on my lap and started reading. It was about Mark Spitz trying to make a swimming comeback at the next Olympics. He trained very hard every day, swam laps, watched what he ate. I got very excited thinking about training, what it would be like to work out hard every day, how good you must feel about yourself. I decided then I would take up swimming, buy a pair of goggles, and swim laps in the pool at my apartment complex.

I ended up not peeing. I flushed anyway because what would he think I was doing in here all this time if I didn't.

When I went back into the bedroom, Davis was dressed and ready. He wore a blue Polo shirt, khaki pants, and a tweedish sports jacket. His leather overnight bag was slung over his shoulder. 'You almost ready?'

'Take me one minute.'

'Okay, I'll see how Mark's coming along.' He dashed down the hallway.

I was dressed in less than a minute. I made the bed, tugging the fluffy down quilt into place. Then I sat on the edge of the bed and waited, reading the article. I noticed notations in the margins in Davis's handwriting. *Ken Olin as Mark Spitz? Jamie Lee Curtis as wife?*

'Ready?' Davis leaned in the doorway. 'We're ready.'

'Can I borrow this magazine?' I asked. 'I want to finish an article.'

'You have two forms of ID?'

We dropped Mark off at Davis's sister's house in Newport Beach, then we drove to LAX, which took about forty minutes.

'You don't have to wait,' he said. 'You can just drop me off at the curb.'

'I'll wait.'

He smiled. 'Good.'

We had coffee and donuts in the airport cafeteria. We held hands across the table. Granules of salt or sugar from previous customers ground under our wrists. We talked about actresses who'd had breast implants, then we talked about Denver, where he'd never been.

'All I know about Denver is what John Denver sings,' he said.

365

'Did you know John Denver's real name is John Deut-schendorf?' I said.

'Someone gave him some good advice to change it.'

'You don't mind someone changing their name?'

'Hey, that's show business. Who's going to take him seriously if his name is Deutschendorf? Makes him sound like a Nazi collaborator.'

'It means "German village".' He gave me an impressed expression. 'I had two years of German in high school.'

When we got to his gate, he hugged me close. His breath smelled like coffee. 'I'll be back in a day or so.'

'I'll be here.'

'I'll call. God, I don't want to leave you.'

'Don't.'

He sighed. 'Thanks for making it easy on me.'

'I'm sorry, I'm being selfish. Have a good flight. Get everybody's life story while you're there so you won't have to go back every time somebody commits a crime. Say hi to Mr. Deutschendorf. Have a Rocky Mountain high.'

He started to say something, then stopped. He shook his head and said, 'I'm afraid to say anything. I mean anything real. Like you'll have a clever comeback and I'll feel stupid.'

I started to say something like 'If you think what I'm saying is clever, you've been in Hollywood too long.' But I stopped myself. Instead I just leaned against him. He wrapped his arms around me and squeezed hard. It was like being back in that down quilt again, or standing in the shower under the skylight, the hot morning sun warming your face, water washing you clean.

*   *   *   *   *

The drive back to my apartment went quickly. I listened to a talk radio station where they discussed the water shortage in Lourdes. Five million pilgrims visit the city

366

each year to drink from the holy waters or bathe in them. For the first time, Lourdes is rationing the water to protect its 400-million-dollar annual income.

'Try the shower at Davis's house,' I said aloud. 'Same effect.'

Then I started thinking about Byron and how he'd marched into my classroom and taken over. That goofy drawing exercise of his had actually been a good idea. I thought of his face, battered and scarred, my own contributions on his chin. Jesus, what a life. What had he and Wren had in common? What had gone wrong?

I checked my rearview mirror for the white Subaru. Nothing.

Still, what Byron had done had helped me at the time. I had been falling apart. Robby was going to be a father. How many hours had he and I discussed that very issue. When we would have a child, what conditions were necessary for us to do a good job. How often we'd debated as to who would be the better parent. I'd voted for Robby. So had he.

Suddenly, while changing lanes on the 405 Freeway, I realized I wanted a baby. I wanted one right way, right that moment, or at least the inevitability of one. If an all-night insemination clinic were open, I'd have driven right in, spread my legs, and said, 'Okay, shoot me up with a kid.'

I pulled into an all-night drugstore instead. The store was brightly lighted and the aisles were packed with plastic-wrapped goodies. I found a pair of swim goggles in the sports department. They only had one kind, with blue lenses, so I bought it. Then I went to the jewelry counter and looked at the watches. I picked a man's Casio with all kinds of functions and dials. It cost eighty dollars, which I charged. It was a gift for Byron.

I was kind of excited now as I drove into the complex and parked the car. Byron had lost everything, including his watch, gambling. This would show him how much I appreciated what he'd done for me.

As I approached the front door I could hear Ethan's guitar upstairs. His windows were all closed, though, so I couldn't hear what he was singing. I couldn't even make out the melody clearly.

I entered the front door, quietly tiptoeing across the living room. The alarm clock/radio next to Byron's bed was playing some tinny music, jazz, I thought. Good, he was still awake. I could surprise him with my gift.

I sneaked into the kitchen to put down my purse, maybe grab a couple beers to set the spirit. But when I walked into the kitchen I saw the bird cage back in the middle of the floor, one of Wren's designer sheets thrown over it. I hoisted up the sheet and discovered Motown nodding off on his perch. What the hell was he doing back?

Footsteps.

I backed up behind the swinging door just as it eased open. The room was dark so it was hard for me to recognize anything more than a human form moving toward the refrigerator. Then the door opened and the refrigerator light snapped a beam of light on the figure.

She was tall, over six feet, slender through the waist and narrow at her hips. Her skin was dark, her thick braided hair hanging down her back to her waist like a black eel. She looked Native American.

Also, she was buck naked.

27

'Who the hell are you?' I said.

She didn't look up from the refrigerator. She studied the contents a few seconds, reached in for a couple cans of beer, and closed the door with her hip.

'I asked who you are?' I was shouting, I don't know why. I mean, what difference did it make who she was, I had a pretty good idea what she was doing and with whom. Even so, what did I care?

She still didn't answer me. When she turned toward the kitchen door with her beers, she noticed me and jumped back, startled. But she didn't say anything.

The kitchen door swung open and Byron entered, wearing those ratty volleyball shorts I'd first seen him in the day he ambushed Davis and me. The day he stepped on that snail. His shorts were on backward, which indicated the haste with which he'd dressed. His long hair was disheveled, no longer pulled into his ponytail. His dragonfly earring was not dangling from his lobe. He looked at me. 'Oh, hi,' he said.

The woman, more beautiful then I'd realized before, smiled at me. She handed a beer to Bryon and offered the other one to me with a gesture.

'No, I don't want a goddamn beer,' I snapped. 'Christ!'

The woman didn't say anything. She shrugged, popped the tab, and sipped some beer. Her dark nipples seemed enormous, like brown thumbs.

'No point in yelling at Shawna,' Byron said. 'She's deaf.'

'And mute, I suppose.'

'Yup.'

Shawna put her beer can on the counter and made some rapid hand gestures at Byron. He made some back. Shawna laughed. Her laugh was like a dry cough.

'You know sign language?' I said to Byron.

'ASL. American Sign Language.'

I don't know why, but this angered me even more. He had so many secrets. I only had one and he knew it.

'I took it in college as my second language,' he said. 'I thought it would be easier than Spanish.'

'Seems like your whole life has been seeking the path of least resistance.'

'Works for water, doesn't it?'

'How zen of you.' I looked over at Shawna. She drank from her beer can without any display of modesty. Not that she had anything to be modest about. Her body was perfect in ways you never thought existed outside airbrushed magazines. It made me want to put on more clothes. 'Doesn't she want to get dressed or something?'

He gestured at Shawna. She responded.

'What did she say?'

'She wants to know what you're doing in my apartment.'

'Your apartment, huh?'

'I thought I'd explained everything to her. Guess my sign language is a little rusty.'

I looked at Shawna and she smiled again. Her teeth were perfect slabs of light, white marble doors to some exotic palace. A drop of condensation dripped from her beer can, bounced onto her stomach, and rolled into the thicket of black pubic hair. She caught me looking and her smile widened. I looked away, embarrassed.

'What's the bird doing back?' I said. 'I thought you lost it.'

'I did. To Shawna.'

'Then who beat you up? Shawna?'

'Someone else. It's complicated.'

That was it. I was standing in my own home being treated like a child too stupid to understand the big bad world. No more. I grabbed his shorts by the waistband, pulled them open, and stuffed the Save-on Drugs paper-bag with the watch and goggles down the front. 'For you,' I said. 'Thanks.'

'Owww,' he jerked away from me. He reached down and pulled the bag out.

I straight-armed the door open and marched out of the kitchen and down the hall toward Byron's room. 'I've had it with all this mystery bullshit. It's complicated? Let me help you simplify it.' I stormed into his bedroom, grabbed a handful of clothing from the closet, and carried it to the front door. I opened the door and tossed everything onto the sidewalk. 'There, does that make things simpler?'

Byron was strapping on the watch to his wrist. 'Hey, a new watch. Thanks.'

'That's okay,' I said. I returned to the bedroom, opened a drawer, scooped up an armful of underwear and socks, and carried them back to the front door. Heave ho. Onto the sidewalk.

'It's got a stopwatch too,' he said with delight. 'Cool.'

'I'm glad you like it.' Back to the bedroom. Shawna was in there now, pulling on her jeans without any underwear. When she hiked the jeans over her hips, her buttocks didn't bunch up around her spine like with most women. The jeans just slid over the dark, solid muscle. She slipped into a sweatshirt, not bothering with a bra. I dug into the next drawer and came up with an armful of T-shirts. She came over, pulled open a third drawer, and picked up a couple of new sweaters.

We formed a mini parade out to the living room. Byron was sitting in the front stoop reading the directions for his watch. His clothes lay scattered across the sidewalk five feet away. 'It's got three alarms and counts laps when you swim. Are the goggles for me too?'

I tossed my armload onto the sidewalk. Shawna did the

371

same thing. On the way back in I snatched the goggles from his hand.

Shawna laughed her hoarse laugh and gestured at Byron. He gestured back.

'What?' I said.

'She says you must know me pretty well to dislike me this much.'

'Did you tell her who I am?'

'Who's that?'

'Don't play zen master with me, okay? Did you tell her I was your wife Wren or your roommate Luna?'

'What's the difference?' he said. 'You afraid she'll talk?'

'You're sick.' I was suddenly exhausted from throwing his stuff out. I went into the living room and flopped onto the sofa. Shawna went to the kitchen and brought me a beer. 'Thanks,' I said.

'This is thanks in ASL,' Byron said, sitting on the floor across from me. He brought his hand up to his lips as if to stifle a yawn, then pushed his hand away and down. 'See?'

I repeated the gesture to Shawna. She extended her hand palm up out to the side and sliced it inward toward her waist.

'That's "welcome,"' Byron said.

I sipped the beer and closed my eyes. What was I doing here? I had been carefully creating a perfect life for myself, sketching in a proper profession, painting a rich background. Okay, so I was borrowing a bit from Wren, not unlike an artist imitating a better artist's style. A homage really. Truffaut imitating Hitchcock. The only problem was my work was being populated with characters from someone else's weird imagination. Byron, the battered gambler. Shawna, the deaf and mute beauty. Motown, the soul-singing bird. And, of course, Hector. The cat.

Byron stood up and closed the front door. He'd made no effort to retrieve his clothing. That made me edgy, as

372

if I'd somehow littered and everyone passing by would know.

'Don't you want your stuff?' I said.

He looked up from his watch, which he was still toying with. 'I know where it is.'

'Someone might take it.'

He shrugged. 'They'd have to be pretty hard up.'

'These are hard-up times.'

He laughed heartily, made some gestures at Shawna. They both laughed together.

'What?' I said. 'What's so funny?'

'What you said. "These are hard-on times."'

'I said hard-up not hard-on.'

He shrugged again. 'Oh. I thought you said hard-on.'

'Aren't you going to tell her?' I pointed to Shawna. I didn't want her thinking I'd said what I hadn't.

'Why ruin the joke?' he said and sat down on the floor next to Shawna.

There's a strange helplessness in having someone in the room with whom you can't communicate. It makes you feel like you need to be on your best behavior because if they can't understand your words, they would try to figure you out by observation. I caught myself gnawing my cuticles and lowered my hand.

The other thing that bothered me was that Shawna and I were both women, but the only way we could communicate was through a man. There was something sinister in that. Something wrong.

'You mustn't think very much of me to have her over and not even close your bedroom door,' I said to Byron.

'You told me you wouldn't be home tonight, remember? What happened to Davis?'

I didn't answer. Hector slinked into the room, walked around rubbing against everyone's leg, then left.

Shawna stood up, gestured, and followed Hector into the kitchen. I heard her opening a can of cat food.

'What is she, some kind of Indian?'

'Italian. But she likes to cultivate the whole Native

373

American image. It's cooler to be Apache than Italian.'

'Where'd you meet her?'

'She's a player.'

I made a skeptical face. 'Why is it so hard to believe anything you say?'

'No one else has a problem believing me.'

'Maybe they don't know you.'

He laughed harshly. 'You don't know me.'

'I know you didn't learn sign language in college. You're too good, too fast for someone just looking for easy credits. That takes years of constant practice, like playing the piano.'

'That's very good. Okay, you caught me. You wanted some truth, okay, here's some truth: My father was deaf. He wasn't born that way, it happened to him in high school. Got an ear infection and that was that. He was an art director for an advertising agency. He died in a hotel fire at a convention because he couldn't hear the fire alarm. Smoke inhalation.' He smiled. 'But I really did take ASL in college. I pretended I didn't know any so I could get the easy language credits.'

'Why didn't you just tell me that in the first place? Why this constant Man o' Mystery act?'

His face got serious. 'You want to know why I don't tell you anything? I'll tell you why. Because my life isn't just background for your impersonation. I'm not just a prop so you can be more and more like Wren. What you're doing is sick.'

'Gee, moral lectures from you really carry a lot of weight. I'm sure your pals at the prison appreciated it as much as I do. Did you hold sermons in the showers?'

'Don't feel so fucking superior to them. One call to the cops and you could be in a cell yourself.'

I jumped up and started screaming. 'Don't threaten me in my own home! You want to make a call?' I marched over to the phone, picked it up, and threw it at him. The receiver flew off and clipped him on the shoulder. 'Then just fucking do it! Do it! Do it!'

I was trembling, knees shaking, eyes burning. I was scaring myself.

He looked at me for a long time. Then a slow grin spread across his face. 'I didn't know you were such a screamer. From what I heard of you and your boyfriend this afternoon, you're more of a moaner.'

I froze, my face flushed. My voice went small. 'You were here?'

'Just for a quick nap. I'd been up all night playing. But how could I sleep with the two of you in the same house. Don't you know that bathrooms magnify sound?' He laughed.

'You're a pig,' I said. 'It's no wonder Wren dumped you.'

His face tightened. I'd hurt him. Good. 'You don't know shit about what happened between Wren and me. You think you do, but you don't.'

'I know she never wanted to see you again. If you're so fucking wise, Confucius, how come you couldn't hold on to her?'

His jaw clenched the way Davis's had earlier when I'd hurt him. Only this time I didn't feel sorry.

Byron unstrapped the watch from his wrist and tossed it to me. 'Here. I didn't come into your classroom to help you. I just didn't want you to ruin Wren's name any more with your pathetic performance.'

My mouth tasted like a toxic waste dump. I was dizzy with anger. 'You don't want this watch?' I said calmly. I put the watch on the floor and started stomping on it. I looked down but I could see it was still working. I jumped on it with all my might, but the shockproof cover wouldn't break. I picked it up by the strap and started whacking it against the edge of the coffee table. Finally the cover shattered. I tossed the broken watch back at him. 'Check your warranty.'

Shawna came back in carrying Hector. Hector was licking his lips.

I put my hands together as if to pray and pressed them

against my cheek to indicate sleep. Shawna laughed and nodded understanding. She waved. I went to my room and closed the door.

I washed my face, brushed my teeth, and peed. I undressed to my panties and climbed into bed. My body was still trembling with emotion. I pulled the covers tight around me, using the edge of my hand to tuck the blanket along the outline of my body. I smoothed out every wrinkle.

I was scared. This wasn't me. I wasn't sure it was Wren either. I had never acted with such manic passion before, not even when Robby left me. It was as if I'd tapped some underground oil well and my bile was gushing all over the wildcatters. Or like a science fiction film. I was the nice scientist trying to create something good for humanity, only to have my creation turn into something horrible: half human/half fly; half human/half wolf; half human/half Luna.

I tried to sleep. But every time I'd nod off some horrible nightmare would jolt me awake. At 3:18 A.M. I was still staring at the clock.

Down the hall I heard noises. Bedboards creaking. Mattress bouncing. Grunting. Strangled cries. I listened, watched the clock. 3:23. 3:35. 3:42. The noises didn't stop.

At 3:45 I reached down under the covers and slipped my panties off. I slid my fingers between my legs. I was a little sore from having had sex with Davis twice today. But I didn't stop. I couldn't have stopped.

28

In my dream, I was walking down a long hospital corridor.
But there were no doctors or patients. At first I thought I
was alone, but then I felt the pressure of a pair of strong
hands holding on to my waist and I knew somehow that
Davis was behind me and that Byron was holding his waist
behind him and that Robby was behind him. I didn't know
who else was back there, but I was certain they went on
for several miles like an enormous cha-cha line.

I turned quickly to try to see Davis, but as soon as
I moved, they all swung behind me so I couldn't see
any of them. I took another couple of steps, pretending
to ignore them, then I suddenly whirled around to catch
them off guard. But they must have whirled too, because no one was there. I was like the head of a long
fat caterpillar, I could never see my body. I looked
down at the hands gripping my waist. One was female,
the other male.

'Oh, I get it,' I said aloud. 'This is some sort of yin-yang
thing, right? Some male/female conflict, right side of the
brain battling with the left side? Right?'

'One, two, cha cha cha . . .' someone in line behind me
answered. It sounded like Paul Simon.

But then I walked into a hospital room. It was a birthing
room, one of the new kind made to look like a bedroom.
Wren was there. And Esther. Esther's cat, Sphinx,
was on the white bed. They all looked happy to see
me.

'Get in,' Wren said, gesturing at the bed.

377

'Will we all fit?' I asked, hooking a thumb over my shoulder at my entourage.

She laughed and helped me into the bed. The cat curled up on my lap. Esther expertly injected me with a shot in the arm and Wren began attaching tubes to my arms, legs, and nose.

'This is just like the dream sequences on *St. Elsewhere*,' I said. 'Remember that show?'

'I could never stay awake that late,' Esther said. She stifled a yawn.

'What's going on?' I said.

'You want to be just like us,' Wren said. 'The doctor will help.'

'I don't want to be like BeeGee,' I said. 'No offense, Esther.'

Esther had nodded off. She snored to the melody of 'I Whistle a Happy Tune.'

I started scratching the cat's neck. I felt so happy to be there, like I could relax for the first time. No secrets.

'You guys look good,' I said.

'Think so?' Wren said. She grinned and nodded at my hand that was scratching the cat. I looked down. My fingers were covered with blood and matted fur. I'd scratched the cat's fur off his head as if it were a mask. Sphinx turned and looked at me, his face a bloody clump of muscle and bone. A bullet was lodged in his cheek.

Wren reached up and pulled off her own face. She nudged Esther awake with an elbow and Esther also began yanking her face off. Beneath their rubbery masks were the same wide-eyed bloody messes of bone and sinew, like in an anatomy book

'The doctor's here, Luna,' Wren said. 'Now you can be just like us. For real.'

Season Dougherty walked into the room wearing a doctor's green operating uniform, only hers had big prison stripes on them. She carried a shotgun.

378

'Hi, Wren,' she said to me. She aimed the shotgun at my crotch. 'You may feel a little discomfort.'

She fired.

*   *   *   *   *

That's pretty much how the rest of the night went. I couldn't sleep most of it, and when I did manage to drift off for a few minutes, I'd get sucked into another nightmarish horror that shocked me awake with cold sweats.

I tried reading once, finishing that article about Mark Spitz I'd borrowed from Davis. Afterward I managed to kill twenty minutes wondering how my life might have been different if I'd have won a gold medal in something at the Olympics.

About five in the morning I actually got up and put on my swimsuit. I figured that if I couldn't sleep this was as good a time as any to begin my new swimming program. I even tried on my goggles and looked at myself in the mirror. The blue lens made everything seem as if I were already underwater. Anyway, I never made it out of the bedroom. I stripped down and went back to bed.

At 6:45 A.M. I was working on a plan to murder Byron and hack up the body into cat food that I would feed to Hector. Maybe when he was gone I could rent the room to Shawna. When she wasn't fucking like an Amazon warrior-queen, she was pretty quiet. I could learn sign language and she and I could go to lunch and gossip about people at the next table without them knowing. We could 'talk' in the movies and no one would tell us to shut up. We'd be like secret agents, living undercover among the unsuspecting suburbanites, acting like them, eating the same foods, wearing the same clothes. Until our government activated us.

God, is this how BeeGee had lived for so long? All those years without proper sleep, night after night, her mind rambling on and on. I was nuts after only one night.

I guess the question isn't what caused Esther to finally snap, but what took her so damn long?

'*"I saw a stranger with your hair/Tried to make her give it back . . ."*'

I opened my eyes. The music was faint, but distinct.

'*" . . . So I could send it off to you/Maybe Federal Express . . ."*'

I looked at my clock. 7:12 A.M. I must have dozed for a few minutes, I dragged myself to the edge of the bed and sat there, unable to get up or even focus my gritty eyes.

The phone rang. I reached for my nightstand, only to remember that I was no longer living in the bedroom with the phone. Didn't matter. The ringing stopped.

'Hey, Wren,' Byron hollered from down the hall. 'For you. It's the Academy Award people. I think you've been nominated.'

I pulled on some sweatpants and a T-shirt and pattered off to the kitchen phone. When I opened the kitchen door, Motown, whose cage was no longer covered by a sheet, started singing, '*"Baby love . . . baby love . . ."* awwwk.'

I picked up the phone. 'Hello?'

'Tell me you miss me more than anything in the world or I'll kill myself with a rusty razor.'

'Who is this?' I said.

'Very funny.' Davis chuckled. 'You're not very romantic in the morning.'

'Rough night. I didn't get any sleep.'

'At least lie and tell me it was because you were missing me.'

'It's because I was missing you.'

'You're lying.'

I laughed. 'Not entirely. I do miss you. The only time my life has any sanity to it is when I'm with you.'

'If that ain't love, what is?'

'You know what I mean. You run off in the middle of the night, but at least you're honest about it. There are no secrets. I'm tired of secrets.'

There was a pause. 'You okay, sweetheart? You don't sound so hot.'

'I'm just tired. I didn't sleep all night. Did I already say that?'

'Yes. Maybe you should stay in bed today, rest.'

'No can do. I've got Season Dougherty sitting in a cell waiting for me to come over and rip her guts out with some of my insightful yet subtle questions.'

'You can take a day off,' he said. 'Lie to your boss.'

'My boss would know. He knows everything.' I was touched by the compassion in his voice. 'When you coming home, Red Ryder?'

'I don't know yet. Negotiations are tricky right now. Lots of lawyers smelling money. State laws prohibiting criminals to profit from their crimes. Et cetera, et cetera. Probably won't be back till tomorrow.'

'Oh.' I let my disappointment come through. He would appreciate it.

Byron walked into the kitchen. He was wearing nothing but those same stupid shorts. As he passed me I could smell the moist scent of sex. A couple of the stitches next to his ear had come out. He stopped at the bird cage, reached a finger in, and started scratching behind Motown's neck. Motown bent his head forward and snuggled up to Byron's finger.

'Say something romantic to keep me going,' Davis said. 'If you can't be romantic, dirty will do.'

I turned my back on Byron so he couldn't overhear me. I lowered my voice. 'Hurry home, okay? I miss you.'

'I miss you, too.' He paused again as if to say something. He sighed. 'I miss you. I really do.'

We repeated ourselves a few more times and then hung up.

Byron was still scratching the bird's neck. Just looking at Byron made me angry again. Certainly he was to blame for my not sleeping. Still, this was no way to act. One of us had to be mature.

381

'I didn't know you could do that,' I said. 'Scratch them like that.'

'They love it.'

'I figured they'd bite your finger off.'

'Only if you do it wrong.' He held up his right hand and wiggled his stump.

'Is that how you lost your finger?' I was just trying to make conversation, be friendly. I didn't even care anymore how he lost his stupid finger.

He ignored my question anyway and started singing to Motown. 'Love child, love child . . .'

'You really are an asshole,' I shouted. 'Why can't you just act like a normal human being for five fucking minutes? Would it kill you, you obnoxious piece of shit?'

Motown sang, ' "*Love child . . . love child . . .*" '

Byron opened the refrigerator, took out a carton of orange juice, and walked out of the kitchen without responding to me. I was so furious that I looked around for something to throw at him, a knife or a hammer. All I could see at that instant was the folded sheet that had covered Motown's cage overnight. I grabbed it from the table and burst through the kitchen door in a rage. He was walking down the hall drinking from the juice carton. I hurled the folded sheet at him, but it blossomed open like a parachute and fluttered harmlessly to the ground before reaching him.

He stopped, looked over his shoulder at the sheet, at me. He snorted and went in the bedroom.

I had never in my life wanted to kill anybody. Until that moment. If there'd been a shotgun in my room, within twenty minutes I'd have been in the cell next to Season Dougherty.

I looked around for something to break, but I didn't see anything that I wouldn't later regret having smashed. I went back to my room. It was later than I'd realized so I had to skip my shower and get dressed as quickly as I could. I didn't want to be late for my meeting with Season. I had a feeling that she looked forward to our conver-

382

sations. I don't know if we were friends exactly, but I think we trusted each other somehow. Maybe because I didn't judge her, maybe because she sensed I wasn't in a position to judge her. I actually felt good sitting there with her, the way I used to feel sitting with Wren and BeeGee, munching microwave popcorn, watching David Letterman on the TV in the refrigerator.

On my way out of the apartment I heard the familiar creaking of bedboards and the muffled throat spasms of Shawna's orgasms. Hector was waiting for me at the door. I noticed the smashed Casio watch I'd bought Byron was fastened around Hector's neck along with the flea collar. He sat next to the door as if he couldn't wait for me to go so the real fun could begin.

I opened the front door. Byron's clothing was still strewn across the sidewalk. I walked on top of it, grinding my heels into the fabrics with each step. That felt good.

When I arrived at the police station, I realized that in my hurry to get out of the apartment I'd pulled on a sleeveless sweater. My clean-shaven underarms, freshly sealed with Arid roll-on, were exposed. Season might balk at them, refuse to see me, demand I drop my pants so she could check the stubble on my legs. That wouldn't do.

I searched the car for another sweater or sweatshirt, something I might have crumpled into a corner unknowingly. I found a muddy white sock and half a pack of Life Savers, a balled-up pair of panty hose from my first meeting with Season. But no shirt.

A red Honda pulled into the space next to mine. A cop in his twenties got out wearing his uniform. He leaned into his car and brought out a hanger draped with freshly pressed civilian clothes still in the dry-cleaning plastic wrapper.

'Hi,' I said to him. 'I know this may sound stupid, but I wonder if you have a T-shirt or something I could borrow for a couple hours while I'm visiting someone. I get so cold in there and I forgot my sweater. I'll give it back. I promise.'

383

He looked me over. 'You the one who visits that woman who shot her husband? You're writing the book.'

'Yes.' I offered my hand. He shook it. 'I'm Wren Caldwell.'

He nodded. He looked at me as if trying to decide whether or not to make me walk a straight line, touch my fingers to my nose.

'You can hold on to my driver's license,' I said. 'Or a credit card.'

'No need,' he said, laying his clothes carefully across the roof of my car. 'Let's see what I've got.' He popped his trunk and rummaged through some golf clubs, a tennis racquet, a stack of *Newsweek* magazines that were bound with twine. He finally dug out his nylon sports bag and pulled out some wadded clothing: socks, jock strap, shorts, T-shirt. He sniffed the shirt. 'Still a little ripe. I wore it a couple days ago to play basketball.'

'That's fine,' I said, reaching for it. It was damp in a couple places and smelled like the produce drawer of my refrigerator. Season wouldn't notice through the glass. 'It smells like you won.'

'Yeah, we played hard.' He picked up his pressed clothes and pointed at the building. 'You can just drop it off at the desk when you've done. Tell them it's for Hirsh.'

'Thanks, Hirsh,' I said.

'Gary.' He waved and trotted off.

I pulled on the moist shirt and noticed the front said in bold black letters: 'WERE IT LEFT TO ME TO DECIDE WHETHER WE SHOULD HAVE A GOVERNMENT WITHOUT NEWSPAPERS OR NEWSPAPERS WITHOUT A GOVERNMENT I SHOULD NOT HESITATE A MOMENT TO PREFER THE LATTER' Beneath the quote it said: THOMAS JEFFERSON . Beneath that it said: SUPPORT THE FIRST AMENDMENT ACLU.

A cop with an ACLU T-shirt? Was he kidding or what? As I walked into the police station wearing this T-shirt, I felt as if I had a huge red target painted on my chest. I forced a big smile on my face and walked up to the guard, Officer Cooper, who usually brought Season out and sat in attendance while we visited. He sat behind his desk with his Scientology pamphlets open.

I asked him which he'd rather live without, his wife or the carpet. He decided it was petty after all.

'Hello, Officer Cooper,' I said. I nodded toward the door that led to the cells where Season was waiting. 'Once more into the breech.'

He gave me a nervous look. 'Uh, could you have a seat please, Ms. Caldwell. My captain wants to speak to you.'

'Sure,' I said, trying to sound calm, even cheerful.

He turned and disappeared through the door. My stomach felt as if someone were doing heavy spadework inside. What was wrong? My T-shirt? Or maybe they found out about me. They ran some kind of fingerprint check on me, discovered who I was, and were coming out to arrest me. I should run, jump in the car, and keep driving. I knew what I was doing was illegal. Last week I saw on the news they'd arrested some twenty-five-year-old guy in Los Angeles who'd dressed as a girl and enrolled in high school. He even joined the cheerleading squad as a girl. They'd interviewed students at the school. They all said he was very popular and funny. A couple were more suprised that he was twenty-five than that he was a guy. The police charged him with criminal impersonation.

Still, I didn't run. Maybe it was nothing important. They wanted to know how I would portray their department in my book. Maybe something like that. I sat next to Officer Cooper's desk and started browsing through his Scientology stuff. There was a pamphlet. On the cover was a cluster of photographs of smiling well-dressed people, most of them shot through some filmy lens. At the bottom was their motto: Improving Life in a Troubled World.

I opened the questionnaire. You could answer either (1) yes or mostly yes, (2) maybe or uncertain, or (3) no or mostly no. *Do you make thoughtless remarks or accusations that you later regret?* Mostly no. *Is it hard on you when you fail?* Mostly . . . Hmmm. Uncertain. I skipped ahead. *Do you rarely suspect the actions of others?*

The door opened and Officer Cooper and another man came out. The man was in his forties, slightly paunchy. His mustache was thick as my wrist.

'Ms. Caldwell?' he said politely.

'Yes.' I stood up. I watched his hands, expecting handcuffs to come flashing out.

'I'm Captain Hernandez.' His hand came out, but nothing was in it.

I shook it. 'Is there some problem?'

'Well, yes. I'm afraid Mrs. Dougherty committed suicide early this morning.'

I stared at him stupidly. 'She's dead?'

'Uh, yes, the suicide was successful.'

'I don't . . . I'm not . . .' I couldn't think how to finish any sentence.

'Perhaps you'd like to sit down.' He nodded at Officer Cooper, who quickly pushed a chair behind me. I backed away from the chair, but Officer Cooper followed behind me with it. I spun away from both of them. 'I'm fine, really. I don't want to sit.'

Captain Hernandez nodded at Officer Cooper. Cooper put the chair back where he got it.

'How did she do it?' I asked.

'She hung herself,' Officer Cooper said.

'Hanged,' Captain Hernandez corrected. 'Pictures are hung; people are hanged. Am I right, Ms. Caldwell?'

I didn't feel much like participating in a grammar lesson. I nodded. 'Yes.'

'Hanged herself,' Officer Cooper said.

'She used her jumpsuit,' Captain Hernandez said. 'Twisted it into a rope and did it. Very unusual.'

'Aren't there people who watch her? Other prisoners who could see her?'

He shook his head. 'She did it while the others were asleep. Or if they saw her, they didn't bother to stop her.'

386

I didn't know what else to say. I tried to force myself to think like a reporter. What would I do next?

'Do you want to see her cell?' Captain Hernandez offered. 'I mean, for your book.'

'Her cell?'

'It's no problem. We cooperate thoroughly with the press. We have nothing to hide here.'

'No. I don't think so. Not right now.' I started to leave.

'Just a moment, Ms. Caldwell. Mrs. Dougherty left something for you.'

I turned around. 'She left something for me?' I spoke in slow and stupid tones. I felt as if I were in the next room overhearing our conversation. Who is that idiot woman in the baggy T-shirt?

He opened the drawer to Officer Cooper's desk and took out a manila envelope. Wren Caldwell was handwritten across it.

'She left a suicide note,' he said. 'In it, she stated that she wanted you to have this book.'

I opened the manila envelope and slid the book out. *Modern Plaque Removal Techniques*. I looked at Captain Hernandez with puzzlement.

He shrugged. 'She didn't say anything else, just to give that to you.'

I leafed through the pages, looking for a note she might have stuffed in there, or maybe some writing in the margins. Nothing. The inside covers had been slit and clumsily taped back together.

'We gave it a thorough going over,' he said. 'We didn't find anything either.'

'Thanks,' I said.

'Investigators will be in touch, Ms. Caldwell. They'll just want a brief statement from you about Mrs. Dougherty's state of mind, that sort of thing.'

I nodded and started to leave again.

'See you're wearing Hirsh's shirt,' he said jovially. 'Hell of a basketball player. Can't shoot worth shit, but he's fearless on the rebounds.' He acted as if he thought Hirsh and I were dating and he needed to put in a few good words. 'Can't think of anybody I'd rather have on my team. Pound for pound, he's the best.'

* * * * *

The car was hot. I didn't roll down the windows. I didn't start the engine. I sat there leafing through the pages of *Modern Plaque Removal Techniques* for the fiftieth time. I'd returned Officer Hirsh's T-shirt to the cop at the front desk, but my sweater still retained some of the pungent ammonia odor. The heat inside the car made it worse. Still, I kept leafing.

I didn't know what I was looking for anymore. There were drawings and photographs of teeth in various stages of decomposition. Some very nasty-looking gums. But no code words written on the teeth, no pleas for understanding, justifications for suicide. No nothing.

Then why give me this stupid book?

Maybe this was a professional message. Something was wrong with my teeth. I adjusted the rearview mirror and bared my teeth. I pulled back the lips and studied my gums. They looked fine. Or was that a speck of something cancerous near my incisor? I held up the book and looked back and forth between a drawing and my teeth.

A speck of light flickered through the page.

I pasted the page against the windshield where the sun was blasting through. A tiny pinprick of light flared next to the page number. Page 61.

Again I thumbed through each page, holding each up to the light. I found more pages with pinpricks next to the page numbers. Each page that was marked had a different number of pinpricks, which I assumed indicated the order of the numbers. Page 61 had one hole. Page 95 had two. Page 55 had three. Page 182 had four. Page 9 had five.

6195551829.

A locker combination? Swiss bank account?
A phone number.
Even the dead have secrets.

* * * * *

When I arrived back at my apartment, Byron's clothes no longer covered the sidewalk entry. The house was clean, the dishes done, the carpet vacuumed. I didn't see anybody, though, so I sneaked down the hallway and suctioned my ear to Byron's bedroom door. I could hear splashing in the bathtub and his laughter, the kind caused by two people being intimate.

I tiptoed to the kitchen, picked up the phone, and dialed the mystery number. It rang for quite a while, ten or fifteen rings. I was about to hang up when it stopped ringing and a little girl's voice said, 'Hello?'

Jesus. Season's daughter.

'Jamie?' I said.

She didn't answer.

I heard rapid footsteps on the other end. A woman whispering harshly, ' . . . told you never to answer when I'm not here . . .'

' . . . thought it might be Mommy . . .' the little girl whispered back.

'Hello?' the woman said firmly. 'Who's this?'

I hung up.

I wandered into my bedroom and closed the door. I dropped onto my unmade bed and pulled a pillow over my face. The pillow smelled like Hector, dank and earthy. I sat up and noticed muddy paw prints across my sheet, a patch of shed hair on the pillowcase.

I did the right thing hanging up, I thought. What did I hope to gain by talking to them? There's nothing that they could say that would make any difference. Season was dead. Why had she bothered going through such an elaborate ruse to give me the phone number? What did she

389

think I would do? Did Season think I would try to figure out why she killed herself? I didn't really care about other people's secrets. I had my own to nurture.

I picked up another pillow, studied it for cat hair. None. I sniffed it. It smelled like Finesse shampoo. I flopped back and smothered myself under its dark softness. I pulled it around my ears.

I tried to imagine Season hanging in her cell. I pictured dangling legs, like they show you on cop shows because it's TV and they can't show you the strangled face, swollen tongue. I read somewhere they vacate their bowels. If Season used her jumpsuit as a rope, what was she wearing? Did she dangle there in her prison-issue bra and panties, her urine and shit dripping down her legs. I pulled the pillow closer against my face. Breathing was very difficult.

Why had Season entrusted the phone number to me when she'd fought so hard to keep it a secret? Did she kill herself because she feared she was cracking, that she might end up revealing her daughter's hiding place? Her husband was dead, why keep the girl hidden anyway?

'Fuuuuuuck!' I screamed into the pillow. The feathered stuffing absorbed my holler like a silencer smothers a gunshot. Fuck sounded like aaaaaawk. I sounded like Motown. Maybe I could take over his life next, sit in a cage and sing Supremes' titles all day. It was bad enough to be tightwire-walking through Wren's life, now I was thrust into Season's.

This wasn't me. I was no crusading reporter, the truth and I weren't even on speaking terms. Now that I thought about it, I never pursued Esther's death, never looked into why she might have killed herself or even why she shot Wren and me? I just passed it off as an insomnia-induced breakdown, visited her grave, and left it at that. Did I even bother chasing down the reasons Robby and I broke up? Not really. I focused on the effects. What it did to me physically, as if the shock were so great that I was actually taking another step in evolution, the way cockroaches adjust to radiation. I don't look for meaning or insight, just clarity. It's kind of like watching TV; I'm the one who keeps adjusting the contrast, the color, the tint for a better picture, not really caring about the quality of the show. I just take things as they are.

The front door to the apartment opened. I sprang out of bed and peeked out the curtain. Byron and Shawna were walking to her car in the parking lot. Byron was dressed in black jeans, a white shirt, and a black knit tie. His hair was combed and pulled back into his ponytail. He looked like he was going to court. Shawna wore cutoff jeans and a white T-shirt knotted at her belly. Shawna was carrying the iron bird stand, Byron was carrying the bird cage. Inside the cage, Motown kept pacing sideways along his perch to compensate for the rough turbulence. Hector followed them, trotting like a show horse, his tail sticking straight up in the air.

Shawna kissed Byron on the cheek and got in the car. The casualness of that peck seemed somehow more intimate than if I'd stood next to their bed and watched them screwing all night. They exchanged hand gestures through the open window, then she drove off.

Byron waved at her until she was out of sight. I watched, waiting for him to come back in. I was going to have it out with him once and for all, no punches pulled.

But he didn't come back. He started across the parking lot toward the street that ran parallel to the complex. Hector didn't follow. He sat on the curb and watched.

I made a decision. I would follow Byron. Get in my car and follow him to where this gambling thing took place. I would find out what he was up to, undoubtedly illegal, then I would have more leverage. I could kick him out and he couldn't talk to anybody lest I do some talking of my own. Maybe it wasn't a shotgun blast to the crotch, but it would be the next best thing.

I grabbed my purse and hurried for the front door. As I rounded the corner into the living room, the phone rang.

I hesitated. It rang a few more times. The machine answered, playing my announcement.

'Sweetheart, I just heard,' Davis's voice said. He sounded breathless, as if he'd just run a couple of blocks. 'Are you there? Pick up, Wren.' Pause. I looked over at the phone. My feet started toward it, but slowly, too slowly to actually reach it. I didn't want to talk, I wanted to follow Byron. I wanted to get the liars out of my life.

'Okay, you must know about Season by now,' Davis continued. 'Jesus, that's terrible. I wish I were there with you. I just don't want you to worry, everything will be okay. The book deal is still on, so you're okay there. I know that sounds very Hollywood of me, but right now I'm more interested in your well-being than anything else.' Another long pause. 'I'll call you later, sweetheart. I don't know what else to say . . .' He hung up.

I walked out the door and jogged to my car. If Byron had walked to the main street, that meant he was taking the bus. The bus stop was at the end of the block.

I nosed my car as far out of the driveway as I could without actually turning onto the street. I saw Byron at the bus stop talking to a Hispanic woman carrying a large shopping bag. The only Hispanics I'd seen so far in Irvine were domestics who came by bus in the morning, cleaned the houses, condos, and townhouses, and left by bus in the afternoon. Some lived in permanently, but they usually wore uniforms.

I waited in the driveway with my car idling. When another car came up behind me to exit, I waved it around me. The drivers would always peer in at me as if I were crazy. Finally, Byron's bus came. He helped the Hispanic woman in, holding her bag for her.

'Count whatever you had inside your bag,' I warned her.

Then Byron climbed aboard the and bus took off.

I followed it with ease for about two miles. That's when I looked into my rearview mirror and noticed that I too was being followed. By a white Subaru.

392

29

The exhaust from the bus was bitter. I pulled the front of my sweater up over my nose to filter the air, but my sweater still smelled of Officer Hirsh's sweaty T-shirt and last weekend's basketball game. So I alternated between carbon monoxide and ammonia.

The Subaru dropped back a couple of cars, but I could still see him back there, keeping pace, darting in and out of line to see what I was doing. My attitude was surprisingly calm. I wasn't angry at him any more than I was angry at Byron. I simply had a job to do here, some house-cleaning in my life, and I looked on the Subaru and Byron as stubborn stains in the middle of an otherwise spotless carpet. My only concern was removing those stains from the shag pile of my life.

In the case of the Subaru, a little elbow grease was required. And I knew just how to apply it.

Byron's bus grumbled down Jamboree Street like a Rose Bowl float, pulling over to suck up a couple of passengers or belch out a couple. Whenever it stopped, I stopped, pulled my sweater up over my nose like a bandit, and waited. Other cars always pulled around me and sped off, shaking their heads at me or flipping me the bird, something editorial like that. The white Subaru, without the shield of cars, had no other choice but to sit it out right behind me and wait too.

We were all idling there in the slow lane at the intersection of Campus and Jamboree: the bus, me, the Subaru. The car that had been between me and the Subaru, a blue

Mustang, had pulled out with a screech. As he passed me, the balding driver yelled, 'The pedal on the right makes your car go forward!'

I looked in the rearview mirror. The Subaru didn't inch forward the way cars do when someone leaves a lane. Traffic abhors a vacuum. But not him. So I shifted into reverse, eased off the clutch, and stomped the gas pedal. My car rocketed backward twenty-five feet until it smashed into the front end of the Subaru. An explosion of glass and the sound of crunching metal echoed dully through my car. My body snapped forward against my seat belt and rebounded backward into my seat.

I checked the other driver in my mirror. He looked stunned, his eyes glazed and his expression disoriented. Blood dripped down from his mouth into his beard.

I unbuckled my seat belt and leapt out of the car. I ran back to his car. It was the same man Ethan and I had chased away the other night. 'Are you okay?' I asked.

'I bih mah tug,' he said, holding his striped tie against his mouth to soak up the blood.

'You bit your tongue? I'm sorry. You shouldn't follow so closely.'

'Closely. I wass twety-fahv feeh away!'

'Then I guess you shouldn't follow at all.'

He groaned and rubbed his neck. On the seat next to him were half a dozen empty cans of diet Slice and a box of Vanilla Wafers.

The bus carrying Byron pulled away from the curb and lumbered down the street.

'You can wait for the police if you want, maybe tell them why you're following me. Why are you following me?'

'I'b nah followin you. You cwazy.'

I slapped him hard on his sor. mouth. He hollered in pain, his eyes tearing up instantly. That's when I reached in and pulled his keys out of the ignition. I tossed them across the street, on the other side of six lanes of steady traffic. Not a bad throw, really.

I ran back to my car, jumped in, and took off after Byron's bus. Something rattled at the back of the car now, but it was worth a little body damage to see myself handle the situation so capably. Just like in the movies. Sigourney Weaver blasting aliens left and right, all the while standing around in her underwear.

But who was I now? Wren? Season? BeeGee? Wild sex, ramming cars, slapping people, following convicts. That wasn't Luna of the lifeless hair and steel-rimmed glasses. Whose life was I leading now?

Eventually Byron transferred to another bus, which I followed down Pacific Coast Highway to Laguna Beach. He got out and walked a couple blocks to a small restaurant that had a few tables corraled outside. He walked up to a man about his age who was already seated and sat down. They immediately leaned close and began talking in a hushed huddle.

I pulled my rattling car against a no parking red curb and spied on them for a while. The new guy wore slacks and an Oxford button-collar shirt. He kept pulling papers out of a battered suitcase and showing them to Byron. Byron studied them, nodded, pointed at various things on the pages, and they talked. What were they discussing? Drug deals? Fencing stolen goods? Blueprints for a house they intended to burglarize?

'Hey,' someone said next to my car.

I turned and looked up at a uniformed cop. 'Hi,' I said.

'You can't park here. It's a red zone.'

'I'm just waiting for a friend . . .' I looked at the stores along the curb. Hardware, bank, frozen yogurt. 'She's just making a deposit in the bank.'

'Sorry, but you'll still have to move it.'

'Okay,' I said. I started the engine and pulled away. He stood in the street and watched me until I was all the way down the block. I circled the block and returned down the same street. Byron and his friend were no longer sitting at the table.

'Shit!' I said. 'Goddamn it!'

But then I spotted them coming out of the bank. Byron handed him a thick envelope. The man opened it and I could see that it was stuffed with money. He counted through it. Byron said something and the man shrugged, looking disappointed. Byron said something else and laughed. The other guy, very studious-looking, laughed too. They shook hands and left in opposite directions.

Now I wasn't sure who to follow. In *All the President's Men*, when Woodward and Bernstein were busting Watergate, Deep Throat told them to 'follow the money'. That seemed to work for them. Maybe I should follow the Oxford shirt and see what he does with the money.

But I stayed with Byron. I had a hunch that he hadn't come all the way down to Laguna Beach just to meet with this guy, not when there were other restaurants and banks more convenient to our apartment.

Since there was no way I could follow him in a car without him spotting me, I crawled along for a few blocks until I found a parking place to tuck my car. Now we were both on foot. I stayed a block behind him, sometimes more depending on the number of other pedestrians I could use to shield myself. I also hung close to the buildings, where I might suddenly duck into a doorway or pretend to window-shop if he got suspicious and turned around. He didn't, though, so I started to feel pretty confident with my shadowing technique. I was surprised at how much practical stuff I'd actually picked up from watching billions of hours of cop shows over the years. I'd disabled the Subaru and now I was following someone on foot.

Byron was walking away from the beach toward the residential area up on the cliffs. The streets were winding higher and higher, with each inclination offering bigger and more expensive houses. The lawns became larger, the gardens more bountiful. We passed several Hispanic gardeners blowing leaves with their loud machines.

Finally, Byron found the house he was looking for, a two-storey mansion with white columns and a brick front, a bizarre architectural hybrid of colonial farmhouse and gothic mansion. Byron marched down the sidewalk to the front door and just walked in the house without ringing the bell or knocking. Apparently, he was expected.

I stood looking at the house for a while. What should I do now? Just stand here all day in the hot sun until Byron came out again? I wouldn't really know anything more about him from the safety of this sidewalk, nothing I could use as counterblackmail. I needed to get closer.

I looked around the neighbourhood. These were million-dollar homes, each with lots of trees and blooming flowers. Fancy mailboxes with iron-stenciled names attached. Cars in driveways: Volvos, BMWs, Accuras, Mercedes. Safe cars. Safe neighbourhood. What could happen to me here?

I started down the cobblestone walk toward the house. I found myself straining to hear a bird chirping. I knew I'd feel better about all this if I could hear some birds chirping. No one would hurt me in a neighbourhood where birds were chirping. I heard something, but it could have been a cricket. Crickets didn't make me feel safe.

I raised a fist to knock on the front door. No, that would be stupid. I was here to spy, not visit. I tiptoed off the front porch and sneaked around the side of the house, stooping next to the well-trimmed bushes that surrounded the house like parsley around lamb chops. I guess the idea of bushes around the edges of a house is to make the building look like it has no edges, as if it just blends in with nature. But it doesn't. A house is just a mixture of cement and wood and plumbing pipes and electrical wires and skylighted showers and down-quilted beds. I didn't know why I was thinking that as I crept around the huge house. Maybe because I was beginning to suspect I was never going to live in such a house in such a neighborhood where cul-de-sacs were plentiful and children let out from school could play unthreatened. This wasn't a house where criminals like Byron should be allowed to just walk in and run whatever illegal activity he was involved in. It was a place for families. Where little Bobby builds a fort out of dirty laundry, or precious Amy traps a spider under a glass and studies it there until it suffocates and she cries all night over the loss.

I felt a yank in the pit of my stomach, a longing to be at a mall selecting wallpaper for the bedroom of my someday-to-be-born child. I made a fist and punched myself in the stomach twice and the longing disappeared.

I heard voices. Men. I raised myself up enough to peek through the window.

'Looking for something,' the voice behind me said. I felt something hard and pointed pressed against my spine. For lack of any other response, I put my hands up.

PART THREE

How To Have a Near-Love
Experience

30

'She's mine. I'm gonna take her,' he threatened.

'Go ahead, take her,' Byron said. 'Go crazy.'

'I'm gonna do it, man. You think I'm kidding?'

'Then do it. Time's running out.' Byron pointed to the clock next to him. Two clocks, really, attached to each other in a wooden case. He started tapping his finger against the card table like a metronome.

The other guy sucked his lower lip between his teeth and started gnawing. I could see tiny white scars crisscrossing his lip from decades of gnawing. 'Fuck you, man. I'm not gonna be psyched out by your bullshit. She's mine.'

Byron shrugged. 'Your choice.'

The other guy reached across the wooden chess board between them, picked up his white bishop, slid it diagonally across the board, snatched up Byron's black queen between his last two fingers, and set his bishop down on the vacated square. Instantly he slapped the silver button at the top of the two-faced clock beside the board.

'I just fucked your queen, pal. Stew on that. I humped and bumped and pumped her and she loved every juicy minute, man. "Oooh, yes," she kept saying. "Take me, Willie. Take me." Hey, what's this? Time running out? You got twenty-two seconds and no fat-assed queen. You're as fucked as she is, man. Bye, bye, Byron . . .'

The man kept up his steady stream of patter while Byron stared at the board with a calm gaze, as if this were a meal he was indifferent to eating. Captured chess pieces lined both sides of the board. There were only eight pieces left on the actual playing surface.

'How's this feel, your royal heiny?' the man said, thrusting his hips back and forth in his chair. 'You like a little more of this, queeny?'

Byron reached over, airlifted his castle across the board, and snapped it on a square with a loud smack. 'Check.' Byron tapped the silver button on his clock. He got up and stretched, not bothering to look at the board.

His opponent glanced nervously at the clock and instantly retreated his bishop back between the attacking castle and his defenseless king. He slapped his clock.

From his standing position, Byron jumped his black knight down two spaces and over one into a position near the white king. 'Checkmate.'

'Shit! Where?' The man with the scarred lip studied the board. 'Just a second. Just a fucking second.' His eyes darted from piece to piece, his hand hovered over one, then another, like a fussy hummingbird selecting a flower. Finally, he just tipped over his king, jumped up, pulled a wad of twenty-dollar bills from his pocket, and threw it down on the chess board. Some of the pieces flew onto the floor. He stomped out of the room toward the kitchen. He stepped on a king, snapping off the cross on its head.

Byron counted the money and slipped it into his pocket. He showed no sign of triumphant glee or proud accomplishment. He looked as unmoved as someone who'd just bussed a dirty table.

'I found her outside,' my beefy guardian said to Byron. He gripped my upper arm and shoved me forward. 'She says she knows you.'

'She thinks she does,' Byron said.

'She was spying on us through the window.' He nodded toward the window where he'd caught me. 'Want me to boot her out? When I boot, they stay booted.'

Byron looked me over as if considering that alternative. Finally, he shook his head. 'Not yet. Thanks, Leo.'

Leo shrugged and came out from behind me. He tossed

up the sharp object I'd assumed was a knife. It was a pointy-headed bishop chess piece he'd held against my back while he kept me in the foyer until Byron finished his game. He caught it in his palm and closed his fist around it. He walked off into the large living-room. There were about twenty men in the room, all playing chess.

'So, you followed me,' Byron said.

'It wasn't hard.'

He gestured around the room. 'Was it worth it? Did you discover something to blackmail me over? I mean, that is the point, right? To get some dirt on me to neutralize my dirt on you?'

'That's the point.'

'Help yourself. Look around. Talk to people. Pry.'

I looked around the room. Men of all ages huddled over flimsy card tables with chess boards and chess clocks. Cigars, cigarettes, a few joints. A wispy layer of smoke clung to the ceiling. Lots of beer cans, a few coffee cups, one man chugging Evian water. Some of the tables had little piles of money. Over near the sofa was a nineteen-inch Sony TV still in its box. Next to it were a couple of VCRs and CD players, also still in their boxes.

'Well, for starters,' I said, 'there's illegal gambling going on here. That's something the cops might be interested in.'

'So, call the cops,' Byron said. He turned to the other men and announced loudly, 'She wants to call the cops on you, boys. Illegal gambling.'

There was some laughter, some annoyed looks. A 'fuck you, lady' chorused with a 'dumb bitch'.

One of the men who was watching a chess game in progress, gray-haired and overweight, sucking on a stubby cigar, reached into his baggy shirt pocket and pulled out a small black wallet. He opened it and showed me his gold badge. He winked at me. 'Don't worry, ma'am. I'm working undercover.'

Everyone laughed.

'What about those boxes,' I said angrily, pointing at the appliances. 'I bet they're stolen.'

'They are,' Byron said. He pointed at a little man across the room. The man was hunched over his chess game, slapping his pieces down, then smacking the clock. He looked as if he wanted to eat the pieces, the board, the clocks, his opponent. He had a tattoo on one arm that ran all the way from his wrist, up the entire arm, disappearing under his T-shirt sleeve. 'That's Grudge. He stole the stuff from his brother's warehouse. You know his brother, Bonkers Bob, does those commercials where he throws TVs out of windows, runs over stereos with his car because they're priced too high. This is Bonkers Bob's house.'

I gave an appreciative turn. Despite the card tables and hunched men and acrid smoke, this one room was larger than my entire apartment and worth more than everything I owned or ever would own. A white grand piano dominated one corner. Someone had pyramided a dozen Coors cans on top of it. A marble coffee table separated two white leather sofas. The table hosted two different chess games, and a pile of wadded Kleenexes from one of the guys who kept sneezing. I looked down at the carpet, an off-white weave that one usually sees in model homes. The walls were filled with various colorful and abstract art works, all of them originals, all of them undoubtedly expensive.

'Where are the owners?' I said. 'Mr. and Mrs. Bonkers.'

'A cruise. The Mediterranean, I think.'

'How convenient for all of you.'

'Doesn't matter. When they come back, the game moves somewhere else. Last week we were in a movie theater in Anaheim. One of the guys is an usher. Before that we played for two days in a courtroom, I showered in the judge's chambers.' He pointed to a black man slapping his clock. 'He's a security guard at the courthouse. Most of the guys you see around here don't really even appreciate where they are. They don't notice that this place is worth a lot, not unless they're professional burglars or something. They're just here to play chess. Sunny, rainy, doesn't matter. Hot, cold, they don't care. Everything's chess.'

I looked around the room again, this time ignoring the furnishings and concentrating on the men. Byron was right, there was an odd fanatical concentration about them, the same one you see on the faces of computer nerds discussing software. They stared at the boards and slapped pieces down with feverish energy. They looked like patients at a tuberculosis sanatorium, pale and hopeful. Even when they talked it was only about chess, either at their own bad move or their opponent's. There were so many games going on that the room had an odd melody to it, the clacking of pieces snapped against the wooden boards, and the smacking of the clocks next to their games. Games kept ending, payoffs made, new ones beginning, all within a brief time.

'They play so fast,' I said. 'I haven't played much, but I remember it always took us a long time to move.'

'This isn't chess,' Byron said. 'It's blitz, or speed chess. Not the kind you'll read about in the papers or see on TV. Every game lasts from between one and ten minutes, depending upon what the players agree to beforehand. After that, it's a race with the clock as well as against the other player. This is the game where all the big money is made.'

We walked by a table where two men were furiously slapping chess pieces, then their clocks. One of the players wore a white shirt and a tie. His suit jacket was carefully hung on his chair, his briefcase was tucked neatly under his chair. His opponent had a thin blue tattooed line that ran across the top of his forehead like the coastline on a map. There was about two inches between the blue line and his receding hairline.

Byron whispered, 'The suit is a lawyer, represents about a third of the guys in this room.'

'He's young.'

'He's also not very good.' Byron gestured at the other player. 'Billy there had that line tattooed on when he was in high school. Back then it followed his hairline exactly so you couldn't even see it.'

'Why? I mean, why'd he have it done?'

'His girlfriend was worried that he'd go bald someday and wouldn't sleep with him because she didn't want to marry a bald guy. He promised her he wouldn't go bald and to prove it, he had the tattoo done.'

I laughed. 'Did they get married?'

'Yeah. Twice.'

Neither player seemed to notice us watching. They picked up pieces and smacked them down with a crack and instantly slapped their clocks. The pieces on the board were wonderfully ornate versions of cowboys on one side and Indians on the other. I glanced around the room and saw other chess pieces, equally complex and intricate in design.

'The chess pieces are beautiful,' I said.

'Something to show your art class, huh?'

He led me to another table where two men were setting up the pieces. One side of the board was lined with familiar biblical figures, each brightly painted: the king was a carving of Moses with a staff in one hand and the Ten Commandments in the other, his gray hair swept back from an imaginary wind; the knight was a golden calf on a platform; the rock was the Tower of Babel; the pawns were frogs and locusts, representing the ten plagues, I guessed. Across the board a modest Jesus Christ occupied the king's square; a demure haloed Mary was the queen; the bishop was Peter, complete with a fishing net across his shoulder, the pawns were robed beggars, each leaning on a wooden crutch, carrying a Bible.

'Christians versus the Jews,' one of the men said. 'The way it's always been.'

'Karl here's a bit of an anti-Semite,' Byron explained. 'Right, Karl?'

'If that means do I hate the Jews, no, I do not. I do not hate Jews or any other religion. I just think they are misguided.' Karl did not look up at either Byron or myself. He kept his eyes down and chewed frantically on a wad of gum.

'Did you make these?' I asked him.

'Yes, ma'am, every last piece. Made 'em while serving my fifty-eight months for armed robbery and I thank Jesus that he gave me that opportunity. Because it is while incarcerated that I discovered both the Lord and chess.'

'The pieces are very beautiful,' I said.

'Thank you, ma'am. Perhaps you'd appreciate this extra little feature the others only seem to find amusing.' Still without looking at me, he reached over and touched a button at the back of his Christ figure. The arms, which had been at Jesus' side, shot straight out into a crucifixion pose. 'That's for when I lose.'

Byron led me away, pointing out the other chess sets that each man had carved while in prison: Civil War pieces, street gang pieces, movie star sets. One person had one side as the characters from the *Threepenny Opera* versus the characters from *My Fair Lady*. As I looked around at the colorful imaginative pieces, they seemed like what little boys would use as currency if they owned their own country.

'Hiya, Bud,' Byron said, waving over my shoulder.

I turned and saw a red-haired spaniel winding his way under the card tables, sniffing the carpet as he crawled through the room. He had a bandage wrapped around his hind leg and he walked with a limp.

'Hey, Bud,' one of the men said. 'What's shaking?'

'Howya doin', Bud,' another said.

'C'mere and hump my leg for good luck.'

Every person Bud came near stuck out a hand and gave him a scratch or a pat as he passed by. Bud licked up a broken pretzel from the carpet and hobbled out another door.

'Come on,' Byron said, taking my hand. 'I'll give you the ten-cent tour.'

I jerked my hand from his. 'I don't need a crossing guard.'

'I didn't do it to be romantic. I'm letting these guys know you're with me so they don't start hitting on you. Chess players are the most sexually starved species on the planet.'

'Present company excepted, of course.' I didn't give him my hand, but I followed closely. Where else would I go? I suppose I could have just walked out of there, driven home, called Davis, asked him to come home and hold me, make me feel better. But Byron's arrogance nettled me. He couldn't be touched and he knew it. But wasn't this where the bad guys in the movies always went wrong, showing the captured secret agent around their domain like Dr. No and Goldfinger? Maybe there was something he'd overlooked, something illegal I could still nail him for. I still had Detective Diesel's number.

'You play chess?' he asked as we walked down the sunlit hallway. Overhead skylights let the bright sun spotlight our path to the kitchen.

'Some, like I said. But not *play* play. Robby taught me. He liked to sit there with Bach in the background, a pipe in his mouth, and take two hours to move one piece. I got so bored he finally took to bribing me to play with him. Thank goodness for those computerized chess games. He finally had the perfect partner.'

'Computers are nice toys, but when it comes to blitz, there's not a person in this house today who couldn't cream a computer nine out of ten times.'

'Why? What's so special about blitz.'

'The speed. You don't have time to figure every variation of every move. And there are so many traps and pitfalls. Your opponent is just waiting for that rash move, that's when he crushes you. It's kind of like having a live grenade strapped to your chest that's going to explode in one minute. Now, if you can run across that field to that toolbox, you can disarm the grenade. Only trouble is, the field is loaded with hidden mines. And, oh yeah, someone's shooting at you the whole time. Ready, set, run. That's blitz.'

We entered the kitchen. The appliances were heavy-duty stainless steel, the kind you find in fancy restaurant kitchens. The refrigerator had a sliding glass door so you could see what was inside. Cold cuts, beer, a couple of buckets of fried chicken, potato salad. The kitchen was large enough to include a small family room with complete electronic entertainment center. A couple of guys were eating sandwiches and watching the big-screen TV, reruns of *The Flintstones*. A couple of other guys were playing chess while munching pretzels at the cooking island with their chess board over the butcher block. The rear wall of the kitchen was glass, which looked out onto a large pool and bubbling spa. Two pale guys with flabby guts sat in the spa playing chess. Several white wrought-iron patio tables with umbrellas dotted the poolside area. Every table but one had at least two chess games in progress. At that one table without chess, five men played poker. One chess game ended and the loser pushed his money across the table to the winner. The winner stood up, pocketed the money in his swimsuit, took off his sunglasses, and dove into the pool. He swam across, hoisted himself up on the other side, tossed his soggy money on the table, and started a new game with someone else.

'Who are all these people?' I asked.

'Ex-cons mostly. A cop or two. Leo, the guy who brought you in, he's a retired guard from Chino prison. Not a bad player, though he gets a little cautious when you pressure his queen. No bluff to his game. Cops and guards are like that. They play like they've got something to lose. Makes them easier to beat.'

'Who did you have lunch with at the restaurant?' I didn't care about this chess crap. I was after something tangible. I looked in his eyes for a reaction.

He didn't give me one. 'A friend.'

'And the money you gave him?'

'What beady little eyes you have, Grandma.'

'It's the company I keep.'

He laughed. 'It was a loan.'

'That was a big envelope.'

'It was a big loan.' He grinned at me. 'You need a loan too? Oh, that's right, you've got that $50,000 deal you're working on.'

My skin chilled. 'What deal?'

'I don't know the details, but from what I've been able to piece together from listening to your phone messages and the tapes you bring home every day from jail, you're doing some kind of article or series of articles, though for that kind of money more like a book, about Season Dougherty.'

'You've played my fucking tapes!'

'You figured to take the money, which I suppose your boyfriend Davis is paying you since this is his kind of game, and start Wren's little ego magazine.'

'You went into my room and played my goddamn tapes, you pig!'

'Only Season went and hanged herself this morning and now you're feeling sorry for yourself, so you figured you'd follow me and try to take me out of the picture. What happened, Luna-slash-Wren? Now that Season's dead you've decided to take on *her* identity and come at me with a shotgun?' He pointed at his crotch. 'Fire away, baby.'

I gave him the cold stare, the one he'd been giving me on and off since he'd arrived. But it didn't seem to have any effect. Finally, I just sighed heavily. I felt so tired and heavy.

'How'd you know Season was dead?'

He made a sweeping gesture. 'Look around. We've got cops and lawyers and cons. This place goes twenty-four hours a day, just like a Vegas casino. The only thing these guys like more than chess is gossip. Anything happens to do with prisons, we know about it first.' He slid open the refrigerator door and pulled out a couple cans of Pepsi. He handed one to me. 'No diet, sorry.'

I took it, popped the tab, and sipped. 'I'm living dangerously these days.'

A loud smacking thud nearby startled me. I jumped back, my heart pounding. 'What was that?'

'Jesus Christ,' Byron cursed. He left me and marched over to the sliding glass door that led to the pool. A wet smudge blotched the glass at eye level. He pulled open the door and bent over.

I followed. I stepped outside behind him and watched him examine the still bird.

'What you got there, great white hunter?' one of the cons who wasn't playing yelled from poolside. Those who were playing didn't even look up.

Byron picked up the bird, a sparrow, I think, and carried him over to the plastic trash cans, lifted the lip of the lid, and shoved him in with the beer cans and pizza boxes. He looked at me as he returned to the kitchen. 'This is not going to be one of those broken-wing-nurse-to-health-in-a-shoe-box stories.'

'What happened?'

'They don't see the glass sometimes.' He went over to the sink, opened the cupboards, poked around, then closed them. Next, he tried the refrigerator. He slid open the door, moved some stuff around, and pulled out a can of whipped cream. He shook the can as he walked over to the large glass doors. He began spraying the doors with whipped cream, a zigzag pattern from top to bottom.

'Hey, whatta you nuts?' Grudge said, walking into the kitchen. One fist was filled with money, mostly fives and ones, not the twenties that Byron had won.

'I told you to put some masking tape over the door.'

'A fucking X out of masking tape. You kidding me or what? That stuff leaves sticky shit on the glass when you take it off. My brother's coming back soon. You think I want to be jacking around here scraping sticky tape shit off the glass with my fingernails?'

Byron shrugged. 'One of these birds may eventually crack the glass. You want to replace it?'

'I'll take my chances, okay. Meantime, you shoot your wad on anything else around here and I'll fucking kill you, okay? Am I clear or what?'

Byron aimed the whipped cream nozzle at Grudge's face and squirted a small puff of cream onto the tip of Grudge's nose. 'Kill that.'

Grudge wiped the cream off with one finger and deposited the white glob on his tongue. 'That reminds me, bunch of gay guys sitting in a Jacuzzi, somebody spills some whipped cream in the water.'Nother guy sees it and says, "Hey, who farted?"'

Byron reached over and wiped the remaining dot of whipped cream from Grudge's nose with his palm. Neither man said anything, nor did they laugh at Grudge's joke.

'Prison humor,' Grudge said to me.

I nodded, not really anxious to engage him in conversation.

'Grudge, this is Wren.'

'Yeah your wife. We talked before, right? On the phone?'

I nodded. He acted as if our conversation had been a pleasant discussion of the weather rather than his onslaught of swearing and threats against my life. Again, I noticed the tattoo scribbled across the entire length of his arm. It wasn't the usual dragon or naked woman. It wasn't a picture at all. Just words. I looked closer. They were names. A single column list of names that ran from his wrist up under his sleeve. Daryl Carson. Stevie the Jinx. Swingshift Jackson. Homer Borden.

'Those are the names of the people Grudge has marked for death,' Byron said. 'Right, Grudge?'

Grudge nodded. 'Every single motherfucker guaranteed to die. My word on it.'

I didn't say anything. What could I say? How nice for you?

Byron laughed. 'See, Grudge's whole scam inside was telling people he was mobbed up, connected with the Mafia. Anybody does something he doesn't like, he tells them he'll have them killed. Of course, no one but the new fish took him seriously—'

'Bullshit! Lots of guys took me serious. Lots got outta my way, didn't fuck with me.' Grudge was a head shorter than Byron, about my height. But he had a compacted muscular look, as if he were wound up real tight and one little nudge would send him expanding to twice his size.

'Yeah, right,' Byron said. 'Anyway, one day some guy Grudge threatened actually died. Autopsy doesn't reveal cause of death, but Grudge is strutting around like he knows something. After that, everybody gives him a wide berth, just in case.'

'Just in case, shit. I know what I know.'

'So next, he starts tattooing names on his arm. Names of everybody who he thinks crosses him or who he wants to do him a favor. He tattoos your name on his arm, then you're dead. That's the idea, right, Grudge?'

'Sooner or later,' Grudge said. He pushed up his sleeve past his bicep. Third down from the top of the list is BYRON CALDWELL.

'That's you,' I said.

'Yup. Grudge claimed I bumped into him on the stairs.'

'He wanted to kill you for that?' I said.

Grudge took a step toward me. He smelled of sweet cologne. 'Lady, inside you kill somebody if he stares at you too long. Don't matter the reason, you let somebody get away with something, anything, then soon they got you down on the shower floor and twenty naked guys are kneeling behind you, your asshole the size of the Lincoln Tunnel. You get the picture?'

'Vividly,' I said. But I was thinking about Mark, my old student who came to visit me after I'd been shot. His tattoo. These men around me with their crude tattoos. What were they trying to mark, to measure?

Grudge looked at me in the eyes, stared hard. 'You

413

don't get it.' He looked at Byron and shook his head. 'She don't fucking get it.'

'Give her time,' Byron said. 'She learns quickly.'

'What do I give a shit what she learns?'

I was fed up with this prison mystique bullshit. 'What do I give a shit what you give a shit about?'

'How'd you like to wake up one morning and find your fucking head in the toilet? Huh? How'd that suit you?'

'That's how I do my hair now, so what's your point?'

Byron laughed. He returned the whipped cream to the refrigerator. 'Hungry?' he asked me.

I shook my head.

'I could use a sandwich,' Grudge said.

Leo the ex-prison guard came in and knocked on the counter. 'Hey, Byron. Shawna's here.'

Byron's face changed. He tensed up a little. The smile was still on his face, but it was a prop now, not genuine. 'Business, kids.'

He walked out of the kitchen, following Leo, without waiting for me or Grudge. The guys over watching TV got up and followed. Outside around the pool, men were talking rapidly and those who finished games or were just watching got up and came inside, walking past Grudge and me into the living room. The poker game broke up and the players also came inside.

'What's going on?' I asked Grudge.

'Rematch. Shawna took Byron yesterday three out of five games. She cleaned him out. First time he's lost in a straight-up match.'

'Straight up?'

Grudge sighed impatiently. 'Jesus, straight up. Where Byron don't spot any pieces or time. He's so good that usually to get anyone to play him for money, he's got to take away a couple of his pieces, a rook and a bishop maybe. Or he's got to play with less time, like he's only got two minutes on his clock, his opponent has five or ten.' He scratched his tattooed arm, his fingers digging in

414

around CLANCY ROBBINS. 'But he played Shawna head to head and she kicked his ass.'

'I'd like to see that,' I said.

He grinned at me, his lips kind of crooked, like half his face was shot up with novocaine. 'Yeah, he said you would.'

31

I walked behind Grudge into the living room. Those who were in the midst of a game continued, but once each game finished, the players got up and moved over toward the grand piano, where the crowd was thickest. I couldn't see Byron or Shawna.

Grudge scratched at his tattoo again, stopping suddenly so that I stepped on his heel.

'Sorry,' I said.

'You think my tattoo is stupid, right?' He was angry.

'No,' I said.

'Sure you do. You think I disfigured myself like some asshole just to sound tough. Now I got the names of guys I don't like strapped to my skin for the rest of my fucking life. Am I right? That's what you think.'

'I don't think about it at all.'

'The fuck you don't. First time you saw me you had me pegged as some turd at the bottom of the shit pile.' He shrugged and seemed to calm down. 'Hey, that's okay. What do I care what you think, right?'

'Right.'

He gave me another hard look, eyeball to eyeball. I thought he was going to try to kiss me. Then he took a step backward and just pointed his finger at my face. 'When you're inside, you don't think the consequences your actions will have once you're outside. You follow me? Inside is inside. That's the whole world. And you do whatever you have to to survive. It ain't like the movies, no matter how bad they make it seem. It's worse.' He rubbed his face with his palms, as if his skin were cold. 'Hell, you know. Your husband told you.'

'Like what happened to his finger.'

Grudge nodded enthusiastically. 'Exactly. Jesus, man. I ain't never seen nothing like that. Byron is cornered in the weight room by some 300-pound brain-dead mother-fucker named Connie. I'm not using that description lightly, this guy *really* fucked his mother—after he cut off her head, though. Connie's suddenly decided he wants an intellectual type for his fuckmate and he's got your hubby up against a wall fumbling with his pants.'

I began rubbing my thumb along the seam of my sweater. Grudge's eyes seemed glazed, trance-like as he told the tale.

'Good thing Byron was smart enough not to try to hurt Connie, because then Connie would have killed him and then fucked him. It wouldn't have been the first time since he'd been inside.'

'Where were the guards? Didn't anybody see what was going on?'

Grudge laughed. 'I had a pretty good view, sure. Front row center. Me and about twenty other guys.'

'And you didn't do anything?'

'Yeah, I watched.'

'I mean you didn't help? There were twenty of you.'

Grudge looked annoyed. 'I thought Byron told you how it was inside.'

'He doesn't like to talk about it much.'

'Yeah, that's true. Me, I love talking about it. I'm like one of those old farts at a Veterans of Foreign Wars meeting. Wear some funky hat and talk about all my battles for the rest of my fucking life.'

More people were huddling around by the piano. For a moment I had a vision of Shawna sitting down playing the white grand piano and suddenly singing in a beautiful voice. That whole sign language thing was probably some practical joke they played on me.

417

'We better be getting over there,' Grudge said, starting away.

I grabbed his tattooed arm and held it. 'Finish your story. Please.'

'Not much to add you don't know. Byron sticks his own finger in his mouth, bites the end clean off, and spits it out on the floor. Then he looks down at Connie's crotch and grins that fucking grin of his. I mean he still has blood all over his teeth.' Grudge laughed. 'You shoulda seen the look on fucking Connie's big face. He's looking at your hubby like he can't fucking believe it. "You're fucking nuts," Connie says and walks away.'

'He bit his own finger off!'

'Sure, what'd he tell you?'

I started toward the crowd. Grudge followed.

'Nobody bothered Byron after that. I mean, nobody wants to fuck with someone like that. Me, I admired his balls. If I'd have thought of it instead of this fucking list, I'd have bit three fingertips off. Shit.' He scratched his arm again.

The crowd was thick as dough around the piano.

'Coming through, assholes,' Grudge said, elbowing ahead of me to break through the men. 'This is Byron's wife. Move it, man, before I have a couple guys come over and chainsaw your flabby ass off, you fucking moron. What're you looking at, fuckhead?'

No one seemed to take Grudge too seriously, but they moved aside just the same. When we got to the front of the circle, Byron and Shawna were setting up their chess pieces on the board. The pieces were simple, carved from wood.

Shawna leaned on the piano with one arm and used her free one to set up her pieces. She looked even more beautiful today than last night. Her black hair dropped straight down the sheer face of a shale cliff. Her expression was serene, as if she were mentally composing a song.

Byron's expression was more intense. His hair, pulled

back and tied at the nape of his neck, seemed more severe than a couple minutes ago. I watched his left hand, studied the stub of his little finger, tried to imagine him biting off his own finger and spitting it out. Was it courage or desperation? The act of a brave man or an animal gnawing off his own foot to be free of a trap?

'What are the stakes?' I whispered to Grudge.

'Whatever they want. They play a series of five games. The first one is ten minutes. Then seven, five, three, and finally a two-minute game.'

Byron reached into his pocket and pulled out the wad of twenties I'd seen him win earlier. Then he reached into his other pocket and pulled out another wad, even larger. He counted out all the bills. Three thousand dollars.

Shawna, not at all impressed, opened her tiny black purse and pulled out thirty crisp one-hundred-dollar bills. She placed them on top of Byron's thicker but dirtier pile and patted them twice, as if assuring them that they would soon all be safely back in her purse where they belonged.

'What does she do to make all that money?' I asked Grudge.

'Well, she wins a lot of it from dopes like us. The rest she makes running her dad's bail-bond business. That's her dad over there.' He pointed to a tall, chubby man with white hair and a kind face. He wore a plaid shirt that yesterday had been one of Byron's. He winked at his daughter and she smiled at him.

'I don't get it,' I said. 'If they want to bet, why not take it to the track or Vegas and put it all on red?'

''Cause this ain't gambling. Chess is one of the few games in the world that doesn't have any element of luck. No dice, no cards, no sun or wind. Life within your own control without chance to fuck you up. No new alarm system you're not prepared for, no flat tyre on the getaway car, no snitch who rats you out. Just thirty-two pieces, sixty-four squares, and your skill. It's like . . .' He brought his hands together and squeezed them until his fingers turned white. 'It's like you can hear that clock ticking in your head, like your fucking life is running out, but if you make the right move, the exactly right move, you can win more time. Like you've done something divinely good and you'll be rewarded. That's how it feels to me and I don't even play half as good as Byron. I can't imagine what the fuck he feels like when he's running the board. Like he's a god or something, like he can fucking fly through walls.' He shook his head with envy. 'I don't know. Shit, I'm just a guy who loads appliances in his brother's warehouse, did some time for passing bad checks. Don't ask me to explain nothing.' He scratched his arm.

I noticed that at the same time he was scratching his arm I was rubbing my thumbnail along the seam of my sweater again. We were, in fact, scratching and rubbing at the same pace, matching strokes. He noticed and looked at me, no hard stare this time, more like recognition. He turned away embarrassed at the intimacy.

'Give 'em some room, assholes,' Grudge said, stepping foward and shooing the crowd back a few steps. 'They gotta breathe too.'

Byron looked at Shawna and made some hand gestures. She nodded. They each set the clocks to ten minutes. They leaned across the white grand piano, their butts sticking out, elbows propping up their heads, like mirror images of each other.

Grudge took a light pawn, put both hands behind his back, and brought them out again as closed fists. Shawna tapped his left hand. He opened it and revealed the pawn. She replaced it on the board and turned the board around so the white pieces were in front of her.

The game was rapid, pieces cracking against the board, clock spanked into motion. I noticed a tiny scar on her jawline, which she occasionally touched when it wasn't her turn. Bud came in again, limped around the room, but gained no sympathy, no strokes. He sniffed the pile of tissues the man with the cold had left, found a half-eaten bagel on one of the card tables, grabbed it, and trotted out, his limp much less noticeable now.

'What happened to Bud?' I whispered. 'That limp?'

'Ssshhh,' Grudge said. Everyone in the room was concentrating on the game that clacked off before them.

Byron and Shawna seemed to exchange pieces evenly, so I didn't see that anyone was winning. Plus, they moved so quickly I never got a chance to figure out what I might do.

Suddenly I saw Byron tip over his king. He reached across the board and shook Shawna's hand.

The crowd went into instant murmur mode, discussing mistakes that Byron made, what they would have done, etc. Some ran for the kitchen and returned with cans of beer they distributed to others.

'It's over?' I said, staring at the board. 'But he's not in checkmate.'

'Checkmate in three,' Grudge said.

I looked at the board, confused. He walked over and started moving pieces. 'He moves there, she moves here. Check. He moves there or there, in which case she moves here or here. Check. That only leaves him here or there and she's there. Checkmate. Bam, bam, bam.'

Shawna's father handed Shawna and Byron each a beer, which they began to drink. The three of them gestured to each other, laughing or looking serious. Shawna's father went to the board and arranged the pieces a certain way that I guess they were at during the game. Then he went through some options and they all gestured some more.

'Bud got in a fight,' Grudge said. 'Got the shit clawed out of him from some fucking cat. Jesus, big dog like that let some weasely little cat fuck him up. He's the biggest wuss I've ever seen. Can't fight worth shit.' He started setting the pieces up on the board for a new game. 'Anyways, he comes in a week or so ago, limping like crazy, bleeding all over the place. Byron fixes him up. He's good with animals.'

So that's the dog blood on the money he gave me. At least now I could spend the money and stop holding it as evidence. My case against Byron was slipping away. His big illegal activity was chess, the missing finger was his own doing, the blood was a dog he administered first aid to, the mysterious phone calls involved chess matches. Compared to him, I was the major criminal. Wait, I still had his prison record. He was in there for something, something that involved Wren losing her teeth. I still had hope.

The second game began with seven minutes on the clock. They moved even more quickly this time, but after a while a little flag on Shawna's clock popped up and the game was over. She'd run out of time and lost. The usual post-mortem went on around us and everyone fell silent when the third game started. The clocks were adjusted for five minutes. Pieces were moved with the same mechanical speed, same clacking. Before I even knew what was going on, Shawna tipped over her king.

She made some hand gestures and Byron nodded. Shawna disappeared down the hall.

'Ten-minute break,' Byron announced and everyone scattered. Some went back to their boards to replay the games they just saw. Others threw money on the table and played a challenge game for real. Everyone's intensity made the room swampy with tension. I followed Shawna.

She went into a bathroom and shut the door. After a couple of minutes I heard the toilet flush, the water in the sink run, then she came out. At the moment she opened the door, before she'd prepared for the world outside, I caught a glimpse of her expression. Tired eyes, rimmed with red. She may have been crying. Mouth smeared with fresh lipstick, but the lips tense and frowning. She came out, caught me staring, and smiled. She laid a hand on my arm and squeezed like we were old and dear friends. Then she walked back toward the living-room, shoulders high, head back. Confident.

The three-minute game was played in a flurry of blurred moves. Captured pieces were tossed to the ground in the rush. Pieces were moved so quickly it didn't look to me as if any thought at all was put into the move. Yet some moves brought oohs and aahs from the crowd.

Suddenly Byron slapped a piece down, made a hand gesture, and pushed himself up from the edge of the piano. Shawna studied the board for a few seconds, smiled, and nodded. She curtsied to him and everyone applauded. Byron cut the money into two piles and shoved each pile into a separate pocket. Shawna came around the piano and kissed him on the cheek. He smiled for the first time since the match had started.

The crowd of onlookers rushed back to their games, looking newly inspired. Pieces were set up, clocks adjusted, and suddenly everyone was playing chess. I had to admit, I even felt like pulling up to a board and slamming a few pieces around. The atmosphere was exciting.

Byron walked toward Grudge and me. As he walked, he took a couple Tylenols out of a bottle in his pocket and popped a couple in his mouth. He snagged a beer can from one of the tables, shook it to see if there was anything in it, and washed down the Tylenol with whatever was left.

'Was it good for you?' he asked me.

'From what Grudge says, you just conquered time and space, you were flying, and winning one for the Gipper all rolled into one.'

Byron shrugged. 'It's just a game.'

'Fuck you, man,' Grudge said. 'Just a game. Just a game my ass. It's just a game when some of these patzers play. Not when you and Shawna play. Not when I play neither.'

'Patzer?' I asked.

'A patzer's a hack,' Byron said.

Grudge punched Byron in the arm. 'You can be such an asshole sometimes. If I had room, I'd scratch your name on my arm again.'

'Just don't put a heart around it.'

I looked past Byron and saw Shawna sitting at a card table playing chess with her father. She was plucking one of his pieces from the board and replacing it with her own. She smacked her clock button.

The doorbell rang. No one seemed to notice. Except Leo, who hauled himself off the sofa where he'd been watching a game and marched off to the front door.

'I'm outta here,' Grudge said. 'There's still some money to be made.' He walked off and started talking loudly to some guy returning from the kitchen with a sandwich. 'Don't take a bite, fatso. I'll play you a two-minute blitz for it. What is that, ham and cheese? You put mustard on it, asshole? If I win you go back and put some fucking mustard on it.' They sat down at a table and started setting up the pieces to play for the sandwich.

'Does that make you even with Shawna for beating you yesterday?' I asked Byron.

'No, that puts me ahead. We had a little side bet. She owes me a couple grand for Motown, the parrot, and a grand for the clothes she won.'

I looked at his face. One of his eyes was bloodshot, tiny lightning bolts of red etched through the white. 'You look awful. You okay?'

'Headache. It'll go away.'

'Do you get these headaches often? I mean, are we talking tumor or something?'

'Nothing so romantic. I just get them when I play chess. It's kind of like blowing out your knee in basketball, only there's nothing you can do about it.'

'You can not play.'

He didn't say anything. He looked over at the entranceway to the foyer where Leo stood with another man, an even bigger man than Leo.

'You must need the money pretty badly to play if it does this to you. What do you do with all your winnings? Other than make loans?'

'I don't give interviews,' he said without looking at me. His eyes were fixed on the man Leo brought in, the man who was now walking toward us, smiling sadly at Bryon. I didn't realize how big he was until he walked by the other men in the room. Their heads barely peeped above his shoulders. It seemed to me that the men in the way purposely moved a little quicker to get out of his way, though no one looked directly at him or acknowledged his presence. Except Byron, who stared into the man's eyes.

'Jesus, Byron,' the man said as he approached. 'Jesus. Why are you making it so hard on yourself? Fuck that, why you making it so hard on me?'

They shook hands. Byron turned the man's hand over to examine the knuckles. 'I guess my face didn't do much damage.'

'My wrist is a little sore. You better not have fucked up my tennis game. Laura and I are in a doubles tournament next week. She'll kill both of us.'

They both laughed.

Byron turned to me. 'This is my old cellmate Jerry Kirn.' He paused, smiled at me. 'Tell him who you are.'

Jerry waited, Byron grinned. What name did he think I'd give?

'Wren,' I said. 'Nice meeting you, Jerry.'

'Aaah,' Jerry said. 'The wife.'

'My current cellmate,' Byron said.

'Am I being dense here or something,' I said to Jerry. 'Did you just say you're the guy who beat Byron up yesterday.'

'That was me,' he said in a chipper voice. He reached out and clutched Byron's jaw in a motherly way, turning it side to side. 'Not bad, not bad at all. Mostly for show stuff, bruises and cuts, but no real damage.'

'I hate men,' I said.

Jerry laughed. He was the most good-natured man I'd ever met. 'We are a dumb bunch of chromosomes, aren't we?'

'Jerry works for Landry,' Byron explained. 'Landry told him to knock me around until I agreed to play a blitz match with his boss.'

'I'm surprised you didn't just chomp off another finger,'

I said. Byron looked startled that I knew. He fired a menacing look across the room at Grudge.

'Wouldn't work,' Jerry said. 'Landry's seen the finger bit already. Hey, "the finger bit", get it?' He chuckled at his own joke.

'So you knocked Byron around and you're still pals, right?'

Jerry shrugged. 'That's my job. Byron knows that. Besides, I could've made it worse. This way it looks like he took a real beating and all I did was throw a few well-placed shots.'

'Jerry's an artist,' Byron said without irony.

Jerry's face went serious. 'Of course, that only works once. Landry was not happy about you refusing him again. I think this time you're gonna have to accept, Byron. I mean it, man.'

Byron shook his head. 'Can't do it, Jerry. The guy's a pig.'

'I don't know. Pig's a matter of perspective. He pays me on time, treats me like a professional. I got no complaints.'

'Can't do it, man. You know that.'

Jerry frowned, looked pained, like he might cry. 'I gotta break something this time, man.'

'Like what?'

'I dunno, he just said not to touch the right arm or hand so you can play.'

Byron looked down at his own body. 'It would be hard to get to a bus on crutches, so how about my left hand? That sound good?'

I couldn't take it any longer. 'Are you two crazy? You're discussing which limb to break because he doesn't want to play a game of chess with your boss. What's the big deal? Play the guy!'

'I think she's right, Byron. It were me, hell, I'd just play him. You know he's not gonna stop hounding you till you do. You know why.'

Byron looked at me. I don't know what he thought he

426

saw, but there was a sadness and gentleness in his expression I'd never seen before. For a moment, I thought he was waiting for me to do something or say something. And, crazy enough, I wanted to, maybe touch his face, smooth his hair, pat his hand. Some gesture as simple and clear as the sign language he spoke with Shawna, the movement of a chess piece. I wanted to do something.

Then the moment passed and he said to Jerry, 'Tell Landry I'll play him.'

'Don't dick me around, Byron. That would only make things worse.'

'Tell him I'll call with details.'

Jerry looked both relieved and disappointed, like he saved a friend but lost a hero. 'I'll tell him.' He turned and walked away.

Before Jerry was out the front door, the room was loud with discussions of what had been overheard. There was excitement and awe and a kind of nervous anticipation.

'Let's get out of here,' Bryon said.

Somehow I got the feeling that he'd taken the match because of me. Somehow I got the feeling that was a big, big mistake.

32

'Where are we going?' I asked. I'd been driving about thirty minutes along the 91 Freeway toward Riverside.

'Keep going. I'll tell you when we get there.'

I'm not the kind of person who generally accepts that as an answer. But this time I didn't argue. I drove.

'Why is Landry so hot to play you?'

'There's a McDonald's. Pull off.'

'Sure you can afford it, big spender?'

He looked at me. 'Who said I'm buying?'

We coasted through the drive-thru lane and picked up our bag at the second window. The girl in the headphones said, 'Four thirty-eight.' I refused to reach for any money. So did Byron. 'That'll be $4.38,' she repeated nervously. I didn't budge. The car behind us nosed closer. A car behind them honked twice. I stared out the windshield. Finally, Byron dug into his pocket and handed me a twenty, which I handed to the girl. 'Keep the change,' I said to her and sped away. I saw her puzzled look in my rearview mirror as she hung out the window, the twenty-dollar bill clutched in her hand.

'Guess they don't get tipped much here,' I said.

He reached into the bag and handed me my iced tea. He shoved a few shoestring fries into his mouth.

'Landry's a loan shark,' Byron said. 'He was in prison the same time Jerry and I were. He fancies himself as something of an intellectual. A gentleman crook, like David Niven or Cary Grant.'

'He was part of your little chess club?'

Byron shrugged, popped a McNugget into his mouth.

I laughed. 'Prison isn't what I imagined. I mean, I envisioned sweaty guys with bad teeth settling arguments with the sharpened end of a toothbrush.'

'Yeah, that's the rule generally. Everything you've ever imagined it to be. Only worse. The gangs, the murders, the rapes. You tell a joke and somebody doesn't get the punchline, he may just kill you for the insult. But even within that there are little groups of aficionado. The weight-lifting group is out there every day pumping iron until their necks look like inner-tube mutations. You know what the Hillside Strangler and the Freeway Killer and those mass murderers do every day? They play bridge. Swear to God, the bastards have a little bridge club, mass murderers only need apply.'

'Sounds cozy.'

Byron slurped his root beer. 'It passes time. More than that it gives meaning to time, structure to what seems like an endless stream of minutes passing you by. They take their games very seriously.'

'But you don't, right? Like you said, it's just a game.'

He looked over at me and smiled. 'That's right. It's just a game. For me, a way to pick up some money.'

A couple of cars coming the other way had their headlights on and I noticed it was starting to get dark. I switched on my headlights too. 'Landry. You were telling me about Landry.'

'No big secret. He's a loan shark looking to step up in the world. Like I said, he fancies himself an intellectual, a mastermind. He's very ambitious and something of a publicity nut. He'd like to be planning major heists, the kind of stuff that makes headlines, like the Brinks job, or the Lufthansa heist, or the Great Train Robbery. Naturally, only those in the very top positions would know he's responsible, but that's enough for Landry. Thing is, to do something that size you need to get permission from the local organized-crime heads. And that you can't get unless they think you've got a hell of a good chance of pulling it off.'

'Are we still talking about chess or did I take a wrong turn somewhere?'

'Be patient, Luna.'

When he said my name, I felt a strange tingle across my scalp. I hadn't heard it in so long it felt kind of nice. Luna. Say it again, I wanted to say. Luna. Luna. Luna.

'For the crime bosses to give Landry permission, he needs to convince them he can do the job and not bring any heat down on them. To do that, he needs top talent, the kind of professional talent that is hard to come by. Why would any of them hook up with a loan shark like Landry? Unless he can convince them he's a smart guy. He thinks beating me at chess will be favorable P.R. for him among the criminal community. First step on the thousand-mile journey.'

'Is that as stupid as it sounds?'

'What, you think crooks are wise old men who spout proverbs and play boccie ball? They're criminals. If he were such a genius, why'd he go to prison in the first place?'

'Why'd you?'

He didn't answer. He finished his root beer and started chewing his ice. So did I. For a couple miles there was no sound in the car but the crunching of ice.

'Pull over,' he said, pointing to the side of the road.

'You sick?'

'Yes.'

I snapped on my turn signal and eased across two lanes until I was able to safely pull off the freeway. Cars whooshed beside us, the force of their speed rocking the car a little. Byron sat straight up staring out the windshield.

'Don't you want to get out or something? Hang your head out the window?'

He turned in the seat and flicked on the overhead light. He reached into his jacket pocket and pulled out a little wooden box, which he unfolded, releasing tiny black and white chess pieces onto his seat like bombs.

'What the hell are you doing? I thought you were sick.'

'I am sick of listening to you talk about things you don't know shit about.' He quickly stuck the pegged chess pieces into their holes and set the board between us. I was white. Then he snatched up from his side a rook, a bishop, two pawns, a knight, and his queen. 'Fair enough?' he asked.

True, I didn't play chess that much with Robby, but I wasn't an idiot either. By the time we were divorced, I played well enough to beat Robby a few times. Head to head, I knew there was no way I could beat Byron. But with half of his pieces gone, especially his queen, I figured I had a better than even chance.

'How about this,' he said. 'You can have one full minute for each move, I'll move within three seconds. That better?'

His arrogance dug into my chest, making my bullet scar ache. 'Yes,' I said. 'That's better.'

'Your move.'

I did, playing a basically sound game, moving my queen's pawn out, then developing my knights to control the center of the board, then castling to protect my king. I moved cautiously but deliberately, showing him no lack of confidence. He moved like a robot, his eyes never leaving the board, but as if he knew all of his moves ahead of time and that none of my moves interfered with his plan the least bit. I started to panic a little, watch the clock when it was my move.

'Time,' he said.

'What?'

'Your minute is up.'

'No it isn't.' I looked over at the car clock but I couldn't remember when my time had started. I moved a piece and he took my rook. My heart was pounding in an unnatural rhythm, like reggae steel drums. My thumbnail was sore

431

from being rubbed against the edge of the seat. I moved again and again he took my piece, a knight.

'Check,' he said. 'Mate in two.'

I studied the board, tried to see the mate in two. I put my hand on my queen, then on my rook, back to the queen.

'Time,' he said.

'Jesus, stop it.'

'You want another minute?'

'Fuck you.' I moved my queen to cancel his check.

He unpegged his knight and pegged it so that it could take either my king or queen. 'Check.'

I had no choice but to move my king, which I did without taking much time. He slid his rook across the board into the same file as my king.

'Checkmate.'

I stared dumbly at the board, looking for his error. Impossible that I could be checkmated so rapidly by his crippled army. Sweat thickened my skin. My throat felt ashy, my teeth were coated with something gritty that hadn't been there before the game started.

He sat back and stared straight ahead out the windshield. 'You feel humiliated, right? There's nothing you'd rather do right now than crush my skull with a hammer. Except maybe play me again. That's the only way you can get a little shred of self-respect back, isn't it? I mean, think about it. I had no queen, for God's sake. One rook, one bishop, one knight, and only six pawns. I moved in three seconds. Three. One thousand one, one thousand two, one thousand three. Pow. Checkmate, stupid.'

'It's just a game,' I said and started the car. I pulled back into the traffic. But the thing was, he was right. I felt stupid, humiliated. And the fact that I knew it was stupid to feel that way only made it worse. I wanted to hurt him for putting me through this.

Byron swallowed another Tylenol. 'Now you know how Landry feels.'

The sky was completely dark now. Headlights crawled by in an ominous procession.

'I came out here with you because I felt kind of sorry for you before,' I said. 'I don't feel that way any longer, so I'm turning around.'

'We're almost there,' he said.

'Almost where?'

'You want to know where the money goes, right? My winnings?'

'I couldn't care less. Why would I care?'

But I kept driving and we kept chewing ice.

The man was running toward us yelling before I'd even braked the car to a stop: 'What the hell are you doing here? Who is she? Were you followed?'

I recognized him from his lunch with Byron earlier that day, the guy to whom Byron gave the envelope stuffed with money. He was short and thin, with wire-rimmed glasses similar to mine. He wore an orange T-shirt and baggy shorts that hung to his knees, making him look a little like an over-age skateboarder. My headlights spotlighted him jumping up and down and waving at us so that he looked like he was doing a kind of crazy dance on a stage. Byron laughed at the sight.

I parked next to the dusty black Jeep in the gravel driveway. A thick cloud of road dust that the tyres had kicked up rose up around the car like smoke. Byron got out and stretched.

'Byron. Christ.' The man shook his head as he trotted toward us, distraught. He peered back down the deserted road that we'd just driven on. 'Are you sure you weren't followed?'

'Relax,' Byron said.

'I'll relax when I'm sure you weren't followed.'

'I don't see any headlights,' I said. I was just trying to calm him down.

'Their headlights wouldn't be on if they were following you,' he snapped. 'That's the whole point. Stealth.' He shook his head. 'Shit!'

'Gee,' I said, 'maybe we should sweep the car for hidden transmitters that might be beaming back our location to a secret helicopter.'

'I've already taken care of that. I've planted four electronic tumblers out there—' he pointed in four compass directions at the vast desert around us— 'that scramble any low-frequency signals for a five-mile radius. Kills bugs dead.'

I looked at Byron for some explanation of what we were doing here and how dangerous this guy might be, but Byron was walking toward the ancient two-storey white house next to the driveway.

'I have to use the john,' he announced. 'Zeno, that's Luna. Luna, Zeno. He knows all about you, so relax.'

Zeno and I watched him walk away, then we looked at each other like children abandoned in a supermarket. We quickly hurried after him.

'This is crazy, Byron,' Zeno said. 'You shouldn't be here and she *especially* shouldn't be here. You're jeopardizing everything. I want that to go on record right now.'

'So recorded.' Byron went up the splintered, sun-dried stairs, across the porch, and into the house. The screen door clattered behind him.

Zeno held the screen door open and waved me impatiently inside. He stared out into the darkness one last time for stealthy cars before closing the door behind him.

Byron stood in the bathroom with the door open and pissed into the toilet. Zeno averted his eyes. I didn't. I could see the steady stream shooting down. The sound was loud and kind of soothing. 'I brought some more money, Zeno.'

This perked Zeno up. 'How much?'

'Not enough. Six thousand.'

'That's not enough. Not nearly enough.'

'That's what I just said.' Byron finished, shook himself, zipped up, washed his hands, and flushed. I thought it odd that he flushed *after* washing his hands. I guess I even thought it odd that he washed his hands at all.

'Where are we exactly?' I asked.

'You don't need to know,' Zeno said.

'Forty miles past Palm Springs,' Byron said. 'Desert all around us for hundreds of miles.'

'Christ,' Zeno slapped his hip. 'Why not take an ad out?'

'We can trust her.' There was something in the simple way he said it that made me ashamed. After all, I was here for dirt, not trust. But Byron knew that. Why then did he bring me here, to the lair of his secrets?

'So far there's not a whole lot to trust me with,' I said. 'An old house in the desert. Did you guys find some gold or uranium or something?'

'Better,' Byron said.

'Much better,' Zeno added. His attitude seemed to change suddenly. Now that he accepted my presence, he got excited and talkative. 'This is bigger than precious metals, and potentially worth a lot more. We're talking about something that will change the world for centuries to come. Nothing will ever be the same.'

I sighed. 'Desert desert everywhere, but not a decent shrink.'

'What's that supposed to mean?' Zeno asked.

'It means you two need some professional help. Byron's playing chess every day, taking an occasional beating to his head. You're holed up here in the thousand-degree heat working on some secret formula or something. Didn't I see this movie already? Jeff Goldblum plays both of you.'

Byron laughed. 'Let's show her, Zeno.'

Zeno looked petulant. 'Screw her. Let her believe whatever she wants. Who cares what she thinks?'

'I care.' Byron led the way through the house and out the back door where we stood in front of a large makeshift greenhouse covered with clear plastic sheets. The building was the size of a barn.

Oh, Christ, I thought, drugs. They're growing some new potent marijuana. The feds probably have the place surrounded and now they think I'm part of the gang. Any second now guys wearing jackets with DEA AGENT in big white letters on them will come rushing in waving heavy rifles.

'Come on, don't be scared,' Byron said. 'It's all very legitimate.'

He held the door of the greenhouse open and I entered. The air was thick and moist, it smelled somehow tropical, the dank-sweet scent of decaying leaves. Warm flannel air clung to my skin like Velcro. I found myself breathing deeply to make sure I was getting enough oxygen.

The room was laid out very simply. Three rows of wooden troughs filled with plants lined the greenhouse. They didn't look like marijuana.

'Bamboo,' Zeno said.

I walked up one aisle and down the next. At the back of the greenhouse was a laboratory bench with all kinds of chemicals and tools and microscopes. 'Bamboo,' I repeated, nodding. 'Just bamboo.'

'Yes,' Zeno said sarcastically. 'Just bamboo.'

'And this is what's going to change the world? I hate to tell you boys, but bamboo already grows in a lot of the world. They been sticking bamboo splints up people's fingernails for centuries. Accept no subsitute.'

'There are over 500 species,' Zeno said. 'Throughout south-eastern Asia, through India, all the way across to Korea and Japan. Even though it's technically a grass, it can grow over 135 feet tall. Amazing, isn't it?'

'Stupefying,' I said. 'What's the point?'

Zeno shook his head and looked at Byron. 'God, you were right about her.'

I looked at Byron too. 'Oh? How so?'

'I told him you sometimes confused being a smart-ass with being smart.' I started to protest, but Byron waved at Zeno to continue.

'Anyway, bamboo isn't just a convenience, millions of people depend on it to literally stay alive. Bamboo hay has four times the protein content of hay from fodder grasses, which means the entire livestock population of most of those countries is dependent on bamboo. No bamboo, no food. The paper made from bamboo in China is far superior to newsprint. Even more significant, bamboo is responsible for much of the housing material in these countries. They depend on it for food and shelter.'

Byron hopped up on a shaky wooden table stacked with bags of soil. 'Problem is, most bamboo has a very long period between flowerings—fifteen years, thirty years, sixty years, even 120 years. This makes it very difficult to use consistently and can cause famine and homelessness in some countries.'

'That's true,' Zeno said, looking annoyed with Byron's interruption. 'Because you have whole stands of bamboo flowering at one time, they also die at the same time. This leads to the collapse of entire forests at once, which often results in vast forest fires as well as rat infestations as they gather to eat the seeds. That means disease and thousands of deaths.' Zeno began tucking his T-shirt into his shorts, assuming a more professorial appearance. He adjusted his glasses. 'Scientists all over the world have been trying to quicken the gestation period of bamboo to make it flower faster.' He looked at Byron and grinned. 'I found a way.'

'Not entirely on your own,' Byron reminded him.

Zeno looked embarrassed.

Byron continued, 'Zeno and I met in prison. He was tutoring illiterate prisoners, teaching them how to read in exchange for cigarettes and whatever other prison currency he could get.'

'Were you a part of the chess club too?' I asked.

'Me? No way. Chess is a stupid game. Waste of time.'

Byron didn't seem to take any offense at that. 'Before prison, Zeno was a lab assistant at a university, doing some key research in plant genetics.'

'The guy I was working for, Dr. Palomar, is one of the big shots in plant genetics. He pioneered acceleration of flowering of the loblolly pine and day lily as a result of tissue culture. Quite fascinating methodology if you—'

'Keep it simple, man,' Byron said.

'What were you in for?' I asked Zeno.

Zeno looked confused, as if he didn't remember being in prison. 'I stole library books and sold them to collectors.'

'You stole books? You went to prison for stealing library books?' I laughed.

'How much did you make a year stealing library books, Zeno,' Byron asked, but he was looking at me.

'Depends. I mean, I had to travel a bit to various university libraries, so there were travel expenses to deduct.'

'Net profit.'

Zeno shrugged. 'Fifty to seventy-five thousand dollars a year.'

'Impossible,' I said.

'Not really,' Zeno said. 'There's actually quite a market for antiquarian books. You'd be surprised.'

'Surprised? I'm dumbfounded. Seventy-five thousand dollars a year for used library books. Christ.'

'Not just any book. They have to be rare, that's the challenge.'

I sat down on a couple of burlap bags of soil. 'Why'd you do it?'

He looked surprised. 'Money, of course. Dr. Palomar abandoned the bamboo project because he was afraid he couldn't get another government grant. Everything is run on grants in the university. So, always sensing grant opportunities, Dr. Palomar applied for a grant to create a smokeless, nicotineless, cancerless tobacco for cigarettes. The money poured in and the bamboo was scrapped.'

'So, Zeno here saved what papers he could from the project, and stole library books to finance his own experiments.'

I looked at Byron. 'And now that he has no more income, you play chess to make enough money to finance this whole thing.' I gestured to encompass the greenhouse.

'We're very close to success,' Zeno said excitedly. 'The idea is adding cytokinin and coconut milk to the tissue-

439

cultured shoots. The coconut milk supplies the inositol and cytokinin oxidase inhibitors that then allows the cytokinin to promote the plant maturation.'

'That's good?'

'Good? Jesus, I've already gotten them to flower after only three subcultures. This is an innovation equal to the Salk vaccine, discovering penicillin . . .' He waved his hands, his mouth open chewing air, searching for an appropriate metaphor.

'Refrigeration,' Byron offered.

'Exactly!' He pointed at Byron. 'Refrigeration. We're talking about not only eliminating one of the world's greatest plagues, but actually increasing food and building supplies. Within a couple generations, a heartier, faster flowering species of bamboo will be growing everywhere.'

I stood up, brushed the loose soil from my pants. 'Thanks for the tour. Your secret is safe with me. I'd like to go home now.'

Byron hopped off the table. 'Zeno, can we borrow your Jeep.'

'Sure, yeah. What for?' He tossed the keys to Byron.

'I want to show Luna something.'

'I don't want to see anything else,' I said. 'I've seen so much. My eyeballs are on full. Really.'

'You want to know about Wren, don't you? What happened to us? About my evil criminal life? Her missing teeth? I mean, isn't that the mystery piece of the puzzle, the information that will make your performance, your impersonation of her all the more complete?'

I looked at him for a while. His face didn't reveal anything, just stared back with that blank wall expression while he fingered his dragonfly earring. All around us mutated bamboo shoots were growing unnaturally fast. That made me nervous, as if I expected them to suddenly shoot a root thick as a cable out of the sod, wrap it around my neck, and drag me back under the ground until I was mulch.

Did I really want to know what happened between

Byron and Wren? If Wren had wanted me to, she would have told me. Besides, I was getting out of the Wren business. Out of the Season business. Just as soon as Davis came back, I was telling him everything. I owed him the truth. I owed someone some kind of truth.

'Never mind,' Byron said. He tossed the keys back to Zeno and started walking back to the house. 'She's just talked herself out of it.'

I marched over to Zeno and grabbed the keys from his hand. 'Let's go, bucko. Show me what you've got.'

34

'Insects,' he said.

'Insects? As in bugs?'

He smiled. 'One and the same. Technically, Insecta.'

'Insecta? Sounds like a Japanese movie. Some giant mantis head crushing a lot of cardboard buildings.'

We were bouncing through the cool night air across a dirt path through the desert. Byron drove what seemed to be much faster than was safe, given the low visibility and lack of clearly defined road. He didn't look worried. He wrestled the steering wheel through turns and curves like someone who knew this land by heart. Every bounce cinched my seat belt tighter against my bladder and I was wishing I'd gone to the bathroom back at the house.

'Insecta is a class of the largest animal phylum, Anthropoda. They used to be called Hexapoda because of the three pairs of legs at the thorax. There are over one million known species and they constitute about eighty three per cent of known animal life on this planet. Impressed or should I babble on?'

'Impressed,' I said. 'Okay, so you were a bug major in college.'

'Entomology.'

'Did you have a specialty, like an English major might specialize in the nineteenth-century British novel?'

'You mean did I have a favorite bug?'

'Right.'

'I was partial to the Hymenoptera.'

'Why, because it had hymen in it?'

He laughed. 'I hadn't thought about it, but you may be right.'

If I concentrated on staring up at the stars, the bouncing of the Jeep didn't bother me as much. Even though we were zipping around like a drunken jackrabbit, the stars overhead stayed in one place and that made me feel better. 'So what is the hymen bug?'

'Hymenoptera. It's an ant. I like ants.'

Now I laughed. I don't know why, it wasn't especially funny. But I felt suddenly giddy, like I had a secret pact with the stars to keep me safe. Or maybe it was the pressure on my bladder.

He must have interpreted my laughter as a response to his love of ants. 'Ants are more complex than people realize,' he said defensively. 'There are 8,804 species of the family Formicidae. They do things we can't fully imagine. For example, they build nests that can go twenty feet deep and have over a thousand entrances. The weaver ants use silk thread from larvae to bind leaves together for penthouse suites. A species in Malaysia keeps livestock in the form of mealybugs. Get this, the mealybug eats sap rich in amino acids and sugar, then passes it on to the ants in the form of drops of excrement.'

'Jesus.' I made a face and swallowed dryly.

'In exchange for this service, the ants protect them from other predators. And when the sap dries up, the ants use their jaws to carry the mealybugs on to new plants. Kind of like being carried in a shark's mouth.'

'Fascinating, Byron,' I said, hoping that would end it.

'It's more than fascinating, it's fucking cosmic. You've got a carpenter ant that has no reproductive organs. You know what it has instead?'

'Cable TV?'

'That space instead holds poison-filled glands. One of these ants gets into a fight, in order to protect the nest, it will purposely rupture this gland, exploding its own body so it can spray the poison on the enemy. God, that's interesting.'

443

I turned in my seat to look at him. His face was boyish and happy. 'I just realized,' I said. 'You're the same type of nerd as Zeno back there. His face looked just like yours when he was talking bamboo sprouts and coconut milk. I mean, you play chess and wear an earring and bite off your fingers, but basically you guys are a lot alike.'

'I don't take that as an insult.'

'It wasn't meant as one. It's just an observation, that's all.'

'Do you have any insight to go with your observation?'

'I don't do insight. I'm not Wren, as you so often point out, just an imposter.'

We were silent for a while. Except for the stars, there were no other lights. I had no idea even what direction the house was. Hell, what direction Los Angeles was. All around us was desert dirt and wiry bushes and a crisp smell that was almost sharp enough to slice your lungs.

'So how did you go from bugs to prison?' I asked.

'I was working for the U.S. Department of Agriculture, developing a program to match beneficial insects with specific crops as an alternative to insecticides. We were trying different breeding methods to make enough insects to keep up with the demand.'

'Like a bug bordello, huh?'

He ignored me. 'We were raising the green lacewing, the cryptolaemus, certain predatory mites. And with the pesticide scare going on, we were in demand.'

'Where does Wren fit into all this?'

'Wren,' he said softly. He shook his head as if he were having an internal discussion.

'Wren,' I repeated.

'I worked with the bugs during the day, but I worked with EarthWorth at night. Secretly, of course.'

'EarthWorth? You mean those guys who chain themselves to the redwoods so the loggers don't cut them down, that sort of thing?'

He frowned at the reference. 'Yeah, that sort of thing. We were a monkey-wrench activist group, like Earth First

444

or Greenpeace. That means we didn't just talk about the environment, we took some corrective action.'

'Like chaining yourself to a tree.'

'I didn't chain myself to a fucking tree, okay? I wasn't a tree hugger, I was an environmental activist. We did things like hammering spikes into trees so the loggers would break their saws. Once we dug a trench across a logging road, filled it with quick-drying cement, and stepped into it to form a human severe-tyre-damage line.'

'Sounds like tree hugging to me.'

He sighed. 'We sabotaged some heavy equipment when they wanted to build condos out here and ruin the ecosystem balance.'

'None of this sounds like Wren.'

He stopped the Jeep. The headlights shone against a sheer rock wall of mountain. We'd been following the hills for a couple miles but I hadn't noticed us getting so close. He jumped out of the Jeep and started foraging in the back. He found a blanket and some matches. 'Go over there,' he said, pointing at some gnarled bushes. 'I'll build a fire.'

'Why do you want me to go over there? So I won't learn the secret of fire, Prometheus?'

'So you can take a leak. You've been squirming in your seat for twenty minutes.'

I walked over behind the bushes, pulled down my pants and panties, and squatted.

'Watch out for scorpions,' he called. 'They're all over the place.'

I looked down at my exposed opening only inches from the ground and lifted myself a little higher. When I finished, I dressed and returned to the Jeep. A few feet away Byron was tossing wood onto a pleasant little campfire.

'Doesn't this destroy the ecosytem balance?' I said, sitting on the blanket next to him.

'Yeah, but I plan to sacrifice you to the god of the desert and spill your blood into the sand, so it all evens out.'

We both stared into the fire the way people always do,

445

like they've never seen one before, dumb expressions on their faces as if their life forces were being extracted by the wiggling flames. Sitting there, not knowing which direction was which, how far we were from civilization, only twenty feet from a wet spot on the ground where I'd just urinated, I felt relaxed. I wasn't even anxious to hear about Wren.

'Wren didn't like my nocturnal activities. Neither did the Ag Department. They fired my ass as soon as a photo of me appeared in *Time* magazine with my feet stuck in cement.'

I tried to imagine Wren with her feet stuck in cement. Somehow I couldn't.

'She thought our behaviour too extreme. We fought about it.'

And you popped her one, right? I thought. Knocked her teeth out, then fell to your knees begging forgiveness.

'Wren liked to watch, to observe. To judge. She was good at it. Analyzing what people did, why they did it, what they meant by it. But she didn't really *do* anything. Did you know she wasn't even registered to vote?'

I shook my head. That surprised me. She always had very vocal opinions about every political issue and candidate.

'For all her articulation, Wren didn't really want to participate. She didn't live life in the fast lane or the slow lane, she lived in the bus lane. Safe and above the others, with someone else driving.'

'That's bullshit,' I said. 'Wren didn't let anyone drive her. She did what she wanted, she was in complete control. Everyone knew that, everyone who really knew her.'

He shrugged. 'She was a better actress than you.'

I stood up angrily. 'You really piss me off. You come out of the woodwork without even seeing her for two years and you start telling me what she was like. Well, maybe you didn't know her as well as you thought. Maybe you didn't know her at all.'

'Maybe,' he said quietly. He tossed a rock into the fire

446

and some sparks flew up. 'One evening I'd talked her into going on one of our little raids.' He pointed out into the darkness. 'Just a few miles over there where people came here to drive their all-terrain vehicles, chewing up the land and killing off a lot of necessary wildlife. I guess I shamed her into it, calling her a fence sitter, a moral Peeping Tom. That sort of thing.'

I sat back down and watched him. He looked right at me, not with his cold prison-yard face, but with lost eyes and a sad turn to his mouth.

'We went in at night to plant some big deep rocks in the paths where they usually did their racing. Wren and I were digging a hole when we heard loud engines suddenly start up and bright flashlights shining on us. Somehow they found out about our plan and had come down and hid out, waiting for us. They started chasing us in their ATVs, armed with baseball bats. I dragged Wren out of there. We were running together when some yahoo drove by us and swung his bat into Wren's face.'

'Jesus.'

'Yeah.' He flicked a small rock from his thumbnail and it sailed over the fire. 'I took her to the hospital. The cops arrested me while I was waiting there. I got two years.'

'For what? Did you kill the bastard who hit her?'

He laughed wryly. 'We never found out who did it. I was sent up for destruction of property and trespassing. I was an example.'

I laid down on my side and propped up my head with my arm. 'That's it, huh? You didn't smack her around?'

'Sorry to disappoint you. Anyway, she wouldn't speak to me after that. She blamed me for what happened, for talking her into going in the first place.' He looked at me. 'I guess she was right.'

Staring into the fire and listening to Byron's voice made me sleepy. Now that I knew there was nothing sinister about him, I could relax even more. But part of me was disappointed. I had set him up as my adversary, the man

I would defeat. I guess it was a lot like having a chase scene, the way my student described. Having Byron as the villain gave some meaning to what I did. Without him in the garden, what good was paradise?

'Why did you tell me all this now?' I said. 'I asked you plenty of times before.'

'I told you. I wasn't going to help you impersonate Wren. And that's the only reason you wanted the information, to add to your shrine.'

'What's different now?'

He flicked another stone from his thumbnail. It arced up high and dropped into the fire. 'You're different.'

I didn't see any difference. As far as he knew I was still pretending to be Wren. Nothing had really changed. So I had to think of some other reason he was telling me all this. It didn't take me long. Money. I had some and he needed some.

'How long before your bamboo project is done?' I asked.

'Hard to tell. We're still running experiments. That takes money. So, as long as I keep winning, we're still in business. But that's going to get harder. I'm going to have to give away too much from now on just to get someone to bet money. Too many pieces, too much time. That will catch up to me.'

'How much money do you need?'

He shook his head. 'Zeno figures another hundred grand. But, considering we're going to make millions, it's worth the investment.'

I sat up. 'Is that what this is about? Making millions?'

He laughed. 'You mean, am I in this for the bucks or to carry on the altruistic spirit of tree hugging?'

'Yes, that's what I mean.'

'Can't I do both? Save a tree and still make a few bucks?'

'A few million bucks.'

He leaned forward and gently laid another piece of gray wood on the fire. 'You're making $50,000 writing a book pretending to be Wren. Does that mean you cared any less for Wren?'

'It's not the same.'

'Sure it is. I hugged trees, you hugged Wren. We both got burned, now we're both in it for the bucks. I can accept that, why can't you?'

I had a mental image of Byron and I standing side by side in a clearing. He had his arms wrapped around a skinny sapling of a tree. I had mine wrapped around a white pine coffin. Inside I could feel Wren's weight pulling the coffin toward the ground, but I wouldn't let it fall.

'You sure must see things a lot different than you used to,' I said.

'Two years in a small cell helps you see the big picture. Two years of looking at things through a snitch mirror you hold outside your bars changes your perspective a little. After you see things in reflection long enough, when you see them without the mirror they look funny, fake.' He whistled a couple notes. 'Yeah, I see different. More clearly.'

'What about EarthWorth? Maybe they'd be glad to invest for such a worthy cause?'

He looked up from the fire straight at me. 'What are you trying to say?'

'I'm saying that I have no intention of giving you any of my money. I'm saying that this whole trip to the desert to meet your wacky pal and see your little greenhouse doesn't mean shit to me. And this cozy chat around the campfire won't get you a cent.'

'That's what you think this was about? Getting your money? Jesus, you're worse than I thought.'

'Right. Like you don't want my money. Were you after just part of it or the whole fifty grand. Did you really want the money for your project or just to keep me from publishing Wren's magazine and making it a success?'

'That magazine is a failure no matter how popular it becomes.'

'Yeah, right. More prison parables from the Monk of C Block.'

He stood up and brushed the dirt from his pants. 'Forget it. I don't weep at the extinction of species, I don't wince at dolphins in tuna nets, I don't lecture passers-by on smoking. The whole world is dying anyway, heading toward extinction. That's as inevitable as the sun flaming out.' He kicked dirt onto the campfire, smothering half the flames.

'Is that your big insight? Two years of looking through a mirror and that's it? Maybe you should have Windexed your mirror, pal. We already know the sun will nova. In a few billion years. Meantime, I still plan to keep up my subscription to *People* magazine.'

'Under whose name? Or is Luna Devon an extinct species.'

I don't know, something about the way he said it, phrased it maybe, I don't know. My skin tightened as if I'd just stepped inside a freezer. I threw a couple more pieces of wood on the fire and blew the flames back to life. I needed warmth.

'Let's go,' Byron said. 'Now that you know I wouldn't take your fucking money, there's nothing to stay for.'

His moral tone bugged me, so I marched back to the Jeep, snagged my purse, and returned to the campfire. I dug out my checkbook and wrote a check for a thousand dollars. I tore it off and handed it to him. 'Here. For your bamboo. No strings. Consider it payment for information received about Wren. For her sake, it was worth it.'

He studied the check a moment, then smiled. He folded it in half as if he would stick it in his shirt pocket. Then, still smiling, he reached the check into the fire, let a flame jump to the edge of the paper, and held it between us while it burned. The flames ate across the paper to his fingers, but he still held it. Finally he just crushed out the flames in his hand and tossed the scrap of check and black ash into the fire.

'Not enough?' I said. I wrote another check for two

450

thousand dollars. He tossed it into the fire without looking at it. My face was burning with anger as I scribbled another check, now for five thousand dollars. He balled it up without looking at the amount, put it on the end of a stick like a marshmallow, and roasted it to ash in the flames.

Before he was even done roasting that check I was writing another one for ten thousand dollars. I was so furious, my penpoint cut right through the paper as I signed my name. 'You might want to look at this one first.'

He didn't. He balled it up, stuck it on his stick, let it catch fire, then flung the burning ball at me. The flaming paper struck my breast and bounced onto my lap. I quickly brushed it away. I attacked my checkbook again. I was practically choking with hate as I scratched twenty-five thousand dollars into the amount line of the check. I knew this bastard could be bought, and I would buy him. That would prove something. I tore the check from the book, crumpled it up, and threw it in his face. It caught him in the corner of the eye because that eye teared up instantly. He rubbed it, but didn't pick up the check.

'Go ahead!' I shouted. 'Let's see you burn it. Let's see you burn $25,000.'

He picked up the crumpled check, looked at the amount. His smile widened. 'This one I think I'll keep.' He smoothed it against his thigh, folded it neatly in half, and stuck it into his shirt pocket.

'You lying cocksucking motherfucking son of a bitch,' I said.

He nodded. 'But then, you knew that.'

451

35

After he stamped the fire out and scattered the ashes, the darkness seemed too loud. Just standing there my ears seemed to pick up some night melody from the darkness. Or else I was going crazy. Certainly sitting around with Byron could drive one over the edge.

I could barely see him, just a shadowy gray ghost moving about. From the sound, he was shaking out the blanket, folding it. I leaned against the Jeep, let the cool metal anchor me. In this kind of darkness, one was liable to float away.

'Here,' he said, suddenly behind me.

I turned quickly, my head smacking his chin.

'Ow,' he said.

I didn't say I was sorry. 'What's here.'

'What?'

'You said "here". What's here?'

'Here, take this.' His hand touched my arm, felt its way down to my hand, opened my fingers, then stuck the folded piece of paper that must have been my check in them. He closed my fingers around the check. 'I wasn't looking for your money.' He paused. 'You're more like Wren than I thought.'

'You don't sound like that's a compliment.'

He didn't answer. But he didn't move away either. I could hear his breathing, see a blotch of face, a glistening in the eyes. His shirt smelled like the campfire. His breath rhythmically puffed into my hair.

Then I saw the darkness around his face shift and sud-

452

denly he was kissing me and I was letting him and I thought about Davis and I thought about Robby and I thought about Wren, but I let it happen anyway. And then I was kissing him back and I didn't think about anything else but how that kiss felt. I imagined our lips pressed against each other magnified a billion times. The crevices and lines were craters and gulches. Then I saw our giant tongues leaping over our lips into each other's mouths like thick pink whales at play. Or plump dolphins bumping bellies. And while I thought of this I felt my blouse come undone and my bra open and strong fingers pulled at my nipples like little mouths. Then he was gone and I heard the snap of the blanket opening up like a flag. And somehow we were naked and on the ground, the rough texture of the blanket scratching my skin.

Even without his clothes he smelled like the campfire and I liked that. I buried my face against his chest. His skin was moist with sweat. I heard a noise in the distance.

'What if we're attacked by a pack of wild coyotes?' I said.

'Maybe we'd better work fast.'

'Not too fast,' I said.

He laughed, his head thrown back looking a little like a coyote, I thought. Then his head disappeared and I felt the nuzzling between my legs, the soft attention of his tongue. I opened my eyes and looked straight up into space. The stars were so clear and sparkling, like they just came out of a dishwasher. What I didn't understand was how I could stare off into space and see things billions of miles away so clearly but the man who was nibbling between my legs was only a dark ink blot. I couldn't even see my own hand, though I could still feel the crumpled check in it.

He lifted my legs up over his shoulders so he could plunge his tongue into me. His hands slid up my side and I winced when he hit a ticklish spot, but he went past that until he was cupping my breasts. He unsheathed his tongue from my vagina and licked his way up to my clit-

oris. His tongue swirled in circular motions like he was
trying to keep an ice-cream cone from dripping. I liked
thinking of my clitoris that way and smiled as he continued. Soon I was gasping and bucking and I could feel
myself being dragged toward climaxing. But I didn't want
to come without seeing him. I grasped his head and pulled
him up on top of me. I reached down and planted his penis
at my opening and he thrust forward and into me.

I looked right at him, our faces not more than six inches
apart, as he rocked back and forth, first slowly, then gathering speed. I still couldn't see his face clearly, though
having the stars behind him at least made the outline of
his head sharper. He made love differently than Davis or
Ethan or Robby. I hadn't realized this before, but there
had been something familiar about the others, as if they'd
all read the same sex manual. It wasn't that Byron did
anything especially different, there was still only the obvious combinations of tongues and vagina and penis. Yet, it
was different. More personal. Like someone making you a
birthday card rather than buying one.

Then he was ramming into me hard and I wanted him
to do it even harder. I dug my nails into his hard buttocks
and pulled him into me. Images burst into my mind as I
felt myself nearing climax. The darkness exploded into
white, like an old-fashioned flash bulb that blinded me at
first, then the white drained away and I could see things.
Flash! Me ramming that white Subaru, crunching his fender. Flash! Me smashing Byron's watch against the table,
jumping up and down on it. Flash! Me throwing checks at
Byron. All the moments of passion I'd been accumulating.
And then the flashes stopped and I was moaning and my
hands were gripping Byron's hair. He was grunting in my
ear and he pumped against me and I didn't give a shit
about anything else in the past, present, or future except
what would happen in the next couple of seconds.

'Luna,' he said. 'God, Luna.'

I was so close, so close, so close, soclosesoclose. I flung
my hands out to the side to arch myself better. One hand

hit the blanket, the other hit the sand, and the one that hit the sand suddenly caught fire.

'Aaaahh!!' I screamed. I looked over to see why my hand felt as if a nail had been pounded through it. But I couldn't see anything. 'Goddammmmmmmn!'

And Byron, thinking I was coming, I guess, pumped even harder.

'No!' I said, hitting him on the head with my good hand. But I felt him spasm and his come shooting into me. 'I'm hurt!' I cried. 'Something bit me.'

He pulled out of me instantly. His penis was still leaking sperm, because I felt the trail drip down my thigh all the way to my knee as he sat up. 'Where? Where are you hurt?'

'My hand. Jesus, it feels like it's burning up.'

'Don't move,' he said. He stood up and ran over to the Jeep. He started up the engine and for a moment I thought he was just going to drive away and leave me here, yelling something like 'Hold on, I'm going for help.'

But all he did was turn the Jeep around so it faced us and switched on the headlights. The light bounced off my naked body making it look even paler than it actually was. I didn't care. My hand hurt too much to care about anything else. I sat up and examined the hand. There was a red hole on the back of my hand and serious swelling around it. The veins stood out and looked kind of bluish. I looked around the blanket I was on for what caused it. I didn't see anything.

He stood up on the driver's side and leaned over the windshield. His penis was mashed against the windshield. 'What's it look like?' he said.

'Like a flattened worm,' I said, pointing.

He looked down and smiled. 'I'm talking about your hand.'

'Red and swollen.'

'Teeth marks?'

'A little hole.'

He nodded and sat down. He switched off the engine

455

and the headlights. I heard him rooting around in the back of the Jeep.

'What the hell was it?' I asked.

'Scorpion.'

'Scorpion?' I pulled my legs tighter and hugged my knees. I let my wounded hand lie on the blanket as if it weren't a part of me. It throbbed horribly.

'Shouldn't we keep the lights on so we can see them?' I suggested.

'Lights won't help,' he said. 'At least not the regular kind.'

Apparently he found what he'd been looking for, because he climbed out of the Jeep, or at least that's what it sounded like.

'Shouldn't we be rushing me to the hospital or something? Don't people die from scorpion bites?'

'By the hundreds,' he said. 'The symptoms resemble strychnine poisoning. The tongue gets thick, muscles twitch, you start sneezing and frothing. Then convulsions and a bluishness in the extremities.'

'What the fuck are you doing? Get me to a hospital!'

'But those symptoms are rare and you would already be slurring your speech if it was going to affect you that way. Mostly people experience a sharp burning sensation, followed by a needles-and-pin tingling like when your foot falls asleep. At least that's how it affected me when I was stung.' I heard his voice coming closer, but I couldn't see him.

'Where are you?' I asked.

'Here,' he said. 'I'm shining a flashlight so I can see the scorpions without stepping on one.'

'Either one of us is crazy or you need some fresh batteries, because I don't see any flashlight shining.'

'It's a black light. You can only spot them under an ultraviolet beam.'

'Look, my hand is doing the samba on hot coals and you're doing your Dr. Frankenstein number. Let's just get out of here, okay?'

'There!' he said. From his voice, I could tell he was standing right next to me, but I still couldn't see him and I didn't know where 'there' was. Then I felt his hand on my arm. He was kneeling beside me, his arm around my shoulder. 'There,' he said softly and I turned.

'Jesus,' I said. 'Jesus, what the hell is that?'

His ultraviolet flashlight was aimed at the cliff wall fifteen feet away. The entire face of the rock was covered with neon greenish-blue outlines of scorpions. 'It's just a photochemical reaction to the black light,' Byron said. 'Beautiful, isn't it?'

That struck me as off, because I expected him to say, Scary, isn't it. That's probably what I would have said. But it wasn't what I was thinking at that moment. I was thinking, Beautiful, isn't it. Though I didn't know it until he said it. Gazing at the cliff wall was like seeing hundreds of zodiac signs. In fact, they reminded me of stars, so clear and precise.

He shifted the flashlight away from the cliff and shone it on the ground around us. Nothing. He aimed it at our pile of clothes. Nothing.

'They're very shy,' he said, as if describing a pet. 'They like to hide.' He picked up a stick and poked my panties. A neon blue-green scorpion scuttered out from under them.

'That's sick,' I said.

'Just be glad he wasn't in them when you put them back on.'

We got dressed—carefully—and drove back to the house. Byron took all of Zeno's ice and packed my hand in it for the drive home to Orange County. We didn't speak much during the trip. He asked how my hand was. Better, I said. Did I feel okay? Fine, I said.

I was busy thinking. Thinking about Davis. I had betrayed him. What did I know about Byron except what he told me. How could I trust that? Even if it was true, even if it was true, so what? I had feelings for Davis. I knew who he was, what he did, what he was about.

457

'What are you thinking about?' Byron asked me after a long stretch of silence.

'Nothing.'

'Come on.'

'Scorpions,' I said. 'How we could be out in the middle of hundreds of scorpions doing what we were doing without knowing they were there.'

'I knew they were there.'

'Then you should have warned me.'

'I did, earlier. I said watch out for scorpions.'

'Yeah, but you said it like "Watch out for falling meteors." Like it was only a remote possibility.'

He shrugged. 'If I'd have shone my black light around beforehand, would you still have made love?'

'I don't know what I would have done.'

He didn't say anything for a while. 'That's not what this is about. The guilt's set in. You're wondering if this has been a mistake. You followed me in the first place to get rid of me and now that you fucked me, you're wishing you'd just gotten rid of me instead. Right?'

'Don't tell me what I think, okay?'

He didn't speak the rest of the trip. We arrived at the apartment and he carried the dripping icepacks to the kitchen sink and tossed them in. There was an envelope under the front door mat addressed to Wren and Byron. I opened it. Inside was a note from Ethan asking us to call him. The phone number was a Los Angeles area code. I tossed the envelope on the sofa and went to the refrigerator for a soda. I was dying of thirst.

'Drink water,' he said. 'It'll flush your system out.'

I popped the Dr Pepper and drank.

He just smiled sadly and sighed. 'Okay, I've been debating about whether or not to tell you this. Before I figured it was none of my business. Maybe it still isn't.'

'What?'

'You know the bookmark you use in that flight magazine?'

458

I thought for a moment. The magazine I brought home from Davis's. 'Yes. What about it?'

'Nothing. If you know, you know.' He turned and walked down the hall to his room and shut the door.

I went to my room, holding the cold can of soda against the back of my swollen hand. I found the magazine on the back of the toilet where I'd left it. For Byron to have known about it, he must have searched my room again. Like I had done to his room, I reminded myself.

I opened the magazine and looked at the bookmark. It was Davis's boarding pass. But I already knew that. So what? He'd just gone to Hawaii last week. But I looked at the boarding pass more closely. Destination: Los Angeles. Departure: Denver.

I sat on the toilet. My hand throbbed and burned even more suddenly, as if my heart had somehow been washed out of my chest and got snagged inside my hand. He hadn't gone to Hawaii, he'd gone to Denver. And if he'd gone to Denver, he'd gone before this man had shot the woman. What if Davis had made a deal with the guy based just on his hounding of the poor woman who'd received the transplant? What if the man, knowing he had a deal, decided to do something more dramatic, something to make the story even better? We're not talking about a stable personality here, we're talking a disturbed man trying to get back to his wife's body parts. He views this woman as a surrogate, as if his wife were growing inside of the other woman. But he can't get back to his wife until he kills the surrogate that's in the way.

I didn't really know what had gone through the man's mind. Any more than I'd known what had gone through Davis's mind. He'd signed a contract with Season Doughterty and she'd killed her husband. That had become his big break. Did he now go searching for people on the verge of exploding and signing them up before the violence so he had exclusive rights? Jesus, think about it.

I stood up and walked out of my room. I didn't bother to switch on the lights. I knew my way through darkness by now. I imagined scorpions lining the walls, the floor. I didn't care. I knew one thing was for sure, I was throwing Byron out. He had always picked at my scabs, tried to lift the corner of my mask, shine his white and black lights at me, expose my neon self. But now he had taken away the one thing I had left in my life. Davis. I hadn't asked for the truth and I wasn't grateful for it. Byron was out of here. Tonight.

I turned the knob on his bedroom door and flung it open. The room was empty. I walked around it, opened doors, the closet. Everything was gone. I searched the apartment for Hector. He was gone too.

36

While waiting for Davis, I sat on the park bench next to the artificial lake and watched an old man shoot baskets. The old man was thin and bony, his pale legs sticking out of his baggy shorts seemed wobbly and coltish. His hair was thin and white and lifted with each puff of wind. He stood at the free-throw line, made sure his toes were lined up, bounced the ball once with both hands, and lofted it at the basket. I'd watched him toss at least twenty shots and he'd missed every one of them. The ball usually bounced off the rim and rolled into the grass that surrounded the small cement court. He walked in slow small steps after it, picked it up, and carried it right back to the free-throw line. He didn't dribble the ball or spin it on the end of his finger. He carried it in front of him as if it were a fragile globe. Bounce. Toss. Miss. Retrieve.

'I'm not late, am I?' Davis said. He came up behind me and kissed me on the neck.

'You're not late.' I was still watching the old man. I knew that once I took my eyes off him and faced Davis, everything would change. 'He doesn't dribble.'

'What?'

'Watch. He never dribbles the ball.'

Davis watched the old man for a minute. 'He's a lousy shot, that's for sure.'

'Yes, but he doesn't dribble. Have you ever known anyone to walk across a court with a basketball and not dribble it a couple times. You can't help yourself.'

'That's true. I hadn't thought of it before.'

We watched the old man shoot a couple more times, never making the basket, never dribbling the ball.

'God, he's a bad shot.' Davis laughed.

I turned to face him. 'My name's Luna Devon, not Wren Caldwell. Wren and I were best friends. She died.'

'Pardon?'

I told him everything. About Robby, the Bat-Faced Girl, my father, Byron. I didn't tell him about the bamboo. When I was done, I leaned back against the bench and sighed. I'd expected to feel somehow different. Purer, maybe. I didn't. I looked around for a sign that the world had changed because of my great revelation. Perhaps the old man would now sink a basket. But his shot ricocheted off the rim, bounced over the top of the backboard, and rolled off until it hit a water fountain.

Davis laughed. 'Is this a pitch for a script? Because I love it. Kind of a Jane Austen meets *Twin Peaks*.'

It was funny to think of your life as a synthesis of two works. As if your life isn't real unless it can be compared with two unreal things. I tried to think of what movies or novels I'd have picked. *Anna Karenina* meets *Attack of the Killer Tomatoes*?

I flexed my hand, which was still sore from the scorpion sting. 'Not a pitch, Davis. Just my life.'

'Jesus,' he said, slumping. His face went pale as the old man's legs. 'Jesus, Wren.'

'Luna.'

'Luna.' He nodded. 'It may take me a little while to get used to.'

'Davis, when you went to Denver this time, you'd already had a contract with this guy who killed that woman, didn't you?'

'With Roger Clemens?'

'Yes, the murderer.'

'Well, that hasn't been proven. I mean, Roger did kill Christine Palmer, but whether or not it's murder, that's going to be the tough call. Legally speaking.'

'Davis, this isn't a press conference. We're talking, that's all.'

He chuckled. 'Right. Sorry. Yes, I had a contract with Roger. When I read about the restraining order last week, I flew to Denver to talk to him. He was very lucid, very intelligent. No blithering madman. He said, yes, he'd been trying to contact Christine Palmer, at first, out of grief over his wife's death, but later, as he got to know more about her, for Christine herself. He made quite a convincing case.'

'So, you had no idea he was capable of anything like this. Of murder.'

Davis shook his head. 'No, not really.'

I stared at him for a minute.

'What?' he said.

'I'm not sure whether you're lying to me or to yourself. Either way, it's a lie.'

'What are you talking about?'

'You go to some guy who's emotionally unstable and you give him money and tell him you're going to make a movie out of his life—'

'Whoa. I didn't promise any movie. I optioned the rights to his life story, but I made it clear that any movie was a long shot.'

'And you think he heard that? He's not in the business, for chrissake, and you know it. Average guy has a movie producer fly in to make a contract and give him money, they expect a goddamn movie. Real people don't expect to get paid money for nothing.'

Davis held up his hands. 'I explained everything to him.'

'Come on, Davis, at least play fair with me. You know what I'm talking about. He was unstable, no matter how lucid he sounded. You went to this unstable man who was already overwrought about his wife's death and you offered him immortality. On the screen. And you don't think that affected him? You don't think that somewhere in his confused mind he didn't come up with a plan to ensure the movie would be made. Hell, he decided to write the ending himself. With a gun.'

Davis looked off at the old man for a couple of minutes. 'I've never seen anyone miss so many shots. It must be mathematically impossible to miss that many, don't you think?'

I didn't answer.

'So, what are you saying? I'm to blame here? I'm responsible for Christine Palmer's death because I wanted to make a movie? Jesus, Wren . . . Luna . . .' He shook his head.

'Why'd you lie to me about going to Hawaii?'

'Shit, we're not going to start comparing lies, are we? I mean, I'm a tadpole in the pond compared to you.'

'I'm not bitching about you lying. I only want to know why you did it.'

He looked off at the old man again, cupped his hands, and shouted, 'Bend your knees. Bend your goddamn knees.'

The old man stopped in midshot, looked back at us, waved, and shot again. He did not bend his knees. He missed the shot.

'Jesus, is that guy stupid or what?' Davis rubbed his hands together and glanced over at me. His face was sad and he looked tired. 'I have tax troubles. And I'm being sued by another video company I did business with over some ridiculous crap.' He waved his hand, dismissing it. 'I was a millionaire before I was twenty-eight, and I did it legally, without selling drugs, junk bonds, or anything like that. I just worked hard. Everything I dabbled in was a success. Then things started going wrong, nobody's fault. Lawsuits, tax problems, depressed economy.' He smiled at me. 'Baby, I need another success.'

I slid over and touched his hand. He saw the bandage on the back of mine.

'What happened?' he asked.

'Scorpion bite.'

He started laughing, laughing loudly. The old man

464

shooting baskets turned around with an annoyed expression, as if we were throwing off his game. He threw the ball up, it missed, and he looked at me and scowled as if it were my fault.

'I don't know, Luna,' Davis said, still chuckling. 'I still say you sell me your story and we both clean up. Jesus, scorpion bite.'

I didn't say anything. I kept my hand over his. I didn't know what I was feeling then, I wasn't even sure what I was going to do. I had no plan, no ultimatums, no speeches. I was winging it.

He sighed heavily. 'Gaaaaaawwd. Shit. I don't know. I didn't think he'd kill her. I really didn't. I figured he'd do something crazy, I guess, and she'd have him locked up and I'd have my story.'

The old man picked up his ball and started walking away, around the edge of the lake. I expected him to do something dramatic, like throw the ball into the water, but he didn't.

'I thought he was going to chuck the ball into the lake,' Davis said. 'He didn't make one basket the whole time we've been here.'

I was startled that we'd had the same thought.

'You want to say something,' Davis said. 'The suspense is killing me.'

'I don't know what to say. I guess, I'm going to say something high schoolish, like we should stop seeing each other.'

'Something like that or that exactly?'

I hesitated, uncertain. I groped ahead through the darkness of my feelings, looking for scorpions. 'That exactly.'

'See, I don't think that makes sense. Not really. Not when you think about it. We still care for each other. Okay, I didn't tell you because maybe I felt guilty and you didn't tell me because you felt . . .' He stopped, unsure what I felt. 'What? Inadequate? I don't know.'

'Inadequate sounds right.'

'Whatever the reason, that's past. That's gone. Isn't

465

that what relationships are all about, adjusting, making some mistakes, readjusting? Right?'

I shrugged. 'You're asking the wrong person for definitions of relationships.'

'Well, help me out here, Luna. What would it take to make things right? Tell me, I'll do it.'

I took my hand off his and leaned forward, my elbows on my knees, my head in my hands. I tried to imagine myself under Davis's warm quilt, showering under his skylight, braiding his daughter's hair, teaching his son to clean his room. I looked good in that picture. 'Thing is, Davis,' I said, 'you fell in love with me as Wren. It's kind of like a kid falling in love with an actress on the screen. Wren's a role I play well and now that I know how effective it is with you, I may resort to it without even trying. I'm not sure I'd ever get out of it.'

He didn't say anything. He looked around for the old man, but he was long gone. He turned, saw some Asian kids playing on the swings, their young mothers sitting nearby talking rapidly and laughing. 'People from other countries, they laugh differently. Did you ever notice that? Like laughter was part of their language and had to be pronounced just so. You wouldn't think there'd be a difference.' He stood up. 'I talked to New York this morning. Our deal is still good on the Season Dougherty book. You think you can handle it?'

I looked up at him, shielding my eyes from the sun. 'Yes.'

'Okay, then. You might want to interview the cops who found her, some of the inmates who knew her, that sort of thing. Her attorneys, maybe the prosecuting attorneys. You know what to do.'

'Yes.'

He stood there, hands in pocket, nodding. He didn't seem to know what to say or do. 'You need any help, any doors opened, call me. Or call me just because you want to. I'm not convinced this identity crisis thing won't just blow over.'

'Yes.'

He took a deep breath. 'Meantime, I got some writers to hire for the Roger Clemens story. Paramount has already offered me a preemptive bid. Looks like this one's going to the big screen.'

'Congratulations.'

'Thanks.' He leaned over and kissed me on the mouth, our lips barely touching. Then he walked off. I didn't watch him. I stared out at the lake and listened to his shoes shoosh against the thick grass with each step. Shoosh, shoosh. Shoosh, shoosh. Shoosh . . .

37

'I shouldn't be talking to you,' she said.

'You don't have to,' I agreed.

She studied me from behind the crack in the door. She started with my face, my hair, then down to my clothes and my shoes. I was wearing jeans and black Keds, a blue jersey; my hair was straight and limp, still a little damp from the shower I'd taken before driving down here. I didn't look too threatening.

'Okay,' she said. 'Come in. But when I say leave, I want you to leave. Got it?'

'Yes.'

'I mean it. I'm serious.'

'I'll leave.'

She opened the door and I entered her apartment. The name on the mailbox said Wendy Clove, but her real name was Carla Lasher. Season Dougherty's missing sister. I'd called her after my meeting with Davis and she'd agreed to see me.

'I don't know why Season gave you this number,' she said. 'But if she did, she must have trusted you. I guess I owe it to her to talk to you.'

'How do you like Del Mar?' I said.

'It's fine. Nice beach community. Jamie and I go for walks along the ocean every evening after dinner.'

'Does she go to school?'

'Every day.'

'Aren't you afraid someone will recognize her? Her photo's been on TV a lot.'

Carla shrugged. 'I cut her hair into a bob and dyed it brunette. She wears those contact lenses that change the color of your eyes to brown. They're all looking for a blond, blue-eyed girl with pigtails. Anyway, now that Season's dead, they'll stop looking.'

She sat on the sofa and I took the nearby armchair. The apartment was neat and very clean, but the furniture looked worn and the walls needed paint. The neighbourhood had probably once been a lovely place with cottages and bungalows for the inland wealthy to spend their summers near the shore. Now there were a lot of FOR RENT signs in dirty windows and a general atmosphere of decay.

'Our neighbours are mostly surfers, five of them renting one apartment, or stable hands working the racetrack. So don't mind the noise.'

'Okay,' I said, though there wasn't any noise.

'It's not bad now, but the moment the sun goes down . . .' She shook her head. Carla was about five years younger than Season, but not nearly as attractive. Every feature that had made Season beautiful seemed to have the opposite effect on Carla. Her face looked somehow underbaked.

'Where's Jamie now?' I asked.

Carla hesitated. She looked out the window, thinking. Finally, she sighed. 'Well, Season's dead, isn't she? I guess there's not much left to be secretive about.' She turned and faced the hallway. 'Tanya, come here, sweetheart.'

'Tanya?'

'We had to get used to calling each other our madeup names so we didn't slip in public. I guess I'm still used to it.'

'Who picked Tanya?'

'Season. Her little joke. It was the name Patty Hearst used when she was kidnapped and inducted into the SLA.'

'I remember.'

'Our last name, Clove, she got from clove oil, one of

469

the main things dentists use to take away pain. She had a sense of humor, my sister. Oh, here's my little angel.'

Maybe because of the Tanya name and the image of Patty Hearst, I half expected Jamie to come out dressed in army fatigues, a beret, and brandishing an AK-47. She didn't. She wore red shorts and a T-shirt with a drawing of crayons arranged to spell out Kid's Club.

'Hi, Jamie,' I said.

Jamie looked at Carla.

'It's okay, Jamie,' Carla said. 'This lady knew your mother.'

'How are you, Jamie?' I said.

'Fine.' She hopped onto the sofa next to her aunt and stared at me, waiting for the questions to begin. She was used to being asked questions by adults.

'She knows her mother's dead,' Carla said, hugging Jamie. 'She knows her mother's gone to a better place. No more jail, no more pain. That her mom's waiting there for her.'

'In heaven,' Jamie offered.

'Of course,' I said. I rubbed my thumbnail along the cushion seat of my chair. 'I'm writing a book about your mother. About how she took care of you.'

'She sent us down here to live.' Jamie pointed out the window. 'The ocean is two blocks that way. I can go there anytime I want.'

'What will you do now?' I asked Carla.

'Go home. Believe it or not, I had a steady job and a house mortgage. I lost the job, but I still own a house in Mission Viejo. My ex-husband still keeps making the payments on it since I went into hiding, bless him. He calls me almost every day to make sure we're okay.'

'Maybe you two will get back together now that this ordeal is over.' I smiled encouragingly.

Carla laughed loudly and I could hear the echo of Season's voice in that laugh. 'Why would I want to do that? Larry's a great guy, but we can't stand being married to each other. That much hasn't changed.'

I guess I'd been looking for some happy endings. Fat chance.

'Jamie will come live with me, just as we've been doing. I suppose the district attorney could bring charges against me, but my attorney doesn't think that will happen now.'

Jamie pointed at my bandaged hand. 'What happened?'

'Scorpion bit me.'

'Cool!' She smiled. 'Did it hurt?'

'Lots. Kind of like scraping your knee and squirting onion juice in the wound.'

'Yeeeech.'

'That's what I said.'

Carla kissed Jamie's cheek. 'Honey, why don't you go off to your room and play for a little while. I want to talk to the lady alone.'

Jamie slid off the sofa and walked to her room.

'Bye, Jamie,' I called after her.

'Bye.' A door closed behind her.

Carla faced me with a stern expression. 'Go ahead and ask what you came here to ask. Let's just get it over with.'

I didn't know what I'd come there to ask. I guess I was trying to figure out why Season wanted me to come here. Why she thought it was so damn important.

'You must have loved your sister very much to go through all this,' I said. 'Uproot your life, go into hiding.'

'I was a legal secretary at a title search company. Doesn't sound like much, especially when compared to Season being a dentist. A dentist, a mother, beautiful.'

'That's a hell of a legacy to live up to.'

'Actually, it was quite easy. No one expected me to do as well. I mean, she was after all Season. So whatever I did, no matter how lame, it was celebrated as if I'd won the Nobel Prize. Lots of parties when I was a kid. Plenty of encouragement. And no expectations. I think my parents thought it unfair to expect much from me when God had given them such a winner in Season.' She laughed. 'Some kind of Catholic voodoo, I guess.'

'Where are your parents now?'

'Arizona. My mother has Alzheimer's. She's in a home. My father has an apartment nearby. He has his little routine. Visits Mom once a day, visits the church once a day to pray for her, and plays golf the rest of the time. He just won his club's championship for the second year in a row.'

I was thirsty, but since I hadn't been offered anything, I didn't want to ask. Carla was fidgeting with a loose threat on the sofa cushion. She glanced at her wristwatch, holding the pose long enough for me to see and take the hint.

'Look,' she said, 'you seem like a nice person. I'm sure Season must have trusted you or she wouldn't have given you this number. She didn't even give it to Dad. So, go ahead and ask.'

Ask what? I wondered. Why was I missing what was so obvious to her?

She sighed impatiently. 'Christ, maybe I'm not Season, but I'm not made of glass. You want to know about the molestation, right?'

I nodded.

'Well, it never happened. There wasn't any.' She'd said it quickly, like a secret she'd been holding in too long. Now that she'd said it, her face relaxed in such a way I could see a resemblance to Season again.

I guess I wasn't really surprised by what she said, because once she said it, I just kept nodding. 'No sexual contact at all?'

'None. Philip wasn't a bad guy. He and Season had their problems, but he adored Jamie and he was always very good to me. I should be so lucky to find a guy like Philip.' She looked up at me quickly, like someone who'd just dribbled her soup down her blouse. Then I knew. The sexual contact hadn't been between Philip and Jamie, but between Philip and Carla. She continued, 'Philip used to give Jamie baths when he had custody. They played volleyball on the beach and they'd come home sandy and hop in the tub, take off their sandy bathing suits, and wash off. Philip wasn't embarrassed by nudity and he didn't

472

want Jamie to be either. It was all harmless enough.'

'And Jamie testified to that?'

'About a hundred times. But Season was convinced she was lying because she was afraid of her father. I tried to talk her out of it, but she got caught up in the whole martyr business and she just couldn't see straight.'

'So, out of loyalty to your sister, you followed her wishes and went into hiding with Jamie.'

Carla's mouth twisted into a bitter smile. 'Yeah, out of loyalty and guilt.' She looked me in the eyes and knew that I knew about her and Philip. 'And because there are millions of women who are fighting a real battle for their children and if people knew the truth about Season's case it might screw it up for a lot of authentically molested children.'

Why had Season sent me down here? To find out the truth she wasn't able to admit, even to herself? What good did this truth do me? I didn't need it or want it, except to write it down in a book that would sell at grocery store checkout stands along with *TV Guide* and *Soap Opera Digest*.

I left Carla's apartment and walked numbly down the sidewalk. I had to be the worst journalist in the world; I hated truth. I didn't want to write a book that would make Season out to be a monster, Carla an adulterer, Jamie molested more by her mother's delusions than her father's innocent showers. Shit, maybe I wasn't the right person for this job after all.

A bearded man was leaning against my car, a big man in a foam neck brace. I looked around for his white Subaru but didn't see it.

'You follow me on foot?' I asked as I nudged him away from the driver's door.

'New car,' he said proudly. He swept his hand toward the car parked behind me, a white Honda Prelude. 'Subaru was a piece of shit. But this baby is luxury and speed.'

'You like white.'

'People don't notice it as much when you follow them.'

'Guess not, I didn't notice you.'

'You probably would have on the way back. You're more paranoid than most, which usually means something to hide, but you're not who I'm after. That's why I'm approaching you like this. I don't want any more accidents like the last time.' He patted his neck brace. 'You know how much these things cost? Don't ask. I'm still dicking around with my insurance company over medical costs. I'm thinking of suing the whole fucking bunch, make enough to fish for the rest of my life.'

I got into my car and closed the door. He rapped on the window with his knuckle. I rolled it down an inch and locked the door.

'I'm not after you. Like I said, I was just following you because you're shacked up with Byron Caldwell. And he's a known associate of the guy I'm after, Zeno Harris. You know Zeno?'

'If you're a cop, let me see your ID.'

'Hey, lady, if I were a fucking cop, I'd have shot you by now, okay? I used to be a cop, but I'm retired. Nerves.' He held out his hand to show me how it shook a little. He grinned like a man who'd put something over on someone. 'Now I do some consultancy work. Private investigation stuff. Like on TV.'

'For whom?'

'Whom? Whom, I like that. For the University of California Library, that's whom. Seems our boy Zeno stole a few rare books since he's been out and they want me to track him down and get the books back so other patrons of the arts may also enjoy them. That *whom* enough for you?'

I started the engine.

'Hey, come on,' he whined. 'Help me out. It's not like you wouldn't be doing a good deed in helping a library.'

'Why not follow Byron? He's the known associate.'

He shook his head. 'I tried. Half a dozen times. You know how easy it is to follow someone who takes a bus?

474

But the son of a bitch always spots me and always shakes me. He's just one of those guys you can't follow unless you've got a team of three cars.'

I closed my eyes and leaned my head back against the headrest. Why hadn't it occurred to me before. Byron had let me follow him. He'd wanted me to. What for? To show me his bamboo sprouts so I'd invest money? To fuck me? Both?

I could just tell this man where Zeno was and let him sort out the ethics of who's doing what to whom. What did I care?

'Just tell me where Zeno Harris is, okay? Then you never see me again.'

I didn't say anything. He waited, but when it became clear I wasn't going to speak, he started back to his new Prelude. I watched him in my rearview mirror. I beeped my horn. He looked up, grinned, walked back to my car.

'Yeah?'

'You work for the university, right?'

'Right. The Board of Regents.'

'I have their phone number. Who's your boss, the guy who hired you? I want to call him first.'

'Tanner. Dr. Felix Tanner.'

I looked up into his wide face. His expression was serious and honest. 'There is no Dr. Felix Tanner,' I said. 'I just did a story on the university and I know every person on the Board of Regents and the administrators.'

He shrugged, looked confused. 'Maybe he's new or something.'

I'd been bluffing, but now I knew he was lying.

He was undoubtedly with some corporation out to steal or destroy Byron's bamboo experiments. So what? What did I owe to Byron, really? Nothing.

I shoved the shift into reverse, stomped the gas pedal, and popped the clutch.

'*Nooo!!!*' he hollered.

My little Rabbit flew backward into his Prelude and

smashed the front end with a chorus of shattering glass and crunching metal.

'You fucking cunt!' he said.

I drove off. Finally, I knew where I was going and what I was going to do.

476

38

'I'm Luna Devon,' I said. It was the first time in so long I'd introduced myself by my real name, I felt as if I should follow it with, 'And I'm an alcoholic,' or something equally confessional.

'Yes?' the woman said, meaning 'so what?'

I looked over her shoulder, down the hallway. I saw no one, just Bud sitting there with a fresh bandage. I heard no snapping of chess pieces, no rumble of men's voices. The room behind her was clear of hazy smoke. A man came down the hallway carrying a bowl of ice cream. I recognized him from his TV commercials. Bonkers Bob.

'I'm looking for Grudge,' I said.

Bonkers Bob came to the door, spooning chocolate ice cream into his mouth. He was tall and good-looking, so was his wife. They had deep tans. They were both in their mid-forties, both dressed in tennis outfits.

'Hi,' he said.

'I'm looking for Grudge,' I repeated.

They both seemed startled, looking me over as if searching for obscene tattoos. Mrs. Bonkers slipped away without saying anything.

'Jimmy's at work today.' He stood in the doorway, making it clear I was not going to be invited inside.

'Do you have a number where I can reach him? It's important.'

He held his bowl and stared at me. 'I don't know. Jimmy's on parole, you know.'

'I'm not a convict, if that's what you're getting at. He

477

won't be breaking parole talking to me. I'm a reporter with *Orange Coast Today* and I'm doing a story of the local chess scene. I was told he knows something.'

Bob relaxed, spooned another glob of ice cream into his mouth. 'Hell, yes. Jimmy's a chess whiz. Plays all the time. Belongs to some chess club, bunch of retired folks, I guess. Helps keep him away from those punks he used to hang around, keeps him out of trouble. Sport is our best defense against crime, I say.'

He gave me the phone number of his warehouse and I drove to the nearest gas station and called him.

'I'm looking for Byron,' I said.

'I'm not his keeper, babe.'

'When I hang up, I'm going right to the parole office and telling them everything I know about you. Gambling is certainly a violation of your parole, so is associating with known felons. All cops can't all be chess players who are willing to turn their backs.'

'You go there,' he growled, 'and I'll have your fucking heart cut out and stuffed in your cocksucking mouth, you bitch. Then they'll fuck the hole in your chest. You hear me? You're dead!'

'Is that a no?'

There was a long pause.

'Twelve-eighteen Baker Street. Pick me up at midnight.'

'Midnight? Give me a break.'

'Hey, that's when I finish my shift. I can't just walk off, my brother would fire my ass and then I'd be back in the joint.'

'Why don't you just tell me where he is?'

'Because I don't know where he is. But I do know where he'll be at one A.M.'

'Where?'

'Playing chess with Landry for all the marbles. I gotta go. See you at midnight.' He hung up.

*　　*　　*　　*　　*

'You sure this is the place?' I said.

He gave me a disgusted look. 'Feel free to drop me off and look somewhere else by yourself.'

I turned off the engine and stared at the synagogue. It was dark. The entire neighbourhood was dark, no lights anywhere except the outside lights of the synagogue that shone on the large stained-glass window.

'I didn't know synagogues had stained glass,' Grudge said. 'Aren't Jews against that sort of thing?'

'Guess not,' I said. Theological discussions seemed out of place right now. 'I don't see anybody.'

'Well, if you saw them, then this wouldn't be a good place, would it?'

We got out of the car. I found myself tiptoeing down the sidewalk.

'Don't be a jerk, okay?' Grudge said. 'Just walk normal. We're not here to rob the place, for chrissake. Just to watch some chess.'

'It's still illegal entry,' I whispered.

'What're you, a fucking lawyer? Don't sweat it so much. It's not that big of a deal. The Jews probably wouldn't press charges even if they found out. They're a pretty sporting bunch, I hear.'

The name of the synagogue was carved in the stone archway around the front door. Ohev Sholom. Grudge knocked on the heavy wooden door. The door opened a crack, a face studied us, then the door opened the rest of the way.

The doorman was close to seven feet tall but couldn't have weighed more than 150 pounds. He wore coveralls and a khaki shirt underneath. A black skullcap sat on his head.

'Hey, Blinky,' Grudge said.

'Don't start with that Blinky shit, you got me?' The man quickly closed the door behind us and locked it. The foyer and hallway was dark. 'I don't know you,' he said to me.

'She's with Byron.'

'Oh, she's the one.' He nodded and gave me an extra

appreciative look that stripped me naked, bent me over, and had me begging him for more.

'How's the eye, Blinky?' Grudge said.

'Very funny.'

'I once tossed a glass of 7Up in Blinky's face and told him it was acid. You shoulda seen him screaming and blinking.' Grudge laughed, blinking his eyes rapidly in imitation.

'Very funny,' Blinky repeated. He handed Grudge a white skullcap from a wooden bin. On the inside, in gold letters, was written: *On the occasion of the bar mitzvah of Barry H. Levinson, October 12, 1991.*

'What am I supposed to do with this?' Grudge said.

'You wear it, moron.' He pointed to the one on his own head. 'It's a yarmulke.'

'I'm not Jewish, asshole.'

'Neither am I. But these people think it's important that you wear one and they gave me a job when no one else would, so I'm gonna make sure everyone else wears one. You don't put it on, you're not getting in.'

Grudge's face twitched at the challenge. He didn't actually move, but his body seemed to crouch under his clothes. Blinky looked more than happy to oblige and even an old score.

'You boys settle it,' I said. 'Meantime, can you point me toward the chess game?'

Mentioning chess seemed to remind them what they were here for. Grudge put the skullcap on his head and struck a model's pose. 'How do I look? Jewish enough for you?'

Blinky pointed down the hall. 'Go through those doors.'

I walked off toward the doors with Grudge following. 'The guy's a fucking janitor, right away he thinks he's Moses or something.'

I pushed through the door into what looked to be a gymnasium. The floors were hardwood with the painted stripes of a basketball court. But there were banquet tables set up in long rows, all facing the far wall, where three long tables were elevated on a platform. All the tables had white tablecloths on them, though they were all dirty, stained with various foods and wine. Crumbs sprinkled the tops of many tablecloths. Men and women were sitting at the various tables, some brushing the crumbs away, others just talking. Most of the people were still milling around, discussing intently.

'They had a bar mitzvah here Saturday,' Blinky said behind us. I hadn't even heard him come up. Next to me, Grudge jumped slightly, also startled. The grin on Blinky's face indicated that was why he'd done it.

'Jesus, Blinky,' Grudge barked. 'Nice way to get yourself killed.'

Blinky ignored him and spoke to me. 'Name's Terry Dern,' he said. 'This jerk's the only one who calls me Blinky.'

'Hi, Terry. I'm Luna.'

'Gotta go. This is a conservative synagogue, which means they're kind of strict about all their religious mumbo jumbo. Still use mostly Hebrew in their services and such. Problem is, they've been losing a lot of customers to the looser reform bunch. That means less money for expenses. That's why I'm the only janitor.' He smiled proudly at his knowledge of the intricacies of Judaism.

'You a chess enthusiast?' I asked him, but I was scanning the crowd for Byron.

'Play every day with the rabbi here. He hates blitz, though. Says it ruins your game, keeps you from becoming a grandmaster.'

'Like you really need to worry about becoming a grandmaster, Blinkmaster.' Grudge chortled. 'Yeah, I think I'm gonna have you killed by having chess pieces shoved up your ass until your colon explodes. How's that sound to you?'

'Like your sexual fantasy, jerkoff.'

481

Grudge spun around with his fists clenched. 'Right now, asshole!'

Terry made fists and went into a crouch and I realized these two men were about to start swinging. I was surprised at how quickly they had escalated from insult to action.

'You guys start something,' a calm voice said, 'and I'll be forced to finish it.'

The three of us turned around. Jerry Kirn, Byron's ex-cellmate and Landry's current strong-arm man, stood there smiling. He was a surprisingly handsome man, and dressed in his knit shirt with a fashionable cardigan sweater blousing over his huge chest, he looked very much like a successful athlete-turned-entrepreneur. He patted Grudge on the shoulder in a friendly but firm way. 'Make it easy on yourselves, boys.'

Fists were relaxed into empty hands.

'I'd better check on some things,' Terry said and drifted off.

'Nice seeing you again,' Jerry said, nodding at us and disappearing into the crowd.

Grudge watched him wend through the men and women, staring but not saying anything. I'd expected a threat, a description of the death he planned for Jerry Kirn. But then, maybe Jerry Kirn wasn't the kind you threatened without being able to instantly back it up. His presence here gave the whole atmosphere a dangerous tinge. I felt like I was in an old speakeasy and a rival mob might come busting in at any second and start shooting.

'Where's Byron?' I asked.

'I don't see him.' Grudge pointed at the three tables on the platform. Two men were setting up chess pieces. A third was sitting down, cleaning his glasses and smoking a pipe. 'That's Landry. Son of a bitch just started smoking a pipe. Thinks it makes him look smarter. Same with the glasses. Guy told me they're just regular window glass.'

I studied Landry. He finished polishing his glasses and put them on. They did make him look smarter. He puffed on the pipe and waited patiently, looking every bit the thoughtful fortyish economics professor rather than the bone-busting ex-con loan shark. He didn't dress in the shiny suit I'd expected, or the dark shirt and darker tie I'd envisioned. He wore pleated khaki pants and a button-down cotton shirt straight from a Land's End catalogue. His hair was longish on top, mussed strategically. If I'd seen him sipping cappuccino at a café, I might have found him attractive. I asked Grudge, 'How good is he?'

'He's good. Not as good as me, maybe half as good as Byron.'

'Then Byron can beat him?'

Grudge laughed. 'That's not the point. The point is, Byron's not going to beat him. They'll play five games of blitz, all two-minute games. Byron will win the first one, lose the second one, win the third, and lose the next two.'

I looked at him. 'You already know this? Did Byron tell you?'

'He doesn't have to. This whole thing isn't about fucking chess. He told you that much, didn't he?'

'Yes. Landry wants to start moving up to big heists. He's hoping to prove himself the mastermind by beating Byron at chess, thereby attracting more quality thieves. That about it?'

He stared at me. 'Yeah, but you can drop the fucking sarcasm. Sure, it sounds stupid to you. You want a job, you just apply. Doesn't work that way out in the organized crime world. See, Byron has a reputation, not as a criminal but as a bright guy. I mean, let's face it, all that monkey-wrench bullshit he pulled was fucking amateur hour. Cementing your feet in a ditch?' He laughed. 'I crack up every time I think about that. Anyway. Byron's a yutz when it comes to real crime, okay? But he is the guy who thought up all those raids where they broke into places and damaged the logging equipment, stuff like that. And no one from his group ever got caught. The guys respect that kind of brains. Now do you see? Landry kicks Byron's ass tonight and he gets the rep.'

'But don't people know it's fixed?'

'Sure, but it doesn't matter how you win. If you win through brains, fine; if through intimidation, even better. The fix part will be forgotten anyway. Crooks just remember who wins and who loses. The details don't fucking matter.'

'So this is just a show, like professional wrestling.'

'Basically. More like a ceremony.'

'Doesn't anyone remember that Byron got caught? That's how he wound up in jail.'

Grudge waved a dismissing hand. 'Sure, but that's only because his old lady needed help. He could've made a clean getaway, instead he took her to the hospital. Even after he took her there he could've split, but he just sat there and waited for her, waited with her, even though he knew the cops were coming. Yeah, it's stupid, but crooks got a romantic streak in them. They don't hold it against a guy if he does something like that.'

I thought of Wren lying in the hospital, her teeth knocked out by a baseball bat. Probably unconscious from sedatives. Byron sitting next to her while she slept. I thought of myself in the hospital bed, a bullet tunnel to my heart, waking up to the nurse I thought was my mother.

What was I doing here? Earlier, when I'd been driving home from visiting Carla and Jamie, everything had seemed so clear. I would find Byron and . . . And then what? What had I been thinking would happen? I closed my eyes, felt my head throbbing. I put my hand on my aching bullet wound and felt my heart beating. My head and heart were synchronized, pounding a message of sympathetic pain to each other. What was my plan again?

'There he is,' Grudge said excitedly. It was odd to hear the excitement in his voice, as if he didn't already know the outcome.

I opened my eyes. Byron walked up to the platform, shook Landry's hand, and took a seat opposite him. The chess clock was placed between them so it faced outward. Everyone began swarming toward the platform.

'What does Byron get out of all this?' I asked Grudge as we moved forward with the crowd. 'Except not beaten up anymore?'

'He places a bet on the game, something nominal like five grand. When he loses, Landry keeps the money, but turns around and loans him, interest free, a hundred grand. Landry gets his reputation boosted and Byron gets to finish whatever he and that asshole Zeno got cooking. You know what it is?'

He asked in such an offhanded way I almost told him. But I stopped myself, remembering Zeno's hysterical face when he saw me invade his little nest. 'No, I don't know.'

He turned and grinned at me. 'You're getting the hang of this, aren't you?'

I saw Shawna at the front edge of the crowd. She was gesturing to the man next to her, her father. Their gestures seemed more frantic than usual. I recognized others from the Laguna Hills house yesterday. But there were a lot more people here tonight. Some people were standing on chairs, on tables, angling for a better look. People were genuinely excited, bouncing with anticipation. Even Grudge seemed edgy. It was as if, even knowing there was probably a fix in, maybe things would turn out differently than they knew it would. Perhaps the more certain the outcome, the more excited people get at the potential for an upset. Futility seems to fuel hope more than anything else.

With all the people surging around me, I could hardly see Byron or Landry. I pulled a folding metal chair out, brushed off some bread crumbs, and climbed atop it. Now I could see them clearly. I also saw a table at the front where people were betting money on the game. Thousands of dollars was stacked up.

I stuck out my leg and tapped my toe against Grudge's shoulder.

He looked back and up, annoyed. 'What?'

I stooped down and whispered, 'If it's common knowledge Landry's going to win, why would anybody bet?'

'They're giving good odds. Thirty to one against Byron.'

'But they know Byron's going to lose.'

He shrugged. 'You never know. Not really. Besides, it's hard for gamblers to pass up good odds, doesn't matter what they know.'

I shook my head and stood back up. The colors had been chosen and the game was starting. Byron had white. He shoved his piece out. The game took less than a minute, with Byron handily crushing Landry. Landry smiled, shook Byron's hand, and started polishing his glasses. There was a break while more people made bets.

'God, he's good,' Grudge said. It sort of just popped out and he looked around embarrassed to have said anything so envious. He noticed me looking and slouched into his usual cynical attitude. 'Forget this next game, it'll be a snooze. The only interesting thing will be how Byron manages to lose without making it look too obvious. He has to be careful not to humiliate Landry by lying down too easy. Landry'll bust his legs for that too.'

The second game started and lasted almost the entire two minutes. They seemed neck and neck, swapping pieces evenly all along. For a moment I thought Byron was going to win, but toward the end of the game he made a bad move and allowed himself to get pinned. Landry won.

'They'll make it go all the way to five games,' Grudge said. 'Just to give the boobs their money's worth. This game could go either way, but I figure it's a better show if Byron wins.'

Which is exactly what happened. Byron rolled over Landry's pieces like an avalanche, snatching pieces left and right while Landry faltered and seemed confused. The game was over and Landry just kept staring at the board. Byron got up and went to the bathroom.

'He'd better cool it,' Grudge said. 'That's just the kind of thing that'll get him a permanent limp.'

Bets continued to be made at the table in front of the

platform. The white tablecloth on the table had a long purple stain splattered across it where someone had probably knocked over a wineglass.

Byron returned, took his seat across from Landry. Landry's face was no longer the calm expression of professorial detachment. He looked angry.

I climbed down from my chair and pushed my way to the front of the crowd. 'Excuse me,' I said, hacking my way with forearms and elbows through the thicket of people. Finally I made it to the betting table. 'A thousand dollars on Landry,' I said loudly and looked up at Byron.

He stared down at me, his face tight and grim. He shook his head at me in disappointment.

I took out my checkbook.

'This is a cash kind of business, lady,' the guy behind the table said.

'All I have are checks. They're good.'

'Right. They always are.'

'I don't have any cash.'

'Sorry, honey.' The man taking bets shrugged.

'She's okay, Mike.' Jerry Kirn appeared out of the crowd, signaled Mike, the bet taker, and floated away again.

Mike sighed heavily. 'Fine, fine. Everybody knows my business. Fine.' He waved me in impatiently. 'You got a credit card number we can take your check.'

I wrote the check for a thousand dollars and handed it to Mike. 'Kind of a stupid bet, lady,' Mike said. 'You're risking a grand when all you can win is $300 plus your grand back. That's not smart. You bet Byron there you stand to win $30,000. And he's already two games to one ahead. I mean, it's none of my business, I'm just trying to help you out.'

'Put it on Landry,' I said. I glanced up at Byron. I didn't know what was in his face or in his head. He just stared at me.

I didn't know why I'd bet the money exactly. I thought I had a reason when I'd started for the table, but by the time I'd made my way through the crowd, all I remembered was my goal, not the reasoning. Still, it seemed like a good idea to go through with my plan. At least it was a plan, I was doing something.

Then the fourth game began. Smack, smack, smack. Pieces were flying again. Sometimes they didn't bother to pick up a captured piece, they just knocked it off the board. I had to admit, watching them attack the board like that had my adrenaline thundering through my body. My headache and heart pain were both gone. Smack, smack, smack. I felt the vibrations of each move pass through me like an earthquake aftershock.

Then it was all over.

Landry won.

'Two games apiece,' Mike announced.

Their was a marked letdown in the crowd. Few people bet now. Most looked disappointed, defeated themselves. Anyone who had doubted the outcome of the match before now knew what would happen.

'Come on, come on,' Mike encouraged people. 'Thirty to one. One more game, one more game. Thirty to fucking one.'

Jerry Kirn swam up out of the crowd, whispered to Mike, then drove back into the crowd and disappeared.

'Forty to one! Jesus, forty to one odds, folks.' Mike acted as if he couldn't believe what he was saying.

A few more people stepped up and placed some small wagers.

Landry looked more relaxed now, beneficent. He puffed on his pipe, looking down on the gathered throng as if they were here to pay their respects to him. I guess in a way they were. They had come to acknowledge their role in the grand scheme of the food chain. Like that scene in Robin Hood my students had talked about.

Yes, I thought, just like that scene.

I stepped up to the betting table. 'Five thousand more on Landry, Mike,' I said. I wrote a check and handed it to him.

488

He groaned. 'The odds have changed, lady. You bet this on Byron and you could win $200,000. You have any idea how much money that is? Better odds than the goddamn lottery.'

'Five thousand. On Landry.'

He took the money, handed me a receipt. Then he went back to trying to drum up more business. No one else bet.

Byron glared at me, his look no longer confusing. I had touched him all right, touched him deep and hard. Now that I thought of it, I guess that was my plan all along.

The final game began.

39

Smack, smack.

Smack, smack, smack, smack.

Smack, smack, smack, smack, smack, smack.

Smack, smack, smack, smack, smack, smack, smack, smack, smack, smack, smack, smack, smack.

And it was over.

No one said anything at first. They just watched the two men on the platform stare at each other. Watched Landry reach for his pipe, light it, sucking the flames to life. Watched Byron, face grim as a gravedigger, rise, shake hands with Landry. Watched Landry paste a phony smile on his face and raise Byron's hand in the air.

The winner.

Then everyone spoke and moved at once. The betting table was swarmed by people waving receipts. Others pulled out pocket-sized chess games and began replaying each game. I could see the triumphant look on everyone's face, as if they had all just come out of an uplifting movie.

Byron took the money that was stacked in front of the board and quickly shoved it into his pants pocket. With his glum expression and bulging pockets, he looked like he'd just won the marbles championship but was about to be scolded by his mother for coming home late. Landry, still smiling sharkishly, whispered something to him. From the way Landry's lips flexed. I could tell it was not something pleasant. Byron shrugged and walked away. As he entered the crowd, people closed around him, slapping his back, shaking his hand. He nodded politely at them, accepting their adulation without encouraging it.

'Jesus fucking Christ,' Grudge said, sidling up beside me. 'I can't believe he did something so stupid.' He was counting a handful of money.

'Where'd you get that?'

'I won it.'

'But you knew it was fixed.'

'Like I said, the odds were too good to pass up.'

Byron broke through a ring of the loyal, their hands reaching out to touch him as he brushed by them. He snagged my arm without slowing down and trawled me alongside him.

'What are you—?'

'Do you have your car?' he asked. People talked to him, offered their hands. He ignored them now, picking up speed as we headed toward the exit. I was trotting to stay up with him.

'Let me go,' I said, trying to pull away. His grip was too strong. I felt a pain shooting up my arm as he tightened his grip more.

'Do you have your car?'

'Yes, I have my goddamn car.'

'Show me.'

We shoved through the gymnasium doors and were hustling through the lobby. Blinky was polishing a glass showcase that displayed fancy skullcaps, candle holders, and such. A little white sign said AVAILABLE AT B'NAI B'RITH SHOP. Blinky hooked the spray container of Glass-Plus onto his waistband and reached for the large ring of keys clipped to his belt.

'You were great, man,' Blinky said. 'Great.'

'Thanks,' Byron said impatiently. We stood in front of the exit door waiting for Blinky to find the right key.

'I wish the rabbi could have seen you. He's a pretty cool guy. I think he might give you a game. Not in blitz, of course, but like a regular game. You wouldn't think a guy that old, being so religious and such, would have such an

491

aggressive game.' He unlocked the door and Byron pulled me through it.

'Where?' he said. 'Where's your car?'

I pointed.

'Get your keys out. Now.'

As we jogged toward my car, I dug through my purse for my keys. I slowed down to rummage.

'Hurry up,' Byron urged. He was already standing at the car, pulling on the locked door and looking nervously at the synagogue doors.

I stalled, pretending to not be able to find the keys. Things were going just as I had planned, I had to keep them that way.

Byron ran over, yanked my purse from my hands, and dumped it on the hood of the car, emptying it completely. The keys clattered out among tissues and my wallet, a movie ticket stub, lipstick. He snatched them up and ran for the driver's side.

I took as long as possible shoveling my stuff back into my purse. When I had everything in it, I slung my purse over my shoulder, marched over to the driver's side, pulled open the door, and said, 'I'm driving.'

'Just get in,' he said, hooking a thumb at the other door.

'It's my goddamn car and I'm driving.'

'Get in or I'm leaving you here.'

I climbed into the driver's side on top of him and gripped the wheel as hard as I could. He tried to push me aside, but I hugged the wheel to my chest and ground my butt into his lap.

'What the hell's wrong with you?' he said. 'Are you crazy?'

'It's my car and I'll drive.'

I had to drive if I was going to make this work. And we couldn't leave yet, not until the rest of the cast had assembled.

'Fine!' he said. 'You fucking drive.' He wiggled out from under me and scooted over to the passenger seat. 'Okay? Happy? Can we get the hell out of here now?'

'Whoa there, pardner,' I heard.

My stalling had worked. Jerry Kirn and another man ran up to the car. Byron sighed and swore under his breath.

'Byron, buddy, you weren't leaving already?' Jerry asked. 'The party's just starting. You're the man of honor.'

The man with Jerry was even larger, no more than twenty-three, his round face set in a permanent scowl of a football lineman trying to intimidate his opponent. Somehow the white skullcap still sitting on his head looked like a dunce cap on him.

'Hell of a game you played in there, buddy,' Jerry said. 'Hell of a game.'

Byron said nothing.

'You mind?' I said. 'We want to celebrate alone.'

Jerry looked at me with a curious expression. 'You lost some bucks tonight betting against our boy here.'

'The check's good. I'm not stopping payment or anything.'

He laughed. 'No, I know you aren't.' A sharp threat was sheathed in his tone. 'I'm just impressed with how well you take losing that kind of money. Not only that, but then you go off with the guy who you bet against. I don't know, it just looks funny, I can't figure it out.'

Byron angrily flung open his door and jumped out of the car. Jerry Kirn's partner tensed for action. Jerry just stood there, hands in pocket, completely calm.

'Look, Jerry,' Byron said. 'It just happened. I didn't plan it.'

'You double-crossed Mr. Landry,' Jerry's partner grunted.

In a blur of motion, Jerry's hand snapped out and slapped his partner in the mouth. The calm, almost bored expression never left Jerry's face. 'I do the talking, Trent.'

Trent nodded, then touched his fingers to his lips. When he took them away he saw the blood on his fingertips.

Jerry took a couple steps toward Byron. Byron didn't flinch or move. Jerry put his arm around Byron's shoulder and spoke quietly. 'Christ, Byron, what do you have against me that you keep putting me in a position where I've got to hurt you?'

'What are friends for?'

Jerry laughed. 'See? That's what I mean. I consider us friends.'

'I do too, Jerry.'

'Yet you back out on your word and you stomp my boss to pulp in front of all the people he's trying to impress.' He shook his head. 'Tell me, at least, it's not because of her.' He pointed at me. 'It's not because she goaded you by betting all that money against you. Please tell me it's not that stupid.'

Byron looked over at me. 'It wasn't because of her.'

Jerry laughed. 'Shit, even Trent here doesn't believe that and he's stupider than his own fist. Aren't you, Trent?'

'Yes, sir, I am.'

'Well, where does that leave us? You know I'm going to have to do some damage this time.' Jerry looked up at the sky, his face suddenly angry. 'Jesus, you make me mad sometimes, Byron.'

'Go ahead and do it, man,' Byron said. 'What's it going to take to satisfy him?'

'A broken limb, at least. Maybe two. Probably a concussion, though a coma would be better. You know, it's got to be visible enough that people, the people who count, can spread the word about what happens when you fuck with Mr. Landry. I can leave your face alone, I suppose, though a nice deep scar would sure be to my benefit. You mind a scar on your face?'

Byron shrugged. 'I'll leave it in your capable hands. Go ahead.' He braced himself.

'Not here, putz,' Jerry said. 'Not now. We got a nice quiet neighbourhood, we got a synagogue full of witnesses. The potential for getting snitched out is too great.' He

494

patted Byron on the arm. 'But it'll happen, don't worry. I'll find you later.'

'Excuse me,' I said. 'Which is your car?'

Jerry looked confused. 'My car?'

'Yes, I'm curious what kind of car you drive.' Most men have an instinctive reaction to that question. If it's a clunker, they shrug and talk about how sick and tired they are of a culture that places so much value on something as shallow as a car. If they have a hot car, they can't wait to point it out, their chests all puffed up like an adder.

He pointed across the street. 'That red Miata.' His chest puffed up.

'You like it?' I asked.

'What's not to like? She handles great, is fast as a bullet. It's the perfect car.'

'Get in,' I said to Byron.

Byron didn't move. He and Jerry exchanged sad looks.

'Go on,' Jerry said. 'I'm getting stinking drunk tonight. Then I'm going home and catch hell from my wife. But tomorrow, Byron . . .' He let the threat hang. 'Don't make it harder on me by running, man. You know that's only going to cost you more pain.'

Byron got into the car and closed the door. Jerry and Trent started walking slowly back to the synagogue. Jerry reached over and straightened Trent's skullcap.

'That was close,' I said, starting the engine.

'What's the difference, tonight or tomorrow? Same results.'

'Well, if there's no difference, then there's no time like the present.' I gunned the motor, popped the clutch, and squealed away from the curb. I shot across the street and sideswiped the red Miata hugging the curb. The metal collapsed in a dent that ran the entire length of the car.

'What are you doing?' Byron shouted, grabbing for the steering wheel.

I pushed Byron's hands away and looked over at Jerry's incredulous face. His eyes studied his car, the dent, the scraped paint, then swung over to fix on me. I idled the

495

car in the middle of the street, waiting. Jerry and Trent suddenly dashed for my car.

'Go, go, go!' Byron yelled. 'This isn't the mood I want him in when he catches me.'

I waited until Jerry and Trent were almost on us before peeling out down the street. I waited at the intersection. In my rearview mirror I could see them jumping into the Miata. Byron was twisted around, watching them.

'Either you're completely deranged or this is the most serious case of PMS I've ever seen,' Byron said. 'Let's get the hell out of here. These guys aren't going to be so polite now. And I wouldn't count on your being a woman as any protection.'

'It never has been,' I said. 'Anyway, I'm just raising the stakes.'

'What stakes?'

'For the chase, Byron. We can't have a chase if there's nothing to lose.'

'Oh, God,' he said, clutching his head. 'I knew better than to sleep with a woman who pretends to be my dead wife. I know the Golden Rule of Males, never sleep with a woman who has more problems than you do. I know it, I broke it. But isn't this punishment worse than the crime?'

The Miata was rocketing toward us. I pulled away from the intersection.

The chase was on.

40

Byron tapped his finger against my gas guage. 'Maybe next time you engineer a car chase, you can remember to fill up the tank first.'

We were empty.

'I didn't engineer it. I was inspired, like an artist.'

'Oh, come on. You hunted Grudge down and blackmailed him into bringing you, right? I mean, that's the only reason he'd have done it unless you had sex with him.'

'I didn't have sex with him.'

'Okay, then it was blackmail. Then you bet against me in the chess match, knowing it was fixed. Grudge would have told you that much. You goaded me into winning that last game. Now, I don't blame you, that's my own fault for letting you affect me. That's the part I still don't get myself. That, and why it was worth six grand to you to see me win. Do you want me dead that much?'

'I don't want you dead.'

'Well, you enraged Jerry back there, forced him into following us. Tomorrow he would have found me, broken a limb or two, put me in the hospital for a week. Nothing worse. Hell, he would even have driven me to the hospital. Now . . .' He turned in his seat, saw the Miata racing behind us. 'Now he's going to do worse. Much worse.'

'We won't let him. That's the point of a chase. We out-run them.'

'Without gas?'

'An oversight. I didn't exactly plan this ahead of time.'

'No shit.'

I didn't tell him, but I was forming details to my plan as we drove. Okay, maybe the chase stuff was a last-minute revelation, but everything I'd done since leaving Carla and Jamie had been leading to this. A white whale hunt, only we were the whale. Driving an empty Rabbit.

'What did you hope to accomplish?' he said. 'In fucking up my life like this.'

'I'm not fucking up your life. I'm fixing it.'

'Jesus, If it's not broke, don't fix it. Haven't you ever heard that before?'

'Is that one of those guy sayings?'

'I'd like to give you a couple good guy sayings,' he grumbled.

'Look, one of us has to be authentic. One of us has to be the genuine article, the person we really are. I'm too far gone, but you aren't.'

He laughed. 'Luna, I've been a prisoner for two years. A convict. That's not who I really was, but I learned to adapt, to live like one, be one. Because, to everyone else, that's who I really was. So I became what they saw me as. Same as you.'

'You don't understand,' I said.

'Yes, I do. And you know it. That's what bugs you.'

I saw a gas station and pulled in. The Miata pulled in behind us, then veered into another slot beside a different pump. Trent hopped out of the Miata as I got out of my car. I walked to the cashier inside the glass booth. He was a kid, maybe nineteen with a series of moles on his cheekbone. A cigarette burned in a glass ashtray next to the cash register, filling the interior of the booth with white smoke. I could smell the bitter scent seeping through the pay slot. It made me want to smoke again. I gave him a twenty and told him the pump number. He took the money and nodded, then looked up at me. Something behind his eyes shifted, because he smiled slightly and said, 'Thank you.' I looked at my blouse to make sure it wasn't

498

unbuttoned or something. It wasn't. I guess he just liked my looks, the way guys used to react to Wren.

Trent walked up behind me, stood there breathing like a bull. I didn't look back at him, just walked back to my car. I heard money being slid into the pay slot, Trent saying, 'Pump three.'

When I got back to the car, Byron was already pumping the gas.

'Give me Zeno's phone number,' I said.

'Why?'

'Just give it to me. We don't have time to argue, Ike and Tina are on our butts.'

He looked over at the Miata. Trent pumped gas and glared at us. Jerry sat behind the wheel reading the newspaper in the dim yellow light of the station, not even looking our way.

Byron gave me the number and I ran over to the phone booth and made a call. Zeno finally answered after the eighth ring. He complained, argued, grumbled, but in the end, he listened.

I ran back to the car and found Byron sitting in the driver's seat. I climbed in on the other side. 'Did you get the change?' I asked.

'Sure,' he said. 'I'm just waiting for our free Star Trek glasses and Dick Tracy coloring book.' He shook his head and pulled out of the station.

The Miata was right behind us.

'Okay, what's the plan?' he asked.

'Drive, she said.'

'Where?'

I gave him a look. 'Follow your heart.'

He laughed. 'God, if only you weren't crazy, you'd make a good convict.'

'If only you weren't stupid, you'd make a good man.'

We looked at each other and did an exaggerated Laurel and Hardy nod.

'Head out to the desert,' I told him. 'It's time for a little nature trip.'

'That's your plan? Head out to a desolate place and make it easier to hide our bodies?'

'Pretty good plan, huh?'

He kept driving. I didn't offer any more explanation because I didn't want him to know how half-cocked all this was. Even using the word plan seemed to give too much credit to my idea, as if I'd thought it all through or something. I was improvising, adapting to the circumstances, like some form of rapid evolution. I had a notion that we could lose these guys if we pulled a quick switch of cars with Zeno down the road. They'd end up following Zeno, eventually realize their mistake, and just go back home. If I told this to Byron, he'd find things wrong with it and probably come up with a better plan and talk me into using it. But this wasn't his chase scene; it was mine. He was just part of the cast, a featured player, perhaps, but not the star. That was me.

I found a tape in the glove department. I thumbed it into the cassette player. The music started in the middle of a song.

' . . . Wash your hands in dreams and lightning
Cut off your hair, and whatever is frightening . . .'

Byron stabbed the Eject button and yanked the tape out. He opened the window and tossed it out. 'I'm sick of Paul Simon. You know how much Wren used to play him?'

'You know how long it takes for a plastic cassette like that to decompose? You know what it does to our environment?'

He rolled his window back up. 'You're right, I should go back for it.'

'That's not the point, Mr. EarthWorth, Mr. Monkey-Wrench Gang, Mr. Tree Hugger, Mr.—'

'I get the point, subtle as it is.' He drove without speaking, though after a couple of miles he started humming the

500

Paul Simon song he'd thrown out. He caught himself and started humming something else, Crosby, Stills & Nash, I think.

'Don't you feel guilty?' I asked.

'About what?'

'About throwing that tape out. Forget that it was my private property. But what you did, littering like that. I mean, you just spent two years in jail for protecting the environment.'

'Ecology is the new civil rights,' he said. 'The earth as nigger. It's the perfect middle-class cause, it can't resent us later for our help.'

'Well, it's effective. I feel guilty about everything my body does. If I eat I'm killing something, if I shit or piss I'm spoiling something else. I have a period, my tampons are adding to the landfills. I'm either consuming or polluting.'

'Yup, that's the cycle all right. And no way out of it. Even dead, your body feeds the undertaking industry, also polluters. At least the corpse feeds insects.'

'So I have to wait until then to do some good?'

He looked over at me with a strange expression, like he'd noticed something different he hadn't seen before. It kind of reminded me of the gas station attendant's look and I thought once again maybe I should check my blouse buttons. 'I haven't thrown anything out of a car window since I was thirteen. When I saw you betting that money against me, I wanted you to lose it so bad I went against my survival instinct, an instinct that I honed through two long fucking years in prison. Every day for 730 days I was scared shitless. But I played it cool. No emotion. I had guys three times your size, guys who carried razor blades in their mouths try to get a rise out of me and fail.' He shook his head. 'You bring something out in me, Luna, I'm not sure what. It can't be good. Not if it means being chased by Jerry Kirn through the desert at three in the morning.'

'You give me too much credit.'

501

'You know what I think? I think people haven't given you enough credit.'

I had no idea what that meant. I didn't want to pursue it, either. 'Turn off that same road we took to where you have your greenhouse.'

'I'm not taking those guys near the house. Forget it.'

'We're not going there. Just do it, okay?'

He did. I directed him, giving him the same route Zeno had given me on the phone.

'So tell me, Byron. Once you and Captain Zeno perfect your flowering bamboo, then what? Sell it for millions and retire to a pollutant-free biodegradable life-style on Maui?'

'This conversation is a little too predictable. You looking to trap me into confessing some hypocrisy? Reveal me for a burnt-out radical who's caved in to the system, trying to get my piece of the pie and split? Or crap to that effect.'

'Yup, that's the effect.'

'Forget it. That's some bullshit yuppie mantra: "What have you done for the revolution lately?" Hey, nature isn't all it's cracked up to be, anyway.'

'Here it comes, the speech of the disillusioned. Dim the lights, dust off the Judy Collins albums.'

'You know me so fucking well. As well as you knew Wren?'

He had me there. I thought I'd known her as intimately as a sister, but I hadn't at all. Only what she'd revealed, not what was in her heart.

'You ever hear of the cuckoo bird?'

'Like in those Swiss clocks, right? They pop out all night and keep you awake.'

'You want to hear this?'

'Turn there.' I pointed.

He turned. We were off the freeway and driving down a dark road. In the distance, a faint cluster of lights. 'Cuckoo birds lay their eggs in other birds' nests. The cuckoo hatching is usually bigger and more aggressive

502

than the hatchling that actually belongs to the nest, so the little cuckoo pushes the smaller bird out of the nest. Then, when the parents return, they feed the cuckoo and ignore their own child because he isn't in the nest. In essence, they're feeding their own children's murderer.'

'Bullshit,' I said. 'You saying that these birds don't notice the difference?'

'Or they don't care. They have a set rule: feed what's in the nest, ignore what isn't. Every creature marks its territory. Like the booby bird. Sailors named it that because they were so tame you could walk right up to one and catch it for dinner.'

'It's straight ahead,' I said. 'When we get there, we're going to have to move fast, so just follow my lead.'

'What lead? What are we doing?'

'Just relax. Tell me about the booby. It's tame. Sailors ate it.'

'They have something called the guano ring.'

'Guano,' I said, thinking. 'That's birdshit.'

'Exactly. They use it to make a circle, then they hatch their young inside the circle. If there's plenty of food, the baby birds leave each other alone. If there isn't, the biggest chick pushes the other chick out of the ring. Once the chick is outside the ring, the mother ignores it and won't feed it. Her child can cry and cry only a foot away, but she'll let it starve to death.'

'Is there a point to all this, Bwana Jim? Other than to depress me?'

'I'm saying, people make their own circles, they draw a circle in the dirt and say, "This much I care about. This is my family, my home, these are my friends in here. Anything outside is not my problem." It doesn't matter the type of dirt, the size of the circle, everybody does it. The rest of their lives is just keeping an eye on the perimeter.'

'Are you saying that's good or bad?'

'Neither. It just is. A person has to recognize their own perimeter, the edge of their own circle. You try to extend that circle or step out of it, there's no way back inside because the perimeter goes on forever. You're up to your eyeballs in birdshit.'

'I think you've been looking at the world through a snitch mirror too long, pal. It's just as distorting as looking at it through mall store windows.'

He didn't say anything for a minute. He looked over at me with an odd expression. 'You miss my point. I'm talking about love here, too. Two people get together, they draw their own circle in the dirt, say to everyone, this is our life. This is where we make a stand against the world. In here we combine our concerns, our goals, our lives. That's love. A circle in the dirt.'

I snorted. 'You're a hell of a romantic.'

'I'm not talking romantic love. I'm talking reality. Think of the most repulsive man you can, both physically and spiritually. His eating habits are gross, he has no personal hygiene, and he thinks women are pigs. We stick the two of you on a desert island for the rest of your lives. You and I both know that sooner or later you two will learn to love each other as much as, if not more than, you have loved anyone before. I've seen it in prison: two men who outside the walls would have killed each other over a ball game, inside are living like man and wife. Love is circumstances, nothing more.'

'Christ, I should've left you back there for Jerry and Trent. You deserve each other.'

'You think you did me a favor here? Fuck, before they were just going to bust me up a little. Now they're going to bust me up a lot.'

This whole thing wasn't working out as I'd planned it. The significance of the chase scene is to have the stakes high enough so that it matters if you're caught. I'd done that. But you also need a little cooperation from the co-chasee. There has to be a feeling of shared worth, like living actually is desirable. After listening to Byron, I'd lost some of my spirit for the adventure. Maybe he'd just sobered me up, made me aware that this whole thing wasn't a game, after all. Those guys were serious. For the first time, I was scared.

'Up there,' I said.

'That's a minimart gas station.'

'Right. It's open all night.'

'We still have gas.'

'We're not stopping for gas.'

He sighed. 'Just trust the Force, Luke.'

We could see Zeno standing in front of the minimart eating a donut. As soon as he saw us, he jumped into the Jeep and started the engine. He left his door open.

I turned to Byron. 'Okay, as soon as we pull in, you put on the emergency brake and hop out. Leave the motor running and the door open. You run into the Jeep and duck down out of sight.'

'And what happens? Zeno gets in this car and the two of you drive away, hoping Jerry will follow?'

'It'll work,' I said. 'You just turn down that street and circle behind the station before turning into it. While we're making the switch, Jerry and Trent will be blocked by the building. By the time they clear it, Zeno and I will be driving away and they'll have to follow. It'll work.'

He thought about it. 'Yeah, it probably will.'

'Thanks.' I smiled, feeling some of that chase spirit returning.

'Except I'm not doing it. When they catch up with you guys, and they will catch up, they'll just take it out on you and Zeno. You can take it, but Zeno can't.'

'You sweet talker, you.' I pointed. 'Okay, turn here, then circle around the building as fast as you can. This has to be done fast.'

'I told you, I'm not doing it.'

'I can take care of myself. I'll take care of Zeno too.'

'Goddamn it!' he said and stomped the gas. The car squealed around the curb and shot the length of the quiet desert road, then he turned to circle the gas station. 'I'm not going without you, Luna.'

I looked at him. He kept his eyes on the road, but I

could see the glint in them, the soft sadness. 'What are you saying, we're the two most repulsive people on the planet and we've just been marooned on a desert island?'

He yanked the steering wheel and we slid around another corner. One more corner and everything would happen fast. Too fast to make any mistakes. No turning back.

'I'm saying this is my circle in the dirt, my guano ring, baby.' He glanced at me. 'And you're on the inside.'

I laughed. 'See, you can be romantic after all.'

He laughed too and I felt a sudden lightness about me. A happiness, I guess. But not like any happiness I'd ever known before. Maybe because it didn't seem like a shared happiness as much as just my own, like eating a whole pint of ice cream by myself. Like I knew who I was and where I was and what I was doing for the first time. I mean, for the first time ever. I had always lived in someone else's house, someone else's routine, someone else's life. I thought of Robby then and there was no longing, no sense that I was missing a part of me. I suppose I had always been missing a part of me, since way before Robby.

The man by my side had seen me do some pretty crazy stunts, had lived with me while I pretended to be his dead wife. He had seen me smashing watches. He had made love to me while I'd been stung by a scorpion. He had seen me at my most extreme. I had no secrets left to hide from him.

I popped open the glove compartment and searched through the shreds of old parking lot tickets and gas credit and receipts and broken eyeliner pencils until I found a tattered book of matches from the days when I used to smoke. I stuffed them into my pocket. I leaned over the back seat and rummaged through the magazines, newspapers, empty Butterfingers wrappers. Finally I found what I'd been looking for, my old balled-up panty hose that Season had made me strip off that first day. I crammed them into my other pocket.

'Okay,' I said, plopping back in my seat. 'I'm in the

circle. Anyone else comes in, we peck the shit out of them. That the deal?'

'That's the deal.'

We screeched into the gas station and both of us leapt from the car. Zeno ran out from behind the idling Jeep and jumped into the car. 'Hey,' he said to me. 'I thought I was taking you?'

'Change of plans,' I hollered over my shoulder. 'Drive on home, they won't follow.'

He took off, missed the driveway, and shot over the curb, bouncing my car onto the street. He disappeared into the darkness.

Suddenly the red Miata was sweeping around the curb and shooting into the gas station. By now Byron and I were strapped into the Jeep. Byron jammed the gas pedal and we swung aound in front of the Miata and blasted out of there, flying off the curb and blasting down the street. Jerry Kirn did a neat spin with his car and was right on our tail the whole time.

'We're not going to lose them,' Byron shouted because the wind whipped around us so loudly. 'And we sure as shit can't outrun them.'

'We're not going to try. Just take us to that place where we had sex. Remember?'

'The place or the sex?'

I swatted his arm. He laughed. His laughter sounded different now, somehow richer. Edgeless. As if before he'd always laughed in mono and now he laughed in stereo. Hearing him laugh was like listening to a song that made you want to sing along or drum against the steering wheel or do something to be involved with that sound.

'Okay,' I said. 'I guess we need a plan now.'

'It's your chase. I'm only the bait.'

I hadn't thought about that, but I guess he was right. I had wanted them to follow, but if it hadn't been them, it would have been someone else. Maybe I would have sped by a police car and given them the finger. Or sideswiped a car with six gangbangers cruising around. I don't know, something. I liked that he recognized that and didn't try to interfere or reshape what I was doing. My art.

'How's this sound?' I told him my plan, every crazy detail. When I finished I smiled and said, 'Simple and direct.'

He looked over at me. The wind was tugging at his hair, flipping his ponytail around like a floundering fish. His dragonfly earring twirled like a weather vane. I leaned over and kissed his cheek. He leaned into me. It was the smallest of gestures, yet it felt so damned complete, just that little kiss, his light nudge. The sex had been consuming and heated, but it had been missing something. Whatever that something was, I felt it then.

'Your plan doesn't call for us to pull over to the side of the road and make love, does it?'

I shook my head.

'Then you need a new plan.'

We drove through the dark desert, leaving a plume of dust to wag in the Miata's face. I looked behind us and saw only the dim headlights surrounded by the gritty fog of brown dust. Up ahead were the rocky cliffs where Byron and I had made love.

'Ready?' I asked.

'Are you?'

We exchanged looks.

'Go!' he shouted. I unfastened my seat belt and climbed into the back of the Jeep. I found the ultraviolet flashlight but I couldn't find a container. I emptied the small toolbox, dumping everything on the floor. I returned to my seat.

'Got it,' I said.

Byron began zigzagging the Jeep, kicking up even more dust. Then he slowed just enough for me to leap out with the empty toolbox and ultraviolet flashlight in hand. I hit the ground at a run and kept running, veering away from the dirt cloud. Then I dropped to the ground, face first, and waited for the Miata to drive by. Once it had, I walked over to the cliff face and shone my black light on it.

The constellation of green-blue scorpions lit up the rock face the same as it had the night before. Some scuttled across the rock like shooting stars arcing across the sky. Most just sat there, clinging, waiting for something. Whatever they were waiting for, it wasn't me. I wondered if one of them was the one that stung me. I looked for a guilty face. They all looked sufficiently guilty, their eyes staring blankly.

I opened the small silver toolbox and began scooping scorpions into the box. I scraped the lip along the cliff and brushed the reluctant ones in with the tip of my flashlight. When I had about thirty or so piled three deep in the box, I closed the lid and waited. I could feel them moving around inside the box and that made me feel creepy. While I waited, I kept pointing the black light all around my feet, making sure there was no scorpion rescue squad heading for me.

About five minutes later, I heard Byron's Jeep returning. I ran out and waved at him. He pulled off the dirt road and hopped out of the Jeep.

'Ready?' he said.

I nodded. But I was scared. I hadn't felt scared up until now. I'd felt excited, elated, nervous, depressed, all kinds of things. But scared was new.

The Miata braked to a stop and Jerry and Trent got out. They walked slowly toward us.

Jerry's face was grim and menacing. 'You know, Byron, from everything you ever told me about your wife, she was supposed to be smart. A real genius.' He gestured at the Jeep, the Miata, the desert itself. 'This was not genius. This was dumb.'

'This isn't my wife,' Byron said.

'Thanks for that resounding defense,' I said.

Jerry gave me a look that said I wasn't even there yet, but when he decided I was there, I'd better watch out. I had a feeling his wife experienced that look a lot. 'Thing is, Byron, now I've got to make things right, not just for Landry, but for me. Christ, you know I don't want to. Why couldn't you just stick to the rules? You know the goddamn rules.'

'I figured we were out of prison.'

Jerry shook his head. 'Unh-uh, I'm not getting suckered into one of your fucking philosophical discussions. Let's just get this over with, okay? I'm pissed, I admit that. That's why I'm going to let Trent do this job.'

Trent, face arranged into his most intimidating scowl, started toward us.

'Don't you know karate or something?' I said to Byron.

'I wrestled in high school until some guy dislocated my shoulder. If I take him down I can get two points.'

Trent stomped closer.

'Do something, Byron,' I said. 'Bite off a finger or something.'

'Fine. Give me your hand.'

Now Trent was within a couple yards. Close enough.

I opened the toolbox and displayed the contents. 'Trent's liable to get a face full of scorpions. And they're pissed.'

Trent halted, his scowl melting as he stared at the writhing tangle of scorpions. I shone the ultraviolet light on them to make them look even scarier. Trent blanched and took a step backward.

Jerry looked disappointed. 'You don't think that's going to stop us, do you, Byron? You've seen me eat worse shit than that in the prison cafeteria.'

'Then come and get 'em,' Byron said. 'They're the fresh catch of the day.'

Jerry started slowly toward us. Trent, nervous but taking his boss's cue, also started toward us. It was like having a pair of pliers closing on you. Byron and I backed up a couple steps until we were pinned against the fender of the Jeep.

Jerry walked closer, rolling up his sleeves with each step. Trent was snorting again.

510

'I think they just entered our guano circle,' I said.

'You do have a backup plan, right?' Byron asked.

'Yup. Dine and dash.' I heaved the toolbox's contents and half of my scorpions became airborne. Trent covered his face and backpedaled. I tossed the rest of the scorpions at Jerry. He casually sidestepped the flock. They belly-flopped to the ground and scuttled away.

I dropped the light and the toolbox and ran like hell. Byron jumped into the Jeep and tried to start it, but they were on him before he could escape. I heard the crunch of knuckles against bone, the thump of fist against body. And still I ran.

I dashed around the big rocky cliff, circling all the way around the thing until I came out next to the Miata. I crouched down so they couldn't see me crawling up to the little red car. The gas lid was locked, but I managed to jimmy it open with my keys. I tried not to listen to the thumping and cracking of the two men beating on Byron. I had to concentrate on what I was doing. I pulled the ball of panty hose from my pocket, shook them loose, and stuffed them part of the way down the gas tank. Then I removed the matches and stood up.

'Hey, boys,' I called out.

Jerry and Trent turned and looked at me. Byron, who was slumped over the hood of the car, slid to the ground and lifted his head. His mouth was bloody, but otherwise not too bad.

'What kind of bullshit is this?' Jerry said, annoyed.

I lit a match and waved it near the panty hose hanging out of his gas tank. 'Now we see why panty hose are a fire hazard.'

'Don't be stupid. You're even stupider than I thought. You light that and you'll get blown up with the car. You'll die.'

'I've been dead before. It's not that bad.' The thing was, I meant it too. I mean, I wasn't trying to be dramatic or even threatening. I was actually being honest. Dying wasn't part of my original plan, but I didn't mind. That's when it occurred to me that I wasn't afraid anymore.

Jerry appealed to Byron. 'Tell her, man. This isn't a life or death thing we're doing here. I don't carry a gun. Trent doesn't carry a gun. We're not killers. We're just going to bust you up a little so people know how to do business with Landry. We're not out to kill you, either of you.'

I thought about that a moment. 'Maybe you should.'

Byron wiped the blood from his mouth with the back of his hand. 'The opinions expressed do not necessarily reflect those of the management.'

'I mean it, Byron,' I said. 'These guys want to hurt you as a lesson. And you are willing to let them. Some lesson. Life and death. Maybe if more things were life and death, things would have more value. I don't know.'

Trent looked at Jerry with confusion. Jerry stared at me, trying to decide how far he was willing to go, how far he thought I'd go. He looked at my face, my matches, his car. He shrugged, pushed his rolled-up sleeves down. 'Fuck it. It's not worth it.'

Trent whispered something to Jerry, his face puffed up with deviousness. Jerry shook his head. 'Forget it. This isn't the right time, that's all.'

I stayed next to the panty hose, a match pressed against the sandpaper stripe, ready to strike it to flame. Jerry and Trent didn't even look at me as they got in the car, started it up, and drove away.

Byron and I watched their red taillights fade into the night.

'Think they'll be back?' I asked.

'Not tonight.'

'Whew.' I sat down on the ground and breathed deeply. Now that they were gone, the old fear curdled my stomach.

Byron limped over to me, holding his side and wincing. He stooped beside me. 'You okay?'

'I feel as if someone had scraped his feet across three miles of thick carpet and just touched my heart with his fingertip.'

'Is that fear? Or something else?'

I shook my head. 'I don't know.'

Byron kissed me on the cheek and stood up. He walked around to the front of the Jeep and popped open the hood. He lifted the hood up as high as it would go. 'You meant that whole thing, didn't you? About life and death and stuff.'

'At the time. Don't ask me to repeat it.'

'I was impressed,' he said.

'Really?'

'Yeah. It sure wasn't Wren saying all that.'

'I'm not sure it was me either.'

'Must have been you. Your lips were moving.'

I laughed and looked over at him just as he gripped the edge of the heavy metal hood of the Jeep and slammed it down as hard as he could on his forearm.

41

The emergency room wasn't very busy. When I brought Byron in, they seemed relieved to finally have something to do. Nurses and a woman doctor fussed over him as they ushered him to a back room. I waited in the lobby, reading *National Geographic* and sipping diet Pepsi. I looked for familiar faces in the *National Geographic*, booby birds, cuckoos, dragonflies, scorpions, bedbugs, any of the creatures great and small that had scuttled through my life lately.

When they gave Byron back to me, his left arm was in an orange plaster cast. He was groggy from sedation. The doctor handed me a prescription.

'That was a bad break,' she said. She was about my age but her eyes were so close together she seemed to be constantly staring at the tip of her own nose.

'He was fixing the car,' I explained. 'The hood came down.'

'Hell of a hood,' she said. 'Caught him in the mouth and eyes too. And I think one of his ribs is cracked.'

'You know guys, they always think they're more mechanical than they are.'

She nodded. 'Handy is to men what sexy is to women.'

I drove Byron to Zeno's. Zeno gave us his bedroom and he took the couch. During the next day, Zeno worked in the greenhouse. Byron mostly dozed. I made some lunch for Zeno and me and we chatted while Byron slept. Zeno was a pretty funny guy actually, now that he wasn't afraid of me. He chattered enthusiastically about bamboo for over an hour, with digressions to the art of stealing rare books from libaries. He went back to work in the greenhouse and if I hadn't pulled him out for some dinner, he probably would have just kept working through the night. After dinner he went back to the greenhouse to 'make a few notes'. I went to bed at eleven o'clock and he was still in there.

Byron was awake when I went into the bedroom. He was stretched out on the bed in his underpants. His broken arm lay at his side like a club. He was watching the news on the tiny black and white TV Zeno kept on a chair near the bed.

'Feel better?' I asked.

'A little drugged.'

'The doctor might have gotten overzealous. She thinks you're either accident prone or I've been beating you up.'

'I forget. Which is it?'

I laid down next to him on the bed. I could see his hardened penis straining under the white underpants. 'Apparently she didn't sedate you enough.'

'I'm just excited, the weather forecast is about to come on.'

I put my hand on his good arm and stroked him. 'I've been thinking real hard since last night. I mean, I know I'm no genius, but I'm not an idiot either. Still, I can't figure out what the fuck you think you were doing by breaking your own arm. Some sort of delayed stress syndrome? What? Tell me.'

He watched the weatherman point at a projection of the California coast, poke his finger at a cloud mass moving toward southern California. Expect rain, the weatherman said, but not enough to dent the drought we've been having.

'I mean,' I continued, since Byron wasn't answering. 'I mean, after all we went through to keep you from taking a serious beating. It's like it was all for nothing.'

He didn't take his eyes off the TV. 'It wasn't for nothing. Don't think that. I probably have never been happier or more in love in my whole life than the moment I saw you standing there next to Jerry's Miata, your panty hose hanging out of his gas tank. It was the most perfect moment. Everything you did, everything you said, was just right.'

'I was babbling.'

'No,' he said, reaching over to hold my hand. 'You weren't.'

'The panty hose in the gas tank, you knew about it. That was part of our plan.'

He shrugged. 'I knew, but I didn't know how it would feel. You know, like sex with someone new. You know how it's going to feel, but sometimes it surprises you, it feels better than you'd ever imagined.'

'Does it?' I said.

'Sometimes,' he said. 'If everything is just right.' He reached over and pulled me on top of him. We kissed. The kiss lasted a while, I'm not sure how long. Long enough to make my skin ache to be rubbing against his skin. We broke apart. He lifted his broken arm the way a lobster with a pegged wrist might. 'This,' he said, 'this is the payment for witnessing that perfect moment. Jerry won't have told Landry anything about what happened. Neither will Trent, he's too afraid of Jerry. Jerry didn't have to leave last night, he could've stayed. He probably could have even taken away those matches and yanked out the panty hose without any damage to his car.'

'You knew that going in?'

'Sure. I've seen him take out three guys at once. He's not afraid of anything, certainly not us.'

'Then why'd you go along with my plan?'

'Because I didn't care if it worked. That didn't matter.' He sat up more adjusted his pillow. 'Besides, I knew Jerry. He wasn't going to risk anything over us. We're not worth it. He knows he'll find me later and finish then. That's how it is. By breaking my own arm, I allow him to save face with his boss, because now everybody sees me walking around in a cast, they know why. Now Jerry

516

doesn't have much reason to do anything more to me. In that way, I've probably saved myself a lot worse pain. Just makes sense all around.'

We both stared at the TV screen. Some time during our conversation, Johnny Carson had replaced the news team. Johnny was sitting behind his desk. Loni Anderson was sitting next to him. We watched them talk for a few minutes, then Loni left. She wore a tight dress that clung to her hips and her exit drew a lot of applause and a few whistles.

'Here's a bright new comedian,' Johnny said. 'Very funny guy. Ethan Brand.'

'Jesus,' I said. 'Look. It's Ethan. Our Ethan.'

Indeed, it was Ethan emerging from the curtain, carrying his guitar and smiling at the audience.

'It's Ethan,' I repeated, sitting up. I remembered the note he'd left us to call him. Probably about this.

Ethan began talking about the TV shows he grew up on and how the theme songs weren't appropriate to the way he perceived the characters. Which is why he'd written some more pertinent lyrics. Like this, he said, and began singing: *'It's the story of a dork named Brady . . .'*

'That's your song,' I said to Byron. 'Cleaned up a little, but otherwise the same.'

But Byron was laughing. 'He's very funny. I didn't realize.'

Ethan did a couple other songs, takeoffs on the *'Beverly Hillbillies* Theme' and the *'Love Boat* Theme'. He was funnier than he'd ever been the times I'd heard his other acts. Byron and I laughed until Zeno came in to see what was going on. He sat on the bed, watched Ethan, and laughed too. When it was over, Zeno looked at us, grinned, and returned to his greenhouse.

I shut off the TV.

Byron and I kissed. He had a slight medicinal taste in his mouth, probably from the sedatives. I didn't mind. During that kiss I could suddenly see the future again, the way I had been able to when I was with Robby. Only it

517

wasn't the same. I didn't see me old, I didn't see Byron old. I didn't see a quiet house, tucked safely away somewhere. I saw us making love in about five minutes. I saw me slipping his underpants over his hips and burying my head in his lap. I saw me finishing my book on Season. I would tell the truth about her, because that was the truth about me, about many women. I knew the future, not because of Robby being there or Byron or anyone else. I knew it because I knew *I* would be there: I couldn't be sure exactly who I'd be in the morning, part Wren, part Season? I couldn't remember who the old Luna was, what she liked, how she felt. It's not so wrong being someone else for a while. We're always in the state of becoming something or someone else. Like shedding skin, evolving into some other creature altogether. Yesterday I was a fish, today I suddenly have legs and scurry across the mud. Tomorrow I may walk upright.

I guess I'd just have to wait and see.